# THE SUMMERTIME ADVENTURES OF THE SEWARD SCHOOL BOMBERS

by J.E. Tooley
illustrated by José A. Rodriguez

To Travi —
From all the gang!
Enjoy

# DEDICATION

To all the sons and daughters who want to know what their parents'
childhood was like, and to all the parents who have forgotten.

# CONTENTS

# ACKNOWLEDGMENTS

I'd like to thank Gracie for lending me her Disneyland notebook to get the novel started, Jimmy for helping me with all this computer stuff and Ali for giving me the incentive to finish the book by saying there was no way I'd ever do it.

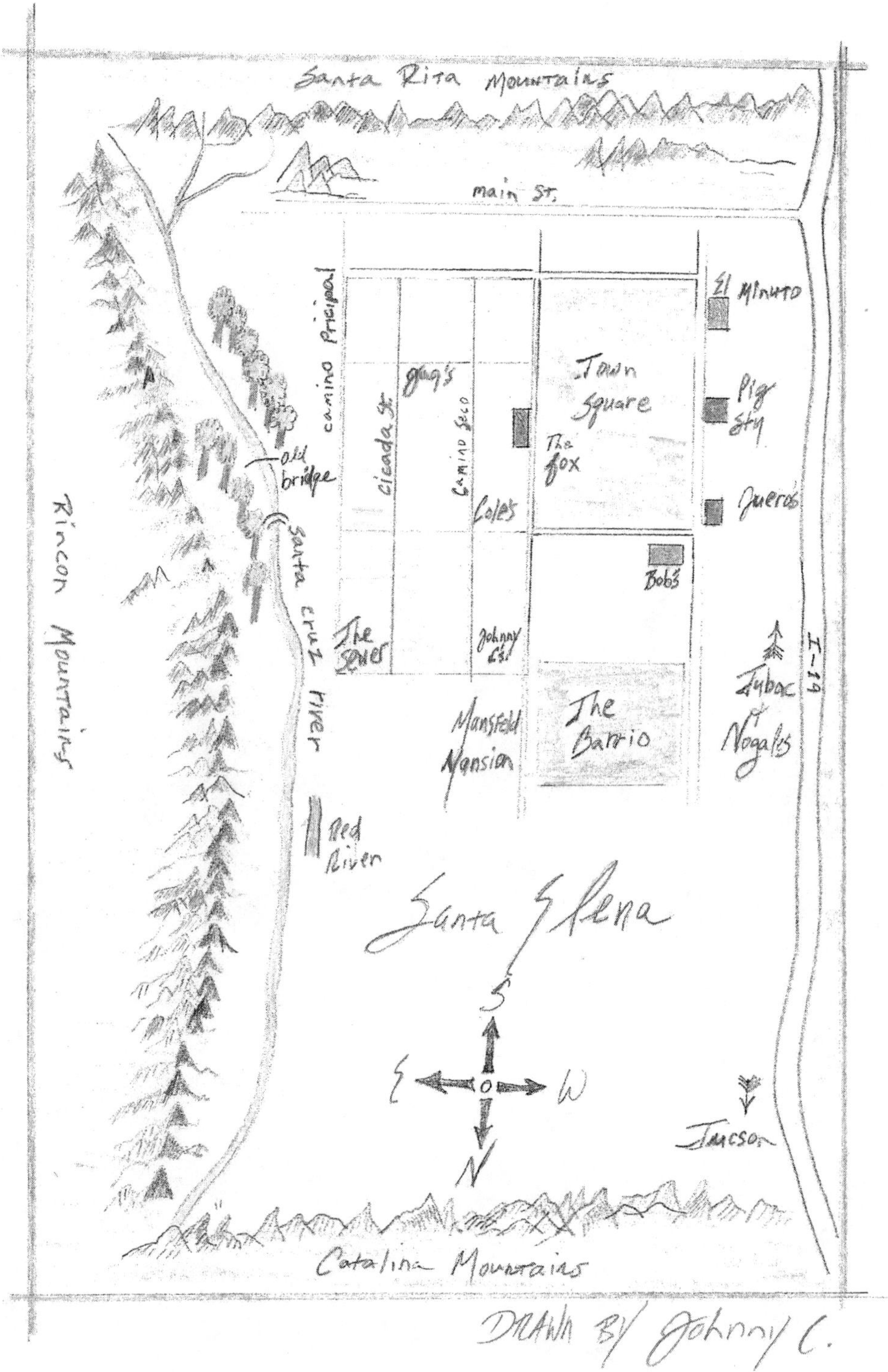

Santa Rita Mountains

main St.

Rincon Mountains

Santa Cruz River

old bridge

camino Principal

Cicada St.

Camino Seco

gary's

Cole's

The fox

Town Square

El Minuto

Pig Sty

Jueros

Bob's

The River

Johnny G's

Mansfeld Mansion

The Barrio

Tubac

Nogales

I-19

Red River

Santa Elena

Tucson

Catalina Mountains

DRAWN BY Johnny C.

# Chapter One

## RED RIVER

"The only chance you got of making it across, Jag, is if God almighty Hisself came down and flung you. And even then it'd be close! Understand!" I yelled out as I squinted to see across the wide, bone-dry *arroyo* we all called Red River.

He didn't understand nuthin'. Never did. That's the problem. Jagger didn't give a darn about being what they call logical. Nope, come hell or high water, once he got some hair brain idea in that thick scull of his, nuthin' was gonna suck it out. Not if you drilled a hole in the side of his head and set your ma's Hoover on high.

"You remember what happened last time, don't ya? You couldn't sit down for a week!"

The last time old Jag tried riding his beat up black Schwinn down one bank of Red River and up the other, it wasn't a pretty site. He hit bottom so hard his seat flew off and he kinda impaled hisself on the post. It took us close to an hour to drag him and Bullet, which was what he called his rattle-trap two-wheeler, through the desert and up to his house on Camino Seco Street. He had to bring a nice fluffy pillow from home to sit on in class for the rest of the school year, which caught 'im a lotta grief from the guys as you could imagine, and Ira said he walked like he had a corncob stuck up his butt for more than a week.

Still Jag didn't waiver one sec as he looked across at Ira on the other side of the gully. He was dead set against letting that old red clay wash beat 'im again. *This* time he was gonna show it who was boss, no matter what. But that's pretty much the way he handled all his problems, and for being

1

just a kid, I guess he'd already had more than his share.

First off it seems he was born with one of his kidneys all shrunk up and not good for much of anything, and had to have an operation to yank it out when he was only just a baby, although none of us found this out 'til much later. Of course, he told us the jagged scar on his belly was from a crocodile bite he got swimming across a mote, trying to escape from Mother Higgin's Reform School for Wayward Children the year before he moved to Santa Elena, which made 'im an instant hero of every second grade boy in the neighborhood.

Because of the fact that he now only had one kidney worth a snot, he was absolutely, positively forbidden by his folks from doing any rough-housing, or hardly playing anything the least bit dangerous. This rule he wholeheartedly and enthusiastically ignored to the fullest. In fact, of all the screwballs around these parts, and there were plenty believe me, Jag was probably the screwiest of all when it came to doing life threatening sorta stuff.

Another thing was, he had this eye problem that made his right one wander all over the stinking place when he tried to stare at somethin'. We all thought this was entertaining as all get out, and Jag was more than happy to give us a show anytime we liked, 'til in third grade the dead beat doctors over in Tucson ruined things by making him wear a patch over his good eye so his crazy eye would straighten itself out. It worked for the most part, I guess, and all the guys were plenty disappointed for a while, 'til we realized that patch he was wearing was a whole lot cooler than his goofy eye, anyhow. Jag started liking it real well, too, and commenced to tell all the kids in third grade at William H. Seward Elementary School, better known by us guys as, "The Sewer," that his pop was really a pirate, and all the men in his family had to start wearing eye patches at the age of nine or they'd be forced to walk the plank. This was accepted by everyone as the gospel truth, no questions asked.

After awhile that eye straightened out decent, but the vision never was too keen, so whenever Jag had to really concentrate on somethin' hard, he'd turn his head just a tad so his good eye would see it dead on, and that's how ya knew he really meant business. After the patch came off last year he got this pair of black horned rimmed glasses he was supposed to be wearing all the time, but they didn't last long. He said, "they encumbered his free spirit," whatever that meant, and because of that "free spirit" them glasses had been busted up so many times that when he took them off they were in the shape of a "Z." I mean there's only so much that Elmer's glue and electrical tape can do to save a pair of specs, right?

That wasn't all the bad stuff that had happened to Jagger, neither. You see his pop was gone, drafted last year into the Army, him being one of them docs that knocks people out in operating rooms before they get cut up. I guess they needed 'im real bad over in Vietnam, and my pops said he was in somethin' called a MASH unit, which was supposedly a pretty dangerous place to be. It had to be hard on Jag not having his father around and all, but he never showed it, not even once, he was way too tough for that.

Oh, there was one more thing that set old Jag apart from the rest of the gang that I forgot to tell ya. He stuttered. Now that might throw some folks for a loop, but me and the guys had hung around 'im so long we hardly even noticed no more. It wasn't one of them awful stutters, neither, where the poor kid squishes up his faces in all kinds of hideous contortions trying to shove a word out, but more like he just had a hard time spitting out certain sounds at the start of some words. For example, he might say, " I'm gonna k-k-kick your b-b-booty," which was somethin' he actually said quite often, or maybe, "N-n-no way, Jose." He also liked to say, "Well," at the beginning of sentences a lot, but I ain't sure why, 'cept maybe it gave 'im a second or two to concentrate so as the rest of the words came out smooth as silk. Like I said, us guys didn't hardly notice the stuttering much, but strangers, they were sometimes kinda startled, and once in while would even laugh. That was a *big* mistake. I don't know if it was all he'd been through or what, but Jagger was one tough hombre, and didn't take too kindly to people messing with him. Now with his pals, he was easy going and even lovable in a goofy kinda way, but if someone he didn't like hassled 'im even a bit, sure as I'm telling you this, there'd be hell to pay. We were all plenty aware of his temper, and tried to avoid those types of situations whenever possible.

Anyway, there he was sitting on Bullet like he was in a trance or somethin', with his head turned just so to get that best eye a good look, and staring straight down at the red clay sides of that gully, baked by the Arizona desert sun 'til they were hard as cement with deep crevices scattered here and there every few feet. Right then, outta his mouth came noises like a hot rod engine revving up loud, and knowing that was a real bad sign I stepped up my pleading for him to reconsider. Ira, on the other hand, being the major pain in the rear that he was at times, started egging 'im on for all he was worth, by taunting as only *he* could.

"Come on, little Jag. Don't be a wussy. My grandma could make it across this little dip here in her twenty-year old wheelchair! What's wrong? Are ya chicken?" He then started to stomp around on the other side of the gully flapping his arms and making clucking sounds like some lunatic 'til Jagger's face got blood red over every inch, and his eyes bugged out so that I felt for sure they'd blow outta his head any second!

"I ain't dragging you home this time, you moron! Do you hear me?" I yelled, knowing it wouldn't do no good, anyhow, and then I just shook my head and looked away, not wanting to see what would happen next.

Well he had that nutty grin on his face, the one that made his front teeth look like a short white picket fence on account'a all the spaces, and his eyes got all squinty like they always were when he was about to do somethin' screwy, and then he reared back hard one time, and was off!

Now the banks of Red River were jagged and steep and the bottom still had nearly a foot of loose sand in some areas left over from last year's rains, and anyone with an ounce of brains in their head, which obviously didn't include Jagger, could see right off he had about as much chance of making it across as he did of winning this years Junior Miss Santa Elena Beauty Pageant.

"Geronimo!" he yelled out as he and Bullet vanished from sight, straight down.

His stubby arms were moving a mile a minute as he did best he could to avoid all them rocks and divots on his way, and his goofy grin got even wider and goofier as he smashed head on into the sand at the bottom and started making his way through. My hands were covering my eyes by now, and I peeked through the cracks between my fingers to see Bullet shaking and rattling so hard that I thought she'd surely break up any second, but somehow that old bike held together and Jag kept right on trudging along. Then he started *laughing*, a kinda high pitched cackling sound, as he peddled like a madman to build up the speed he knew he had to have to make it across the bottom and start up the other side. I looked on, flabbergasted that he had made it this far still alive, and I started to realize he might actually have a chance! Just think of it, Jagger, my best pal, could become the first boy ever in the long history of Santa Elena, to make it across that no good Red River gully that had caused so many of us so much pain and suffering over the years. He'd be the most famous kid for miles around and his bravery would become legendary, but best of all, no one would ever again be able to call 'im a chicken for the rest of his life, and that's mighty big for any kid getting ready to start Junior High, if ya know what I mean.

Just then, Ira started to sense Jag had a real chance, too, and as he stood on the far bank looking over the edge with his mouth opened wide and his eyes even wider, he started hopping up and down, waving his arms and nodding his head like crazy, and though he'd sure never admit it 'cause that was just his way, I could tell deep down, he was pulling hard for old Jag just the same.

Now Pop always says that sometimes in life things just don't turn out the way they should, no matter how bad you want it, or how right it would be, and this, unfortunately for Jag, was one of them times, as his luck started to turn bad, and then started to stink to high heaven. First off, Bullet hit the stump of an old Palo Verde tree that was mostly hidden in the sand, causing 'im to lurch violently to the right like an old rag doll, and his left foot to slip off the peddle for a split second or two. He managed to straighten hisself out all right after that, but lost a bunch of valuable speed in the process. Then, like a scene from one of them bad disaster movies, wouldn't ya know it but here comes a darned dust devil whipping straight down the ravine towards him, and kicking up a mess of dirt and trash and such along with it. Jagger didn't notice nuthin', being too busy dodging rocks, stumps, lizard holes and the like, but Ira and I seen it just fine and knew it'd probably cost our pal any chance of success--or maybe even survival! It sure wasn't one of them cute little baby dust devils you sometimes see on the playgrounds, neither. You know, the ones little kids like to run after and try like the dickens to get in the middle of, but never quite make it. Nope, this one was a monster, big as a house; and it was coming right for 'im!

Bullet was already starting to lose steam as Jagger tried as he might to climb the far side, and Ira started making all kinds of wild hand jesters to try and alert our doomed friend as the twister was closing in, but he had his head down, determined to go where no kid had gone before, and just kept peddling away as fast as his muscular little legs could go. The dust devil was bearing down somethin' fierce by now, and as my hair started to blow and the dirt flew in my face I yelled, "Faster! Faster!" to try to get 'im up and over the other side before it was too late. But it warn't no us, I could tell sure as I'm telling ya this, the jig was already *way* up.

So just as he was reaching the top of the opposite side, and one of the greatest victories of kids over nature of all time, that nasty twister hit 'im broadside with all of its ferocious force. Jagger quickly jerked his head away from the wind and sand and other crud that was sailing around 'im, instinctively turning Bullet's front wheel sharply to the right---and, I'm sorry to say, that was all she wrote. That old Schwinn stopped short like it had hit a brick wall, and Jag flew head over heels over the handlebars like he was shot out of a cannon. He let out a hideous scream as he flew through the air, did a perfect somersault and hit hard, face first, with a loud *thud,* on the upper slope of Red River.

His body went limp as he slowly slid down into the bottom of the wash, and Bullet came tumbling after 'im, landing in a heap just a few feet away. I don't think I've ever been more scared in my whole life than when I saw old Jag's body slap against that sun-baked desert dirt, and Ira and I slid down on our butts to where he was lying all sprawled out, lickety-split.
"Jag, you okay? Say somethin' kid! Will ya?" I shouted in his ear but there was nuthin', not a peep. He just lay there on his stomach with his arms and legs all twisted up and pointing every which way. "Jagger can you hear me?" I yelled again without no response. "Help me, Big I, we need to try and

rouse 'im before he goes into one of them life-threatening commas or somethin'."

So we started jabbing 'im, and pinching 'im, and pulling at 'im, and even kicked 'im a little; but nuthin' seemed to work, and it started to look to all the world that my best pal was a goner at only twelve years old. How was I ever gonna tell his poor mother about this one? I mean he had got hisself plenty banged up and broken in the past, but, let's face it, dead was a whole different ball game, and with his pop being at war and all, it might be just a little more than she could handle. And even though she had three other kids to worry about, I knew for a fact she'd be all in a terrible tizzy, even considering the fact that poor old dead Jag wasn't such a prince, if ya know what I mean. But that's just the way moms are when it comes to their own, I guess. I mean you could be the most low down, good for nuthin' piece of rat turd to ever walk the planet, and sure as you know what, your ma would still love you and dote all over you and treat you like you were the sweetest saint there ever was. It all has to do with instincts. We learned all about it last year in science. Nope, there was sure to be plenty of crying and screaming and carrying on like you never seen before, and I knew it. Oh, why didn't I stop that imbecile when I had the chance?

But just when it seemed all was lost, and I was sitting there in the dirt at the bottom of that gully with my head in my hands, feeling like someone had knocked the stuffing outta me, Ira says, "Wait a sec Johnny C., I got one more idea before we call the mortuary," and he bent over Jag's limp body, put his hands in his arm pits, and started tickling him like there was no tomorrow.

Well I sat there dumbstruck, thinking Ira had completely lost it as he kept on going to town on poor Jag's limp body and getting no response at all, when outta the blue came the tiniest puff of dust out from under Jagger's nose! I snapped my head up quick, not believing what I saw, but then Jag started twitching, barely noticeable at first, and then before ya knew it he was wiggling and twisting and then laughing and jerking hard as he could.

"S-S-Stop it Big I! Stop ticklin' me, I'm b-beggin' ya!" he screamed out.

"I knew you were faking it, you big fat turd," Ira said with a hard jab to the ribs that Jag hardly noticed. "It'd take more than a fall like that to break that thick skull of yours."

"I g-g-guess you're right about that," Jag answered as he lifted his face outta the dirt, rubbing his noggin, and then shot us one of them big goofy grins that showed all of his top teeth and most of his bottoms.

"Jag, you got crap for brains, ya know it!" I barked out in disgust.

He thought about that one for a second, rubbing at his chin, and then said, "Well, I guess th-th-that accounts for that stinky smell I been n-noticing lately," and then started up grinning all over again.

Me and Ira finally agreed after some pathetic pleading to help pick him up outta the dirt and help dust him off best we could, but he was still a disgusting mess, worse than usual, I mean. His hair was sticking up every which way and his shirt was pretty much shredded and barely hanging on, and his glasses were so bent up that the lenses were looking in two completely different directions at once. None of this seemed to faze him one bit. Things like that never did. He said he didn't much like that shirt to start, and now that it was all torn up, it made him look more like a pirate, which was, after all, his family business. He didn't give a lick that his hair looked like a rat's nest, neither, since he never could see no reason for getting it all slicked down since it was just gonna get all messed up again after sleeping, anyhow. No skin off his back about the glasses, either, 'cause he didn't really look *through* them, they was so scratched up, but only around 'em in the first place. We all had a good laugh at that, and Ira said now he knew why Jag hadn't even got one hit or caught one fly ball in Little League all last season.

Now good old Jagger may not've cared much about hisself, no doubt, but there was one thing he'd sure give his life for, and that was his old bike Bullet, and I'm sad to say she was nuthin' but a mangled mess of metal and rubber. Her handlebars were twisted all cock-eyed and her front wheel was bent to look a lot more like the letter G than the letter O. The seat was pretty much facing backwards and the playing cards that were clothes-pinned to the front wheel forks to make that sweet *flappety-flappety* sound against the spokes, were nowhere to be seen and probably all the way to Mexico by now along with the rest of the junk caught up in that nasty dust devil. After taking a good long look at his trusty old pal, you could tell Jag was a little shook-up, and I swore I saw his bottom lip start to quiver just a tad. Now ya gotta understand, no living being had ever seen Jag cry before, no matter how bad things got. Not even last summer when he almost became one off them tunics after sitting on some electric hedge clippers, but he got pretty darn close when we yanked old Bullet outta the dirt.

He straightened hisself out right quick though, and after blinking tight a couple'a times and having a good hard swallow, he said she really didn't look all that bad after all, and with a little work here and there, she'd be as good as new in no time. Ira said it was gonna take more than just a little work to get that "old rat trap," up and running again, but Jag gave him a nasty snarl and told 'im to shut the heck up and help pull her outta the wash. Ira was all set to let Jagger have it for being ungrateful and all, but thought better of it and grabbed onto the front of the bike and started to pull.

After a mighty struggle, we finally got back on the desert trail towards, "The Sewer" and home, with Ira and I peddling nice and slow, and Jag half pushing, half pulling old Bullet along. The air was starting to smell nice and fresh and moist, the way it always did right before the rains came following a long dry spell, and although everyone knows it sure don't rain much in the desert, when the rainy season does finally come, them storms were quick and brutal. The "monsoon season," named after some wicked bad weather they got over in Arabia or somewheres, always started up in mid July and then petered out in late August, and every morning during that time, it'd be crystal clear 'til about noon, when a few of them extra fluffy clouds, the ones that look like big globs of vanilla frosting, started rolling in over the Santa Rita mountains down south. They'd keep right on coming, slowly turning darker and darker and butting into the ones in front 'til by three or four, a lumpy grey blanket would be covering every inch of the sky. Then a soft breeze would start to blow, just a gentle tickle against your face at first, but it would keep building, slow but sure, 'til it was so strong it felt like it could rip your clothes clean off, and the dust got so thick you couldn't make out Marilyn Monroe two feet in front of your face. The trees would start to sway, nice and gentle at first, but before you knew it they'd be bending back so low they almost touched the ground, and the windows in the house would start to quiver and shake, and all the street signs would be rocking back and forth, this way and that, and finally, like the guy who shoots a gun off to start a big race, there'd come a loud *"tha-wack!"* and a dazzling flash of lightning, and then, like Pop always liked to say, all hell would break loose. Right then and there the clouds would open up and millions of gallons of water would be dumped over our little desert town. It'd rain so hard, the sound would be deafening, even inside your house, and the drops would get so big they'd actually hurt if they hit ya square. Forget trying to drive a car in it. People would just stop dead in their tracks on the side of the road and wait it out, 'cause there ain't no windshield wipers in the world fast enough to keep up with them monsoon raindrops; not the ones on my mom's brand new Buick, and definitely not them little puny ones on Pop's old Chevy. The temperature would dip close to 25 degrees in less than five minutes, usually from around 100 to almost 75, and then all of a sudden everything would quit just as quick as it had come, with the whole shebang lasting no more than twenty minutes. The skies would open up, the sun would shine through, and the hot, dusty, desert town would be changed into a cool, moist, lovely oasis for the rest of the day. The next afternoon the whole crazy cycle would start up all over again--you could bet the farm on it.

Well, it was getting late in the afternoon as we crept our way through the desert, and it was looking mighty clear that them nasty monsoons would soon be paying us their first visit of the summer. The desert creatures could sense it, too, and the lizards and horny-toads were starting to scurry back and forth all nervous-like, and once in a while a tarantula would stick his hairy head outta its hole to watch us go by and take a peek at how the skies were shaping up. It was pretty plain old Jag was feeling plenty sore from his doomed attempt at becoming the town's supreme daredevil, but being the way he was, he wouldn't let on much, and just kept trudging along with a wince here and there and a low moan every once in a while that gave 'im away.

As we closed in on Camino Principal, the street that pretty much was the border between eastern Santa Elena and its western part, and ran right down the front of the school yard, the sky started to darken with clouds and the wind started to howl.

"We better get our butts to the ramada before the darn storm hits," Ira shouted, squintin' up his eyes from the dust as he checked out the clouds overhead.

We agreed and started to pick up the pace and crossed the street with our heads down and pointed in the direction of the front lawn of Seward School. The big grassy area was bordered on two sides by lovely red and yellow rose bushes, which were the only hint of color in the otherwise drab grays and browns of the Sonora Desert, and in front by gigantic junipers, maybe fifty feet high, and probably planted when the school was first built. They were a pretty magnificent site, to tell ya the truth, shooting straight up to the sky like huge green spears on a normal day, but right at the moment they were blowing this way and that like all get out. The school itself was built in 1927, the same year Pop was born, and had a red tile roof and adobe walls that were covered over with white stucco that had browned plenty over the years from the sun and such, and was chipping away here and there to show the burnt orange colored bricks underneath. It had big wood doors and window frames made outta mesquite, on account'a it was the only wood growing around these parts back then that was worth a darn according to Pops. All the desks inside were made outta mesquite too, and a bunch of 'em were as old as the building itself. I even found one in old Miss Runion, "The Onion's," class that my pop had carved his initials in back in '35.

Anyways, we made our way across the front lawn to the porch along the main building and through the chain link fence that surrounded the little kids side of the playground, as the wind started whistling all around us but good, and then outta nowhere there was an ear-splitting *"crack!"* and a blinding flash straight above where we was standing that made us all quick duck down low and the hair on our arms stick straight up. We all knew what was coming next, and it sure as heck did! It started with nuthin' but a light pitter-patter of raindrops, but before you could say, flash flood, it was falling in buckets, and we still had about fifty yards to make it to shelter.

"Ouch!" "Woo!" "Dang it!" we yelled as them killer drops smacked hard against our skin, and I hollered out at Jag to leave Bullet there and I'd give 'im a ride on my handlebars the rest of the way. He slid on kinda gingerly as I shifted my Stingray into first to handle the heavier load, and we high-tailed it outta there fast as my skinny legs would take us. Ira had already made it to the ramada, and was starting to shimmy up one of the poles to get to the wood rafters in the ceiling and keep from getting drenched. It didn't do no good just standing under the ramada, 'cause the wind blew so darn hard it turned the rain sideways so it shot right on in, and a kid could still get completely soaked to the bone.

After we jumped off my bike and I set her down real gentle in a nice grassy area, I took a look around to see how the storm was shaping up. The wind was swirling the rain like mad by then, and I had to put my hand in front of my eyes to keep out the dust, but I could tell there was still a good ways to go before this monsoon had reached its full strength. I could make out to the south what looked like a black wall blowing straight our way. Boy, this was gonna be a doozy I thought, and I was already dreading the tongue-lashing I was in for once Ma and the rest of the "Gestapo" (My Grandma and Aunt Leah) got a hold of me and my soaking wet body at home. Ya see, like all the rest of the kids around these parts, I was strictly forbidden from being outside during the monsoons storms, no ifs ands or buts.

Me and Jag, we latched onto the nearest poles and started to shimmy up quick like a couple of polecats when I heard Ira shout out up above, "Hello girls!" which was the way he normally greeted Jag and me, but then I realized he was talking to someone else. As I looked up, I could make out the shadows of too other kids, one kinda puny and the other one enormous, sitting in the dark on the cross beams with their legs dangling down.

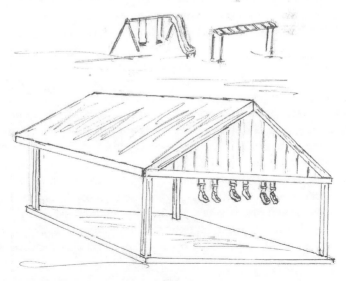

11

"You wish, lover boy!" came the reply from one of the heads, and I immediately recognized the voice of our old pal Emeliano De la Rosa. Rosie's what all us guys called 'im though, partly 'cause it was kinda tough to pronounce Emeliano, and partly 'cause "Rosie" described his personality to a "T". He was probably the nicest kid any of us had ever known, always having a sweet smile on his face and never, ever saying nuthin' the least bit nasty about nobody. Pops said he was like that on account of how he was raised, and I guess I can buy that 'cause Mrs. De la Rosa was about the kindest, most gentlest, wouldn't-hurt-a-fly kinda lady you ever did see.

Rosie had dark curly hair and a big round face and, well, pretty much big round everything, if you know what I mean. To put it bluntly, he was a pretty big fatso, and kinda touchy about it, too, and later on he earned the nickname "Big Rosie," not on account of his size, neither, but 'cause of something even more remarkable, but I guess you'll just hafta hang around to find out about that if you're interested. He also was the only Mexican kid we hung out with 'cause he was the only one living on this side of town, and I heard his pop was some kinda bid wig with the state in the Department of Urban Refuel, whatever that was. I also heard through the grape vine that some of the Mexican folks in town gave his pop a lotta grief about moving to the east side, like he was too good for them or somethin', and it really hurt his feelings bad. Now I don't get that one bit. Seems to me a family should live wherever they darn well please. This is the land of the free and the home of the brave after all, ain't it? Sometimes I just don't understand grownups.

One of the best things about being friends with old Rosie was that Mrs. De la Rosa was just about the best Mexican cook in the whole world, and there was nuthin' she liked more than trying to prove it. During the summer we'd always swing by Rosie's place around lunchtime to see what he was up to, even if we knew darn well he was busy doing chores or was sick or somethin'. We made sure to walk in looking real hungry and weak and pathetic as possible, and before ya could sing "La Cucaracha," there'd be Mrs. De la Rosa laying out a Mexican feast fit for that Emperor Max-a-million we learned all about last year in Mr. Fulgensie's history class. She'd have chili con carne and cheese enchiladas, and carne seca and caldo de queso, and even somethin' called "mole aye," which was a cross between chocolate syrup and hot sauce, that sounds kinda putrid, but take my word for it, it's "muy delicioso!" We'd wrap it all up in piping hot tortillas and stuff ourselves silly 'til we was filled to the brim. The whole time we were shoveling the stuff down our throats, good old Mrs. De la Rosa would be hovering over us like a mother hen trying to cram *more* food on our plates 'til we had to practically beg her to stop. No wonder poor Rosie was so *gordo!* We'd all roll outta there content as can be, and she'd see us off, standing at the doorway with a big smile on her sweet round face and saying stuff like, "Mis hombres pequenos," and a bunch of other Mexican words we didn't understand. We'd just wave back and say, "Gracias!" about a thousand times and then be on our way. The only problem was that after a meal at Rosie's house, we were so stuffed that we couldn't do much of anything 'cept lay under one of the big mesquite trees down at the schoolyard and wait 'til the old digestive juices kicked in but good.

Anyways, Rosie was a swell kid and we were plenty happy to have 'im living with us right here in the "White Ghetto," which was the name Ira thought up for our quiet little neighborhood a few years back. He said the name would make us sound a lot tougher, since all the west side kids thought we were nuthin' but a bunch'a pansies. He said everyone knew that the roughest, toughest kids in the country lived in the ghettos of New York and L.A., and just 'cause we lived in puny old Santa Elena didn't mean we couldn't have one too. He said that if we didn't start living like we was in the ghetto real quick we was destined to grow up a bunch of no good weenies, and he for one wasn't gonna sit around and just watch it happen. That Ira, just when you were sure he was as shallow as the kiddie pool at Highland Vista Park, he'd surprise the snot outta ya and come up with somethin' phillysofical as all get out.

We all agreed that a "ghetto" was definitely the kinda neighborhood for us, but we had one major problem; on T.V. all the official ghettos had a bunch of Negro kids, and we didn't have even one. We thought about trying to recruit some, but no one could even remember seeing any for miles around. Ira found out about some official negro club on the nightly news called the N.A.A.C.P., and he gave 'em a ring, asking if they knew of any Negros maybe wanting to join the new ghetto we was starting up in Santa Elena, but the lady got real nasty and slammed the phone shut for some reason, and Ira didn't have the guts to call back. Well, we still had Rosie who was pretty dark brown all year round, and me, being Italian, I tanned up real nice in the summer time, so we decided that we'd hafta do for now.

We were pleased as punch with our new tough image and decided to use the term "ghetto," any chance we'd get to describe the stuff we were doing. We always played "ghetto ball," instead of plain old basketball, for example, and always played by "ghetto rules," which meant you could slap each other around silly before a foul was called. We went on "ghetto patrol" when we rode our bikes around the neighborhood, and never conducted ourselves in any manner "unbecoming of the ghetto," which pretty much meant no sniveling in public.

Anyways, as me and Jag pulled ourselves up them poles and outta the rain, the kid sitting on the rafters next to Rosie barked out, "Well if it ain't The Three Stooges; Meat ball, Matzo ball, and Goof ball!" No doubt about it, that had to be Neil.

"Shut up, Nelly!" Ira shot back.

"No, you shut up!"

"No, you shut up!"

"No, you shut up!"

"Why don't you try and make me?"

"I would, *Little* I, but I forgot to bring my pacifier!"

Neil was a funny kid to try and figure out. One minute he's your best pal and next minute he was cutting you down so low you could walk under one of them miniature wiener dogs without messing up your hair. Pop said he must'a had a screw loose somewheres, which was probably true, but the one thing about Neil that you could always take to the bank, whether he was making fun of you or not, was that he was about the wittiest kid you ever met. I mean the stuff he came up with was completely off the wall, mostly, but it would make you laugh, no doubt. And not just a little snicker, neither, but hysterical, pee-in-your-pants laughing, so hard you couldn't catch your breath and you'd start coughing and sputtering and your nose would run and your eyes would water and there was nuthin' you could do to stop yourself no matter how idiotic you looked. The problem was, he was a complete and utter screw up in just about everything else in life he tried. He was lousy in school, mostly because he was always goofing off and trying to be funny, he was rotten in sports 'cause if he wasn't automatically the best player he'd say the game was stupid and then wouldn't even try, and he was pretty well despised by everyone at the Sewer besides us, 'cause when he wasn't picking on the other kids, he was usually making up insulting names for 'em.

Come to think of it, I'm pretty certain he's one of them idiotic savants, you know, those kids that are retarded as all get out, but could do *one* thing better than anyone in the whole world. I saw a special on PBS once about 'em last summer. It was way out! This one poor fella, who hardly knew where the heck he was, could listen to a Baytoevan conchairtoe just once, and then, lickety-split, play the whole thing, start to finish without missing a note! Another guy, who spent the whole day sitting in a chair mumbling to hisself and drooling, could figure in his head the most difficult math problems you ever heard, all in about two seconds. So I figured that's gotta be what old Neil is, a comic idiotic savant. He uses all of his brainpower to think up hilarious stuff all day so there wasn't much left over for nuthin' else.

Some of his "masterpiece" nicknames for the kids around here were, "Outta" for this big dorky guy whose last name was Bounds, who always dribbled the basketball off his foot during pick up games, "Pissy" for Missy Stan, this girl in our fourth grade class who had a weak bladder if ya know what I mean, "Lockjaw Louie" for this kid that always froze up something horrible every time he was asked a question by the teacher, and "Ego Trip" for Mike Tripolet, this hot shot high school kid who thought he was better than everyone else in just about everything. He also came up with "Iceman" for Ira because he was so *cold* to people sometimes, and also, "Irene," 'cause although he'd deny it somethin' fierce, Ira was the spitting image of his little sister, Rosie for Emeliano which I told ya about before, and a bunch'a others you'll hear about later. Jagger was also one of his ideas, although a swell nickname like "Jagger" don't just come outta nowhere, but gotta evolve over a long period of time, like a fine wine, something like this: first Neil started calling Jeff "Ungowa," 'cause that's the sound he said all the surfers made when they were riding the big ones in Hawaii and Jagger loved to jump on his raft off the side of the pool down at the park and ride her as long as he could before he wiped out.

"Ungowa" got shortened to "Gowa" after while, and then just to "Gow," and then that changed to "Jow," but I don't remember why. Neil added "ger" on the end of "Jow," 'cause that's the noise Jag made when he was playing football to make himself sound real mean, but mostly it just made us think he was an idiot. Then Jow-ger turned into "Jagger," probably 'cause it was easier to say, and "Jagger" lead to a bunch of other spin-offs like, "Jaggertino" after the great lover Rudolf Valentino that Granny was always yapping about, whenever we thought Jag was getting sweet on a girl, and "Jaggernese" when he'd get all serious and squint up his eyes which made him look like one of them Chinamen characters on the Saturday morning cartoons, and "Jaggerissimo," when he was trying to act all tough and in charge like the "Generalissimo."

There was one other thing Neil wasn't too shabby at now that I think of it, and that was working up devious plans for us to carry out to drive the folks living in the "White Ghetto" nuts. To be totally honest, some of his ideas worked out just swell, and others were real stinkers, but right then as the wind and rain were whipping like mad, and me and Jag were settling into our seats on the last open crossbeam, he leaned over, and speaking loud enough to be herd over the storm all around us, let on that he had come up with a doozy of an idea for tonight that would rival the great military battle plans of Neapolitan and Patton. He wouldn't let on no more about it yet, 'cept for the very important fact that there'd be plenty of firecrackers involved, which was all we needed to hear, and we all quickly agreed to meet in the alley behind Jagger's house at seven o'clock for further details.

# Chapter Two

## WAR PLANS

As the wind and rain finally started to peter out, we shimmied down from the ramada roof, with Rosie bringing up the rear as usual, needing two or three spotters below to make sure he didn't fall and break his neck. We all prayed to the good Lord he didn't slip and squish us like ants. After he made it down safely, we walked across the playground to the gate that opened on to Cicada Street. For those of you who don't know, a Cicada is a large beetle that comes out in the desert at night in the summer time and makes the most God-awful buzzing sound you ever heard, by rubbing its back legs or wings or something', but whatever it was, when it really got going to town, it sounded like someone was using a drill to bore a hole through the side of your head. I heard they made that sound to try and attract a girlfriend, but I ain't buying that, 'cause it don't take a genius to see that any self respecting lady cicada that got within ten yards of all that racket would surely turn tail and run!

Along the way Jag gathered up poor Bullet, and we pushed our bikes passed the jungle gym where we used to play "King of the Hill" when we were just little kids. Those games got pretty ruthless at times, and more than one kid got a one way ticket to Tucson Medical Center after losing a battle for the top wrung. The bars were all wet now from the rains, and the water slowly dripped off and into the sand below. As the sun broke through the clouds, it shined down on that old metal contraption and set it to sparkle and shine so it looked a lot like that new "Lunar Lander" thing-a-ma-jig they been talkin' so much about on the news lately. As we kept on, I took in a deep breath and thought to myself that there isn't nothin' sweeter in the

16

whole world than the smell of the desert after a big rainstorm; clean, cool, and refreshing—like the smell of a new car, as Pop always says. I just love the feel of that cool wet air creeping up my nose and down my lungs, felling so clean and refreshin' all along the way, compared to the hot, dry dust we normally had to put up with around here.

After making it through the gate and saying so long to the guys, I walked up the hill towards home watching the water trickle down along the curb 'til it almost reached the school crossing at the bottom. I found a leaf, stuck on a little black beetle that happened to be crawling by, and set them in the little stream. "There ya go little buddy. How about a lift on the Seward School Express?" I said as I watched 'im float along. Then I started thinking about how cool it would be if *I* was floating down some big roaring river instead of that lucky beetle, maybe the Amazon or something, and then maybe I'd run across a terrifying tribe of hungry cannibals while I was just floating along minding my own business, and what if they started shooting poisoned darts at me with those cool blowguns they all have and throwing spears and flinging nets and chanting up some nutty tune like those cannibals always did in the movies. And all the while, I'd also have to maneuver through nasty rapids, and dodge rocks and trees and ticked off hippopotamuses and giant anaconda snakes that get long as a fire hose and twice as big around, and I knew dang well that if I fell in, every ounce of my flesh would be gobbled up by a swarm of bloodthirsty piranhas, and there'd be nuthin' left of me but a picked clean bag of bones to send home to Ma.

After awhile a car went by, splashing me in the face and waking me outta my swell daydream, and I decided I'd better get my rear home quick, seeing it was closing in on dinnertime and all. I jumped on my Stingray, shifted into first gear, popped an awesome wheelie and headed down the other side of the hill. The Schwinn Stingray, in case you didn't know, was the most far out bike ever invented, especially if you had the three-speed stick. Mine was metallic blue with chrome monkey bars, a banana seat, a big slick on the back and an 8- ball shift knob. It was my pride and joy and I babied it to no end. Neil had me one up with his boss "Orange Crate," model that had all the swell stuff mine did but was painted bright orange and had longer front forks with shock absorbers and a baby front tire that made it look just like one of them cool chopper motorcycles you see in all the movies these days. I gotta admit, it was bitchin'! Come to think of it, all the guys rode some kinda Stingray or another 'cept Jag, of course. He insisted on riding that old black clunker, Bullet, and whenever we pressed 'im about it, he said she had, "sentimental value." I didn't have a clue what he meant by that, 'til later on I found out it was the last thing his pop had given 'im before going off to war.

Anyway, as I reached my house, I hopped off my bike and pushed her up the incline quiet as a mouse. I'd seen Granny and Aunt Leah's green

Rambler parked out in front and was hoping they might all be distracted and I could somehow make it back to my room and avoid the Spanish Imposition they'd love to put me through for being outside during the storm, *and* late for dinner to boot. But, of course, I had no such luck. Soon as my big toe touched the floor, before I even stuck my head through the door for crying out loud, I was attacked head on, without mercy! Just like one of them old Chicago mob bosses that got ambushed by about ten Tommy guns all at once, soon as he stepped outta some mom and pop Italian joint.

"Well, look what the cat dragged in! Soaked from head to toe, just as I thought," Aunt Leah started the assault, throwing her hands in the air for added dramatic effect. "He is going to catch pneumonia!" That was her favorite line whenever you went outside with even an ounce of water still in you hair after a shower, or dared to not wear a sweater when it was less than 90 degrees out. "Get me the Vicks right now!" Which was her cure for everything from chicken pops to lumbago. Aunt Lee was my Mom's sister *and* my Godmother, which gave her the authority, she often reminded me, "to make sure I didn't turn out to be a good for nothing hooligan like all the other boys in the neighborhood." She didn't have no kids of her own, lucky for them, so she concentrated all her motherly instincts on me, I guess.

"Look at him Frieda, he doesn't even have a jacket on!" Granny added.

She was Ma's mom, a short stocky lady with a long hooked nose, flaming red hair, or red wig, I should say, and a thick Boston accent. Her favorite saying was, "If it weren't for me, none 'a yas would even be he-ah!" She always seemed to have it out for me, too, ever since I was a little kid and apparently kept walking up to her and saying, "too-pah eeya," over and over. Everyone thought that was real cute 'til one day when I started talking a bit clearer it came out, "stupid idiot!" and our relationship's been going downhill ever since.

She was sitting at that kitchen table, smoking her cigarette and looking out the bay window just like always, and her wig was laying on the table right next to her ash tray, which wasn't too bright seeing that they were highly flammable and she'd already burnt three of 'em to a crisp over the years by flicking her ashes a bit too brisk.

"I don't need no jacket, Granny. It's the middle of summer for gosh sakes."

"Don't talk back, ya he-ah!" she growled, her voice gravelly from smoking all them Camels. "Yous should always take a jacket just in case. Do ya understand? Huh? Ansa me when I'm talking to yas."

I started to say something but she cut me off quick, " Are yous talkin' back again?" she croaked, as she glared down that ski slope of a nose at me.

I was about to say, "How in the heck do you expect me to answer, if you won't even let me get a word in edgewise?" But I couldn't see no advantage in it, and decided my best move was to just clam up and hope for the best.

"Giovanni Giuseppe Caruso, just look at you!" (Giovanni's *Italian* for Johnny, and don't tell nobody about my middle name if ya don't mind) Ma shrieked like she had just seen Frankenstein or something, as she turned from the gas stove.

Well, I guess I was a bit of a mess at that. The wind had blown my hair all crazy and covered me in dirt, and then with the rain and all coming later, I was pretty much spackled in mud from top to bottom, my clothes were dripping dry, and my shoes and socks were soaked through from sloshing in the puddles all the way home.

"I couldn't get back in time Ma, I swear. Them dang monsoons hit quick, *real quick!*" I pleaded, looking for a little compassion, for a change.

"Don't you tell me about the storms, young man. I know all about the storms in the summer and so do you. We both know they come right at four o'clock every day, and that is exactly why you are supposed to be home at 3:45, right?"

Well, she had me there and I knew it, but as I looked around for some help outta this mess, all I got was Granny and Aunt Leah shaking their heads and starring a hole through me like I had just committed the crime of the century. Just then my lamebrain dog Dodger came out from under the table where he was searching for some crumbs, and started licking the dirt off my shoes. I bent down to pet 'im to try and break the mood but it didn't do no good. They all three just kept letting in to me, telling me how I needed to be more responsible and how I wasn't a baby no more, and how I needed to learn to follow rules or I'd never amount to nuthin'. I had to stand there and listen to what a sorry example of a young man I was becoming, and how that little weasel Ronnie Thompson, the town goodie-goodie, would never disobey *his* ma like I had so blatant, and all kinds of other garbage 'til I felt about knee high to a horny toad. I gave 'im all my sorriest look, still trying to catch a break, but that didn't work, neither. They just kept on riding me to no end.

Finally, when I just couldn't take it another second, a deep, booming voice came roaring in from the living room, "Aren't you three hens finished yet? You're giving me a headache. Stop picking on the boy!" It was Pop. Thank the lord he must've got home a little early.

All three of the storm troopers stopped yapping at the same time and froze stiff like some alien had just shot 'em with a stun gun. Well, I saw my chance and I took it, and made a mad dash through the kitchen and into the living room to safety.

"Hi, Pop," I said as I stretched out my arms. "Boy, am I glad to see you!" I raced over and gave 'im a big hug around the neck for all I was worth. He was sitting there in his chair, like always, with a tray on his lap and a dish towel tucked up into the neck of his shirt like a bib, so he wouldn't spill nuthin' on hisself, although he always did anyhow. He was having some soup ma had fixed up, and sure enough he had dripped on just about every inch of his shirt, *except* for where that old dish towel was hanging.

"Damn!" he said, as he looked down at the mess he had made. "How do I always do that?"

He looked at me with a small frown on his face that quickly turned into a big, bright grin. He was such a funny guy. He was the most relaxed, laid back and loveable person you ever knew when he was at home, and the greatest dad ever, but catch 'im over at his produce warehouse and he was quick as a whip and sharp as a tack, and definitely not the kinda guy you'd want to cross. The thing about Pop was he didn't care a lick what anyone thought about 'im 'cept his family, I guess, and he basically did the best he could. If you didn't like it, tough turds. He always told me it didn't matter a hoot what other people thought of you, only what you thought of yourself. When I looked at 'im kinda blank after that, he said that someday I'd figure it out. All I know is he was always there for me in a pinch, and I loved 'im for it.

"How's my little man?" he said as he gave me a big kiss on the cheek and patted me on the rear.

"I'm great, Pop. Thanks for saving my life."

"Well, they were ganging up on you pretty good, so I thought I'd give you a hand. But Johnny, I want you to listen to your mother. You know she worries a lot."

"I know Pop, but it was just a little rainstorm, I mean, big deal."

"Well sometimes they can get pretty nasty with the wind and the lightning, so just be smart, understand? I don't want anything to happen to my son, in whom I am well pleased."

He liked to say that last part a lot, "my son in whom I am well pleased." I think it's in the Bible somewheres, but I ain't sure. After that he told me to go change into some dry clothes and then come and get some supper and we could watch some T.V. together for a while.

I went down the hall and into my room feeling much better about my situation, and I closed the door and plopped down on my bed, letting out a long sigh of relief. There's nuthin' in the world like being in your own room surrounded by all of your most best stuff to make you feel nice and warm inside and forget about all of your troubles. There was Sandy Koufax and Don Drysdale up on one wall, right where they're supposed to be, and the shelf with all my Little League trophies against the other, my mini basketball hoop hanging over the closet door, angled down just a tad from too many slam dunks, and a complete set of World Book Encyclopedias collecting dust over in the corner. Yep, it was just how I liked it. *My* room, where *I* was the boss and nobody could tell me what to do. Well, that wasn't entirely true but I could at least kick my little sister Gracie out if I felt like it, although she'd for sure go crying to Ma and I'd probably get a licking for it. I could try to make Dodger do whatever I pleased, too, but that never worked very well, neither. The problem was that stupid mutt was five years old already and hadn't come close to learning one darn thing yet, 'cept where the treat jar was, but *boy* did he have that down pat! Not only that, but if you really tried to teach 'im something cool, like how to play dead, or somethin', after awhile he'd get real ticked off at you for bugging 'im and start biting. If you tried to stop 'im from doing that, that numbskull would think you were playing, and bite you even harder. Then if you tried to run away, and this was his favorite thing to do, he would chase you down and bite you right on the rear end as hard as he could. Believe me, I got plenty of teeth marks on by butt to prove what a bad dog he is. The problem was, he could be so darn lovable at times it was hard to stay mad at 'im for long, no matter how rotten a thing he did, and before you knew it you were back down on the ground petting and playing with 'im. It sure would be nice if he at least *tried* to learn a simple trick or two like all the other dogs in the neighborhood. I mean, after all, it was getting kinda embarrassing, and just the other day when Neil was over he came up with a nickname for 'im that I'm sure is gonna stick; Dumb-ger.

I put on a new T-shirt, wiping my face and hands off on the old one, threw on a pair of shorts, traded my soggy PF Flyers for some dry ones, and was pretty much ready for dinner. I was hoping by now that Ma and her two side kicks would have eased up on me, so I walked back down the hall, spitting on my hands to smooth down my hair as I went, and then strolled into the living room. I plopped down on the burnt orange couch, the one with the material that felt like burlap against your sensitive skin, and looked across at Pop in his big black leather chair. That chair was humongous, like a throne or somethin', and I guess in a way Pop was like a king sitting there and ruling over his castle. The only thing that sorta ruined the whole image was the dishtowel bib and that trail of soup from his chin, down his shirt, and all the way to the bowl sitting on the tray in his lap.

"How's the new T.V. Pops?" I asked glancing over my shoulder to see if Ma was giving me the evil eye.

"Johnny, you'd swear those actors are standing right in the room with you," he answered with a cock-eyed smile, the one he always gave you when he said somethin' *he* thought funny as heck. I was asking 'im about our new Zenith *colored* T.V. complete with "Space Age" remote control and everything! After watching that little cartoon guy on the commercials singing, "I got color T.V. Prettiest thing I ever did see!" about a zillion times over the last few months I finally talked Pop in to one. We bought it from Fitzgerald's up in Tucson just last weekend, the first of its kind in the entire white ghetto. Now that's somethin' a kid could be mighty proud of! Ma, she didn't care much for T.V., saying it was a "horrible waste of a mind," and that a person could be doing a lot more useful stuff besides starring blankly at some picture tube. What a load of garbage! Hello! This is the twentieth century calling. She obviously never experienced the utter satisfaction of watching a great western or maybe one of them new outer space shows with those mind-boggling special effects? How do they make those people "transport" from one planet to another right before your eyes? Amazing! I knew if she would just stop wasting all that time cooking and cleaning and washing and *disciplining*, she'd have a lot more time to enjoy the finer things in life, like, say, color T.V., for example. I really don't understand it.

Anyways, that "Space Age" remote control that I told ya about earlier, was a way out, super cool new invention right up there with the light bulb, the telephone and the slip'n slide, as far as I was concerned. It didn't look like much, I gotta say, just a small, plastic, brown box with a little screen on one end and two long shiny buttons on top that said "up" and "down," but when you pushed 'em they made a sound like someone dropping their change all over the floor, and the channel knob on the T.V. would magically start to turn to the next show! It was almost too good to be true. Especially now, with the new "independent station" outta Nogales giving us five full channels to pick from. The only problem was that it wasn't quite perfected yet, and sometimes when you actually *did* drop some change on the ground, or anything else for that matter, that made a loud "clank!" that channel knob would hear it and start spinning like crazy.

This "living color" business wasn't perfect, neither, and sometimes the folks on T.V. would have this pulsating pink glow all around 'em that followed wherever they went, kinda like that dust cloud around Pig Pen. Just for fun, me and Pop started pretending it was a mega force field like the one we'd seen on an episode of "Lost in Space." Now *that* was somethin' that your average black and white characters could only dream about!

I know that new Zenith was pretty much just a big brown formica box on four skinny legs with a small piece of gold material stuck on front to cover up the speaker, but to me it was a real thing of beauty; five channels of heaven, that is if you count PBS as a channel, of course.

Well, it was five-thirty, and me and Pop started watching old, "That's the way it is," Cronkite to see what was up. He was talking in that phony-baloney low voice of his about a bunch of long hairs, as Pop called 'em, making a big hullabaloo on some college campus again.

"You know, if those kids spent half as much time studying as they did belly-aching, they'd all have masters degrees by now," Pop said to himself, shaking his head. Pop didn't care much for hippies; lazy people and whiners, neither.

After a bit, here comes Ma with a big, piping hot bowl of lentil and spinach soup. Oh yum! Just what the doctor ordered when you were half-starved from a long day of bike riding, Parcheesi, and capture the flag.

I sadly stared down at my dinner of brown goop with assorted green slim balls as Ma said, "Eat that all up young man and maybe, just maybe you won't catch your death of cold."

I glanced over in the kitchen and saw the two executioner's helpers giving me the evil eye. Maybe that was the plan? They would make me eat a dinner so horribly disgusting that I would barf myself to death! Boy, what I wouldn't do for a chilidog or two. I thought about trying to sneak some to Dodger who had his no good begging head stuck between my legs just like always during dinner since he was always up for a bite of anything no matter how vile, but I couldn't come up with no way to sneak him soup 'cept to let him just stick his face right in the bowl. That seemed too chancy, already having two strikes against me, so I just picked up the bowl with one hand, held my nose with the other, and poured that lousy liquid down my throat in two or three big gulps.

After breaking out in a cold sweat and almost upchucking a time or two, my poor insides finally stopped doing the twist, and I leaned over and asked in a pitiful, weak voice, "Hey Pop, do ya think it'd be okay, if I went over to good old Jag's tonight for some fun?" It was getting near seven and I didn't want to be late for the big meeting.

"You might be pushing it tonight, pal, if you know what I mean," he answered and kind of waved his hand towards the kitchen.

"Yeah, but it's the beginning of summer vacation and all the guys are going out to horse around a little," I kinda whimpered as I bent over to scratch Dodger's ear.

"I know Johnny-boy, but you kind of messed up, and Mom's not going to forget about it that easy. She's probably going to say no this time, champ."

I shot a quick glance back through the kitchen to see if Biggy Rat, Snidely Whiplash, or Commander McBragg had caught wind of our conversation. Luckily they were side tracked, gossiping about the new second grade teacher and the amount of facial hair she had.

"I guess I understand," I said real pathetic-like, while continuing to pet the mutt. "But what do *you* say, Pop?"

With that I looked up real sheepish and gave 'im a little half smile, and after a few seconds he smiled back real wide and said, "I say you better high-tail it out that front door before your mom catches on, and make sure you are back by nine."

Well that's all I needed to hear, and I jumped up and lit out for the front door fast as I could. Dodger got spooked and chased after me and tried to bite me in the butt but I was too quick, and as I dodged his sharp teeth I turned and yelled, "Thanks, Pop!" and slammed the door behind me.

I was across the street, through the gap between the Nelson's and the Monroe's, and into the alley before the three war lords in the kitchen ever knew what hit 'em, and though I figured once in the alley I was pretty safe, I kept up a slow trot for another ten or twenty yards just to make sure.

It was one of them desert summer nights when the moon is full and it looks like a giant communion wafer sitting way up high in the sky. I'd never told Ma that, though. She'd have about two hemorrhages and call me sack-religious and make me say about a thousand rosaries or somethin'. She's real touchy when it comes to any church kinda stuff, if ya know what I mean, and I soon came to realize it was best to avoid the whole subject if at all possible.

There were still some thin wispy clouds in the sky and once in a while they'd float across that moon and darken things up a good bit, giving me a case of the heebee-jeebees. It didn't help that them obnoxious Cicadas were chirping up a storm way off in some Palo Verde trees, making it sound like you were walking right through some gigantic buzz saw. The air had that musty desert smell from the earlier rain, and every now and then I could hear one of them nasty Colorado River Toads, the ones that looked like giant green cow pies with eyes and are poisonous to dogs, croaking their disgusting hearts out as I got closer to the wash that ran along Chantilly Street. It reminded me of the time when I was just a kid and Dodger just a pup, and one of them toads got in the back yard while we was playing. Well as me and Dodge went over to check 'im out, here comes Ma, flying outta the kitchen like some escapee from the nut house or somethin', screaming at the top of her lungs at us to stay away, and then with one quick swat with her frying pan, splattered that frog to smithereens and then flung it over the wall all in one fluid motion. It was pretty impressive, I gotta admit. As you can see, Ma didn't take too kindly to any of her own being threatened no how.

I slowed on down to a nice relaxing pace now, and picked up a few good throwing stones along the way to try my aim out on the old Saguaro cactus that sat aways off in the middle of the vacant lot. It was huge, maybe forty to fifty feet high with all kinds of arms sticking out all over. I heard somewheres them Sahuaros only got one new arm every hundred years or so, and if that's true this monster gottta be from the Dark Ages! A few weeks back some of the cackling hens down at the town square were saying how it won some kinda award from Arizona Highways Magazine as the largest Saguaro in southern Arizona. I guess us guys should maybe show her more respect, but she was such a nice target. After four or five tries I tagged her pretty good and solid, and a cactus wren flew outta one of the holes and straight at me, squawking and flapping its wings over head to try and scare me off. I figured she must've been sitting on a nest and was none too happy about me banging on her nursery.

I ran off down the alley and turned up the street towards Jagger's, and then after a block or so here comes Ira up from the schoolyard saying he heard from some of the littler neighborhood kids that last weekend Neil and his family had gone down to Nogales on the Mexican side just south of Santa Elena, and he had smuggled in a mess of fireworks. Word was it warn't just some little black cats, neither, but bottle rockets, cherry bombs, Roman candles and maybe even an M-80's or two, which were rumored to pack as much punch as a quarter stick of dynamite and had a water proof fuse to boot! That made 'em perfect for underwater operations like neighborhood swimming pools, city fountains, or even the school toilettes when you absolutely, positively had to have the next day off.

After hearing the news I couldn't hardly contain myself and me and Big I raced all out toward Jag's. Ira licked me, as usual, him being the fifty-yard dash champion of Seward School and all, but he sure wasn't the only three-time Presidential Physical Fitness Award winner around these parts, now was he? Not by a long shot, 'cause that would be me, and I had them cherished patches sitting right on top of my shelf to prove it. Now the other fellas could handle all the push-ups and sit-ups and long jump and stuff, 'cept for Rosie who just didn't have the right "body habitus" for that sorta stuff according to Mr. Starr the P.E. instructor, but the softball toss was the event that separated the men from the boys, and I just so happened to have a cannon for an arm. You could ask any kid in Saguaro Little League. Pop says it's a God given gift and not somethin' that you could learn or acquire in any way. So I had that going for me, which was pretty cool.

Anyway, Ira and I turned down Jag's alley at full speed, and there sitting behind the tall oleander hedge that ran along his back wall was our pride and joy, the Tash-ma-hall and Buckingham Palace all rolled up into one, the official clubhouse of the S.S.B.'s, the Seward School Bombers. That's what we called ourselves, in case you've been living in Siberia or Bisbee or somewheres, and hadn't heard of us, yet. We came up with the name one day during recess, when we were kicking balls as high as we could, trying to make 'em come down and konk kids on the head. We discovered this was loads of fun and took quite a bit of skill, too, plus the playground monitor couldn't prove you were up to nuthin', 'cause we could just say we were kicking the ball to one of our pals that was strategically placed next to our potential victims. One day there were so many of them red, blubbery kickballs in the air over the playground that Neil said it looked like one of them bombing raids from World War II, and the Seward School Bombers were born.

The clubhouse I was telling ya about, was made mostly outta old wood slates we got from lettuce crates I'd swiped from Pop's produce warehouse. It was about four foot high and maybe eight feet across and had a roof made of aluminum siding we'd snatched from the alley over behind old Mrs. Simpson's house after she got through remodeling last year. We painted it up bright red, mostly 'cause it was the only color we could find, and always gave it a brand new coat the first day of summer vacation as a kinda ritual. Sitting proudly above the little door were the letters "S.S.B." that we had "borrowed" from different mailboxes around the White Ghetto, and right under that, "No Sissies Allowed!" in blue chalk. I guess it might not've looked like much to just anybody, but to us it was just swell, a home away from home, and a place to call our own.

As me and Big I crawled in, there was, Jag, Rosie and Neil, looking none too happy with us for keeping 'em waiting, and two other kids that you haven't met yet. The first one's name was Bampu Boto, or somethin' close, and he was new in the neighborhood. He was kind of a goofy looking kid, to tell ya the truth, small and wiry with curly black hair, humongous buck teeth, and horn-rimmed glasses thick as the bottom of mason jars that made his eyes look like two big black olives when you looked at 'em head on. After awhile, though, the thing about old Bampu that really stuck out, was that he was a complete, and hopeless nervous wreck. He'd fidget nonstop, adjusting his glasses this way and then that or smacking his lips or blinking his eyes real hard, over and over, and the whole time scratching up a storm. It could get real annoying after awhile if ya know what I mean, and before you knew it *you'd* start itching all over and carrying on, just from watching 'im. Sometimes when things really got dicey, he'd just take his glasses off, not wanting to see what was gonna happen next. He had just moved here from one of them far off countries like Pakistan or Indiana, where the folks all looked white but only had this real dark brown suntan, and talked like they had a mouth full of marbles or somethin'. Some of 'em even walked around with what looked like a "red hot" stuck in the middle of their forehead for some unknown reason, and that's the God's honest truth--I seen it once on P.B.S. When we first seen old Bampu hanging around school we got real excited, thinking we finally got the negro kid we needed to make our "ghetto" official, but Neil said he didn't count. After hanging out with 'im a little these last couple of weeks there was one other thing that hit you like a ton of bricks; he was sharp as a tack. In fact he was so smart that Neil said it was darn right *"creepy"* and guess what, the name stuck. Creepy could figure out all kinds'a cool stuff, like how long it would take for somethin' to hit some kid on top of the head if you dropped it from a certain height, or how high you needed to throw a water balloon to make it come down smack dab on top of the school principal's car as it was going down the street. Really useful information that a kid needed to go about his day. He said it all had to do with X equals one-half A-T somebody, how hard gravity pulls at ya, the laws of taking a physic, and some guy named Newton that Rosie recognized right off as being a world famous cookie maker. He was just plain amazing. His dad was a professor at the University of Arizona up in Tucson and he had two brothers that were a lot older than he was that already had kids of their own, and were supposed to be big shots at some top secret government scientific program. I figured right off old Creepy was there tonight to help with the details of Neil's plan, which we were all eagerly waiting to hear. I guess you could call 'im a special technical advisor to the S.S.B.'s.

The other kid that was sitting in the clubhouse I could barely see, 'cause he was hiding behind his best pal Rosie, as usual, and his name was Mark Cooper. Coop had one special trait too; he was scared stiff of everything, didn't really matter what, bugs, girls, the lunch lady, you name it. Not only that, but as soon as things got kinda touch and go, he got a horrible case of uncontrollable hiccups! In fact, Ira said that of all the chicken-sh!#s (I ain't allowed to say cuss words, but you get the picture) in the world, Cooper was the chicken-sh!#iest, and that earned 'im one of Neil's classic nicknames--Chicken Coop. He was an average size kid with long stringy blond hair that hung down in his eyes, with a few freckles scattered here and there, though it was tough to tell where the freckles left off and the dirt began. He was a pretty odd kid with a bunch of odd ways, like when things weren't going his way he tended to start banging his head against the nearest hard surface. I ain't sure why, Ma says it was a way of trying to "externalize" his frustrations. Last year in math he "externalized" so hard during a pop quiz, he nearly knocked hisself silly, and now he's gotta have a pillow strapped to his desktop at all times, which is kinda embarrassing and all, but he says it comes in right handy for a quick cat nap during slide show presentations and history movies and such. The one other thing about Coop, I can't ever remember a time when he didn't have chapped lips, and I've known 'im since he was three. Not just the little dry and flaky kind, neither, but the full-blown, cover half your chin and all the way up to your nose from non-stop licking kind! You know what I mean? Seems there's always at least one kid like him in every neighborhood. Don't it? His pop was the pharmacist in town which was a good thing, on account 'a the fact that he was always sniffling and sneezing and rubbing his eyes, and talking all stuffy, like someone had shoved a French fry way up each nostril, and he could sure use some pills to help 'im out once in a while. Too bad it seems medical science hadn't quite caught up to what was ailing old Coop just yet. He never said much of anything, either, not wanting to call attention too much to hisself, I guess, but when he did, it was usually somethin' straight outta one'a his favorite cartoons like, "Sufferin' Succotash!" or, "I'll make mincemeat outta that mouse!" which was probably for the best on account'a the fact that poor Coop was about as dull as Creepy was sharp, if ya catch my drift. But even for all that, and God only knows why, I had a good feeling about old Coop, like one day if the chips were down and we really needed 'im, he'd somehow come through. I truly doubt any of the other fellas shared these same thoughts.

Now that we were all here, Neil knelt forward, cleared off a part of the dirt floor in front of 'im with the palm of his hand, and while shining a flashlight down, motioned for us all to gather round.

"Listen up girls, here's what's up," he said. But as I took a closer look at 'em I noticed his hair was all wet and stuck straight up.

"What's with the boofont hairdo?" I asked, much to his dismay.

"Oh, that tallywacker of a big brother of mine got sore at me for wearing his love beads and pretending I was Gina Lollabrigida, so he gave me a twirly. (A twirly was when some big kid grabbed you by the heals and stuck your head in the toilet and then flushed it.)

"Gross! Man that guy's a real animal!"

"Tell me about it. I almost puked three times! Anyways, hush up, 'cause here's what's what, we're hitting back at that pissant Nancy Cole and her mutant family, and we're hitting back hard! Her days of making our lives miserable are over!"

So *that* was it. Nancy Cole, just the name sent shivers down my spine, like a hideous shriek in a horror movie. She was queen of the class tattletales and totally despised by every boy that bent the school rules even just a little. The last week of school, for example, she single-handedly ruined a swell plan that Neil had cooked up to sneak out at lunch break and go over to El Guero's taco stand to eat some fresh green corn tamales instead of the purple roast beef and canned spinach they were serving at the Sewer. This, of course, was strictly forbidden along with just about any other activity that could possibly be the least bit fun, and once old Nancy got a whiff of it she went straight to El Generalissimo, which is what we called our battleaxe of a principal, Mrs. Wagner. Neil had spent days working out the finest detail, leaving nuthin' to chance. He brought wire cutters to school, and each day at recess would cut just one link in the fence so as not to call attention to hisself, eventually making a space big enough to crawl through, and mapped out the movements of the playground monitors to know when his best chance to sneak out would be. When the big day finally came, he yelled out, " There's a dead packrat in the girls bathroom!" for a sure fire diversion, but as he turned to run something strange happened, his legs were moving like crazy but he wasn't going no where. That was because El Generalissimo had snuck up behind 'im and was now lifting 'im off the ground by the belt loop of his jeans, with one hand!

Well, they headed off to The Dungeon, what we called her office, just like that, Neil's legs and arms flailing away, and Mrs. Wagner carrying him along with about as much effort as if she was carrying a newborn kitten or somethin'!

He never would say what kinda punishment he got, although we had a pretty good idea when he came back from her office with his nose running like a sieve, and his eyes beat red, and him squirming in his seat like a worm on a fishhook the whole rest of the day. Yep, it was pretty clear to us all that Neil had received the capital punishment of elementary school; butt swats. Rumor had it that El Generalissimo's got herself a custom made paddle, big as a garbage can lid, with it's own custom carrying case and a special grip that fit that fat hand just right. There were holes all down the middle for the air to go through for less wind resistance, according to Bampu, so as she could swing it just that much harder, inflicting the most pain per swat possible. It was also said that it was painted black with a red skull and crossbones square in the middle, and the words, "Payback Time" written all along the edge. So now you know why Neil had it in for good old Nancy, and if I know him, he was gonna go for the juggler.

"I guess ya have to admit, Neil, you haven't exactly been Prince Charming when it came to Nancy, neither," I said smiling his way. "Remember the day she wore those red high heels to school that were so small her fat feet hung out all over the sides, and you said she must go to the same shoe salesman as Porky Pig's girlfriend! She was so embarrassed she didn't come to school for a week." That got the guys to chuckling.

"Sure, but that was an honest mistake, Johnny C., you know that. Anyone would'a noticed the uncanny resemblance," he answered, laughing, and giving me a wink. " Now here's the deal," he said, turning to the rest of the guys. " I plan to throw everything I've got at that big mouth twit and her weasely family, and this time I ain't just whistling Dixie." With that Neil took out a brown paper bag from under his shirt and dumped it all out in front of us. Well, there was a loud gasp of amazement at the haul of major explosives we saw lying there in front of us in the dirt, and Neil started up one of them big, low evil-scientist type laughs as he pointed out the black cats, bottle rockets, cherry bombs and Roman candles he had managed to smuggle outta Mexico.

"I don't believe it!" I screamed. "That's enough fire power to wipe every commi off the face of the planet!"

"Exactly", Neil answered. "And that's just what we're going to do to the Coles! We'll make sure that little maggot thinks twice before she messes with the S.S.B.'s again. Okay, now pay attention 'cause here's the plan to end all plans. First, we stake out the house and try to figure out what rooms Nancy, her mom and dad and that snot nosed little brother of hers are smelling up. Then, we put black cats with delayed fuses at each one of those windowsills."

"What in the heck's a delayed fuse?" we all asked.

Neil got this sinister smile on his face all over again, and pulled out a pack of cigarettes that he had lifted from his big brother Barry for just this occasion. We all looked at him and then at each other with blank stares.

Seeing we weren't catching on, he turned to Creepy and said, "Professor, will you please explain the details of the delayed fuse to the special ed class."

"Well it is quite simple actually," started Bampu with that weirdo, garbled, sing-songy accent. "We know the tobacco burns at a constant rate that I have earlier calculated as five millimeters per minute. Therefore, we make a hole large enough for the fuse of this specific firecracker along the shaft of the cigarette at a predetermined distance from its tip, and then pass the fuse through the hole, as such," he continued as he demonstrated with one of the cigarettes he had already fixed up, while we looked on dumbfounded. "Then, we light the cigarette thusly, and give it a few small puffs to get it started," which he did, followed by horrible spastic coughing which gave us all a good laugh 'til Neil shot us the evil eye. "And then we can reliably estimate when the fuse will ignite and the firecracker will explode," Creepy finished up with a small, satisfied grin, then adjusted his glasses and started itching hisself all over again, as Chicken Coop blurted out, "Wow, just like Professor Whoopee!"

"How come we always hafta do everything all backasswards? That's what I'd like to know," Ira scoffed in his usual disgusted tone. "Why don't we just light them firecrackers, throw 'em through the front door and run like heck, just like always?"

We all nodded our agreement.

"Man, you guys don't know sh!# from shinola!" Neil barked back.

"What the hecks shinola? Rosie asked.

"Well I ain't certain, but apparently it don't look nuthin' like sh!#" Neil answered quickly, and then went off on us again. "I don't know why I keep banging my head against the wall trying to come up with these bitchin' plans, just to waste 'em on a bunch of retarded ingrates! *Your* ideas are little kid's stuff. *This here* is soo-ffisticated military technique. This way, we place the explosives exactly where we want 'em, and then take cover and watch the show from a safe distance, just like real army generals. Also, we can stagger the times that the black cats go off, so when Nancy and her lame-brained family come out looking for us, they'll be racing from one explosion to the next, and we'll be nowheres to be found!"

A smile started to creep onto all the guy's faces.

"And that's not all," he said in his best game show host voice. "After all the firecrackers go off, we'll deliver the knock out punch before they can recover with all the bottle rockets and Roman candles we can place around the property," Neil finished, crossing his arms over his chest, nodding his head and looking mighty proud.

"That's b-b-brilliant!" Jagger shouted, giving Neil a hard slap on the back that he didn't look too crazy about. "One of your all time b-b-best."

"Thanks, Jag, I appreciate it," he said, "But it's all in a day's work, ya know."

"Let's give one big cheer and get this show on the road!" I said as I stuck my hand in the middle of the group with everyone else doing the same, and with a rousing, "All for naught! And not for long!" which was our official club motto, by the way, we anxiously crawled out the door of the clubhouse and started down the alley.

We were all in a pretty giddy frame of mind, thinking how we would finally get even with that bigmouth Nancy, and all, but as we got closer it was starting to look like Rosie and Chicken Coop were a little less enthusiastic than the rest of us, which was pretty much the norm when we were doing anything not completely on the up and up.

They were walking along with their heads down, dragging their feet real slow at the back of the pack, and finally Rosie got up his nerve and said, "Neil, are you sure about this? We can get in big trouble if we get caught. And besides, I'm not allowed to play with matches or fireworks, and I'm not supposed to be anywhere near cigarettes."

Chicken Coop slowly poked his head around the side of Rosie's huge shoulder, nodding his agreement.

Neil stopped dead in his tracks, whipped around and glared at Rosie, who also stopped short, and then backed up a few steps to shield hisself from what he was afraid was coming.

"Are you kidding me? You've got to be kidding, Rosie, right? Don't you want to get back at Nancy for always ruining our fun?"

"Well, yeah," Rosie mumbled. Chicken Coop was nowhere to be seen.

"Don't you remember how she told on you for eating that candy bar in class?"

"I sure do," he answered, a little louder.

"What about how she ratted on you for shooting spit wads in the cafeteria?

"She's got a big mouth," Rosie said firmly, with Chicken Coop sneaking a peek at Neil from behind 'im.

"And how about when she blabbed to everyone in class how much you weighed after our school physical?"

That did it. Rosie looked up with fire in his eyes, clenched his teeth, puffed up his flabby cheeks and screamed out, "Let's get that little maggot!"

We all cheered out loud once more, even Cooper, and were back on our way. Rosie sure was touchy when it came to his glandular problem.

# Chapter Three

## WE GO ON ATTACK

As we made our way to the Cole's place, we stuck mostly to the alleys and breezeways between houses to keep from being spotted. Neil said all top-secret military operations were run like this and we went along okay with it for a while, but the garbage hadn't been picked up that day and with the rain and all, the smell was getting pretty rancid. As our stomachs started to turn and our faces turned to green, against our commanding general's advice, we decided to try our luck in the streets and just ditch quick into the desert if anybody happened to come along. Neil said it was our choice, but if some spy happened to see us we'd surely have to bound and gag them, and if they didn't swear allegiance to the S.S.B.'s on their mother's *and* grandmother's grave (Just in case their ma abandoned them when they were a baby and they were raised by their grandma. That Neil sure thought off everything) then we'd have no choice but to have to kill 'em.

"Are you sure we gotta kill them? Ain't that a little severe?" I asked.

"Of course ya gotta kill 'im! Man, don't you guys know nuthin' about commando warfare? This ain't "Ring around the rosie," ya know."

We were all moving along pretty well now, really hoping not to run into any spies, and thinking about how nice it was gonna be to make old Nancy squirm a little for a change, when all of the sudden Jagger turns to me and said, "Hey, watch it!"

"What's wrong?" I answered, my heart jumping into my throat.

"You almost stepped on m-my moon shadow."

"Your what?"

"M-m-my moon shadow. Look," he said, as he pointed down at the street.

He was right, he did have a shadow, and all of the rest of us did, too. A kinda grey and hazy one stretching out to the west, not dark and sharp like a daytime one. It was funny, but none of us had ever noticed one before at night. Jag said his dad had told 'im before he went to the war, that moon shadows were something very special and that only kids had 'em, and if a kid ever stopped acting like a kid, getting too serious about stuff and all, then his moon shadow would disappear and never come back. But as long as you did have one, it would always keep you safe when you were out at night, and, here's the most important thing, you should never, ever step on one 'cause that was terrible bad luck and somethin' horrible would happen, sure enough.

Well none of us had ever heard any of that before, but if old Doc Howell said so, who were we to doubt it. Anyway, it was pretty neat having a shadow just for kids, and to tell you the truth, we could use all the help we could get tonight.

Of course, the first chance I got I pretended to stomp all over Jagger's moon shadow just to get 'im ticked, and he chased me all around a while and gave me a pretty nasty Indian burn on my arm before Neil yelled at us to cut it out before we completely blew our cover.

We kept plodding along, walking single file so as to be harder to spot, and every once in a while diving into the bushes to avoid a car. Once, old Mrs. Simpson came creeping down the street with her miniature wiener dog Bella, or Bella-Lagosi as we called her 'cause she was such a terror and about the most obnoxious yapper that there every was, and we all crouched

behind an oleander hedge at the corner of Camino Seco and Pantano. We thought we'd given 'em the slip, but Rosie's big rear end was sticking out a bit, and that good for nuthin' Bella caught sight of it, which wasn't all that hard to do, and made a bee-line straight for poor Rosie's butt, barking up a storm, and snipping around a little too close to his manhood for comfort. Rosie, being on all fours, didn't dare turn around, but with beads of sweat popping up all over his forehead, shot us a worried look, not knowing what that screwball dog was gonna do to 'im back there. We tried to shush her and pet her, and I even bonked her on the nose with a pebble, but nuthin' would shut that little rat up. Well, just as the old lady started to walk over to see what all the commotion was about, Rosie reluctantly pulled outta his pocket a graham cracker he'd been munching on earlier, and flung it in the middle of the street. That did it! Bella went for the tasty treat like she hadn't eaten for a year, and before she could get back to harassing us, we crawled down the back of the hedge and then ran the rest of the way up Nancy's street. We heard her start to barking all over again as we were well away, and Neil said to remind 'im to come up with a plan to get back at that pipsqueak pain in the butt, too.

We stopped in the cul-de-sac in front of Nancy's house to check out what we were up against, a gigantic adobe place with wood beams sticking outta the top, and a flat roof, just like most of the houses in the neighborhood, with one 'a them red wood plank fences all around the sides and back with the spaces between the slats that were just big enough to sneak a look through. There was a big roomy carport stuck on the east side of the house and two wide picture windows on each side of the heavy mesquite front door. In the back was a large sliding glass door opening from the family room, a long red cement covered porch, and Nancy's pride and joy, a built-in swimming pool, the only one around these parts as Nancy was sure to always remind ya. Us guys all had whatcha call above ground pools, you know, the ones that have them tin frames that ya put up first, and then this big plastic lining that looked like a huge garbage bag, that fit down in the middle. The problem was, that frame wasn't too strong and was always buckling and letting the water spill out, especially if some blubber-butt jumped in, or the plastic lining, sure as I am saying this, would tear and spring a leak that was impossible to patch and would end up flooding the whole backyard before you could do anything about it, killing all the grass and ruining your summer all in less than twenty minutes! That was, of course, if your pool was lucky enough to make it through all the crazy monsoon storms. When that howling wind got a hold of it, before you could say, "I ain't in Kansas no more," your beloved pool, the only escape a kid had from the deadly desert heat, was a mangled pile of sheet metal lying in the corner of your backyard. Nancy, naturally, never had to worry about none of that, but did she ever invite any of us over for a nice refreshing swim after we had nuthin' left but a wet spot and fond memories? Not on your life!

Neil and Creepy were standing off a few feet away from the rest of us chatting it up, and after finally ironing out a few last details, they walked over to us and Neil said, "Men, I know this is a dangerous mission and some of you may not make it back alive."

I looked over at Jag and he started up with that big goofy grin again, and I started to chuckle a bit 'til Neil gave a big "U-HUM," and shot me this *very* dirty look. After that our heads snapped forward and we stood at attention best we could.

"That's better", Neil continued. "Now as I was saying this is a dangerous and complicated mission and it will take complete team work to pull it off. If anyone thinks they will not be able to do their duties, for whatever reason, they should back out now."

Everyone's eyes turned toward Chicken Coop, who took a big swallow and then started to hiccup a bit, but before he could say a word, Neil said, "That settles it, we're all in, just as I always expected of the S.S.B.'s. Now listen up and listen up good," and he started giving us our combat instructions. We were gonna work in teams of two, with me and Jag, and Rosie and Coop as the bottle rocket brigades. For any of you that ain't aware, a bottle rocket is basically a firecracker on about a ten-inch stick, and when you light 'em, they shoot out about fifteen feet and then explode over your target, so you can use 'em like artillery or guided missiles. You didn't want to hold 'em after they were lit on account of the thrust coming out the back could scorch your fingers pretty good, so we usually stuck 'em in a pop bottle that was propped up at just the right angle to hit what you were shooting for, and then lit 'em. Our mission was to set 'em up in strategic spots along the front of the house, and Creepy handed us five bottle rockets apiece, and Jag and I took the east side of the house with Rosie and Coop taking care of the western front. Creepy and Big I made up somethin' call a "special tactical force brigade," and they were responsible for setting the black cats with the delayed fuses all along the front windows of the house. Neil said he'd set up the roman candles and then head over to "H.Q." which stood for "headquarters," a big mesquite tree right across the street, and "coordinate the attack." Then he pulled out a pack of cigarettes, the black cats and a lighter he also swiped from his big brother Barry, and said, "Let's roll!"

We all scattered to do our jobs, staying low and quiet to avoid being detected by the enemy. Jag and I found the soda bottles we needed in no time flat lyin' around the alley and desert behind the house, and started to set 'em up in a half-moon kinda pattern around the front and side of our target. Jagger whispered, "This is g-gonna be great!" and I nodded back and gave him a quick wink. We could see Rosie and Coop finishing up their work across the way so that the whole front of the house would be pretty much covered, and I'm glad to say the hiccups coming from Chicken Coop's way were getting fewer and farther between. Creepy and Big I began their covert activity by first crawling up to the front of the Cole place, and then poking a hole in just the right spot of the cigarette, gently weaving the fuse through and placing the entire contraption on window sills around the house. Neil said that by having them black cats explode outside the glass, it would make for a bigger blast inside the house, and the windows rattling up a storm would be an extra scary effect. He really was a devious little devil, when you came to think about it, and I was glad he was on our side, at least for now.

After about twenty minutes we were all ready for action; Lieutenants Johnnie C, Rosie, Coop, Big I, and Jagger, with Supreme Commander Neil, as he *insisted* we all call 'im. The anticipation was getting unbearable as we waited for Field Marshall Creepy to light the cigarettes. I could see 'im, fidgeting all over like a madman, take a little puff on the last one at the far end of the house to make sure it was good and hot, and then start having a conniption fit or two trying not to cough. Finally, after the feeling had passed, he covered up his mouth and hustled back over to where we was all slouched down in the cul-de-sac behind a particularly pesky patch of prickly pear cactus. Our "Supreme Commander" then ordered us back to the alley to set up our observation post where he said we could watch, "in glory," the enemy's defeat between the slats of the old wood fence. All but one of us, that was, on account of he needed a volunteer for the most dangerous job of all; lighting the bottle rockets and roman candles along the front of the house after Nancy and her folks came outside to snoop around, already p.o.'ed to the max and ready to scalp someone. We all quick stared down to the ground and started to squirm after hearing that, not being too excited about maybe getting caught, completely humiliated by Nancy, and likely grounded for the whole summer by our own folks. Everyone 'cept Jag, who stepped forward without so much as a thought saying, "I'm your m-m-man, sir," with a crisp salute and a click of his heels.

Neil answered, "Well done, mister!" while standing at attention and returning the salute, then pulled him aside, presented him with his brother's lighter like he was giving him the Congressional Medal of Honor, whispered some instructions in his ear that caused Jag to get that same old goofy grin on his face, and off he went.

The rest of us headed back to the alley, crouched down nice and low, army style. I looked back over my shoulder at Jag as he crawled along in the opposite direction and gave 'im the thumb's-up, knowing darn well this could be the last time I'd see my pal 'til school started up if he got nabbed. He just waved the lighter back at me, cool as a cucumber, the moonlight reflecting yellow in his mangled glasses, giving them the look of some cool night vision goggles, before he slipped back behind a creosote bush. He was really some kinda kid.

We made it into the alley without too much commotion, 'cept when Rosie accidentally gave Neil a flat tire and received a nasty monkey bump for his efforts, and took up some good spots behind the back fence to watch all of the action. From there we had a clear shot through the big sliding glass door off the back patio, and sure enough there was Mr. Cole, Nancy, and her dweeb of a little brother Timmy in the living room, peaceful as can be. Mr. Cole was resting in a recliner, reading the paper and puffing on a big fat cigar, whose smoke was collecting overhead like his own personal rain cloud. Timmy and Nancy were sitting on the floor, eating ice cream and watching some T.V. show that looked like, "Rat Patrol," but it was darn hard to tell with the screen flickering like mad from this distance. Ever wonder why that happens?

Every now and then, Timmy would take a break from his dessert and start picking his nose, and then Nancy, being the dainty thing that she was, would reach over and slug 'im a good one, square on the shoulder. Timmy would let out a screech we could hear all the way out where we was, then punch her back, and after a pretty good pounding Mr. Cole would yell something and they would both straighten up and get back to eating before the whole show would repeat itself a little bit down the road. There weren't hide nor hair of Mrs. Cole anywhere, and we figured she must've been in the kitchen finishing up the dinner dishes.

Just about then, Creepy pulls out his Timex and started up a ten second count down to when the first delayed fuse would explode, and Neil turned to us and said, "Men, you will all go down as heroes of the White Ghetto, and will do the S.S.B.'s proud tonight."

We still weren't completely certain of all that was supposed to happen once the attack got started, so Neil said to sit tight and follow him when he gave the signal. Old Creepy was finishing up his counting and we all glued our eyes on that back window and waited, but when it got down to "three, two, one, zero!"…There was nuthin'. We kept watching, giving it a little more time to get the show on the road, but still there was nuthin', and by this time poor Creepy was looking mighty hot around the collar. We didn't want to look back over our shoulder at our Supreme Commander in fear that he might go ballistic any second, and I'm sure Creepy was thinking he wished he was back in Indiana with the "red-hot heads," but just as Neil was reaching for the Creep's neck…KABOOM! Every window in the house shook as we watched with our eyes peeled and our mouths wide open, as first Mr. Cole's newspaper and then the kid's ice cream bowls went flying so high they near splattered the ceiling! Mr. Cole's cigar dropped outta his mouth and landed in his lap, almost starting his pajamas on fire, Timmy leaped almost as high as his dessert with his finger pushed so far up his nose he was close to giving hisself a frontal lobotomy, while Nancy's eyes got big as saucers and she looked truly horrified for a few glorious moments, but in no time flat her eyes snapped back to those sinister slits that we had all come to know, as her devious little mind was already figuring out what was up and who was probably responsible. After that they all started screaming and hollering and carrying on, and making all kinds of crazy hand gestures at each other, although we couldn't hear hardly any of it being outside and all, which made the whole crazy scene that much more funny. Mrs. Cole came racing into the room drying her hands on her apron and trying to console little Timmy, who continued to run in circles over and over again, crying and flinging his hands every which way. Then Mr. Cole, after calming his frantic family down a bit, said somethin' to them all and they all headed for the front door. That's when Neil whispered, "Okay Men, follow me," and we all slithered along the fence to the east side of the house towards the carport and side door.

We found a good spot behind that same oleander hedge we had used to ditch old lady Simpson and Bella on our way over, and I could make out with the help of the porch light, the Cole's all standing in the front yard and peering hard out into the darkness. They were trying their darnedest to catch a glimpse of whoever was responsible.

Then Mr. Cole says, "Who's out here?" with as much authority in his voice as he could muster and Nancy says, "That better not be you, Neil Wales!"

We all shot a look over at Neil who whispered that he was expecting that kind of reaction since he got blamed for everything that happened in the neighborhood even when he wasn't responsible, which, to tell ya the truth, wasn't very often. I tried to spot Jagger back behind the Palo Verde trees along the front of the house but he must've been hunkered down pretty good 'cause I couldn't catch a glimpse of 'im, no how. The Coles started inching up all huddled together, toward where I figured Jag was hiding, and I started to think my old pal was a goner, when all of a sudden there was another monstrous "KABOOM!" as the second black cat went off just in the nick of time against the front window. The whole family jumped up in the air in unison and after regaining their wits they all raced over, mad as a pack of hornets to see if they could catch whoever lit that one, but, of course, there weren't nobody there. Them delayed fuses was working like a charm, and after another few moments of the Coles scratching their heads and looking totally bewildered, the last black cat went off around the other corner of the house, causing them all to shriek and leap up again, and then fly around the side of the house and outta sight. I looked over at Creepy, and he was all smiles, like a crazy professor whose experiment had been a great success, and I was thinking that he had surely cemented his place as a permanent member of the S.S.B.'s with his impressive technical help on this strategic mission.

The Cole's came out from around the side of the house, looking as confused as ever, except Nancy, who looked just plain ticked. That last black cat must've been Jigger's cue, I guess, 'cause all of the sudden I spotted him scurrying out from under cover toward where we had started setting up them bottle rockets on the far side of the property. The Cole's must've seen somethin' too, 'cause they all turned quick and glared out into the darkness to their right, straining their necks and squinting up their eyes. Jag was racing along, lighting the bottle rockets and roman candles for the last part of our assault, but so far nothing had happened and Mr. Cole started walking right for where Jigger had been crouching. By then Jag was almost to this side of the house, and we could see 'im plain as day. Just after he lit the last bottle rocket in front of the carport, and Mr. Cole was snooping around where Jag had lit the first, it went off. "P-S-S-S-T KA-POW!" It flew straight over Mr. Cole's head and exploded right above where the rest of the family was standing. It was a joyous sight to see as the explosion lit up their faces to show an expression of utter horror from this new attack. Mr. Cole scurried back over to them with arms flailing all around, and they began to slowly move all scrunched up close as they could toward the carport and side door. That's when the second and third bottle rockets went off along with all the roman candles, sending them into a full, frantic sprint, with their hands on their heads and yelling enough to wake the dead! The fourth, fifth, sixth, seventh and eighth rockets flew over and

exploded, practically chasing 'em around the front of the house, into the carport and through the backdoor, which slammed behind 'em just as the last bottle rocket went off right above it.

Neil put his cupped hand under his armpit, brought his elbow down hard by his side to make the sound we all recognized as the S.S.B.'s call to retreat, and we all lit out fast as we could, still in awe at our resounding triumph over tattletales everywhere, and feeling just about as good as a kid could possibly feel. But as we raced away, Nancy, not ready to admit defeat that easy, stuck her fat head out that same backdoor, and screeched in a high pitched, frustrated voice, "I will...If you...Don't think..." and then, "I'm telling!" and then slammed the door again.

We took the alleyways back to the clubhouse, the rancid smell of the garbage not bugging us near as bad anymore, with Ira out front, and Rosie, bringing up the rear, huffing and puffing pretty good, but still with a big grin on his face.

Once we made it back safe, Neil said, "Job well done, men. You've done your platoon and your families proud this evening with your brave actions against such a horrible and formidable opponent," and then he gave us all a sharp salute.

I said I was happy how the whole thing went off mostly, but it still irked me to no end how that no good Nancy had that swell swimming pool all to herself for the whole summer, and us with nuthin' to splash around in 'cept what amounted to oversized garbage cans in our backyards.

Neil looked over at me with a satisfied smile and said, "Don't you worry your little head there, Johnny, my boy, I got that covered too. You see me and the Creep found a big bottle of laundry detergent in the carport and before you guys placed the firecrackers along the front of the house, I poured the whole darn thing into the pool filter. I figure by tomorrow them soap bubbles will be high as the house and it'll take 'em 'til Christmas to clean 'em out!" We all gave one more big cheer at this delightful news, and started to head home, when our Supreme Commander gave us one more piece of advice, "Keep your eyes peeled, and remember that enemy patrols could be around every corner."

By "enemy patrols," he meant good old Mengo, the chief of police of all of Santa Elena, which wasn't saying much, and his only deputy, cousin Pato, who was mostly deaf, and widely known to be scared stiff of anything that didn't have a skirt on, and even then only some of the time, according to Pop. They weren't all that tough to spot coming, driving around in the red and black '58 Chevy Impala squad car that Mengo's Uncle Chango left 'im when he died a few years back from something called botched-u-lism he caught from eating a bad batch of Mexican cheese. It had only one headlight that worked, the left front hubcap had rocks in it so it sounded like a cement mixer coming down the street and the only thing louder than the cherry bomb mufflers that they welded on was the Mariachi music that was always blaring from the radio with Mengo and Pato singing their lungs out right along with it. All in all, crooks and juvenile delinquents had it pretty easy in Santa Elena, I guess, but no one took too much of an advantage, not wanting to ruin a good thing.

On the way home, I walked down Chantilly street and looked over to see if I could catch a glimpse of what was going on in front of the Cole's as I passed by, being careful not to call any attention to myself. I didn't see nobody, but I could make out the muffled sound of Nancy's annoying voice screaming something about how she was going to get us, and how she'd never rest 'til we paid double for what we had done, which brought another big smile to my face and made me feel real warm and fuzzy inside.

From there I ran as fast as I could back home and snuck in the back door, tiptoeing past Pop, who was asleep in his chair with the tray still sitting on his lap, and the T.V. blaring. I noticed his dinner plate had been licked clean, and I gave Dodger a stern look as I passed by 'im, but he quickly turned away, laid his fuzzy yellow head on that green shag carpet and stared at me like he didn't have a clue what I was so upset about. Mom was already in bed, and I knew she had been asleep for a good hour or more by now, she being a true believer in the whole, "early to bed and early to rise" thing. Problem was, she insisted everyone else buy into it too, and I argued long and hard for my theory of, "sleep in late, end up great," with very little success.

I slipped past Gracie's door and into my room, took off my clothes and slid into bed, and thanked the good Lord for watching over me and the guys during our time of need, and then closed my eyes, snuggled down deep in my pillow and fell asleep as visions of bottle rockets danced in my head.

# Chapter Four

## THE BIG GAME

The next morning was glorious; the sun was out, the birds were chirping and Nancy had been taught a lesson that she wouldn't soon forget. Now I guess we all knew that sooner or later the Coles would be calling our folks to complain about last night's little fireworks show, but when you get right down to it there ain't no hard evidence against us, so the way I see it we had a fairly good chance to go scott free, for a change. Even if we was convicted, hey, it was well worth it to watch those trouble makers run around like a bunch of chickens with their heads chopped off. But as I lay there thinking them good thoughts nice and cozy, I suddenly remembered something even more wonderful if that was possible, today was Saturday and that meant baseball!

You see, Little League was a plenty big deal around here and just about all the guys played. There wasn't any football or basketball league for kids, and none of us would be caught dead playing one of them girlie sports like soccer. I mean what kinda man's game is that where you run around in bright colored outfits and knee socks for crying out loud, and if ya dare push a guy from the other team, even just a little, he immediately starts rolling around on the ground like he's gonna die any minute and here comes the referee in a get up that looks like a tuxedo with the arms and legs cut off, to politely give you a pretty colored greeting card. I ain't kidding, neither, I seen it once on Wide World of Sports! Now hockey looked pretty cool with all them fights and blood spurting all over the place and teeth getting knocked out and all, but the problem was there wasn't an ice rink for more than a hundred miles, and even if there was, nobody here would have a clue how to ice skate.

So baseball was pretty much it, and that was just fine by me. It was the All-American game after all; what's not to like? And I knew for a fact that someday I would be the next great southpaw pitcher in the Los Angeles Dodger's rotation, seeing that old Sandy's retired and opened up a spot. I'm a huge Dodger fan, you see. Partly 'cause they were a real class act, as Pop always said, and partly 'cause the Dodger games were the only ones you could get on the radio in Santa Elena. As it was, it really was a Tucson station, but on a clear crisp night, and if there weren't no thunderstorms brewing, I could pick up the signal just swell on my transistor.

I spent most of my summer nights just lying in bed with all the lights out, listening to good old Vin Scully telling his stories in between pitches about today's players and yesterday's players, and things that had happened in baseball that would make you laugh, or even make you cry, and pretty much giving a kid a great bedtime story while letting you know exactly what was going on in the game that night, just as good as if you were sitting in the stands yourself, maybe better.

Sahuaro Little League, that was us, didn't only take in teams from Santa Elena, which wouldn't be much of a league at all, but also from other small surrounding towns like Bisbee, Tombstone, Nogales and Benson. Little Beaver's Kindergarten was our team, and although the name was a bit embarrassing as you might have guessed, they were really pretty darn good folks and shelled out plenty of dough for some swell uniforms every year. They weren't just them cheap T-shirts with stuck on letters that fell off half way through the season, neither, but real, honest to goodness, button-up jerseys, just like the big-leaguers wore. They had red piping and a mean looking beaver on the front, with big old front teeth and a red cap on his head, and he was swinging a bat like he was ready to park one. We had red sleeves to wear underneath, too, but I can't remember a game that wasn't too hot to wear 'em, although Ma was always trying to force me, on account'a the one in a million chance there might be a cool breeze. We all wore red stirrup socks that were pulled up so high ya couldn't even see the top part no more but only the side, which was the style these days, in case ya didn't know. We still caught plenty of grief about our name, especially early in the season with teams saying lame stuff like, "Beavers are nuthin' but big mice", or "Isn't it nap time, Little Beavers?" But after awhile, and a few good beatings by Jagger, they pretty much kept it to themselves. It also helped that we were darn good. It kinda makes it less fun to make fun of the other team when they're beating the snot outta ya.

The best thing about the team, though, was all us pals were on it, even Neil, who swore that he couldn't stand baseball, but I guess he didn't want to miss out on the fun of beating the tar out of the rest of the league; that was right up his alley. Now some of us were better than others, no doubt about it, but that didn't really matter none, we all pulled for each other just the same and had a pretty swell time overall. Since I was kinda tall and lanky and a lefty to boot, I always played first base, ever since I was old enough to hold up the "professional size" Willie McCovey model mitt Pop bought me when I was only five. But although it was sweet playing first with all the action, and all, there was really nuthin' I loved better in the world than pitching. Just being out there on the mound with all of my guys yelling for me, and all the other guys yelling against me, and looking that batter in the eye and going at 'im with my very best stuff. That's what I'm talking about! I didn't leave nuthin' to chance, neither, and spent plenty of spring days in the backyard firing a hard ball against the wall, trying to hit a trash can lid that I had hung up with a long piece of copper wire. I figured it was pretty close to a twelve year old kid's strike zone, and I developed some pretty good heat on my fastball by throwing over and over, in and out, and up and down, and even breaking off a curveball once in a while, but not too many, I didn't want to hurt my arm at this age and throw away a sure fire hall of fame career, ya know.

Sometimes when I'd go into the stretch and stare down that old trash can lid, I'd get it in my head that it was the bottom of the ninth of the seventh game of the World Series, and it was always the Dodgers against them hated scum-bum New York Yankees, and I was the young kid reliever brought in with the bases loaded and nobody out and a one run lead to hold up. Usually, I'd just strike out the side, blowing the ball right by Ruth, Gherig and Mantle, or some other group of Yankee Hall of Famers, and then just mosey on off the mound at Yankee Stadium, cool as a cucumber, and smile real sweet and wave my hat while their obnoxious fans were balling like a bunch of babies. Sometimes, just for fun, I'd have my least favorite hotshot Yankee hit into a game ending triple play, leaving them same fans in an even worse state, and ready to commit suicide or something.

Now Pop always told me the key to pitching was just like real estate; location, location, location. And after awhile I got a fairly good idea of what he was talking about. Believe me, you didn't even want to think about throwing one right down the pipe to one of them monster kids from the West Side, no matter how much zip it had on it, or that ball wouldn't come down 'til it reached the Grand Canyon.

Like I told ya before, our team was made up mostly of kids from the white ghetto that had all been playing together since peewee league, and to tell ya the truth, we were starting to gel pretty good. I played first and pitched, Rose was catcher on account'a the fact that he was the slowest and the *widest*, Big I used to pitch, too, 'til he got the yips last year, outta the blue, in a close game against Linda's Lingerie (and we thought our name was bad!) and now played center, being so fast he could pretty much could cover the whole outfield if he had to. Jagger played third, though he couldn't catch a ground ball to save his life since he had hands like two rocks, and having that one crazy eye didn't help 'im none no matter how far he turned his head to the good side, but he was so darn tough that he would simply knock down a grounder off his chest, even a roaring rocket, and then throw the kid out at first. Creepy, to everyone's surprise, turned out to be a pretty slick fielder and so we stuck 'im over at second, while Chicken Coop played right, if you could call it that, all the while he and us both praying that the ball wouldn't come his way. Neil, who could really pick it when he felt like it, was the team shortstop; that is when he decided to show up and grace us with his presence. In left field we'd take turns playing Ricky De la Rosa and Dougie Howell, Rosie and Jag's little brothers. They were only ten and couldn't play a lick but they were nice kids and Ira kinda covered for 'em out there whenever possible.

Jag's pop who played varsity ball over at the University of Missouri way back when, had always been our coach, but since he was at the war and all, Mr. Goldstein, Ira's dad, was filling in this year. He was a little bald guy, 'cept for a little ring of hairs that were still hanging on for dear life around the edges so it looked like he had on a permanent halo, with the biggest set of forearms I had ever seen that weren't on a cartoon character. He told us he had played minor league ball in the old days with the Cubs organization and said he got them muscles from swinging a thirty-six ounce Louisville Slugger, but after a while Ira let on that was a bunch of hooey, and he really got 'em from putting together toilets in a factory back east when he was a teenager. The other funny thing about them forearms of his was that they had tattoos of half naked ladies on each side. Once Neil found out, he'd always pestered 'im to have a look at his *big muscles*, which flattered coach Goldstein to no end, but after a while I guess he caught on that warn't all we was looking at, and he started to wearing long sleeve shirts from then on, even on blazing hot days. The funny thing was, them ladies on his arms didn't look nuthin' like *Mrs. Goldstein*, not even a tad, leaving us to wonder who in the heck they were. Jagger thought maybe they were his sisters, but that didn't figure, them being half naked and all, so we were in a bit of a quandary over the whole thing, but nobody had the gumption to ask old Ira, figuring it could be a kinda touchy subject.

All of the teams played on Saturdays and usually once during the week before it got too dark, but never on a Sunday. When I asked Ma about it she said it was because God said that was the day of rest and all. I tried to tell her I got plenty of rest during all the other days of the week just fine, but she just gave me a dirty look and I decided not to ask no more about it after that.

Nope, there was nuthin' sweeter in the whole world than Saturday morning at the ballpark. We'd usually roll in about eight, still rubbing the sleep from our eyes, and there to meet us was the sweet smell of watered down infield dirt mixed with hot dogs cooking and popcorn popping over at the snack bar. There was the sound of umpires, mostly teenage boys working the early games and yelling out in their best manly voices, "You're out!" or "Stee-rike three!" and there were moms and dads cheering, and little brothers and sisters crying, and big dogs chasing little dogs, and little dogs chasing cats, and teams from all over warming up for their big games. There were only two teams from Santa Elena, it being so tiny, Little Beavers and the team from the west side of town, El Charro Mexican Restaurant, our biggest rival. It was made up mostly of big strong Mexican kids, some already bigger than their folks, and the ones that weren't all that big had rockets for arms and could run like the wind. They were tough, really tough, but even though they could intimidate most of the other teams in the league, being a Little Beaver meant you didn't back down to no one, no how, no time, and it just so happened we was playing them today, with the winner having a lock on the major's championship, and the all important town bragging rights for the whole year. Seeing that we had already split our first two games with El Charro, this would be the rubbery game, and coach Goldstein, a real Nervous Nelly to start, was already in quite a tizzy as he gathered us around the old cottonwood tree out past the left field fence to give us our pre-game pep talk. He had on his usual plaid Bermuda shorts that came down way past his knees, since he wasn't much taller than we were, a long sleeved flowery shirt, and leather sandals, which we all wished he'd stop wearing 'cause his feet were so uncommonly hairy they was giving some of the younger kids nightmares. Creepy and Coop flat out refused to sit next to him in the dug out because of them, saying every time they looked down they thought there was a tarantula getting ready to crawl up their leg! He had on his red cap with the white "B" on the front that was way too small for his enormous head, even though the elastic in the back was stretched to the limit, and no matter how many times he pulled that thing down, before you knew it, it'd start to slowly slide back up, and there it'd be, sitting on top of his bald head like a big cherry on top of a vanilla sundae.

By now, coach was stomping around considerable, waving his hands and yellin' about how big a game this was and how much was at stake and all the usual stuff that Little League coaches think their teams wanta hear. Every once in a while his cap would fall off and he'd curse and pick it up and jam it back on his head. He kept on about "winning strategies," and "goals of the game," and such, but to tell ya the truth, after a few minutes we kinda tuned it all out and started thinking more about what kinda soda and treats we was in for after the game was over. We all knew he was finished when he yelled out, "lets go get 'em men!" 'cause that's the way he always finished them talks, so we got in a circle, put our hands in the middle and screamed, "Little Beavers!" and then made some mean beaver faces by wrinkling up our noses sticking out our front teeth far as we could, and then curled up our hands like little claws out in front of us and ran out on the field looking like a bunch'a nuthouse escapees.

The game before ours went extra innings so we didn't have no time to take infield, and just ran out to our positions since we were home team that day. There was a polite smattering of cheers from our kids' parents that had managed to show up, and since I was pitching, I walked up to the mound, grabbed the game ball and started rubbing it between my hands for all I was worth. I gotta admit I ain't quite sure what that was supposed to do, but I knew all the big leaguers did it so I was gonna darn well do it, too. Mengo and Pato, the town sheriff and his trusty deputy, I told ya about earlier, doubled as Little League umps on Saturdays to make a few extra bucks, and were standing at the backstop behind home plate, talking real sweet-like to Señora Ochoa's younger and much skinnier sister, Señorita Castellano, the one with the false eyelashes so big they looked like a couple 'a monarch butterflies stuck to her face.

Rosie waddled out from the dugout to behind home plate looking, just like always, in his catcher's get up, like some giant trying to wear little kids stuff. The chest protector barely covered half of his belly, which was hanging so low he could've been walking around all day with his fly open and nobody would know the better of it. His head was so big that his cheeks squished out between the bars of the catcher's mask like Play-Doh through your fingers when ya squeezed a big clump, and that mask squinted up his eyes so, that I ain't sure how he was able to see out at all. His legs were so big around that Mrs. De la Rosa had to add longer elastic straps to his shin guards just so he could buckle 'em up.

I started lobbing a few balls into him to loosen up a bit and then Rosie crouched behind the plate and I kicked and scratched at the mound with my cleats to get it just right. I was the only southpaw pitcher in the league, so the mound was all cock-eyed from how I liked it, with the ups and down just opposite. Of course, them silly rubber cleats that they made us kids wear were nuthin' but useless when it came to diggin', not giving any more traction than if ya had your P. F. Flyers on, which some kids did, come to think about it. We warn't allowed to wear proper metal cleats 'til Senior League on account'a some pantywaist decided we might hurt ourselves. The infield was taking grounders from our first baseman, a kid I forgot to tell ya about earlier named David Tune, and Neil dubbed 'im "Looney" first time we met 'im. He was a long drink of water with a butch haircut and freckles and a kinda raspy voice from a "chronic post nasal drip" that made 'im sound real mean even though he looked like Howdy-Doody. Looney Tune was the only kid around with braces on his teeth on account 'a his dad was the local dentist, which made 'im a kinda celebrity, but unlucky for him, it seems each and every game he'd find some way or other to take a ball right to the chops and with all that metal in there, it'd look like the inside of his mouth had been through a meat grinder. There'd be blood spurting all over the place, and we'd hafta get ice from the snack bar and slap it on quick or his lips would swell up so the poor guy would look like one of them duck-billed platypussies.

Anyway, I started throwing a little harder, trying to get in my groove, and was feeling mighty strong, being careful not to throw full tilt. Last thing I needed was some smart alec lead off hitter timing my fastball, if ya know what I mean. We weren't officially supposed to throw no curve balls yet 'cause, like I told ya, they could hurt your arm if you're only a young pitcher and all, but I'd break off a little cutter once in a while, which was pretty much just a fast ball with a bit of a flick of the wrist at the end, causing it to break an inch or two. It was enough to throw the hitter off, but not enough for the umpire to catch on, and I hadn't been found out yet. Now, I did have a secret weapon, a pitch so unbelievable and mysterious that no hitter could touch it, not even a foul tip in three years. No one knew about it 'cept for me and Rosie, and we decided to call it my "sleeper pitch," on account'a hitters just stood there at the plate, frozen, like they were in a trance every time I served one up. It was really pretty amazing, if I do say so myself, and

I saved it for only those life or death situations when we absolutely had to have an out. Now I can't rightly let on how I threw it, it being top secret after all, but lets just say that it's a cross between a knuckler and a splitter, with enough shakes, twists and shimmies to make one of them A-rab belly dancers green with envy. It's pretty much unhitable, you could ask any of the poor kids that seen it, and I plan to use it plenty in the big leagues to help return the Dodgers to their rightful place as world champions. To signal for the sleeper, Rosie would make this loud snoring sound, causing everyone to look at 'im like he was nuts.

I finished up my warm up tosses, Rosie fired a bullet down to Creepy at second, and after the infield threw it round the horn we were ready to play ball. I glanced into the dugout at coach Goldstein, who was pacing up a storm and wiping the sweat off his forehead every few seconds, and after he spit out "set 'em down one, two, three," in between nervous contractions, I had to look away before I started laughing and lost my concentration. I peered up in the stands and there was Pop in his usual spot, right behind home plate, with a hand full of salted pumpkin seeds, his absolute favorite snack in one hand, and a soda in the other. He had that real contented look on his face as usual, like there was no where else on earth he'd rather be, which was the truth, and he gave me the thumbs up as he popped another pumpkin seed into his mouth. Boy, what a great guy! Even though he worked like a dog down at that produce warehouse six and one half days a week, I can't remember him ever missing even a practice, let alone one of my games, and he warn't one of them obnoxious dads, neither. You know, the ones that was always riding their kids to no end whenever they made the least little mistake, and even when they done something good, it could always have been better. Pop, he never said nuthin' to me 'cept "Good game, son," no matter if I was the hero or if I stunk up the place to high heaven.

About then, Mengo yelled, "Peetch the ball!" and slid on his mask, which went on silky smooth due to all that grease he wore in his hair, and I wiped the sweat off my forehead with the back of my mitt and looked in for Rosie to give me a sign. The El Charro fans started up with their singing and dancing and carrying on, just like always, as they turned up the mariachi music on the radio full blast. Some were ringing cow bells and hollering out in Mexican, "Arriba, Arriba!" and somethin' about "la palota!" and a bunch of others were yelling, "Meeho!" whatever that meant, along with all kinds of other stuff I didn't understand, and pretty much just having themselves a ball. They started up with their favorite cheer, their very own version of the old, "Two bits, four bits, six bits, a dollar, all for our team stand up and holler!" but theirs went like this, "Two bits, four bits, six bits, a *peso*, all for El Charro stand up and say so!" Well, that just killed 'em, and they went completely nuts all over again. After watching the show for a while, I glanced over at our fans, not making a peep, like they were at a funeral, and all of 'em staring at them El Charro folks like they each had three heads or something. I looked back and forth at the two sides a couple of times and started to realize there might be no better place in the whole wide world to study the differences between cultures than a Little League baseball game.

The lead off man for El Charro was this little, wiry kid named Tavo, who was fast as lightning and just as dangerous, and I knew for sure I needed to keep that little piece of desert doo-doo off the bases or he'd steal us blind. As he stepped into the box he flicked the knob of the bat against the plate so it flipped right back into his hand, causing the crowd to go nuts all over again, then shot me a smile full of bright gold teeth, and he was ready to hit. I settled on an outside fast ball, stared into Rosie's mitt, and with the whole team screaming, "Hey, batter, batter!" did my best Sandy Koufax wind up with a leg kick straight up in the air and my left hand almost dragging on the ground, and then fired the ball for all I was worth. Good old Tavo's eyes got bit as saucers when he seen it coming, took a pretty big hack, and smashed a worm burner right at Looney Tunes. I cringed, knowing exactly what was gonna happen next, and I'll be darned if that ball didn't take a bad hop, hitting poor old Looney right smack in the kisser, just like always. I mean it was the first stinking pitch of the ballgame for gosh sakes! With no time to waste, I hustled over toward first, grabbed the ricochet off 'a Looney's dental work, and tagged the base just a hair ahead of Tavo. By then, bad luck Looney was rolling around on the infield grass with blood spurting outta his mouth like water out of a fire hydrant on a hot summer day. Coach Goldstein had a big bag of ice already on the bench for just this occasion, and he came running out of the dug out, hairy feet and all, and slapped it on his mangled mug. Dr. Looney, the dentist, always had some of his tools at the ready during our games, and he was already on the field trying to coerce his hysterical kid to open up his mouth for a quick look see.

We all crowded around, trying to get a better view of the carnage, when Neil, fed up with the whole situation said, "You moron, Looney, why don't cha try using your mitt instead of your face, for a change!"

Well that started the poor, miserable kid to blubbering even worse, and after some nasty looks from all around, Neil skulked back over to shortstop, kicking the infield dirt and mumbling to hisself all the way. Rosie came over and told Looney not to feel too bad 'cause this kinda thing even happens in the pros sometimes, although I couldn't for the life of me think of any pro players who wore braces, and then Creepy added that the odds of this type of thing happening again this season would be greater than 10,000 to 1. None of this helped to snap 'im outta it, and after while, Coach Goldstein and Doctor Looney Tune decided to simply drag 'im off the field, still bawling, swollen lips and all, and laid 'im over on the bench where he stayed for the rest of the game.

That left us in kind of a bind over at first base, and after pacing up and down a few dozen times in front of the bench and chewing his fingernails something fierce, coach decided on a chubby faced, toe-headed, rosy cheeked ten year old kid named Barry Brunenkant to fill the spot. Problem was, little Barry couldn't even catch a cold, if ya know what I mean, plus his mom insisted on lathering 'im up with so darn much sunscreen all the time that it was always dripping into his eyes so he couldn't see, neither. I decided then and there, I'd hafta cover first on any ground balls to the infield, and told Barry to just get the heck outta the way if he saw me coming, which he seemed more than willing to do.

I must've been a little bit shook from seeing all that blood, 'cause I walked the next batter on four straight pitches. I took a little stroll behind the mound and rubbed up the ball some more, trying to regain my composure, like Pop always told me to do when the chips were down, and it worked just swell 'cause I fanned the next kid without breaking a sweat. That brought up the El Charro clean up hitter, Armando "Ten Ton" Tenejo, the biggest, strongest, meanest twelve year old in all of Southern Arizona, and probably the world. He made Rosie look small by comparison. At five-foot, seven inches and pushing two hundred and fifty pounds, he was almost as wide as he was tall, with squinty little eyes that were way too small for his gigantic head, and a turned up nose that always whistled when he breathed in and out and made 'im look a lot like one 'a them enormous, prize winning pigs you'd see at the Cochise County Fair each spring. Of course, nobody was willing to point out the uncanny resemblance to good old Ten Ton, although Ira liked to let out a loud snort whenever Tenejo was up to bat, just to try and get a rise outta him. The El Charro fans always went especially bananas when he came to the plate, cranking up their transistors to a deafening pitch, ringing them cow bells like there was no tomorrow and screaming out "El Gigante!" and "El Gordito!" 'til Mengo had to ask 'em to settle down, which did nuthin' but start them yelling another word I didn't know; "Cabron!"

Now I had faced Ten Ton plenty over the years, and knew he could knock the ball clean into the next county if he got a hold 'a one, but he didn't scare me none, I still had my secret weapon, didn't I? Well, here he comes, waddling up to the plate with his thighs rubbing, his uniform buttons barely holding on for dear life, and swinging a thirty-inch bat that looked like a toothpick in his hands. He took off his hat and bowed to the crowd, dug his huge right foot into the batter's box with authority, turned and said something nasty to Rosie and then looked out at me, puckering up his lips like he was gonna give me a kiss. He squinted up his already pee-hole in the snow sized eyes, and his nose started whistling up a storm as he wig-wagged his bat back and forth, daring me to throw one anywhere close.

I glanced over at Neil who said not too softly, "Strike out blubber boy and let's go hit, would ya."

So I reared back and fired a fastball down the pipe and Ten Ton took a vicious cut, almost coming outta his shoes, but he came up empty. Next, I decided to give 'im some high heat and threw one up around his eyes that he couldn't hold back on for strike two. Old Tenejo was plenty steamed now, and stepped back into the batters box with them beady eyes staring a hole right through me. I swear there were little puffs of steam coming outta his piggy nose as he waited to cream my next pitch. The El Charro fans were getting restless, too, and letting Mengo know about it. Rosie was frantically giving me the sign for the "sleeper" pitch, figurin' we'd been lucky to get by with two fast balls up to now, which was probably the God's honest truth, but I kept shaking 'im off, not wanting to show my best pitch too early, knowing darn well that it could come back to haunt me in the later inning's when I really needed some help. Rosie would not take no for an answer, though, and kept snorting his nose to beat the band until Mengo finally asked 'im if he was having a seizure or something! I decided to go along, and grabbed the ball with my top-secret grip, and then flung that thing up there, not too hard, and not too soft, but just right. Well, everything seemed to move in slow motion as the ball floated up to the plate, dancing in and out and up and down, and slowly twirling all along the way, and Ten Ton expecting another fastball, just stood there like he was hypnotized, watching that ball just flutter along, and by the time he woke up it was already in Rosie's mitt and Mengo barked out, "Stee-rike tres!"

Tenejo pounded the dirt with his bat and clenched his teeth, glaring out at me as he slowly dragged his feet back to the dugout. I gave 'im a little wink that threw a little fuel on the fire, and then trotted off the field.

Coach Goldstein wiped the sweat off his forehead, pushed his cap back down on his head and stammered, giddy as can be, "Nice job, Johnny! Make sure you keep it down on that guy next time for sure."

"No problema," I said with a smile as I slapped hands with the rest of the guys.

"Ten Ton is *p.o.ed*, Johnny," Rosie said, plopping hisself down on the bench next to me. "He'll be out for blood next time up."

"Relax, Rosie," I said. "I got 'im right where I want 'im," and patted his big old thigh.

He looked at me and nodded with his eyes rolled back in his head, and I could tell he thought I was nuts. Then he stood up, put on a batting helmet, and gave it a couple of whacks on top with the bat to get it to fit over his huge head, and handed the Louisville Slugger to Ira, our lead off hitter.

"Start us off now, Big I, be a hitter, hum babe!" Coach Goldstein yelled as Ira walked to the plate. Then he turned back to us on the bench, "Come on guys, show a little enthusiasm, will ya. We *gotta* win this one!"

As soon as he turned his back to us, Neil jumped up, sprayed his face with the water bottle to look like he was sweating all over, too, stuck out his belly, blew his cheeks up, and set his hat on top of his head so he looked just like a miniature coach Goldstein. Then he started mimicking everything coach had just said, with perfect copies of his hand jesters and facial expressions 'til we were practically rolling on the dirt floor laughing. This kid really had talent, I gotta admit. He kept it up 'til coach looked over his shoulder to see what all the commotion was about and gave Neil a dirty look, who quickly ran to the end of the bench, sat down, and pulled his hat over his eyes.

Ira rolled the first pitch slowly up the third base line, and then beat out the throw to first by a whisker. He let out a "Whoop!" shook his butt at us in the dugout, and made a couple of loud snorts toward Tenejo behind the plate. We all responded by making our mean beaver faces and gnashing our teeth and hissing. Normally Ira was a cinch to steal second with all his speed, but not with Ten Ton behind the plate, he had a rocket for an arm and nobody had swiped a base on 'im all season long. Big I didn't see it that way, of course, and was practically pleading with his pop to give 'im the steal sign so he could show up old Tenejo. Coach instead turned to Jagger, our number two hitter, and wiped his hand across his belt for a bunt. Now Jag didn't have much pop at the plate, and he'd be the first to tell ya that, and I suppose it was partly on account'a he was kinda lacking in what they call "fine motor skills," and partly 'cause of that no good eye, but that led 'im to practice his bunts every chance he got, and I swear he could handle the bat better than any kid I ever saw. He warn't just good at sacrifice bunts, neither. He was also proficient in push bunts, drag bunts, suicide bunts and slash bunts. I asked 'im one time how he got so good when sometimes he saw double and all, and he said that when he did see two balls coming at 'im he always tried to bunt the one that was higher, that way he stayed on top of the ball and didn't pop it up. I thought he might be feeding me a bunch of bull, as was often the case with Jag, but then you were never quite sure, and he'd hardly ever let on when he was. Anyway Jagger picked up the sign, rubbed his nose to let the coach know he'd seen it, stepped to the plate and turned and said something to Tenejo that really got his goat and he jumped outta his crouch and got right up in Jag's face and start jabbering back. Mengo made 'em break it up after a bit, and old Jag shot a glance over at the bench with a wink and that big-toothed grin of his, which started up our goofy beaver faces all over again.

I told ya before Jag warn't afraid of nuthin' so I figured he must'a said somethin' to Ten Ton and try to get 'im to lose his cool and mess up, or better yet, haul off and slug Jagger one and get hisself thrown outta the game. Either way it would be to our advantage. Sure enough Tenejo was so steamed that the first pitch to Jag got by 'im all the way to the backstop, letting Big I swiped second without a throw. Jag bunted the next pitch just lovely down the first baseline and moved Ira over to third with one out. As I walked to the plate I gave Jag a pat on the helmet, and asked what he had said to Ten Ton to get 'im so ticked.

"N-nuthin' much," he answered, shrugging his shoulders. "Just c-c-congratulations, I didn't know you were p-p-pregnant!"

Old Tenejo was in no mood for messing around now, so I kept my mouth shut and lifted a nice easy can of corn to medium left field on the first pitch. Ira tagged up and scored, no sweat, but as he crossed the plate, Tenejo stuck out his knee and clipped Ira's right leg, sending him flying head first into the backstop.

"You're a low life, Tenejo!" Ira yelled, as he picked hisself up outta the dirt, but Ten Ton just rubbed his eyes with his fist like a baby does when he is crying and jammed his helmet back on his fat head.

If Mengo would'a seen what happened, Tenejo would'a been gone, but it just so happened that during the play he was back making eyes at Señorita Castellano up in the stands and missed the whole dang thing. Coach Goldstein ran out to argue, but it didn't do no good 'cept to rile up the El Charro fans to no end, and after kicking dirt all over home plate and having his hat pop off several times, he walked back, dejected, to the bench and plopped hisself down on the end next to Looney.

Rosie grounded out to end the inning but not before he got the usual grief from the Mexican folks in the stands for playing for our east side team instead of for them. It happened every time we played these guys. They started yelling out, "Coconut!" which was something Mexican folks around here called other Mexicans when they thought they were acting too "white" inside but were really "brown" on the outside, and a bunch of other stuff in Mexican that I'm sure warn't too complimentary on account'a Dr.and Mrs. De la Rosa, who were sitting to the left of home plate, were getting plenty steamed.

Anyways, we got one run in the first, which is always nice, and I was determined to make it stand up. I was starting to get in a groove, hitting my spots just swell, and I set 'em down one, two, three in the second and third and was cruising right along causing the El Charro faithful to get their undies all tied up in knots, 'til the fourth inning when the top of their order came back around.

"Stay tough Johnny C, don't lose your concentration now," Coach hollered out, his voice cracking, as he wiped some more sweat from his forehead with the back of his hand. Some of it splashed on Looney Tune who was still lying at that same spot on the bench with an ice pack on his mouth, and he made a muffled, disgusted, whining sound. Coach bent over and apologized and then looked back onto the field and rolled his eyes. Well that little turd Tavo was up again, and he put down a real nice push bunt on my first pitch. I knew if it got by me, Creepy wouldn't have a prayer of making the play from second, so I dove flat out to my left and knocked the ball down just barely, then got to my knees and flipped it gentle as I could to little Barry over at first, who had one hand covering his eyes, not wanting to see what might happen next, and the other one in his useless mitt, stuck straight out in front of him, palm up. That ball floated in the air for what seemed like forever, and then, with the baseball gods looking over Little Beaver's Kindergarten that day, landed nice and soft in the pocket of his glove.

"Chore out!" barked Pato, as little Barry Brunenkant slowly peeked out between his fingers and started to realize what had happened.

Once it set in, he began to jump up and down and pump his fist in the air, and wave wildly to his mom and pop in the stands, who were waving back so hard I was afraid that any minute they'd fall over the edge and break their heads open. Then Barry, not finished celebrating his great feat yet, threw down his mitt, grabbed his hands over his head, and started pumping 'em like he just won the heavy weight championship of the world or something. Well, this was getting darn right embarrassing for the team after a while, so I walked over and grabbed the ball outtta his mitt and told 'im to stop acting like he had never caught a baseball before. Problem was, it *was* the first time he'd ever caught one, so that didn't slow him down none, and he kept right on going, strutting back and forth and flexing his puny muscles, all to the delight of his proud parents, for pretty much the rest of the game.

After the next kid popped out to Neil, here comes Ten Ton, and there was no doubt in my mind that he was thinking nuthin' but trying to tie the game with one big fat swing, literally. I took my hat off and wiped the sweat from my face with my sleeves, then looked over at Rosie who was nervously pointing down at the ground, the sign to keep the ball down. I looked up into the pure baby blue sky, feeling the slow burn of the mid morning sun against the back of my neck, and hoped the Big Guy upstairs might look out for us poor old Little Beavers just a tad longer before getting on with His more important business of the day.

I glared into that catcher's mitt real ferocious like trying to intimidate Tenejo, which I realized was a real long shot. He just spit on the ground, scratched his big butt, and waved at me to throw something up where so he could crush it. I threw my first pitch belt high and he jumped all over it, hitting a rocket to left field that would still be going sure as I'm telling you this, if not for one of the craziest things that to ever happened in the history of Little League. As the ball was flying outta the park like it had jet engines for a game tying homer, it smashed head-on into a thick branch of the old cottonwood tree that hung over the left field fence. As the ball struck it made a loud, "Tha-wack!" and ricocheted all the way back to the infield, landing right behind Jagger at third base. Tenejo was still standing in the batter's box like a big fat statue, with his mouth wide open and his squinty, pig eyes trying their darnedest to open up big and see what the heck just happened. Jag just turned around, picked up the ball easy as can be, and tossed it over to me covering first for the out.

"P-p-piece of cake," Jag said as he brushed by Tenejo on his way back to the dugout, whose face by now had got red as a beet, and with his teeth clinched and his nostrils flared and whistling like all get out, he let out an ear-piercing scream as his coach came out and had to lead him back to the bench. The El Charro fans were dead silent for the first time in the game, maybe history!

It was still one zip in the top of the sixth when another devastating blow to our slim chances came outtta nowhere. Neil, with two outs and nobody on, laced one down the first base line and tried stretching it into a double, before being nailed on a bang, bang play. We all cringed as Neil began ranting and raving, and kicking, and throwing his helmet, and cussing up a blue streak, which, just like we all figured, got 'im promptly tossed by old Pato, who at least heard good enough to catch the insults being thrown his way. The El Charro fans exploded into another round of blissful cheers and high pitched cackles as coach Goldstein came trudging out on the field, fast as his pudgy little legs would carry 'im and started pleading frantically with Mengo and Pato to reconsider. He knew darn well that with Looney still outta commission and Chicken Coop having a double hissy fit at the first sight of Ten Ton, we were left with only eight players, and the El Charro folks, also picking up on this, started screaming for a forfeit right off. The umpires huddled together trying to figure out what to do next as poor old coach paced back and forth in front of them waving his arms and getting his two cents in where ever he could, all the while trying to keep his hat from popping of his head.

Finally, after about ten nerve wracking minutes, Mengo says, "Choo boys can estill play, pero solamente con ocho players."

That lead to a bunch of hoots and hollers from the El Charro side, and a few polite claps from ours, and although it was better than a forfeit, with Ira moving into short, it meant we'd only have two, practically paraplegic ten year olds in the outfield for the last inning in the biggest game of the year. Well, all the guys were plenty ticked at Neil for shooting his big mouth off and leaving us high and dry, but nobody said nuthin' seein' how he was already feeling lower than a run over rattler.

'Course, he wouldn't apologize, it warn't in his nature, and he only said, "That Mengo and Pato ain't nuthin' but a couple'a butt-wipes, and them El Charro punks can kiss me where the sun don't shine, and I hate baseball anyway!" Then he plopped hisself down at the end of the bench, almost sitting square on Looney's still bleeding face.

Coach Goldstein, seeing we was in pretty dire straits, gave us a quick pep talk, saying all we needed was three more outs and the championship was ours, and then, "Let's show them our mean beaver faces!"

But no one felt much like it, and the best we could muster looked more like a bunch'a scared mice, to tell ya the truth. Then, he looked over at me kinda worried like, and asked, "How's the old arm feeling Johnny?"

I lied and told 'im it was swell, even though it felt like it would fall off any second, but the poor guy had enough to worry about, and besides, I figured I had the whole rest of the summer to rest up, right? I gave 'im a little wink and said not to worry, and that I'd put these guys down lickety-split and we'd all go home champs. He looked a little more relieved after that, and after wiping the sweat off his forehead, he gave me a pat on the rear, which left a big wet spot on the seat of my pants, and said, "Go get 'em, kid!" then hid his face in his hands and walked down to the end of the dugout like he was afraid to watch.

Needless to say, I warn't feeling too confident at that moment myself, with only two out- fielders, neither one of 'em with the foggiest idea how to catch a baseball, Barry the bumbler at first, my arm feeling like a piece of spaghetti, and the top of the El Charro lineup coming to bat. Rosie strolled out to the mound and asked me what I thought, and I told 'em I thought we were in deep doo-doo and better mix up the pitches a whole lot more and hit some corners 'cause I probably couldn't break a pane of glass with what I had left on my fastball. He nodded, pulled a piece of dirty beef jerky outta his back pocket, and after giving it the once over decided it was still edible, and popped it in his mouth. Then he mashed his catcher's mask back on his head and trudged on back behind the plate.

The El Charro fans started whooping it up for their final at bat, yelping in high-pitched voices, "A-yee, a-yee, a-yeeee!" as the first batter stepped in. I looked up at Pop in the stands, and he calmly gave me a wink and a nod like, "You can do it," and I took a deep breath and looked into Rosie for a sign.

Now there was no room for mistakes, and I couldn't let either of these first two guys on base knowing Ten Ton Tenejo was lurking in the hole, and the last thing I needed with my arm giving out, was for him to have a chance to win it with a homer. I got Tavo to hit a dying quail over to Creepy at second on a low and away fastball, if you could call it that, and high-tailed it over to first to take the throw, not trusting little Barry to pull of two miracles in the same day. The second guy popped up to Jagger at third on a cutter, but not before old Jag did a juggling act with the ball a circus clown would'a been proud of. I watch in horror from the mound while he slapped the ball up no fewer than five times and then fell flat on his back as the ball landed luckily, square in the middle of his chest. I'm telling you, that kid's hands were like two bricks, and not just regular old bricks, but ones that had been hardened in the desert sun for twenty years! Well, that brought up your friend and mine Tenejo batting for all the marbles, which sent the El Charro side of the stands into complete hysterics. You would'a thought you were at a mariachi festival on Cinco de Mayo in the middle of the Mexican Revolution with all the racket going on. It was giving me a headache for crying out loud, but as I looked over at Mengo to complain I noticed he was doing a little jig behind home plate to the song they were blaring, so I figured that warn't no use. Our fans on the other hand looked like figures outta that Madame Two-Sods wax museum. Nobody said a word, not a peep. The only people moving at all were a couple of moms trying on each other's lipsticks, Bampu's dad doing some kinda math problem on one'a them new calculating machines, and Mr. Chicken Coop tapping his watch over and over and then putting it up to his ear to see if it was still running. Unbelievable!

Anyways, Ten Ton had this fierce look of determination as he stomped outta the dugout, still steamed over what happened last time up, and he was surely looking to set things right. He pounded his feet into the dirt of the batter's box, making his big belly jiggle all over like Jell-o on springs, then slammed his bat on the plate, causing a puff of dust to rise up from underneath it with every *"whack!"* Then he looked straight out at me, no fooling around this time. This time he meant business. I looked down at Rosie and Tenejo standing side by side, like two monstrous kids, with huge arms and legs, and big round heads and even bigger bellies, and it suddenly dawned on me that they looked just like Tweedle Dee and Tweedle Dum-Dum, and I let out a little chuckle. I couldn't help myself. This accomplished two things, it made me relax a bit in a tight spot, which was good, and it made Ten Ton madder than a hornet 'cause he thought I was laughing at *him,* which I was.

Well, he was fit to be tied, and I reared back and fired an inside fastball, jamming 'im pretty good, and all he could do was hit a little dribbler off the handle foul past third. That worked so good, I thought I'd try it again, which was a mistake. There's an old saying in baseball that ya can't go to the well too many times, and Tenejo was sure ready, turning on that inside pitch and absolutely crushing the ball down the left field line, just fowl by inches as it soared over the fence by fifty feet. My heart did about three somersaults when that ball left the bat and I glanced over at coach Goldstein, who looked like he was about to faint. His face got white as a ghost and he moved real wobbly-like as he grabbed onto the fence for support, eased hisself down on the bench, and grabbed the ice pack off Looney Tunes face and slapped it on his forehead.

I realized I'd dodged the bullet with that one, and decided then and there that if I was gonna get beat, he was gonna hafta hit my best pitch. The fans were going completely bonkers as Rosie started to snort up a storm for the sleeper, and I closed my eyes, said a little prayer, and let her fly. From that point on everything was back in *double* slow motion, and all the noise melted into a low drone, as the ball gently floated up to the plate and then, about half way, started to sink. Ten Ton's squinty eyes were trying like mad to bulge outta their chubby sockets as he recognized the sleeper a tad late, and he was well out in front as his monstrous cut made contact. He lifted a fly ball about a mile high but not all that deep, to dead center field, and I realized right off we was in trouble as our two kid outfielders started running around in circles trying to get under it. Tenejo, seeing what was going on, started motoring around the bases fast as his fat legs could carry 'im, and was half way to second when the ball finally came down, square on the top of little Dougie Howell's head! Ira and Creepy sprinted out to center fast as they could to try and help out, but they both tripped and fell flat over poor Dougie who went down like a sack of potatoes.

Ten Ton was rounding third by the time Big I finally chased down the ball, and then wound up and fired a frozen rope toward the plate, and as I stood there on the pitcher's mound watching the ball sail through the air, it suddenly hit me what was about to happen, and I really didn't want to watch. Ya see, Ten Ton was chugging like a freight train towards home, yelling at the top of his lungs as he went, and determined that nuthin' on God's good earth was gonna stop 'im from scoring that run, and poor old Rosie was standing a couple of feet up the line toward third, with every ounce of concentration he could muster just trying to field Ira's throw so he could make a clean tag. Well, like I told ya before, everything was moving real slow, and I could see perfectly clear that the ball and that tub of lard Ten Ton were gonna make it to the plate at exactly the same time, causing a colossal collision of preposterous proportions, the likes of which had never, and never will again, be seen at Palo Verde park, or any other little league park across this great nation for that matter.

Everybody else at the game had figured out what was about to happen, too, 'cause all of a sudden things got real quiet, almost eerie-like, and even the fans from our side, stood up to watch the historic moment. I caught a glimpse of our dugout outta the corner of my eye and could see Looney Tunes sit up to get a better look-see, and coach Goldstein trying to cover up the poor kid's eyes to keep 'im from being so traumatized twice in the same game. Neil was standing next to them, looking out with his face smashed against the chain link fence, with a big grin on his face, anticipating the catastrophe that was about to occur.

Well, here comes Ira's throw, and here comes Tenejo, and just as Rosie snagged the ball in his mitt and turned toward third, Ten Ton plowed right into 'im! It was real weird though, 'cause instead of a loud *"Bam!"* like ya would'a thought, it was more of a *"Boing!"* as their big fat bellies collided, kinda like the sound it makes when you throw one 'a them big red bouncy balls against the wall hard as you could.

At first the two huge kids kinda moved towards each other as all that blubber around their middle started to cave in, and then they both bounced backward; Ten Ton toward third and Rosie towards home. It was the weirdest thing you ever saw! Tenejo staggered back a step or two and then fell flat on his back, kicking his arms and legs in the air and looking to all the world like one of them big stink bugs that fall over and can't get back on their feet without you giving 'em a flick. Rosie, poor guy, did a half conscious peer-o-wet and was lying face down in the dirt in the left-hander's batter's box, and making this pathetic, half-whining, half-groaning sound. Mengo, figuring he'd take care of first things, first, was frantically looking around for the ball in order to make the final call, and to tell you the truth, with all the excitement going on, I kinda forgot the game and the whole league championship was on the line. Mengo and Pato were searching high and low, but there warn't no sign of that baseball nowheres at all. Pretty soon, here comes both coaches and a bunch of the players to help, but they couldn't see hide nor hair of that little devil, neither! They were all standing around home plate scratching their heads, when Neil blurts out from over in the dug out, "Why don't ya check under De la Rosa's big fat belly?" And then he added, only partly under his breath, "Ya bunch'a morons!"

Now that seemed like a pretty good idea to Mengo, so he and Pato tried rolling old Rosie over, but couldn't budge 'im an inch. They tried pulling on his arms and legs and rocking him back and forth and even twisting his neck and feet 'til his face and toes were practically facing in the wrong direction, but nuthin' seemed to work. Finally, with Coach Goldstein and one of the El Charro coaches helping out, and a lot of teeth gnashing and swearing, and a, "One, two, three, heave-ho!" they finally managed to slowly flip 'im over.

Well, I know it don't seem likely, and if I'm lyin' I'm dyin', but there she was, trapped between his mitt and chest protector, and resting ever so gently on his big soft belly.

"Chore out!" Mengo hollered. " El juego ees over!"

Me and the guys let out a huge cheer, threw our mitts in the air and ran over and made a big dog pile on top of Rosie who was still laying there in the dirt, only half conscious.

The El Charro coaches went ballistic, jumping up and down, screaming and yelling, throwing their hats down in disgust over and over, and calling poor Mengo and his family all sorts of stuff unsuitable for innocent ears. But Mengo kept his cool, being the keeper of law and order that he was, and said if Rosie still had the ball pinned to his chest, he must've made the tag before Ten Ton reached the plate, and so he was out, no ifs ands or butts. But them coaches weren't about to give up that easily, not with the whole season on the line, and I swear they were practically crying as they pleaded, first with Mengo, and then with his half deaf, dim-witted cousin Pato, who just stood there smiling, pretendin' like he didn't have a clue what they was saying. Then, all of a sudden, the El Charro fans burst onto the field; moms, dads, grandmas, and grandpas, you name it, just about trampling old Ten Ton who was still laying on his back, still kicking his arms and legs, and pretty much being completely ignored. Then *they* started arguing with Mengo and Pato, and each other, and some of 'em were looking straight up to the sky and yelling and pointing like they were arguing directly with God hisself.

Our fans, on the other hand, were just staring out at the field and all the hubbub, with their mouths open wide, and their eyes peeled back, and generally appalled at the whole disgusting scene. They were saying stuff like, "Oh, my stars!" and "Some people!" and "Well, what do you expect!" All except Pop, that is, who was still sitting there in his same old spot, calm as can be, eating his pumpkin seeds just like always, and just gave me a little wave and a smile soon as our eyes met. That was just the way he was. He never got hisself too worked up about stuff. He said he didn't see no advantage to it.

There was so much confusion by now, that we finally gave up trying to give a cheer to El Charro, and coach pointed for us to go down the right field line to hear his post game talk while them fans and coaches kept on ripping poor Mengo and Pato up one side and down the other. A bunch of us guys helped Rosie to his feet and gave 'im a bunch of, "Hip-hip-hoorays!" as he shook his head to get the cobwebs out and started to come back to his senses. It would've been nice to have carried 'im off the field on our backs like you're supposed to with sport heroes, but we knew there weren't a chance in hell of that happening, so we just surrounded 'im and patted 'im on his huge back a bunch of times, and told 'im over and over how he saved the game and the championship and all.

We were all sitting out in right, when Coach Goldstein, who looked like he could use a long vacation on a beach somewheres, started telling us how great we had played and what an honor it was to be our coach and all that end of the season kinda stuff. Jag looked over at me and said he sure wished his dad was here to see our team win, and how proud *he* would be.

I gave 'im a little pat on the back and said, "Jag, this championship is really for him. You know that. After all he's been our coach since we were only eight years old." After that he just stared down at the grass, not looking up for a long while, and I knew he must'a been missing his pop something fierce.

Coach Goldstein was still yaking about the game, and the season, and how great we all were, but by then, to tell ya the truth, we couldn't care less and started thinking only about the snack bar and what kinda free drink we were gonna get.

"If I only had a Big Hunk, I know I'd feel *much* better," Rosie blurted out in the middle of one of Coach's sentences, and he realized it was no use to keep on talking, and just said, "Have a great summer, boys!"

Everyone let out another big cheer after that, and we tore off fast as we could towards the snack bar. Rosie, of course, was last getting there, but we all agreed, even Neil and Ira, that today he definitely deserved the honor of being first in line, and as he took his rightful place at the top of the rickety wooden steps of the little trailer that was our snack bar at Palo Verde park, and held up his soda and candy bar to the cheers of all his teammates, it seemed as though he would burst with all the pride he was feeling inside, and as I looked up into that chubby face and saw all that joy, I knew right then and there I never would forget the "Great Collision at the Plate of 1968."

# Chapter Five

## RELIGION

The next morning was glorious all over again; in fact, I couldn't recall, in the entire, distinguished history of the S.S.B.'s, two finer mornings in a row, ever. I was just lying there in bed, feeling content with my lot, and mullin' over our great victories over Nancy, the nasty nincumpoop, and the notorious El Charro baseball team, when the whole lovely mood came tumbling down with a loud *"Bang!"* on my bedroom door.

"Get up Johnny, now! Mom says we're leaving for church in fifteen minutes! No excuses!"

It was my darling little sister Gracie, and the horrible news was even harder to take when it came with her ear piercing, someone drilling a nail through your eye, voice. I had completely forgot it was Sunday, being summer and all and not having school days to remind a kid about the weekend. I was totally unprepared for wasting a whole day at church, and already had started planning out my day with the guys; lizard hunting in the desert, pitcher's-hand baseball down at the Sewer, maybe some Mexican delights for lunch over at Rosie's, and then sneaking into Highland Vista neighborhood pool for some atomic canonballs to finish off the afternoon when it got too hot to do anything else. But all them plans were right down the toilet, now, and instead, we were gonna spend half the day listenin' to old Padre Moreno remind us of what a group of ungrateful, unworthy and thoroughly useless louts we were, and how none of us had the slightest chance of getting to the good place unless we changed our evil ways, and even then he wouldn't put no money on it. Just like always. It was enough to send a twelve year old kid into a terrible state of depression, and I told

# Religion

Ma so, too, but she said Sunday mass was, "The most righteous and uplifting experience in one's week," and that if we didn't learn the difference between right and wrong real quick, we were, "Destined to burn for all eternity in damnable hellfire." I tried to tell her that I had a pretty good idea of the difference already, and that I wasn't so sure it was necessary to be reminded so often, but she just said I was a lost lamb and needed to be brought back to the shepherd. I had no idea whatsoever what the heck she was talking about, but I didn't let on 'cause I figured I was *supposed* ta know all about it, and if she thought I didn't, I'd be exiled back to Sunday School or Bible Study of some other kinda God-awful horror a kid could hardly endure.

At least I knew she couldn't send me back to catechism class on account'a I was too old, thank the Lord. For those of you who haven't had the pleasure of attending catechism, thank your lucky stars 'cause let me tell ya, it's a kid's worst nightmare. Ya see, it's a religious class for Catholic kids that didn't go to Catholic school, and it was every darn Saturday morning, no if, ands, or butts, from eight to twelve, and here's the kicker, that's the exact same time of all the best Saturday morning cartoons. You know, the ones you'd wait for all week long to watch. Why couldn't they have it any other time during the week, like say Wednesday night, nuthin' fun ever happens on Wednesday night. I'll tell ya why, 'cause that wouldn't be good enough torture! That's why. The whole four hours was spent learning everything from turning the other cheek even when some worthless nimrod treats you like a piece of crap, to making sure not to *cover* your neighbor's wife, whatever the heck that means. None of this stuff was taught by no sweet little college girls or kindly, soft spoken grandmas, neither, but instead by the nastiest, most ornery, black-hooded nuns, this side of the Spanish Imposition! I guess they were plenty sore about being exiled out here to the middle of the God-forsaken, Sonora desert, and were more than happy to take out their frustrations on us poor little lost souls with a ruler straight across the knuckles, or worse. One unfortunate member of the flock, Lefty Leftwich, had the horrible luck of blurting out the "S" word, right in front of Sister Mary Josephine, after stubbing his toe against her desk. The poor guy spent the rest of the day in the bathroom having his mouth washed out with Palmolive detergent. When he finally got back to class, he had a distinct, green hue to his face that lasted the whole rest of the week and part of the next, and for the next three days every time he said, "Wow," a cute little soap bubble would float outta his mouth! Let's just say I was very grateful that that part of my religious upbringing was over and done with.

Well, I dragged myself outta bed, realizing I didn't have no choice, and walked down the hallway real slow, like I had chains on my feet or somethin', and into the kitchen where Ma was making the morning coffee.

I tried looking pitiful as possible, and whined, "Ma, do I hafta go to church today? I'm real tired, probably coming down with stripped throat or somethin' and was planning on just staying home today and maybe cleaning my room." (I decided to really give it my best shot.) "Anyways, I haven't missed a Sunday all year, and most've the guys don't even go to church 'cept maybe Easter or Christmas Eve so I figure I'm a little bit ahead of the game."

She didn't even look up from the percolator, apparently prepared for my feeble attempt to shirk my responsibilities.

"First of all, I don't care one iota what your friends do. You are *my* son and *my* responsibility and you *will* do what I think is right for you. Secondly, aren't you ashamed of yourself? All God asks is to give him an hour or two on Sunday morning to show our respect for all he has done for us. And when you are thinking about the little time you are giving up, I want you to remember that Jesus sacrificed his whole *life* for you."

Well, ya gotta admit, that was pretty hard to argue with, and actually *did* make me feel kinda ashamed.

So I headed on back down the hallway, and as I passed Gracie's room, she gave me this big fat smile and said, "You better hurry, Johnny, you don't want to be late now, do you?"

"Stuff a sock in it, you little twit!" was the best I could come up with, considering the low down state I was in.

After that I decided to head into the master bedroom and try my luck with good old Pop, surely he'd listen to reason, although his credibility on the subject ain't too great. One time when I was a kid, he told me if I wanted to be a great left-handed pitcher some day I should go to church and pray about it every Sunday just like Sandy Koufax did; after more than a year and a whole lotta praying I come to find out old Sandy was Jewish.

I let into Pop anyways with my pitiful pleas for mercy, but he just shook his head, put his thick hand on my shoulder and said, "Your mother knows best on this one, pal," which meant he wasn't about to cross Ma on such a sensitive subject and get hisself in the doghouse, too, even though I knew for a fact, that he warn't all that crazy about sitting in church all Sunday, neither, when he could be home watching football. In fact, one time I overhead him talking to Mr. De la Rosa after mass, and saying he'd given his eye teeth to have been able to stay home that day and watch the big Rams and Colts game on T.V., and Mr. De la Rosa said he felt exactly the same way. That was, of course, before the ladies walked up, causing them to change their tune real quick to how lovely the alter was fancied up. It was pathetic! Ain't nobody gonna stand up against this horrifying scheme to make our lives miserable every Sunday morning? Don't look too promising, if ya ask me.

Beaten again, I went on into the bathroom, splashed some water on my face, mashed down my hair best I could and brushed my teeth, even though

I hadn't eaten nuthin' yet. Of course, a person couldn't eat no breakfast and then receive communion, that was against church rules aimed at making it's folks even more miserable, so not only were ya bored to death, just sitting there on them rock hard pews, unable to move or say a word, or even give a little wave to one of your buddies, but you were also half-starved and feeling like you'd pass out any second from malnutrition. Gracie, she'd always get a jelly doughnut or English muffin with peanut butter or somethin' before we left to hold her over, on account'a Ma saying she was too young to go without food for that long. But do you think she'd ever consider for one minute to sneak her poor starving older brother even a tiny morsel to help hold 'im over? Not on your life!

I put on my Sunday best; a pair of black pants, grey hush puppies, and a starched white shirt that was so stiff you'd swear you'd rip the sleeve clean off if ya raised your arm too quick, with a collar that felt like a straight razor cutting into your throat every time you took a look around, and headed back to the kitchen where Ma was waiting to perform her official inspection.

"You hair looks like a rat's nest, Johnny!" she said, as she pulled a comb outta her purse and started tugging at the tangles I had missed like a lion yanking the flesh off of his latest kill. Now this hurt considerably and I longed for the days of crew cuts once again, but too bad for us guys, them four singing morons from England had ruined hair styles for boys forever.

"Watch it Ma, that hurts!" I cried, as she continued to rip at my poor scalp.

"Well, I am sorry, but no son of mine is going to San Xavier Mission looking like a ragamuffin."

San Xavier Mission was the oldest church in Arizona, just South of Tucson and close to 45 miles away. We couldn't just go to St. Joseph's, which was the Catholic Church right down the road where all the sane people of Santa Elena went, oh no, we had to go the *mission* ' cause that's where the *Bishop* said mass. No regular priest's for our family, no sir-e-bob. Now I gotta admit the mission was a pretty cool place, all made outta adobe bricks and white stucco and all, with saguaro rib ceilings and mesquite beams, and the whole thing sat out on the Papago Indian reservation, being one of them missions built by old Padre Kino in the 1700's. We learned all about 'im, along with a bunch'a other very forgettable stuff during Arizona History Week over at the Sewer; the most boring five days of the year. I mean let's face it, after Tombstone, there ain't much else to get excited about in the "Valentine State," for gosh sakes. The Grand Canyon? Big deal! A huge hole in the ground. Give me and the guys a few M-80's and a couple'a shovels, and in a week we could give ya the same darn thing out in the desert behind my house. No problema.

Anyways, seems Father Kino was sent up from Mexico to try to civilize

67

the Injuns and teach 'em about Jesus and all, and to get them to quit acting like a bunch'a blood thirsty savages, only some of them decided they liked they way they were just fine, and tried to scalp the Padre instead. They must've been the ones who found out about having to go to Catechism in advance, I figured. The mission never was finished, neither, with one bell tower left only half done, on account'a before the good Indians were done building the place, a bunch'a them no good, heathen Indians went on the warpath, and cut up the good Indians somethin' fierce. After that the good ones said, "The heck with it," and decided the place looked just fine as is. That's the God's honest truth. You could look it up.

After Ma finished making me presentable, we all loaded into the Buick and headed on out. After awhile of staring outta the window, I got to thinking about religion and all of them different kinds around the world, and so I asked, "Pop, who are the Jewish people, anyways, and what do they have to do with anything?"

Well, I think I caught him off guard, 'cause it took him a minute to start up, but then he says they were the original *chosen* people of God to pass his word around here on earth, and I said that was pretty special, and he says, "Yup." And so then after thinking a bit, I asked 'im, how they was different from us, and he says that when Jesus was alive some of the Jewish people believed he was the son of God and some thought that was a load of huey, and the ones that believed became the first Christians and followed Jesus all over the place, not letting the poor guy outta their sight for even a second, and wrote down everything he said and did and ate and drank, and then stuffed it all in the Bible after he was gone. So then I asked 'im who the Jewish people that are around today think Jesus was, and he said they think he was a special person, but not the Son of God. And then I asked 'im what they thought about the Pope, and he said they didn't think much about him at all. I asked 'im how ya could tell if a person was Jewish, and he says you can't 'cept for sometimes their last names might end in "berg" or "stein" or somthin' like that.

"Hey, my friend Ira's last name is Goldberg. Is he Jewish?"

"He sure is," Pop replied.

Well that kinda floored me 'cause I knew Big I practically all my life and never thought for a minute he was any different than me or the other guys.

Finally, I asked, "How come he don't wear one of them swell beanie caps like some of the Jewish people I see on T.V."

"Well, only some of them wear those caps all around, and they're called Orthodox Jews."

I was getting kinda confused so I asked, "What about the Bible? Do they read that too?"

"Only the first part called the Old Testament, that deals with Cain and Abel, and Moses and those fellas."

"Well then who's the most important guy in *their* religion?"

"Oh, probably Moses, I guess," Pop says. "You know who he is, don't you."

"Sure I do. He's the guy that split the river in two with his big stick so all his friends could walk across, pretty as they please, and then slammed it shut on all the bad guys when they tried using the short cut too."

Pop chuckled and said, "Yup, that was one heck of a nice short cut."

After another long while I asked, "How 'bout all them folks in China that worship the statues of that little chubby guy with the big smile on his face."

"You mean Buddha?"

"Yeah, that's the guy, and what's he always smiling about?"

"Well, Buddha is supposed to be someone who is all knowing and comes to earth every once in a while to help save humans when they start to go bad."

"You mean a real smart guy, like Creep, er, I mean Bampu, to help ya figure out stuff?"

"No," Pop shook his head, "more of a spiritual guy, to show you how to run your life."

"Oh, I get it," I answered, although I was getting more confused by the minute and was starting to wonder why everyone didn't just agree on one religion and just leave it at that. Then I asked Pop if he thought that would ever happen, and he said not a chance since every religion thinks they are right and they weren't about to change their minds.

"Well, is that all the different religions then, Pop?"

"No, not by a long shot. There's Moslems, and Hindus, and more than you could shake a stick at."

I started to realize I was never gonna know everything there was to know about religion, unless I was willing to put a whole lot more time in it, which I wasn't, but I did have one more question, "What about them Atheist people you hear about on the news all the time complaining about this and that. What do they believe in?"

"Well, they don't believe in God at all."

"Whatdaya mean?"

"They think there is no God or spiritual being, whatsoever."

Now that really threw me for a loop and I couldn't say a thing for a minute, being so amazed at the notion. Finally I blurted out, "Well, where the heck do they think we came from then?"

"They think we evolved from single cell organisms that lived in swamps millions of years ago."

"You mean like them slimy protozoa things we learn about is science class?"

"Exactly," Pop said, and shot me a glance over the back of the seat.

"You gotta be kidding! They think we developed arms and legs and brains and everything from that!"

"They sure do." he replied.

"How about the earth. Where do they think *it* came from?"

"Most of them think it came from an explosion of one huge planet that broke up millions of years ago."

"So where did that big planet come from, then?"

"They don't know."

Well I tell ya what, I wrote off them Atheist folks right then and there, 'cause none of that stuff made sense to me in the least. Me and the guys related to some pond water scum? Come on! And after all, the way I see it, and I ain't no genius, the big question still is, why is there something here instead of nuthin', right?

We were nearly to the mission by the time my lesson on religion was done, and I didn't feel no closer to understanding all the different types, than Dodger was to figuring how to put a man on the moon, so I just went back to something I was good at--feeling sorry for myself. Gracie was all jacked up to play, "slug-bug," but it wasn't in me, and besides, we hadn't passed ten cars *total* on the way over, let alone V.W.'s, so it wouldn't't'a been no fun, anyways.

We turned off of I-19 and onto the Papago reservation towards San Xavier and things started looking real shabby right off. Most of the houses were nuthin' but tin sheds, or mud huts with a door and a window and a bunch of old dried palm leaves on top for a roof. There was no sign of running water, let alone air-conditioning, and the little Indian kids were covered from head to toe in the red clay that was common around these parts, most of 'em only half dressed and barefoot. It was a plain pitiful sight, and it made me think how lucky we was back in the white ghetto, and how much we took for granted and all. I could hardly stand to look, and I couldn't figure out why Mom insisted on coming all the way over here and forcing me and Gracie to see such a sad state of affairs. There were a few Indian men walking around, too, but they didn't look much like them Indians you saw on T.V. or in the movies, not by a long shot. There warn't a cool eagle feather headdress or a swell bow and arrow to be seen nowhere, and none of 'em wore those neat leather loin clothes or deerskin moccasins, neither. Pretty much they dressed like most Americans, just not as nice. It was real disappointing. I mean, how could your ancestors have such bitchin' getups, and you settle for Levis and a T-shirt? You could forget about seeing any way out war paint on their faces, too, there warn't even a smudge to be found. Some of the men didn't even have long hair, for crying out loud. I just didn't understand it. Them Papagos weren't too keen about mingling too much with the white folk walking around the mission, either. They pretty much just stayed to themselves, although some of 'em were selling their turquoise jewelry out on the front steps, all laid out nice and pretty on colorful blankets. But even them Indians didn't say much, and just sat there with their eyes down and looking sad, I thought. In fact, that's exactly how they all looked, even the kids—just plain sad.

We walked through the huge carved mesquite doors and into the entrance way where there was a humongous painting of Padre Kino sitting on his horse and surrounded by a bunch'a grateful, adoring Injuns he'd just taught all about Jesus, I suppose. There weren't no little kid Indians hanging around 'im in the paintin', I noticed, they probably were already shipped off to catechism class. There was two swell carved wooden statues of Mary and Joseph standing on each side with about a hundred candles sitting at their feet, and their light flickering up and down all over 'em. They were hand painted and real old and the paint was wearing off in places and burned off in others, but nobody cared ' cause the rest of the church was kinda old and worn too, and to tell you the truth it gave the whole place a nice sincere feeling that was kinda touching really. If you think about it, Jesus being born in a manger, surrounded by nuthin' but a bunch of smelly farm animals, I ain't so sure he'd go for all them gaudy churches with their gold and silver, and marble and all. Nope, I think that old mission with its worn wood floors, hand-carved pews and stained stucco walls would suit Him just fine.

After dousing myself with as much holy water as I could get my hands on to try and stay cool before getting the back of Ma's hand across the side of my head, we walked on into church real polite-like, and I spied good old Rosie stuffed in one of the middle pews with his folks. I gave 'im a quick wink, but he didn't look none too happy about being there, neither, not being able to eat breakfast on top of everything else, and could only manage a sick looking little smirk in return. Mrs. De la Rosa, on the other hand, she was grinning from ear to ear, and let out an excited, "Como estas?" Mr. De la Rosa's didn't rightly share her enthusiasm, and just raised his eyebrows a tad in recognition as we made our way by. Rosie's family was the only other one from the neighborhood nutty enough to come all the way out to timbuktoo for mass.

We headed down the aisle a bit further, and then it hit me, the *only* thing that could possibly make wasting a perfectly good Sunday a little easier to swallow; Jenny Darling. There she was in all her radiant beauty, sitting up in the first pew like always, looking like one of the angels herself, with her luscious red hair flowing all the way down to her waist, done up just right in a big pink bow. She had this terrific milky white skin that I didn't see too much of in my family being Italian and all, and these cute little freckles running across the bridge of her nose. She was all dolled up in one'a them little girl sailor dresses, with the big flap over the back and baby blue stripes down the sleeves. Boy was she a sight for sore eyes! She was real sweet, too, not bossy or a know it all like every other girl I knew. Nope, Jenny was a real lady, through and through, and to tell you the truth, I guess I was a little sweet on her. I mean, how could you help it, just look at her.

Now, I know I was only twelve and all, and if the guys got wind of my feelings about Jenny I'd hafta leave town and change my name and have all kinds of plastic surgery, just to keep 'em from making my life a living hell, but I couldn't help myself. It was weird. Kinda like when you're a little kid and your ma absolutely forbids you from crossing the street, but your best pal just got the new Johnny-7 OMA assault rifle, so ya do it anyways. Understand?

There was only one small problem with our relationship the way I saw it; Jenny hardly knew I existed. But what was I supposed to do? I mean she went to St. Joe's instead of the Sewer, and pretty much the only time I ever even saw her was in church, which wasn't exactly the best time for chatting up girls, if ya know what I mean. As a matter of fact, if I said two words during mass that weren't in the miss-a-let, Ma would give me a whack so fast it'd make your head swim.

My folks decided on a pew about half way down the aisle and I sat down, all the while keeeping my eyes on the back of Jenny's lovely little head and hoping she'd turn around just once so I could maybe give her a little wave, or somethin', but no such luck. So I settled in for the hour's worth of agony that I knew was coming, and there wasn't a darn thing I could do about it. I thought about asking to go to the bathroom, and then trying to get good old Rosie to do the same, since, like they say, misery loves company, but Ma had heard *that* one so many times that lately she's been insisting on going with me, which not only ruined any chance of having fun, but also was down right embarrassing! And if the boredom warn't bad enough, I also had to put up with my evil little sister Gracie, who would poke and pinch and kick me to no end, and pretty much keep up her own style of Chinese water torture for the next sixty minutes or so. But God forbid, if I so much as touched one hair on her bratty little head, 'cause she'd start wailing like she dropped her favorite stinking ice cream cone, and I'd be completely grounded for the next week without the slimmest chance for parole.

Just about then the bell in the one finished tower I told ya about earlier started ringing it's head off, and all the folks stood up nice and straight, and the organ started playing that song about Gloria, and here comes old Bishop Moreno walking real slow and unsteady-like down the aisle, holding on to his staff for dear life, and being followed up by a bunch'a them goody-goody altar boys and one of those helper priests. The whole procession took a good while, on account 'a the fact that the Bishop wasn't no spring chicken no more, and Ma took the opportunity to point over at the altar boys and give me one of them big phony smiles like mothers always do when they want ya to know they really like something. Well, I knew where she was going with that, and so I held my nose, and shook my head right back at her, which, needless to say, she didn't take too kindly to, and if we had been anywhere but church she would'a hided me good, but instead, she just glared back, grinding her teeth, with her face turning redder than a rat's eye. Now I was a reasonable kid, willing to do any *reasonable* thing to make my folks happy, I mean look at all the crazy stuff they do for us. But a guy's gotta draw the line somewheres, right? Everybody knows that only guys named Francis get pounded more than alter boys, and I mean *pounded*, on a daily basis at school, and lets face it, walking around in them robes that look awfully close to a lady's valentine's dress didn't help their cause none.

The Bishop, he made it up the steps to the altar alright, but only with some help from his sidekick, and then sat hisself down behind the altar facing the rest of the congregation. Now the chair he sat in warn't really no chair at all, but more like a throne, and I mean a monster, maybe ten feet high, with the back all hand carved mesquite and with massive arms in the shape of lion's paws and legs that ended in what looked like eagle claws. The seat itself had to be four feet off the ground if it were an inch, and the Bishop, being kinda shrimpy to begin with, and now shrunken up even more with age, couldn't come close reaching the floor with his feet so they just kinda dangled there in the air. It hit me then and there that he looked an awful lot like some little kid all dressed up and sitting in his high chair, waiting on his ma to bring 'im a treat. That got me to chuckling, though I did my best to hold it in, but I swear that darn woman could read my mind, 'cause before you could say, "Roseanna in the highest," Ma leaned over and whispered, "You better show some respect, young man, or you are going straight to hell. Do you understand?"

It was uncanny, that sixth sense that Moms had. I mean, how do they do it? Is it on account of you being in their bellies for nine months and all that makes 'em able to know everything your thinking or gonna do even before you do it? Maybe a little piece of your brain swims up and sticks in their's while your nuthin' but one of them lizard-looking embryos, and acts like a radio receiver or something from then on, picking up every darn thought that pops into your head for the rest of your pathetic, completely controlled, life. Heck, I don't know how it happens, but there ain't no denyin' it, neither. Some folks say they don't believe in them clara-buoyants that you see on T.V., but I sure as heck do, on account'a I'm living with one!

After that I tried keeping my thoughts about the church to a minimum, and turned my attention back to the back of Jenny's head. She still wouldn't turn around, though, not even once, 'cause I suppose that would be considered rude, and she warn't that kinda girl, like I told ya before. So I gave up on Jenny Darling after a bit and started looking around the old church to see if there was somethin' the least bit interesting that might catch my eye and help me pass the time a little less painful. Over on one wall there hung a huge painting of the last supper, and it was a pretty swell job, too, with all twelve apostles sitting at the long wood picnic table with Jesus in the middle with his arms outstretched like he was asking whoever looked at the picture to come over and give him a big hug, which in a way, I guess he was. There were a whole bunch'a different plates of food on the table scattered here and there, but nuthin' that looked all that appetizing, just some apples and oranges and berries and stuff, and a few pieces of that flat, round bread over in the corner of the table, the kind that Arabs like to eat. Not a piece of pizza or a hotdog to be seen, nowheres. Judas, that scumbum, was down on one end of the table where he belonged, with his head slung down lower than everyone else, to show what a low down, lying turd he was. There was good old doubting Thomas on the other end, and you could tell it was him by the way he was turned towards one of the other apostles with his hands up like he was saying, "What the heck was that all about!" I tried naming all the apostles in my head to waste a little more time, but could only muster eight, no matter how hard I tried, unless Freddy was one, then I got nine. I felt a little ashamed after that, and decided I'd better start reading my Bible soon as I had some extra time. Maybe even next year.

On the other side of the church there was this big table all covered up real fancy with lovely blue silk with lacy edges, and on top of it was lying this lady who was dressed in a long beautiful robe and she had a golden halo made outta wire stuck on top of her head. I guess she was supposed to be the Virgin Mary, but I ain't quite certain what she was doing just lying there 'cept maybe taking a nap and waiting for one of those big shot angels to come and tell her what to do next. Anyway, the really weird thing about her was that church folks, especially them old Mexican ladies, had pinned a million little trinkets all over her. I'm telling you she was covered from head to toe! They weren't just any trinkets, neither, but special little medals that looked like a heart or a leg or an eye or some other part of your body. I didn't have a clue what that was all about, but figured it was another one of them weird Mexican traditions from way back when, and believe me, they had a bunch of 'em, and if ya hung around Santa Elena long enough you'd get an eyeful. Like the time I was over at Rosie's house and his aunt had just had this baby and she was changing a sopping wet diaper, when outta the blue she starts to wipe her face with it, happy as a lark! Well, it almost made me lose my lunch and I was about to run out of the room screaming, when Mrs. De la Rosa grabbed me and said it was only an old Mexican custom that ladies believed made their skin extra soft and lovely after having a baby. Okay, if that's true why don't they just stick their head in the toilet 'til they look like Miss America! Or hows about we collect all the wet diapers in town for a year, wring 'em out in a bottle, and sell them in one of them fancy department stores in New York City and become zillionaires. We could call it, "Pee Pee Potion," or maybe, "Ur-ine for a treat," or something catchy like that. After all, Pop always said ladies will buy anything if they thought it'd make 'em look pretty, but I figured *this* might be pushing it. And believe me, if you think that's bizarre, you ain't heard the *half* of it.

Anyway, after a bit, I nudged Ma and asked her what was up with all the stuff stuck all over poor Mary, and she said that if someone was sick, Mexican folk would get one of those medals called a "me-log-rows" or something, of whatever needed fixing, and then stick it on the Virgin with a special prayer to help the person get better. I guess that made sense, 'cause if you think about it, Mary had her hands plenty full just trying to keep the people of this planet from going straight to hell in a hand basket, so it couldn't hurt to have one of them medals to remind her of your special problem once she got around to it. I wonder if they got one of those medals for little sisters?

About that time Bishop Moreno eased his way up to the pulpit, which was made outta wood with that famous picture of the Virgin Mary with that little guy sticking his head out between her feet carved on the front, and started in on reading us the gospel. The gospel was always a letter written by one of the apostles, letting some bunch'a no goods like the Samarians or Californians have it for not having a clue what was what, or a cute little story that Jesus hisself had told about the right way to do this or that, or sometimes about some miracle that Jesus had done to prove to all the lamebrains out there he was the real deal. Today's reading was the one about the potty-gal son. I had heard this one about a thousand times over the years in catechism class and Sunday mass, but for the life of me it still didn't make no sense at all. The way I see it, there's this one swell son who stays home and works like a dog, doing every little thing his pop asks him to do to try and make him proud and all, and then there's this other good for nuthin' son, who left his family high and dry and pissed away all his dough on all kinds of useless stuff, and didn't do an honest day's work in all his miserable life. But guess who gets the big shindig when he drags his lazy butt back home one day after he's all tapped out? That's right, the worthless bum! Now the loyal hard working son gets pretty ticked off at all this, and rightfully so if you ask me, but when he asks his pop what the heck's going

76

on, all he gets is some lip service about how his brother was "lost and now is found." I mean what kinda answer is that? How about a little get together for the guy who's been doing right his whole life and then a good old fashioned butt whipping for the useless slacker? I got so riled up just thinking about it, I was this close to raising my hand and saying something to the old Bishop, but then thought better of it because if I did, I'd probably be the one getting the good old fashioned butt whipping.

As the ushers got set to pass around the collection basket, the choir went into a rousing rendition of, "Come, tell it from the mountain," probably trying to wake up the men who by then were looking less than chipper so they'd be able to find their wallets easier. That Bishop Moreno, he still had a few tricks up those way too long sleeves of his. Gracie started begging like mad to be the one to put the envelope in the basket, she was still at that real childish age when it came to stuff like that; you know, pushing the button in the elevator, being first in line for ice cream, that sorta thing. Anyway, I thought I'd have some fun with her, and started to remind Ma that it was my turn to put the envelope in, when she dug her knuckles in my ribs so hard I let out a little screech and had to pretend I was holding in a sneeze just to save face. One thing about old Gracie, she wasn't about to give up something so important without a fight, and pound for pound, she could inflict more pain than Dick Butkus, if she had a mind to.

The alter boys started ringing them bells to signal mass was winding down, and the Bishop, he commenced to mumble over the wine goblet and communion wafers like always, which got me to thinking about how hungry I was. Remember, I hadn't had even a crumb all day! I was being mercilessly starved outta respect for the lord, which didn't seem all that Christian if ya ask me, which nobody ever did. We all recited the, "Our Father," and then had to start in with the, "Peace be with yous," to every Tom, Dick, or Harry that happened to be sitting near ya even if you'd never set eyes on 'em before in your whole life. The worst part, though, was that some folks couldn't just *say* it to ya and let it lie, but had to *touch* you just the same, especially if you were a kid, and it was mostly the crusty old ladies with about an inch of rouge on their cheeks that looked like the first layer had been set back in 1933, and a mouth that you would'a swore had a pair of them red wax lips from Halloween stuck in it. A quick look around told me I was in for it 'cause there was nuthin' but blue hair, pink cheeks and rosy red lips as far as the eye could see, and after they finished mauling me I looked like one of them hideous clowns from your worst nightmare, with my hair sticking up every which way, and old lady make-up smeared from ear to ear. It was down right embarrassing, and there was no way I was gonna let Jenny see me like this, so I decided to try to make a run for the bathroom as our row started filing out for communion, but just as I turned to make my escape, Gracie ratted me out and Ma grabbed me by the collar quick as a cat and twirled me back around toward the altar with the rest of the lot. That meant I was gonna hafta pass right in front of Jenny Darling on my way, and I knew my only chance of saving face was to try and hide myself close behind Pop best I could, and just slide on by undetected. Well, that plan went about as well as the rest of the day, 'cause just as we was passing by where sweet little Jenny was sitting and saying her prayers to herself nice and quiet and all, my darn foot caught on the back of Pop's heel, giving him a nasty flat tire and throwing me sideways with a lerch. As I flung my hand out to catch my balance, I instead knocked Mrs. Darling's hat clean off and halfway to the confessional, and then practically collapsed right into Jenny's lap! She was so shook up she let out a little screech and threw her Bible high up in the air, which, wouldn't ya know it, whacked the littlest altar boy square in the kisser, causing him to drop the bell he was carrying on his foot and let out a scream you could hear all the way to Mexico! I mumbled some lame apology to Jenny, looking up at her from down between her legs, and then Pop grabbed me by the belt and jerked me back to my feet. By then the whole nosey congregation was standing up and stretching their necks, trying to see what all the commotion was about. I was so embarrassed I couldn't think of nuthin' but running, so I did--- straight down the aisle towards the front door and freedom. As I flew by the pews, I caught a glimpse of good old Rosie, staring at me in horror, with his mouth wide open and his chubby forehead all wrinkled up like a huge prune. I slowed down just enough to splash a bit of holy water on myself as I went by the little cup on the wall, figuring I was gonna need all the help from the Lord I could muster after Ma got a hold'a me, and then kept right on running all the way to the car, where I jumped into the back seat, slammed the door, laid down flat and waited 'til the rest of my completely humiliated family showed up to take me home.

# Chapter Six

## BAZOOKA WARS

I laid low the next couple of days, hoping to ride out the barrage of humiliating comments I knew were headed my way from the guys on account'a me practically mauling poor Jenny Darling in church on Sunday. Now Rosie was a good friend and all, but even he wouldn't be able to keep something this juicy to hisself, and ya couldn't blame him, really, and even if he did, half of southern Arizona was at San Javier and seen the whole disgusting thing for themselves, so I was pretty much S.O.L., as Pop always says when he's in a tight spot, although he wont tell me what that stands for. It might be "Sort of lousy" but I ain't sure. Anyway, can you imagine the stuff Neil's gonna have in store for me with this kind of ammunition? It ain't gonna be pretty, let's face it.

So I decided to hang around the house 'til things simmered down a tad, working on my pitching, playing board games with Gracie and trying to teach Dodger the easiest dog tricks I could come up with, which was still a complete waste of time. Golden Retrievers might be kinda cute I guess, and at times even sweet, but take it from me they are definitely not the Einsteins of the dog world.

Ma was actually being pretty cool about what happen. I suppose she felt that no matter how big a jackass I made of myself, at least I was in church like a good kid, which didn't make *me* feel a whole lot better, to be honest. Anyway, towards the end of the week, I was sitting at the kitchen table having a nutritional breakfast of Pop Tarts and Lucky Charms when the phone rang.

"Why, hello Jeffrey. How are you?" Mom always called Jag, Jeffrey.

"How is your Mom getting along with your father away at that terrible war? You tell her if she needs anything at all, don't hesitate to call. Okay? Hold on now Hun, I'll get Johnny for you."

I wasn't too keen on taking the call, but knew I was gonna hafta face the guys sometime, so I grabbed the phone and before I could say a word, Jagger screams out, "Ba-ba-bazooka wars!"

"Are you nuts?" I yelled back, after my ear stopped ringing and then turned to see Ma stretching an ear to try and hear every word I was saying, so I took the phone over to the couch and sat down. "Don't you remember what happened last time?" I whispered, trying to look real nonchalant.

"Don't b-b-be a w-w-weenie! That was six m-m-m-months ago, and anyway, K-K-Kemery is an idiot."

Bill Kemery's the only other member of the S.S.B.'s that you haven't met yet on account'a he's been in California with his folks on vacation all summer. He's a nice kid and all, and real funny, but he is a little screwy, if you know what I mean. Like he doesn't have a shred of common sense sometimes. Now everybody does something dumb once in a while, 'cause that's just how kids are, but Kemery, he really takes the cake. Like the time at his slumber party he left all our grilled hotdogs on the picnic table to go get some mustard and when he came back all the hotdogs were gone and in their place was his little mutt Yogi lying on his side with a belly big as a basketball, or the time in science class last year when he poured the whole test tube of sulfuric acid into a bottle of chlorine powder and they had to shut down the entire school for two days to get all the poisonous fumes out. Anyway, he was famous for that sort of stuff, even though he never did nuthin' on purpose, and I could vouch for 'im, 'cause I was there.

Now last Christmas vacation we all decided to make tennis ball bazookas outta tin cans, which I'll tell you all about later, and Kemery's just wouldn't work. After trying and trying to get it to fire, he got real ticked off and decided to take a look down the barrel to see what the heck the problem was, when "KA---BOOM!" That tennis ball came flying out about a mile a minute, and hit the poor little numbskull square in the head, almost putting his eye out. His face swelled up all purple and blubbery, and before it was finished it looked like he had an eggplant growing outta his forehead! Word spread to all the moms in the white ghetto faster than chicken pops through a nursery school and that was pretty much that as far as tennis ball bazookas were concerned, until now, apparently.

"G-G-Grab your stuff and m-m-meet at the clubhouse in thirty!" Click!

He obviously didn't want to hear no moaning about last time and all, but I knew down deep this warn't a good idea. After the Kemery fiasco, I knew if Ma found out, the rest of my summer would be spent on dog poop patrol and playing dolls with Gracie, but come to think of it, bazooka wars were one of the coolest ideas we'd ever come up with, and I figured the combat training we were getting could really come in handy if we ever had to protect the white ghetto someday from an all out attack, from say, Mexico.

Anyway, I couldn't resist and went quietly around the house in search of all the supplies I'd need for battle: six tin cans, four or five old tennis balls, duct tape, lighter fluid, a lighter and a football helmet. I grabbed a trash bag and started to fill her up. Mom suspected something was up as she watched me rifling through closets and cupboards, but she couldn't quite put her finger on it, and I sure wasn't gonna give her any clues. The tennis balls, the cans and duct tape were easy, it was the lighter and lighter fluid that were going to take all my conniving and finagling skills, 'cause Ma wasn't about to leave them kinda things out in the open. Not with little kids like Gracie around.

"Ma," I said, real sincere. "I sure am happy Pop stopped smoking. Ya know they're finding out all kinds of horrible stuff cigarettes can do to you."

"I know, Johnny, your father will live a lot longer and happier life now that he has quite that disgusting habit."

"I do kinda miss that big old green glass ashtray, though, you know, the one you used to have sitting out on the coffee table. I used to like looking through the bottom of it and then watching T.V. It made the people look all squiggly and green like scary monsters. What cha ever do with that thing, anyhow?"

"I put it away in the cupboard above the ice box in the kitchen so as not to remind your father about smoking."

"That was real smart, Ma. I bet you did the same thing with that old gold lighter he had too, the one with his initials engraved on one side and the flag of Italy on the other."

"You bet I did, son. I hid *that* in the top drawer of my dresser."

I was off down the hall almost before she had finished her sentence and found the old lighter right where she said it was, stuffed behind some old brassieres. It wouldn't light so I figured the wick must'a been dried out from sitting so long, after all, Pop quite smoking more than two years ago. The flint looked okay, so now all I needed was to find some lighter fluid and I'd be home free.

I didn't want to try to scam Ma a second time; she was way too sharp for that, so I decided to start looking through the shed, but no luck. I searched high and low, in boxes and on shelves and under rags but there was no sign of that stinking little can. Finally, it dawned on me that a huge worrywart like Ma would never leave something dangerous like lighter fluid outside in the heat, especially where I could reach it, so I decided to check that same cupboard in the kitchen where she hid the green ashtray. I had to wait 'til she was distracted, though, and it started getting kinda dicey since I was supposed to be at the clubhouse in ten minutes and Jag was a real stickler when it came to being on time for official S.S.B.'s meetings, but lucky for me just then the phone rang and it was Aunt Leah calling to gossip this time about how horrible the dress was that old Mrs. Saloom had on at the Fourth of July extravaganza down at the town square. That reminds me, don't let me forget to tell ya what Neil did to the mayor and his new toupee with two sparklers and one of them pellets that oozes out what looks like dog poop during last year's big independence day speech.

Anyways, when Ma and Aunt Leah start gossiping about the ladies in town, World War III could break out and they wouldn't have known the difference, so with Ma in the family room yapping away, I slowly dragged one of the kitchen chairs over to the refrigerator and climbed on up. I opened the cupboard and reached up to feel around 'cause I still wasn't tall enough to see in. I could feel that dumb old ashtray all right, but not much else. The lighter fluid *had* to be there, I thought, it was the only logical place for her to hide it. I stretched way up on my tippytoes, trying to feel all the way to the back when the chair started teetering, and as I frantically grabbed at something to balance myself, my fingertips slid across something smooth. I quickly reached back up, and with a little hop was able to snatch it. There it was, that beautiful yellow and blue tin can with the little red top! I kissed it, which tasted kinda yucky on accout'a some old fluid dried on the outside, stuck it in the back pocket of my Levis, jumped down and slid the chair back to the table. Then I grabbed my trash bag full of stuff and slammed my football helmet on my head as I raced through the laundry room toward the back door.

"See ya, Ma. I'll be back before dark!" I yelled as I slammed the door, threw the bag over my shoulder, jumped on my Stingray and took off down the hill for the clubhouse.

I flew down Jagger's alley and jammed on the brakes while pulling hard right on the front wheel, and did a pretty respectable fishtail for only having one hand on the monkey bars, if I do say so myself. I gave the secret knock, which was the drum solo from "Wipe Out," but don't tell nobody or Neil says we gotta take your first born son, (don't ask me what we want some snot nose kid for,) and the door was unlatched from inside and swung open.

"Where the heck ya been!" Ira barked. "Don't tell me your mommy hid the lighter fluid again."

"Well, yeah. But come on, I'm not *that* late, so eat me!"

"No thanks," Big I shot back. "I want a meal not a snack."

"Ooooh!" All the buttheads groaned.

"Just don't trip and land face first in my crotch like ya did to sweet little Jenny at church, you animal," Neil sneered, without even looking up.

"Chopped low!" the rest of my supposed best pals all yelled out as they made a chopping motion with one hand against their arm.

That was the official S.S.B. way of saying you'd been totally humiliated, and I knew that was coming sooner or later so we may as well get it out of the way now.

"Shut up, Neil! That ain't how it was at all." I said, as I gave Rosie, who wasn't having no luck trying to hide his fat self in the corner, a real nasty look.

"That's not what I hear," he answered in a real serious voice. "I heard you mauled her pretty good and there's a good chance she could be scarred for life, may even need to see a *shrink* for awhile. I mean if you *really* needed a big hug and a kiss, why didn't you just ask?" He said as he looked at me, puckered up his lips and made some loud smooching sounds.

Well, that was all I could stand, and I lunged for 'im hard as I could, but just before I reached his throat with my outstretched fingers, a hand like a steel trap grabbed me by my collar and yanked me back on the seat of my pants.

"S-s-settle down there, J-Johnny boy. W-w-we've got work to do," Jagger said, "You two c-can settle this on the f-f-field of honor, like gentleman, soon as we f-f-finish up our g-g-guns.

I sat there for a minute or two, huffing and puffing, with my heart pounding away, then I crawled over to Rosie and gave 'im the nastiest Indian burn on his arm that I could muster. He let out a little yelp, but didn't say another word, knowing darn well he deserved it, and worse for opening his big fat mouth. After that I felt a lot better, even though Neil kept winking at me and puckering up every chance he got, so I set my sights on making the best stinking tennis ball bazooka ever, now that I had a lot more reason to inflict as much pain as possible on some of my best pals.

Well, in order to build these contraptions, in case ya didn't know, ya had to cut the ends outta three tin cans for the barrel of your gun, which warn't as easy as it sounds considering we didn't have no can opener, and instead had to poke about a million holes all around the edge with an ice pick and then kinda pry the piece out. Problem was, those jagged edges were sharp, which lead to a lot'a mangled, bloody fingers. Then ya had to smooth out all the rough parts, but couldn't use a rock or nuthin' to bang 'em flat, 'cause that would bend it all outta shape. Nope, ya had to use something round to do the job, like, say a Coke bottle. You just stuck it in the end 'til it was nice and tight, and then spun it real slow back and forth 'til them edges were smooth as good old Steve McQueen. The cans had to be nice and straight, too, without any dents or dings, or else your aim wouldn't be worth a snot. After them three were finished, the next can in line was by far the most important, on accout'a it was the, "combustion chamber," where ya dripped in the lighter fluid through a tiny hole on the side, and it mixed all up just right with air and fumes and stuff, so when ya lit it, there'd be enough force to shoot that tennis ball at warp speed straight at the head of your no good, back-stabbing buddies. For this amazing miracle of playground science to come off, one end of this can stayed solid and the other end, the one facing the barrel, had a hole cut about the size of a quarter smack dab in the middle, which, take it from me, took a heckuva lotta concentrating to do a sweet job with that lousy ice pick. That's where we separated the men from the boys, 'cause if that hole warn't dead on size-wise; too big and most of the fumes from the lighter fluid would leak into the barrel and the ball wouldn't do diddly squat, too small and not enough of the force would explode down the barrel leaving ya with a shot Nancy Cole could throw harder.

I looked up and saw Creepy huddled real serious with Neil, and he was using a funny looking ruler with a half moon shape stuck on top to make marks on his cans, and then jotting down a bunch'a numbers in a notebook. I heard 'im whispering something like, "Fifteen degrees of projectory," and then, "use point five sissies or ten drops of Ethel Nowl."

It was plain to see Neil didn't have a clue what he was jabbering about neither, and finally he says, real irritable, "Stuff a sock in it, will ya Creep! You're giving me a migraine with all this scientific mumbo jumbo. Just build the dang gun and tell me what to do when the time comes, got it!"

Well, that rattled old Bampu to no end, which, quite honestly wasn't hard to do, and he started getting all fidgety again, blinking his eyes non-stop, biting at his lips, and stretching his nose up and down and side to side, 'til I had to turn away to keep from cracking up.

Finally, Jag says, "S-s-settle down, Bampu, kid, before ya sh-short circuit yourself! Anyways, I th-th-think you're doing a b-b-bang up job."

After that Creepy was able to calm hisself, mostly, and went back to his figuring.

I poked the tiny hole on the side of my combustion chamber can, which was where ya had to hold your lighter 'til blast off, duct-taped it to the barrel, making sure the whole get-up was straight as a whistle, and then added two more cans after that with an old dish rag I snatched from the kitchen taped to the end for padding against my shoulder. Believe it or not, if everything was just right, these babies could have a pretty nasty kick. I added a piece of twine on each end that I swiped from Rosie's bag to act as a shoulder strap and declared that I was ready for combat.

We filed out of the clubhouse, one by one, carrying our heavy artillery, and showed off our work, which pretty much fit each kid's combat style. Take Chicken Coop, for example, he was too afraid to come out from cover long enough to actually aim at somebody, so he added two sticks to his gun to act as legs and made it into a kind of mortar to lob shots in your general direction. Jag, the psycho, liked going on kamikaze missions, saying only weenies needed to hide behind stuff, and always used a gun with a short barrel and no padding that you could shoot from the hip and was easy to handle. Rosie was also kinda yellow, afraid to get too close to the action, and besides he was too big and slow to run away from a full frontal charge, so he slapped one of the sights off his father's hunting rifle on his gun and became a long range sharp shooter. Ira didn't care what his gun came out like 'cause he said the whole thing was stupid and he could throw a ball better than the bazooka could shoot 'em, which may have been true, but not near as much fun, and the only reason he played at all was to watch us make complete fools outta ourselves. Neil, on the other hand took bazooka wars real serious, saying any time ya had a chance to inflict pain on another human being you should do the best job you possibly could. He had come up with some pretty evil ideas in the past, like the tennis ball grenade that had a black cat stuck inside and could be used to flush out the enemy from their bunkers, and the paint bomb which was a torn up tennis ball filled with paint that would splatter ya from head to toe if ya got hit, but as he crawled out of the fort with his, "Chief Engineer," Creepy, close behind and held up his new creation over his head in triumph, it was obvious that he had outdid hisself this time.

"Behold fellow warriors, I bring twice the fire power, twice the pain, twice the fear. I give you my latest master piece, TWIN KILLING!" he yelled and then started up one of them phony mad scientist laughs.

"No way, Neil, you know the rule has always been only one gun per player, so forget it!" Ira snapped.

"This *is* one gun, numbnuts, it just has two barrels like a double-barreled shotgun." And then he aimed the contraption at Ira, point blank, and shouted, "KA-POW! KA-POW!" and started up his evil laugh all over again as Creepy started to fidget.

"That could be real dangerous," added Chicken Coop, moving slowly over to his big pal Rosie for support. "It'd be a lot harder to dodge two shots at once."

"It's dangerous for you to look in the mirror, Cooper, so shut the heck up!" Neil growled back.

"What do you think Jag?" asked Rosie, obviously not too comfortable with the situation, either.

"W-w-well, I guess it is only one g-g-gun, so I guess the only thing to s-s-say is—THIS MEANS WAR!" He yelled this last part out with all his might, and we all held our guns over our heads and cheered, then grabbed our ammo, jumped on our bikes and peeled out for Red River.

There were still a few skinny clouds hanging around from last nights rainstorm, and they were just enough to blot out a few of the blazing sun's rays, leading to a lovely cool breeze in our faces as we rode along. It warn't too often ya felt anything cool in Santa Elena in the dead of summer, 'cept maybe when Señor Ledesma, the *paletero*, would open up the back of his ice cream wagon just to give us kids a break from the sweltering heat, even if we didn't have no *dinero* for a bullet or drumstick, or even a little carnation cup.

We rode single file down alleyways choked with cattails and desert broom from the rains and it always amazed me how them tiny seeds just waited underground all summer through the miserable heat real patient for a few precious drops of rain, and then—Pow! Them plants practically leaped outta the dirt and just kept on growing to beat the band. Sure they'd shrivel up in a couple'a months, who wouldn't around here under this kinda heat, but next July there they'd be again, doing there best to add at least a little bit of beauty to this God-forsaken desert.

We tried avoiding the streets as much as possible, 'cause any moron could see what we was up to, and ever since the Kemery debacle, every mom and little sister in the neighborhood was on the lookout for anything remotely looking like a tennis ball bazooka. The alley still had that soothing moist desert smell from the night before, although an occasional whiff of wet garbage put a damper on things. After a block or two Rosie pulled out a little clear plastic pouch from his back pocket with some black tarry looking stuff inside. This was a new one on me, and I watched along with everyone else, dumbfounded, as he ripped one end open with his teeth and started squeezing the black goo into his mouth.

"What the heck are ya eating now, Roseola!" Neil barked, disgusted.

"This?" Rosie answered. Caught by surprise by the grossed out looks on the faces starring back at 'im. "It's *pulpa de tamarindo.*"

"Looks more like poop-a de Tammy and Ringo," Ira barely managed to spit out.

"I scraped stuff off the bottom of my shoes that looked more appetizing than that!" I added.

"No. It's good. They make it in Mexico by mashing up the beans in the pods that fall on the ground from mesquite trees," he said with a big grin, like that was supposed to make us feel better, or something, and then he said, real enthusiastically on account 'a he already knew for sure what the answer would be, "Any body want some?"

When the alley opened up to Cicada Street, we made a beeline for the schoolyard and raced straight across like a bunch'a commandos on a secret mission behind kraut lines. We had forgot summer recreation was going on in the auditorium, which, anyway ya cut it, was pretty much a babysitting service for the little kids in the neighborhood, although I'll have to admit there were days that we'd hang out there when there warn't nuthin' better going on. They had an old ping-pong table with a cracked ball, paddles made outta cardboard and popsicle sticks, and a net that drooped way down low from being whacked so many times by kids trying to slam one against their opponent. The shuffleboard court was drawn with chalk on the front walk and the "pusher stick" was nuthin' but a broom handle with a wire hanger taped to the end, which was pretty good for goosing kids but not much else. The arts and crafts table had paper mache that was perfect for turning your pals into mummies, and that salty white dough stuff that didn't taste half bad if you missed lunch, for making ashtrays and pottery and such that your ma would always pretend that she absolutely loved.

We knew we'd better avoid old Coach Holstrum who was in charge of the whole mess. He was a retired high school football coach with a long handlebar mustache, calfs as big as fire hydrants, and deaf as the day is long, which probably explained why he was able to keep up this job so long with all them screaming meemie brats running around like lunatics. To tell ya the truth, he was a pretty swell guy most of the time, and was always glad to see us, 'cept Neil, of course, who had already wore out his welcome this summer for playing tic-tac-toe with a green marker on little Russell Covey's shaved head, but old coach was still an adult, and absolutely could not be trusted in a situation this sensitive.

As we rode up close to the front of the Sewer there were kids everywhere; chasing each other, beating each other, playing keep away, and never stopping for one second, just like little kids always do, and Jag decided our best bet was to try to just creep right along undetected through the whole wild bunch seeing they was so preoccupied.

Things were going along smooth enough at first and I thought we might just luck out, when that little pecker wood, Timmy Cole, Nancy's brother, spotted us and yelled out, "Hey, where are you guys going, and what's all that stuff you got?" Well, you'd've thought Santa Claus hisself was walking by the way every kid on that playground stopped dead in his tracks and raced over to us to see what was what.

"What'da'ya guys got behind your backs?" sweet little Timmy asked, wiping his nose on the sleeve of his shirt and edging closer to us. Nobody said a word but just kinda scowled at 'im, hoping to scare him off, before Coach Holstrum got wind of us.

"Is that you Ira?" it was Sue, his nagging little sister. She always strung out his name, "*Eye-eee-ra*," in a scratchy, whiney voice to be as annoying as possible. "Does *mom* know where you are?" Big I, embarrassed as all get out, pretended not to hear her.

Now the rest of the little maggots were crowding us pretty good.

"Come on! I demand to know what you're hiding!" Timmy blurted out with his hands on his hips, and sounding eerily like his delightful big sister.

Well, that was more than Neil could stand, and before I could stop 'im, he says, "You really want to know what we've got you little twerp? Well take a real close look!" and he pulled out his double-barreled bazooka and stuck it right in little Timmy's face, point blank.

Well he and all the other mini-maggots let out this blood-curdling scream all at once, and started yellin' "He's got a gun! He's got a gun!" and ran off to tell the old coach all about it.

"Let's book!" Jag said frantically and we all high tailed outta there, across Camino Principal and into the desert.

I glanced over my shoulder just in time to catch a glimpse of poor old Coach Holstrum, all frantic, racing through the front door led by a mob of screeching kids, and shouting out, "Don't shot, don't shot, they're only children!"

We didn't stop peddlin' 'til we made it to Red River, which was close to 200 yards from the school, and too far off for any of the summer rec weenies to follow.

"You're a real stinking genius, Neil!" I said, right to his face as we all kinda made a circle with our bikes in front of the wash. "Now everybody in the county's gonna know what we're up to."

"Yeah, well, tough turds! You guys can do what ya want, but I'm not about to stand there and take any crap from that little twit Timmy. I only wish I had my gun loaded 'cause I would've loved to have bounced a couple of tennis balls off his fat head."

Jagger started laughing that same retarded, "Hee-hee-hee," and said he wouldn't've minded seeing that himself. Well, nobody could argue with that, I guess, and we all had a good laugh, thinking about the horrified look on his puss when Neil pointed, "Twin Killing" right between his eyes, and we took turns doing our best, "petrified Timmy," face. That lightened the mood up considerable and got us feeling a whole lot better about things, all except Ira who hadn't said a word, knowing he'd be first to pay the price when he got home, now that sweet little Sue was on to 'im.

It was time to start the war preparations so we all slid down on our rear ends into the wash and started gathering up stuff to make our bunkers. Some of the guys liked digging foxholes in the sand left over from the recent floods, and some guys favored using cardboard boxes and such to make above ground "pillboxes." I liked the combination of digging down about two feet deep, just enough to lie face down and not having anything important sticking out for target practice, and then ringing the whole thing with the biggest rocks I could find for shooting through. The spot you picked was real important, too. When we played teams, it didn't really matter much, but in a free for all, if you were too close to somebody else, you were either dead meat, or you could be pinned down the whole battle, which warn't no fun at all. The battlefield usually took the shape of a huge ring, although it took a lot of convincing to get Rosie and Chicken Coop to set up within firing range, and Creepy would've been right along with 'em if not for Neil insisting that he hang out with him as his "tactical analyst." No one was allowed to dig in on either bank 'cause he could cause some major carnage shooting down from above, but after the battle started up, there was no restrictions, and the last man standing was the winner. After about half an hour, we were ready to go.

"What do ya call that," Ira laughed, as he pointed at my spot, obviously feeling better about his upcoming jail sentence.

"It's my desert fox hole. Designed for easy firing from every angle." I shot back with some pride.

"Looks more like a shallow grave, just what the doctor ordered after I plaster you in the first minute," Ira laughed, along with the rest of the guys. He gave me the, "Chopped low" sign, and then fell over on his back with his hands folded on his chest like he was dead.

"O yeah, Big I. Well, I won't even need to waste a shot to bring down that mud hut you made. Probably a good *sneeze* would do the trick!"

Ira had piled up as many big dirt clods as he could find to make a little wall and was gonna make his stand behind 'em.

"That reminds me," said Neil. "Did any of you guys hear about the Mexican Navy's submarine that kept sinkin'?"

We all shook our heads no.

"Yeah, I guess the adobe wall kept falling in!"

That gave us all another good laugh, all 'cept Rosie, who was getting kinda touchy about all the jokes about Mexican folks around here. Funny thing, most of the time it was some Mexican person telling it.

"You g-g-guys are a bunch 'a w-w-wuses," Jagger said. "Here's all the fort a real soldier needs." And he pointed to a small boulder, no more than 2 foot by 2 foot. Jag didn't waste much time making fancy digs 'cause first of all he wasn't too good with his hands, and second he was so nutty and fearless he spent most of the battle running around like a mad man.

"Hey, Neil and Creepy, why don't you two go home and hide behind your mother's skirt and get it over with?" Ira yelled out as we all were looking at the elaborate fortification of mud, driftwood and cardboard they were building at the south end of the wash. Neil just glared at Ira over the top with The Creep kinda cowering behind.

"We'll see who's gonna be crying for their mommies in a few minutes, Irene!" he growled.

Rosie and Cooper weren't taking no chances. They found themselves two big cardboard boxes, stuffed themselves inside, and then just cut two little holes to see through. The one Rosie found used to hold a refrigerator, and had just enough room for him to squeeze in.

The time had finally come for war, and we decided to start with a free for all, each man for hisself, and we hunkered down in our bunkers ready for the command. I stuffed that Baltimore Colts helmets on tight and started to load my bazooka. First, I looked for a nice old tennis ball, since they didn't have none of that fuzzy stuff left on 'em any more to slow 'em down, then I put three drops of lighter fluid down the barrel, stuffed the ball in, shook it up real good to get the fumes all mingled just right, put another drop on the small hole on the side of the combustion chamber can, and then wiggled my way down as low as I could in my fox hole with my lighter at the ready.

"Ready! Aim! F-f-fire!" Jagger screamed as tennis balls whizzed trough the air in every direction. I took my first shot at Jag to start the game, like I always did, and just missed beaning 'im but good. Instead, it hit the top of his boulder and bounced about 50 feet straight up.

"You were almost dead meat, punk!" I screamed while peeking over the edge of my foxhole.

"Almost d-d-don't count, Johnny C. 'cept in horseshoes and hand g-grenades. But f-f-eel free to try again s-s-sometime!" Jag yelled back as he stood straight up, and stuck out his tongue with a big goofy smile, knowing darn well I couldn't load up fast enough to take another pot shot at 'im.

"BLAM! BLAM!" Neil's first two shots were right at Rosie's cardboard box and they hit it head on, knocking it over and leaving poor old Rosie sitting in the sand defenseless. He let out a horrid screech and his eyes got big as baseballs, and we all had a good laugh as he scrambled on all fours fast as he could, which for Rosie, warn't too quick at all, to get back in his box. Unfortunately, for him, Ira had saved his first shot for just this kind of opportunity and nailed the poor guy hard, right in the butt, before he could get to safety.

"You're dead, fat boy." he said proudly.

Rosie collapsed face first in the sand, spread eagle and didn't move a muscle. He was the first casualty, and out of the game.

The rest of us reloaded quick and got ready for round two. Now nobody wanted to waste a shot 'cause the rule was you were only allowed three balls to start with, and after that ya had to scramble to find more ammo wherever you could, so it was kind of a cat and mouse game for a while as everyone was waiting for a nice, wide open shot. I could tell Jag was getting kinda antsy behind his rock, on account'a it went against his grain to hide for too long, so I set my sights over on him and waited. Just then I heard this sort of sizzling sound coming from Neil's way, and sure enough here comes a firecracker grenade landing right next to me! I had no choice but to leap outta my fox hole or get blown to bits, when, "BLAM! SPLAT!" Neil's paintball bomb whizzed past my head and splattered a lovely shade of green against the side of the wash. I steadied myself, aimed, fired and nailed Creepy right in the chest as he stood up a little too high to see if their shot had hit its mark. He let out a sickening yelp as the tennis ball smashed into his ribs, staggered backwards a few steps and fell over on his back. There was no time to gloat over my great marksmanship, so I dove for my hole as Big I and Jagger took their best shots at me; both sailing high.

"Nice try, retards!" I yelled in triumph as they all grumbled over their missed opportunity. All except Chicken Coop, that is, who hadn't made a sound the whole battle, probably hoping we'd forget he was out there at all. Well, that wasn't gonna happen, and as soon as Neil was reloaded and wanting to take out his frustration on an easy target, smashed a ball right through Coop's box with a direct hit. Chicken Coop got spooked and stood straight up, still carrying the cardboard box over the top part of his body and started to run as fast as he could. The problem was, he couldn't see where the heck he was going and tripped over a piece of driftwood and fell flat. Neil then nailed 'im square in the back with the ball in his second chamber as Coop tried to crawl into his box and hide.

"Aaaah!" he screamed.

"Your gone, Chicken Poop," Neil answered with another of them sinister laughs, and just then, "BLAM! OUCH!" Jagger nailed Ira in a leg that was sticking out too far, as he got careless watching poor Coop's execution.

That left me, Neil, and Jag as the last commandos alive in the battle of Red River, and things were pretty much a stalemate for the next twenty to thirty minutes as we kept scrambling for balls, but nobody could quit hit the guy in the open. Jag did his best to keep everyone entertained while gathering up his ammo, running around like a chicken with its head cut off, doing summersaults, rolling in the sand, and all the while making these loud, "Whoop! Whoop!" sounds. He got Neil and I laughing so hard we couldn't shoot straight.

Finally, Neil decided to use his last "Grenade" to flush Jag out for an open shot, and rolled it over behind his boulder. The problem was, Jagger was so crazy that instead of running away from the grenade he actually picked the darn thing up, firecracker and all, and flung it right back at Neil before it exploded. Well, Neil dove outta *his* fort like he was shot out of a cannon, and Jag nailed 'im while he was still in the air: with a really bitchin' shot, and he landed with a thud, gasping for air as the tennis ball plugged 'im right in the solar plexus.

"Hey, N-N-Neil, if you d-d-die, can I use your g-g-gun next game?" Jag asked, real sincere-like.

"Never, buffalo breath!" Neil spit out in between gasps and then took off his helmet and flung it hard as he could at Jagger, who by now had run out into the open and was doing a little samba-style victory dance around Neil.

Rosie and Chicken Coop were sitting at the edge of the bank watching the action along with Creepy, and they were laughing and clapping and egging Jag on, happy as clams to see Neil squirming around in defeat. But they all had forgotten one real important thing, and that was that I was very much still in the game. I had Jag dead in my sights, but waited patiently for just the right moment for him to stand still, and I got my chance as he stopped in front of Neil to shake his butt in his face. I raised up on one knee, took aim and flicked my lighter. KABOOM! SMACK! My shot hit Jag dead center in the back of his helmet. He stopped dancing, staggered forward a couple of steps, did a 360 as he grabbed his head with both hands and fell face first in the mud. There was complete silence for a few seconds and then everyone started laughing and clapping all over, with Neil being the loudest, obviously tickled at how the worm had turned.

"J-J-Johnny C," Jagger groaned in a low muffled voice, his facemask still stuck in the mud. "I c-c-can't believe you'd shoot your old p-p-pal in his moment glory."

"Yeah, well, believe it," I said, as I ran over to my victim and put my foot on his back as I raised my gun over my head in victory.

"All's fair in love and war, ya know."

"Well you ain't never gonna find out about love, Johnny, if you keep mauling Jenny every time she's around." Ira added with a big smile.

That got all the guys to laughing at my expense all over again.

"Alright, alright, am I ever gonna hear the end of that one?" I asked pleadingly.

"Probably not," Ira said. "What do you think Neil?"

"Nope, never," he answered, and everyone kept on laughing and hollering out "Chopped low!" for a good long while.

Well, we all just hung out talking about the battle for a bit and how Rosie wasn't gonna be able to sit down too comfortable for a few days, and how Jag's ears would be ringing for a while, when out of the blue came a bright flash and a loud, "BOOM!" A huge bolt of lightening! I guess we got ourselves so caught up in our bazooka war we hadn't noticed the clouds rolling in. It was already black as the ace of spades over the mountains to the north and the winds were getting to whip around but good. We knew that weren't a good sigh, and the rains weren't far off so we started walking toward the old tree stump we used to haul ourselves outta the wash. After a few more lighting bolts off to the north, we heard another low rumbling noise starting up that seemed to be slowly getting louder. Nobody was quite sure what the heck it was, and we called out to Creepy, who had already hustled up to the top of the bank, to ask if he could see anything.

"Don't see a thing, Johnny C," he said as he took off his glasses and wiped 'em on his shirtsleeve. When he put 'em back on and took another look, his mouth dropped open and he turned three shades of white.

"O my God! Get out! Get out quick!" he screamed at the top of his lungs, and then started waving his arms up and down like a madman. We all turned to look behind us to see what he was all worked up about, and as the rumbling sound got louder and louder we started to see a little trickle of water coming down the wash about a hundred yards away. Then outta nowhere, a five-foot wall of water came flying down right toward us! Everyone let out a yell and ran fast as our terrified legs could go.

"It's a flash flood! Oh my God! Oh my God! Hurry. *Hurry!*" Creepy kept yelling over and over as he watched us scrambling for the tree root while that wall of water was getting closer and closer.

"Come on! Come *on*!" he screamed, as Neil and Cooper started to scramble up.

Ira, the fastest of the group, wasn't even there yet, and I looked over my shoulder to see that he had fallen and tore up his knee pretty bad. Jagger and Rosie helped 'im up and then were on their way. That water kept on coming hard and was only about fifty yards out as I made my way up. Ira started up next, bad leg and all, and yanked himself up and out, moaning in pain the whole while. Rosie and Jagger were the last ones left as the wall of water rushed on, but that meant trouble, 'cause Rosie being as heavy as he was, could never make it up in time without help, and Jag knew it.

"You g-g-go first Rosie, and I'll help hoist you up," I heard Jagger say over the roar of the water, which was about a foot deep where they were standing by now.

"No Jag, you won't make it in time! You go ahead and save yourself!" he answered and then started to cry.

"S-s-snap out of it!" Jag yelled as he gave Rosie a bit of a shake. "There's no time for that. G-g-get your butt up there right now!" Jagger leaned over, clasping his hands together to make a foothold for Rosie to use.

The water was rising fast now, closing in all around Jagger, as he strained to hold Rosie's weight, and then braced himself against the wall of the wash as Rosie stood on his shoulders to start to pull himself up. I laid on my stomach looking over the edge of the bank and with Neil and Ira holding onto my legs, grabbed onto Rosie's arms to help pull 'im up. When I looked back down, my heart sank, there was no sight of our friend in the wall of water that had rushed by and was already twenty yards down the wash.

"Jagger! Jagger!" I screamed, but there was nuthin'. "He's been swept away!"

I looked back at the guys and they were all sitting there stunned, with their hands on their heads, crying and carrying on and unable to look up, but just then I heard a kinda gurgling sound from over the edge, and I looked back down into the wash to see the top of Jagger's head barely sticking up outta the water. He had grabbed that old root and was holding on for dear life, but his head kept going in and out of the water and he was trying to catch his breath the best he could. The current was pulling at 'im something fierce, and even with all his strength; his grip was starting to slip.

"Hold on, Jag! Hold on!" I yelled down to him. "Guys he's still there! Lower me down." Rosie grabbed hold of Neil and Ira's ankles and bolstered himself behind a big rock that was sticking up about three feet from the edge. Then Ira and Neil each held onto one of my legs and started lowering me over the side of the bank.

"I'm coming, Jag!" I screamed as I made my way down.

The water was roaring by, real choppy, so you could see little white caps all over. Jag had a hold of the tree root with both hands but it seemed he had slipped down a couple of inches lower than he was before. His body was almost sideways in the water as the current kept pulling at 'im, but he was able to keep his head up just enough to get a breath every once in a while. His eyes met mine for just a split second and it seemed to me that he didn't really look scared at all, but instead calm and kinda serene, the look of a kid that didn't have a worry in the whole world, while I was scared to death and trying to keep the tears in my eyes from blurring my vision as I reached for his hand.

"Lower Rosie! Lower!" I yelled back, and I could hear him groan under the pressure of holding all three of us.

I reached down as far as I could with my left hand but it was still a few inches away, and Ira, Neil and Rosie were screaming that they couldn't hold on much longer. Cooper and Creepy were crying and screaming and praying and running around completely out of their wits.

"Hold on! Gimme one last try!" I yelled, and I grabbed that darn tree root with my left hand and gave it a tug with all my might. It was enough to raise Jagger up the couple of inches we needed as his head popped out of the water, and he saw my hand and was just able to grab on. I clamped on with both hands now for all I was worth, and hollered for Rosie to pull us up, but nothin' happened. Rosie was completely spent and he was crying that he couldn't hold out another second.

"Dammit, De la Rosa," Neil said through clenched teeth. "If you wimp out now I'm coming back there and beating the living snot outta you, understand! Just throw your fat butt down on the ground and that should be enough to get us outta here."

After that Rosie mustered up all of his strength, stood straight up using the rock that was sticking up for leverage, and with sweat poring down his face, threw his enormous body backward. Well, Neil was dead on, and with that we all came flying outta there like a bunch of rag dolls. Thank God for good old Rosie's glandular problem!

We all just laid there in the dirt sucking air for a while, too exhausted to say anything, as the rushing water roared in the background. Chicken Coop and The Creep came running over to Jag, and started pawing at 'im and wiping his head and patting his back to no end, 'til finally he said if they didn't stop he was gonna throw both of *them* in the wash. About fifteen minutes passed 'til we gathered up enough strength to get on our bikes and started to slowly peddle back home, our clothes, ripped to shreds and filthy from our ordeal, and our bodies scraped from head to toe. Still nobody said a word, being sorta numb, I guess, as the horrible thoughts of what *almost* happened started to sink in. Poor Jag was the most beat up from the flood water pounding him over and over into the side of the wash, but he was too tough to complain, and although he winced in pain a couple of times, he just kept peddling, staring straight ahead. Still, not a word had been spoken as we passed through Seward School and went on our separate ways. I rode along with Jag as far the big saguaro, which was silhouetted in front of us as the sun began to set over the mountains to the west. As we split apart, I stopped and watched as he rode slowly away.

"You could have drowned back there, and you weren't the least bit scared, were you?" I said after a second or two.

"N-N-Nuthin' to worry about, Johnny C.," he answered without looking back. "I knew you guys wouldn't let me down." He turned his head back just enough for me see that goofy big tooth grin of his, and then he winced once more in pain and continued to ride on and outta site.

# Chapter Seven

## THE OLD PUEBLO DEBUTANTES

I don't hafta tell ya that the word spread about our little adventure at Red River faster than grain through a chicken, whatever that means, and not only regarding the strictly forbidden Bazooka wars, neither, but also about the brilliance of horsing around at the bottom of the wash in the middle of flash flood season. It was for sure a "Twin Killing" of a screw up, and we were gonna pay twice as dearly for it, no ifs, ands or butts. Thank the Lord nobody ratted about how one of us almost drowned out there, or it would'a been the St. Valentines Day Massacre all over again, only with crazed moms instead of murdering gangsters, which was definitely more horrifying and gruesome. Give me the quick death of a Tommy gun anyway to the slow agonizing torture of an angry mother's scorn.

The next week was a nightmare, with me and the guys prosecuted to the fullest extent of the law. That meant no T.V., no phone calls, no playtime, no nuthin'! And you were only allowed to read books without any pictures! I mean this made death row look like a summer afternoon at Disneyland. Even Neil's folks, who usually didn't give a rat's patoot what kinda low life shenanigans he was up too, threw the book at 'im. I'd gotten the third degree from Mom, Granny and Aunt Leah all at once as they waited in ambush for me after our little incident, which I was fully expecting, but when Pop let me have it pretty good, it really got to me, on account'a I knew it wasn't in his nature to ever holler at us kids, and it was probably harder on him than me. That made me feel lower than a run over rattler, and I decided I'd make it up to him soon as I was able.

The first two days of solitary confinement were just awful, and then got *worse* as Ma decided there wouldn't be no radio, neither. I mean, I could live without the other stuff, but now I had no way of following how the Dodgers were doing, and the pennant race with them stinking Giants was getting tight, real tight. I was going nuts just sitting in my room all day playing paper football, shooting baskets with rolled up socks and having to listen to Gracie out in the hallway trying to teach that peckerhead, Dodger, how to roll over for the one thousandth time, but just when things seemed to hit rock bottom, the commandants came up with a new scheme to torture their sons even further; The Old Pueblo Junior Debutants. It was one'a them goody-goody training classes that all the sissies went to in the big cities so as they could get "cultured." A few of the more hateful moms started it up a few years back after Scooter Mamana got in a knock down, drag out fist fight with Misty Higgenbottom out in front of Ratty's ice cream parlor, and although it seems that Misty pretty much cleaned old Scooter's clock when all was said and done, the fine ladies of Santa Elena figured that their girls *and* boys needed to start acting a lot more like little ladies and gentlemen.

"Why ya always forcing me to do things I hate?" I pleaded as I tugged at the tie Ma was trying to strangle me with. "I hate girls, I hate dancing and I hate learning about manners."

"How about you stay in your room and stare at the four walls the rest of the summer?" Mom calmly asked.

It really ticked me off when she wouldn't even consider my feelings about stuff.

"You *will* learn to be a gentleman and you *will* like doing it. Do you hear me?"

I heard her all right, like a jet engine roaring at the threshold of pain. I kept my head down thinking about how ridiculous I must'a looked in this get up she had me in, and how crummy the rest of the day was gonna be. I mean summer vacation was supposed to be fun for crying out loud!

The Old Pueblo Junior Debutantes was run by an old spinster named Miss Hausman, who was a tall, thin, grey haired old biddy, with dentures that were so off kilter they'd smack together something horrible every time she spoke so you'd've swore an old horse was clopping along outside. Now I ain't sure if she had always been single, or if she had married some poor soul in the past and then nit picked 'im to death, but she sure warn't married now, and anybody meeting her could plainly see things were bound to stay that way. She had a bunch of annoying things about her besides the choppers too, like the way she saved her Kleenex, using 'em over and over again, and then stuffing 'em in her sleeve for safe keeping. Problem was, once in a while one of them dirty snot rags would come loose from its storage spot and fall on ya while she was barking out her ridiculous commands. A booger bomb as Neil called 'em. Absolutely disgusting! Just ask poor old Brian Frazier who caught one in the mouth and spent the rest of the class in the bathroom puking up his guts.

When she wanted to get the whole group's attention she'd snap this little metal clacker that she always carried around, but the darn thing sounded so much like her dentures clicking together that you didn't know what was going on. God help the kid that didn't stop what he was up to when that thing went off, cause she'd walk over behind you and smack the top of your head so hard you'd be seeing outta your belly button! Then, after she practically maimed you for life, she'd lean over and say in a real sweet grandma sorta voice, "Excuse me, Mr. so and so could you please pay attention now? Thank you." She was a tough old girl, no doubt about it, and dead set determined to turn us into a group of upstanding young gentleman--no matter what the cost. The only thing was, she ain't never had to convert a group like the S.S.B.'s before.

All the guys showed up about the same time in front of the Santa Elena Convention Center, which was the name the town council gave the place on the outskirts of town, even though no one could ever remember 'em ever having anything close to a convention there up to now, not even one of them corny little ones for say the National Association of Horny Toad Lovers or something. I guess they thought the name made it sound like a real important place to hang out, but it really warn't no more that four walls and a toilet, that over flowed most of the time, and gave the whole place a real "special fragrance" that was half mildew and half—you know what. Each of our moms gave us one last going over, making sure our ties were straight, our sport jackets were just right, and our hair was slicked down nice and pretty, and then practically pushed us out of the car, threatening us to be on our best behavior or else. Ma said if I got in hot water with Ms. Housman I could kiss the rest of vacation goodbye, but I told her not to worry 'cause by the end of this class I'd be so gosh darn gentlemanly it'd be downright nauseating. She just rolled her eyes and pointed to the door.

The old stucco place must've been somebody's house way back when, 'cause it had a lawn out in front and one of them old red cement porches with a couple of well worn steps leading up to it. The roof was flat with a rusty old swamp cooler chugging away on top, and you could see the adobe peeking through on the front walls where the stucco had cracked and fallen off. Neil and Big I didn't look too thrilled to be here, to say the least, and behind them crept Chicken Coop, Creepy and Rosie, all looking more scared than anything else, like ya do when you're walking down a dark alley and ya think someone might be following you. Rosie had on this crazy plaid sports jacket that must've been his pops 'cause it was way too long in the sleeves so they covered up his whole hand, and the bottom practically came down to his knees. It fit around his belly just right, though. He came along slow, doing the Rosie ramble, where his upper body turned way around one way while his lower body turned the other, and his pants made this loud swish-swish sound with each step as his thighs rubbed together. His arms didn't hang down flat by his side neither, but stuck out considerable on account'a all that flab in his armpit area.

"Hey, where's your tie, De la Rosa?" Neil barked, thinking Rosie was trying to pull a fast one.

"What da ya mean? It's right hear," he answered as he pointed to his neck.

Problem was his neck was so chubby that one'a his chins had completely swallowed up his bow tie and there weren't hide nor hair of it to be seen.

"Well, I suppose we'll just have to take your word on this one, old boy," Neil said with a laugh as we all turned toward the door that was looming ominously in front of us.

There was a sweet little receiving line starting up as we got closer to the building and Miss. Hausman was there, greeting all of the new inmates as they arrived. Did she have to look so stinking excited about the torture she was about to spring on us? What a sick-o! But just then I spotted good old Jagger at the front of the line looking mighty dapper in a black and white herringbone jacket, blue polka dot tie and grey trousers, but as he shook hands with Miss. Hausman I saw something that almost made me puke; that rat pulled out a red rose from behind his back and handed it to her with a big phony smile and a little bow.

"Did you guys see that?" I said, shocked. "Jag just gave that old bat a rose for crying out loud!"

"Why that stinking little brown noser." Ira said. "First he gets us all in this mess with his hair brained idea of a bazooka war during flash flood season and now he's kissing up to the Dragon lady to make *us* look bad. Wait 'til I get my hands on that little twit!"

We all muttered our agreement with Ira and continued up the line with the new found energy of the double-crossed. When I finally got up to the door, there was the old battleaxe patting me on the shoulder and saying in this very phony English accent, "Well, well, Mr. Caruso, don't you look handsome this fine day."

"Thanks a million." I answered without looking up and just kept on moving.

"You're looking very dapper this afternoon also, Mr. Wales," she said to Neil, who was next in line.

"You ain't looking half bad yourself, sister." Neil answered, and then gave her a big wink.

The old girl got this shocked as all get out look on her face and put her hand up to her mouth as she blurted out, "Well, I never!" to which Ira, who was next in line answered, "That's pretty much what we all figured, lady."

Well, that sent old Miss. Housman staggering back a step or two, gasping for air, and we really had her on the ropes for a second, but too bad for us, she snapped outta it just before she went belly up, and was soon back to the greeting line, yakking away. It looked like she was gonna be a pretty tough nut to crack.

We all scampered through the front door after that, disappointed that our initial assault wasn't a knockout blow, but Neil and Ira slapped each other on the back anyway in recognition of their gallant try. Then we made our way to the "main ballroom," which was nuthin' but the original living room of the old house, and there we saw something so terribly horrifying that it stopped us dead in our tracks; almost twenty girls in their Sunday best, giggling up a storm! As soon as they spotted us they started waving and batting their eyes, and saying, "Hello handsome!" It was enough to turn your stomach! What's wrong with girls, anyways? Are they normal human beings like the rest of us, or are they really those ancient astronauts from a different galaxy that I heard about on that show, "The 21st Century." That's gotta be it.

Once we realized what was happening, we immediately looked down to the ground and made a beeline for the refreshment table to try and drown our sorrows. After about a hundred glasses of punch, one of them hostess moms came over and told us to back off, so we made our way over to the boy's side of the room where Jagger was waiting patiently for us.

"You b-b-boys sure looked civilized," he said with his usual big toothy grin.

"Shut up, President Peabrain!" Ira shouted back. "If it weren't for you, we wouldn't be in this mess. Let's have a bazooka war. *Great* idea! Oh, and for the grand finally, maybe we'll all almost drown, just for fun! You are the king of the planet Moron."

Jag just laughed. "It was a p-p-pretty good adventure though, you g-g-gotta admit. Right Rosie?"

Rosie warn't in the mood for saying nuthin' on account'a the way too close call at Red River, and from the look of things, his folks must've laid into 'im somethin' fierce 'cause he just stood there staring off, all catty-tonic.

"L-L-Loosen up Rosie, kid," Jag said, punching 'im on his enormous shoulder. If it weren't for you, I p-p-probably wouldn't b-b-be here. I owe you one, b-b-big guy."

That made Rosie feel some better right off, and he let out a little chuckle that made his chubby cheeks jiggle and his big belly bounce.

"Thanks, Jag," he said, kinda sheepish-like.

"I don't care what my folks or that old bag with the clacker says, ain't no way I'm even getting close to one'a them," Neil said, pointing across the room at the group of junior debutants.

"They're monsters!" I added. "Just look at 'em. Where did she find 'em so big?"

It was true. They were gigantic. I was the tallest of the guys by a long shot, pushing five foot two with my sneakers on, and each and everyone one of them debutants had at least five inches on me. It was a little scary to tell you the truth, though none of us wanted to admit it. And not only that, but besides Rosie, they easily outweighed each us by at least 20 pounds! Now that I think about it, I guess one reason us guys hated girls so much was because we knew deep down inside, if they really had an inkling, they could probably beat the living snot outta us any time they wanted.

We were giving them a good looking over by then, kinda evaluating the enemy, but making sure we had a nasty sneer on our faces so they wouldn't get the idea that we was interested in them by any stretch of the imagination, when Chicken Coop says, peeking out from behind Rosie, "What the heck are they so happy about?" It was true too. I knew something wasn't right with the picture I was seeing but couldn't put my finger on it. Them nutty girls were acting *glad* to be here! In fact they acted like there was no place in the universe they'd rather have been at that moment than right here at Old Pueblo *stinkin'* Junior Debutantes. This warn't no punishment for them, it was fun!

Creepy peeked out from his hiding spot behind Rosie's other side, and took hisself a peek. "The fact that they are enjoying themselves immensely is incontrovertible."

Neil squinted up his eyes like someone had just ran their fingernails along a chalkboard and shot old Creep a real dirty look. Then Ira whacked 'im on the back of the head and said if he couldn't speak proper American then don't speak no more at all 'cause he was embarrassing himself and his family. Old Bampu adjusted his glasses, started fidgeting all over and slid back into hiding.

"Don't you numbnuts know that's just exactly how girls are?" Ira said, disgusted. "I got an older sister, remember. Let me tell you, they live their whole stupid lives for this kinda garbage. They actually *enjoy* putting on all those fancy clothes with miles and miles of lace and ribbons that swish all over the place whenever they move an inch, and them pointy black shoes that mash your toes all together with hardly no sole at all that gotta make ya feel like your walking on nuthin' but bare concrete. And don't forget them skintight stockings that they just couldn't live without, with all that special needlework up and down the sides, and all other kinds of under things that you wouldn't even believe. They got at least ten layers of stuff on underneath them dresses, swear to God, and for no darn good reason at all, 'cept for the fact that they *like* wearing it. It's enough to make ya suffocate just to think about it!" He said, as he pulled at his collar and stuck his tongue out like he was choking or somethin'.

# The Old Pueblo Debutantes

We all circled around Big I and listened close as he kept up his tirade against womankind. "And what about their hair. Do you think all those curly cues grow all by themselves? Not on your life! They spend hours and hours getting their hair set just right, with their combing and spraying and combing and spraying and pinning and curling. It is absolutely insane!" He said as he demonstrated the technique like he was looking in mirror. "Heck, my sister Fay uses so much of that lousy hair spray, you can't go into the bathroom for at least an hour 'cause the air's so thick with that crud if ya took a deep breath in, it sticks your nostrils together!"

We all gave a big shudder, took in a big sniff and kept on listening.

"But, I tell you what, that stuff will do the job. I swear she could be right smack dab in the middle of the typhoon of the century, and not one precious little hair would be so much as a millimeter outta place. It's unbelievable! And don't forget all that make up, and perfume and such. You think them rosy-red cheeks and lips come natural? Not by a long shot. That takes a whole nother hour or two of hard work in front of a mirror getting things just so. And any old regular mirror just won't do, neither. No sir-e-bob! They gotta use this special *magnifier*, that makes your nose look as big as your foot! Scared the living daylights outta me first time I seen it, I ain't ashamed ta say! But not them. Not for a second. They *like* looking in it. Spend all day doing it if they could. It just ain't natural, I tell ya!" Big I yelled out in frustration.

"Mark my words fellas, it ain't nuthin' for them to tie up your bathroom for the whole damn morning, and once they do finally let ya in, you wished they hadn't. It looks like the A- Bomb went off in there! With powder over here and rouge over there, and lipstick all over the towels and foundation smeared on the sink. It's absolutely nauseating! And what about them new curling iron things. They're lethal weapons! I kid you not. If you ain't seen one, it looks just like a steel cattle prod, only when ya plug it in it gets about a thousand degrees and can burn the outer layer of your skin clean off in a flash. And *that's* one of their favorite tools. Never go so much as across the street without it. And I haven't even started on the eyebrow plucking! (Serous whincing all around.) The really sad thing about all this is that their moms, instead of straightening 'em out right quick, actually encourage 'em to keep making fools outta themselves, and seem to have themselves a grand old time helping them do it!" After Ira finished, he rolled his eyes, pursed up his lips and just shook his head. The rest of us were speechless, not realizing the horrible conditions our pal had been forced to endure at home. No wonder he was always so stinking p.o.ed.

"If ya ask me, the more stuff they do to themselves, the more hideous they end up looking," Neil said pointing over his shoulder. "I mean, just take a gander at that group of mutants standing across the way."

We all shot a quick glance over at the girls and then looked back at Neil and nodded in agreement.

"The other thing I don't get about girls," Ira continued, "is the way they're always so darn interested in what we're doing all the time. I mean, I couldn't give a flying fudgicle what they're up to, but there they are, always snooping around and wanting us to play with them in the idiotic games they're endlessly coming up with. Take that rancid Nancy Cole for example; have we ever hung around her to see what she was up to? Not a chance! But *she's* gotta always be sniffing around and listening in on our plans and finding out what we are up to, so she can go and rat to El Generalissimo. Ya wanta know what I really think the problem is? Girls ain't smart enough to come up with any cool stuff to do for themselves, so they gotta try and ruin it for us so we can't have no fun neither."

It was amazing! Ira had hit it right on the head when it came to girls, and I gotta admit I was pretty impressed. Never before in my recollection had he ever shown this kind of deep thinking.

"Take that disgusting Hairy-Carrie Lewis, you know the one with the back that looks like Mayor Troncoso's toupee, do you know she had the gall to call my house the other day, right out of the blue, just to ask me what I was doing? I couldn't believe my ears! I told her it was none of her freaking business and hung up in her face. Can you imagine that? Invading my privacy like that and I don't hardly even know her. I'll tell you one thing, it'd be a cold day in Santa Elena in the summer time before I'd ever let her in on my plans for the day, that prissy twit!"

Now that was quite astonishing, 'cause none of us had ever been called by a girl before. In fact it never even entered the realm of possibility. It was low down enough for them to be snooping around us all the time at school, imagine the nerve of 'em trying to spy on ya in the privacy of your own home like that. It was downright shameful! We all looked back across the floor and gave 'em the meanest, most ferocious look we could conger up. They just giggled, batted their eyes and waved back. They just don't seem to get it! We all hated their guts. What's *wrong* with them, anyway?

Then just as I was getting ready to give 'em my most disgusting face, the one where I turn my eyelids inside out, two of the larger specimens stepped aside, and there, hidden behind them, was a much more dainty example of their species. She was looking down and her long red hair was hanging in her face, but as she raised her baby blue eyes, I felt a bolt of lightning shoot through my body. It was Jenny Darling.

Well, I guess my expression must'a immediately changed to one of utmost joy and happiness at the sight of her lovely face, 'cause before I realized what I was doing, Ira blurts out, "What's Johnny C. so happy about, all of a sudden?" And all the guys shot a quick glance at me, and then one across the way at what I was looking at. I was busted.

"Oh, your sweet little Jenny is here. Isn't that just peachy. Why don't you go give her a big old wet smoocherino on the lips. You big sissy!"

Ira was really asking for it this time, and I was raring back to give 'im a good roundhouse right in the solar plexus, when all of the sudden, "Clack! Clack! Clack!" Miss. Hausman walked into the room.

"All young ladies and gentleman gather round here, please," she said as grand and sophisticated as she could muster, in this kooky high voice.

"I'm gonna pound you, Ira." I said as we walked over.

"You and whose army?" he shot back.

Clack! Clack! "All ears and eyes directed at me, if you please," she said with a quick dirty look at me and Big I. "I need your undivided attention." She was an amazingly annoying old girl with a voice that was whiney and kind of gravely at the same time. Her head looked like it had been chiseled out of some kind of grey stone, and absolutely nuthin' on her face ever moved 'cept her jaw, and that only went up and down slightly when she was talking, kinda like one of them ventriloquist dummies. She had deep set eyes that were black as an eight ball and eyelids so wrinkly they looked like a prune with a slit down the middle. She didn't have no lips at all, just teeth, or I should say dentures, but that sure didn't stop her from using her share of lipstick though, not in the least. In fact, she used the most God awful bright red stuff you ever seen and plenty of it, to give the *illusion* of having lips, I reckon. A goodly portion of her lipstick got stuck to her teeth, too, probably on account of the fact that she didn't have no lips to hold it up, and that gave her an especially frightening look when she smiled, which wasn't often.

"I would like to personally welcome you to this year's Pueblo Junior Debutantes and Young Gentleman's Academy," she kept up her yapping with her dentures clacking away. "Our ultimate goal is to slowly mold each and every one of you into a fine young gentlemen or lady by the time the course concludes." Well that sounded kinda painful, and got us all to wincing a bit, but not them lamebrain girls, they actually started jumping up and down, clapping their fool heads off.

"You shall be well versed in manners toward the opposite sex." Ira started to chuckle after the word sex, for which she shot him a quick look, which sent a shiver through his spine and made him snap to, right quick.

"You shall be tutored on the finest points of ballroom dancing" (Another round of jumping and clapping from the girls. What was *wrong* with them?) "And you will be trained in proper etiquette with regards to fine dining." After the words dining, Rosie perked up considerably. "Let us all have a joyous experience as we bask in the ways of high society!" More thunderous applause from you know who.

"I'd like to give her a high society right where the sun don't shine." Neil mumbled as we made our way to the corner of the room for our first etiquette lesson.

She was supposed to learn us the proper way to open a door for a young lady, 'cause I suppose they're too uncoordinated to do it themselves, and you'd think this couldn't be too tough, right? Wrong. In Miss. Hausman's nutty world, every stupid little detail was a matter of life or death, and you had to do the darn thing over again a thousand times if need be 'til it was just so. For instance, a fella couldn't just open a door for some girl and let her out. Oh no! You hadta open the door nice and wide, ya see, and no matter if you was at an outhouse or the White House, you hadta make a sissy little bow and wave your left hand across that open doorway so she'd see just where to go, saying, "After you, mademoiselle." It was downright humiliating, it was. And it wasn't as easy as it sounds, neither. Poor Rosie was supposed to be opening the car door for Julie Baker, but he swung his left hand out a little too late and smacked her up side the head so hard she went flying half way across the floor. She didn't stop crying and carrying on for the rest of the class, and every time poor old Rosie tried to apologize she practically spat at 'im. Coop had his problems with the maneuver, too. Seems he bowed down a little too low as he opened the door for old Lynn Perry, who was a good 5' 8" and 160 pounds, and she cold-cocked 'im with a knee to his forehead that knocked 'im senseless. The poor guy laid there on his back making funny snorting sounds with his eyes wandering crazy all over the place before he finally came to, but not 'til Neil whispered in his ear to get his butt off that ground pronto or he'd beat him senseless hisself for embarrassing the S.S.B.'s by getting his lights knocked out by a girl.

After we all performed that maneuver to Miss. Hausman's liking, we moved on to the proper way to help a young lady get her coat on. Now this warn't quite as complicated as the door thing, 'cept for the fact that the girls were so darn much taller than we were that we practically had to jump to get the lousy coat over their shoulders! Things were going along okay, I guess, "left arm in first, then right arm, then gently raise the garment over the young lady's shoulder," 'til Jag had some trouble helping Missy Stand, better know as Pissy on account of her lovely disposition, find that right arm hole. She was fishing around for quite awhile and getting mighty frustrated, so when she finally *did* find it, she shoved her fist through with all her might and smacked poor old Jag right in the family jewels! Now no one else was paying much attention, but I was, and I saw him stagger back a couple of steps, bite his lip as hard as he could to keep from screaming, and watched as his face turned five shades of green. But just as I figured, that kid never shed a tear and never said a word, but just took his sweet time walking back to our side of the room with his knees locked together and his hands in his pockets, thinking that no one had seen what had happened.

Soon as I had a chance I leaned over to Jag and whispered, "That Pissy Stand is kinda fresh, wouldn't ya say?" and gave him a little wink. Well, he hauled off and slugged me in the shoulder as hard as he could, which under the circumstances wasn't much more than a tap.

"Nice try," I said, knowing darn well that as soon as Jagger was back up to it, he would pound on me good and hard.

Our next lesson in being gentlemanly was on the proper table manners at some fancy schmancy dinner party or banquet or some other boring event which none of us had ever been invited to and never would want to be, but we went along with it anyway 'cause we heard through the grapevine that the main course, at the end of all the dribble, was gonna be a big piece of strawberry shortcake. Rosie got so excited thinking about it that he raced over to be the first one sitting down at the dinner table, but Miss. Hausman let loose with a loud, "Clack!" right behind his ear that almost caused 'im to jump outta his skin, and then gave 'im what for on account of having the gall to sit down before any of the young debutantes had a chance to stick their big butts in a chair. Rosie slowly stood back up and walked kinda sheepish back to where us future gentlemen were lined up.

That table was really a sight to see, I must say, with a fine linen tablecloth with fancy needlework lace all around the border and matching napkins to boot. They weren't just folded into triangles you might see on any average dining table, neither, no these were made into a shape that looked a lot like that hat that the Pope wears at especially holy shindigs, only smaller. It was sitting right there in the middle of our salad plate which was itself sitting on top of our dinner plate. Me and the guys marveled at them and asked Mrs. Hausman how she had done 'em but she said that knowledge was beyond the scope of our curriculum, whatever that means, and so we were left to figure it out for ourselves. There was all kinds of other finery on the table too, like silver salt and pepper shakers and matching gravy boats, which didn't look like any boat I'd ever saw, but more like a silver Aladdin's lamp or somethin'. Mrs. Hausman let on that the silverware wasn't just something you picked up at the five and dime but was, "the finest Grand Baroque" and there was plenty of it. There was a fork for your salad and a fork for your main course and a fork for your dessert and even a tiny pitchfork to try and snag your butter with. There were all sorts of knives and spoons all around at strategic places too and God forbid you would use the wrong one for the wrong thing at the wrong time - that clacker of hers would be in your face so fast, it would make your head swim.

I raised my hand and told old Mrs. Hausman that I thought all these utensils was a great waste of fine sterling silver and that I could get by just fine in any meal with maybe just one fork. The guys stood around me and all nodded their agreement with what I was saying. I said, "For example, if you were having soup it was just as easy and much more pleasant to simply slurp it up at the corner of the bowl after you lifted it up to your mouth. This was a lot easier to control then those silly soup spoons that usually dripped a steady stream all along the tablecloth and up your shirt until it got to your mouth where there wasn't much soup left to eat any longer anyhow. And besides that, this gave you the added advantage of using your front teeth as a sort of strainer to keep out unwanted stuff like green beans or peas and such." Mrs. Hausman's mouth gapped wide open as I continued to talk. I could see my common sense approach to things was making a lasting impression on her. I shot a quick glance at Jenny to see if she was listening, and she sure as heck was, and her eyes were big as saucers with the same kind of expression on her face as old Miss. Clacker. Seeing how well I was doing I decided to continue. "Say you're eating a steak, you don't need to use a sharp fancy knife that could slip and cut your finger clean off," and I pretended to slash my index finger and then bent it back at the knuckle, and held up my hand like I was in terrible excruciating pain. "Not on your life. You could just spear that piece of meat with your fork, bring it up to your mouth and then gnaw a perfect little piece just as easy as pie." The guys again enthusiastically nodded their agreement with me and I was feeling pretty satisfied with my efforts and I knew that Jenny had to feel the same way, too. I was just about to start up on my ideas on the best way to eat your piece of lemon meriangue pie when I noticed that Miss. Hausman was starring at me like I was from some other planet. There was a long silence as she looked at us in disbelief and my smile started to fade as it became obvious she wasn't in total agreement with my common sense approach to fine dining etiquette after all.

"What is wrong with you boys!" She finally screamed. "Were you raised by wild animals in a cave somewhere? I have never seen anything like it in all my years!" Then she got right up into our faces and pointed her finger at each of us individually with her dentures chattering up a storm and said, "You boys *will* learn the ways of a gentleman or so help me, I will have your mothers bring you back every Saturday morning for the rest of your lives. Do I make myself clear?"

That was plenty clear for us. Mighty frightening, too. So we all straightened up and took our assigned seats at the table, after helping them demented debutants with their chairs, that is. The moms there, absolutely giddy over how lovely and gentlemanly we was all carrying on, served up a big old piece of strawberry shortcake to each of us, but said that we should pretend it warn't no cake at all, but instead some fancy dish like oysters rocker fella, or chicken fountain blue, and we should let on like we was eating supper at the royal palace in London, England where they got them guards with the red outfits and the big hats whose chin straps is so short it catches 'em right up under the nose. Personally, I didn't see nuthin' wrong with that there strawberry shortcake, being one to usually call a spade a spade, if ya know what I mean, and anyways that other slop they mentioned didn't sound too appetizing at all.

Miss. Housman, she started whining and carrying on all over again about them confounded forks and knives and dishes and spoons, and said we couldn't, "commence dining," 'til she was good and finished and satisfied we'd learned everything just so, according to some hotshot named Amy Vanderbutt.

She was really pushing it this time, on account'a none of us had nuthin' to eat substantial for way past an hour, not counting a cookie or two we swiped before class started, and all this gentlemanly activity could really work up a kid's appetite. Now if it was tough on me, it was *murder* on poor old Rosie, and on top of everything else, strawberry shortcake was one of his all time favorites. He started eyeing that piece of cake mighty hard, and licking his lips and sniffing at it like an old dog at some strange lady's crotch, and all the while Miss. Hausman kept jabbering away about how to pass the salt and pepper shaker and the "genteel" way to butter your bread, and blah, blah, blah, but I kept my eyes on poor Rosie, hoping he wouldn't crack and take a big chomp outta that cake before she gave the word. That stinking Ira caught on to what was up, too, and started to egg on poor Rosie by pretending like he was already eating *his* piece, and he started liking his lips and rubbing his tummy like he had practically died and gone to heaven 'cause it tasted so good. That was more than Rosie could take, and the sweat started pouring down his chubby cheeks as he starred down at that plate like he was hypnotized or somethin', all the while Miss. Hausman kept up with her obnoxious yakking.

I started shaking my head at 'im somethin' fierce, knowing what a fix we'd be in if he broke, but it was no use, he was too far gone. When old Rosie was hungry, which was pretty much all the time, a team of wild javalenas weren't gonna keep him from his dessert, and as soon as that nutty old broad turned her back to demonstrate how a proper lady was supposed to flatten down her dress before she parked her caboose in a chair, Rosie plopped his face right down into that cake and took a monstrous chomp outta it. That got Ira to laughing out loud, which broke Rosie outta his trance, and he shot straight up in his chair, trying his darndest to wolf down what he had in his mouth. Problem was, when he stuck his face down in that plate, he came out with a big glob of vanilla frosting sitting right on the end of his nose, and he didn't have the slightest clue it was there! Ms. Hausman, hearing Ira crack up, turned around as quick as a cat and screeched, "What, pray tell, is all the commotion about, now?" Giving me and the guys the evil eye all over again.

"It was nuthin' lady, I mean Ma'am," Ira answered. "Just Cooper down there making funny faces behind your back."

Poor Chicken Coop, he'd been doing all he could the whole day trying to stay in the background to escape any kind of trouble, and now this. The Nazi moved towards 'im causing his eyes to start bulging almost clean outta his head! He started to quiver all over, but real soon that quiver turned into out and out convulsions, and before you knew it, here come the hiccups. It was pretty pathetic sight to tell you the truth. Then Coop started stammering and coughing and choking and pointed over at Ira while shaking his head somethin' furious to try and show his innocence, but no matter how hard that kid tried he couldn't manage to spit out one darn word.

She kept coming right for 'im, with her jaw locked and her eyes piercing and her dress swishing so fierce that you'd swear a fire would break out between her legs any second. Old Coop was a complete basket case by then, and was getting ready to dart under the table to hide, when all of the sudden she stopped dead in her tracks, smack dab behind Rosie. Somethin' had caught her eye, and she started searching up and down the table for what it was she'd seen. The sweat started rolling down Rosie's cheeks all over again and he began tugging at his collar for air. His eyes were squeezed shut as tight as he could make 'em and you could tell he was mumbling a little prayer to hisself to help 'im out of this jam. Well, I guess God was busy with some more trying problems, 'cause sure enough Ms. Housman noticed that mangled piece of cake sitting in front of 'im, and spun his chair around to face her in a flash, which was pretty impressive considering who's big butt was stuck in it. Poor Rosie kept his eyes shut tight and the mumbling got faster and louder, but there was no denying it, she'd already seen the one undeniable piece of evidence that a kid had sure been eating cake - frosting on the nose! Ms. Hausman gasped at the sight and started clicking her clacker like mad right in Rosie's ear, who put his hands up to the sides of his head to try to muffle the obnoxious sound. Realizing that one of our fellow Seward School Bombers was in deep doo-doo we tried to create a diversion to take some of the pressure off of 'im. First, I took a big bite out of my cake, chewed it up a bit, then asked the old girl if she wanted to see a train wreck in a tunnel as I opened my mouth up wide and pointed to the mush inside. That got her to stop her clacking, and she was just about to give me what for when down at the other end of the table Jagger let loose with an impressive display of what I believe proper gentleman call flatulence, and then he stood up and took a real nice bow. *That* made her forget all about me *and* Rosie as she made a B-line for Jagger like she was gonna strangle him or somethin', but when she went by where Neil was sitting, he stood up and yelled out, "Wait! Wait! Wait! I just have to know if this is proper party etiquette," and then he proceeded to grab his piece of cake and shoved it right in the face of the young debutante sitting next to him. Well, that did it! An all out food fight broke out between the fine young gentleman and the prim and proper debutantes, the likes of which may never be seen again at an Old Pueblo Juniors Etiquette class, or in the whole of Santa Elena for that matter. It was absolutely brutal, but in a really good way, if ya know what I mean. There was cake flying through the air from one end of the table to the other, so thick you could hardly see, and punch being splattered from head to toe so that there wasn't a drop left in a cup anywhere to be found.

Mrs. Hausman watched in horror for a minute or so and then started screaming for us to, "Cease this instant!" and started clacking away to beat the band. But I guess it was more than the old girl could take, 'cause all of a sudden she got to looking mighty pale, and before you knew it, her eyes rolled back in her head, she did about two 360's, and then slumped dead away in a chair against the wall. After that, everything stopped and we all just stared at her limp body sitting there. The debutantes, well they started crying and carrying on right off, and said that she was dead for sure and how me and the guys had murdered her, and all other kinds of hysterical girl yapping, 'til finally Neil got fed up and said, "She ain't dead, you panty waists, watch!" And with that he grabbed an ice bucket full of punch, walked over to where she was drooling all over herself, and flung it in her face, hard as he could. Well, that brought her around sure enough, and she began to make some pretty gnarly gurgling sounds and then started moving her arms up and down and turning her head from side to side, and we all gathered close around her to see if she was gonna pull through.

Finally, she let out this humongous yawn and slowly opened her eyes to see all of our faces covered in strawberry shortcake and doused with fruit punch leaning over and peering right back at her. Once she realized what was what, she shot straight up in that chair and started wiping her face and fixing her hair and straightening her skirt, which had managed to hike itself up to a very unladylike height. After a few more seconds she started to mumble somthin' about there would be no more lessons necessary today, and that everyone in this class now had a good foundation to set right out and be young ladies and gentleman and pillars of society. We all just looked at each other kinda dumbfounded, but knowing it'd be rude to argue with a lady of her stature, just lined ourselves up for dismissal, still dripping from head to toe, and Ms. Hausman, obviously still shook up from what she'd been though, handed out our, "Certificate of Proper Etiquette," one by one as we walked outta class.

I gotta say, that even though them pieces of paper were mighty smeared with strawberry filling and punch, they still looked real impressive, and I got a real satisfied feeling of accomplishment when I accepted mine. Ms. Housman, she made a special point of telling me and the guys that it warn't necessary for any of us to never, ever return to her class again, and we all thanked her and told her how much we had learned and we knew it was gonna make us more gentlemanly by a long shot.

As we were filing past her, Jag stopped and said, "T-T-Thanks, for the s-souvenir," and then he pulled her clacker outta his pocket and started making the most obnoxious clackety-clack sound with it he could muster. She started feverishly searching through all of her pockets, but could only come up with a couple'a dirty snot rags, and then made a quick move toward Jagger but thought better of it and just snapped, "Goodbye, forever!"

He just waved back at her, pleasant as could be and kept right on going. That little sneak must've lifted it off her in all the confusion while she was lying there, dead to the world. I was very upset with Jagger for doing somthin' so underhanded to a poor old lady, especially since I didn't think of it first!

I walked over to my Ma who was waiting in the car out in front, and proudly handed her my certificate with a big smile on my face. After looking it over once or twice to make sure it was authentic, she got a little teary eyed and gave me a huge hug and a big sloppy kiss on the cheek and told me how proud she was of her "Little gentleman." Then, as if waking up out of a trance, she looked me up and down and said, "What happened to you, you are *filthy!*"

"I slipped," I said and jumped into the back seat.

# Chapter Eight

## THE LOSERS

The grass on the big kids side of the field at Seward School was still moist from last night's cloud burst, and the morning breeze felt almost cool, instead of like a blast furnace in your face as usual around here during the dead of summer. Several glorious days had passed since we all become official young gentleman of the white ghetto, and our moms were proud as peacocks and pouring on the rewards. Jagger reported he had hamburgers and french fries for dinner every night this week, and Ira said he was allowed to watch T.V. as long as he wanted, any channel, without having to make up the time reading some boring book as usual, and I hadn't had the slightest snide remark from the "Gestapo" for nearly five full days and even had a ding dong for breakfast yesterday no questions asked. Yep, life was as good as it gets around here, for a twelve year old that is. To tell you the truth I didn't mind all that much doing some of that high fallooting stuff for Ma, like opening the car door and all. I mean, let's face it, it didn't take all that much effort on your part, but boy did it pay off big in the long run, if you know what I mean. Pop gotta big kick outta watching me do all that sissy boy stuff too, and he said if I learned to treat all ladies with respect, pretty soon I'd have 'em all eating right outta my hand, which was a thoroughly disgusting thought, and I told 'im so, too.

Pop just laughed and said, "Give it time, son. Give it time." Well, I didn't want to argue, and I gotta admit that Pop's advice was usually dead on, but on this particular point he was way out in right field, in fact he was in the bleachers!

We all met down at The Sewer and were sitting in a circle in front of the

Ramada, getting ready to wrestle for captains for a little ghetto baseball, when crazy Jag got a wild hair up his butt. Seems he decided it wouldn't be a bad idea at all to try and jump from the roof of the Ramada as far as he could and then catch hold of the big branch of the cottonwood tree standing next to the basketball court, right before he splattered his brains all over the cement slab below. It didn't help matters that Big I had already double dared 'im to do it as he heard the ridiculous idea, and said Jag wasn't man enough to even get up on the roof, let alone jump off of it. That's all it took, and he was already standing up there, straddling the peak and eyeing his path, looking like he didn't have a care in the world.

"Jag, don't do it! You ain't got a prayer and I'm not gonna scrape you off the cement after you miss, understand?" I said, just like I always did when he got one of his suicidal ideas. And just like he always did he didn't seem to hear a word I said.

"He ain't gonna do it, 'cause you know and I know he's too yellow to even jump off his mommy's bed," Neil answered as he turned his back on Jag altogether.

Now *that* brought a slight smirk to Jagger's lips, but he just kept right on staring at the challenge in front of 'im. Problem was, I'd seen that look plenty of times before and I knew what it meant, and it never was good.

We all squinted up our eyes to get a good look on account a' the sun was settled straight back from where Jag was standing, as he counted back exactly eight giant steps from the end of the roof and stopped right there. He started jiggling his arms and legs and head all over to get out the kinks, just like them swimmers did in the Olympics me and Pop seen on T.V. from Mexico City, right before they had a big race.

"He ain't gonna really try it, is he Johnny?" Rosie whimpered.

"Afraid so. The kid's sure as shinola's gotta screw loose," I answered shaking my head, "Ya better get ready to run down and let Mrs. Jagger know the latest stunt her genius son has pulled, while I try and revive 'im after he cracks his head open on the basketball court."

I looked over at Cooper and the Creep just standing there with blank faces, unable to understand whether this was tremendous bravery or sheer stupidity. I had already made up my mind on that subject regarding Jeffrey Howell many moons ago. Anyway, after a few minutes Jag was ready to roll, and he started rocking back and forth to get a little momentum going.

"Forget it Jag, you're gonna kill yourself!" I screamed out with Rosie as he got that all too familiar nut-case look in his eyes.

"Come on Jag, don't be a big weenie. My little sister could make that jump in her tutu!" hollered Neil.

"My grandma could make it *without* her orthopedic shoes!" added Ira, with a sinister smile.

Jag rocked back and forth a couple more times, gave us the thumbs up and took off in a sprint, no holes barred. We all stood up at once to get a better view of what was sure to be a horrible but memorable scene, just like them folks do when they slow down and crane their necks to take a gander at a car wreck they was driving by.

Jag was trying his darndest to pick up the launch speed he was gonna need to reach that tree limb, but the problem was it's pretty darn tough running smack dab on top of a pitched roof, and he was staggering from side to side, like a drunk chasing a beer truck. You could tell right off he was probably in for it, but then on his last step things went straight down the toilet as his foot caught the final shingle that was propped up just a tad from the storms, and he lurched forward, letting out a loud "Whoop!" as that retard flew head over heels off the end of the roof.

I put my hands over my eyes, not wanting to watch as my best friend turned himself into a human hamburger patty, and all the rest of the guys, even Neil and Ira, turned to look away. He obviously didn't have enough momentum to reach the big branch he was shooting for after stumbling like he had, which meant he was going straight for the basketball court, head first.

"Cowabunga!" he screamed as he flew through the air, and then, and then - there was nuthin'. No crash, no splat, no hideous thud, and definitely no horrible crying out in pain. I slowly pried my fingers apart to catch a quick peek at what was going on, and I as I took in the scene in front of me, I couldn't believe my eyes! It was another Jagger classic.

There he was, dangling from the tree, about five feet above the cement, with one of the lower branches of that cottonwood stuck through his belt on the back of his jeans. I mean, what were the chances? His eyes were closed and his arms and legs were just hanging there and he looked just like a giant spider hanging from the end of his web. He slowly opened his eyes, looked down at the ground, started feeling his body all over to make sure he was all in one piece, and then started laughing like a looney bird.

"You are the luckiest little S.O.B. in the whole world! Ya know that, Jag?" Neil said, disgusted he'd been cheated outta seeing some real blood and guts.

"Just how I p-p-planned it," Jagger answered smiling away, his eyes little slits in his head.

Rosie, Chicken Coop, and the Creep just stood and stared with their mouths wide open, and Big I simply smiled and shook his head, for once speechless.

"Oh, by the way," Neil said. "The governor just called to say they're starting a new town just for dumb-asses and he wants *you* to be mayor!"

After a few more minutes of the guys letting Jag have it about his latest suicide attempt, he said, "All right, All right. J-J-Just help me d-down and then we'll play some ball."

"Eat me, Jag!" barked Big I. "You're so darn smart, get yourself down, or you can rot up there 'til Halloween for all I care!" Then he stomped off toward the drinking fountain with Neil close behind.

"Aw, come on guys! L-L-Lighten up. C-C-Can't a guy have a little fun once in a while?"

"You're so full of it your eyes are brown!" Rosie screamed, ticked off at being scared out of his wits once again by our old friend, and he walked off in a huff with Creepy and Coop in tow, leaving me as Jag's only hope for a little sympathy.

"Johnny C, I know you wouldn't l-leave your old p-pal hanging from a limb, now would ya?" he said with his familiar smart alec smirk.

I just stood there staring up at 'im for a bit, swaying ever so slightly from the end of that branch, completely helpless, like some baby in a swing waiting for his mommy to come and get 'im. I was gonna tell 'im what he looked like, too, but thought I better not push it. After all, he was gonna get down eventually, and when he did, he'd still be the strongest kid in the white ghetto.

"Forget it, Jag," I said. "I think it'd do you some good to just stay up there for a while and think about how idiotic your ideas can be sometimes!"

I turned my back on 'im and went off to meet the rest of the guys that were now sitting on the bars of the jungle gym pretending like Jagger didn't even exist. As soon as I got to 'em I climbed up and sat on the absolute top rung, hooked by legs around the bars so as not to lose my balance just like I'd done so many times before. After awhile of not doing nuthin', we started starring back out at the old cottonwood tree, and there was our dejected friend, still just hanging there limp, his head down and arms and legs sticking straight down like dead weight, a totally defeated player in the game of amateur daredevilism.

"Look at him. He's pathetic," Ira said, disgusted and turned his head away like he was looking at somethin' your cat coughed up. "He's so pig-headed! He ain't never gonna learn, and he ain't never gonna change."

"Hey, he's *Jagger*," I said. "Do you really want 'im to change?"

We all sat quiet for a bit more just watching 'im, and by then the summer sun was high over head and beating down on us pretty good. The morning breeze had died off and we were settling in to another blazing day in beautiful southern Arizona.

"Maybe if he had landed on his head, it would'a done 'im some good." Neil said, as we all climbed down the jungle gym and stopped by the drinking fountain to pour water over our baking heads.

"Doubt it," said Rosie, as we ambled back toward the helpless head case.

Along the way I started thinking about all the times, good and bad, I spent playing on that field. After all, it'd been six years since I started at

Seward School and I must've spent a thousand hours or so down here doing one thing or another. I thought about the time in second grade when me and Tubby Thomas were wrapped up in a mean game of tetherball before school even started, 'til old Tubby threw all of his substantial weight behind a vicious slam and the ball caught me square in the mouth and knocked me out cold and chipped both my front teeth. Boy did Ma have a cow and a half after that one! Then there was the time in fourth grade that Jagger ripped the sleeve clean off my brand new dress shirt during an after school football game. I tried *gluing* it back on with some rubber cement which was the only thing that I could find in the janitor's storeroom, but needless to say, that didn't fool Ma for a second, and my football career was put on hold for a month or so. And how about the most embarrassing time in my life, the thing that almost ruined my reputation forever, when in forth grade I ran into Nancy Cole's elbow during a come across game at the ice cream social, giving me the worst shiner you ever did see, and she, of course, blabbed to everyone that would listen how we had gotten into a fist fight and she had clocked me but good! Boy, do I hate her guts! I remember my teacher Mr. George asking, "What happened Caruso, did some big guy tell you to shut up and you thought he said stand up!" Well, that got the whole class to laughing nice and loud and long, like they'd split a gut, or somethin' all at my expense. It was a whole year, and several trips to El Generalissimo's office for fighting, 'til the "Nancy boy" jokes started to die down.

When we reached Jag he was still hanging there without even a twitch, and his eyes were closed and his mouth was open and he was drooling all over the place - mostly for effect.

"Okay, listen up Charlotte (that's the only spider name I could come up with quick) we decided to save you from your nutty self one last time, but not 'cause we think you deserve it, but only on account'a we need another player for lob ball to make the teams even. Got it?" I said. This actually was the case since old Creepy warn't no help at all to the team he was on, 'cept maybe if ya needed 'im to figure the exact bat speed to hit a dinger or somethin'. But in his defense I guess they didn't play no real baseball where he came from, only that sissy form of it named after some insect, "Beetle" or "Caterpillar" or somethin' like that, where the players wear them dressy white get-ups that make 'em look like a bunch of milkmen, and slap the ball around with what looks like a giant fly swatter.

So, after a bunch more attacks on Jagger's manhood and mental capabilities, Ira, he got on Neil's shoulders and I climbed up on Rosie's, with Chicken Coop giving us each the heave-ho, and I grabbed on to Jag's ears and Ira took a hold of his feet and we started pushing and pulling at 'im, and twisting and turning, and jerking and jostling trying to set 'im free free, and all the while he was yelping, "W-w-watch it!" and, "Stop! You're kkillin' me!" We didn't pay no mind, we only kept on about our business. The only thing was, that branch wouldn't budge. It was lodged under his belt for good, it seemed. We had to stop for a bit 'cause Neil was cussing up a storm about how his back was gonna break, and Rosie's face was getting beat red and the sweat was pouring off it faster than the water slide at Larry's Lagoon water park down in Rio Rico. We thought and thought about what other way we could possibly free him up, and decided that our only chance was to climb the tree and saw that branch off. Jagger, of course, didn't like that notion one bit, seeing that it meant a painful fall of almost ten feet, flat on his face.

"What are you worried about, Jag?" Ira asked. "Your brains can't get any more damaged than they already are, and falling on your face may actually improve your looks."

That made Jag laugh. He always appreciated good humor, even when he was the butt of it. Then he said, "K-K-Kiss me where the sun don't shine, okay Big I?" (One of his all time favorite comebacks.)

Cooper, who lived the closest, was all set to book home and grab his dad's hack saw, when Creepy blurted out, "Why don't you just undo his belt," and then threw his hands up like, "What's wrong with you people!"

After we finished slapping each other on the head for being such retards, I said, "Atta boy Creep! That's what we pay ya for, kid." It sure is nice to have a brainiac around when ya need one.

Now Jagger, he didn't see things quite the same, once more realizing that as soon as that buckle was undone he'd fall like a rock, so he yelled, "I'm g-g-gonna pound you Bampu when I g-get down from here, comprendes?"

After that poor Creepy started fidgeting all over like he had ants in his pants, and shot behind his old pal Rosie for safety, like always. Since he was already standing there, I had 'im give me a hand back up on the big guys shoulders, which tuckered him clear out. Rosie had recovered pretty well by now, with the sweat running down his face slowing to a small stream, plus he had scarfed down a couple'a handfuls of M & Ms he had been hoarding in his pockets to give him extra energy.

"Hey, how 'bout a few of them for your old pal?" I asked, my stomach so empty it ached.

"Sorry, all gone," he mumbled, his mouth so full that his cheeks bulged out like that crazy trumpet player Dizzy what's his face. When I looked down it was obvious his pockets were still stuffed to the brim.

As we moved in closer to Jag's belt buckle, he started kicking his legs and flailing his arms and warned us to stay away from him if we knew what was good for us. But he couldn't quite reach us if we came in from the side, hard as he tried, and God knows he was giving it his all.

"Now, Jag, that ain't no way to treat your old pals trying to help you out of a tough jam, now is it?" I said as I reached for his belt.

"G-G-Get away Johnny, I swear!" he yelled, half mad, half cracking up with laughter.

"Too late, Jag." I said, as I pulled the leather through and gave it a good yank.

"Whoosh!" That belt went flying through the loops on his jeans quicker than a jackrabbit on greased roller skates, and then all of a sudden, "Twang!" the branch snapped back hard toward the sky, as Jagger let out an ear piercing screech followed by a sickening, "Thud!"

We all huddled around to see how bad off he was, all except for Bampu who was already halfway to Red River, but he wouldn't let on none, playing it up for all he was worth as usual, and just laid there not moving a muscle. Then, after a bit, he slowly started to shake hisself to get the cobwebs out, looked up, gritted his teeth, flared his nostrils, and let out a yell to wake the dead! With that he leaped up and pealed out after us like a raging lunatic. We scattered right quick and took to our heels. Chicken Coop, already figuring Jagger's unpleasant state of mind, and knowing darn well he wasn't one to tangle with when he was plenty p.o.ed, already was climbing the jungle gym, trying frantically to get to the top rung and to apparent safety. Big I ran straight for the gate, and seeing that he was the fastest of the guys, had better than average chance to stay alive as he tore down Cicada Street. Neil went for the Ramada, and was shimmying up the pole to the rafters where he felt he could avoid the carnage best. That left Rosie with me *still* sitting on his shoulders, who first started running around in circles flapping his arms, screaming at the top of his lungs and choking on the M & M's he had stuffed in his face, and begging Jag to leave us alone. I figured we were sitting ducks right off, but I couldn't just jump off Rosie at full stride without causing myself considerable bodily harm, so I just hung on his big fat ears for dear life, closed my eyes and hoped for the best. Now, it turns out the best warn't no good at all, 'cause Jag, seeing the easy prey, was all over us like flies on you know what as he threw a nasty body block at Rosie and knocked us both flat. The big guy just laid there face down, playing dead and hoping for mercy and I tried to crawl away as fast as I could which wasn't near fast enough to avoid an irate mad man. Jag was on me in a flash, grabbed both my feet and dragged me like a rag doll back to where Rosie was lying. I tried twisting and turning with all my might to break his hold, but that little fart had a grip like steel, especially when he was pissed, and this time he was *really* ticked off.

Once he got me up along side Rosie, who was still lying there stiff as a board, he put one foot on my back and one on our fat friend, then reached down and grabbed on tight to the waistband of our underpants.

"Don't do it Jag!" I screamed, seeing all too well the sick idea he had in mind, but it was no use. As he took a deep breath, he squatted way down and then jumped up as high as he could with a loud grunt, giving them jockey shorts a monstrous yank.

"Aaah!" we both yelped in agony as my underpants were nearly ripped clean off, and in the process giving my poor privates such an eye watering wallop, that for the first and only time in my life, I wished to God I was a girl.

Jag, that low life, still had his foot stuck in the small of my back, so I couldn't flip over for the life of me, although right at that moment I probably didn't have the strength to shoe away a gnat, but I sure could hear his goofy giggle from up above. What I didn't hear was any of the other guys making any smart alec comments for a change, knowing darn well if they did, they'd be next.

Then Jag says, "I guess that'll t-t-teach you to m-mess with the Great Umgowa!" as he held his arms over his head with his hands clasped, the way professional wrestlers do when they win one of them big time phony matches. Then he jumped off of us, looked around real quick to see if anyone else was in need of a good thrashing, and when he seen there were no takers, walked over real proud-like to the ramada and plunked hisself down with a loud sigh.

When it looked like the coast was clear, Neil slid down from the rafters, Ira sneaked a look through the corner gate and came on back in, Rosie and I rolled over on our backs and tried to adjust ourselves the best we could through the front pockets of our jeans, not wanting to suffer any more embarrassment than we already had by having to pull our pants down, and lastly, the Creep and Chicken Coop slowly made their way down back towards us, the whole time keepin' a close eye on Jagger's attitude.

We sat around in the shade for a while trying to decide on fair teams for lob ball, which was more difficult than negotiating a nuclear missile agreement with them no good commies, mostly on account'a nobody wanted poor old Creepy.

"I don't understand it," he finally yelled out in frustration. "Are my skills that inadequate?"

"Well Creep, let's put it this way," Neil answered, coming over and putting his arm around 'im. "Ya know how they say old Willy Mays is the world's first four skill player? Well you, my little brown friend, may be the world's first *no* skill player. You can't run, you can't catch, you can't throw, and you sure as sh!# can't hit. Now do you get it!"

"Unequivocally."

Then outta the blue Cooper blurts out that he just remembered how he had heard from Brian Frasier, who had heard from Gloria Messina who had heard from Lenore Gillette, that Billy Garber had found a huge stash of sand rubies over by the kickball field last week. Sand rubies were a mighty precious commodity to kids like us, right up there with fools gold and mica chips, maybe more, so we all high tailed it over there to stake out a claim and start sifting. It didn't take long at all to realize that good old Billy had found the mother lode this time, too bad there won't be none left by the time he got around to checking on it.

"Easy as taking candy from a baby," Big I said as Rosie shot an excited glance his way at the sound of "candy," and in not more than fifteen minutes, we each had a small handful of precious gems safe in our pockets for later when we'd store 'em in the little vials we swiped from last year's science fair.

After that, I said, "Hey, I heard Shlosh and some other high school kids saying over at El Guero's, if ya sucked real hard on one'a them sprinkler heads in the middle of the playground, you could get water to come spurting out."

Well, we had to see about that, and in no time we were in the middle of the field on our hands and knees and sucking our brains out. After a bit we started hearing a distant rumbling, gurgling sound making it's way up through the pipes, and we knew we were really on to something, when Neil has to go and ruin it all by saying he just remembered seeing Nancy Cole's obnoxious dog Corky peeing all over this same exact area yesterday afternoon, *after* the monsoon! That little tidbit lead to frantic spitting and wiping and washing out of mouths over at the drinking fountain 'til we was satisfied we were rid of any dog piss germs.

"Come to think of it," Neil added as he scratched his head, "I think I saw him pinching a few big tootsie rolls over there, too."

That got 'im a couple of quick monkey bumps on the shoulder from Jagger before he could move, and we all laughed as Cooper squatted down and did a perfect imitation of old Corky relieving himself, scared look on his face and all. Ira said Corky probably couldn't even drop a decent load if he wanted, on account'a the fact that he was too constipated from being such a tight-ass like everyone else in that family.

"That's why he walks all knock-kneed. Didn't ya ever notice?" And with that he got up and started tip toeing around, squeezing his butt cheeks together with his hands hard as he could.

I said that instead of being constipated the poor guy probably had a severe case of the runs 'cause living with the Cole's would hafta tie anyone's stomach in knots. Then I did my best impression of someone sitting on the pot with the worst case of diarrhea this side of the Mexican border, sound effects and all. That was more than the guys could pass up, and pretty soon every last one of 'em were doin' *their* best impression of someone with a horrible case of the squirts and basically having a great old time.

It was close to eleven o'clock by then and we were all getting pretty hungry and thought we better get started with that lob ball game or we'd never get it in. We'd already made plans to head on down to Dairy Delight for a cowboy burger, some onion rings and a chocolate chip malt with extra chocolate syrup, the S.S.B. special we liked to call it, soon as we finished up.

"I hope old Isabel ain't working the counter today, I don't think my stomach can handle sucking on a piss covered sprinkler and that thing growing on her face in the same day," Ira said.

He was referring to Isabel Duarte, a pretty nice lady and a decent waitress if you didn't mind the greasy hairnet she never went without, and the even greasier looking cigarette that was always hanging halfway down her chin. But them things were minor nuisances compared to the mass on her nose that was shaped like a head of cauliflower, and was darn near as big! I mean it was getting so outta control that her nose was starting to look more like a lobster! Only in Santa Elena, like Ma always said.

Anyways, we were getting back to the business of picking teams, when from outta nowhere there came a beautiful sound, a sound like no other, like music to the ears of twelve year old boys everywhere. It started kinda faint off in the distance, and slowly but surely got to growing louder and louder. Pretty soon you could start to make out a mellow burble, and then a belch and braaap. It was the lovely song of notes from a two stroke Briggs and Stratton lawn mower engine, and the best part about it was that it was powering our pal Larry's bitchin' new minibike.

Ahh, the minibike, every boy's dream, the closest you could get at our age to riding a real motorcycle. There was nuthin' like the glorious feeling of pull starting the engine, twisting the throttle and hearing that wonderful, "Braaap!" "Braaap!" behind you as the wind blew in your face and you drove, yes *drove*, yourself, free as a bird, wherever you wanted to go, as long as it wasn't on city streets or public property, of course. That was strictly against the law and could land you in Juvi, which was what everyone called the Cochise County Juvenile Center, faster that you could say Hell's Angels. But nobody really worried much about all that 'cause the chance to ride a minibike was just too great to pass up, no matter what the risk. Would Evil Kneivel weenie out on a big jump just 'cause there was some silly law against it - heck no. He would thumb his nose at those cops, rev up his engine and let her fly!

Larry rode his magnificent machine in the gate, like a prince on a white stallion coming to rescue us from our summer boredom, across the basketball court and right up to where we were sitting.

He shut it down, got off triumphantly and said, cool as can be, "Well, guys, what do ya think?"

He knew exactly what we thought, and that was that he was the luckiest kid in town. Larry knew it too, but the cool thing about him was that he wasn't stuck up about it at all. The only one that had anything against 'im was Cooper, but that was only on account'a the first time they met Larry asked 'im if he'd like to see the nutcracker, and Coop, thinking he was talking about the Christmas play down at the Fox said he'd love to, and then old Larry reared backed and hit him hard right in the nards. Coop needed to get over it.

It turns out Larry's family was really loaded, both his folks being doctors, and according to Pop they were really raking it in, although he said it weren't right for women being doctors in the first place. He said her real job was to be with her kids at home, and anyway what's a guy gonna do if he has a problem with his private parts and in walks some lady doctor. It just wasn't natural. He also said it seemed to him that all of Larry's folks were doing was throwing money at him to try and keep him happy on account of the fact that they were never really around to raise him. Well, I got to thinking that for ten bucks a week, which was old Larry's allowance, I could hire myself someone to teach me what I needed to know, and still pocket enough to cover anything my little heart desired. None of the guys ever held a grudge against Larry neither, on account of the fact that he was really a very generous fella and was always treating for ice cream if someone was short of dough, or springing for the extra nickel at hot lunch if you wanted a chocolate milk. That sort of stuff. Lately, everyone liked Larry because of his new minibike, Freedom, he called it, and also for the fact that he would let you take it for a little spin all by yourself and not nag at you like so many other kids would while you tried out their stuff by yelling, "Watch this!" or, "Be careful about that!" But would only stand back and smile real big and proud and look sincerely happy that he was giving so much joy to kids less fortunate than hisself. Come to think of it, I didn't know why us guys didn't hang out with Larry more often. I guess it was just that he only moved to town a couple of years earlier and never really became one of the gang, and also for the fact that he really didn't like to play sports which made 'im seem kinda odd in everyone's eyes. Neil, of course, said Larry must be queer or somethin' but that was just because he was jealous, and everybody knew it. Another reason, I guess, we didn't hang out much with old Larry was on account of his unfortunate last name, which may sound really silly 'til you hear what it is -- Lipshitz. I mean, you gotta be kidding me! If that don't conjure up all kinds of disturbing sites in your mind's eye, I don't know what will. Larry Lipshitz, the fortunate kid with the unfortunate last name. It's funny how God works ain't it. Neil was so taken aback when he first heard it that he thought Larry must be joking. When he finally realized it was for real, he thought and thought but finally said, "That name is so bad already that no matter how hard I try there ain't no way to make it worse!" And so gave up trying. It was the first time any of us could remember Neil being stumped.

"How cool's my new sissy bar?" Larry asked, again knowing the answer as he pointed to the tall chrome tubing he had screwed on the back of the rear seat.

"A sissy bar for a real big sissy," Neil answered under his breath, but nobody paid no mind. We were in too much awe of his new addition. A sissy bar, in case you're from some other planet or a weenie or somethin', is to keep you from sliding off the back of your seat after you popped a major wheelie, but mostly it just looked bitchin' rising up from behind along with the high rise monkey bars and chrome exhaust tip he had added earlier.

"Larry, old pal, hows about a ride?" I asked, unable to control myself any longer.

"Sure, Johnny C. Go for it!" That Larry sure was one heck of a guy, and before the "it" was outta his mouth, I threw my leg over the seat, pulled hard on the starter rope, gave the throttle a twist and the engine came to life. That lovely engine burble sound was coming up from behind me now as I slowly pulled away with the feeling of sheer joy and power that few experiences could bring to a kid, 'cepting maybe jumping from the cliffs at little Acapulco along the Salt river, but that's getting' into a whole nuther adventure.

As the hot wind blew through my hair and the landscape started to fly by, I had to squint up my eyes to keep them from drying, and I made it to the end of the playground in nuthin' flat. I was completely in command and feeling pretty confident, so I decided to open it up and leaned back on that sissy bar with full throttle, and popped the most humongous wheelie of my young career! I managed to ride her about ten feet, much to the amazement of all the guys looking on, when outta nowhere the back wheel hit a divot which got me a little squirrelly and before I knew it I was flat on my back with the bike landing in a heap a few yards away. Rosie, Creepy and Chicken Coop raced over to see if I was all right, which I was 'cept for my pride, while everyone else had a real good laugh, and then remembering that the mini bike was now free started fighting over who got the next ride.

Well, everyone got their turn, eventually, Larry being the fine fellow that he was, and pretty much everyone ended up wiping out one way or another. Neil ran into the drinking fountain, Ira hit some loose dirt, did a doughnut and flew off face first, Creepy stopped after the first twenty feet, saying he got motion sickness, Rosie gave it his best shot and so did Freedom, but under the enormous strain, and I do mean enormous, that poor little lawn mower engine just didn't cut it, and the mini bike warn't no faster than Rosie's own two wheeler, causing him to lose interest pretty quick. Coop actually refused to ride saying his mom strictly prohibited him from riding "all mechanized forms of transportation," to which we all replied, "Join the group." When it came to Jagger's turn, he refused, of course, to just drive the bike around and enjoy himself like any sane kid would, oh no, he had to try to *jump* over somethin' like them daredevils riders you see now and then on, "Wide World of Sports." Only with Jag at the controls you just knew it wasn't gonna end up with the "Thrill of Victory."

After a bit of considering he settled on trying to jump the sandbox under the rings, and made us start looking around for stuff to make a little ramp. Within minutes we'd come up with some bricks and an old piece of plywood that seemed like they'd do the trick, although it was more than a little bit wobbly once set in place. That didn't deter Jag none, as he got a long running start and was really flying low as we began chanting "Jagger, Jagger" over and over while standing in two rows for him to ride through. When he tore by his teeth were clenched, his eyes small slits, and his head down in the fork of the monkey bars, as he tried to cheat the wind and pick up a few more miles per hour. He hit that ramp square and stood straight up, just like them other nuts on T.V., but could only muster a few feet in the air before the front wheel came down hard and sunk deep in the sand, causing him to promptly do a head first summersault in the air straight over the handlebars and land with a thud, flat on his back just on the other side of the sandbox.

He just laid there moaning for a while, his poor body absorbing a second terrible beating in less than an hour, as we cracked up watching Neil and Ira do their uncanny impression of him flying through the air.

After a few minutes, Jag sat up, scratched his head and said, "Oooh, not enough lift, I guess."

"No sh!# Sherlock," Neil answered, "and don't forget not enough brains either!"

Well life didn't get much better than this in Santa Elena in the summer time; Jagger making a fool out of hisself over and over, finding a major stash of precious sand rubies, sucking on some peed on sprinkler heads, and riding Larry Lipshitz's minibike to our heart's content. I mean, what could be better? The problem was, as Pop always said, good things always come to an end, and our good time came crashing down real quick as Bubba Lane and his ever present sidekick, Miguel "El Rey" Dominguez, better known to us as Loser Lane and El Estupido, came strolling in the far gate.

They were the well known and much feared leaders of a bunch of scum bums that lived on the outskirts of town, which in Santa Elena, meant about two blocks in any direction from where we were standing, and their whole gang was made up of some of the finest high school drop outs ever to frequent the halls of the Cochise County Juvenile Center. In fact, I hear they have a row of cells there reserved just for them at all times. They manage to keep the entire Santa Elena police force, meaning Mengo and Pato, on their toes with plenty of broken windows, little kid poundings, old lady harassing, and other real sophisticated crimes. Mengo makes no bones about it, if it weren't for The Losers or, "Los Delinquents," as he calls 'em in his typical Santa Elena Spanglish, our little pueblo probably wouldn't need no police at all and he and Pato would be out of a swell job. So in a way, I guess, he's kinda grateful that they're around. I also heard 'im say one time that they're directly responsible for more than half of the law enforcement money we receive from the state, so they got that going for them also, which is pretty impressive if you think about it.

They walked straight for us, if you could call it walking, you see they were way too cool to actually lift their feet off the ground and just kind of slid 'em along as they went, and we instinctively huddled together and took a step or two back, except for Jag, who stood his ground and even had a little smirk on his face as they came towards him. Loser Lane was tall, maybe five foot ten and skinny as a pogo stick. His long blonde hair was stringy and greasy as usual and stuck to the side of his pointy, pimply face. Stuck in the corner of his mouth was a toothpick, that he must put in there before he gets outta bed in the morning since I can't ever remember seeing 'im without it, and he was wearing one of them skin tight Mexican gauze shirts that go for about a buck and a half down in Nogales. His hand me down bellbottom jeans were so big for his frame that he had to cinch up his belt real tight to keep 'em from falling, and the ends were all frayed and tattered as he decided to *walk* off the last couple of inches instead of having them hemmed like a normal human being. On his feet were an absolutely essential part of any tough white kid's wardrobe around these parts; a pair of "you know what" kickers. The dark brown, square-toed dingo boots with the little brass buckle on the side of a two inch-wood heel.

El Estupido, on the other hand, was your typical Pachuco. He had a round pock marked face, with skin like brown shoe leather and a set of teeth that looked like candy corn. He had a thick mop of stick straight, jet black hair, just like every other Mexican I ever saw, that was all slicked down and topped off by one of them lovely hairnets that old lady waitresses wear at greasy diners. There was a tiny tuft of whiskers below his bottom lip and a couple of other stragglers below his chin, but the rest of his body was completely hairless, even on his arms.

El Estupido, and take it from me, he earned every letter of his nickname, always wore only black, kinda his trademark, I guess. The guys thought it was to make 'im look tougher, by I had a hunch it was to make mixing and matching his wardrobe that much easier. He didn't look like the type with much fashion sense, let's face it. His Mexican wedding shirt was bulging at the seams, not because he was so muscular, but on account of it was cut for about an eight year old, with the sleeves rolled up high as they'd go, and, of course, a pack of Camels tucked in on the right side. His black Wrangler jeans were so tight that he couldn't take a full stride and instead had to kinda swing his legs forward and walk slightly bow legged to keep from having a permanent wedgy. He was sporting a lovely pair of black leather boots, the ones with the chain around the ankle, I guess to make it easier for the police to shackle your legs together, and they had a sharp pointy toe covered with a shiny piece of chrome, the preferred foot wear for the Mexican Macho men of Santa Elena.

"Well, if it isn't *Fagger*," Loser Lane said, as he got right up in Jag's face.

"Pendejo" said El Estupido as he spit on the ground, speaking in one-word sentences as usual.

"I see the rest of the little dwarfs are hiding behind you as usual," the head Loser snarled as he slid his filthy blonde hair behind his ear. "Let's see, there's Dopey and Sneezey and Sissy and Weenie and Pansy, and, of course, Lardo!"

"Chiquitas," El Estupido squealed in a high voice with a wide grin that showed off the lovely greenish hue of all his teeth, except, of course, the solid gold one out in front.

"Well, well, well, poor little rich kid Lipshitz made his way down from his castle on the hill. Isn't that nice?"

"Gracias," said El Estupido as he bowed toward Larry and then

"Cabron!" under his breath.

At that point Cooper started hiccupping like a madman the way he always did in situations like this, and Creepy started scratching so hard you would'a swore he was having an epileptic fit. Then quickly ripped off his glasses and slid them in his pocket the way *he* always did when he was too scared to see what was gonna happen next. They both took a giant step backward and slid in behind Rosie who wasn't looking too keen about the situation neither.

"What the hell's that noise?" Loser said as he glared at each of us with his beady little eyes.

"Th-that's just Cooper," Jag said. "He has a s-s-spastic diaphragm."

"Huh?"

"Que?" grunted El Estupido.

"You know, the diaphragm muscle, the one in your chest that has to contract to help you breath," Big I explained.

Loser Lane and El Estupido looked at each other with their heads slightly tilted, exactly the same way your dog does when he doesn't know what the heck you're talking about.

"Well, you see, if the diaphragm muscle goes into a spasm, it can cause you to hiccup, and that's exactly what Cooper's problem is, get it?" I said as I stepped slightly forward. "But then I know I don't have to explain something so elementary to a couple of valedictorians like you."

The two Losers just stood there, staring out into space for a minute with their eyebrows all wrinkled up and scratching their heads. Then Lane said, "Oh, I get it!" Like someone flipped on a switch. "He's a big chicken sh!#"

"He actually prefers chicken poop," Neil answered, with a wink that neither of our unwanted guests appreciated much.

"Comè caca," El Estupido grunted.

"Hey, c-c-correct me if I am wrong, since my S-S-Spanish ain't too good, but wasn't that two words in a row? Good job Miguel!" Jag said and gave El Estupido an enthusiastic thumbs up.

Well even these two Neanderthals were smart enough to know when they were being made fools of, at least part of the time, and they didn't take too kindly to kids half their size giving them the business. As they crowded Jag, so his face was practically right in their chest, Loser Lane barked, "You think you're smarter than us, you little stuttering twit?"

"N-N-Not at all." Jag replied, not flinching in the least. "I'm absolutely certain that you two are b-brilliant. I mean, it's obvious. Come on!"

El Estupido smiled real proud at this fine compliment 'til Loser Lane shot 'im a menacing look and jabbed 'im in the ribs with his elbow, causing him to realize he was being duped, and start scowlin' all over again.

"Baboso," he said and spit on the ground.

Things were getting a little dicey now, and I could see Jag was gonna be in need of some help pretty quick, so I slowly circled around behind Lane as he and Miguel closed in on the gang. I gave Jag a wink looking over Lane's shoulder and he nodded and smiled back. That really ticked off the head Loser and he said, "What are you smiling at you little peckerhead? Don't you realize I am gonna pound your face in?"

As he reared back to clock Jagger with a big right hook, I threw myself down on my hands and knees directly behind 'im and at the same time Jagger ducked and pushed that Loser in the chest as hard as he could, causing good old Bubba to flip over my back and land hard, head first, on the sun baked dirt with a loud, "Thunk!"

"Run!" screamed Jag as we all bolted for the gate.

El Estupido stunned for a second, at the sight of his leader, lying dazed on the ground, quickly came to his senses and reached out to grab me from behind, when Big I threw a vicious body block into his side.

"Ay! Mi Madre!" Miguel yelled as he crumpled to the ground, holding his knee in agony and rolling from side to side.

"Escusame, señor," Ira said in his best Mexican accent and then gave him the chop low sign as we turned to make our getaway.

# Chapter Nine

## THE GREAT ESCAPE

We booked out the gate and into the street like no tomorrow and scattered so as to be harder to track. Jag and I went right along Cicada Street and then turned up the first alley we saw. I looked over my shoulder to see Loser Lane just starting to stand and trying to shake the cobwebs out of his head, while El Estupido was hopping up and down and hollering out more cuss words in Spanish than I knew ever existed.

"Man, are they gonna be p.o.ed!" I said to Jag as we ran along, not sure if I was glad or scared to death.

"Yeah, ain't it g-great," he answered with his trademark grin.

I wasn't so sure. You see The Losers included some pretty bad mothers, not just your everyday, garden variety delinquents, but some honest to God, can't miss, future death row inmates. They included Felix "El Raton" Munoz, who got his lovely name by gnawing off some kids ear in a gang fight when he was ten; Leroy "The Surgeon" McKnight, who, kids say, can carve his initials in you with his Swiss Army knife like lightening, and don't even ask what he does with the corkscrew that comes with it; and Oscar "Chile con Carne" Cervantes, who can pound your face so bad that it looks like a big heaping plate of the stuff when he's finished. None of this, however, seemed to bug Jagger one bit, but, I guess that really didn't surprise me all that much, seeing who we were talking about.

We ran down the alley almost as far as the Munroe place and then doubled back towards the clubhouse, figuring everyone would end up there eventually, if they were still alive that is. I was most worried about Rosie, 'cause even with El Estupido's one leg outta commission, and Lane's concussion, they could still probably run him down. The other guys, I figured, were either quick enough or scared enough to make their way to safety.

We kept behind hedges and between houses as much as possible to stay outta view and after about half an hour of heart pounding terror, finally ended up in Jag's alley. Instead of going straight for the clubhouse, which would be the obvious place to ambush us, we decided to hide out behind the oleander hedge and waited for the other guys to show up. I kept my eyes peeled for any of the other Losers sniffing around, 'cause I knew it wouldn't take long for their reinforcements to be called up after the humiliation their leader had suffered. As we pushed through a clearing and started to sit down we heard a soft, "Psst, Johnny is that you?" and we turned quick to see Ira and Neil huddled behind the hedge about ten feet down from us.

"Yeah, it's us. Me and Jag. How about the others?"

"Saw Rosie and Cooper running like two mental patients, if you could call it running, on their way towards Main Street. They kept smacking into one another and screaming at the top of their lungs. It was an embarrassing sight to tell ya the truth. Good thing them Losers were out of it, or they'd have been dead meat."

"That reminds me," I said. "Nice crack back lock on the El Estupido, Big I."

"Thanks, I think I might've broke a rib or somethin' but it was worth it. I saw Jerry Kramer of the Packers use that same move against some little defensive back from the Colts last week. Almost knocked 'im into the second row. Thought I'd give it a whirl. I doubt "El Rey" will be chasing down any old ladies for a while."

"Did you see the look on Loser Lane's face while he was flipping over Johnny?" added Neil. It was priceless, a real Kodak moment! He went from being Mr. Macho to looking like a little girl who had seen a ghost, in about a tenth of a second. I guess he just couldn't believe that any of us kids would have the juevos to pull a stunt like that on him.

"Well, that's our 'Fearless Leader,'" I said as Jag lifted his arms and made his biggest muscles, which were pretty impressive for a kid, I gotta admit.

"Hey, where are you guys?" a frantic voice called out from behind the fort.

"Over here, Rosie," I whispered, "And not so darn loud."

"Thank God!" he answered as he moved quickly towards us, his inner thighs scrapping up a storm, and the sweat pouring off his forehead like Niagara Falls. When he got close I could see Chicken Coop cautiously poking his head out from behind his pal to make sure it was really us.

"We seen a group of Losers walking towards the school down Cicada Street. They must've planned a meeting of the whole gang down their today or somethin'. Looks like we're gonna have to deal with more than just Lane and El Moron," Rosie said.

"It's El Estupido, dammit!" Ira said, "Get it right."

"Whatever, that dude is dumb, that's all I know, but I guess you don't have to be a genius to slit somebody's throat!"

"Good point," Jag admitted as Coop poked his head out from around Rosie, nodded in agreement as he made a slashing motion across his neck with his fingers, gave a big shudder and slipped back behind Rosie again.

"We were afraid them other Losers might've spotted you guys. I mean they would'a pounded our faces in just for fun, even *before* they found out what we did to their leader."

"How many of the upstanding young gentlemen did you see?" I asked.

"Couldn't tell for sure. I was too busy being scared to death. The only way Coop and I managed to avoid 'em was because I heard the tall, skinny, zit-faced one with the tattoo that says, "Have a *knife* day," on his shoulder singing some Mexican folk song at the top of his lungs while he walked. Might've been "El Rancho Grande", come to think about it. Anyway, I figured nobody in this neighborhood would be singing that song 'cept maybe me, so before we even caught sight of 'em, we ducked in behind Mr. Star's crusty old Coupe de Ville parked on the side of his place. Good thing he didn't leave for the dog track early today. To tell the truth, that wetback's voice wasn't half bad. I would'a enjoyed listening to 'im sing for a little while longer if I wasn't about to pee in my pants from fear. He might actually have a future in the mariachi business someday."

"Oh yeah," Neil agreed. "He can sing the lead in the Spanish version of 'Jail House Rock' with the Mariachi del State Pen."

"Hey, where the heck's Creepy?" Ira asked with a start.

"What da ya mean? He's not with you guys?" Rosie answered as a look of fright came over his face.

"Prairie sh!#" Neil blurted out. "With all the excitement we totally forgot about the little fart. This ain't good. You know he would'a made a beeline for this place, first thing, sure as hell. If he ain't here by now, somethin's up and it ain't good."

"Poor little Bampu, can you imagine what those animals would do to him?" Rosie cried out.

"He's gonna look like a jigsaw puzzle after the surgeon's finished carving him up." Ira said sadly.

"Didn't anybody see 'im after he took off?" I asked, kinda annoyed. "What about you Coop? He's usually stuck to you like a Siamese twin when things go bad."

"Let me see," Chicken Coop thought out loud in between hiccups.

"Seems like I remember him taking off his glasses when things started getting kinda tense, you know the way he always does when he's so scared he don't want to see what's gonna happen next. He did that the whole way through "Abbott and Costello Meet the Wolf Man," over at the Fox last month, bet he didn't see more than five minutes total of that picture show. Anyway, after Jag yelled, "Run!" I looked back and saw him take off like all get out, but now that I think about it he was carrying them stupid glasses in his hand, and was heading straight for the big cottonwood tree next to the Ramada. O my God! Ya don't think he ran into that tree trunk and knocked himself out cold do ya?"

We all looked down and shook our heads knowing that was probable *exactly* what happened.

"We better call Mengo and Pato on this one," Ira said, matter of fact. "With some luck, they'll get to him while his parents can still identify the body."

"M-M-Mengo's outta town, Jagger said in a low voice. I heard he's up in Phoenix b-bartering with the state legislature for m-m-more money due to all the problems those Losers been causing him."

"Well at least he's not barking up the wrong tree this time," I said. "But I guess that means we're on our own."

"I say just leave the little turd," Neil barked disgustedly. "That's what he gets for taking off his glasses. I swear sometimes the smartest kids got the least amount of common sense, and I for one am getting damn tired of having to always bail another idiot out. Everyone knows the Creep's blind as old Mr. George without his specs!" (Mr. George was the janitor at the Sewer, and his eyes were so bad that he wore these glasses that had little microscopes glued on the outside so that it looked like he had a set of binoculars strapped on his head all the time, I kid you not. You had to be careful not to look straight into the lenses 'cause they made his pupils look about the size of a Kennedy half dollar, and it'd scare the life outta ya. Once he sorta snuck up on me in the library, and when I wheeled around, he freaked me out so bad I left a little somethin' extra on the floor for him to clean up! Even *with* them things on the poor guy still had to feel his way around, mostly, and needless to say, our school never did get very clean, which just added to it's well deserved nick-name.)

"I mean," added Neil, "He practically had to *try* to get caught after the way we took out those two scum bums."

"Come on," Jag said, fed up with Neil's attitude. "We c-can't just l-l-leave the poor little guy. We're supposed to be a team, remember? W-w-what about that 'All for one stuff.' Don't that m-mean nuthin'? Anyway we may n-n-need old Creepy to do some f-f-figuring on something important down the road some time."

We really couldn't argue with that, since none of the rest of us was especially well known for their high intellect, if you know what I mean, but none of us were too eager to have to take on those Losers again, neither, and this time they were gonna be plenty ticked off and at full scumbag strength.

"It's probably too late to save 'im anyways, Jag. Let's face it," Neil said. "They must've beat 'im to a pulp by now."

"I doubt it," I said. "It ain't little Bampu they're after, it's us. They'll just use him as bait to try and lure us back down there. We're the ones who have the *cajones* to stand up to them, and they're gonna want to cut them off to teach us a lesson."

"Well, I'm kinda fond of my *cajones* and I'd like 'em to live and prosper right where they are, thank you very much," Ira said as he grabbed his groin and gave a big smile.

"That's good to hear Big I, 'cause I heard through the grapevine that you was about to have one of them new surgical procedures that guys like you need."

"What the heck are you talking about?"

"You know," Neil laughed. "An add-a-dick-to-me!" ("Chopped lows!" all around)

"Well, I heard *you* were the first in line, Nellie!"

"Hey, Hey!" Jag said, trying not to laugh too hard himself and stepping in between the two guys, "We're g-g-getting off track here. W-W-What about Creepy?"

"Okay, let's get down to business. How many Losers did you see going toward the school, Rosie?" I asked.

"Four, I think."

"You said the guy who was singing was tall and skinny with a tattoo. Did he have a long pointy nose and kinda slanty eyes?"

"Yep."

"Okay, that's 'El Raton,' all right. What'd the other guy look like?"

"One was short with this huge round head and real bushy eye brows and one of them little 'Contiflas' mustaches." (Contiflas was this *muy* famous Mexican actor that had this very corny little mustache that looked like two pieces of brown rice stuck to the corner of his mouth.)

"Okay, that's your friend and mine Chile Con Carne. Who else?"

"Another guy was about medium height with monster biceps and a big hoop ear ring, and he wore one of those leather bands with spikes all around on his wrist."

"Hmmm," I thought for a bit. "That don't ring a bell, must've just been paroled or somethin'. Was there a white dude with droopy drawers and taps on his boots, sucking on a Marlboro?"

"Bingo! How'd you know?" Rosie asked.

"Darn! That's The Surgeon. I was hoping he might be busy cutting up some other middle class kids today. Oh well, guess we'll just have to deal with them best we can."

"And how, may I ask, do you suggest we do that without committing suicide?" asked Ira.

"Look," I answered, "We got no chance against 'em if we're on equal footing. That's a no brainer. So we have to get an edge. Something that will put us at an advantage."

"What the heck are you talking about?" asked Cooper with a blank stare.

"Well," I went on, "what do the Losers love to do even more than beating the snot outta little kids like us?"

"Smoke dope!" the answer was quick and unanimous.

It was a well-known fact that smoking marijuana was the national pastime for the Losers. It was like it was one of their four basic food groups for crying out loud; meat, vegetables, grain and San Samea. Ya see, the "wacky tobaccy" was everywhere around these parts, being so close to the Mexican border and all, and although none of us had tried it, we used to make fun of the stoners all the time by pretending to take long puffs off an imagined marijuana cigarette and then saying stuff like, "This is good sh!#," while holding our breath in long as we could. We learned all the correct lingo from Neil's older brother, Barry, who was known to smoke his share. He had this far out looking green glass bong in his room, right out in front of his parents, for crying out loud. It had two big brass bowls, instead of just one like the others I'd seen, and he called it a "Power Hitter." He told his mom that it was a fancy flower vase which she thought was awful nice, 'til one day when she had a big dinner party and decided to use it as part of the centerpiece on the dining room table. Seems she got some mighty funny looks from some of her guests, and according to Neil, none of them would ever return her phone calls after that.

Anyways, I asked the guys what *always* happened to the Losers after they'd been smoking dope, and they all yelled at once again, "They get paranoid!"

"Exactly," I said. "And that's gonna be our edge. We gotta create some kinda diversion after they're stoned to the bone, and then sneak in and snatch Creepy. If we're lucky, we'll get some help from a real nasty monsoon that seems to be brewing off to the south in about an hour or so."

Dark grey clouds were rolling in real nice, and a breeze had already started to pick up as we began to make our plans for the great escape. We decided to use wrist-rockets to shoot at the enemy from hidden combat positions at all different angles, to cause as much fear and confusion as possible. Neil said we should try and time our shots with the thunder to freak 'em out even more, and I suggested that the best marksman, who just happened to be me, should take the first shot from the best vantage point, and try to blast "The Surgeon" square in the *cabeza* and therefore, take out the biggest psychopath of the group right off the bat. We weren't too concerned with "El Estupido" on account'a his bad knee, or Loser Lane for that matter, who would surely be stoned to the bejeesus, and had a concussion to boot, which can't be too good for your reasoning ability - not that it was anything to write home about in the first place.

We decided the old cottonwoods surrounding the playground would be our best firing positions, and I reminded the guys that it was curtains for poor old Bampu if any of them low lifes got so much as a whiff of any of us before the shooting started. Finally, after all the shooting stopped, we decided that Ira, being the fastest of the gang and all, would race through their totally fried and hopelessly confused group, whooping and hollering, to decoy them into following him, so I could slip in and carry the Creep off to safety.

After finishing up the final the details, we all looked at Jagger, him being our president and all, and after thinking on the plan long and hard, he nodded his approval, and that was that. We came out from behind the hedge into the alley next to the club house and made a little circle around Neil who yelled out our official cheer, "All for naught!" and back we hollered, "And not for long!" It was a lot like the one used by them Three Mouseketeers, in case ya didn't know, and after racing home to get our slingshots, we were on our way.

We moved on down the alley staying low and keeping our voices down in combat mode, with our eyes peeled for any lurking Losers. There was a real look of determination in the guys' faces I hadn't seen too often, and it made me feel real proud they were able to forget about their fears and differences when one of us had his butt in a sling. Could it be that we were finally maturing into that dedicated, focused and unified platoon just like them guys on, "Rat Patrol." Did we finally have what it took to keep the white ghetto a safe place for our friends and family like we'd always talked about? Were we *finally* changing from little boys to men, or at least big boys? Well, I ain't sure I'd go that far, after all Coop was still hiding behind Rosie and there was a distinct wet spot around the fly of his Levis, although he did poke his head out a little more than usual, and Neil was still mumbling about how Bampu was the world's biggest numbnuts to take his glasses off the way he did, but at least he was going along on the mission, which was more than I expected. So, I guess if we were able to pull this thing off, and that was a pretty big if, then maybe the Seward School Bombers warn't just a bunch of silly kids horsing around no more, but something much more important and mature, something that all men would someday give their eye teeth to be a part of, like say the Moose Lodge.

The lizards and horny toads scampered into the weeds, and under trashcans, and into old brick piles as we marched on by single-file and double-time, on our way to the battlefield. We searched for nice round stones no more than the size of a cat's eye, to use as ammo in our wrist rockets, on account'a they shot more true than the flat ones, and we knew how important accuracy would be if we were gonna get our new pal back in one piece. Coop was mumbling, "I fight to the finish, cause I eats me spinach," as we reached the end of the alley that opened onto Cicada Street. We were now smack dab across from the little kid's playground gate, so we hugged close to the back wall of the Sutton place on our left. The wall, and the whole house for that matter, were made outta old, wind worn adobe bricks that still felt wonderfully cool to the skin even on a hot summer day, having soaked up plenty of rain water from the storms. Doc Sutton was the only podiatrist in all of Santa Elena and probably the whole of Southern Arizona as far as that goes, and did pretty well for hisself according to Pop. He was built like a clothes hanger, with a mess of jet-black hair and skin the color of a 'Nilla Wafer.' He never did say much and smiled even less. In fact, he looked more like a mortician than a doctor, which wasn't too comforting when you were sitting in his office with an ingrown toenail the size of an elephant heart plum, and he was coming at ya with a foot long needle to *supposedly* numb you up, just like I was last month. Well, I tell ya, he was digging around down there for what had to be an hour, yanking and jabbing and cutting and cussing under his breath. I looked at Ma for some comfort, but she was blubbering worse than me for crying out loud! What the heck was she all bent outta shape about? I was the one in so much pain that the top of my head felt like it was about to blow clean off! Take it from me, if you ever get an ingrown toenail, just have a friend chop the dang toe off and go about your business. I guarantee it's less painful than what I went through.

The other funny thing about the Suttons was that they were the only Mormon family in all of Cochise county, but I wasn't too sure what to make of that since all I knew about Mormons was that back in the old days a man could have as many wives as he darn well pleased, which Pop said sounded to him more like a penalty than a privilege, and that they were supposed to keep a big old stash of food hidden in their house somewheres so when Armygetton hit they'd be able to ride it out, no sweat. But little Sammy Sutton let on one time, he'd secretly raided their pantry so many times his family would be lucky to last out an afternoon. Said he just couldn't resist a can of Hormel chile when he got the urge, no matter what the consequences. Anyways, old Doc Sutton's place was coming in mighty handy now since the backyard wall had little port holes in it every three to four feet which gave us a chance to check out the enemy camp without being spotted.

Jag gave the signal and we all hopped over into the backyard easy as pie and picked out a hole to spy through, all 'cept Rosie who gladly accepted the position of "special alleyway liaison" which Jagger made up to help 'im save face. What we saw when we peered out across the playground was a scared outta his wits Creepy with no shirt on, and no shoes or socks, neither, tied to one of the poles of the Ramada. What looked like a tube sock was stuffed in his mouth and the elastic band from his jockey shorts was hanging around his neck, probably ripped off after a painful number of double Melvin's. Even from where we stood you could see every muscle in his body twitch like some invisible man was giving him electric shocks, and his head kept jerking quick from side to side like he was trying to catch a glimpse of somebody sneaking up on 'im or somethin'. It looked like they gave the poor kid an atomic pinky, too, 'cause his tummy was beet red with the outline of fresh handprints. Poor little Bampu, he might never be the same after this, even if we do get 'im out alive.

The good news, if there was any, was that The Losers, just as we predicted, couldn't resist celebrating their great victory over a poor defenseless kid by smoking themselves into oblivion. Loser Lane was on his back staring up at the sky and giggling all crazy like a little girl playing with a puppy. The Surgeon had his pocketknife out and was having a sword fight with an invisible opponent. El Estupido was just sitting there with a completely blank expression, not all that different from normal, probably trying to remember who he was and where he was, and how he was gonna get somethin' to eat. The rest of the "National Honor Society" were content to just smile at nobody in particular and wait their turn for the wacky tobaccy to come back around their way.

The monsoon was starting up just as we had hoped, as the wind began to blow and the clouds got dark and thick, rollin' in over the Santa Rita Mountains from the south. We picked out the cottonwoods we'd climb closest to the Loser's position that had good sturdy limbs to stand on so we could get off nice straight shots. We told Rosie to just stand behind the widest tree trunk of the bunch and shoot from there for obvious reasons. It was decided that Jagger and Neil would make a wide arc around the school and take up the position in the trees on the far side of the playground while Cooper and Rosie would stay on the near side. Ira was gonna sit outta site here in the alley 'til it was time for his dash through The Losers, and I was gonna try to somehow make my way to the roof of the Ramada, where I would have the cleanest shot at The Surgeon, and be able to whisper to Creepy about our plan to save his butt. I'd give a sign to the guys to open fire and Ira would bolt on through after the second or third round and try and get 'em to chase him all the way to Red River if he could.

Jag pulled a shiny new ball bearing outta his pocket and handed it to me for the first shot. He said he'd been saving it for rabbit hunting with his pop when he got back from the war, but figured this was more important. Then he shook each of our hands, said, "Good luck men, and m-make your family and p-p-platoon proud!" and we were off.

Neil, Jag and I doubled back down the alley a bit and then cut through some houses to get south of the playground. Then we headed back toward Camino Principal where we parted ways. Jag and Neil kept on towards their position on the far side of the field, and I headed on back toward the Sewer 'til I hit the alley closest to the Ramada and Creepy. I crouched low as I peered into the playground to see if the enemy's position had changed at all, but, of course, it hadn't. By this time they were having a hard time just standing up, let alone moving around much. I spotted Rosie, Cooper and Ira over behind the Sutton place and gave 'em the thumbs up as I slipped quietly through the gate and behind some creosote bushes and weeds growing along the old mesquite fence, then I worked my way down, nice and easy, 'til I was smack dab behind the Ramada and Creepy, about twenty feet away from the closest pole.

Just then the wind started to really kick up and I could see a few lightning bolts flashing off in the southern sky. It looked like this was gonna be a doosy of a storm, which was just what the doctor ordered. I could see Creepy now, poor kid, clear as day as I slithered in right behind 'im. His head was sunk down low and he just hung there real limp with his hands tied behind 'im around the pole with a pair of shoelaces. Off to my right I caught a glimpse of Jagger and Neil slipping in behind two of the bigger cottonwoods along the east side fence. So far things were moving smooth as silk, but I knew enough not to count my chickens 'til all the foxes were long gone, and now the hairy part was just about to start. I had to somehow race over to the Ramada across nuthin' but open space, shimmy up one of the back poles, and then pull myself up on the roof, all without being spotted, and for the first time since we split up my heart began to pound and little beads of sweat sprung up on my upper lip. I knew for certain if them Losers got even the slightest whiff of what was up it'd be a slow painful death for me and the Creep, no matter what the rest of the gang did. I told myself to stop thinking so much and just react, like I'd been taught a million times while playing ball, the only problem was in baseball the other team doesn't try to *kill* you if you lose.

Just then I caught a big break as a humongous black raven, flying low to cheat the wind, made his way over the field and let out a loud, "Caw! Caw!" The Losers all rubbed their eyes looked up, kinda dazed and confused, and followed the black bird's flight as it glided off to the north. I saw my chance and took off like a shot for the pole right behind the Creep, using his body as cover best I could. When I reached the Ramada I climbed up like a pussycat chased by a Doberman, then grabbed the overhang of the roof and flung myself over the top. Because of the pitch in the roof I was completely hidden from view. I made myself thin by blowing all the air outta my lungs, and lay flat on top of that tar paper kinda stuff with the sand stuck all in it, which made for really good grip, but scraped the living daylights outta my elbows. I sat stiff as a board for a second and listened to see if I had caused any commotion, but the only thing I heard above the wind was some giggling, coughing and an occasional, "Chingalo!" or "Pendejo!" so I figured no one was the wiser.

"Psst, Bapu. Can you hear me? Don't look up. It's me, Johnny C."

I heard a low, muffled groan from down below and took that to mean a yes.

"Listen, we got these animals surrounded and we're gonna get you outta here, got it? So just hang tight!" A little whimper sound came from down below, exactly like the sound that Dodger makes when he wanted a piece of your steak and there weren't no chance you were giving it up. In fact, after I heard it, I instinctively looked over my shoulder to make sure that stupid mutt hadn't followed us out here somehow, but he was nowhere in sight. Thank God.

I crawled to the top of the roof, having to hold on tight on account'a the wind was really starting to swirl. I peered over the top to my left, and saw Coop had climbed up into position, and there was Rosie's big butt sticking out for the whole world to see, behind the widest tree trunk on the street. Man, does that kid got a caboose! Ira had slid down close to the gate where I had just come in and had crammed hisself between two garbage cans and a water meter where he could get a good look at the action.

I slowly raised the lucky ball bearing Jag had given me over my head as a signal to the guys that it was time to get ready, and snuck a look over at The Losers to pick out my target. Not much had changed in their position 'cept for now, the one I hadn't seen before, with the biceps like two holiday hams and the pantyhose hat, was standing up and looking around like an old dog that was sniffing in the wind. Maybe he sensed somethin' was up. Come to think of it, I hadn't seen him smoking like the rest of 'em, neither. He *definitely* could be a problem. Anyways, I seen I had a clean shot at The Surgeon who was standing still as a statue with a cock-eyed grin on his face as the evil weed was kicking in. I knew for sure I had to hit 'im dead on, first try, to take full advantage of the element of surprise, and I lifted my head over the peek of that roof nice and slow, like one of them three toed sloths on a lazy day, and brought my sling shot up to eye level, glancing from side to side to make sure the others were doing the same. I looked up to the sky for some help, and at that moment the first, and always the nastiest, lightening flash of the storm went off to the north, lighting up the whole Catalina Mountain Range. I knew that was my chance, so figuring the bolt was about five miles away, I counted out five Mississippis, stretched them rubber tubes on the wrist rocket for all I was worth and then let her fly.

At that exact same moment there came a thunderous "Kaboom!" echoing off the mountains, and then a sickening "Tha-Wack!" as my shot nailed The Surgeon square in the back of the head. He did a nice little pirouette with his eyes rolling back in his head, and then fell over like a hundred pound sack of potatoes. Before them Losers knew it, shots were coming at 'em from every direction as our plan started to take shape. They started kicking their feet and flailing their arms, and slapping at their backs and grabbing their personal parts, all while trying to cover their heads, and then threw themselves on the ground hoping for cover. I reloaded quick and kept on firing, and all the other guys did too, and before you could say, "*Aye, Chihuahua!*" their whole goofy group had melted into a mass of Loser humanity in the middle of the field. It was a pretty pathetic sight to tell ya the truth. They kept on squealing and squirming and rolling around on the ground as the shots kept whizzing through the air all around 'em, and didn't look nuthin' at all like the baddest bunch of *"pachucos"* this side of the border. All but Mr. Biceps, that is, he just stood a bit off to the side, cool and collected, taking in the whole crazy seen. Who the heck is that guy?

After the fourth or fifth round went off, Big I sprang into action. I caught sight of 'im outta the corner of my eye as he took off like Speedy Gonzalez through the gate and straight for The Losers, yelling at the top of his lungs like an escaped mental patient or somethin'. The shooting stopped as he came into view and The Losers all looked up to see what all the ruckus was about, though they were too spooked to lift their heads off the ground more than an inch or two. Once they seen it was Ira, they came to their senses and within a few seconds were all in full chase as Big I headed straight for the desert. That gave Jag, Neil, and Coop a chance to jump down from their trees, and they, along with Rosie, beat it outta sight. I threw my legs over the top of the roof and was easing my way down the other side to free good old Creepy, thinking how swell my plan had worked and how p.o.ed them Losers were gonna be about being duped twice in one day by us wimpy rich kids, when all of a sudden Pantyhose head stopped dead in his tracks and turned quickly around. There I was, plain as day, flat against the roof like some pitiful spider stuck in flypaper. I froze stiff, my thoughts suddenly changing from glee to horror, and watched hopelessly as he got a sickening smile on his face, showing several different shades of green, and started walking real nonchalant back towards the Ramada. He didn't even take time to call for the other delinquents to stop, I guess he figured he could handle this little ass-kicking hisself, and they could find their own fun.

I frantically weighed my options as he moved slowly towards us. I figured I could probably jump down and haul out the gate before he could reach me, and then it'd be pretty much a cat and mouse game to try to make it home before getting murdered, but that would mean leaving the Creep alone to take the full brunt of The Losers anger for being shot at like a bunch of fish in a barrel. I could jump down and try and fight 'im off, which really wasn't much of an option seeing that each of his arms was bigger than my waist, and it'd sure be *"adios amigo,"* in about two seconds, and I really couldn't expect any help from the other guys 'cause they were probably back at the clubhouse by now, waiting for me, Creepy, and Ira to show up and start the celebration. All them thoughts were racing around my brain as he kept getting closer and closer with the wind beginning to roar through my ears and the early, big raindrops started to smack the ground. I was *this* close to leaping down and running for my life when I heard a faint whining sound coming from below. It was Creepy, the sock still stuck in his mouth pleading to me for help. I shot a glance quickly over at the gate and then back at Pantyhose, and knew it was now or never if I had any chance of getting outta there alive, but I just couldn't get myself to do it. I mean, how was I gonna live with myself if I didn't even try to help poor, defenseless Bampu. I decided to just stay put, being the major ignoramus that I am sometimes, and do whatever I could to keep the both of us from being slaughtered in what I was certain would be a very unpleasant way.

The big armed freak continued to close in and as he got nearer his grin revealed the absence of several teeth here and there, and that along with his squinty, coal black eyes, big round head and slick backed hair gave his head a distinctive Jack o' Lantern look, which made me chuckle to myself in spite of the hopeless situation we were in. The squealing coming from below started getting louder and more frantic as he got to about ten feet of where Creepy was tied up. I still couldn't see my pal from where I was on account'a the overhang of the roof, so I lowered myself down careful trying not to slip and fall and hasten my own death.

"Hola, gatitos bonitos. Quiere jugar?" he croaked.

My hands were covering my face by now, and I was peeking out through the cracks between my fingers as the sound from below became a high pitched squeal as that low down, vile, piece of pond scum moved in closer and drew back his fist in front of Creepy's face. But just then, as I looked on, scared outta my wits, a glorious and most unexpected thing happened. Creepy, the chicken hearted, the little lamb among wolves, called up all the bravery he could muster in his scrawny little body, and hauled off and kicked that Loser as hard as he could square in the *cajones!*

There was a loud and lovely thud as his foot hit it's mark, and the look on that low-life's face changed from cool confidence to sheer agony as his eyes buggered out and then rolled back, his mouth dropped open and he slumped to his knees before falling face first into the mud with a splat. I was so shocked by what had just happened that I lost my grip and slid off the roof, landing hard with all my weight smack dab in the middle of that lousy Loser's back. He let out an ear piercing, "*Aye, mi madre!*" and kept on squirming in the mud with both hands grabbing at his manhood. Creepy and I just stared in amazement in what we had accomplished for a second or two 'til I came to my senses, untied my little friend and together we ran off for the clubhouse, leaving our beaten opponent in a heap on the ground.

We made it to the oleander hedge in Jag's alley where the rest of the gang was hide out in about ten seconds flat, like we were floating on air or somethin', and they all wanted to know what the heck had took us so long. Even Big I had made his way back by now after leading The Losers on a wild goose chase half way to Nogales and back. After I caught my breath and calmed myself down, (my heart was still beating a mile a minute) I told 'em the whole sensational story, but they didn't believe one word of it, and even started to get kinda ticked off at me for thinking they'd go for somethin' so ridiculous. But after insisting it was true, and having Creepy show 'em just how he done his dirty deed, they all came around and let out a monstrous cheer in the Creep's honor, slapped 'im on the back so hard he almost fell over twice, and congratulated him on his great triumph over juvenile delinquents. As the ultimate sign of appreciation, equal to the Congressional Medal of Honor as far as the S.S.B.'s were concerned, our President Jagger played a rousing rendition of "Wipe Out" on Bampu's head, and Neil cupped his hands in front of his mouth and made some of the loudest "pops" of the summer.

From that day forward Creepy was never quite the same. It was hard to put your finger on, and don't get me wrong, he was still a world renowned weenie, but he was somehow different, a more *confident* coward may be the best way to put it, I guess. And also from that day forward his new official white ghetto nickname changed from Creepy to B.B. And not on account'a him being shrimpy, neither, like most folks might've thought, but instead on account'a him being an A-1, champion ball-buster, that's why! That nutty little Creep from Indiana, whoever would'a thunk it?

# Chapter Ten

## BETTY ANN PATRICK

Betty Ann Patrick, or BAP as Neil had dubbed her by her first week in Santa Elena, was one'a those girls who Moms like to say is, "Way too advanced for her age," if ya know what I mean. Her physical attributes were plain to see, even to a blind man, but she also had a real special way about her; the way she walked, the way she talked, heck, even the way she ate a Hostess Ding Dong could make a guys innards get all jumbly and legs turn to rubber! Well, you can imagine it didn't take Neil long to take notice, and it warn't long before a lot of the men in the neighborhood started noticing BAP, too. There were plenty of times I saw for myself, wives shooing their husbands into the house as she made her way down the street, swaying back and forth nice and easy, like a well oiled gate on a breezy afternoon.

"Boy, look at that sweet swing set!" Neil would mutter as BAP floated on by. He was one hundred percent, drool down your chin, head over heels in love with her since the first day she showed up in homeroom two months ago, sitting there in her swell red, white and blue striped hip huggers and lovely purple eye shadow. He warn't the only one, neither, but nobody else was about to admit it, not with Neil so obviously laying his claim. Seems BAP had been exiled to Santa Elena by way of Chicago on account of "activity unbecoming to a young lady," according to the Santa Elena branch of the CIA, better known as Ma, Aunt Leah and Granny. She came from what they called a broken home, with her ma working as a waitress all day and, "god knows what all night," and then Betty Ann started hanging out with "people from the wrong side of the tracks." Her grandparents, Mr. and Mrs. Gianninoto were I-talian immigrants, and were eighty-five years old if they were a day, but even though they'd been here for half their lives, they never bothered to learn more than a couple of words of American. They lived over on the outskirts of town, high up in the foothills, and I guess they agreed to take their granddaughter in to teach her right from wrong, and most important, keep her away from boys at all costs. Neil had other ideas.

Now Neil had always rode all of us unmerciful if we even thought about a girl for any reason other than to humiliate them in some way, and God knows I caught my share of grief for just being civil to old Jenny Darling, but I guess BAP changed all that. The thing was, to tell it straight, it wasn't so much *girls* that Neil all of a sudden was gaga over, it was their breasts. He was getting absolutely nutty about 'em, and Betty Ann definitely had some Grade A, U.S.D.A. choice ones. It didn't matter to Neil one bit what kinda breast a girl had, neither; big or small, high or droopy, firm or bouncy, he

liked 'em all. The thing was, I knew for a fact he'd never even seen a breast before, not a real live one, anyway. Our only experience with the female anatomy came last summer when we found some girly magazines in the trashcan out behind Damon Timmons's house, a college boy visiting his folks over break. Jagger had gotten an inside tip from Wade Sutton, a third grade neighborhood kid who had overheard good old Damon say one day while he was shooting some baskets down at The Sewer, that his mom had found his stash of Playboys and threw a conniption fit and a half, so he was gonna have to toss the whole lot of 'em. We staked out that guy's stinky garbage around the clock for a week, each of us taking a four hour shift, 'til we finally hit the jackpot; a complete 1967 twelve edition set, in perfect, mouth-watering condition. It even included the full color calendar, for gosh sakes! It was a darn shame we had to give old Wade the Gala Christmas Issue for his part in the find, but I guess you shouldn't get too greedy with your pals when it came to quality entertainment for men.

Like I said, those magazines were my first real exposure to the female anatomy, 'cept for the time I accidentally walked in on Ira's older sister, Jean, as she was getting outta the shower. Problem was, she covered up so quick with the shower curtain I didn't even get a glimpse of anything good, and then she proceeded to beat me with the back scrubber so viciously I was lucky to escape from that bathroom with my life! I gotta admit, I found the female body much more interesting than what we got. I mean they had all kinds of stuff sticking out here and going in there, and though I didn't really understand why, just looking at those pictures always put a big smile on my face.

That summer we would set aside at least thirty minutes a day for our viewing pleasure. We treated those magazines with the utmost care and respect they deserved, always careful to not tear or even bend any of the pages, and soon after we found 'em Coop was banned from touching the pages on account'a his hands were so sweatie he'd smudge the pictures. It was decided that only one issue would be enjoyed each day, that way, according to Neil, "our relationship with the girls would never get stale," whatever that meant, and that issue would be carefully set on a clean hand towel in the middle of the clubhouse floor with us guys sitting in a circle all around it. Jagger had the honor due to his high rank to gently turn the pages, rotating the whole magazine slowly so we'd all have an equal chance to view the loveliness right side up, and then after all the pictures were done, he'd move on to the cartoons; my favorite being the Vargas girls, Jag preferring Little Annie Fannie. After that, Ira would carefully remove the centerfold by first bending the staples back, and then with a ceremony fit for a king, he would parade it around the clubhouse and then tack it on the wall next to last month's playmate while the rest of us sang a rousing rendition of Elvis' "Hunka, Hunka, Burnin' Love."

Every day we'd stash 'em away in a metal cash box Jag had clipped from his Pop's desk, and then set 'em in a hole in the ground under an old piece of carpet in the corner. That was, every day 'cept for the fateful one where we got spooked after hearing Mrs. Howell coming down the alley with the trash, and high-tailed it outta there before putting them up. Just our luck, that night was a monstrous downpour that lasted more than two hours, with pelting rain and winds howling worse than a pack of coyotes with a nasty case of constipation. Next day when we showed up for our usual "thirty minutes of anatomy class" as Neil had dubbed it, what we found, to our utter horror, was eleven girlie magazines and a calendar soaked through and through and floating in a disgusting puddle of mud, due to our less than water tight roofing job. We worked fast and frantic to do what we could as gentlemen to save our girls, but it was no use. It was one of the saddest sights any of us could remember. The ink from one picture had run all over the next, so you couldn't tell Miss April from Miss November, even though we had their exquisite features memorized down to the smallest beauty mark! The hanging centerfolds, once the most lovely angels of our affection, looked more like the grotesque, deformed aliens from one of them outer space shows, although still naked, of course.

We tried wiping 'em with our t-shirts, but that just smeared the ink worse. We tried blowing 'em dry, but that didn't do nuthin' to get rid of the mud. We tried drying 'em out in the sun, but that just made the pages swell up and get all wrinkly, which had the nauseating effect of making our lovelies look like a bunch of porky naked grandmas. We finally realized there was nuthin' we could do to bring back our little treasures, but we couldn't just throw 'em in the trash after all we'd been through, and so we decided we'd have a little ceremony and bury the whole lot of 'em in a small grave site just outside the clubhouse door. Neil gave a real swell eulogy about how Miss January through Miss November had played such an important roll in our young lives, and how we'd never forget them, and although we'd never had the chance to thank 'em properly in person and all, he was sure they were well aware just how much they really meant to us and all young boys around the world. It was really kinda touching to tell ya the truth. Then Coop drew a pretty nice rendition of the Playboy bunny on the side of a slightly used paper plate for a headstone, and that was pretty much that.

Well, that was all well and good, but Neil wasn't about to give up that easy on his quest to become the foremost authority on breasts in the whole of the white ghetto, and it seemed from that day forward, every female we came across, 'cept maybe a blood relative, received some kinda comment about their chest size. He just couldn't control himself. Sometimes it was just a subtle, "Nice ones," under his breath as some lady walked by, or

"Magnificent mounds!" if a blouse was strectched a bit tight, but sometimes it was a, "I've seen a lotta honkers in my day, but I ain't *never* seen nuthin' like them before!" loud enough to wake the dead. It was getting down right embarrassing! Once in a while he'd feel kinda musical and start singing his rendition of that old love song, "Memories," but he instead used the word "Mammaries" and it completely changed the feel of the piece, if ya know what I mean. The thing was, Rosie probably had bigger breasts that any of the girls we had known before, if ya got right down to it, but all that changed when Betty Ann Phillips bounced into town.

Neil started right off making daily trips over to BAP's place to torment her grandparents and try his darndest to get a few seconds alone with her. We'd usually tag along to watch the show and also to make sure he didn't get away with lying about any great achievements. I guess we were getting to the age where that kinda stuff was important and nobody wanted to get left behind. We all knew Neil would be the first guy to make up some wild story of sexual adventure if he had the chance, but that sorta thing was gonna take hard proof to hold any water, and we figured there was nuthin' better than seven eye witnesses.

By now poor Neil had completely convinced himself that BAP was head over heels in love with him, on account 'a the way she always smiled real sweet and pretty whenever they'd cross paths. The problem was, everyone *except* Neil noticed she acted exactly the same way anytime she met any guys at all, no matter who they were. Heck, I even saw her giving the hairy eyeball to old Señor De La Vera the mailman, and he was three hundred and fifty pounds, bald headed and had eczema so bad that if you stood right next to him you'd swear it was snowing!

The point I'm trying to make is that Betty Ann wasn't too picky when it came to her suitors, and we pointed this out to Neil a bunch of times, trying to be subtle and all, so as not to burst his bubble too bad, but he wouldn't have none of it. Instead, he read us the riot act and said, "You're just jealous 'cause she ain't in love with any of you maggots," and said we should be ashamed of ourselves for not being happy for him, a fellow S.S.B., and his, "Manly success of nabbing the most exquisite female in all the world," or at least, I guess, in eastern Santa Elena. After that we decided to put a sock in it and let the chips fall where they may, which we all suspected would probably be right on top of Neil's hard head.

One Friday evening, we were all just hanging out behind Jagger's after dinner and having a contest to see who could get the most dogs barking by kicking an old Folgers can down the alley, when Neil says, with this dreamy look on his face, "I wonder what Betty Ann is up to tonight?"

"Probably locked in her bedroom like every other night," I answered, as I stepped up to take my turn.

"C-c-come on Neil, not again," Jag said, knowing what was coming next. "Them G-g-gianninotos are like p-prison wardens, kid. They w-won't let ya within twenty yards of her!"

"Yeah, but maybe this time will be different. Maybe this time we could sneak her out just for a bit, and her and I could go for a little walk in the moonlight, and then maybe I'd reach over and give her a little peck on her lovely cheek and then maybe she'd say that that wasn't enough and then grab me and plant a big wet one right on the lips, and then, then…Oh man! Those breasts!" he screamed out and then sunk down to the ground like he couldn't live another day without her.

"I don't know, pal," Big I said. "You better get yourself some mountain climbing equipment if you're gonna tackle a body like that! I got some rope and a carabineer or two you could borrow if you want."

"Just like the Grand Tetons!" Chicken Coop said as he cupped his hands in front of his chest, doing his best B.A.P. impression, but then quickly remembered himself and cut it out before Neil got sore.

"Actually the Grand Tetons are substantially more than 20,000 feet at their pinnacle," said B.B. as he took off his glasses to wipe them with his shirttail. "I would estimate that Betty Ann's mammary glands top out at six or seven inches, max."

"Yeah, you'd like to find out, wouldn't you Mr. Wizard?" Neil said as he shot old Bampu a dirty look, which got him to fidgeting, and us to cracking up. After a few more minutes staring out in space Neil said, almost inaudible "Can you even imagine her beautiful brassiere?"

"What?" asked chicken Coop.

"Her lovely lingerie," said Neil.

"Huh?" grunted Rosie.

"Her over-the–shoulder-boulder-holder!" Neil screamed.

"Oh. Why didn't you say so in the first place?"

"Anyways, I've been doing my hand strengthening exercises real regular with an old rubber ball, and practicing my hooking and unhooking on some old fasteners I found in mom's sewing box, so I feel I'm ready to accept the challenge." And with that Neil turned to us, shot us a quick, sharp solute as he clicked his heels, and started off towards the foothills and Betty Ann's, with the rest of us trudging along behind, having nuthin' better to do.

What a lovely night it was turning out to be, as the sunset shown pink and gold through the western sky silhouetting the Rincon Mountains and lighting up the large fluffy clouds so they looked like huge pieces of cotton candy floating across the sky. The moisture in the air from the rains that made it so sticky and miserable during the day, now, as night began to fall, added a welcomed refreshing quality to the faint breeze blowing in our way from the Catalinas. The recent rains brought life back full force to the usually barren desert, making the plants look less frightening, and almost pretty. The Palo Verdes were practically dripping in bright yellow blossoms that were startling against the mostly gray surroundings, and the small red flowers and vivid green leaves on the ocotillos made you realize they weren't just dead sticks coming up from the ground after all, as they had appeared most of the year. The white rubbery flowers on top of the saguaros gave them the look of tall, skinny, bald men wearing bad toupees, and the shimmering leaves of the large cottonwoods that lined the Santa Cruz River made me dream of living in a place where there was lush green shrubs all year 'round and you didn't have to be rushed to the hospital if you happened to fall into one of 'em!

Around this time of year there was actually a few feet of water in the normally bone dry riverbed, and we could hear its soft flowing sounds up ahead as we raced through the trees and then slid to a stop on our butts on the bank, peering down at the rushing water below. There really was something mighty soothing in the sound of a running river, and Jag and I laid back and closed our eyes and just listened for a while. Neil and Ira were trying to skim rocks across which almost never worked, and then got into a knock down drag out argument about who was dumber, Dudley Do-Right or Chumley from Tennessee Tuxedo, while Rosie, B.B. and Coop were searching up and down for a piece of cardboard to make a boat, and some unlucky bugs to make up a crew. After finding the remains of an old "Shake and Bake" box caught in the branches of a giant Creosote bush, they set her in the water along with three ants, two dazed grasshoppers and a stink bug, christened their boat the "Queen Elizabug," and launched her with a drum roll and a glorious three burp salute. Unfortunately she capsized after hitting some rapids ten feet down stream and I am sad to report that all aboard were lost.

After a few more delightful minutes just listening to the slow stream carrying precious water to the dried out dessert, like a dying man's bloodstream bringing the nutrients he needed to survive, it was time to move on and we started off along the west bank toward the old suspension bridge about a quarter mile down river. That rickety old thing wasn't the fastest or the safest way to cross over, not by a long shot, but what kinda kid in his right mind's gonna use a new cement overpass, when you could use a fifty year old wood and rope contraption that swayed so bad and was so flimsy, it might just collapse at any second! Besides, we were all strictly forbidden from using the old bridge, which made it all the more irresistible.

We continued up along the banks of the Santa Cruz which, by the way, I had heard was the only river in North America that flowed south to north, and according to Pop, fit right in, being "backasswards" like everything else around these parts. I guess it must'a been a kinda big deal to some of them outdoor freaks, 'cause on more than one occasion I had seen strangers jump outta their cars and look over at the river excited as a screwy school girl at a Beatles concert.

A good sized road runner with a baby lizard in his mouth for dinner ran out from under a creosote bush just up ahead of us and when he saw us coming he made that weirdo "Thump, Thump," sound that ya had to hear to believe, and then raced off.

"That reminds me," said Rosie, real sincere. "I'm getting awful hungry."

"You know you got a real problem there De la Rosa." Neil said in disgust.

"I can't help it," Rosie said in a sad voice. "My ma says I have one of those glandular problems."

"Yeah, you got a bad glandular problem, alright," Ira shot back. "It's that big fat one between your ears!"

We threw just about anything we came across into the water as we went along just to watch it float away. The silt that had washed down from the mountains after the monsoons had settled in layers at the side of the banks, and was made up of all different colors that flowed, one into the other, like one of them pretty sand paintings that the Papagos sold out in front of San Xavier Mission on Sunday mornings. Outta nowheres came a loud, "Caw! Caw!" and looking up we saw two big black turkey vultures with their sickening, scrawny red heads stretching straight out and circling above us.

"Hey Rosie, don't lie down, kid," said Neil. "'If they think you're dead, we'll have every damn vulture in Arizona over here for the big feast."

"Gosh Neil, I'd think you'd be excited to see all of your relatives in one place like that," shot back Rosie, real calm and collected.

Well, that caught Neil off guard, not being used to being out done, let alone by someone low key as old Rosie, and he just stammered a bit under his breath, and just gave 'im a nasty, curled lip look. It was nice to see Neil put in his place once in a while, and we took turns quietly congratulating Rosie on his success. We decided to hang out under, "Los Amigos Bridge," for awhile, the new one made outta concrete I'd told ya about before, to listen to the cars rumble overhead which made the whole darn thing quiver and creak.

"Darn good thing there ain't no big semi-trucks in Santa Elena or this thing would crumble to nuthin' but gravel!" I said as a slug bug went across.

"Heck, this thing might collapse from a fat guy on a bicycle!" Ira snapped.

"Especially if he let out a big fart!" Cooper added with a grin from ear to ear. After we got over the initial shock of hearing somethin' fairly quick-witted like that coming from the Coop, we all had a good laugh at the image it conjured up.

"Coop's right!" said Jagger. "And they should have a s-s-sign on each end that says, 'Caution! If you've had f-f-frijoles last night, p-please avoid the bridge.'"

"Or they could just have a sign with a circle around a big fat butt and a line through it to signify 'No Farts Allowed!'" Neal added as he started to giggle.

"Speaking of farts, I'm smelling somethin' pretty rancid right now, Rosie," Ira said, squeezing his nostrils.

"Hows come every time someone cuts the cheese I get blamed?" Rosie asked in a truly hurt voice, and then looked around real quick to see if anyone was close enough to his behind to tell it really was him. "And anyways, he who smelt it, dealt it!" We all popped our hands in front of our mouths to signal our agreement, and gave Ira the "chopped low" sign like mad. We started to move on, but not before we agreed to do our part to keep the town safe by making a few, "No Farts," signs soon as possible and nailing 'em up on each end of the bridge one day before Mengo and Pato did their early morning patrol about two in the afternoon.

"Come to think of it, Penny Boyce would be the perfect model for the sign," Neil said. "She's got the biggest butt in school."

Penny Boyce was this chubby red headed girl who sat in front of Neil last year in Mr. George's class. She was really pretty annoying, to tell you the truth, always turning around and telling him to, "Shush!" or eavesdropping on what we were talking about, and Neil hated her guts. One day she made the terrible mistake of wearing a denim shirt to school with a big pink pig embroidered on the back. As soon as Neil noticed it he got this twinkle in his eye, and I knew exactly what he was thinking and as soon as old Penny sat down after the "Pledge of Allegiance," Neil tapped her on the shoulder and asked in a voice loud enough for everyone in class to hear, if she had done a self portrait on the back of her shirt! We all laughed hysterical, but old Penny got hysterical the other way and started blubbering up a storm, and then ran off to the restroom followed closely by her best pal and fellow pain in the rear, Nancy Cole. Less than five minutes later we all heard the horrifying, "swish, swish, swish," from down the hall of El Generalissimo's thunder thighs rubbing against each other. All the color went outta Neil's face as he realized what was up, and he tried hiding out in the art cabinet, but with all our paper mache globes in there he didn't quite fit, and she stuck her big mitt inside, grabbed him by the ear, and drug him outta class, kicking and screaming, up the hall to her torture chamber that was mistakenly labeled, "Office."

We didn't see hide nor hair of Neil for the rest of the morning, and once he did show up he wasn't looking too chipper, if ya know what I mean. His hair was a mess and his eyes were red as beets, and he walked real slow and gingerly, like his butt was made outta fine china and he was afraid it would brake at any second. Rumor had it that his naked rear end was the first to feel the wrath of El Generalissimo's new custom made paddle, although he still won't talk about it to this day and none of us are about to bring it up. Jag says he heard she had it made to fit her big fat hand just right by Señor

Montejo, the high school wood shop teacher. He says he heard that she had 'im drill a bunch of small holes through it for less wind resistance, allowing her to reach maximum paddle speed with every swat as she threw her considerable weight behind it. And that's not all she had in her agonizing arsenal, neither. Ray Bidagin, a scrawny, buck toothed kid with a hair lip, that always had to go home too early after school, taking his ball with him and ruining whatever game we were playing, said he just happened to be walking past the back window of the torture chamber last year, when he heard a blood curdling scream and took a quick glimpse in. What he saw changed his life forever. Old Ray crossed his heart *five* times, and then swore he saw some poor kid, he was too shook-up to remember who it was, lying on his back with some contraption strapped to his feet that was slowly pulling each and every one of his toenails out! All the while El Generalissimo was sitting at her desk, cool as a cucumber, eating a fudgesickle and powdering her hideous face.

We marched the next two blocks to the old bridge, arm in arm, hollering out "Hey, Hey, get outta our way, we just got back to the U.S.A." the way all the World War II G.I.s used to do. By the way, did I tell ya that Pop was in the Occupation Army over in Japan after we dropped the bomb? While he was there he said he sold a bunch of stuff at a place called the "Black Market," and he sent so much money home to his ma that she thought he was a General or something. My Pop was something you call a, "Natural born business man," according to just about anybody who knew 'im.

We were lined up smallest to biggest, with Rosie on one end and B.B. on the other, all still arm in arm, and all of a sudden Rosie stopped dead in his tracks and yelled out "Merry Go Round!" and before we could let loose, he started spinning his big old fat self fast as he could, snapping the rest of us around like a bunch of rag dolls and darn near flung old Bampu right in the river. He would'a, too, but just as his feet came out from under 'im, and he looked a lot like a scrawny version of Superman flying through the air, he grabbed hold of the back pocket of Chicken Coop's Levis and yanked 'em clean down to his knees before coming to a stop with a thud, face first in the mud on the edge of the river bank, his glasses hanging from his left ear all cock-eyed and spattered.

"Pulling boys pants down again, Creep? I'm startin' to worry about ya, kid." Big I said shaking his head.

"Nice Dudley Doo-right undies there, Coop," Neil added. "Are you guys *ever* gonna grow up?"

Chicken Coop pulled up his trousers with one hand, and helped his old pal outta the mud with the other, and then after washing his glasses in the river Bampu stuck 'em back on his face and we were off again in search of real live breasts.

"Do you think BAP might be aroused by a man with a lovely flower in his lapel?" Neil asked as he picked one of them yellow blossoms that grow on weeds and stuck it in the top buttonhole of his shirt.

"W-w-well, I don't know about her, b-but I think you look dee-vine." Jag said in a high girly voice, while batting his eyes big and pretty.

"I always knew you were a big homo, Jag!" Neil snarled.

"You w-wish, Nelly," Jagger answered, using Neil's hated nickname that only he had the guts to say to his face, bringing on another rousing round of hand popping and "Chopped lows!"

The old bridge started to come into sight, and I gotta tell ya it looked a heck of a lot more worn out and dilapidated than I'd remembered. I guess we hadn't tried crossing it for more than a year now, which was the last time the Santa Cruz had any real water flowing in it, and the last twelve months had sure been tough on the old girl. I'd heard that the big windstorm we'd had a few months back, the one that was set off by a hurricane down in the Gulf of Mexico and nearly blew the giant ice cream cone off the top of the Dairy Delight, had whipped her around something fierce and nearly snapped some of her rope like it was kite string. Looking closer I could see that a bunch of the wooden planks had been splintered as well, and the whole thing was held together by nuthin' but a lick and a prayer.

"Maybe this ain't such a good idea," Chicken Coop squeaked, sliding in behind Rosie as we drew near.

"Don't be such a weenie," Neil barked, "Your skinny little butt shouldn't have no problem making it across, anyhow."

"What about me?" Rosie asked sheepish, looking over his shoulder, as if we had forgotten how big *his* butt was.

"W-w-well, Rosie, my man, let's j-just say your chances ain't quite as good. You go last," Jag said, grinning big and goofy while he patted 'im on the back.

"It's been real nice knowing ya, Emiliano," Ira said, shaking poor Rosie's hand. "You're really one helluva guy, 'cept, of course, for that nasty habit of not sharing your treats."

"Let's go! Times a'wasting. Did you guys forget they're beautiful breasts, ripe for the taking, practically begging me to come and visit them right across that river!" Neil yelled as he ran up the bank to the bridge and started to walk across, completely ignoring the big red sign saying, "DANGER. KEEP OFF!"

He hung on tight to what was left of the side ropes, and edged along slow and sure, keeping his feet wide since the center of the planks were mostly split through and through, and the old girl creaked and groaned and swayed something awful with every move. I shot a glance at the ropes that anchored the bridge to the bank, and they weren't nuthin' to write home about, neither. Neil didn't pay no mind, spurred on by the burning desire to get to Betty Ann and her real live womanly attributes. I just didn't get it. Neil risking his neck and *ours* for some dumb girl he never even said so much as a word to. Now I could see going out on a limb for something *really* important once in a while, like the time we snuck down to Tubac on the Southern Pacific for the Mexican jumping bean festival for instance. But this! Come on. All I could figure was it must be one of those puberty problems Ma was always talking about, and if that's the case, I'd just as well stay at twelve years old the rest of my life and save myself a lot of trouble. Thank you very much.

We all watched close and quiet as Neil slowly crept across and then turned to holler at the rest of us to quit being such panty-pansies and get a move on. Jag decided we'd better send B.B. and Coop over next on account'a the fact they were the littlest. Plus, if they were left 'til last, let's face it, there's a good chance they'd just turn tail and run. At first they absolutely refused to move a muscle and just held on to each other for dear life, staring over the edge at the rushing river below. Then the fidgeting and the sniffling and the hiccuping started up like nobody's business 'til finally Ira got sick of it, and threatened to throw both of 'em over the side then and there! Well, that got 'em started, and they crawled on their knees the whole way, looking back over their shoulders at Big I every few feet, and not stopping their whimpering for a second.

Big I and me, we made it to the other side without too much excitement, though I slipped once or twice as the breeze started to pick up giving the bridge a nudge from side to side. I got a little weak in the knees when I stopped in the middle and looked down at the water roaring along. I ain't sure what it is, but I'm scared to death of heights. I never told the guys, of course, but any time I get higher than say, six or seven feet off the ground, my legs may as well be made out of Jell-O and my head feels like a watermelon on a twig.

Anyway, we were all across 'cept for poor Rosie, who was standing all alone on the other side looking over at us with big, sad, basset-hound eyes, and probably thinking serious of just packing it in, but being too ashamed to just walk away.

"Come on big guy, you can do it," I yelled. "Don't look down, grab onto the ropes, and haul butt!"

He just stood there with a blank stare on his face, like a big, fat statue. Jagger, sensing that Rosie was about to cave, and then would have to hear about it for the rest of the summer, started to chant, "Rosie, Rosie, Rosie," real low at first, but then louder and louder. The rest of us joined in, "Rosie, Rosie, Rosie! Rosie!" And then as we were stomping our feet and yelling at the top of our lungs, "Rosie! Rosie! Rosie!" his eyes got big as Oreo cookies, he let out a big honking yell, and then started running across the bridge fast as his big fat legs could carry 'im. The ropes were stretched to their limit and making a high squealing sound, and the planks were snapping right and left, but on he came; teeth clenched and eyes shut tight.

"Rosie! Rosie! Rosie!" we kept on.

"Aaahh!" he screamed as he trudged along.

Then with only about five feet to go there was a loud a *"Crunch!"* as two large planks split in two right underneath the big guys weight, and at that instant Rosie leaped with all his might for the bank, landing hard, face down in the dirt as a large cloud of dust flew up around him.

We stood over him, and with the old, "Heave ho!" rolled him on his back, but he just lay there with his eyes still clamped shut.

"You made it Rosie, you big dork," I yelled in his face. "You're alive!"

"I'm alive? I made it? Are ya sure?" he asked as he started touching himself all over to see for hisself, but still not opening up his eyes even a slit.

"Yeah, I'm sure, tubby," Ira said, wincing in pain. "Cause you landed right on my foot and smashed it to smithereens!"

Rosie got this huge grin on his face, opened his eyes and sat straight up. We all helped him to his feet, congratulating him on his great bravery and then headed on down the path through the cottonwoods and toward the hills, feeling pretty good about the adventure that was shaping up so unexpected. All except Ira, that is, he was limping and cussing under his breath and not feeling too festive right at the moment.

Our shadows started to stretch mighty long and the mountains in front of us took on a kind of shimmery look as we finally turned up the short dirt road where the Gianninoto's lived. Neil was getting antsy as all get out and licked his hands to slick back his hair over and over, blew into his hands to smell his breath, and then tried to smell if his armpits were stinky. We all watched, amazed at how some idiotic girl could turn the meanest, most hard nosed and cold-blooded kid in all the white ghetto into a big bowl of mush, just by the thought of *maybe* getting a little glimpse of her. It was unbelievable, and a little bit scary, too.

"Now remember," I said. "If ya do get a look at her bare breasts (which I knew was a million to one shot) don't stare right at 'em too long, it could be dangerous. Just take a quick glance and then look right away."

"What the hell are you talking about?" Neil barked.

"He's right," Jag added. "It's a w-well known fact that the n-n-naked breast can burn a man's retina, just l-like looking at a s-solar eclipse!"

"Kinda like being snow blind," said Rosie, and Jagger and I nodded our agreement.

"Grow up, will ya! That's the most ridiculous thing I ever heard," Neil snapped back. Then he turned to Bampu and asked, "Isn't it Creepy?" Old Bampu just stared at him in disbelief, and then rolled his eyes in response to the incredible ignorance that continued to surround him.

As we reached BAP's place Neil stopped and turned to us, "Listen, when we get up to the door, do me and yourself a big favor and let me do the talking. Got it? Just do what I do and say behind me," then we walked through the front gate and up the steps to the red cement porch. BAP's house is one of the original ten or twelve built in Santa Elena in the late twenties according to Pop. It was made outta adobe and thickly plastered and whitewashed all over. It had a flat roof with big old wood beams sticking out near the top. The windows were deep set with a nice ledge for flowerpots and such, and there was a huge mesquite door with an equally huge wrought iron knocker.

Neil took a deep breath, pulled back on that heavy piece of rusty metal and let her fly. "Clang!" it went, practically shaking the whole darn house, and then after slicking his hair back one last time he smiled widely as we all fell in behind him, to watch the show. The door opened real slow like and creaked loud on its worn hinges, and through the crack in front of us was the unmistakable face of Mr. Gianninoto, a thin, gray-haired old guy, slightly stooped at the shoulders and with glasses so thick that they made his eyes look like billiard balls. On top of that he had on one of them cool old-fashioned hearing aids, ya know the ones that had an ear plug with a long wire that went down to what looked like a stinking stereo speaker hanging off his belt. It was one of the wackiest things I'd ever seen! Needless to say, Mr. G. warn't too crazy to see us.

"Hello, Mr. BAP," Neil said, way too soft for 'im to have any chance of hearing.

"What did you say?" He answered in a thick Italian accent as he tried to angle his speaker toward Neil's mouth.

"I just come by for a sec to try and get a good look at your granddaughter's lovely breasts. If that's O.K. with you, sir?" He mumbled softly again, as we all tried to keep from busting a gut.

"What was that?" He said way too loud and really annoyed, as he frantically fiddled with the volume knob of his speaker causing the contraption to let out a hideous screech.

"By the way, how's Mussolini doing? You guys shot the breeze lately?" Neil said grinning from ear to ear and then turning back to give us a wink. Apparently Mr. Gianninoto hated this Mussolini guy's guts and fought in World War II with the Italian underground against him and all his followers that were known as the Fatshits. Pop and I watched a documentary about 'im one Sunday on PBS.

Well, that humongous hearing aid must 'a finally kicked in, that or he read Neil's lips, 'cause all of the sudden Mr. G got spitting mad and started screaming at us to get off his property or he'd throw us off hisself, or at least that's what I think he was trying to say with that crazy accent while using a whole lotta improvised sign language the way his people are famous for.

Neil just stood there smiling nice and sweet while BAP's Grandpa howled in his face, and then to the astonishment of us all, stuck the middle finger on his right hand straight up for all the world to see, and started to wave it at the old guy like it was the most natural thing a kid could do, and then said, real pleasant, "No sweat, Mr. BAP, whatever you say. You and the missus have a real nice evening." Seems Neil had found out that besides not knowing much of the English language, the Gianninotos didn't know squat about American hand gestures, neither. Neil looked over his shoulder at us and gave us another wink and pointed to his hand, and then we all slowly stuck up our middle fingers and waved 'em at Mr. BAP, too, though not feeling too comfy in doing so. The old man seemed to relax a bit after that, and seeing how polite and friendly we were acting, gave us a quick wave back and turned and slammed the door shut.

We all shook our heads and had a good laugh and then Ira said, "Well, I guess that's that," as we all turned and walked away.

"Not a chance," Neil answered, ashamed we'd even consider giving up that easy. "I saw the light on in Betty Ann's room on the side of the house as we walked up, and I mean to check it out."

"I don't know, Neil," Rosie stammered. "That old guy looks a little nuts to me. He might take a shot at us or somethin'."

"Don't be ridiculous. He can't see six inches in front of his face. But if yer that yellow you can say an extra prayer to your patron saint, Saint Francis of the Sissies! Now come on!"

We walked back out the front gate and down the street a bit and then doubled back just in case we was being watched, and after some not so gentle prodding from Neil, Rosie got down on his hands and knees along the side of the house under good old BAP's window and he climbed on his back to try and take a peek inside. The rest of us waited along the wall, anxious for the full report.

"Oh, my God! She's walking around in there stark naked!" Neil half screeched, half whispered.

"No way! Let's see!" "Me first!" We all screamed and then jumped on Rosie's back to have a look, too.

"Hey, watch it! Ouch! I'm not a dang loading ramp ya know," came Rosie's voice from down below. But nobody was paying no mind. All we knew was that here was our first chance to see a real live naked lady and we were going for it.

I grabbed on to Neil's arm and pulled myself up, all the while fighting the other guys off for best viewing spot. I stood on my tiptoes and peered over the ledge, and there she was, Betty Ann Philips, in all her womanly glory, sitting at her dressing table, painting her toenails as her silky blond hair flowed like a river of gold over the soft curve of her shoulder all the way down to her perfectly round behind. To tell ya the truth, she wasn't really naked, neither, but had on some of them thin, lacey underclothes that girls liked to wear, the kind that looked like they'd surely fall right to pieces if ya no more than blew on 'em, but that didn't ruin the vision none, and I was completely satisfied with the opportunity I'd been given.

"Wow!" was all I could spit out as I stared with my mouth hung open.

"Is she really naked, Johnny? Is she?" the rest of the guys were asking eagerly.

"Well, yeah, I mean, for all intents and purposes."

"Look at those breasts," Neil kept repeating as if in a trance, "Look at those bodacious breasts!"

That was about all Jagger and Ira could handle and they reached up and grabbed me and Neil by the belt loops and yanked us down on our butts.

"Hey, I wasn't done yet," Neil cried out as Jag and Big I scampered up Rosie for a little look see.

"Owww! Take it easy would ya," Rosie winced.

"Holy Moly!" Jag and Ira said at exactly the same time as they pressed their noses up against the glass as hard as they could.

You could tell Cooper and Creepy wanted to take a peek, too, and who could blame 'em, but they weren't about to push and shove like the others. I felt a little sorry for 'em, not wanting them to miss this once in a lifetime chance. "Come on you guys, you're next," I said, pushing them up in front of me next to where Rosie was kneeling. "They'll be finished in just a minute, so get yourselves ready for, 'The Greatest Show on Earth!'" I leaned against the cool plastered wall of the old house and closed my eyes and tried to burn what I just saw into my memory forever and ever. I got a slight grin on my face and started getting that tingly feeling all over inside once again when I heard a twig snap beside me. As I jerked my head around to see what was up, there was old Mr. Gianninoto no more than two feet away, with his lips all snarled up and his eyes looking bigger and scarier than ever through them coke bottle glasses, and worst of all, he was holding a shovel over his head like an ax! A scream got stuck in my throat, the way they always did when you're completely scared outta your wits, and as he swung straight at my neck with all of his might, I was just able to duck in the nick of time, as that shovel whizzed over my head and clanged hard against the wall.

"Aagh!" I finally screamed as I started to run, and Mr. G. yelled out somethin' in Italian that didn't sound too hospitable and then struggled to raise the shovel again. Creepy and Chicken Coop were already hauling down the side of the house towards the back alley and Jagger and Ira jumped off of Rosie and took off after 'em. As I ran by, I grabbed the big guy by the collar and yanked for all I was worth to help him up on his feet, and then headed out quick, not daring to look back, even once.

Clang! I heard the shovel hit again close behind us, and then before you knew it we were in the alley and heading back down towards the river, running for our lives! We might not of been the slickest group of kids in the world, but I guess we could at least out maneuver an eighty year old guy who was both deaf and blind. Barely.

When we were about fifty yards from the house, coming up on the big line of cottonwood trees, I looked around and realized that Neil wasn't with us. "What's that idiot up to now?" I thought, and as if on cue I heard from back toward BAP's place, Neil's voice scream out, "Mussolini!" and then in the distance a loud, "Clang!" and then a few seconds later another, "Mussolini!" and then another even louder, "Clang!" We all stopped to listen and just shook our heads. It seemed Neil wasn't ready to give up his vision of BAP that easy and figured he could dodge old Mr. Gianninoto for a little while longer if that's what it took to get a couple more good looks at the finest set of breasts this side of Tucson High.

About a week later, we were all sitting on the monkey bars down at The Sewer, getting some fresh air after another afternoon monsoon, when here comes Neil with his head hanging lower than a baritone in a basement.

"Hey, what's up?" Jag asked as he came within earshot.

He didn't even look up but just mumbled, barely audible, "It's all over. She 's gone."

"Whatdaya mean?" we all asked.

"BAP's mom called for her, I guess, and she said she had to go back home. Seems after talking to the Gianninotos about all the stuff going on in Santa Elena, she figured Chicago wasn't such a bad place for her after all." Then he sat himself down on the bottom rung, which was right about where he felt in life right then, put his face in his hands, and didn't make even one measly comment about breasts for a full day and a half.

# Chapter Eleven

## CHICKEN, THE TOWN SQUARE, AND FATHER KINO

"Who do you guys think's the greatest quarterback, Johnny Unitas or Bart Starr?" Rosie asked while trying to entice a ladybug to crawl up his chubby finger.

"That's no contest," I said. "Gotta be Johnny U. Didn't you hear how he picked apart the Giants in, "The Greatest Game Ever Played?"

"Yeah, but Bart Starr won two Super Bowls," added Ira, nodding assuredly.

"S-so what," said Jag. "Heck, you and me and the g-guys here could beat one of those girly A.F.L. t-teams!"

"That's for sure. What a joke. 'The Super Bowl.' Mark my words, no American Football League team will ever beat a team from the N.F.L. as long as we live," I said.

"How about Don Meredith?" Coop asked, just above a whisper. His pop was from Texas.

"Don Meredith!" we all screamed. "You think a guy with two *girl's* names is the greatest quarterback in the world!"

"What we gonna do today?" I asked lying on my back and chewing on a piece of grass.

"How about something inside for a change, I'm sick and tired of near dying of the heat stroke every afternoon in this God forsaken town," answered Big I, lying right next to me. We were all there, flat on our backs on the little kids playground, just soaking in the morning sun. We always laid the same, biggest to smallest, meaning Rosie on one end and Creepy on the other, so as to never get pinched between two guys bigger than you that could really slap you silly if they got a wild hair up their butt. This way, if things got dicey, you had a fighting chance to push your way past the smaller guy and make a run for it. The only problem was, Jagger, that freak of nature, was one of the shortest, but also, without a doubt, the strongest, not counting if you sat on someone, which put Rosie in a class all to hisself.

"What da ya have in mind fart face?" Neil grunted from down the line. He'd been in an especially nasty mood all morning since his big brother Barry, who was no ray of sunshine, neither, found out about him swiping a few of his precious Marlboros for our little raid on the Cole place, and gave him a good thrashing. That, and he wasn't even close to being over the lovely Betty Ann Patrick and her irreplaceable qualities – *both* of them.

"I dunno," said Ira, p.o.ed about the fart face remark. "But I'm sick and tired of sweating my butt off all day long and then dodging lightning bolts all afternoon - comprende?"

"Too bad it ain't Saturday," Rosie said. "Then we could go down to Marshall KGUN's Lil' Cow Pokes Playhouse at the Fox."

It *is* Saturday, you moron!"

"No kiddin'?" Asked Rosie, kinda confused. "You mean I missed the cartoons this morning to help my ma clean out my closet? She told me it was Friday to keep me from trying to wiggle outta it. I've been had!" And then he reached into his pocket, pulled out a gum drop, picked off the fuzz that was stuck all over it, and popped it into his chubby face to ease his pain.

"Hey, g-g-give me one of them will ya?" asked Jag, reaching over us to get to Rosie.

"Sorry, last one."

"That's w-what you always say. You really got a p-p-problem, Emiliano. You should see a shrink, or s-something."

Rosie just pretended not to hear, looked back up at the sky and started whistling a mariachi tune. I think it was "Rancho Grande," one of Pop's favorites.

"I was under the impression that the remainder of Marshall KGUN's appearances in Santa Elena had been cancelled indefinitely due to the unfortunate incident involving Bucky Strong," said the Creep.

"You mean Bucky Weak," blurted out Neil, real quick. "And it wasn't unfortunate, neither. That retard got just what he deserved."

Bucky Strong was a scrawny fourth grader at Seward with a huge pair of buckteeth, thick curly black hair, a bunch of little dark moles all over his face like he'd been splashed by a mud puddle and forgot to wash, and a brain about the size of a ping-pong ball. He was always pulling some asinine stunt or another, and last month when the old Marshall rolled into town from Tucson, Bucky ran up on stage right outta the blue in the middle of the show and swiped the Marshall's cowboy hat right off his head. With the ushers hot on his heels, he leaped up and grabbed one of them ropes they used to pull open the curtains and started swinging out over the orchestra pit like Tarzan, over and over, all the while hollering out at the top of his scrawny lungs, "Hi Ho Silver! Away!" Well the kids in the crowd went berserk; the boys laughing so hard they peed their pants, and the girls sreaming their fool heads off. Before anyone could snatch 'im down, and believe me they were trying their darndest, racing from one end of that stage to the other and jumping up and down like a bunch of jackrabbits, Bucky's grip finally gave out and he fell like a brick on the cement floor below, smashing a bass fiddle to smithereens, cracking his head wide open and mangling the Marshall's hat so bad it looked more like somethin' the Pope would wear. Speaking of the Marshall, he went a little berserk himself, gnashing his teeth and pulling at his hair, and finally yelled out in a high screechy voice that he'd "Never step foot in this God forsaken place again!" meaning Santa Elena, along with a slew of other real colorful words, most of which I ain't never heard before or since, before stomping off stage and down the aisle, grabbing what was left of his ten gallon hat on the way out.

Ma said she heard from some of the ladies in town that Bucky was recovering just swell over at the St. Joe's hospital in Tucson, and before long he'd be acting just the same as always, which I'm sure was only a mixed blessing to his poor folks. I heard myself some whispering down at the town square, too, that they had old Bucky locked up in one of them padded cells, where he sat in the corner all day reciting his ABC's, but instead of saying the L-M-N-O-P part, he'd kept repeating I-C-U-P, and then would laugh hysterical to hisself for awhile 'til he'd finally simmer down and do it all over again. The head shrink thinks he's got something called "Mechanic Depression." Neil thinks he remembers hearing a Jimi Hendrix song about it, so we're gonna try and find the album and learn more about it.

"Even if that old Codger was coming to town, there ain't no way I'm going to a show for "Lil' Cow Pokes," got it? Neil said in disgust. "Don't you guys have any pride at all?" Then he turned and spit.

Well, he kinda had a point there, I guess, us being at least twelve and a half and all, but to tell ya the truth, we always had a blast at the Marshall's shows ever since we were just little kids when he was one of our heroes. I mean he had his own T.V. show and everything for gosh sakes, every Saturday morning at eight on KGUN, Channel 9 outta Tucson. He was the only television star we'd ever seen in real life, and around these parts, he was way bigger than Bozo the Clown and right up there in the same league with Captain Kangaroo. Since we got older and a lot more sophisticated, he didn't seem quite as cool as before, and Neil started saying he wasn't even a real cowboy. Said he'd swear on his grandpa's grave he'd seen him selling Lazy Boy recliners at a big old discount store in Tucson, wearing a business suit and necktie! None of us were gullible enough to take the bait on that one, thinking Neil was just out to cause trouble as usual. The Marshall in a necktie, that's was just crazy talk. Like saying you saw Santa out sunning hisself in a bikini!

"Anybody got any better ideas?" asked Rosie, a little ticked off.

"Yeah, how about a good old game of chicken?" Neil yelled out and then started to snort and cough and bring up as much thick spit in his mouth as possible. Chicken was this thoroughly disgusting game Neil made up when we were about five, where we all laid on our backs in a row, and then took turns spitting up in the air as high as you could and try to get your loogie to come down and hit one of the other guys, preferably right in the face. If you moved even an inch to dodge it, you were "chicken" and outta the game.

"I ain't playing," said Cooper, in a tougher voice than usual. "On account'a first off it's grosser than all get out, and second, my mom found out about it and said it was a real good way to catch the boob-on-it plague, or something just as deadly and disgusting!"

"Is that so? Chicken *Poop!*" Neil barked back, with a lotta emphasis on the Poop. "Well you can run home and tell your mommy that if you don't play I am gonna beat you so hard that catching some little plague or whatever is gonna be like going to the Dairy Delight for an ice cream sundae. Got it!"

Coop got it just fine, and laid back down next to Creepy keeping his mouth shut and his eyes closed. Rosie wasn't all that crazy about playing, neither, 'cause being three times as wide as everybody else meant three times the chance of getting hit. But after Neil's sweet words to Coop, he'd just as soon lie down and take his medicine.

"I'll start," said Neil with a wide grin on his face, always excited to inflict some kinda pain on someone else, and he took a deep breath in and let that clump of spit fly. We all had our eyes and mouths clamped shut, and prayed to not be the one on the receiving end of the gross glob, when there was a "Splat," and then an, "AARGH!" and we opened our eyes and sat up straight to see who'd had won the grand prize of, "Loogie Lover," but with a quick glance around it seemed we were all clean as a whistle. Then, after a few bewildering seconds passed we finally realized what had happened which gave us all a real warm and fuzzy feeling inside. To the delight and amazement of us all, there was good old Neil, still lying flat and stiff as a three-day-old corpse, with his face red as a chili pepper, and a big green ball of slime smack dab in the middle of his forehead. He had spit on himself! At first, no one made a sound, unable to believe the bizarre twist of fate that had made good old Neil the victim of his own disgusting idea, but after a bit, the laughing was so hard you could hardly catch your breath and had to cross your legs and squeeze tight.

Well, Neil was fuming by then, still lying there with his eyes squeezed tight and his teeth clenched, and then started shaking all over like he was having an eplectical fit or something.

Finally, Ira says, "Don't feel bad, Nelly (Neil hated it when you called him Nelly)," in this real kind and sorrowful voice. "I hear this kind of thing happens all the time, specially to the *retards* in Mrs. Johnson's Special Ed. Class!"

That was more than Neil could take and he let out a high-pitched, blood-curdling, goose bump producing scream, and lunged for Big I at the same time. But Ira had figured on that, and was already on his feet and running like a greyhound with his tail on fire. Neil was up and after him lickety-split and the race was on. They ran under the Ramada and around the basketball courts and wove there way in and out of the tether ball poles and up one side of the jungle gym and down the other, and then through the sand box on the way to the big kids side of the playground and outta sight. All the while Ira was laughing and giggling, and all the while Neil was shaking his fist and yelling about what he was gonna do when he finally caught him. But although Neil was pretty quick on his feet, he was no match for Ira's blazing speed, and pretty soon he realized it too and just let out one last agonizing screech like a part of him was dying, and then stopped and walked back over to where we were sitting, head hangin' low and utterly dejected. You see, Neil wasn't used to being made a fool of, and it was plenty hard on him. He wasn't like any of us who were completely accustomed to being horribly humiliated any number of times each day.

None of us dared say a word, and Creepy and Chicken Coop sensing the possibility of a good pounding in the air, stared straight down at the ground and slowly slide in behind Rosie, just in case. After a few minutes of complete silence, here comes Ira, walking real slow and easy over to us, his eyes glued on Neil every inch of the way. Finally, convinced his life wasn't in immediate danger any more, he sat down, real gentle like at the far end of the line, still huffing and puffing from his great escape. Each and every one of us knew Neil wasn't about to let you off the hook so easy, not for an offense as damaging as this, and Ira knew it too, realizing he'd be needing to do a special service for old Neil to smooth things over to keep from someday being surprised by something especially nasty and painful.

Just then Jag breaks the ice by saying, "Ya know, it has b-been an awfully long time since we paid our old p-pal Marshall KGUN a visit. M-m-maybe we should mosey on d-down to the Fox and say 'Howdy'. W-what da ya say to that Johnny C?"

"I say that sounds just swell partner." And with that we gave a big cheer, all except Neil who just sat there, staring off in space like he was in one of them hip-not-it trances, and then hopped on our bikes and headed on down Cicada Street. Of course we couldn't just ride for the fun of it and let it go at that, but decided to have a contest seeing who could ride no hands the longest before whipping out and turning himself into one big scab. There was just enough loose sand in the street to make the game all the more dangerous and the falls all the more painful. Right off, Jag went head over heals on Bullet, partly on account of hitting a patch of gravel, and partly on account'a the front wheel on that stupid bike was so bent outta shape from all of his daredevil schemes that the thing barely rode straight when you held on to the handlebars with all your might. Next, poor Rosie hit the asphalt pretty hard but bounced right back up, literally, not too much worse for wear. Face it; Rosie's body wasn't cut out for dainty little movements important in balancing yourself while riding no hands. When he shifted his weight, he *really* shifted his weight. Ira ended up winning, which was even more impressive considering Neil was right on his tail the whole time trying to find some way to send 'im to kingdom come.

After that we decided to have a wheelie race, the top of the heap test of bike riding skill and agility if ya ask me, and somethin' each and every one of us worked at long and hard. Any other day Neil would'a whipped us in his sleep on his Orange Crate with the big slick and sweet sissy bar and all, but he was still so down in the dumps from spitting on hisself, he had no more strength than a wet dish rag hardly able to lift his front tire even an inch, and even that tuckered 'im out so much he just hung against them monkey bars like a flag over a dead president's coffin. It was a truly pitiful sight, almost enough to make a person feel truly sorry for him, but not quite. Well, like Pop sometimes says, one person's loss is another one's gain, and I was fixed to gain plenty on this one. I grabbed my eight ball shiftnob, slapped it down into third to take some tension off the pedal, and then flung my skinny self backwards, popping the front tire off the ground just enough to center my weight over the back one. It really was a special art if ya think about it. They should put it in the Olympics if they had any brains. It sure beats the snot outta girls rowing! Come to think about it, it beats the snot outta girls *anything*.

I kept my balance by turning the front wheel a little this way and that, depending, and had clean sailing more than a city block to snatch the White Ghetto Championship by a mind-boggling twenty feet, and then we turned up Tanque Verde, the busiest street in town where you could actually see a car every now and then. No kidding. You truly had to pay attention and couldn't just ride straight down the middle like all the other streets around. It got downright annoying. She had real asphalt, too, not just dirt, although it was mighty rutty all along, and rattled your teeth considerable, and a white line down the center that was mostly worn off now and kinda wavy after

Mengo and Pato tried touching it up one Saturday night a few years back after spending a couple of hours at the Stumble Inn Cantina over in Sahuarita. There was honest to goodness traffic lights to boot, two of 'em, the pride of Santa Elena. And although they weren't new, but just used up ones that Tucson up the road was fixing to throw out, good old Mayor Troncoza, living up to his campaign slogan to "bring Santa Elena into the nineteenth century," got wind of what was up and snagged them for our own. Pop said they were nuthin' but a waste of good electricity and just gummed up the works, but Ma thought they were a nice addition, giving the town a, "Cosmopolitan air," whatever that means.

They had this big unveiling ceremony last Cinco de Mayo in the town square with burritos and chimichangas and fresh menudo from Guero's, and free saladitos for all the kids from El Minuto Market, and the Mariachi Gigante all the way from Casa Grande was playing their sombreros off. It was really some shindig, and the whole town was there all day long and most of the night. They finally decided after a lotta fussing and whining to stick one up at the front of the courthouse, all the grownups agreeing it would be handy for hanging banners and decorations and such for special occasions, and all us kids thinking it would be perfect for one of them tree limb swings ya see in picture books. The other one they put over near I-19, even though there weren't no intersection or hardly any traffic, but that way all the big city folks on their way to Mexico couldn't help but notice it and know right off we weren't no one horse town but a real up and comer. Someday, Mayor Troncoza promised, if he were re-elected, which seemed like a shoe-in in light of this great addition, he'd see to it personal that them lights would actually change from green to red from time to time instead of just blinking yellow on weekdays, and being turned off completely on Saturday and Sunday.

If you know anything about Mexican folks, it's that they don't much care for drab and ordinary looking stuff, and so before you could say, *"Ay! Que bonita!"* they had them signals changed from faded old yellow and black, to the most bright and lovely shades of red, white and green you ever saw, the same colors as the Mexican flag in case ya didn't know. And that wern't all, neither, 'cause before you could say *"Ay! Caramba!"* they had plastic vines with red flowers all up one side of the pole and down the other, and shiny silver tinsel left over from Christmas hanging here and there, and a few baby *piñatas* placed every once in a while, and as the crowning piece, a big bright painting on black velvet of Our Lady of Guadalupe hanging in the place of honor, right up along side them flashing lights. A few of the less extravagant and much more boring town folk tried complaining to the Mayor about the traffic lights swell new look, but seeing that just about every Mexican in Santa Elena was related to him in one way or another, he weren't about to go against their wishes and finally settled the whole brouhaha by proclaiming them stop lights, " Official Treasures of Hispanic Culture," and that was that.

Neil's drooping spirits picked up real quick once we finally pulled up in front of the Fox and he got a load of all the poor, unsuspecting little tikes he could easily torment once we got inside. You see, the moms never stayed with their kids during the Saturday morning shows, no matter how young they were, but instead just dumped 'em off and then sped off like demons, never once looking in the rear view mirror. It wasn't that they weren't

allowed to stay, in fact I'm sure them poor, frazzled ushers, who were just a bunch of unlucky teenagers from around these parts anyhow, would've welcomed the help like a starving man welcomed tater-tots and a malted, but it seems the moms felt as if twenty-five cents for admission and twenty-five more for candy was a *ganga* for a few hours of peace and quiet all to themselves. And speak of the devil, just as we rode up, I saw Ma drop off little Gracie and her snotty friend Marti, then peel out in the direction of Myrtle's Light and Lovely Salon over in Amato.

The two little twits had on their fanciest party dresses and were wearing the most God awful earrings, necklaces and bracelets you ever set your eyes on that they'd made the day before with Gracie's Pretty, Pretty, Princess Jewelry Kit just for the occasion. They sure enough had gotten into Ma's make up drawer, too, and done quite a number on themselves, and even though it looked like Ma had done her darndest to scrape most of it off, they still had big red splotches on their cheeks and around their lips and dark brown circles around their eyes, so they looked like two drunk raccoons. But in their little minds they were convinced they looked absolutely stunning, and strutted along the sidewalk with their noses in the air, turning their heads from side to side and batting their fake eyelashes a mile a minute.

"Hey Gracie!" I said as I gave her ponytail a yank from behind. "Did Ma give ya any money for me?"

"Maybe she did and maybe she didn't," she said as she and Marti giggled up a storm over her smart as heck comeback.

"Come on, I'm serious, I only got a dime in my pocket and that ain't gonna cut it, *comprende?*"

"*No comprendo, Señor,*" she said with a lame, squeaky Mexican accent, which was really pretty cute, to tell you the truth, but at the moment I wasn't in the mood. I snatched her pink vinyl Snow White purse off her shoulder and held it over my head as I rummaged around in it 'til I found a couple of quarters way down on the bottom underneath a mound of mints, lipstick, eye shadow, miniature dolls, and make-up mirrors, as Gracie jumped and screamed and kicked to get it back.

"You boys better not get out of line one iota (Iota. I loved it.) or we're gonna tell," said the annoying little maggot Marti as she put her hands on her hips, stuck her tongue out and then tried to give us the evil eye, which only got us to laughing and her to fuming.

"Take a hike will ya, Farti?" Neil shouted at her little friend, feeling back to his old self, as the girls wrinkled up their noses, threw their hair back the way ladies always do before they stomp off all in a huff. Then through the big revolving doors they went, almost knocking flat poor Pooh Pridey the ticket taker, who got his nick name a few years back on account of a the fact that he was unusual hard to potty train, if ya know what I mean.

The Fox was a grand old theatre with carved marble columns and polished brass showcases out front. It was built in 1927 (it was stamped plain and clear on one of the front corner stones) for something called "fraudville acts" according to Pop, which were, best I could figure, live shows with a lot of singing and dancing and corny joke telling and guys slapping the bejeezus outta each other on stage just to get a good laugh. The whole idea died out a few years later, which ain't too surprising, when the talkies came out, and The Fox has been a movie house ever since. Pop knew just about everything there was to know about the place, and was even there at its grand opening night. If ya didn't believe 'im, he could show ya the photo to prove it. There he was in that old wrinkled up and yellowing snapshot, no more than five years old, wearing one of them old fashioned caps and a cute little tweed jacket and shorts to match, and holding *his* pop's hand, a guy I heard was really something else according to the old folks round here, with a grin on his face a mile wide. I'd stare at that picture sometimes for hours, seeing that it was the only one we had of Pop when he was little, wondering what he was like as a kid. It was funny thinking of him as a kid at all, if ya know what I mean. Parents were grown ups and kids were kids and that was that. Thinking anything else was way too confusing in my mind, and I decided against it. I mean, come on, Pop as some snot nose pipsqueak that didn't know his butt from a hole in ground? Don't seem possible.

Anyway, back to that picture. The marquis over the door was blazing in the background, with lights all around, and smack in the middle in big black letters said, "GRAND OPENING!" and underneath, "WELCOME BUSTER KEATON," whoever that was, and there was about a thousand other people in that picture all milling around the entrance with all the men wearing the same tweed suits and the ladies in sparkly long dresses all the way to their necks, with their hair piled up high on their heads like a triple decker sundae.

Tell ya the truth, nuthin' much had changed at the Fox over the years. It still had the same majestic marquis sign, though a handful off light bulbs were permanently burned out. It still had the same round glass ticket booth out front with the fancy wood top, and the same old colored glass chandeliers and red velvet seats, and it ain't no surprise that it was still the only theatre in Santa Elena, or for that matter anywheres for fifty miles around. I guess that in itself told loads about the great progress bein' made in Southern Arizona over the last half century, huh?

The Fox was the main building on the east side of the town square which was pretty much just four narrow streets paved here and there with old Santa Catalina granite, and they surrounded the old court house, dead set in the middle. All the buildings around looked to have been put up around the same time and were built outta good old baked adobe and plastered all over with thick white stucco that over the years had worn through or flaked off to show the burnt orange bricks underneath. The windows were all bordered in wood and most had mesquite shutters painted in different bright colors for a real cheerful look, even the jail. The roofs were every one, flat with a swamp cooler jutting up here and there, and there was a creaky wooden plank walkway out in front all along. There was even some hitching posts still standing every so often, but instead of horses, they mostly had, "Sale," signs or bratty kids tied to 'em. On one corner there was El Guero restorante, famous for miles around for their *cosido* a kinda Mexican vegetable soup with gigantic pieces of potatoes and green chili and carrots and usually a considerable sized ear of corn swimming around in it, too. "No eetsy beetsy peeces como sopa de gringos," El Guero liked to say when he'd see our eyes bulge out in anticipation as he scooped us out a bowl. He and his boy Chuey had thoughtfully strapped up some colorful zarapes over a couple of wooden picnic tables over on the side of their place opposite the garbage cans, so us kids could eat in the summer without getting heat stroke. On another corner was El Minuto Market, the only grocery store in town and one of Pop's best customers. They had anything your heart desired; Chick-o-stick? You got it. Chuckles? No problem. Them little wax soda bottles that you could chew all day once ya drank the stuff inside? No sweat. Plus they had a swell soda fountain in back where you could get a snow cone with *colores de la bandera* which meant cherry, coconut and lime, or an ice cold glass of *horchata* on a hot day. They also had lots of candy from south of the border, but it wern't what you think. There was lollipops, alright, but with some kinda *worm* stuck inside, and brown slimy liquid in plastic bags with pieces of plants swimming around in it, and a bunch of stuff that was basically one kind of chili powder or another! Even Rosie wouldn't try it. Not even a free sample!

On the south side of the street, right next to Bob's Bargain Barn, was Santa Elena Savings and Trust, a monstrous two-story place, with the name in extra fancy wrought iron letters stuck way up high on the front. It was started up and still run by the Schlossberg family who lived high on the hill overlooking town in the biggest house you ever saw, on land homesteaded by old man Schlossberg back in the day. The new Mr. Schlossberg was a pretty swell guy, always dressed just so in a pin-stripe suit with one of them silly vests inside, a monkey suit Pop called it, no matter how hot and miserable it was, and he always had a swell gold watch on a chain sitting right there in that vest pocket. He'd pull it out now and then to see if it was time to count the money, I figure. He was forever standing out in front of his place greeting folks and passing out candy to all the kids when they'd walked by, which we did plenty 'til he'd finally catch on, and say, "You always have to make a deposit if you want to collect the interest," and then pat us on the head and push us along. Everybody in Santa Elena put their dough in Mr. Schlossberg's bank, no questions asked, that was just the way it was, and Pop said he was a real honest man and all, and that he and his kind were at the top of the heap when it came to handling money.

Christy's Space Age Electronics and Appliance store was the main business on the north side of the square and they stocked some of the most wondrous stuff you ever saw. They had more T.V.'s than you could shake a stick at, but also eight track tape players for your home *and* your car, which meant no more having to listen to whatever goofy stuff they was playing on KTKT-AM outta Tucson, the only station you could pick up decent around here, but instead you could slap in your own tape, pick one or the four tracks, and presto! In no more than five to ten minutes the song that *you* wanted to hear would usually come up. What'd they think of next? Of course, them tapes were kinda hard to come by, and they'd squeakity-squeak 'til you jiggled 'em a bit, and God forbid you left your Pop's favorite Frank Sinatra tape sitting on the back seat in the sun on the way to your little league game, 'cause it would warp up like the brim of a sombrero and then never, ever fit in that little slot again, no matter how much you stomped on it.

They also had them new push button phones, the ones that made that cute little beep when you dialed and made it so ya didn't have to wait all day for the dial to come back around before you picked your next number.

They weren't just the same old clunky square black jobs anymore neither, but came in the new, "Slim Line," which was half the size of the old ones and shaped like a banana to fit in your hand nice and snug. And that ain't all; you could buy 'em in any number of lovely, designer colors. Ma's favorite was burnt orange but she also had a strong inkling for olive green. Heck, the thing even lit up at night so as you could call somebody in the dark without breaking your neck trying to find the light switch!

But the thing that Ma had her underpants all bunched up about most, was the new electric clothes dryer. Lately she'd been hounding poor old Pop to no end, saying that all the high society ladies in the big cities had 'em and that only barbarians still hung their clothes outside to dry. Personally I didn't see no advantage. I mean if you're gonna live in the desert ya might as well use the heat to your advantage when ya could since most of the time it was nuthin' but a big pain in the butt. Ma didn't see it that way, and had about ten conniption fits every time she stood face to face with one of them big square metal contraptions. I mean she practically drooled all over it as she opened and closed the doors and fiddled with the buttons. It made me sad to think that pretty soon we wouldn't have no clothesline out back, I mean where else are you gonna hang up your little sister by the overalls when she started to get annoying. Yep, sometimes the old ways are still the best.

The old Court House, that sat smack dab in the middle of the square was actually kinda pretty in a southwestern, mud hut kinda way. It was all covered up in that same white stucco that had turned over the years, but it was a cool two story design with old stone steps that had started to wear down in the middle a bit, leading up to this monstrous arched mesquite door with heavy black wrought iron hinges. The windows were all arched, too, and were set deep into the walls so there was plenty of room on the sills for pretty flowerpots and a stray cat or two. At the very top was an old bell tower that only rang once a year during the Independence Day Extravaganza, and on occasion on Cinco de Mayo, when one of the Mexican men in town had too many *cervesas* and snuck up there to give the rope a tug or two before Mengo and Pato could drag him down.

Way up on the very tippy top it had a wooden cross with Jesus hanging on it and all, and Pop said some years back a couple of official looking fellas came down from Phoenix and tried to take it off, saying something about churches and states. But before they could, a bunch of the town folk got wind of what was up and completely circled the place, and Mrs. Rodriguez told them fellas that if they touched one splinter of that cross she'd unleash all of God's fury and most of the Mexican women on them at once and when they were finished they could ship what was left of 'em back to Phoenix in a cigar box. I guess those boys seen the error of their ways, and high tailed it outta here with the whole of the Our Lady of Sorrows Saintly

Women's Alter Guild waving brooms and rolling pins and frying pans hot on their heels.

The grounds surrounding the old place were real pleasant, too, with a nice green lawn, or as green as you could get around here, and majestic cottonwoods with their white barks and shimmery silver and green leafs sprouting out all over. There was a bunch of that large leaf ivy growing on the north side of the building and a mess of boganvia on the south. That's that vine that looks pretty as a picture in the summer time with big old heart shaped leaves and bright red flowers, but looks like nothin' but a bunch of dead sticks with nasty thorns sticking out all over the whole winter. Right out in front sat a gigantic bronze statue of good old Father Kino on his horse. He's the Spanish priest I told you about earlier that rode up from Mexico way back when and started up Catholic missions here and there in Arizona and California along the way so as to teach the heathen Injuns about Christianity, whether they liked it or not, but a whole bunch of 'em *didn't* like it all that much and started attacking them churches left and right, burning 'em down just as fast as the good Injuns could build 'em back up. That didn't slow down old Father Kino none, he just kept on preaching and building more and more missions 'til them heathen Injuns finally gave up and all became alter boys. He's the one who started up San Xavier Mission, the white dove of the desert, the place Ma always made us go to mass, and the same place I seen Jenny Darling a few weeks back, and then, right before communion, I, well, you know.

# Chapter Twelve

## MARSHAL K-GUN'S LIL' COWPOKES

"It's show time!" Jag yelped as we raced over to the ticket booth where a million little kids were screaming to see the Marshall. The teenage girl inside looked like a prairie dog at a coyote convention, and we were just able to finagle some tickets out of her before she ran out the back screaming. As we strolled through the revolving glass door and into the lobby, over in the corner stood our old pal Dan Dunn. Boy, did he look sharp in his red usher's suit with shiny gold buttons all over the front of the jacket and fancy gold stripes sewn down the side of his pants. He had some big floppy gold tassels sewn on to his shoulders, too, and one of them flat brown hats on his head that looks like a pie tin with a button glued on top, strapped tight under his chin.

"Duuun!" Neil screamed and then made a popping sound with his hands in front of his mouth as loud as he could muster. "You look deeevine!"

"Gee, thanks guys," he said back, all flattered and kinda sheepish, in a voice way too low to come outta someone his size.

You see, Dan didn't catch on that Neil was yanking his chain as usual, but the poor guy didn't catch on about a lotta stuff. At least not right at first, anyway. We figured out right off that Dan Dunn was never gonna be a rocket scientist, if ya know what I mean, and it weren't long before Neil dubbed him, "Damn Dumb."

"Ya really think so? Gotta look the part if I'm ever gonna make head usher, you know. But in the meantime you fellas will be proud to know you're now staring this very day at the new *chief assistant* usher of The Fox

Theatre," he said and then took a little bow, which caused his pie tin hat to fall off.

"No kidding, Dan? Well, your folks must be darn proud!" Ira said, slapping Dan on the back and then turning around and giving us a wink.

"Yup," he said giddy as all get out.

There's another thing you gotta understand; Dunn was our pal and all, but he wasn't no kid. He was old, maybe twenty years or so and full grown, even though he wasn't much taller than me, and the closest thing he had to a whisker were a couple of uncommonly long nose hairs that hung down over his upper lip. We got to know 'im on account'a the fact that he liked to come down to the Sewer after he was outta work and shoot some hoops with us or play some flies up, and pretty much just goof off like the rest of us. We kicked around the idea of asking 'im to be in the S.S.B's for a while, but decided against it 'cause number one he didn't live in the white ghetto, and two, he was so old that we were afraid that if he got caught doing some of the stuff we pulled he might get arrested. When Ma got wind of us hanging out with Dan, she did some quick neighborhood research and learned from Sunny Sixkiller, the school nurse, who happened to be a one hundred percent, full-blooded Hopi Indian princess and a semi-regular on Mexican Theater, that he had officially been diagnosed by some hot shot M.D. in Cleveland after hundreds of tests as being, "Slow." She said she didn't feel comfortable with us playing with someone that was practically a man, no matter how he acted. Pop stepped in and said she needed to loosen up before she blew an O-ring, and it didn't take long for us guys to realize old Dan was harmless as a heel hound, and about twice as loyal.

On top of everything else, it was pretty handy having a friend who could drive, and just about any time we wanted, which was plenty, we'd hop in the back of his orange El Camino and he'd give us a lift over to Dairy De-light for a Mr. Frosty or to El Minuto for a malty *gigante*, and most of the time he'd treat us all to boot! You couldn't beat that deal, not with a stick. Sometimes, if we pleaded just a little, he'd even let us take turns behind the wheel, though I never told Ma about that part. Yep, all in all Dan Dunn was one heck of a guy, though that didn't stop Neil and Ira from riding him unmerciful at times. But that was just their way. They didn't mean nuthin' by it.

Old Dan had another job, too, I mean besides being chief assistant usher at the Fox. He was a full fledge security officer, or a rent-a-cop as Neil liked to call him. One of those guys you hired if you didn't want a bunch'a yahoos messing with your place after hours, or, say, keep order at a *quinciniera* or something. He had a swell looking uniform for that job, too, with a big silver badge and everything, and sometimes he'd come down to the schoolyard after work still all dressed up, but that didn't stop 'im from playing none. He'd just take off his shirt and boots, roll up his pants, and start right in. He looked pretty goofy, in his old man t-shirt and socks so thin they were held together with nuthin' but a lick and a prayer, but he didn't seem to mind and neither did we.

Another neat thing about Dan, *really* neat, I mean, was that he had his very own forty-five caliber pistol for his rent-a-cop assignments. Or at least he said he had one. None of us had ever actually seen it, even after a pathetic barrage of whining and pleading to try and get 'im to bring it down sometime. Ira didn't buy it one bit and said you had to pass all kinds of exams and jump through all kinds of hoops before you could carry a real life pistol, and there wasn't no way Damn Dumb could even pass a urine test as far as he was concerned--which actually was a pretty good point, I guess.

"Well, it's darn good to see ya, Dan, and way to go on the new promotion," I said, patting him on the back, "But we better get some candy and get ready for the show."

"Alrighty, you little cowpokes. Have fun now!" he said enthusiastically, as he pointed his finger at us like it was a pistol and pretended to pull the trigger.

"Don't *really* shoot anybody, Dan. Okay?" Ira said walking by.

"Don't be silly, Ira. I'm a professional."

"Yeah, a professional moron," Neil said under his breath.

I winced and looked over my shoulder, hoping Dunn hadn't heard, but he was already back to work, patting some little freckle-faced kid on the head and talking his ear off.

Rosie was first in line for candy. Surprise. Surprise. In fact, it seemed that the only time he ever was first for anything was when food was involved, and even then it wasn't so much that he moved real quick, 'cause that was just against all laws of nature, it was more like somehow he'd finagle hisself in the lead and then swing his big butt from side to side like a huge fly swatter, whacking anyone who got too close. As he rumbled on up, licking his lips and staring straight ahead like he was in a trance, there was an unfortunate preschooler at the counter trying to decide between "Goobers" and "Blackcrows" who turned to see that crazy, "I ain't stopping for nothing 'til I get my candy," look, just in the nick of time to escape from being flattened thinner than the "Snow Cone" sign. I don't think Rosie ever even saw him.

The candy counter at the picture show was always something special, even to normal human beings, on account'a they had treats you just couldn't get no where else. I'm talking about real *special* stuff like Raisonettes and Drops, Junior Mints and Boston Baked Beans, Dots and Jordan Almonds and Good and Plenty; and my personal favorite, Flicks. They were bite sized pieces of chocolate, like a big nestle chip that fit just right in your mouth, so you didn't have to break off a piece and maybe lose some precious crumbs, and they came in these cool tubes all coved in bright tin foil that, with a little finagling turned into a swell kazoo you could use to annoy the heck outta everybody with after all the chocolate was gone. In the icebox they had Bon Bons, Drumsticks, and Peppermint Patties if you were more in the mood for ice cream, and, of course, they had popcorn, but we didn't care about that, it was the candy we were after. I mean, if you got an inkling for popcorn, you could always get yourself a Jiffy Pop, and stick it on the gas stove at home anytime you wanted, right? But, like I said before, there ain't no way you're gonna get any of this other great stuff anywheres but here. Ever wonder how come? We did, plenty. And it became a real bone of contention, especially with Rosie.

"How dare they deny us our basic nutritional needs!" He used to like to say. "Kids cannot live on Hershey bars alone!" It sounds kinda corny, but he was dead serious.

It was pretty weird that ya couldn't ever find stuff like Drops or even Raisonettes at the five and dime--and believe me I've tried. Even Kresgee's over in Tucson didn't have 'em, and they had everything, even Bit-O-Honey and Laffy Taffy! We thought on it for a while and then figured it must be some kinda conspiracy by the movie houses to force kids to go to the show, even if it was a real stinker like that sissy, "Bye, Bye Birdie." But I gotta admit, it worked pretty well. There were times I was practically going though withdrawals thinking about JuJu Bees and the like. I can imagine how hard it was on poor Rosie! And those low lifes wouldn't just let ya in the door to get what you wanted and be on your way, neither. Nope, you had to buy a stinking *ticket* if you wanted to get anywhere near the good stuff!

Well, we were all pushing Rosie from behind, trying to get to our favorites, but that was like a swarm of gnats against a hippo, and he didn't pay any mind at all and just kept looking from one thing to the other and licking his lips. We always tried to pick something different from the other guy so we could do a bit of horse trading during the show for something a little different, but the problem with that was Rosie would wolf his whole box of candy down so quick there was nuthin' left to deal. Then he would spend the rest of the day pleading for a handout from the rest of us. We finally came up with a solution a few years back to slow Rosie down, if he wanted to share with everyone else the only candy he was allowed to get was "Dots" on account'a the fact that they were so gummy and sticky that it was darn near impossible to eat 'em quick, even for a professional like Rosie, and so by the middle of the show there'd still be a few left to swap. Rosie accepted this decision reluctantly, and when the girl at the counter asked 'im what he'd like, he turned to look at us with big sad eyes and we all yelled, "Dots!"

"And a piece of beef jerky," he added quickly and with a smile.

When my turn finally came, there was no hemming or hawing, and I ordered up my Flicks and immediately opened one end and popped a piece of the scrumptious milk chocolate in my mouth to let it slowly melt all over my tongue and down my throat. Jag got Raisonettes, B.B. asked for Bon Bons saying that the initials were a perfect fit, Cooper got Sugar Babies, Big I got Red Vines, "Because they can be used to whip the snot outta the punk sitting next to you, *and* are a delicious treat to boot!" and Neil, after oogling the poor concession stand girl for a while, got his usual Jordan Almonds, "Because they hurt the most of any other candy if ya felt like flinging them at someone."

Now we were all set and started walking toward the giant double doors manned by the junior ushers, holding them open at the entrance to the theatre, but as we stepped inside we stopped dead in our tracks. The place was complete and utter bedlam and just up our alley! Every little kid from every two-bit town in Southern Arizona musta been crammed into that place and doing anything their wicked little hearts desired. Some of 'em were jumping up and down on their seats trying to see how high they could get, and some of 'em were crawling over the backs of their seats to see how many rows they could go before falling flat on their heads and cracking their skulls open, which, for the record is no more than two. Some were playing atomic tag up and down the aisle and whacking each other something fierce, while others were in the orchestra pit trying to climb up on the stage to get at the Marshall's props. One especially determined little troublemaker was standing on his pal's shoulders and trying to crawl into the hole in the back wall where the projector was set up.

A little earlier the ushers had handed out tin deputy badges to all the lil' cowpokes, but that was a major mistake, 'cause with the pins on the back they managed to stab themselves and each other just horrible, and they had to be collected, but not before two of the most uncoordinated fruitcakes had to be hauled of to Doc Porecca's house for stitching up. I think I forgot to tell you about the old Doc. He was a swell fella, not one of them stuffed shirts, if ya know what I mean. He was a short, barrel chested Italian guy, yep another Italian, with curly, muddy red hair that he tried his darndest to slick down with a big glob of Brillcream without much luck, and he was always singing the craziest opera songs you ever heard the whole time he was looking you over at his clinic in the back of his place the other side of I-19. He wasn't half bad, with the singing I mean, and a good medicine man, too, and he warn't just a regular doctor neither, but one of them O.D.'s or D.O.'s or something, which meant he didn't just take care of the sniffles and such, but say if you had a nasty crick in your back, he could crack you like a walnut 'til you were looser than one of them marionettes we used to buy over in Nogales when we were kids.

Anyways, back to the Fox. Something wasn't right. It didn't hit me right at first, but after a bit it smacked me right between the eyes. There were no adults to be seen in the whole theater. Not a one! Not only that, but the only sign of authority at all was poor old Jackson Wells, a fourteen year old junior usher in his first day on the job, standing way down in front, frozen stiff and looking terrified. When I pointed this out to the guys their faces lit up like jack-o-lanterns and Jag said, "M-m-man, this is gonna b-be great!" And with nothing but pleasant thoughts we raced down the aisle.

Now Neil had this thing, that no matter what, he had to be sitting smack dab in the middle of the center section, to give him the best shots all around with his Jordan Almonds, he said, and when he found some little kids sitting there already, he didn't think twice before grabbing them one by one by the belt and flinging them into the next row, right on top of a group of unlucky third graders. It made me wince again. I sure wish he'd try and be a little more tactful. I mean, them kids would've ran like rabbits if he'd just looked cross-eyed at 'em, but let's face it, that ain't Neil's style, no matter what it says on his new diploma from the Old Pueblo Junior

Debutantes.

We made ourselves nice and comfy in our seats and started enjoying our treats when the lights started to flicker on and off which meant you were supposed to sit down and shut up 'cause the show was about to start, but all it really did was get the little nuisances even more riled up, and running around and screaming and carry on worse than ever. Finally, the theatre people got fed up and turned the lights clean off, and that led to sheer chaos as kids started bumping into each other and tripping over stuff and crashing into the orchestra pit, and then whining and blubbering enough to wake the dead. Just then the projector started its flickering light, which shown just enough for all but the most retarded of the bunch to find their seats, and by the time Woody Woodpecker finished off his first victim things had settled down to a dull roar.

"Hey Johnny, I th-th-think I see Jenny Darling sitting down in f-f-front with N-N-Nancy Cole," Jag said, way louder than necessary. I had noticed her too and was hoping no one else would, but now with Jagger practically screaming it out, the cat was way out of the bag and the guys were already wrenching their necks trying to get a load of her. Once in a while when the cartoon flickered especially bright I caught a quick peek of her lovely red hair way down in front where all the girls always sat.

"There she is Johnny, down about row five," Rosie said pointing and then smooching up his lips at me.

"Yup, and there's Nasty Nancy stuffing her fat face right next to her. I wonder how she'd like a good old Jordan Almond right in the *cabeza* to start this show off right," Neil said with a big grin.

But just as he drew back his arm to throw, Ira jumped up and grabbed it, saying, "No, wait! Don't do it." Which was a real shocker coming from Big I. Was he going soft or something?

Neil stared at him like he was looking at an alien and said, "Don't tell me you're sweet on *Nancy*!"

Ira looked like he was about to upchuck and yelled out, "Yuck! Are you nuts? You pin head. I was just thinking if you're gonna throw something at such a big prize, you should use one of these," and he grabbed one of Creepy's, half melted Bon Bons and slapped it into Neil's hand.

"Now you're talking!" Neil said, as he stood up and stared down at his target, concentrating real hard with his eyes all squinted up into little slits and his tongue sticking out the side of his mouth, and waiting for just a little more light to take his shot. Chicken Coop started hiccupping like mad, sensing there was gonna be trouble and the Creep started to fidget all over, but Rosie was so into the cartoon, one of his Pop Eye favorites, the one where Wimpy eats about a hundred hamburgers, that you could' a set off the A-bomb and he wouldn't of noticed. Some little kid from behind us made the mistake of shouting, "Down in front!" but before he could get it all out, Neil had 'im by the nose and was twisting it for all he was worth. The kid let out a muffled screech and then slumped back in his seat, and didn't make a peep the rest of the show.

Now I could see that nuthin' but trouble could come outta this situation, especially with Nancy being the target, and all, but I knew there was no reasoning with Neil once he got an idea in his little brain, and even if I tried I knew I'd be accused of trying to protect Jenny and never here the end of it. So I just sunk down in my chair, clammed up and waited for the storm to hit. Well, I guess there are times when a kid should step up and do what his instincts tell 'im is right, because when Neil saw his chance and reared back and fired that Bon Bon across the theatre, not only did it totally miss Nancy's fat head, but it hit square on the side of the face of poor Jenny, splattering chocolate and vanilla ice cream all over her as it did. All the guys ducked down low when they saw what happened, although you could still see a good foot of Rosie sticking up above the seat in front of him. I, being a complete numbskull sometime, stood straight up to make sure Jenny was okay, just as she turned back to look over her shoulder with a real sad look in her eye and saw only me standing there staring down at her. I didn't know what to do exactly, and I couldn't help but think to myself that she still looked awful pretty, even with that vanilla ice cream running down her face, so I just grinned and gave her a little wave. She didn't look none too happy to see me, though, and even tried to give me a dirty look, but on her sweet little face it didn't amount to much, but then I suddenly realized that she thought it was *me* that had plunked her!

My heart began to sink and I started waving my hands frantically at her, while shaking my head and pointing at Neil who was still slumped way down in his seat next to me, but she didn't pay no mind, and only moved down her row and stomped up the aisle to the lobby with a growling Nancy in tow, sticking her tongue out and pointing her finger at me the whole way. I fell back in my seat feeling a little nauseous, and looked over at Neil who turned to me and simply said, "Oops".

"You're a real retard, ya know it?" I spit out in disgust.

"Look, I didn't mean to hit your *sweetie pie*, okay? I was trying to nail that pissant Nancy."

"Well you throw like a girl."

"I couldn't help it, the stupid ice cream melted all over my hand and it slipped," he said showing me his palms and then licking off what was left with delight.

"Hey, Ira, got any more of that red licorice?" asked Rosie oblivious to everything that was going on.

"Yeah, here's one," Ira answered, and then whipped him over the head as hard as he could with it. Rosie lunged for him to try to grab the whole rest of the box while he was off guard and almost squashed poor Creepy who was sitting in between them.

"Settle down, you m-m-morons," said Jag, ticked off. "Or we'll g-get thrown out b-b-before the cartoons are even over."

I couldn't believe what was happening. Here was my chance to maybe visit with Jenny Darling a little during the show and let her get to know what a swell guy I was and all, and even maybe officially apologize for that little San Xavier incident, and now she thinks I'm some kinda lunatic or something! I'd give even money that right this minute that maggot Nancy was giving her an ear full about how horrible me and all the guys were, and how she should never give me the time of day, and from now on I bet she avoids me like liver and onions! I gotta tell ya, what started out as a pretty promising day was quickly going straight to hell in a hand basket.

Just then the projector clicked off and the lights came up and out on stage stepped good old Marshall K-Gun hisself, with six shooters pulled and spurs clanking to high heaven.

"Howdy, Lil' Cowpokes!" he yelled out loud and then waved his big old ten gallon hat way up high.

"Howdy Marshall!" all the kids screamed back, all except Neil, who

hollered out, "Been chasing down rustlers on your Lazy Boy lately, Marshall?" But no one paid him no mind, and after a mean look from Jag he sat down and shut up.

Sauntering up behind the Marshall on stage was his trusty horse, Black Jack, who had been his sidekick long as I could remember. Black Jack really wasn't no horse at all, but really just two guys in a horse suit, and not a very convincing one at that, but the little kids didn't seem to mind none and loved him just the same. Them fellas inside the horse never could seem to get things quite right, though, and when the guy in the head went one direction, it always took a few seconds for the guy in the butt to figure out what was up and start moving too, so that horse always looked like he had a mighty big crick in his back and maybe needed a visit to Doc Porreca's, too. Which would'a been alright since he ended up taking care of most of the animals in town to boot.

"Howdy, Black Jack!" the kids all screamed out hysterical, and that horse, who was rumored to have Mengo and Pato, our trusty sheriff and deputy, stuffed inside, reared back and waved to the crowd with one big front hoof. As he did, a bunch of hard candy thrown from the audience bounced square off his head.

The Marshall whipped out his pistols again, and fired them in the air as all the kids screeched, to show what a swell cowboy he was, but they was only cap guns, not the real thing, and we knew it too because one time after a show, we searched that theatre high and low for any signs of bullet holes, but couldn't find a one. Heck, with all the shooting going on, that place should'a looked like a big piece of Swiss cheese!

"What da ya say we sing some old camp fire tunes to get this show on the road?" asked the Marshall.

"Yeah!" screamed the kids.

"Please, no!" yelled Ira and Neil.

"Alrighty then, hows about we start with, 'Home on the Range.'"

Another ear-splitting cheer.

"Get ready. Get set. Go."

Well, me and the guys had worked up our own rendition of this western classic over the years of coming to see the Marshall's show, and the words went something like this:

Bones, Bones, on the range!

Where the deer and the antelope are slain,

Where often you've heard of disgusting big turds,

And the flies drive you batty all day!

We were real proud of our lyrics, and sang them out loud and clear, certain they were a major improvement over the originals, but we were still drowned out by the rest of them little maniacs. We had our own words to "Good Bye, Old Paint" and "She'll be Comin' Round the Mountain," too, but it might be best not to get those printed up just yet, if you know what I mean.

I was aching to go up to the lobby and see how poor Jenny was doing, and try to explain myself, but I knew it wouldn't do no good, not with everything else that had gone on, and certainly not with that rancid Nancy hanging around to get her two cents in. So I just decided to let it be for now and maybe try to work up something later when the time was right, and let pretty little Jenny Darling know just exactly how I felt about her, if I could get her to keep from calling the cops long enough to give me a chance.

After all the sing-song stuff had stopped, the Marshall announced it was time for the games to begin and the kids answered him back with another sonic boom. I looked over at where Jag was sitting and noticed he had smashed his Raisonettes into the seat back in front of him in letters that spelled "EAT ME." He grinned at me proudly as I shook my head, and then offered me some of what was left, which I gladly accepted.

The first Lil' Cowpokes game was a race with Black Jack from one end of the stage to the other, and any kid that won, which they always did, would get a "Rootin'-tootin' six-gun shootin' prize." Unfortunately, those prizes were usually pretty lame, like a rubber snake or tarantula or something, but hey, they were free, and sometimes stuff like that could come in real handy in the right situation. The theatre turned in to a big looney bin as soon as the Marshall asked who wanted to be first to have a crack at old Black Jack, and every kid in the audience started to hollering at the top of their lungs and jumping up and down in their seats and waving their hands and doing a two finger whistle if they were able, and there was popcorn and chips and all sorts of stuff so thick in the air, the stage looked kinda hazy from where we were sitting.

Neil and Ira started right in, just as nutty as the others, and pleaded to be the ones picked "Because there was no way that phony jackass, Black Jack, could beat 'em in a race." The Marshall, he took his own sweet time in picking the first contestant, and after laying low at first, me and Jag decided to join in, even though we knew that it was real childish, because we suddenly realized that our seat bottoms were spring loaded, and if ya came down on 'em just right, they would fling you back up in the air like a trampoline. We started up our own contest to see who could reach the highest, but had to quit after Jag tried doing a somersault on his second jump and landed hard on his head in the lap of one of those same unfortunate cowpokes Neil had thrown into the row in front of us, sending the kid straight to the first aid station.

Creepy and Coop weren't looking none too comfortable with all the chaos going on around them and Creep started fidgeting with his glasses and blinking his eyes real hard over and over like he always did, and then Chicken Coop slunk down real low in his seat and started mumbling,

187

"Heavens to murgatroid," and before you knew it here come the hiccups loud and quick. Rosie, on the other hand, seeing a great opportunity, stood up and tried his best to snatch some of the edible stuff that was flying around, and with them big paws of his he managed to haul in several Milk Duds, a Bit-o-Honey and half of a Zagnut bar, which he stuffed in his face immediately.

The crack team of ushers came racing in from the lobby to try to restore order, but that was like trying to put out a ten-alarm fire with a squirt gun and nobody paid them no mind at all. Finally, with the anticipation getting down right unbearable and a full fledged riot about to break out, Marshall K-Gun picks Joey Lipshitz, the ten year old brother of Larry, to be the lucky contestant. He was a goofy looking kid with this humongous round head, tiny eyes and ears, a nose that looked like it should've had a ring in it, plus a real nasty case of eczema. Oh, and, of course, that same *very* unfortunate last name.

"Lip-shitz! Lip-shitz" the chant rang out loud and clear as he slowly made his way to the stage, waving to the crowd as he went. The kids kept yelling out his name with extra emphasis on the last syllable since it was the closest you could come to actually cussing in public without getting a licking or hauled off to Juvi.

"You know, if I had a name like Lipshitz," Neil said, leaning towards us, "I'd either shoot myself or move to a foreign country where they had a different word for what comes out of your butt!"

Well, there was no arguing with that, and we all started up our chant louder than ever. The Marshall got this awful confused, almost scared look on his face, not quite knowing what everyone was yelling, 'til little Joey made it over to him on stage, and with the place falling dead quiet, said his full name, loud and clear, straight into the microphone. That set off a whole new round of "Lip-shitz!" making Joey look read proud and the Marshall a bit more relieved.

After a few quick instructions to Joey and Black Jack, Marshall KGUN pulled out his six- shooter and fired a round in the air to start the race with a bang, and they were off. It was pretty much neck and neck for the first two laps around the stage, with little Joey pumping his arms and legs for all they were worth and his chubby cheeks bouncing to beat the band, 'til finally he pulled away for the victory after the person playing the butt end of Black Jack slipped on a piece of melted Hershey bar that had been thrown on stage earlier, causing 'im to slide way out wide and whip the guy in front straight back and over on his side with a loud thud, much to the delight of every Cowpoke in the audience.

After Black Jack untwisted hisself and got back up on all fours, which ain't as easy as it sounds, it was plain to see that the fella playing the front part wasn't too happy about being flipped around like a rag doll, and he kept turning around jostling his head every which way, like he was giving his butt end what for. Well, pretty soon the front part lets out a horrifying screech and leaps up in the air like he'd been stuck with a hot poker or something, and then all of a sudden them front legs started to kicking at his back end like they really meant business, and the back legs started to kick at the front, and before you knew it, Black Jack was rolling on the ground, fighting with hisself, sliding all over the stage and getting so twisted up that the front legs were pointing one direction and the back legs another, and all the while Marshall KGUN stood by with his mouth gaping wide, froze stiff by what he was seeing, and the audience going absolutely berserk!

Then here comes one end of the horse trying to stand up, but before he could right hisself the other end would knock it back down, and then the other end would give it a go and the whole thing would happen all over again. I tell you, it was the darndest fight you ever did see, with the audience going nuts worse than ever and pelting old Black Jack with candy and peanuts and you name it, 'til finally the ushers and the Marshall hisself had to jump in and call a truce, although they weren't able to completely separate the fighters for obvious reasons.

"That Black Jack, he don't know his ass from a hole in the ground", Ira said, real matter of fact-like.

"Yeah, but he's the only animal in history to actually kick his *own* ass," Neil laughed out loud. That got us all to giggling pretty good, and we started watching once again as the ushers left the stage and the Marshall looking plenty shook up, leaned over and yelled something in old Black Jack's ear that didn't sound too pleasant. Then he righted hisself, straightened his hat, smoothed down his vest, and moved to the microphone to announce the next contest.

This was the big one, the Grand Finale, the one every single one of the Lil' Cowpokes would give their eyeteeth to be in on, including us. It was the "Rootin' Tootin' Sharp-Shootin'" contest where some lucky kid got to shoot an actual, real-life Winchester rifle, that shot, honest to God, real plastic bullets at targets on stage. It was the slickest gun any of us had ever seen, way neater than my Uncle Al's Red Ryder B.B. gun, and just like the ones on all the westerns on T.V.. It had a carved wood handle and a hand engraved barrel that was polished so bright that the stage lights glared off of it bright as the sun. It was the Marshall's pride and joy, and he kept it in this lovely velvet lined case, only bringing it out at the end of every show for this here sharp shooting contest.

Well the place went nuts all over again, and as Marshall KGUN held that rifle high over his head the noise reached the level of a hundred jet engines firing all at once, maybe more. We all started jumping up and down in our seats, getting high as we could to get his attention, even Rosie, though he couldn't muster more than an inch or two. Neil was really going gangbusters this time, getting five or six feet up in the air with each jump and yelling "Yaa-Hooo!" with all his might, just like them real cowboys did in the movies when they got their selves all riled up about something. Now this went on for what seemed like forever while the Marshall paced up and down in front of the stage and stared out at all the screwball kids, building up the suspense something ferocious. Then I'll be darned if, outta the hundreds of nutcases there, he didn't pick Neil, the kid you'd least want to give a loaded gun to!

I got a horrible shiver deep down in my bones, thinking about the possible catastrophe that laid ahead as Neil squeezed by us saying "Sorry suckers," with Ira sliding in right behind 'im. He marched down the aisle, arms raised in triumph with a sinister sneer from ear to ear, then slowly climbed the side steps of the stage making his way over to the center. The kids in the audience that recognized him quickly stopped cheering, obviously thinking the same way I was, and I could see Big I moving slowly through the orchestra pit to the front of the stage, undetected by the ushers, so as to get the best view of whatever was gonna happen next. He crouched down low as the Marshall brought Neil forward to introduce him to the crowd 'til they were practically standing right on top of him. I heard Coop start to hiccup all over, and looked over to see Creepy quickly take his glasses off and shove them in his front pocket. Rosie was staring hard at the stage now and although his cheeks were chuck full of gumdrops, he actually stopped chewing, which was a sure sign of just how serious things were getting.

Jag leaned over to me and said in my ear, "This c-c-can't be good, Johnny C."

"You said a mouth full there, sister," I answered as we both turned our attention back to the stage.

"Here's our lucky contestant, boys and girls," the Marshall said, real excited-like into the microphone over a few scattered cheers. By now most of the kids had realized who was up there, and let's face it, Neil was never gonna win a popularity contest with the elementary school kids in these parts that he'd been torturing for most of their lives.

"What's you name, son?"

Neil thought for a second and then with a completely straight face said, "Wyatt Earp."

I looked over at Jagger, and after shaking our heads we both started to snicker.

"What did you say?" asked the Marshall, thinking he hadn't heard right.

"I said, Wyatt Earp, sir."

There was a bit of a pause as Marshall KGUN stood there at a loss for words, while the two teen-age ushers on the side of the stage that knew all about Neil, started looking pretty peeved and tried to stare 'im down.

"You know son, many years back there was a famous law man around these parts by that same name," said the Marshal, trying to manage a smile.

"Why, yes sir, I should say so, since he was my great grand-daddy," Neil shot back lickety-split, without so much as a blink.

Now the Marshall took off his hat, scratched his head and wiped his brow looking mighty perplexed, and them ushers I told you about were shooting daggers with their eyes over at Neil by now. Jag and I tried to keep from laughing out loud and Chicken Coop and Creepy were getting more and more nervous by the second. Rosie wasn't paying no mind anymore on account'a the fact that he was too busy finishing off Coop's Sugar Babies and Creepy's half melted Bon-Bons, seeing that they were preoccupied.

Then Neil started up again, not knowing when to quit as usual, "Us Earps, we all lived over in Tombstone, you know, 'The town too tough to die,' for as far back as the gunfight at the O.K. Corral, but just last year my Pa, Triand Earp, and my Ma, Imagonna Earp, decided to mosey on over to Santa Elena to get away from the constant prying eyes and unwanted attention. I mean it got to be downright ridiculous. Ya couldn't even go to the outhouse without some pushy eastern reporter knocking on the door and then pushing a microphone in your face, right then and there while you were trying to do your business, to ask you a bunch'a personal questions about Grandpappy. I tell ya it can be a real hardship being the kin of the most famous lawman the wild west ever knew, but I guess you understand all about that, sir."

Marshall KGUN was dumbstruck. He just stared at Neil with his mouth open a mile wide and his brow all wrinkled up, not sure what to say, 'til finally he spits out, "That is all very nice young fella," and gives Neil a little pat on the back, "now let's get on with the sharpshooting contest," and then he picked up his rifle off the table, and held it up once again to the crowd.

"This here my young whippersnappers is one very special firearm. It is the very same rifle used by the legendary Buffalo Bill in the stupendous and world famous Wild West shows at the turn of the century." (We knew that was a crock 'cause Don Martin, this very strange fourth grader that Neil dubbed Don "Martian" got picked for the contest last month, told us that he noticed stamped right there on the barrel in big letters, clear as day "Made in 1965.")

"We will now see if our imaginative contestant, ah, Wyatt Earp, has the steady hand and sharp eye of a Wild West rifleman necessary to hit five targets with only five shots."

Old Neil waved real excited to the crowd, when the Marshall said, "Wyatt Earp," and I swear them ushers were *this* close to coming over and ringing his scrawny neck. He snatched the rifle from the Marshall before he was even finished with his schpeal, and then after looking it over top to bottom like he was some expert or something, started to aim at the targets sitting on a table next to the two ushers. From where I was standing on my seat, I could just see the top of Ira's head peeking over the front of the stage with the Marshall only a few inches away as Neil took aim real serious-like, with one eye all squinted up and his tongue sticking out the side of his mouth, and the only sound in the entire theater was Rosie sucking chocolate off the tips of his fat fingers.

After some real serious aiming, Neil stopped and looked back up and said, "I'll be a horsepoop picker at the rodeo parade, but old Wild Bill's gun barrel is crooked!"

Well, that did it for the Marshall and he started gritting his teeth and his eyes started to twitch, and with his face starting to look like a great big pomegranate, he forced out, "That is impossible you lil' cowpoke, that weapon is of the utmost quality!"

"Why don't you just shoot, you little twerp?" said the smaller of the two ushers, loud enough for everyone to hear.

"Why don't you take that bed pan off your heads and put it on your butt where it belongs?" Neil said pointed at their usher's hats.

"If you don't shoot we're gonna beat the snot outta ya right here and now!"

"Do you really want me to shoot?" Neil answered back quick.

"We sure do."

"Are you absolutely positive?"

"Yes!"

"Alright, then maybe I just will."

"Uh, oh," me and Jag both said at the same time as we strained our necks to see what would happen next, while Rosie, Bampu and Chicken Coop hid their heads behind the seats in front of them. I started waving my hands over my head hard as I could and shaking my head "No!" but it was too late. Neil put that rifle back up to his shoulder, pulled back the hammer calm as can be and then "Pow!" and "Ping!" that plastic bullet whizzed through the air and knocked the big mouth usher's hat clean off!

"Why you little creep!" yelled the other usher as he tried to lunge for him, but Neil was ready for him, too, and his next shot nailed him square in the Adam's apple, putting him outta commission at least for the time being.

Poor old Marshall KGUN was frozen stiff as rigor mortis once again, staring straight off into space, as Neil ran over to where Black Jack was standing and jumped up on his back to make his get away, yelling, "Hi Ho Silver!" but the horse just staggered forward a couple of steps before falling flat as a pancake with a loud thud.

The Marshall, seemed to come to his senses after that and yelled out at the top of his lungs, "Wait 'til I get my hands on you, you little brat!" But as he tried to go for Neil there was an ear-piercing, "Aargh!" and then "Bam!"

as *he* fell flat on his face.

I looked real close to see what had caused the fall, and could tell someone had tied the Marshall's spurs together with what looked an awful lot like a red licorice rope. I shot a quick glance down at the orchestra pit, and there was Big I crouching low in front of the stage with his hands over his mouth, trying not to laugh out loud and bring any attention to hisself. Boy, we were really in for it this time!

Everyone kept on watching amazed, as first Neil ran off one side of the stage, being followed closely by the two mad as hornets ushers, and then behind the curtain and all the way across the back of the stage to the other side. They kept on chasing round and round, the whole time Neil yelling and laughing like a madman and the crowd going completely bonkers. Each time around, them three couldn't help but trample all over poor Black Jack in the middle of the stage who kept trying to get to his feet, and when they did he'd yell out something in Spanish, obviously in pain. The old Marshall, he just layer there, face first with his hat pulled low over his eyes, not caring to watch as another one of his kiddy shows went straight to pot.

Finally, Neil dropped the rifle in the center of the stage, hollered out to the crowd, "Th-th-that's all folks!" and jumped off the stage and tore out one of the side exits with Ira hot on his heels. We decided it was high time for us to get lost, too, before anyone remembered we were all together, and we scooted down the row and up the aisle in an all out sprint. We were headed through the lobby when Dan Dunn, completely oblivious to the riot that was going on in the theater, stopped us to ask what was up.

"Some crazy kid tied up Marshall KGUN, shot two of the ushers, and knocked Black Jack out cold!" I said, huffing and puffing as I blew by.

"Oh no, not again!" Dan cried out. "Okay. Nobody panic, I'll take care of this," and he blew his chief assistant usher whistle loud as he could to get the attention of all available re-enforcements and then yelled, "Let's go men!" as he, the ticket-taker girl, and the hot dog guy from the snack bar charged into the theater.

We flew out the front door past a bunch of startled parents there to pick up their little tykes, on past the courthouse and right on toward home, with me and Jag in the lead followed closely by Chicken Coop and Creepy and Rosie bringing up the rear as he ate the last kernels out of the bottom of some kid's popcorn box.

# Chapter Thirteen

## THE MANSFIELD PLACE

Well, the days were flying by way too fast, just like always. Before you knew it summer vacation would be clean gone. I couldn't bear the thought. Pop quizzes, homework, and Nancy all over again! It was more than a boy could bear. We decided our only hope was to come up with some reason for the whole gang to be excused for the entire year, which led to an embarrassing number of the most lame-brained, half-baked, and bone-headed scams you ever heard, with Chicken Coop being in fine form as usual, but there was one that actually had a chance we figured, and that was that we all got exposed to this truckload of high grade radio active plutonium, playing too close to one of the top secret nuclear missile silos, that everybody but the Russians seems to know about, up near Sahuarita. We figured we could tell everybody that mattered, that the Secret Service picked us up and hauled our glowing butts over to some even *more* top secret underground M.A.S.H. unit, like the one Dr. Jagger works at over in Viet Nam, and the folks there said that it just so happens to take exactly nine months, or one whole school year, (quite a coincidence, huh?) for all the nasty stuff to get outta our systems, and 'til then the only people it'd be safe to hang out with would be each other. Not bad, huh? Creepy's working out the final details, so I'll let ya know how it turns out.

On top of vacation being almost over, we were also starting up at a whole new school, Alice Vail Junior High, with a lotta new kids. *Bigger* kids. *Meaner* kids. No more fun filled days at The Sewer, ruling the roost. Nope. Now we'd be nuthin' but worthless seventh graders, low men on the totem pole, and likely to get pounded on a regular basis just for looking at someone cross-eyed. Heck, we didn't even have an official nickname for the place yet, but Neil did call last night to see what I thought about, "Alice Vail Junior Jail." Not too shabby. It has a nice ring to it, wouldn't ya say? That boy surely has a gift. Or maybe it's actually more of a curse. Anyway, I decided not to worry about things 'til the time come, 'cause just like Pop always says, worrying never did nuthin' but give a body a sore head and a jiggle in his insides, and heck, look on the bright side, there was still twenty-two and one half days left of freedom to enjoy!

Having nuthin' better to do, me and Gracie spent the whole morning sitting on the kitchen floor and licking Gold Bond stamps. She was only a hundred and fifty more books from a Barbie wardrobe, and I needed another seventy-five for the James Bond briefcase, the one you could shoot a real plastic bullet outta without even opening it up. How sweet is that! So at this pace I figured we were only about three years away from paydirt.

After a barely edible lunch of leftover eggplant parmijohn, Gracie and I were lying in the den on the green shag carpet Ma had just worked over with her goofy rake, locked in a nasty game of Chinese Checkers. I would've whipped her good and quick, but I had to keep my eyes peeled for that doofus Dodger who kept slurping up my marbles each time I looked away. About then Jag called saying he was in the mood for some big game, sling-shot hunting; lizards, horny toads, maybe even a prairie dog or two, and I said that sounded swell. We decided to meet at the gate to the old Mansfield property soon as the monsoons passed, and have ourselves a little desert safari. That was the best time of day to hunt anyways, on account'a all the desert dwellers come outta their holes for a quick drink from a nearby puddle before it all evaporates, or maybe search for an insect or two for dinner, plus the temperature dips ten to twenty degrees after a big rainstorm, and living in Southern Arizona in the dead of summer, all living creatures, including us, learn to take advantage of such things whenever the chance comes up.

Old Man Mansfield, he was one of the founders of Santa Elena, according to Pop, and he and his wife and three daughters homesteaded all the land around the east side of town, including all the way north to the foothills of the Santa Catalina Mountains. Seems he and his family come out on a covered wagon all the way from Kansas in the late 1800s and plopped themselves down on this God forsaken desert to live for the rest of their days. Don't ask me why, there weren't nuthin' around these parts back then, 'cept maybe Tucson, which was just a small cavalry post, and, of course, the most famous of the wild west towns, Tombstone, to the east. It's sad, but nowadays about the wildest show that ever happens in Tombstone, is when the mayor's wife gets a little tipsy, which happens quite often I hear, and his honor has to fetch her back home, kicking and cussing all the while.

Anyways, back to Old Man Mansfield. He was a cagey old goat, and I guess he learned right off that he could swindle the poor Injuns in these parts outta just about anything they owned for practically nuthin', and that's exactly what he did to the best of his ability for the rest of his days. Seems he practically cornered the market around this neck of the woods on native blankets and carvings and pottery and all kinds of swell stuff, and then set up the biggest trading post west of Santa Fe. He became one of the richest men in all of Arizona territory, a real tycoon, according to Pop, not caring a lick about bamboozling them simple Papagos and Navajos all the while. He got real famous, too, and when they made us a state back in 1914, there he was, proud as a peacock, sitting smack dab next to the new governor at the statehood parade wearing nuthin' but his finest Indian get up.

Now the youngest of his three girls was said to be sweet as pie with a heart of pure gold. Not at all like her conniving, money grubbing old man, and it's said she'd do her darndest to sneak out whenever she could, and go down to the reservation and give them poor Indians, the same ones her father had been thieving all these years, food and clothes and medicine and what not, to try and make amends. Turns out her name was Elaine and on account'a her being so sweet and kind and all, the Mexican folks, being so religious, said she must be a saint. Not like Our Lady of Guadalupe or nuthin', but still pretty swell. It wasn't long before everyone started calling her Saint Elaine, or Santa Elena in Mexican, and that's how the town got its name. Seems her no good, snake in the grass father never did get wind of all her good deeds, and never for the life of him could figure out why everyone made such a fuss about his youngest girl.

A few years after he showed up, Old Man Mansfield built him and his family a considerable mansion outta wood and lava rock, which is common as scorpions and jumping cactus around here on account'a some volcano that erupted in these parts about a million years ago, which might also explain something about the intolerable heat we get. I knew all about his place, or as much as any kid dared, 'cause it sits on what's left of the Mansfield homestead right out behind our back wall. It had a wide, wood plank porch all the way around, and three chimneys made outta stone, with four gables way up high, and two full stories, and I hear tell it was really somethin' to see in its hey day. Too bad that after the old codger passed on in 1920, his wife and daughters sold the trading post, packed up all their belongings, and took off for California, leaving the big house to fend for itself out in the desert, and now it was really showing the signs of all those God awful summers. The white paint on the wood all along the second story was chipped away somethin' horrible, so the brown showed through, mostly, and near all of the windows were broke clear out to the frame. A good number of ceiling tiles had blowed clean off many monsoons ago, so you could see the wood beams, like exposed ribs, all underneath. The whole place was looking real ramshackle, a sad and sorrowful picture of what it once was.

It sat there, smack dab in the middle of about five acres of desert, lonely as can be, and nobody never, ever went near it as far as I can remember, 'cepting the time a few years back when old Morty, the town drunk, was trying to sleep one off without Mrs. Morty finding out, and decided to spend the night. When he came out the next morning, he was babbling like a madman. Ya see, that's the thing, the house ain't just worn and ugly, it's way worse than that—it's *haunted*, no ifs ands or butts, and I mean haunted to the gills with the most sinister, lowdown, blood thirsty spirit that ever lived, or died, or whatever them ghosts are—you know. Anyways, everyone for miles around knew it too, and all about the story of Old Man Mansfield and how when his time come, he fought and fought and became more and more ornery, and how he told the doctors he weren't really all that sick but they were trying to make him so in order to steal all his swell stuff. And when he finally *did* croak, plenty of folks believed his spirit never left that old house that he built with his own two hands, and he's still there to protect his beloved property from any rascals that may try and take it from 'im.

We'd heard from some very reliable sources, like George Morrison, a *fifteen* year old, that the reason his family up and left so quick was because of the fact of his wretched old spirit in that house wouldn't let them be. I swear there were nights when I'd lie in bed with all the lights off peaceful as a pup after double helpings, when outta nowhere here comes the most spin tinglingest, hair raisingest, mournfullest howl from off in the distance that a living being ever did hear. And sure as I'm sitting here, it was old Man Mansfield letting off some steam. It was a low blowing kinda sound, like one of them tug boat horns, and it wasn't just Dodger having a bad dream or gas or somethin' neither. I know 'cause I checked.

Anyways, round about four o'clock here comes the monsoon, right on time, and a mighty forceful one at that. There was wind blowing and rain splattering, and even some hail tapping at the front windowpanes. I'll never for the life of me understand how it could be 105 degrees one second, and ice balls falling from the sky the next, but I guess that's why they got all them sharp as a tack weather men on T.V. Anyway, it was always exciting to see the hail come down 'cause we were never gonna see any snow around here, let's face it. This was the closest we were gonna get! There wasn't any thunder or lightning flashes this time around, and after about half an hour everything was still and lovely. The temperature dropped to seventy-five, just like always and Ma went around opening up all the windows to take advantage of a little fresh air for a change.

I grabbed my wrist rocket, the same one I used to help spring Creepy a few weeks back, and slipped out the back door. The desert smelled so nice and pleasant after all that rain, and I took in a few deep breaths just to clean out the old stale, dusty air that had been clogging up my lungs all day long. I spotted a couple of rusted up tin cans under some desert broom, and went to setting 'em up for target practice. I gathered up some nice round stones to use as ammo on account'a the fact, like I told ya before, they shoot a much truer line, not like the flat ones that get to spinning and flying every which way, and saved the best ones to use for the real deal. I set the cans up on the arm of a dead saguaro, with all the meat worn off and nuthin' but ribs left, and started plugging away. I was having a pretty good go of it when Jag finally rode up.

"W-well if it ain't Annie O-O-Oakley!" he said, and than jumped off Bullet and watched her do a couple of circles before she crashed landed into a barrel cactus. He already had out his wrist rocket and was taking a pot shot at one of the cans still standing, but without much luck.

"W-what the heck! Does that c-can have holes in it or w-what?" he cried out, all astounded-like. Truth was, Jagger, for all his other strong points was a lousy shot, although nobody dared tell it to his face, of course. It might have been due to that crazy eye he had, or maybe because he was too strong for his own good, but whatever it was he was a real stinker.

You see, we had this, Happy Heatstroke Hunting Society between us guys this summer to see who could bag the most lizards and other desert dwellers before vacation was up. The thing was, you had to have another hunter vouch for ya when you did get a kill, and then you would measure it all up, the bigger it was, the more points you got, and then you'd write all the numbers on a little file card 'til school started to see who won. We had to come up with this system 'cause last summer Neil insisted he killed three Kimono Dragons, over four feet long each!

We were all pretty certain those monsters didn't live anywhere near hear, and when we asked Creepy about it, he just gave us another of them, "Don't waste my time you morons" looks. The only reason any of us had even heard about them at all, was on account'a they were featured on Mutual of Omaha's Wild Kingdom one Sunday afternoon a few years back. That's the goofy animal show where that old guy with the white hair is in charge of the whole shebang, and sits off safe and sound in the helicopter or somewheres, while his devoted young assistant does all the dirty work like wrestling hungry alligators or shooting ticked off grizzly bears point blank with tranquilizer guns and stuff.

Anyway, Neil, kept swearing on his brother's grave, which I don't think counts if you only *wish* the person was dead, that what he said was true, and that he should be the winner of the big game hunter prize, which was a pretty swell plastic skull with all the teeth in place that we found out in the alley behind Dr. Looney Tunes house one day last Easter vacation. We tried to press 'im to show us some kinda proof, but he said he was real sorry, he had already skinned those giant lizards to make belts for his cousins for their birthdays, and gave the meat to the humane society so those poor, lonely dogs could have a nice gourmet meal to take their mind off things.

This season I had already bagged three horny toads, two whiptail lizards and a centipede. I had a couple of open shots at some prairie dogs, too, but I didn't take 'em. I knew for sure I'd get to feeling like a lowdown murderer if I killed a cute little bugger like that. Let's face it, killing ugly things doesn't weigh near as heavy on your conscience.

"You ready for some action, Jag."

"Darn right. I feel lucky today," he said as he shot one last time at the can and missed by about five feet.

"Grab a couple more good stones, and let's head on up the trail," I said as I climbed up and over the old wood fence that still stood around the Mansfield Homestead. When Jag came up behind me I asked, "How's your Pop doing? Have you heard from 'im lately?"

"W-w-well, he wrote us just last week and said there was a l-l-lot of bombing around their field hospital."

"Wow! Was he scared?"

"Nope, he n-n-never gets scared. Says nobody's gonna b-bomb a hospital. Not on p-p-purpose, anyways."

"How's your ma doing?"

"Now *she's* scared to d-death."

"My Pop says it's a different kinda war over there," I said. "He says in the big war, we were out to win no matter what, and we showed them Krauts and Japs a thing or two by the time it was all said and done."

"Who the heck are the Krauts and Japs?" Jagger asked.

"Why they're the Germans and the Japanese, you moron. Don't you know nuthin' about World War II?"

"W-w-well I thought we were f-fighting the Italians, too?"

"I'm not certain on that one. Seems I heard that they may have actually been helping *us* out. Anyway, Pop says in Vietnam, we don't know what the heck we're doing, and if American soldiers are gonna fight, they should always fight to win. He says the politicians are running the war instead of the generals like it should be, and whenever those lame brains get into the act, they don't do nuthin' but screw things up. What does your pop say?"

"He says that he sees a l-lot of young g-guys with arms and legs blowed off."

We walked along quiet for a while over one of the footpaths that had been trampled down over the years by kids like us going through the desert brush. All the plants had got a nice long drink from the heavy rains we'd been having and looked all plump and healthy, a nice change from the generally shriveled up and sickly way they were most of the rest of the year. There were a few small creeks running through the Mansfield property that could only muster a light trickle of water even after an especially fierce storm, and they ran down to the east and finally into the Rillito River which was really no river at all, but ninety percent of the time just a big dry wash. Whatever water there was in the Rillito, and it weren't much, made its way into the Santa Cruz way down south of town.

The sound of that water trickling along was real peaceful and pleasant, and Jag and I sat ourselves down on a big rock along the trail and just listened for a while. I could tell Jag was thinking about somethin' else, probably his pop, I figured, so far away and all and with all that shooting going on, and I didn't want to disturb him. Sometimes when somebody's got somethin' on their mind, it's best just to sit there next to them, nice and quiet, 'til they got it all worked out in their own head. There's no need to be yapping about somethin' every dang minute of the day, anyhow. Too bad Gracie hadn't learned that lesson yet.

Finally, like he snapped out of a trance, Jag jumped up and yelled out, "Horny t-t-toad!" as he whipped out his weapon from the back pocket of his Levi's and fired away. I was kinda startled at first, enjoying the peace and tranquility and all, but after a few seconds I saw what Jag was hollering about, a particularly nice specimen sunning hisself on a rock about ten feet dead ahead. Jag had already let off three or four shots, but missed so badly that toad didn't even flinch.

"Prairie poop!" he yelled out in disgust at his lousy shooting.

"Stand back Jag and let the pro have a go," and with that I took aim, pulled back and let one fly. My shot was dead straight but just low, and it smacked into the rock it was sitting on with a loud THA-WACK! I tell you that ugly thing jumped about a foot in the air and was off like a rocket with Jag and I in hot pursuit. He was flying low as we chased 'im through creosote bushes, around barrel cactuses and ocotillos, and over cholla, and I'm sure we looked liked a couple of escaped mental patients chasing that no good horny toad this way and that and zig zagging back and forth and all the time screaming and hollering and shooting like the dickens. Finally, he ran off into a big old pile of jumping cactus and disappeared. Jag was fuming by now and itching to go in after 'im, saying no lizard was gonna make a fool outta him.

"You're nuts, Jag, you'll come outta there looking like a porkypine, and you still won't have nuthin' to show for it. He's probably got ten different holes in there to hide out in and besides there ain't no telling what else you might meet up with in there."

Of course, there just ain't no reasoning with Jagger when he set his mind to somethin' like I told ya before, and this time weren't no different. He wasn't about to let anyone get the best of him, let alone a six inch, cold blooded reptile, so with that same crazy look on his face that he had over at Red River a few weeks back, he started tippy toeing into that cactus patch with his sling shot drawn and ready for combat.

"Jag, you gotta be nuts to go in there!" which I knew he was, but felt it was my duty to at least remind 'im.

I just stood and watched as he winced in pain every now and then when he got stuck with a cactus thorn, but he was way too pig headed to stop, or even squeal a bit, and after four or five steps with his eyes peeled and his head cocked to one side to get his good eye working for him, he spotted his prey and raised up his weapon for the kill. But before you could say, "Desert doo-doo" a sound like someone was shaking a can full of rocks came from just off of where Jag was standing. We both froze stiff as a year old Big Hunk, on account'a we'd heard that sound before and it ain't a good one when you're standing in a desert, if ya know what I mean, especially from only five feet away!

Jagger lowered his weapon ever so slow, so you could count the hairs on the back of his hand, and looked down and over to his left to see what he could see, but I had already spotted it, an ugly head sticking straight up and eyes that were on fire. It was the biggest Diamondback I ever saw, all curled up and ready for business!

"Don't move an inch, Jag, understand? Just hold tight." I managed to squeeze out, with my throat tighter than a pair of hot pants on a hippo's butt, as I looked around for something to throw. Jag nodded ever so slight but kept his eye on that rattling reptile as it started to rear its head back and hunker down a bit. I found what I was looking for, a nice round throwing stone about the size of a coconut. By the way, did I ever tell ya about the time Pop brought a coconut home from his warehouse, and while trying to crack it open for me and Gracie with a hammer, he slipped and broke off half of our kitchen counter! Remind me, later. It was a doosey.

Anyways, back to the cactus patch. After I grabbed that rock I said, "Okay, listen up. I'm gonna try and cold cock that mother with this here rock, so soon as I let fly you turn tail and haul outta there, got it?" Jag didn't say nuthin' but just ever so easy nod his big fat head, and after taking a deep breath and then letting it out nice and slow so as to relieve the tension like all the big league pitchers do, I wound up with my best fast ball delivery and flung that rock for all I was worth, straight for the middle of that snake's horrible head. Well, old Jag, he jumped clean out of that prickly pear patch in one leap that would'a made a jackrabbit proud, and sure enough that nasty rattler jumped, too, but just a hair too late, and right when he begun to spring my throw nailed 'im right between the beady eyes, stopping him cold, and flung him a good ten feet back where he landed with a thud up against the trunk of a Palo Verde tree. I didn't stick around to give him a chance for revenge, but tore outta there, hot on Jag's heels, with my heart pushing outta my throat and pounding harder than a bully on a pipsqueak.

We flew like an F4 Phantom through the desert, fast as our legs would go, not caring what we ran through, getting plenty scraped up along the way, and finally, huffing and puffing to beat the band, came to a stop, not able to go another step. But it seems we couldn't win for losing, 'cause as I glanced over my shoulder and spun Jag around, too, so he could have a look, there staring straight back at us, close enough to spit on, was the Mansfield mansion, big as day but dark as night!

Well, I guess getting the bejeezus scared outta ya more than once in a minute was more than a body could stand, and instead of tearing off again in the opposite direction from our latest life threatening situation, we just plopped ourselves down in a heap right in front of the old place with our chests still heaving and the sweat pouring down our face, not able to move another inch.

"That snake almost b-b-bit me in the b-b-butt as I turned to run," Jag spit out between breaths. "If that would'a happened, Johnny C., you would'a had to s-s-suck the venom out to save my life," he said with that same goofy, picket fence grin I seen so often over the years.

"I got news for you pal. If that snake bit you in the butt, you were gonna die!"

"Why, Johnny C, th-that really h-h-hurts my feelings. I though you were my b-best friend."

"Yeah, well, being friends and sucking on someone's butt is two different things."

We laughed for a bit after that and then I let Jagger have it over and over for going into that cactus patch in the first place. He didn't say nuthin' in return, but just kept smiling to hisself, probably thinking what a cool story it was gonna be to tell the guys. We sat there on that muddy ground for a good while, catching our breath and breathing in that beautiful damp desert smell and laughing all over again about how ridiculous we must've looked running from that snake like a couple of lousy lunatics. Jagger said that was his closest call yet to being bit by something venomous, not counting the time Nancy Cole tried to take a chunk outta his arm after he stuck a Palo Verde beetle in her hair during gym.

"Think about how funny it would've been if that dang snake bit you in the butt and then clamped on for dear life, not letting go for nuthin', and you'd've been running and screaming like a banshee and I would'a been chasing after you trying to grab that rattler and yank 'im off!"

"Yeah, and I c-c-could'a tried to sh-shake 'im off by wiggling my butt fast as I could, l-like this," he said as he jumped up, stuck his butt out as far as he could and then started shaking it a mile a minute.

"Man, you look like one of them goofy Tahiti dancers with the grass skirts that I seen on T.V. Pop says they can make their rear end jiggle so fast it looks like, 'Jell-O on springs.'" Then *I* got up and stood next to Jag and started shaking all over fast as I could, too, and we carried on like that for a while trying to out do each other 'til we were all tuckered out all over and slunk back down on the ground. We just laid there for a bit with our hands tucked in underneath our heads, staring up at the sky and not saying much of anything. Just then a Tarantula about the size of a Buick came crawling outta his hole ten or so feet away from where we were and started sniffing around for some dinner. Jag seen him, too, and we both whipped out our wrist rockets and rattled off a couple of shots before he crawled off real indignant like. To tell ya the truth I weren't too keen on killing the furry guy, anyways. I heard once that the Apaches say that killing a tarantula is not only bad luck, but they will come back twice as big and then hunt *you* down instead! God knows, the way things were going lately I didn't need no more trouble, especially from a ten pound prehistoric spider!

After a bit we heard some Colorado River toads croaking up a storm off by the little wash, but neither of us felt like getting up from our nice comfy spot to try and add them to our big game hunter's list. Anyways, it made me half sick to my stomach just looking at them things, all blubbery and green and slimy with short fat arms and legs sticking out and looking for all the world like one big fat cowpie with eyes.

The sun started to slowly slide down in the southwest sky, and the clouds that were stragglers from the afternoon storm, lit up bright and colorful like God's own chalk drawing. There were all shades of pink and deep purple at first, and then a little later, when the sun began to sink lower, they turned to brilliant reds and oranges, like fire, with a little yellow sprinkled in here and there. Through a break in the clouds, and in a while, you could see streams of sunlight shining down, that looked, close as I could tell, like heaven itself was giving us an early glimpse of it's magnificent beauty. I gotta say, there ain't nuthin' more lovely or peaceful than a Sonoran Desert sunset flowing like a waterfall over the mountains in the rainy season.

Anyhow, Jag and I were still laying there in front of that old house, forgetting how close we were to danger all over again, and enjoying the heck out of our wonderful freedom and solitude, when out of no where, came the most horrible screeching sound this side of Nancy Cole's beautician! My skin started to crawl and the hair on the back of my neck stood straight out like a porkypine, and both of us whirled around quick to see the monstrous front door of the old house swinging slowly, back and forth on its rotting hinges. That place had never looked more frightening than at that moment, as the setting sun's rays shined through the back, giving it an especially ghastly glow. The whole front of the house by now was nuthin' but a silhouette against the darkening sky, and the breeze that blew through the broken windows made it sound like the whole house was moaning in agony. We stood there, frozen stiff, no more than five feet in front of the broken down wooden steps that led up to the porch, and I was thinking how stupid we'd been to stay so close to a haunted house as darkness fell. We both knew all too well, that Old Man Mansfield would be roaming all over his place soon as night came, just dying to catch a couple of tender kids to eat for his nasty nightmarish feast!

"Let's get while the getting's good," I yelled as I turned to run with my legs churning like an egg beater, but my body not budging an inch on account'a Jag had a hold of the back of my pants.

"W-w-well wait just a second, Johnny C.," he said. "The way I see it, this here's a ch-chance in a lifetime to see if that old m-man's ghost really has been hanging around this house all these years."

"Are you nuts? We ain't gonna have no lifetime at all if we don't split right this second. Of course, there's a ghost! The whole town knows it, you imbecile, and he ain't gonna ask us in for no milk and cookies, neither. Now, come on!" I tried to loosen myself from his iron-like grip, but it weren't no use. Once that numskull got an idea in his head there weren't no stopping 'im, but you already seen that, plenty.

"L-l-look, we're never g-gonna get this close to the old place again, right, so I f-figure we might as well try and at least g-g-get a little peek of 'im, right? D-d-don't be such a weenie all the time, Johnny C. Remember you're a d-dang S.S.B.!" And with that he got down on all fours and started to crawl over to the front porch steps.

Well, now I was in a real fix. I couldn't talk Jag outta it, that was impossible, and I couldn't just leave 'im to fend for hisself, although that's what he deserved, so I just sucked it up and scampered over to where he was, staying as low to the ground as I could to avoid ghostly detection and a sure, painful death.

"Now what, Sherlock? Shall we just knock on the front door to see if he wants to come out and play? Maybe we could get a nice group photo with him to show the guys." I said, disgusted.

"N-n-nice idea, but I didn't bring my camera," he answered as he lit out for the back of the house. The rickety old place had this wide wood porch circling all around, with white washed rails and hand carved parts standing up in between. They got a special name, but I forget. Something like ballerina. There was a set of steps in the back of the house, matching up with the ones in front where we had been lying before Jag came up with his newest death wish scheme. We sat up against the side of them steps now with our backs to the house, and all along the sun was slowly fading over the Rincon Mountains in the west.

"Jag, it's getting dark and we're dead meat for sure if that ghost finds us snooping around where we ain't got no business. Let's blow out of here while we're still able," I pleaded. But it was like talking to a rock, and not one of them interesting, sparkly kinda rocks, neither, but just a grey flat piece of old desert granite.

"W-we got our b-b-backs to the sun, so we got an edge. It'll b-b-lind 'im if he tries to get a good look. Get it?" he said with a wink and then before I could tell him how spirits had super x-ray vision and all, and didn't care a lick about looking into the sun, he was up the steps and laying flat and still on his stomach smack dab below one of the big back windows. I couldn't believe what that lamebrain was getting me into this time. Why was it always me that was left to clean up Jag's mess? How come it was never Big I or Neil or even Rosie? I'll tell ya. It's on account'a them fellas would tell him to go straight to you know where, and leave him alone to get hisself outta the fix he seemed to always get into. But not me. I gotta have a gosh darn conscience!

Anyways, I just swallowed hard, looked around good to make sure Old Man Mansfield hadn't already snuck up behind us, and then slithered up them steps slow and whispery quiet as any living creature could.

"Take a l-l-look in that window, Johnny, and s-see if he's around," Jag whispered, his face only an inch or two from the old wooden planks.

"Are you from another planet or something? I ain't getting my head lopped off by some mad as a hornet spirit for you. It's your plan, *you* look."

Well, he started to get that crazy grin all over again, and then nice and easy started to raise hisself up. The old boards began to creak and groan with the pressure and I was cringing with every little sound since even the dumbest ghost was sure to know exactly where we were by now and what we were up to. Jag, he kept on slow but sure raising up 'til the top of his head was even with the windowsill. It was one of them four pane jobs with dividers, and somehow after all these years not a one of them was broke or even cracked. I figured that was good luck for us 'cause at least it would be harder for the ghost to *smell* us out here if by some crazy stroke of luck he happened to be blind and deaf. Jag kept on creeping higher and higher and by now the top of his head was clear as day to anyone inside the room. My heart was pounding so hard my whole body kinda lurched with every beat, and I just laid there watching him and thinking what a weird kid he was to never, ever be afraid of nuthin', no how. Now I had always suspected that before, but this here really cemented it.

Just then there came from inside the house a quick *"Tap, Tap, Tap,"* sound on the floor like someone or something was scampering around. Jagger yanked his head back down quick and stayed there with his face pressed up against the wall under the window ledge.

"What the heck was that?" I was able to spit out after a minute or two of being paralyzed from fright.

"Dunno, m-m-maybe a lizard."

"Pretty big lizard," I said, knowing darn well what it was.

Jag took a deep breath, set his jaw tight, and lifted hisself up so as to see clear through the lower panes of the window this time. The last, bright orange rays of the setting sun were plastering him square in the back of the head as he peered in, and I watched as his eyes quickly darted back and forth and up and down searching for old man Mansfield.

"What da ya see? Is it him? Is he in there?"

"Nope, nuthin' but an old bedroom," he finally answered, dejected.

I got off my stomach and sat up on my knees to have a little look-see myself and although there weren't no spirits to be seen, what was there was still kinda surprising. There was a four-poster bed sitting flush against the far wall, with a canopy on top that was tattered and torn. There weren't no sheets on the bed but it had them ruffles along the bottom that you see in fancy ladies magazines, and there was a tiny vanity up against another wall made outta wood with a little flower design painted on the drawers. A dusty oval mirror was still sitting on top of it and a few knick-knacks and small bottles were scattered here and there where they must have been left fifty years ago. An old highboy dresser that had seen better days stood next to the bed and a fine needlepoint rug in the middle of the room finished things off. It was hard to believe that all this stuff was still there just like the family had left yesterday, but I guess not even the thieves around these parts were willing to risk meeting up with that old man's ghost. That being said, there was Jagger and I, big as life, smack dab in the middle of the place with the sun sinking low and no more protection than a couple of sling shots.

Well, the room we were peering in was pretty clear one of the Mansfield girl's and by the way things looked, they sure enough took off in a hurry, just like Pop had told. Somethin' spooked them big time, and us two geniuses were just asking to find out for ourselves what it was.

"That's it Jag. I've seen enough. Let's call it a night. Anyway, I'm half starved." I thought the food angle might work, but this wasn't Rosie, unfortunately.

"I b-b-bet any money he t-took off for the next room when he heard us coming," Jag said like he hadn't heard a word of mine. "We gotta t-take one more look."

Famous last words, I thought, but maybe, just maybe "One more look," meant that'd be it, so I decided to clam up and play along. We slid on our bellies past the back door and then laid there under the window to the sitting room on the northwest corner of the house, my hands and arms burning from the splinters I picked up along the way.

"Listen, one more look and that's it. Got it!"

"Okay, okay," Jag answered without looking up.

The window to this room had not been as lucky as the other and all four panes were busted clean out with the wind swirling inside sounding like an angry hoot owl. We laid there for a few minutes arguing about whose turn it was to take a look this time, with him saying it was mine and me saying it should always be his on account'a me not wanting to be there in the first place. We finally agreed after a couple of "not its" and a "rock, paper, scissors," or two, we'd do it together, and scooted up on our knees to get set. The sun was almost down by now with only a few small rays still peeking out over the mountain range in the west, and I looked over my shoulder in that direction to see the silhouette of some giant Saguaros in the desert behind us looking like tall, black ghosts with arms reaching up to the sky. Then all of a sudden a different sound was coming from the room, and it was hard to tell if it was just the wind changing directions again, or somethin' a whole lot worse. This time it sounded more like a moan than a whistle, and to tell you the truth, *this* time it sounded a whole heckuva lot like a grown man bawling his eyes out! I got a serious case of the jitters, and in a flash the goose flesh and the porkypine hairs on the back of my neck were worse than ever. Jagger's eyes got big as silver dollars instead of them little slits he normally lived with, but instead of making a mad dash outta there and not stopping 'til the Mexican border like any sane folks would'a done, instead he says with this wide grin, "N-n-now we got 'im!" and before I could make a run for it, he grabbed me by the collar and yanked me up over that windowsill with him.

What happened next warn't particularly clear, but all foggy like, the way things looked when Gracie forced me to play in her idiotic underwater tea party over at Highland Vista pool, but I suppose getting the bejeezus scared outta ya will do that to a kid. Anyways, as we cleared that window ledge and took a long look inside, there he was, big as life, all black and horrible and trembly. The ghost of Old Man Mansfield!

# Chapter Fourteen

## GHOST STORIES

I was froze stiff as a board. My mouth gaping wide and my temples pounding and my eyes bulging so that they started to ache, and I watched that dark, cloudy outline of what once was a man slink slowly across the far wall all floaty-like, up and down and side to side, and all the while yelling out that same woeful howl. My legs were like lead and my chest tight as a drum, and I couldn't move an inch or squeeze out a sound if my life depended on it, which it probably did. I couldn't even muster up enough strength to turn my head to look over at Jag, but I figured he was in the same sorry state on account'a he was stock still and not saying nuthin', neither, for a change. Finally, like someone flipped a switch, our muscles all let loose and we were off like a flash. We flew across the porch, leaped over the handrail and hit the dirt running, racing through the desert like our hair was on fire!

Neither of us said a word all the while, but just kept up a kinda, "Whooa" from deep down in our throats that started off soft and low but built its way up steady to a loud, high-pitched wail. We didn't look back, neither. What for? To maybe see that monster about to take a bite outta our butts? No thank you!

We barreled over barrel cactus, charged through cholla, over ran ocotillo and peeled through prickly pear, and didn't stop for nuthin' 'til we finally reached the old homestead fence. I was leaning on a wood post, sucking air and counting my lucky stars to have made it back alive, thanking the Almighty for once again saving my worthless soul, and promising I'd never, ever, ever think of coming within a mile of that God forsaken place again, when I glanced over at Jag and with this wild look in his eye he manages to slowly spit out between puffing like a freight train, "L-l-let's go back and try to trap 'im, Johnny C. Whatdaya say?"

I whacked the side of my head against my open palm a couple times to open up my ears, 'cause I was sure I must'a been hallucinating from the horrible stress my poor mind had been through, but when I looked over at him again, he just winked and smiled that same Jagger smile, and I realized, incredible as it was, that what I had heard was true!

"Are you from a different planet? Is that it? 'Cause that's the only thing that could possibly explain you wanting to go anywhere near that God-awful place again. No normal human being would even consider it! Didn't we just escape from the most horrible ghost in God's creation by the skin of our teeth, and wasn't that all your fault to start with, and shouldn't you be apologizing on your hands and knees and kissing my feet for forgiveness instead of asking me to go and get myself killed for you all over again? I'm counting my lucky stars that *he* ain't coming after *us*, you bird brain!"

"Is that a yes or a no?" he said with that crazy grin, and then, "Okay, okay, I g-guess I understand, but then I say w-w-we call a code red meeting of the S.S.B.'s Supreme Counsel for t-t-tonight and make our plans while the t-t-trail's still h-h-ot."

"You're serious, aren't you? Don't it mean nuthin' to you that we could all get eaten alive by that thing and our folks not having no clue at all of what happened to their precious little children 'cept maybe a small shred of clothes or a lock of hair or something that the ghost happened to spit up while he was devouring us like so much fried chicken at a ghouls only picnic!"

"D-d-don't be silly, Johnny C.," he said with a little chuckle. "Everybody knows ghosts d-don't eat people, they just *scare* you to d-d-death." I could see once again it weren't no use trying to reason with him once he got an idea in that two ounce, two neuron brain of his, so I just shook my head and ran on home, looking over my shoulder plenty, and scared stiff all over again about what Jag was about to get us all into next.

Jag, he jumped on bullet and took off like a rocket down the street. He had that lunatic look on his face all over again as he peeked over his shoulder and yelled, "I'll c-c-call the guys, be there by n-n-ine!" And then barely audible from about a block away, "Bring a flashlight!"

I went straight home, not slowing down to kick a rock or nuthin', still spooked through and through from my close shave. We were real fortunate, me and Jag, and at least *I* knew it, that tomorrow's headline on the Santa Elena Star wasn't gonna be, "LOCAL BOYS MISSING. NUTHIN' LEFT OF 'EM BUT A FEW DROPS OF BLOOD AND TWO SLINGSHOTS."

My heart was still pumping to beat the band as I slunk in the back door, through the laundry room and into the kitchen, and as sure as the sun sets in the west, there was Granny, with her wig on the table off to one side and Aunt Leah on the other, sitting at the breakfast table having themselves a Winston and jabbering somethin' nasty about Pop's sister Gina and her "seven little delinquents." My gut started to knot up, knowing what I was in for--and here it come.

"Well, well, well, look what the cat dragged in, and looking like a street urchin at that! Don't you know it's after dark and you are supposed to be in more than a half hour ago?" Granny snapped, tapping her cigarette in the ashtray and then pointing at me with the knobby index finger on her free hand. "I *never* seen a boy like this in all my born days" (Only it didn't come out never, but nev-ah on acount'a a that Boston thing.)

Before I could conjure up any kinda defense, sweet old auntie added, "You better not have been in that desert, you hear me. There are all kinds of wild animals in there that come out after dark that would eat you alive, easy as looking at you? Isn't that right, Frieda?" Ma nodded wholeheartedly from over a big pot of steaming sauce on the oven. "Not to mention the snakes, tarantulas, centipedes and black widows whose bite could make a little boy swell up like a pregnant elephant in the summer time." After that she leaned her head way back with her eyes all rolled up and her hands grabbing the side of her head and let out a long mournful sigh to make her point in her usual, ridiculously dramatic style. It was enough to make you upchuck. I heard Pop say one time, after a particularly elegant outburst, that she had truly missed her calling, and that she really should've been an actress on Broadway. He said he'd bet his bottom dollar that within a year she would'a won every award there was to win in the category of, "Best dramatic adaptation of a scene that nobody gave a rat's ass about." Now you would'a thunk with a real fine complement like that about her older sister, Ma would have been plenty grateful and proud, but that ain't how it played out at all. In fact, she was so peeved with Pop that night, she stormed off straight for bed leaving him to cook dinner for Gracie and me, and ever since, fried bologna and Jiffy Pop is one of our all time favorites!

Anyways, I just stood there kinda numb, taking relentless abuse from all sides, but still way too shook to put up any kind of defense. They kept on hammering at me, over and over, but I just stared straight ahead like in a trance or somethin' as all the ranting and raving melted into one long droning sound that swam slowly past my ears. I just had to get outta there, that's all I knew, so I started taking slow, silent baby steps backward one after the other toward the den, where I knew I could depend on Pop to help me out.

"Don't you walk away from me when I am talking to you, young man! Do you understand?" they all seemed to say at the same time, like they'd been rehearsing that line for years, which I wouldn't put past 'em.

"Sorry, ladies, but I gotta go to the can somethin' awful." And with their mouths opened wider than one of them giant groupers on "American Fisherman," I skedaddled into the next room.

"Hey, Johnny my boy! Come on over here and give your tired old man a big, wet smack-a-reeno," Pop shouted from his chair as he put the newspaper down and opened up his arms real wide to greet me. Smack-a-reeno was what Pop called a real big kiss and he just had to have one from you, first thing after he came home from work, before he could do just about anything else. He just seemed to live for them kisses from me and Gracie, saying they gave him all the energy he needed to keep going through the long, hard day of selling moldy produce. I ran over to 'im and jumped in his lap and I planted a good one on his cheek and then he gave me a hug. Not one of them polite pat on the back hugs neither, but a good hard squeeze like he really meant it, the kind where you felt your rib cage start to creek before he let up. It always gave me a real nice sense of security, and considering the day I'd had, I needed it.

I plopped my rear end down there in his lap, which was getting harder to do nowadays on account'a I was growing pretty fast and so was Pop's belly, but I found a nice spot to cozy up into anyhow, and sat there with my arms stretched out around his neck. There ain't no better feeling in the world for a kid than snuggling with your Pop after having the wits scared outta ya, and I ain't ashamed to admit it.

After a good long while of just lying there, I said, "Pop?"

"Yes, buddy."

"Do you believe in ghosts?" I only kinda whispered in his ear, feeling silly I guess, and he reached over to the lamp table next to his chair and turned off Walter Cronkite with a clank of the remote control right in the middle of, "And that's the way…"

"Do I believe in what?" he asked.

"You know, ghosts or goblins, or evil spirits, like the ones you see on T.V."

"No, no Johnny. There's no such thing, honey," he said reassuringly. "That's just a figment of people's imagination," and he gave me a nice little pat on the knee. "Now don't you worry about that kind of stuff, it's all make believe. And if you ever do get scared, remember all you have to do is say a little prayer and God will protect you, no matter what, and you won't be frightened any more." Now that sounded right straight, and I wondered why I hadn't thought of it myself, considering all the church going and Catechism classes I been dragged to these past years. Heck, if that evil spirit wanted to start somethin' down the road, maybe I'd just conjure up some Holy Spirit of my own, or maybe even them four horsemen of the acropolis, and let *him* try a little fire and brimstone on for size. That Pop. Always right on the money.

Feeling a little more easy with things I asked, "Hows about the old Mansfield place, ya think it's haunted?"

"Oh, come on. Those are just old wives' tales, sweetie. You know that. But you haven't been snooping around that old house now have you?"

"Nope," I said and quickly looked down at Dodger who was tugging at my shoelaces.

"Well, make sure you don't, understand? First of all it's private property and second of all that place is so old and dilapidated it's just plain dangerous." It was dangerous all right I thought, but wasn't really paying no mind to Pop's last sentence on account'a I was thinking on what he'd said before about how the Mansfield place being haunted was nuthin' but an old wives' tale, and I gotta say it gave me the shivers 'cause all I know'd was that the old wives, and widows for that matter, around these parts knew way more than that Soccertease fella, and were better at predicting stuff than old Notredamus. So them saying the Mansfield place was haunted was about as rock solid as the Good Housekeeping Seal of Approval as far as I was concerned. Besides I saw that flipping ghost with my own eyes, didn't I!

I slid off of Pop's lap after that with my guts all in a jumble, and threw myself down on the couch in a heap. Pop clanked the Zenith back on and by now the news was over and one of those outer space shows was starting up, but I couldn't enjoy 'em none. My mind kept on coming round to the ghost and the haunted house and how that lamebrain Jagger was gonna get us all killed one way or another by snooping around where we ain't got no business. I laid there a spell, mulling over things while Pop read the paper, and Ma, Granny and Aunt Leah worked away in the kitchen just like everything was peachy keen, and not having a clue that not more than a stones throw from our own back yard all hell was about to break loose.

I was in a real fix, sure as you know what, and I didn't see no way out. The last thing in the world I wanted to do was meet up with that demon once again, same as any person in his right mind, but now with Jagger about to call a Code Red meeting of the S.S.B.'s and all, I had to make a show or else I'd be called such a big weenie I might as well get Oscar Mayer tattooed on my forehead! Like I said before, I couldn't see no reasonable way out of the pitiful predicament I was in, so I figured I'd best just go along for awhile and try to come up with some way of keeping Jagger from turning us all into one big Mansfield Mansion meal!

Just then, Ma carried in a big bowl of piping hot spaghetti and meatballs and set it up real nice on a T.V. tray right next to where I was lying. There was plenty of melted parmesan on top, just the way I liked it, and a big piece of Granny's famous garlic bread sitting right in the middle, but even that couldn't wipe my mind clean, but it smelt so lovely I did manage to wolf down a few healthy bites before my stomach tied up in knots all over again.

I decided to wait 'til a few minutes after eight before heading for bed, not wanting to look too suspicious, and tried to act normal, but after about an hour, I realized that trying to act normal was about the hardest kind of acting there was. I sure weren't too good at it, that was clear, 'cause every member of the Gestapo must've asked me ten times in that hour if I was okay. Anyway, I finally said my goodnights and headed on down the hallway with Dodger right in tow as usual. He was acting a bit under the weather, lately, lollygagging around even more that normal and not biting anyone in the butt for two days running, but I bent down and felt his nose to be wet, and knew it weren't nuthin' serious.

We passed by Gracie's room and I peeked in through the crack in the door to see her bed and her little chubby face peeking out from underneath the covers, softly lit with the yellow glow of a Snow White nightlight that Ma had picked up for her at the five and dime last trip up to Tucson. I gotta admit she looked awfully cute lying there with her eyes closed, all peaceful-like, surrounded by her dolls arranged just so, in order of their importance that day, and it got me to smiling a bit and feeling kinda warm all over. I stood and watched her for a while and then turned up the hall again, and after a step or two I heard her say in a sleepy, little girl voice, "Good night, Johnny, sleep tight, don't let the bed bugs bite."

"Night, Gracie, kid," I answered, thinking to myself that I wished all I had to worry about tonight was a few crummy bed bugs.

I washed my face and brushed my teeth to keep up appearances, and then crawled into bed and turned out the light. Dodger stood there looking at me for a while like I was nuts or somethin' since I hadn't changed into my p.j.'s and instead just pulled the covers up over myself fully clothed. I figured it'd be a waste of time changing and unchanging, and besides the noise might of let on that somethin' was up. I think I told ya before that Ma had the kinda ears that could hear a gnat fart at fifty yards!

Dodger just stood there next to the bed staring at me for a bit, and then forgot what was eating 'im and let out a big "Harrumph," and plopped himself down on the blue shag carpet after circling a time or two to get everything just right. I reached over and gave 'im a little pat and then clicked on my transistor, and the joyful sounds of baseball filled the room. It calmed my worried mind a bit to close my eyes and see myself sitting in the front row at Dodger Stadium with a Dodger Dog in one hand and a bag of peanuts in the other. I could almost feel the cool night breeze hitting me in the face as I watched the guys taking on those low down, good for nuthin' Giants. If ya listened real hard you could hear the crack of the bat, the ball hitting the mitt, and even the beer vendors screaming out their sales in the background. It was awful pleasant to just lie there and listen, and I thought to myself what I wouldn't give to be there watching that ball game instead of here in the mess I got myself in.

About half past eight I heard Pop come up the hallway. Ma had already gone to bed, being an early riser and all, and said her "Goodnights," to Gracie and me about twenty minutes before. Pop stopped at Gracie's room first, like always, to make sure she was sleeping restful and wasn't wanting anything. He always walked into her room tippy-toe, then got right up next to her bed and leaned over 'til his face was right up against hers. I watched 'im one time and then asked why he did it. He said it was just a habit from when we was just little babies and he couldn't sleep a wink 'til he was sure we were still breathing. He even did that to me once in a while still, and on occasion I would sense somethin' and wake up nearly scared to death seeing his face no more than two inches away from mine. He'd just say, "Sorry, Johnny, now go on back to sleep," but that warn't all that easy with your heart racing a million miles a minute, if ya know what I mean. You couldn't really get sore about it though, a grown man worrying about his kids like that.

Anyway, after he finished up with Gracie he came on up the hall to my room and stuck his head in the door. "Johnny, you asleep already, pal?" he said softly. I didn't move a muscle but just started to breath extra heavy and deep through my nose and smacked my lips around a bit to let on I had dozed off. Pop, he walked in and turned off the radio, and patted Dodger on the head. Then he walked on over to me and I was praying he wouldn't try to adjust the blankets the way he always liked to, on account'a he'd sure notice I hadn't changed. But I was safe, he only bent over and gave me a little kiss on the forehead, and then for some reason he just stood there next to the bed and stared at me, or at least I think he was staring because I didn't dare open my eyes even a slit to see what was up. Anyway, after about a minute or two, he just let out a deep sigh, not one of them disappointed tired out sighs, neither, but one of those "boy, life sure is great," sighs, and then walked out, went into his bedroom and closed the door.

Well, I about flew outta that bed, and shook up old Dodger so that he started to let out a little yelp, but I grabbed 'im by the nose before he could muster up much more than a squeak, and then gave 'im a few strokes to calm 'im back down. I slipped on my tennies, grabbed the flashlight I'd hid in my dresser earlier and stuffed it in my back pocket, and then cranked open my bedroom window nice and easy as far as she would go. I had snuck out that way bunches of times in the past without no problem, but I'd grown considerable since then, and I knew this time it'd be a tight fit. I threw my left leg over the sill and out the window easy enough and then started to squeeze the rest of me through, and it was pretty smooth sailing and I was just about home free, when all of a sudden I felt somethin' clamp onto my right foot like a steel trap from inside. I wheeled my head around right quick and whacked it a good one on the window frame as I looked down to see that stinking Dodger standing there with my P.F. Flyer stuck firm between his teeth.

"Let go you stupid mutt!" I said in the meanest whisper I could muster, but he just pulled on it harder, tail wagging up a storm, like we was playing tug of war or something. I couldn't believe what I was seeing. "I'll get you a nice treat when I get back if ya let go Dodge," I said in a much sweeter tone this time to see if that would get through that thick skull of his a little better, but he just kept tugging and shaking and growling and having a good old time. "Dammit, Dodger, you better let go this instant or I'm gonna pound your face in, understand," I said as I yanked with all my might, figuring I'd either finally shake loose or pull that flea bag's teeth clean out. Well, my foot came free alright and I landed with a hard thud, flat on my back in the flower garden below, but as I stood up and brushed myself off, still cursing that blasted dog, something didn't feel quite right, and when I looked down at my feet a knot set up firm in my stomach--there was nuthin' on my right foot but an old tube sock!

I looked around to see if my shoe might'a slipped off in the fall, but no such luck, and as I glanced back through the window, there it was, still stuck firm in the mouth of man's worst enemy, who seemed to all the world to have a little grin on his skinny dog lips as he stared up at me. What did I do to deserve to be stuck with an animal so mean and ornery as this? I ain't some degenerate delinquent who needs to get his do, am I? I mean, wasn't I the Red Cross representative from the whole sixth grade last year, and didn't I turn over nearly all the money I collected even though most of the guys (especially Rosie) wouldn't talk to me for a week on account'a I refused to make a generous contribution with it to the S.S.B.'s ice cream fund. And wasn't I the one a few weeks back, who helped senile old Mrs. Simpson, who's nearly blind and slobbers a good sight, too, to cross the street down at the town square, even though she beat me merciless the whole time with her handbag thinking I was a degenerate or somethin'? It just don't add up. Ma keeps on telling me to do the right thing, and I'll come out smelling like a rose, but I keep coming out smelling like somethin' entirely different!

Now what, I thought. I didn't have time to go back in and try to wrestle my shoe away from Dodger, and even if I did I'd sure wake up the whole house. But with a bare foot in the desert on a summer night and all the nasty thorns, cactus needles, scorpions, centipedes, and gila monsters, I had as much chance of making it without getting mutilated as a porterhouse steak in a tank of starving piranhas. But I couldn't see no way out, and decided to just try to survive best I could and then get even with that old fleabag if and when I ever made it back.

I took off like a shot across the street, between the Monroe's and

Nelson's and into the alley, all the while shining that flashlight in front to keep from stepping on any potentially painful desert life. I was clip-clopping along at a pretty good pace when I practically ran headfirst into Big I. We must be on the same wavelength or somethin'.

"Where in the heck's your shoe, Johnny C?" he asked, first thing, pointing to my sock which was already looking plenty brown and tattered.

"It's a long story."

"Don't tell me it was Dodger again," he said disgusted as I nodded my head slowly. "That dog's a retard. I swear. You should take him back and get a refund 'cause he's definitely defective!"

"Tell me somethin' I don't know," I answered.

"Well, good luck not dying of some kinda poisonous somethin'," he said matter of factly. That Ira, he sure knew how to pick up his pals when they had a stretch of bum luck.

It was an eerie kinda night, with the moon big and bright as a headlamp off of one of Al Capone's old Packards, resting just up over the Rincon Mountains to the east, and skinny strips of clouds slowly creeping by like they were afraid to see what was up ahead. There was just a tickle of a breeze, blowing almost cool in our face as we made our way, and bringing with it the sweet musty smell of rain still some ways off down south. The cicadas were chirping to beat the band, so loud it close to rattled your brains, and off in the distance a coyote got to howling which sent all the dogs and cats inside and a slow shiver down my spine.

We kept on for nearly two blocks when Big I turns to me and says, "So what's Jagger got his boxers all in a bunch about this time? It better be good 'cause my folks still haven't forgotten about the Red River fiasco he got us into, and if I get caught out late I'm dead meat for the rest of the summer!"

"Oh, it's good, alright, believe me," I shot back.

Ira gave me a look with his skinny top lip all curled up and said, "Yeah, I bet."

"Just wait, you ain't gonna believe it."

Just then we reached the oleander hedge out behind the Howell house, and slipped down the alleyway 'til we came to the clubhouse. Creepy and Chicken Coop were just about to crawl in the door and they looked back, kinda startled 'til they saw it was us.

"Hello, ladies," Ira gave his trademark greetings.

"You wish, Romeo," Coop said and then scooted in the door just ahead of Ira's foot.

We followed right behind and took our assigned spaces along the wall, making a kinda horseshoe, and Jagger, seeing everyone was accounted for, slid into the middle and said, "Hear-ye, hear-ye. I hereby c-c-call to order this code red m-m-meeting of the official b-board of governors of the

# J. E. Tooley

S.S.B.s"

"Yeah, yeah, cut the crappola and just tell us what all the hubbubs about, bub," Neil snarled. "And president or no president, I swear I'll pound you if you're just farting around again!" Neil got real testy when he wasn't the one calling all the shots.

"Silence!" Jagger roared, in his best Wizard of Oz voice. "You will all s-s-soon realize the importance of this m-m-meeting, and I dare say n-n-none of your lives will ever be the same after you do!" While spitting out the last word, Jagger leaned way forward getting right up into each and every face.

With that, Chicken Coop, Rosie and the Creep all pushed back hard against the wall, holding their breaths and squeezing in all close, and even Ira and Neil looked just a little shook and began to squirm.

Jag, seeing he'd got under everyone's skin just right, decided to play it up for awhile and just sat there grinning ear to ear, but not saying a word.

After gathering hisself for a minute, Neil finally said, "Out with it then Jag, or else I'm gone, and I mean it! You already led us on enough witch hunts this summer to fill two lifetimes and a half!" All the others nodded their agreement, leaning in towards old Jag again to hear just what was so big that they should gamble this whole summer vacation and probably most of the next.

"Not until you all t-turn off your f-flashlights," Jag demanded, still with the tough guy voice.

"What the heck for!" we all screamed at the same time.

"Because I said, that's why!" It looked like old Jag was gonna really play it up before delivering the goods, and who could blame 'im? No one ever had goods this good before!

Jagger stared down each and every one of the unsuspecting souls 'til each and every light was out and there was nuthin' but complete darkness and silence all around. There wasn't even the tiniest sliver of moonlight to be seen nowheres, and I nearly stretched my eyes outta their sockets searching from side to side, but could see only blackness for an inch and forever. All of a sudden a stiff breeze kicked up, and came swirling through the wood planks walls, setting off an eerie, low whistling sound, which was just what the doctor ordered for Jag and the little creep show he was putting on.

Jag kept his trap shut tight, milking the moment for all it was worth, 'til you could hear the hiss of heavy breathing and the soft thump of hearts pounding. Heck, even I was getting creeped out and I already knew the ending! Nobody dared make a peep for what seemed like forever, 'til finally feeling the time was just right, and with the guys about to jump outta their skin, Jagger snapped on his flashlight. He had it stuck up under his chin so the light splashed over his already ugly face, the way kids always did when they were in the dark telling ghost stories, and it made his whole head glow something fierce, like the butt end of some giant firefly. Still he didn't say nuthin', but just sat there with his eyes closed and with as much expression on his face as a ten day old dead man. A few faint rays of light bounced off of his mug so you could make out the guys circled all around, as they stared out straight with eyelids pealed back and bodies stone stiff. Then, just like that, Jagger opens his eyes with a quick jerk, causing the rest of the guys to snap their heads back like a rear end collision and take in a gasp and a real hard swallow, and to start to wonder if they really wanted to hear what he had to say after all.

Then Jag starts real slow and trembly, with his voice low as his vocal cords would stretch, and says, "I have s-s-seen the ghost of old m-m-man Maaaansfield." He held the "a" sound long as he could for extra creepiness.

Well, I'll tell ya, for a minute or two it was like there were five Michael and Julo statues in that clubhouse with Jag, frozen in total horror with eyes bulging and mouths gaping, and every hair on our bodies standing at full attention on top of their very own little goose bump. Now Jag knew he had 'em right where he wanted and didn't want to break the mood none, so he kept his trap shut and just stared straight out into the darkness, not twitching even the tiniest muscle, like he was in some kind of ghostly trance of somethin'. Then for the grand finale, he slowly raised his hand and pointed the flashlight square in the terrorized face of each and every one of us, and then quick back at his own face that now had on that ear to ear, nutcase, toothy grin with his eyes all wide and wild, darting back and forth over and over like some lunatic, and then suddenly his flashlight light snapped off, leaving nuthin' but eerie darkness all over again.

# Chapter Fifteen

## HOW TO CATCH A GHOST

All of a sudden outta the total blackness came an eye watering screech, no doubt from Chicken Coop, due to the familiar tone quality, and before you could say, "Bielzebug," six flashlights snapped on and lit that place up like Tumamak hill after the annual *Fireworks and Fiesta* on July 4th and the just as annual *Holy Crap the Desert's of Fire!* that followed. Rosie, Creepy, and Coop were huddled together in the far corner all quivery, with their eyes racing top to bottom and side to side like they were expecting that old man's ghost to pop up and grab 'em any second. I gotta admit, even knowing what was what, I still felt all fluttery inside with my skin crawling outside, after all of Jag's horrifying horse manure. Neil and Ira had gathered themselves up by now, not wanting to look the least bit yellow in front of us, and were back to their old snotty selves.

"Jag, you're so full of it you're eyes are brown, and not only that, but it's starting to ooze outta your nose and ears!" Neil snorted. "I can't believe you dragged us out here in the middle of the night for this big steaming pile of crap!"

"That goes double for me, numbnuts!" added Ira. "I already told Johnny here that my folks are just aching for a reason to lock me up for the rest of the summer after almost drowning at Red River, which by the way was another of your pissant president plans! Now you come up with some asinine ghost story that ranks right up there with the time you were "one hundred and fifty percent certain," you'd seen a real live Martian lying out behind El Guero's taco stand, and it turned out to be only Spanky

Smallhouse's pop drunk outta his mind, and colored green all over from the old *chile verde* they'd thrown out back. Remember that one, Einstein? You need help Jag, bad. No kidding. And I mean professional help. Comprende!" Then Ira and Neil started crawl for the door in complete disgust.

"W-w-wait, you non-believers!" Jag shouted, now using his best Sunday morning preacher voice. "It was not only me who saw him. J-Johnny C. was there, too!" Now that was a horse of a different color, and Big I and Neil froze in their tracks as all the guys snapped their eyes and flashlights over at me.

After an uneasy second or two that got my upper lip moist and my throat dry as the Rillito River bed, Rosie managed to stammer, "Did ya *really* see that old man's ghost, Johnny C.? Honest Injun?" He was just about begging to hear that it was nuthin' but another one 'a Jag's famous tall tales, like the one about the crocodile I told ya way back, with not an ounce of truth to be found if ya searched from now 'til kingdom come.

Now all the guys leaned in, this time towards me, waiting for the words that could change their lives forever, and right at that moment, after seeing the anxious looks on all their faces, I realized somethin' about the guys that never crossed my mind before, even though I'd known 'em all since we was practically babies. They *trusted* me. And considering that Rosie, Creepy and Coop were too chicken to think straight most of the time, Neil was always looking for some angle to benefit hisself, Ira was so darn skeptical about everything and anything, and Jagger, with his past history of flakiness was hard to take serious on something as big as this. I guess that left me as the most level headed of the group, which made me feel kinda good for a second, but then lousy all over again, knowing what I was about to say could lead to nuthin' but trouble, and maybe even a horrible, grizzly death to us all!

I looked down at first, trying to conjure up in my mind some way outta the mess I was in, but nuthin' came 'cept how I wished we'd never, ever gone within a hundred miles of that darn old house, and then finally I said, shaking my head and not able to lie to my best pals, "Yup, I saw 'em. Saw 'em clear as day. Not more than ten feet in front of my face."

Well, that knocked the breath clean outta 'em, the breath they'd been holding all the while I was thinking, and they all sunk back, limp, like a bunch of rag dolls, almost lifeless, against the wooden planks that creaked somethin' awful from the sheer weight, especially around Rosie's spot. I shot a quick, kinda sorry glance over at Jag, who had a bit of a smirk on his face and was nodding his head over and over again with great satisfaction.

After a few more minutes of dead silence, Ira finally says, "Okay, Johnny C., let's hear it right from the top." So I started telling the guys how Jag and I started off lizard hunting on the Mansfield property and how Jag chased that lizard into the cactus and almost got snake bit, and how we ran off all crazy, not realizing we was heading right for the front of the old mansion. Then I told 'em about the mournful moaning sound from inside the place, and how we crept up to the window and peeked in to see that horrible creature.

"What'd he look like?" asked Rosie, with his eyes practically bulging out of his head.

"Did he have fangs and long curved fingernails?" added Creepy.

"Did he float across the floor and try to eat ya?" cried out Chicken Coop, and then hid his face in his hands.

"Well, he was about ten feet tall and all dark and dreary-like and he was plastered against the wall with his hands holding his head, making the worst, most spine tingling, groaning sound a body had ever heard in his whole life!"

There was a loud gasp all round.

"Did he *say* anything to you?" asked Ira. Still not sure he was buying any of it.

"Naw, just moaned a lot."

"Did he have any chains binding him up?" he added. "'Cause real ghosts are nuthin' but chained up souls wishing they was in heaven, but too darn ornery in their lifetimes to have a chance, so they're stuck floating around in limbo for all eternity to scare the bejeesus outta any poor kid that might come across 'em."

"Well, I don't remember seeing any chains," I said, as Ira got a real doubtful look. "But I did hear some hideous rattling and clanking going on all around," I added quick. Now I know I stretched that last part a bit, but I didn't want there to be any doubt about what we were dealing with. After all, I'd seen it with my own two eyes, hadn't I?

"I tell ya what I think," Neil said, leaning back on his elbows with his legs stretched out straight in front. I think you two have been watching way too much "*Chiller*." That's what I think!"

*Chiller* was this very corny horror flick show that was filmed up in Tucson or down in Nogales, I ain't sure which, and it played on Channel 9 every Saturday at midnight. It was hosted by this cornball guy called Dr. Ghoul, who wore a long black cape with red satin lining, that didn't quite make it all the way around his considerable pot belly, and had to be safety pinned in the front, which only partly kept a good amount of blubber from peeking through in places. His face was plastered all over with this thick white goo with little blobs of red here and there that was supposed to look scary as all get out, but instead just made 'im the spitting image of a big fat piece of strawberry shortcake. After a minute or two, his make-up would begin to run all over on account'a the hot studio lights, I suppose, and you'd 'a swore the poor guy was starting to melt! Now, *that* actually did make 'im look kinda scary. He was always standing in what was supposed to be this super creepy old graveyard, and right next to 'im was his skeleton side-kick, Slim, who wore an old beat up black chimney-top hat, and had eyes that would glow a fiery red every time Dr. Ghoul said somethin' particularly clever and spine tingling. Stuck to his arm was this mangy looking hoot owl, Screech, that the doctor ordered around to go do this or that horrible thing to kids that were staying up past bedtime to watch his dumb show, and not listening to their folks and all. That always happened right before a commercial to get you extra creeped out, and then when the show came back on, he'd be perched up on his masters left arm, stone stiff, just like always. Neil said that owl was nuthin' but a big phony, just like the rest of the show, 'cause once when the doctor whirled around quick to get his cape to fling way out for added effect, Screech took a nasty shot to the old noggin against an especially tall tombstone that would'a sent a real bird reeling sure as I'm tellin' you this, but he didn't make a sound nor move a feather and just sat there in his spot, only a little lopsided. If that weren't enough to convince you about *"Chiller,"* it was plain as day to anyone with half a brain in his head that Dr Ghoul had much more than a passing resemblance to Buddy O'Rourke, the doofus Channel 9 weatherman, right down to his "Howdy Doody" ears and "spit all over your face" lisp that put a real damper on things when he tried to describe the next movie as having, "Seriously scary scenes," the way he always insisted on doing.

"W-w-well, I guess t-there's only one thing to do then," Jagger said, pleased as punch as Big I and Neil made for the door. "W-we'll all just mosey on down to the M-M-Mansfield place and take a little look see!"

Well, I knew that was coming, but it didn't make me feel no better about running into that evil spirit again, and this time asking for it ourselves.

Jag's idea didn't sit too well, as you might've figured, with the three more cowardly, or in this case, more sensible, members of the S.S.B.'s that were all still huddled up together against the far wall.

"I for one would like to say that I believe each and every word that Jagger and Johnny C. just said," Rosie blurted out, like steam exploding from a hot tea pot, and nodding his head so fast in agreement that he nearly scrambled his brains. "There ain't no need to go rousting out that ghost just for the fun of it, far as I can tell."

"That goes double for us," said two soft voices all trembly from behind him, without hide nor hair of the bodies that went with them to be seen.

"Shut up you three lily livers," Neil barked and then looked over at Jag and me, real hard. "I still ain't buying this whole ghost story garbage, so before I put any stock in it, I say, *prove* it, *comprende?* And last I checked, we're still the Seward School Bombers and not a bunch of yellow bellied sap suckers, so I say we all stick together and head down to that old house and see what we see, got it!" He shouted out this last part, making sure to look each of us square in the eye to show he meant business.

The three huddled back even farther until the wall of the club house started to creek and moan, and then with Chicken Coop and the Creep slowly poking their heads out around the side of their gigantic friend, they nodded with about as much enthusiasm as a guy on his way to his little sister's dance recital. I glanced over at Big I who looked a little queasy, but he wasn't about to say nuthin' now that things had been settled up.

"W-well I guess that's it then," Jag said real satisfied. "Let's go hunt some ghost!" And then he flung open the clubhouse door and crawled on through. The rest of us following behind, some with a bit more spring in their step than others, and Rosie finally squeezing through to bring up the rear, and a pretty substantial rear it was!

We slinked along the alley and on down the street like a bunch of guys headed for a hanging, nobody saying a word but just watching out to keep from kicking a rock or tin can to keep from calling attention to ourselves. There was a stinking full moon, of course, just like always on a night when you already had the heebeejeebees, and we made sure not to take even a little peek at it, not wanting to give any evil spirits the least bit of an excuse to pay us a visit. The guys looked over their shoulders a lot and checked out all alleys before walking by, being plenty spooked after Jagger's little creep show, and as we passed by that grand old Sahuaro standing all alone in its vacant lot with its tall black shape and outstretched arms silhouetted in the moonlight, I realized for the very first time what a horrible and frightening spectacle it was.

"W-w-watch it, Johnny!" Jag yelped suddenly, causing me to jump back quick as a cat and throw my arms over my head and scrunch down low to protect my innards from any invisible attacker. The rest of the guys came to a screeching halt and shot darting glances every which way into the darkness, fully expecting to see old man Mansfield's spirit coming to pay us a little visit. After a second or two of nuthin', I slowly opened my eyes, one, then the other, but the coast was clear far as I could tell. Finally, I stood up straight and pulled my arms down and asked, "What, Jag, what the heck was it?"

"Oh, n-n-no spirits or nuthin'," he said kinda sheepish. "But you almost stepped on my m-moon shadow again." Well that got my blood to boil and I grabbed on to his thick arm with both hands and twisted with all my might to give him the nastiest Indian burn in the history of the white ghetto.

"*That's* what I think about your idiotic moon shadow, you pinhead! You scared the daylights outta me."

"W-well I'm sorry," he answered, without even a wince at my sad attempt to cause him pain. "You b-believe what you want. But I ain't asking for no b-bad luck tonight if I c-can help it."

Well, I suppose that made pretty good sense considering the mess *he* was getting us into, and I got to watching out for my own moon shadow after that, just in case.

We turned up my street and started to get closer to the Mansfield homestead, keeping our flashlights off, mostly. The last thing we needed was some blabbermouth neighbor lady to rat us out and getting each and every one of us sent down the river by our folks faster than grain through a goose.

We were making decent progress and I hadn't heard no whimpering from the back for a while which either meant Rosie, Creepy and Coop had finally got some cajones, or they were so scared stiff they couldn't utter a sound. When we were about a block away, we came up on something crawling slow across the street a couple of yards ahead, and Jag waved at us to hold up 'til he could tell what it was. He moved nice and easy towards it, and when it turned and hissed at 'im instead of running off, it was clear what we was dealing with was no run of the mill lizard, but instead one of the nastiest creatures God ever created; a Gila Monster. Last summer Ma got into it with an especially viscous one in our carport, and instead of running for cover when he seen what he was up against, it actually *attacked* the broom she was pushing at 'im, and bit onto it for all he was worth. He wouldn't let go, neither, not for anything, and after more than a few un-christian type words that Ma latter said she truly regretted and said seven Hail Mary's to make up for, she flung the whole darn kit and kaboodle into the desert, big lizard, broom and all, and that was the end of it. Anyway, we gave it a big wide birth, all the while keeping an eye out for an attack, and then kept on our way.

After a nice long spell of silence while we all were thinking of what we were getting ourselves into this time, Ira stops and says, "So what if we *do* happen to see old man Mansfield's ghost? Nobody this side of the Arizona State Nuthouse is gonna believe us for even a second, anyway."

"Maybe if we ask real nice we can get 'im to sign one of those afterdavids," Neil said, real snotty. We all nodded our agreement 'cause we knew all about afterdavids from *Perry Mason*, and they were rock solid for telling the truth and would stand up in any court, anytime, anywhere. Neil just stared at us for a second with this blank look on his face, then rolled his eyes and just kept on walking.

"*No hay p-p-problema!* I g-got that covered," Jag said as he pulled out his Brownie instamatic camera from the front of his Levis and held it up proudly.

"You can't take a picture of a ghost, you retard. Everyone knows that!" Ira said. "It's like trying to take a picture of thin air."

"I thought they just didn't have no reflection in a mirror," I added, remembering somethin' from an old horror flick.

"No, Johnny C. That's *vampires*," Creepy said in his garbled, mouth full of marbles accent. "And they also will melt if you throw water on them."

"That's not vampires, you little twit. That's the Wicked Witch of the West!" Neil said, disgusted at our stupidity.

"Neil's right, Bampu," said Rosie, he always felt kinda bad calling Creepy, Creepy. "Vampires is the ones that die right off if they get even ten yards of the skinniest ray of sunlight. Ain't that right, Johnny C."

I looked over at Coop who was turning three shades of green by now from all the monster talk, and decided to hold off on what I was about to say on werewolves, and just nodded over at Rosie.

"W-well, I guess w-we-ll just have to see," Jagger said calmly, and shoved his camera back into his pants.

After a few more yards Chicken Coop said, hopefully, "Maybe he's a friendly ghost, like Casper."

"Yeah, and maybe horny toads are crawling outta your butt!" barked Neil, as Coop looked on sadly and then took a quick look behind him to make sure Neil was just kidding.

We moved along at a pretty good clip now 'til we reached the old mesquite fence around the Mansfield property. I looked over to the south about a hundred yards from where we were standing, and could see my house all buttoned up for the night, not a speck of light to be seen anywhere. I told myself that I should be all snuggled in bed right about now, safe and sound, instead of out here in the dark getting ready to trudge through a desert crawling with poisonous critters, searching for a ghost that I didn't want nuthin' to do with, no how, and all that with only one shoe! By the way, did I tell ya lately how much my poor foot was throbbing? I swear I'm gonna skin that no good Dodger alive when I get home. Or maybe I should say, *if* I get home.

We stopped at the fence and hopped up to peer over the top rung, and way off in the distance you could make out the solid blackness that was the Mansfield place surrounded by a faint glow of moonlight. I rubbed my eyes and looked out again, and swore I could see a little flicker of light every few seconds in one of the downstairs windows. I kept my trap shut about it though, not wanting to rile up the others anymore, knowing darn well we were already in for a plenty rocky time of getting Rosie and the Rosettes, which is what Neil started to call Coop and the Creep lately to suck it up and get anywhere near the place. Then Jag told us to gather 'round and began to lay out his plan to snag that old ghost, making sure to point out that if we could somehow pull this one off, we would forever be heroes of all kids everywhere that were chicken of spooks, and our efforts would be legendary. And before you knew it, word would get out of what we'd done and we'd be known world over for being the one and only kids to ever catch a real live ghost, and pretty soon people from all over would be calling on the good old S.S.B.'s anytime some no good evil spirit or such was making a nuisance of hisself and causing nuthin' but trouble for some good folks somewhere, and we'd fly off in our own personal supersonic jet with "Seward School Bombers," painted big on the side to set things right.

After he jabbered on for a while Jag stopped to see if he'd made any head way, which he hadn't much, though it was a pretty decent try, so he kept on about how if we did a special good job of it, maybe we could even get our own T.V. show, and not just some fly by night summer replacement hack neither, but an honest to goodness regular season program. And maybe, just maybe they'd even stick us on Saturday morning instead of them lame "Monkeys" or even "Lance Link Secret Chimp," and wouldn't that stick in old Nancy's craw but good! Just feel how sweet and satisfying it would be when she crawled on her hands and knees, pleading to be a guest on our show and we gave her the heave hoe every time, no matter how hysterical she kicked and screamed.

Well, *that* did it! I mean helping out poor people in the world with their problems was nice and all, but having your own Saturday morning T.V. show was somethin' all together different, and the guys pepped up considerable after that. We listened sharp while Jagger let on how we'd break up in two groups and make our way nice and easy toward the house from different directions so as not to be as easily spotted, just in case that ghost had an inkling to what we might be up to. Jag and I would be the two ringleaders seeing as how we had already been acquainted with the place, and for that matter with the ghost hisself. Ira and Neil insisted on going with Jag "so as to be able to beat his brains in as soon as they realized they were being duped." Jag said that suited him just fine but it didn't suit me in the least, seeing that left me with Rosie, Chicken Coop and Creepy, not exactly the three musketeers when you were in a tight spot, if you catch my drift. I decided not to make a stink about it, though, and accepted my assignment like a man, but I knew down deep that if the going got tough, my men would be going, too, in the *opposite* direction!

So with that settled we split ourselves up and headed out, but before we were out of ear shot Jag reminded us all to keep from using our flashlights 'cept for an "out and out emergency of the ghostliest kind," and then he disappeared into the darkness with Neil and Big I close behind, already jawing at 'im as they went. I looked over my three fine recruits, gave a big sigh, shook my head at no one in particular, crossed myself three times and walked off in the opposite direction according to Jagger's orders. But after no more then ten steps, I sensed somethin' not right, and turned around, to realize I was standing there all alone. I peered into the darkness and could see the outline of the three great warriors all huddled together, not having moved an inch. I let out a loud "Harrumph!" and stared down at them in disgust, and after a good deal of whispering among themselves with a lot of finger pointing, head shaking and foot stomping, slowly but surely, the black blob of bodies finally started to shuffle toward me like a huge dark snail slithering along the desert floor. I looked down at my poor, pulsating, unprotected foot, and then I prayed to the Lord to give me strength to battle that evil demon 'cause I knew for a fact I wasn't gonna get any help from my pitiful platoon. No ifs, ands, or big butts!

# Chapter Sixteen

## WE SET A GHOST TRAP

The desert still had its lovely, musty smell from the rain earlier on, and the Colorado River toads were croaking up a storm, happy to be out and about for the evening. I was kinda grateful for the noise, obnoxious as it was, mostly, on account of it broke some of the creepy thoughts stuck in my head about what we were going up against. I was doing my darndest to act like what we were up to was the most natural thing in the world, instead of the most assanine, 'cause I knew in my bones my troops were just itching for a reason, *any* reason, to go A.W.O.L.

I looked down at my ripped up sock and cussed Dodger, again. My big toe was poking clean through by now, and I knew it was just a matter of time before somethin' real painful was gonna happen to it. Rosie, Cooper and the Creep continued to saunter along slow as molasses, and holding on to each other for dear life.

I was way out in front once again and finally, disgusted, walked back over to 'em, and said, "Look, you guys really need to get a grip, or we'll never get in position. But until you do, I'm going up ahead and I'll meet you at the big Palo Verde tree there off to the left of the Mansfield place," and I pointed my finger in the general direction where you could see the tree tops still outlined against the lighter gray of the western sky. "Try and get there this year sometime, got it!"

They didn't say a word but just stood there all mushed together, one large shivering mass, and Rosie pulled out his *escapulario*, that brown piece of cloth with the Virgin Mary on it that all Mexicans wear around their necks, sqeezed it for all he was worth, closed his eyes tight and started mumbling some prayers, as I trudged off again to do the best I could to hold up our end of the bargain, all by myself if need be. By keeping a keen eye out, I'd managed up to now to keep from mangling my poor right foot any further, but it was tough to fight the urge to flick on my flashlight here and there to have a good look see around. Every once in a while I'd shoot a glance over to see if I could catch a glimpse of Jag and the guys across the way, but there was nuthin' doing. It was hard enough to see being no taller than the average creosote bush, but every now and then a few wispy clouds, stragglers from the afternoon monsoon, would go floating across the full moon, causing the whole darn place to go black as the ace of spades, and my stomach to do about fifteen cartwheels. As I got closer, I took a quick peek to my right and could now see clear that monstrous black shadow of a house sitting there, lonely as could be, in the middle of that dreary, God forsaken desert. I felt the life being sucked clean outta me, like a balloon that got away before it could be tied up proper, and I had to take a knee for a second to gather myself up again.

Till then I had been trying out that "outta sight, outta mind," mumbo jumbo I'd heard Ma and the two storm troopers blabbing about once when they were gossiping on cousin Sherry and her outta town boyfriend, but I guess that just wasn't gonna cut it when it came to haunted houses with blood thirsty tenants! Then something Pop told me once popped in my head. Something like, "There were times in a boy's life when he had to confront his fears head on if he was ever gonna get over them and become a man." Well, Pop, how about walking right into a haunted house just to say howdy!

The moonlight kept flickering on and off as a few rays would sneak through them clouds now and then, and shine off the upper floor windows, those that weren't all busted up, I mean, and made 'em look for all the world like glowing yellow eyes peering out of a humongous black head. The worst part off all was they looked like they were staring straight at me! I jerked my head away as the goose flesh started to crawl like a million fleas doing a tap dance over every inch of my body, but I knew I had to stay in control or my trusty troops would be making trusty poops in their draws at any sign of fear. Speaking of my Medal of Honor candidates, I took a look over my shoulder to see 'em finally coming into view, the smaller ones holding onto Rosie's arms for dear life as they slowly slid forward like some tractor beam from outer space had a hold on 'em, and they were doing everything in their power to resist.

"Glad to see you guys could make it," I said as they finally reached me, and then we all hunched down low behind that big Palo Verde and looked out towards our final destination. I only hoped it wouldn't be our final resting place, if you know what I mean.

"Now what?" Rosie asked, shooting wild glances all around.

"We got to wait for Jag to give us the signal to move in," I answered matter of fact like, trying to stay cool. "He said he'd give us two quick flashes across the front porch when they were ready."

"I got to go pee, Chicken Coop blurted out, hoping that would get 'im a pass back home and out of danger.

"Take your pick. There are make shift toilets all over," I said, as I pointed to the bushes surrounding us. "Just do me a favor and drain it back there aways, so I don't step in it on the way out. Remember, I only got one shoe." Cooper thought about it for a bit, grumbled "Heavens to Murgatroid!" and then figured he'd rather pee in his pants than walk even two feet into the desert all alone.

Every now and then I'd hear a little squeak come outta him and I could tell he was fighting the hiccups off with all of his might. Old Creepy wasn't fairing much better looking like one of them bug-eyed lemurs with glasses, and only peeking out from behind Rosie once in a while to see how close we were getting. The poor kid hadn't said a word the whole night and I guess all them brains weren't much help if you were too scared stiff to think.

I made a motion and we all sat down on that damp ground huddled together, and waited for Jagger's sign. I looked out, at the house again and my heart danced the jig as I swore I could make out a shadowy figure in one of the back rooms as the moonlight snuck through the clouds. I put my hand up to my mouth quick to keep even the faintest squeak from sneaking out, but after that there was no doubt in my mind that old man's evil spirit was still in there, and we, the S.S.B.'s, were gonna meet 'im, real personal like. After that, I felt like someone had stuck their hand down my throat and was twisting my insides the way your ma rung water from a face cloth before she went headlong after your poor ears with it, but I guess that ain't that unusual when you realize you're about to die a horrible death and there ain't a thing in the world you can do about it, unless, of course, you don't mind if everybody in town thinks you're a panty wearing pansy.

Well, my head was all in a fog and my sight started to tunnel up, but just as I felt myself starting to float off, two quick flashes across the front porch snapped me out of it and back into our sorry state of reality. Ya see, Jag's original plan was to circle the house, each of us heading for a different window, and then, all at once shine our flashlights inside like a set of laser beams on high. Jag said this would sure fire throw old Man Mansfield for a loop, and then *he'd* be the one scared stiff, and before he came to his senses, we'd snap us a lovely 8 x 10 glossy of 'im, and be world famous before you could say, "No problem, Mr. President, and you just give us a ring if there's anything else you need us to do for the country." Try as I might I couldn't convince Jag that ghosts didn't get scared, they only *did* the scaring, but he stuck to his original plan, hard headed like he was, saying, "G-Ghosts had to have some feelings, s-s-seeing they was once people, like us. Right? And anyhow, the way I see it, there ain't n-no reason why we can't at l-least startle him up a b-bit and then get our snapshot and be off l-like a shot before anyone got eaten." Everyone went along okay with the plan, but not Rosie. He didn't like what he was hearing one bit, right from the get go, on account of first off he never did nuthin' in his life, "like a shot," and second, him being the plumpest and juiciest of the bunch it was pretty clear that if any of us was gonna be that gruesome ghost's choice for supper tonight, ya might as well start pouring the country gravy over Rosie's head right now, and while you were at it stuff an apple in his mouth, for good measure! He finally came around, but only after Jag swore he'd bring up the rear no matter what, and also that Mrs. Howell had homemade apple pie for desert tonight and there was one piece left with Rosie's name on it after the mission was finished.

After snapping outta my funk, I still wasn't any more keen to face that old ghost again. I knew I needed to live up to my duty as platoon leader and all, and Jag was depending on me to come through, but I mean, come on, couldn't we have just called it a day and at least slept on it before being scared outta our wits *twice* before you could say, *Frankenstein meets the Wolfman!* I tried easing my fears by thinking about our upcoming T.V. show and all, but even that glorious thought was only enough to nudge my body up and outta my crouch, and then take in a long look around. The moon was still doing its peek-a-boo through the clouds, but the clouds was winning, and then here comes a soft, tickly kinda breeze, cool from the damp, and started the goose flesh to crawl all over again. I was bumpy as a plucked porckypine, and just as embarrassed as I looked around hoping the others hadn't noticed, while that same breeze caught hold of the taters of cloth still hanging in the busted out upper floor windows, starting them to float nice and gentle, back and forth, and giving the house a sad, lonely look I hadn't picked up on 'til now. The guys felt it too, and we all just stood and stared for a tad, feeling a little sorry for the place, so grand and cheerful in its hey day, with little children dancing and playing inside and out, and bigwigs visiting, and great big shindigs, the grandest for miles, but now all broken down and ramshackle, no one lifting a finger to help it out for more than a generation. Just then a considerable gust blew right by us, and in through them upstairs windows that now let out a low, mournful, "Whoooo!" as in "Who the heck are you tiny turds trying to sneak up on me?" and after that, any thoughts of pity went right out the window, and we were all back to being scared to death.

Jag set off another quick burst of flashes from the front of the house, this time giving that light a mean jiggle, and then to make sure he got our attention this time, here comes a rock, and I don't mean no tiny pebble, but a good sized lake skipper, sailing straight for us, that would'a brained old

Creepy but good if he hadn't stooped over just then to help Rosie find some Boston Baked Beans he dropped trying to get 'em outta his pants without no one noticing. I told my men to fall in behind me, stay low and no feet dragging as we moved out across the clearing between us and the front porch. We hunkered down good, just like we'd seen them army men on *Combat*, and started off. We were no more than ten feet from where we started when the sniffling and hiccups went into high gear, and as I shot a nasty glare over my shoulder, I saw Rosie, already with his arms around the two small-fries necks', slap his enormous hands over their mouths to shut 'em up, and then give me a little wink like everything was hunky dory.

We made it across without any casualties, dumb's luck, I guess, and as we reached the steps, out popped Jagger, Neil and Ira from the other side.

"Where the heck have you been? We've been waiting for more than an hour," Neil barked.

That really steamed me, seeing that I had to fight the three chicken hearts and my aching foot every inch of the way.

"Why don't ya kiss me where the sun don't shine! First off, we only split up twenty minutes ago and second, how'd you like to be in charge of dragging these three brave souls all the way to a haunted house in the dead of the night?" and I pointed behind me where my men were huddled together once again, trembling, with their hands covering their eyes.

Neil didn't like my tone one bit, and he took a step toward me with his fist pulled back and his teeth clenched.

"G-g-g-ive it a rest! Will ya. W-we got work to do," Jag said, stepping in between us. Now c-c-come on!" and he gave Neil a tug on his arm as he walked by.

We followed 'im over to the north side, that being the safest, on account 'a it having only one window to be spotted from, keeping our heads below that porch line that ran about four feet all around, and did a pretty swell job of it. Well, all but Rosie, who couldn't bend over that far without his knees running into his belly every step, so Jag told 'im to get down on all fours, and then grabbed a tumbleweed that was stuck against the railing and slapped it on his back as cammyflodge.

"All I know is if we don't see old man Mansfield pretty darn soon, Jag, *you're* the one who's gonna be a ghost," Ira said as he pulled some burrs outta his socks that had been biting at his ankles.

Neil was all for that, and added, "Ya might as well get ready for a pounding right now, 'cause you know and I know you ain't gonna get a picture of nuthin' but air with that weenie camera of yours."

"O t-t-thee of little f-f-faith," Jag answered back with his trademark grin, and then pumped his eyebrows all over the place at the two doubting Thomases.

Just then a loud *"Ka-bang!"* from inside the house, not only broke the silence all around us, but smashed it to Smithereens, and the whole lot of us jumped back all together like one big fat scared-to-death kid, and then fell flat, face first on the soggy desert floor, our hands tight over our eyes and my lips mumbling "Our Fathers," fast as I could spit 'em out. No one moved a muscle for at least five minutes and then, after mustering up as much courage as I had left, I slowly slid my hands back to see Neil and Big I glaring right back at me with a look of out and out terror. Jag was the first to sit back up on his heels, to show he was still in control of his limited senses, and after wiping some of the mud from his face, he let out a long, low whistle. I rolled over on my side, and though I was still pretty well shook, I got a real kick outta watching the two tough guys trying to pull themselves back together. First they looked at each other, then they looked at the house, then they looked behind them, and then they said at the same time, "It must've been the wind," and then "Right Jag?" Jag just puckered up his lips, turned his palms up, shrugged his shoulders and tilted his head to the side as if to say, " Beats me." Then they turned and looked at me and said, "Right Johnny C.?"

I thought for a spell and then, just to yank their chain, said, "Funny thing is, I don't remember no wind coming through just now."

That didn't make 'em feel no better and they just stood there blank faced with their mouths open and eyes darting side to side and up and down quick as a cat, and then I noticed a whimpering sound from behind me and wheeled around to see Rosie, Creepy and Chicken Coop still lying face down in the dirt, babbling somethin' under their breaths that we couldn't quite make out seeing that they had their faces smashed down in the mud far as possible, as if they were trying to burrow themselves into the sand like horny toads in a Folger's can. I went over and shook Creepy and Coop, but they just let out a shriek and wouldn't budge. I kept at 'em for a while, but it didn't do no good, they were scared stiff as a Chick-O-Stick, and finally, disgusted, Neil and Ira grabbed 'em both by the collar and yanked 'em straight up.

They practically had three conniption fits and screeched, "Please, don't kill us, Mr. Mansfield!" with their eyes still shut, and I mean locked tight, like when your Ma gets that "gentle" baby shampoo in your eyes that burns like battery acid!

"Snap outta it, you two. It's only us!" I said.

They slowly opened up their eyes after hearing my voice, first the left and then the right, and took a long look around. After realizing they were safe, and there weren't no evil spirits to be seen, they hugged each other and jumped up and down like two long lost sisters. It was pretty pathetic, to tell you the truth.

Rosie, now he was a complete different story. Not only was he a huge chicken, but he was just plain *huge*, and it took all six of us, tugging and heaving with everything we had and almost busting three hernias, just to roll 'im over on his back, and then another two guys at each arm to pry his hands away from his chubby face. But even after talking 'til we were blue in the face, he refused to open his eyes, saying we could still be the ghost, only using our voices that he stole after eating us all up, and he weren't taking no chances no matter how many names Neil called 'im. He said he knew all about it 'cause he'd seen it happen once in a, "Horror Hoedown," moviefest he'd watched on a channel outta Albequercky, New Mexico that he tuned into by putting tin foil on his T.V.'s rabbit ears and bending 'em just right. Well, after pleading with 'im for a while but not making any headway at all, Jag finally got an idea and pulled out a piece of beef jerky from his pocket he'd been savin' for later, and waved it in front of Rosie's nose, just like smelling salts. Well, *that* sure did it! I never seen Rosie move so fast in all my life. He sat up straight in a flash, eyes big as bowling balls, and snatched that jerky outta Jag's hand and stuffed it in his mouth before you could say, "Bone apateet," and all the talk of ghosts was gone just like that.

"Okay, big guy. Let's r-r-roll!" We all huddled back at the front steps and Jag laid out his battle plan for out smarting that spirit, snapping a photo, and us becoming the most famous kids in the world 'cept maybe Alfalfa and his pals, over night. First, we was each to hide outside one of the downstairs windows all around in order to surround that no good ghost and give 'im what for, no matter where he was hiding.

"What if he is upstairs taking a nap?" Creepy asked, matter of fact, all mouth full 'a marbles like always.

"Ghosts d-d-don't take n-n-naps at night, dumb, dumb. Night's when they go to w-work, exact opposite of l-living folks. G-got it! He'll be wide awake in his n-n-night time s-s-scary mode, sure enough," Jag answered back, rolling his eyes at the silliness. It was plain Bampu needed to get his head outta them stupid physics books his pop's got 'im reading and learn somethin' useful for a change.

Then Jag told how he'd be strategically set with his Brownie all ready at the big picture window off the sitting room at the west end of the place, where we'd caught a glimpse of the old man this afternoon. He said he figured that'd be the most likely place he'd hang out on account'a it was the creepiest looking room in the house with it's old lava rock fireplace, dust thick as shag carpet and eerie spider webs all around, and anyway, even if he weren't there right off, he'd probably high tail in there after we scared the daylights outta 'im with our flashlights.

I saw Neil and Ira shoot a quick glance over my way, like "Who's gonna be scaring who?" But I just shrugged my shoulders and went on listening, laughing inside just a little at them two squirming for a change. Jag said when we took our places at the windows to be sure to stay low and not make a peep, and he'd make a little "Coo-Cooing," sound like a dove, for the signal to shine all the flashlights full tilt into the house at the same time. He said, no matter what, we shouldn't stop 'til he said so, on account'a we were gonna flush old man Mansfield away from the light and toward that sitting room, the only room that would still be pitch black. He said everyone knew that ghosts were deathly afraid of light, so his plan had to be a slam-dunk.

"It's vampires that are afraid of light, you doofus! And only sunlight at that," Ira blurted out and then crossed his arms over his chest and stuck his chin way out to show how sure he was.

"All evil s-spirits are afraid of l-l-light. Everybody knows that," Jag answered. "Have you ever saw F-F-Frankenstein or the Werewolf p-parading around in broad daylight? 'Course not. They only come out in the d-darkest, d-dreariest, most m-miserablest nights that they can find. Right? Don't be so s-stupid!"

It was true. I couldn't ever recollect ever seeing any of the top notch horror film creatures doing any of their mischief at any time but the dead of night, and preferably during the worst thunder and lighting storms you ever seen. I guess Jag did have a point.

So we all agreed to go along with the plan, some more enthusiastic than others, but after all we'd come this far and might as well see it on through. But making our way to the house was one thing, ticking off the most horrid creature this side of Transylvania, and just for the fun of it, was another, and I started to get the willys and my stomach felt like it was bouncing on a trampoline as I crawled ever so careful to my spot below the window of the west side bedroom. It was the little girls room Jag and I had peeked in about five hours earlier. Five hours - it seemed more like five days! It was amazing to think that in that little time how my whole darn life had changed. I went from a fun-loving kid, enjoying his last days of summer vacation without a care in the world, to being scared stiff, and within a stinking inch of getting murdered to death, all for the chance to be world famous and maybe even impress a certain red haired girl, and maybe get another red faced girl's goat. Was it really worth it? Maybe. Maybe not. Can't you just see the look of disgust on Nancy's face when we, the S.S.B.'s, get knighted by the President for showing uncommon velour in the face of evil spirits! And what about the look on Jenny Darling's face when she sees me up on that grandstand as the President taps me on the head with that big sword for sticking my neck out to make our small town a safer place for sweet little things like her to live in. Come to think of it, this just might be the *greatest* idea that Jagger ever came up with! If we don't get mutilated in the mean time, that is, and that *if* is about as big as Emilano de la Rosa's rear end.

As I crawled along the porch, I could hear the low creak of the old boards under Rosie's enormous self, and I looked back over my shoulder and put my fingers to my lips, but he just gave me back a sad scowl like, "What the heck do you expect me to do about it?" I started on my way again but after a few feet, I heard hiccupping so loud it sounded like a popgun going off, and knowing darn well who that was, I quickly looked over my shoulder again, but Rosie already had Chicken Coop, face down, with one hand over his mouth and the other one pinching his nose to try to cure him before he tipped off the whole town to what we was up to. Poor old Coop turned three shades of blue, and darn near blacked out before Rosie decided to let up on him. He just laid there close to dead, but his hiccups was gone, so it was all well worth it in the long run. I mean, what's a little brain damage for the sake of the gang, and in Coop's case, nobody was gonna notice the difference anyways.

I made a move with my hand for them to come up, but with my platoon moving in with as much finesse as an octopus with the jimmy-leg, I knew our chances of sneakin' up on the old man were lower than Dodger's I.Q., but somehow, someway, we managed to reach our spots without blowing the whole mission, dumb's luck I guess. Now the problem was that every darn nighthawk, cicada, and river toad from hear to the Mexican border was having an all out competition to see who could make the most obnoxious noise, making it near impossible to hear Jag's signal when the time came. I got my flashlight aimed and ready over the windowsill anyways, and cupped my hand to my ear to try and listen best I could, and then took a look down the south side of the house to see Rosie huddled under his window. As I looked closer I could make out Creepy and Coop stuffed in right beside him, nowheres near where they were supposed to be, but it was too late to holler, and it wouldn't of done no good anyhow, let's face it.

Far off to the left I could barely make out the top of my house, looking nice and peaceful when the moonlight snuck out between breaks in the clouds just right, and my mind started to wander again, as I started thinking about my cozy little room and my soft, comfy bed with my *Jetson's* sheets that felt so cool and fresh after a long day of playing in the blazing heat, and my eyes got kinda heavy I guess, and I must'a nodded off, 'cause next thing I knew, I was rousted outta my lovely peacefulness by a loud, "W-W-Wooo-Wooo-W-W-Woooo----Woo-Woo—W-Wooo!" Well, I knew for a fact there weren't no stuttering doves in Santa Elena. That there was Jagger's signal!

# Chapter Seventeen

## JAGGER MAKES A STAND

Jag's nutty birdcall jostled me back to reality with a jerk, and I snapped on my flashlight and shined it through the window for all I was worth. The whole first floor of the place was lit up like a Christmas tree by then, as the S.S.B.'s were carrying out their duties like the crack outfit that we were. I only had a second to feel pride, though, when somewhere out of the middle of the house came the most blood curdling, spine tingling howl that had ever been uttered by man or evil spirit! Well, that was pretty much that, and our ranks broke and ran faster than the French army during the Blitzkrieg, as my Pop used to say, and I flew past Rosie like he was standing still as I high tailed it down the porch to the front stairs. Creepy and Coop, giving that ghost a run for his money in the scream department, were already racing down the steps, arms flailing and legs kicking in a million different directions all at once. I noticed Creepy's glasses had got all jostled up in the excitement and were now mostly sitting on the side of his head, which didn't matter much, seeing his eyes were closed tight and he was following Chicken Coop's lead by the sound of his screeches. I forgot I had only one shoe on and jumped the whole flight of stairs in one leap, landing hard on my unprotected foot and tearing what was left of that mangled sock clean off. Up ahead I could see Neil and even further up Big I, forgetting all about looking tough for the gang, running for dear life towards the old mesquite fence where we started.

After a few seconds passed, my senses cleared a bit, and although I kept on for all I was worth, I glanced side-to-side and realized Jag and Rosie were nowhere to be seen. Come to think of it I had heard a loud, "Thud!" as I cleared the stairwell, and it started to sink in, to my utter horror, that maybe Rosie had tripped and bit the dust. I slowed to a jog and turned to look back for any sign of 'im, when I saw three quick flashes from the west side porch. Could that nutjob Jagger really still be at his post snapping his brownie like some school photographer on picture day! I couldn't believe what I was seeing! Where did that kid come from anyway? I started feeling cowardly and shameful after that, and thinking I should go back and at least try to help old Rosie out before he becomes a big fat feast for the ghost and several of his closest ghouls, when from outta the house came another sound, a sickening sound, in an eerie, tormented kinda voice, "No May Montay!" It yelled out over and over, and it stopped me dead in my tracks, but I couldn't make heads nor tails from it. Was old man Mansfield using some kinda ancient, super secret ghost lingo to put a nasty curse on us, or maybe call up all his evil pals to come help him finish us off?

I looked back behind me but Neil and Ira had vanished from sight into the darkness. Bampu and Coop were still running like crazy, all zig-zaggy, and still screaming to beat the band, and believe me I wanted to be right there with 'em, but I just couldn't. I knew what I had to do, but I warn't too happy about it. No matter if I was peeing my pants scared, I just had to go back and at least try to help get those guys outta there alive. I mean, knowing me I wouldn't be able to live with myself if I didn't. Not for at least a week, anyway. I figured even if we all got killed by that horrible creature at least we'd be all up in heaven together, and I betcha we could find plenty of fun stuff to horse around with up there for a while 'til the rest of the guys showed up. At least we wouldn't have to put up with that stinking Nancy Cole ever again, 'cause it's pretty plain to me which place *she's* going to.

Well, I shook my head to clear out the cobwebs, took a deep breath, clenched my teeth and raced back toward the last place in the world that I wanted to be. As I reached the clearing around the house, I could barely make out in the darkness a large blob lying still at the base of the steps that I figured had to be Rosie, and I crept on up keeping an eye peeled for any ghostly ambush. As I got closer, I started to notice the big blob wasn't alone, there was a smaller blob kneeling at his side, and it was yanking with all it's might on his arm. Why that worthless ghost was trying to rip off a piece of poor Rosie right then and there for a little midnight snack! Well, that did it, and somethin' snapped in me, and screaming like a banshee I raced right for 'im. I came harder and harder, not thinking like a man but more like an animal, with only one thing in mind, I had to stop that thing before it ripped my pal apart. But just as I came on 'em and was ready to lunge, the smaller blob looks up from his horrifying work and says, "Sh-shut the heck up, will ya? And help me with this m-m-moose!"

Thank the good Lord it was Jagger! I was so happy to see 'im I almost gave 'im a hug, and I would'a too, but as I got closer, he growled at me again to give 'im a hand before we was all goners. So I knelt down and threw one of Rosie's arms over my head, which almost knocked me on my rear, and Jagger did the same, and with plenty of grunting and groaning and almost another three hernias we managed to drag 'im slow but sure outta danger. Over the considerable commotion we was making as Rosie's heels dug two wide trenches in the desert floor, I heard a low, kinda blubbering sound coming from inside the house that gave me shivers all over again, and I knew deep down inside that we hadn't heard the last from old man Mansfield. Not by a long shot.

We tugged old Rosie best we could toward the old fence and safety, rolling over rocks, busting over bushes, and crashing over cactus, and probably more than a few poisonous creatures, we weren't being too particular, and we weren't breaking no land speed records neither, but the big guy still didn't show even the slightest sign of coming around.

Finally, with my back ready to snap and my arms on fire, I dropped my half, slapped 'im a couple of times hard across his chubby cheeks, and yelled, "Snap outta it Emiliano! You're killing us here!"

"I don't want to die. I don't want to die," he started to mumble all squeaky and weepy like.

"You're safe, you big baby, but if you don't come around and quick, me and Jag are the ones that are gonna be dead! Understand!"

He stopped his babbling then and stood straight up but with his eyes still closed, of course. Then as he slowly opened them and saw we was telling the truth, he couldn't control hisself and started blurting out a million, "Gracias a Dios!" and "Gracias a Maria y Jose," and all other sorts of Mexican gibberish that I couldn't make out, and then he started hugging and squeezing us to no end 'til Jag and me felt like a couple of rag dolls with all the stuffing knocked out. Finally, we pushed 'im away and I yelled, "That's enough, Rosie. We gotta get going while the gettings good," and off we went in search of safety and the rest of our trusty troops.

By the time we made it to the fence, my poor foot was so covered over with cactus needles and thorns of every which kind, it looked more like one of them sea urgents than anything human, but the funny thing was, I'd been so darn scared 'til now I hadn't felt so much as a twinge. The bad thing was that now that my wits were slowly coming back, so was my sense of pain, and it was near intolerable! I swore once again I'd teach that Dodger a lesson if I got the chance, and at least now it looked like I might just live another day to give 'im his due. So things were looking up, I guess.

When we came to the gate, there were Neil and Ira looking like somethin' the cat coughed up. Their faces were white, but all smudged with dirt and sweat, and their hair was all crazy, tossed and tangled with small leaves and twigs and their clothes were torn and tattered and reddish brown from the clay that was peculiar to these parts. From the looks of things they hadn't stopped for nuthin' on their escape route, and now had completely lost that look of self confidence they had always been able to keep up at even the toughest of times. To be honest, they were a little hard to recognize, without their tough guy aura and all, and it made me feel a little sorry for 'em, but only just a little. They didn't utter a word as we came up, but just kept staring out, all wild eyed, and when we got within earshot, Jag asked about Cooper and the Creep. I guess he felt responsible for all his men like a good general should, no matter how yellow bellied they'd been.

"They just kept on running," Ira answered, in no more than a whisper. "They ought to be home by now, if they didn't pass out first."

The full moon found a nice open spot amongst the clouds and shined bright down on that damp desert floor. We sat ourselves down with a thud, like the last ounce of energy had been drained outta us all at the same time. It happened like that sometimes when something's got you so berserk you could just about run through a wall, and then when the whole shebang's over your body feels about as sturdy as a wet linguini noodle. We sat there for what seemed like forever, everyone quiet except for the thump of our hearts, and just staring down between our knees. The cicada were still chirping and the toads were still croaking, and even a coyote would howl now and then, but I realized I hadn't noticed any of those sounds for the last twenty minutes or so on account'a my mind was too preoccupied with being scared to death.

After a bit, Neil calmed hisself enough to ask, "Jag, what the heck happened back there after that God-awful scream?" Jagger was lying flat on his back by now, chewing on a piece of barrel cactus fruit and staring up at the massive moon. He pulled hisself up on his elbows and looked at us all for a few seconds, like he was trying to find the right words to explain something that had no worldly explanation, and we all leaned in towards 'im to hear his thoughts.

"W-w-well, first off *m-men*, and I do use that t-term lightly," he said rolling his eyes at us. "I gotta say I've n-never seen such c-cowardice in all my born days! If you'd have run any faster, I w-would've swore you were the Seward School Girls Track Team!" Well, I felt about as worthless as a fork at a soup kitchen and we all dropped our eyes in disgrace. When we finally looked up again there was Jag giving us all that great, goofball grin with his picket fence teeth and eyes squinted into little slits, and you could tell he was just yanking our chains. He knew deep down inside that only a kid as nutty as he was, would'a hung around in a spot like that, instead of trying to save his own skin.

After that he got all serious again, and said we all had to swear not to tell a living soul what we were about to hear, and if you did, the others would hunt you down like a dog, no matter where in the world you were hiding. But instead of just killing you then and there, which would be way too easy a way out for a louse like you, you'd be dragged back to Santa Elena by your ankles and have to dress up like a girl everyday and become Nancy Cole's best friend, and hang out with her and her dimwit twits every minute, and do everything she did all the time and act like you *liked* it, and if you refused, then nuthin' would happen to you, but your family would have to die a terrible death with Chinese water torture, fingernail pulling, you name it, and you'd have to go through the rest of your life a low down, guilt full, Nancy loving transvestite! Well, nobody knew what transvestite meant, but judging from the tone of things it warn't good, and so we all quickly agreed to Jag's terms, and hunkered down to listen to what we knew would be the most fantastic tale of the supernatural and the supernaturally stupid, ever to be told in the town of Santa Elena, or in all of Cochise county for that matter.

"W-well this is exactly h-h-how it h-h-happened," he said as he crossed his heart and spun around three times for effect, showing his fantastic flair for the dramatic when he got a captive, and in this case scared stiff audience. "And if I am l-l-lyin' may a pack of w-wild coyotes chase me down and tear me apart, and g-g-give each one of you one of my still hot organs for a s-souvenir!" (He could be real gross, too.)

"Just get on with it! Will ya?" Big I screeched.

"Okay, okay--so everything was g-going according to p-plan, as I was laying for that good for nuthin' ghost outside the b-b-big room at the east side of the place. I had my f-flashlight r-r-ready and checked the camera to m-make sure the film was set and the f-flashbulb was on tight. I figured you all had enough t-t-time to m-man your post by then, so I let out the "Hoo—Hoo," sign to light that place up."

"We know all that, brainiac!" Ira snorted. "We were there, remember? What happened *after* the scream."

"As I was sayin'," Jag continued, clearing his throat and not paying Ira no mind. "After the f-f-flashlights were l-l-lit, I peeked over the windowsill and into the d-darkness, b-but couldn't see hide nor hair of 'im, but then I heard the terrifying screech, and f-figured the plan had w-worked, s-scarin' the bejeesus out of old man Mansfield, just as I had b-brilliantly reduced."

"You mean *deduced*," I added, pleasant as possible.

"Right," Jag said and then continued. "After that I heard p-plenty of other screams but since they were higher p-p-pitched, I figured they were from all of you girls," and he gave us that grin and had a nice little chuckle to hisself all over again.

"Look, are ya gonna tell us what happened, or am I gonna have to beat it out of ya," Neil said, starting to feel like his old self again and getting sick of being called yellow.

"R-r-r-elax, I am g-gettin' there. Okay, where was I? Oh yeah. W-well t-t-there I was, peeking over that window ledge and waiting to take the p-p-picture that would make us all world famous, but s-s-still there was nuthin'. All I was able to m-m-make out over all your carryin' on was the s-sound of feet flyin' every which way, b-but I couldn't tell for certain whether it was the g-g-ghost or you guys r-runnin' for cover. After a second or two I could tell that those footsteps were c-c-comin' from *inside* the house and could hear s-someone or s-something opening d-d-doors and r-runnin' into a r-room, and then comin' back out and trying another room, over and over 'til I realized that s-spook must'a been tryin' to find the d-darkest room left to hide in. Just like I planned." Again we got the grin and the proud look. "Finally, I seen the d-d-door crack open ever so slight in the corner of m-my room, and some l-l-light shinin' through from behind 'im from one of the f-flashlights that was left pointing down the hallway. And then there he was, big as life, or in this c-case death, right in front of my eyes!"

I could feel the skin start to tighten over my forehead as my ears pulled back and began to tingle, and I leaned in so as not to miss what happened next.

"What'd he look like?" asked Neil, about to pull his hair out if he didn't get some answers, quick.

"W-Well he was hideous, I t-tell ya! He made Nancy Cole look like M-m-miss America."

"Gross!" we all shouted.

"He had a t-tall skinny body with long pointed f-fingers."

"How tall was he?" Ira asked, unable to control hisself.

"Ten f-f-feet, if he was an inch!" There was a loud gasp.

"His head was more s-square than r-round, and had only a few straggly tufts of hair stickin' out now and then."

"Like Frankenstein?" Rosie asked.

"M-m-more like a tall Dracula with a Frankenstein h-h-head."

"Oh, I gotcha!"

"His eyes g-glowed red, like fire, and they s-seemed to look straight through me"

"Like laser beams?" said Neil.

"Exactly. And when his lizard l-lips pulled back, his teeth, or fangs I should say, glowed a hideous green, and the little b-bit of light that hit the side of it's face showed a trickle of r-red from the corner of it's mouth."

"Blood!" we all screamed at once.

"Afraid so," said Jag.

"Then what?" I asked quickly, not able to wait no longer for the final gruesome details.

"W-w-well, when he seen the room was s-s-safe, he c-came creepin' in real quiet-like, and then closed the door nice and s-soft. That w-w-weren't any good 'cause soon as the d-door shut the room went p-pitch black again and I couldn't see a darn thing. Plus, I was the only one who *didn't* have a dang f-flashlight. Well, I knew that m-monster was in there, I just w-weren't sure where, but I figured even though I c-c-couldn't see him, he could sure as you know what see me with the m-moonlight at m-my back and all, so I jerked myself d-down quick and sat there on the p-p-porch with my back to the wall, and thought through my next m-move."

I was amazed. I mean, who ever heard of a twelve-year old kid this brave before in their whole lives. No one. That's who. I'll tell ya one thing, Jag's stock was going up like a rocket ship, and not just in my book, neither.

"Now I was in a fix and I knew it," he continued. "Without that picture, n-no one in their right mind was g-gonna believe our story, and then we w-would'a risked our lives for nuthin', and there goes our one ch-chance of becomin' famous and maybe even g-getting our own Saturday morning T.V. show."

We all smiled and nodded thinking how great things were gonna be, if only Jag could come through. Then we all urged him to continue on.

"If I s-started just takin' pictures helter skelter, there was a g-g-good chance I'd m-miss 'im, on account'a the room was pretty big and I had no c-clue where he was hiding. But then I caught a b-break. All at once I heard this t-t-terrible b-blubbering sound coming from inside, like a cross b-between a man cryin' his eyes out and a ticked off animal trying to call his pals for help."

I felt a quick shudder go down my spine, remembering that creepy sound all too well myself.

"In b-between the whimpering I could almost make out what s-sounded like some words but it was t-t-too garbled up to t-tell for certain. What I c-could make out was the direction that hideous howling was comin' from to help direct my c-c-camera. So I decided to pop up quick as I could, and take a picture in the general d-direction of the b-blubberin', and then some more in the direction of the door, f-figuring that's where he'd head, to try and escape once the flashes started to p-pop. So that's j-just what I did." (What genius under fire!)

"How'd ya know he wouldn't come right for ya and try and bite your head off?" asked Big I.

"I didn't."

Jag never seemed more brave to me than at that very moment, and believe me, I'd seen 'im in some pretty hot water. But, I mean, come on! A twelve year old kid able to keep his cool, facing off all by hisself against the most bloodthirsty butthead this side of the Lock Mess monster! I was darn proud to be his pal, and hoped just a little of what he had inside would rub off on the rest of us pathetic pansies someday.

"Then what happened, Jag?" Ira asked.

"After I started f-f-flashin' like mad, all hell broke loose. First off, old man Mansfield lets out an even more eye watering screech than before, and t-t-tries to scramble to his f-feet, but he was pretty well shook and s-s-seemed to be havin' all kinds of trouble righting himself. Once he did, he l-l-lit out for the d-door just like I figured, takin' a second or two to find the doorknob in the dark. That g-gave me the chance for three or f-four shots in all. Hope at least one comes out decent. After th-that I took off down the porch along the side of the house and f-f-flew over the front steps, but

I tripped over this b-big b-blob at the b-bottom, that turned out to be Rosie, out cold, and t-t-that was pretty much it, I guess."

Well, I guess flabbergasted explains best how we all felt, and proud of ourselves, sure, and the S.S.B.'s and Jagger in particular, to have pulled off such a hairy and scary mission like this. Even *Neil* gave Jag a little pat on the back in appreciation.

"T-tomorrow, I'll t-take the film down to the five and dime and when them p-pictures come out, "G-good by w-white ghetto. Hello Hollywood!" Jag yelled as we all let out a cheer.

"Was there anything else that you can remember, Jag, anything that might be important for the newspapers and stuff, I mean?" I asked as we climbed over the fence.

"W-well there was one thing," he said as he stopped and rubbed his chin and scratched the back of his neck. "As I was f-f-flashing away and that devil was runnin' for the d-door, it sounded like he was screaming out somethin', but I c-couldn't make heads or t-tails of it. Kinda sounded like some f-foreign l-l-language or somethin'."

I told him I had heard it too, but didn't have a clue what it was about.

"Yeah, and he was yelling it through all of his ghostly b-b-blubbering, but he said it over and over---somethin' l-like "No m-me ma tees," but who knows. I'll tell ya one thing, it sure weren't English. S-some kinda g-g-ghost lingo, I figure. Maybe a code or s-s-somethin', or m-maybe one'a them ancient l-l-languages that nobody ever speaks no m-more, like L-latin or Egyptian."

"I can speak Latin," Ira said proudly.

"Pig Latin don't count, it-shay ead-hay," Neil said and just kept walking.

That funny talk will have to wait, I guess, 'cause it was real late now and no matter how scared outta my wits I was a few minutes ago, sleep was starting to take hold and if I didn't get to bed quick, Ma was gonna find me in the street in the morning snoring up a storm, and how would I wiggle outta that one? Sleep walking maybe? Hum, not bad, actually. I gotta remember that one. Anyways the skies finally were clearing, and the full moon shined bright down on us with a flood of light to help us on our way. I was particularly grateful on account'a my foot was plenty sore by now and I wasn't interested in stepping on any more painful desert *anything* if I could help it. There warn't nuthin' left of that poor sock no more, saving just the elastic band still clinging around my ankle with it's two red stripes that matched our Little Beaver's uniforms. I looked over at Jag and noticed the moon shadow just off his left and couldn't help but think that maybe some of that garbage was true he was spewing before about good and bad luck, and how as long as you thought like a kid and acted like a kid you'd always have a nice moon shadow around to protect ya. Anyways, I wasn't gonna argue. Far as I'm concerned, *someone* was looking out for us tonight, and you can take that to the bank! As we started to split up, we decided to meet tomorrow morning and talk over our next move, and then began to head for home.

Before we moved off too far, Rosie turned to Jag and asked, "What was that thing you thought you heard old man Mansfield say again, Jag?"

"S-s-somethin' like, 'No m-me ma tees,' but d-don't hold me to it, it was nuthin' but a garbled mess."

Well, that was that and we split up and went our separate ways. I was still pretty spooked and went quick as my bare foot, that by now had a fair resemblance to Ma's Sunday evening meatloaf, would carry me. I looked over my shoulder plenty, I ain't ashamed to say, after all it warn't every day you crossed paths with a real live ghost, and today we done it twice, just for good measure.

The stars were out tonight fine and sparkly and I tried picking out the big and little dipper to help take my mind off things as I went. They was always fairly easy to see on account'a they actually looked a little like a big spoon sticking out of a bowl---but just a little. But take them other star figures you always heard about, like that Archer guy and Pigasus and all. Well, they look about as much as those things as Mickey Rooney looks like Paul McCartney. I mean, come on. Somebody had a heck of an imagination, and a lot of fun playing connect the dots, to come up with all that mumbo-jumbo. That didn't calm me down none, so I decided to try to come up with the names of all seven of the planets, but could conger up only three, besides Earth that is; Saturn, on account'a it had those cool rings all around, Pluto, 'cause of that silly cartoon dog, and Ur-anus, well, for obvious reasons, I guess.

When I finally reached home, I swung around the front across the lawn on the way to my still open bedroom window. The cool grass with a thin coat of dew felt soft and soothing to my poor, sacrificed foot. Sacrificed. It was kinda, wasn't it? I mean I could'a just whimped outta the whole mess after Dodger ripped off my shoe, but instead I stuck it out, exposing myself to extreme torture for the sake of my family's safety and the safety of all of stinking Santa Elena for that matter; Jenny Darling, Mayor Trancoza, Mengo and Pato, Larry Lipshitz, even nasty Nancy! Well, that made my foot feel better right off, in fact I hardly felt it at all any more. Ain't it funny how that works sometime? Mind over madder, that's what Pop always says.

After that I got to thinking about how proud Ma was of that luscious lawn my foot was enjoying so much, and how plenty of people said it was the nicest for miles around. Truth is there weren't more than two or three houses in the whole town that had grass at all, with most settling for what was called, "Native Vegetation," which was a nice way of saying, the same old desert that was there before you'd done a darn thing to the place, weeds and all. Ma had a different name for it---lazy. Personally, I was fine with the desert stuff, 'cause first off, you never had to miss a great game of Capture the Flag on account'a your Ma made you spend half of the dang morning watering her Assalias, and second, say ya got some weeds, heck you could just leave 'em be on account'a there was a good chance they were prettier than anything else ya already had growing there! People were always asking Ma about her gardening secrets and all, and she got a pretty big kick outta it to tell ya the truth, although she didn't let on, and would only just blush and smile wide and beautiful and say it was "Nothing really," and just something she liked to "Dabble in," and how most of it was just luck and mother nature. But we knew otherwise, 'cause I swear there would be days she'd work her fingers raw digging and hoeing and fertilizing and weeding and edging like a madman. All her hard work paid off though, 'cause once when I was about five the main news station outta Tucson actually came down and did a story on our front yard! I heard Pop say it must'a been a slow news day---but not around Ma, and she was the talk of the town the rest of the summer, 'til that nasty fungus set in that is, and ruined the lovely emerald green grass and Ma's reputation right along with it. She was near a total breakdown after that, and wouldn't come outta her room for days on end. Pop was at his wits end of what to do 'til finally he offered to take her all the way up to Phoenix to shop at some new high faluting department store, the one all the ladies were yapping about outta New York City. Well that did it! She shot outta that bedroom like her hair was on fire and didn't stop 'til she was sitting in the passenger seat of Pop's T-bird, blowing the horn for him to come along before she missed out on all the latest fashions. I still remember the sick look on Pop's face as they drove off.

Anyways, I crept up nice and easy toward my window, first passing by Gracie's room and peering in to make sure no lights were on, and then peeked into my room, to see where that good for nuthin' Dodger was hanging out. And there he was, lying right where I left 'im at the foot of the bed with my tennis shoe still in his mouth and a real peaceful look on his face, 'cause it weren't *his* foot that was torn to shreds now was it? That reminded me that the first chance I got I was gonna whoop him good. I suppose it was a good sign that he was still lying there like that, meaning that nobody had came in my room since I left, 'cause if they had, the first thing they'd have done was take that darn shoe away from him.

I held off outside for a bit so Dodger could pick up my scent all nice and slow. I didn't want to startle him and get him to yapping up a storm that would sure wake up the whole house, and send me up the river for the rest of the summer. But, while I was standing there I swore I heard a little rattle sound coming from the bushes off to my left which was *never* good in the desert southwest, and I kinda half-climbed, half-leaped over that window sill, landing with a low thud on the floor, face to face with you

# J. E. Tooley

know who. I didn't move a muscle and neither did he, and we only stared at each other eye to eye for a few seconds 'til he started up that soft, low growl under his breath, the way he did when he was trying to decide whether somethin' was worth barking about. After thinking on it a bit, and sniffing at me for all he was worth, he stuck out his long slobbery tongue and licked my face up one side and down the other to his heart's content.

"Cut it out, doofus," I said soft and quick and then sat myself up on the bed.

He waddled over to me with his tail wagging so hard it swung his whole body from side to side, and he started with his low moaning sound like he always did when he was happy to see ya. Since he was a retriever, he always had to bring you something to see, no matter how lame it was, and in this case he decided on my right shoe, just to spite me.

"Thanks for nuthin'," I said as I yanked it outta his mouth. "I coulda really used this about two hours ago, you retard." He just stared at me for a while with those big, droopy eyes and then started sniffing me up and down all over. I suppose I had a truckload of new and interesting smells stuck all over me, considering where I'd been, and he kept at it good and long, there was nuthin' you could do to stop him, and finally, after he was satisfied, he laid back down with a big, "Harrumph!" and started licking at my filthy right foot, which I'm sure was a tasty treat in his book. That reminded me that I better clean myself up a bit before I hit the sack so as not to cause any suspicion in the morning, and I figured I'd better bandage up my foot nice and tight to keep from bleeding all over my sheets, which would be plenty hard to explain.

I sure enough looked like something the cat dragged in, as I saw myself in the bathroom mirror, brown with dirt from head to toe and only a few flesh colored streaks on my face where the sweat had run down. There were all sorts of twigs and leaves and bits of cobwebs stuck in my hair, and my clothes looked all reddish from the Sonoran Desert clay. I took everything off, even my jockey shorts, and rolled it all up into a ball and slid it under my bed for safe keeping for now 'til I could figure a way to ditch it all for keeps. I scrubbed my face and hands and fished all the stuff outta my hair best I could, which weren't easy with this mop top my ma had me sporting. I sat myself down on the counter top, like I ain't supposed to, and soaked my aching foot in the sink after mixing in some of Gracie's Mr. Bubble with the water, 'til the pain started to ease off. I patted it dry, real gentle like, and then, after finding some Mercur-o-chrome in the cabinet, practically poured the whole bottle over it. It might'a looked red as a lobster after I was done, but I weren't taking no chances with infection. The last thing I wanted was one of them Pennysillin shots in the rear with the needle the size of a ten penny nail!

After that I made up a pretty swell bandage out of a face cloth and two

250

rubber bands, and then was all set for p.j.'s and bed. I wiped up as much dirt and blood as possible, and then tip-toed back to my room thinking how nice it was gonna feel to snuggle down into my pillow and doze off until late as I pleased, but as I slid into the covers and set my poor aching head to rest, I felt something all crinkly under my pillow, and thinking it could be a scorpion or somethin' even nastier, quickly jumped up, pulled back the pillow, while grabbing my, "How to Pitch" book by Bob Feller off the night stand, ready to smash the sucker to smithereens. But it weren't no scorpion at all, but only a piece of notebook paper all folded up nice and neat, and on the outside was printed in little kid letters, "PRIVATE!" I started to unfold it, wondering, "What now?", and noticed a sticker of a puppy in one corner and a kitty cat on the other and then in the middle the horrifying words, I HOPE YOU HAD A NICE TIME AT OLD MAN MANSFIELDS HOUSE. LOVE, GRACIE.

# Chapter Eighteen

## GRACIE LAYS DOWN THE LAW

Ever get that feeling of complete and utter doom way deep down. Like you were sinking fast in quicksand in the middle of the Amazon jungle with no way out, not even a stinking vine to grab hold on like they always had in the movies, and there was nobody around 'cept a bunch'a man-eating cannibals wearing them crazy masks carved outta coconuts or somethin' and fancied up with bright paint and feathers all over, dancing and "Uga-Chuging" to beat the band 'cause they knew they were about to have a tasty "Buffet of boy." Well, that's exactly how I felt after reading Gracie's note---*only double*. I knew there'd be no stopping that little snot-nosed, big-mouthed, tattle-tailing troublemaker from yapping about something this juicy to the whole world at the first sign of light. I didn't have a clue how she found out what we was up to but that didn't matter none now. All that did matter was that Ma was gonna tan my hide for this one, and it was good-by fellas and hello Sister Mary Joseph, the Mother Superior and number one battle ax of the "San Xavier Mission Summer Church School for kids needing a little extra teaching in the proper Christian ways," such as getting whacked over the head with a yard stick 'til you're loopy for maybe getting just a little mixed up while naming the apostles and leaving out Peter and including, say Scooter or someone. I heard all about her from Jojo Sixkiller, this half Indian, half catholic kid that got hisself sent up the river by his ma last July for not letting the girl know she gave him back too much change from buying a double scoop at Dairy Delight. He warn't sure how she found out, but I guess that pecker head Nancy was third in line that day, so there you go. Anyway, Jojo said the sister made El Generalissimo look like Shirley Temple!

I leaped out of bed and half ran, half hopped on account'a my bad foot, down the hall to the little devil's room to see if she might still be up, but no dice. She was lying there still as can be, flat on her back with her mouth open only a tad with the corners of her lips turned up ever so slight and her little hands clasped lightly over her chest, just like always, and any stranger that seen her would'a thunk she absolutely had to be the sweetest, most gentle of all God's creations, without a thought in that pretty little head 'cept for spreading happiness and joy to all around. Isn't it amazing how outward appearances don't mean diddly-squat sometimes! I just stood there for a while shaking my head not able to understand how such a little thing could always be causing me such *big* trouble. I mean between her and Dodger I might as well be in that Purgastory place that Father Moreno's always warning about. Heck, that might even be a welcome improvement to what I got here!

I figured there was nuthin' I could do right then and there to help patch things up, so I decided to go ahead and turn in, and laid there a long while 'til sleep finally came, even though I was dead tired both physical and otherwise. It's hard to wipe clean thoughts of being eaten alive that easy I guess, and now I gotta worry about Gracie ratting me out to boot. I figured if Jag's snapshots come out, nobody's gonna argue that what we was up to was nuthin' but fine and upstanding, and we'd be let off the hook pretty clean. But who knows? Things around here had a way of not working out the way ya hoped, especially with Jagger in charge, if ya know what I mean.

I had just started to nod off nice and peaceful when I heard Dodger make a low whimpering sound in his sleep, and as I looked down at the moron his eyes were all fluttery and his paws were flipping slowly back and forth, and I could tell he was having one of his doggy dreams, about chasing a cat up a tree or digging up a bone or something idiotic like that. I thought to myself that I hoped my dreams tonight were like old Dodger's and not the more frightening kind, but as I drifted off I heard a faint, low pitched moaning sound coming from outside due north that didn't help things. I tried to tell myself it must'a just been the wind, but deep down I knew better.

That night, instead of suffering through the nightmare I deserved, my dream was something sweet and soft, and, well, dreamy. It started off with me and Jenny Darling sitting in this field of tall, green, soft grass with just enough dew on the tips to make your skin tickle a bit but not get all wet and sticky. Nuthin' like you'd ever see around these parts. And we were eating this sweet little lunch Jenny had fixed up of fried bologna and jujubees, and talking and laughing without a care in the world. Then we started walking through that field that was now covered wall to wall with the most lovely yellow daffydils far as the horizon, and they were swaying ever so slow, back and forth in even waves like the water down in Patagonia lake after a little dingy goes by, and we were just holding hands and looking at each other like it was the most natural thing in the world to do. I looked up to the sky which was a perfect deep blue, like the very best cleary in your marble bag, and there weren't no clouds to be seen nowheres. The mountains rose up tall and majestic all around and the light breezes in our face were cool and moist and almost gave you the shivers. There weren't no ghosts nor haunted houses, or rattlesnakes or scorpions or even Neil or Ira for that matter, but only a swell picture of me and Jenny, happy as can be. We just kept walking for a while and I picked a bunch of flowers to make a bouquet for Jenny, and she was real happy to have it and told me so, and said I was the nicest, most handsomest young man in the whole town, and she was happy as a milkman's kitty-cat to be my best girl. I told her I was plenty pleased too, and how all the other guys might be jealous and all, but that was tough turds. After I said that I realized I kinda ruined the moment 'cause Jenny got this kinda sick look on her face, but I quick mumbled somethin' about how she was pretty as a picture and she started smiling all over again, with her red hair blowing ever so gentle in the breeze to show off her perfect pink and white skin underneath. Then, outta the blue, she leaned over and started kissing my face all over, top to bottom, again and again, and I just sat there with this dumb smile, thinking how wonderful life was as she kept at it. Then suddenly I opened my eyes to see Dodger on my bed staring straight down at me and giving me a bunch of disgusting, slobbery licks!

"Stop that, you flea bag!" I yelled out, trying to push 'im off, but he wouldn't budge, and only thought I was playing, so he started biting at my arms and barking and bouncing up and down like a doofus nutcase, and then fell flat with all his weight on my chest so I could barely move a muscle. Finally, just before I was about to suffocate, and being outta other ideas, I reared back and gave 'im a good old-fashioned head butt, right between the eyes. Well, that dazed 'im a bit, and didn't feel too good to me, neither, but I was able to wiggle my way out from under that dumb mutt and slid off the bed with a thud. Dodger rolled over on his back, pleased as punch that he now had the whole place to hisself, and proceeded to fall fast asleep.

"Someone's gonna get a good old fashioned whooping, and he's big and hairy and yellow!" I said, disgusted as I slowly stood up, still a little woozy, rubbing my forehead. But he didn't pay no mind at all, and was already in doggy dream world with his eyes fluttering and his paws flipping away, happy as can be.

I turned to look at the clock and my heart did a flip. It was eight-thirty! That meant I'd overslept and gave that megaphone mouth Gracie at least an hour and a half head start to cook my goose. I slipped the face towel ever so gently off my poor aching foot and wadded it up and tossed it under the bed with the rest of my filthy stuff from last night's adventure, and then pulled on some socks and my soft, fuzzy, bunny slippers that Granny got me last Christmas. She was always getting me silly, little kid's stuff like that, but this morning I gotta admit, they were just the ticket for my throbbing right foot.

I slowly made my way down the hall trying to walk natural as possible with a half chewed off foot, and then through the den and into the kitchen. I prepared myself for the hammering I was sure was heading my way and decided to use the old, "Helping out a poor friend," defense soon as Ma started in on me. I was gonna say Jagger had been out in his alley playing kick the can, when outta nowhere here comes a pack of wild javelinas running right for 'im, looking like they hadn't had as much as a stinking piece of prickly pear cactus to eat since Cinco de Mayo! He had no time to lose and had to run for his life, but got so darn scared he got all confused and started running *away* from his house. Next thing he knew he was hauling down our street with them crazy, stinky pigs snapping at his heels. When he seen our house he thought his prayers had been answered (I thought the "prayer" thing might soften Ma up a bit) and he made right for it, lickety-split. But being the fine gentleman he was, he didn't want to wake up the whole family, and just knocked on my window to beg me to save his life, running around in circles the whole time to keep from getting caught 'til I gave 'im my answer. I told 'im right off, though, I was sorry he was gonna get eaten and all, but my ma absolutely forbids me from going out at night no matter what, and I would never, ever consider going against my dear mother's wishes. But then Jag started begging and pleading something awful, saying he didn't want to die such a terrible death, especially with his pop being in Viet Nam and he being the only man of the house and all, and he was sure that just this once my Ma wouldn't mind if I broke the rules just a little bit to save my best pal's life. Finally, seeing the horrible predicament he got hisself into, I reluctantly agreed and jumped out my window just in time to help fend off a few of the very nastiest pigs before they made poor old Jagger a nice midnight snack. In my rush to help my poor desperate friend, I forgot one of my shoes, which led to my shredded sock and torn up foot.

As for the Mansfield place, I decided to say that, on account'a poor old Jag being so shaken up and all, he shouldn't go home alone and I decided I'd better go along to make sure he got there safe. In order to throw them sneaky pigs off our scent, we went through the Mansfield property and then on up to Jagger's when the coast was clear. Even though I knew I had broken the rules and felt lower than Sandy Koufax's e.r.a., I was sure that my ma, being the kind and caring woman she was, would not only understand why I did what I did, but would want to reward me for making the absolutely correct decision in a very tough situation! I figured soon as I got a second, I'd break away and call up old Jag and fill 'im in so we could keep things straight during the ruthless interrogation that was sure to come.

I waltzed into the kitchen with all the confidence I could gather and after shooting a quick, angry glance over at Gracie who was already sitting at the table, eating her usual bowl of Fruit Loops with the stuffed Toucan Sam she got from sending in like two thousand box tops sitting right beside her, I turned to Ma who was standing at the sink with her back to me and said, "Good morning. How's the world's greatest mom!"

She whirled around quick to face me and despite my best efforts to remain calm, I winced and took a step back to miss the slap that was sure to come my way. But I'll be darned if all she said was, "Oh, good morning, dear. You startled me so. Why don't you sit down and I will fix you up some nice pigs in a blanket just like you like them."

I blew out all the breath I was holding in one big whoosh, getting a full blown head rush, and seeing all kinds of stars to boot, kinda like a guy facing the firing squad that finds out right after they pulled the trigger that the guns weren't loaded.

"Are you okay, Johnny? You look a little pale, honey."

"Ah, sure Ma, just fine. Still half asleep I guess," and I walked to my chair and sat down a little limp. Now what was up? Could it be that Ma really knew the whole story but just toying with me 'til I cracked and spilled the beans before she even had to say a word? Or did she maybe have an inkling that something was up and was just biding her time 'til she had enough evidence to put me away for life? Or could it possibly be that Gracie, the Olympic gold medalist in tattle tailing, the kid who couldn't keep her trap shut even if it meant every one of her teeth would fall out soon as she opened up, had actually kept this juicy tidbit all to herself the whole morning, and didn't rat me out to Ma the soonest chance she got? And if that was so, then what gives? What could her devious little mind want in return. She sure wasn't doing it outta the goodness of her heart. She ain't got one!

All these thoughts were rifling through my head as I sat there at the breakfast table thinking on my next move in this game of cat and mouse; or in this case, kids and ghosts. As far as Ma was concerned, I decided to play it cool, not saying a word outta the ordinary, no matter how much she piled on the sugar, and hope to God that she really didn't have a clue. If she finally came clean and tried hitting me hard between the eyes with what she knew, I'd spring my wild javelina story on her and let the chips fall where they may. On the other hand, if she really didn't know nuthin' yet, then I had to get to Gracie quick, and find out what the heck she was up to.

"Here you are, dear," Ma said, smiling, as she slid a big plate of pancakes in front of me.

Her voice snapped me out of my deep thoughts and before I could stop myself I blurted out, "Wild javelinas!"

She looked at me real weird and asked, "What did you say?"

"Ah, I said wild javelinas couldn't get me away from one of your home cooked breakfasts," and then I looked down at my plate and just shook my head.

"Well…thank you, dear," she answered, still looking mighty strange. I shot a glance over at Gracie and could make out a little smile coming up from under her pigtails as she kept starring down at her cereal, Sam now in her lap.

Right about then here comes Dodger prancing into the room, no doubt smelling the food, and laid his big slobbery face right in my lap like usual. I looked down at his innocent, pleading eyes, and thought to myself what a big phony he was. I swear, this no good loaf almost causes me to lose a foot last night, ruins my best dream in years, then proceeds to force me outta my own bed just so he can make hisself nice and comfy, and now here he is, acting like my all time best pal, desperately in need of a small bite or he'd surely pass out from malnutrition.

"Not a chance, Buddy!" I said, without no remorse, pushing his slobberpuss off, and then going back at my breakfast with even greater enthusiasm.

He raised the left side of his upper lip just a tad like he normally did when he was about to growl, but then thought better of it and instead put one of his mangy paws on my leg and started to whimper.

"Aw, Johnny. He's giving you the paw. (That's what we called it when he lost all self respect and put his dirty foot smack dab in the middle of your lap to beg even harder.) How can you resist something so darling?" Ma said as she walked over and started to scratch his ears. Ya see, she weren't no help at all when it came to bad dogs, being a huge pushover for that sorta thing. It was just plain sickening. I wish a little of that kindness would rub off when it came to dealing with my less than stellar behavior once in a while. "Give him just a little taste. You know how he likes flapjacks."

"Come on, he'd beg for fried tarantula turds if that's what ya had," I thought but didn't say, and just broke off a piece that that mongrel snatched outta my hand along with almost half of my finger before it even cleared the plate, and then slid under the table smacking his lips, real satisfied.

I cleaned my plate in seconds after that, having worked up a big appetite from hunting ghosts and all, I guess, and not wanting to share no more with you know who, neither. I kept an ear open for any talk of last night from Ma, either straight up or round about, to get me to hang myself, which I'd done plenty in my younger, less sophisticated days. That wasn't gonna work this time. No way, Jose! I was ready for her best shot, and just bided my time, looking innocent and regular as could be. But nuthin' came. No "How'd you sleep last night, Johnny?" or "I heard a funny noise last night. Didn't you, dear?" or "You're looking a bit worn out this morning Johnny. Did you have a tough night?" No, not even a peep from the woman everyone knows is the biggest master of E.S.P this side of "The Famous Kresgee." And it was mind boggling how she knew stuff most times. You'd've swore she'd been there right by your side the whole time! Too bad it was always when you were doing something you could get lynched for, instead of after ya helped Gordito, old Mrs. Vasquez's cat, outta a tree or somethin'. But this time there warn't the slightest sign she'd got even a whiff of last night's activities. Could it be that Gracie wasn't the devil's child after all. Or maybe she'd finally realized the important lesson that sometimes big brothers had special stuff to do that were nobody else's business, and that's just the way it was gonna be around here from now on. Or maybe she was *finally* getting growed up and realized bein' a tattletale was very immature and a low down, good for nuthin' thing to be. Could it be that the era of me and the guys getting fingered every time we stepped outta line even an inch was finally coming to an end? Did this mean that the S.S.B.'s would finally rise up and realize their great potential as saviors of the neighborhood and maybe even all of greater Santa Elena just like we always wanted, without a bunch of nosey moms and little sisters keeping us down?

Well, I was starting to get that lovely, light and airy feeling, you know, when everything seemed to be going your way for the first time since…ever I guess, when all of the sudden the air got heavy as a cement truck all over again as a terrifying thought popped into my brain. What if Gracie wasn't all growed up and mature after all? What if she was actually more evil and cunning than I'd given her credit for? What if she was gonna want something in return for keeping her trap shut. Something much more awful and humiliating than just getting grounded by your folks!

I looked across the table at her with renewed suspicion and disgust, when just then the phone rang and Ma went into the den to answer it. It was Aunt Leah calling, which suited me just fine 'cause that meant about an hour of yakking about the big sale at Bob's Bargain Barn or the new girl working the soda fountain at El Minuto Market, or how embarrassing it was the way old Mrs. Simpson had her slip showing in church last Sunday.

That gave me the chance I needed and I walked around the table to Gracie and whispered in her ear, "I need to speak to you in my room, pronto."

I walked on through the den and down the hall and plopped down on my bed, still deep in worrisome thought. After a few minutes, here she comes, whistling to beat the band and half riding, half dragging poor Dodger as she came through the doorway. I shut the door quick behind her and grabbed her by the shoulders and sat her down on my bed. Dodger immediately jumped up and sat down next to her, just like he wasn't allowed to do, and they both stared at me with the same blank look on their faces.

After pacing back and forth a few times to gather my thoughts, I said, "Gracie, you're my little sister and I want you to know how much you mean to me." I shot her a quick glance to see if that might'a softened her up a bit, but her face was still stiff as a statue. "I know we've had our small differences in the past, but it never did add up to a hill of beans if ya think about it, and anyways, families that love each other and care about one another don't ever do nuthin' to hurt each other, right?" Still not even a hint of a smile from Gracie, although Dodger started getting a bit of a warm, sentimental look, I thought. So I kept on going. "So sometimes somethin' happens that may be very important to someone in this very close family, and if that someone got found out it would cause a lot of unnecessary pain and suffering for that certain someone, and that really wouldn't be good for no one at all. Do you understand?"

With that Dodger rolled clean over on his back with his legs spread wide, and Gracie started rubbing his stomach nice and slow. He was just lying there looking at me, upside down, with his upper lip hanging down low so you could see his full set of teeth. What a goofball of a dog, I thought, but then I decided I better finish up before I lost her attention completely.

"So, having said all that, and you and I agreeing on the fact that we are an *extremely* loving and caring family, I was thinking that maybe the best thing to do about what happened last night was just keep it to ourselves. What da ya think?" I asked quick, and then closed my eyes tight, waiting for the bad news I was sure was coming.

Well, she didn't take no time at all to think it over, and to my complete and grateful surprise, she looked me square in the face and said, "I think you hit it right on the head, Johnny. There ain't no use in telling Mama every little thing that goes on around this house anyhow. It'll just cause her to worry for no good reason."

I threw my arms around that sweet little child and hugged her for all I was worth. I even gave her a big, wet kiss or two on the cheek I was feeling so giddy and proud at her newfound maturity and intelligent outlook on things. Dodger raised his eyebrows and tilted his head as he watched us, the way dogs always do when somethin' just ain't right, but they can't quite figure it out.

"Gracie kid, I'm pleased as punch you and me see eye to eye on this here little matter, and I want ya to know that if you ever need some help to get you out of a fix, just say the word. Got it?" And I gave her another little squeeze around the shoulders.

"Thanks," she said as she pulled up at the corners of Dodger's mouth to make him look like he was wearing a huge grin.

"Is there anything else I can do for you, Crazy?" (Crazy is what Pop always liked to call her on account'a it kind of rhymed with Gracie and also cause he thought she was always acting nutty.)

"Well, there is just one little thing I would kinda like, I guess, Johnny."

I stopped cold in my tracks on my way outta the room and turned slowly to face her.

"You just name it, Sweetie. Anything your little heart desires."

"Really. Do ya mean it?"

"Sure, Cupcake. You just name it."

"Well, I was just thinking how nice it might be, to be able to hang out with you and the boys for the rest of the summer, and especially the next time you go over to the Mansfield place," she said, sweet as pie, without even looking up from the dog for a second.

I swear it was like I was struck by ten lightening bolts in the groin all at once, with a couple of body shots from Casius Clay to boot. The air was knocked clean outta me and my whole body got to trembling from my pinky toe to my teeth. So *that's* what the little monster was up to all along. So much for maturity and brotherly love! I should'a known better than to get my hopes up too high on a screw up this big and juicy. I snapped myself out of the near coma I was in, clinched my jaw, and gave her an ice cold, steely stare, saying, "There ain't no chance in hell you're doing *anything* with me and the guys, let alone going on top secret S.S.B. business. *Do you understand?*"

"Maybe *you* don't understand," she shot back. "If I tell Mama anything about last night, plus the fact that you just swore, your days with the S.S.B.s are over for the rest of the summer. Maybe forever! So put that in your pipe and smoke it!" I hated it when she tried using adult sayings like that. Come to think of it, I hated just about everything about her right about now.

Well, it goes without saying that I wanted to squeeze her neck 'til her pigtails stood straight out, but I knew if I even so much as *breathed* on her hard, she'd start spilling her guts faster than fudge down a fatso. I tried my hardest to control myself, but it wasn't working, especially after the wink and smirk she just shot my way, and I started edging towards her with teeth clinched and nostrils flared. But just before all hell broke loose I pulled back, remembering something Pop once told me. Something like, "When you're in a fix, use your fists if ya gotta, but there ain't no shame in using your head, neither." So instead, I sat myself down on the bed next to Dodger and thought. If Ma found me out, then I ate the big chimichanga

for sure, and I could say "Sayonara" to all the great stuff we were gonna get after it got out about us catching the first real live ghost in the history of mankind and all. On the other hand, if I tried to bring my snot nosed sister along with me, not only would I be banished from the S.S.B.'s forever in disgrace, but I'd be such a laughing stock that I'd hafta move to Siberia or somewheres just so I wouldn't get my face pounded soon as some guy heard my name! I was in an awful tight spot, no doubt, and I searched my brains over and over to try and come up with some way to wiggle outta it, while Gracie messed with Dodger's ears in all kinds of ways pretending to give him different hairdos. Well, I finally figured after almost being put six feet under by that ghost last night and living to tell about it, I'd come way too far to just throw it all away, and besides, I couldn't stand missing out on all the cool stuff coming our way once we were world famous.

"Okay, you can tag along with us, but you gotta promise to keep your trap shut and listen to what I say no matter what. Got it?" I said, almost choking on every sickening syllable.

"Sure thing, Johnny," she said, smiling with excitement and jumping up and down on the bed as Dodger gave her a worried look.

"Alright then, now get the heck outta my room," I said, with my head in my hands, knowing my goose was cooked with the guys sure as I'm telling you this. But just as I was thinking that at least things couldn't get no worse, that little devil spoke up once again.

"Johnny, there's one more little thing."

"Now what?" I asked, too weak to even look up.

"I want Dodger to come along too."

# Chapter Nineteen

## I AM HUMILIATED

That was it. The final humiliation. Not only did I have to take my little sister with me everywhere I went for the rest of the summer, but that worthless, obnoxious, too dumb too even learn one trick Dodger to boot. Well, I'd heard that the good Lord only tried folks to make them strong, bit I tell ya what, if I get through what he stuck me with this time, I'll be the next Sampson! Heck, I already got the ridiculous hair.

My body was totally numb through and through by now, with as much strength left as a newborn chick. By the way, did I ever tell you about the time Gracie and I got baby chicks for Easter. Let's just say that a stuffed one instead of a real live one may be a better choice for kids less than five, and a whole lot nicer to look at after you accidentally step on it! Anyways, I walked down the hall; feet dragging and head hung low, and plunked myself down on the green shag carpeting in the den. I just lay there for a while and stared up at the ceiling feeling lower than a river toad run over by a semi-truck, when the phone rang and snapped me outta my terrible torture.

"Hello," I said, barely able to force the words out.

"Johnny C.?"

"Yup."

"What's the password?"

"Huh? Oh, ah, Nancy Cole is an A-hole," I answered, realizing it was official S.S.B. business.

"Okay, be at the clubhouse this morning by ten for a 'Super Secret Ghetto Gathering', got it?"

"Got it."

Something's was definitely up. I was expecting a meeting this morning to plan out our next step in the Mansfield mess and all, but the voice on the other end of the line wasn't Jagger or Big I or even Neil. Nope. I could'a swore it was Rosie! And if that's what's what, it's the first time I recall him ever calling any kind of anything 'cept, of course one of our famous, "Feeding Frenzies," which came up anytime one of us fixed to "borrow" a tray of *apple empanadas* that were cooling off on the back porch of La Estrella Bakery on the corner of Ajo and Las Palmas, just down from Conchita's Curios. I wonder what the heck Rosie was up to?

I raced down the hall and threw on some cut offs and and baseball sleeves, seeing it was already 9:30 and all, but as I ran by Gracie's room, I heard her call out, like fingernails on a chalk board, "Where're ya off to, Big Brother?"

"None of your business, that's where. Understand?"

"Well, I suppose it doesn't have to do with our little *deal* then?"

I knew what she was getting at, and my blood started to boil, but I sucked it up and said calm as a cucumber, "Nope, just going to the Sewer to play a little ghetto ball with the guys. Nuthin' you'd be interested in." (Ghetto ball was basketball without no rules. You don't hafta dribble or pass or nuthin'. Heck you could even tackle the guy if you felt like it. All you were trying to do was put the ball in the basket anyway possible. Jagger made it up.)

"That's funny, 'cause I could've swore someone just called for a top secret meeting."

Why that little leech had been listening in on Mom's princess phone! "Darn it, Gracie, you're going too far now. Don't push me. Got it!"

"I'm not pushing anyone, but only making sure that you live up to your end of the agreement, that's all. So, of course, Dodger and I will be accompanying you this morning. Let me just put on something appropriate. Come on Dodgie," She said as she jumped off her bed and ran into her closet.

My teeth were clinched near to breaking and the pressure in my head was building like it was the tenth pump on one of those water rockets, and I could'a swore my eyeballs would shoot across the room any minute. I wanted so to beat dear, sweet Gracie to a ragged pulp, but knew where that would land me. Oh, but it would feel *so* nice! How about just a few well placed monkey bumps and maybe an Indian burn? No, no I had to keep cool. But it was so hard!

I fought back the urge and said, "By the way, I forgot to ask earlier, how'd you find out all about what happened last night?"

"Well, first I heard you and Dodger rustling around about something close to nine o'clock (Of course, *Dodger!*) so I started to listen real hard and then heard what sounded like you falling out your window and into the bushes. I jumped out of bed to take a peek outside and caught a glimpse of you running off across the street and into the alley behind the Bradley's place. After that I tried and tried but just couldn't fall asleep 'cause I was thinking about what you were up to and all, so I tossed and turned for a while until around eleven and then heard some noises like screams coming from the desert. I ran into the back yard and jumped on one of the lawn chairs so I could see over the wall, and I peered out and saw a bunch of small lights far off flickering and going this way and that all around the Mansfield place. After that there was a lot of screams and moans and carrying on, and then after all the commotion stopped, I came back inside and wrote you that little note."

Well, if that ain't pathetic I don't know what is. Here is an eight year old girl who didn't even have to break a sweat to figure out every little detail of official, top-secret S.S.B. business. We, I mean, I, was a complete disgrace to the S.S.B.'s, the F.B.I., the C.I.A., and even the A.S.P.C.A.! I deserved what I was gonna get. Let's face it. But, when you get right down to it, the whole stinking mess started with good old, "cause you nuthin' but trouble," Dodger. I'm really starting to despise that mutt. I mean, he's practically ruining my life.

"Ma, I'm taking Gracie and Dodger down to the schoolyard to horse around a while, okay?" I said as we walked through the kitchen. She was standing at the counter laying out some long strips of pasta into her favorite pan to make lasagna for tonight's dinner.

"Why, Johnny, that is awful sweet of you, dear. I'm very happy that you have decided to include your little sister more in your playtime. It is about time you two started to get to be more close. She is the only sister you have, after all."

"Thank God for that," I muttered under my breath.

"Johnny, would you mind terribly pulling me along in the wagon. It's an awful long way for a little girl like me to walk," Gracie said as she looked over at me and smiled. Oh, boy was she pushing it!

"That is a very good idea, Gracie Elizabeth. I don't want you to get overheated. You better make sure you wear a helmet too, just in case you fall over," Ma said.

I got my Baltimore Colts football helmet outta the cupboard, and jammed it on her head, hard, then I dumped all the junk outta her Radio Flyer, grabbed a jump rope and a handful of dog treats and headed out the door.

When we were outta sight of the house, I sat Gracie down in the wagon with the football helmet on as snug as I could get it since it was about ten sizes too big, then I tied one end of the rope to Dodger's collar and the other to the wagon handle, filled my back pocket with dog treats, and started walking down the street again. Soon as he caught the scent, Dodger started to follow me close behind, pulling the wagon along with 'im as he went. Now I know it probably looked real ridiculous and embarrassing and all, me walking along with that stupid mutt smelling my butt all the while, but if I was gonna be put to the unthinkable shame of bringing my baby sister to a big time meeting like this, I sure as heck wasn't gonna pull her myself! Anyways, I figured if that fleabag was gonna hafta come along, too, he might as well make hisself useful.

"This is so much fun, Johnny. We just have to play together more often," Gracie said, while she giggled and bounced along in that wagon, holding on to the facemask, so as to keep the helmet from falling down over her eyes.

"Yeah, it's stinkin' sensational," I muttered, although I gotta admit that seeing her having such a bang up time started to make me fee kinda good inside after awhile. That was, 'til I remembered she was totally *blackmailing* me!

Things were going along pretty smooth for the most part, with me strolling along, breathing in the still cool morning air, and Dodger sniffing my butt and pulling that wagon right along with 'im, real easy like, 'til outta nowhere, here comes that no good Nancy Cole's cat, Chatty Cathy, running right for us. Well, I don't hafta tell ya, all hell broke loose then, 'cause before I could grab a hold of Dodger's collar, he was off after that cat like he was shot out of a howitzer. Little Gracie let out a screech and hung on to the edge of the Radio Flyer for dear life, the football helmet bouncing on her little noggin like a bobble head doll, and then finally falling way down over her eyes so she couldn't see a thing, which was probably best considering what was probably about to happen. I took off after 'em yelling and waving, but that idiotic dog is fast as lightning when he wants to be, which ain't often, and he wanted that uppity Chatty Cathy something fierce.

So there we were, me chasing that wagon like a madman and ordering Dodger to stop, and he not paying no mind at all, and even running faster the closer I got to collaring 'im. I yelled out, "Sit!" and, "Heel!" and, "Play dead!" and every other command I could think of, but nuthin' slowed 'im down a lick. But that ain't surprising seeing he was too dumb to have learned any of them tricks in the first place. I even yelled out, "Treat!" which almost always did the job, but not this time, he was dead set on catching that obnoxious cat and nuthin' in this world was gonna stop 'im.

Gracie kept hanging on, her body jiggling faster than a fat lady's butt on one of them lard shakers over that rough old asphalt, and zig-zagging like mad form side to side as Dumbger was closing in on Chatty at every turn. Her football helmet was all the way covering her face by now, but she didn't dare let go of the wagon to try and push it up. A couple of times that old Radio Flyer went banking up on two wheels and come within an inch of tipping over, only to right itself at the last second, and each time it did, I had about three coronaries, knowing darn well that if Gracie got banged up on my account, I'd be so old by the time I got outta solitary my head would look like a cue ball and my face like a road map of Mexico City!

Anyways, that dog was barking, and the cat was screeching, and Gracie was screaming, and I was yelling, and we all kept running up and down and round and round like a bunch of lunatics, 'til finally that cat lit out for a tall cottonwood tree across from Nancy's house and climbed up quick as, well, a cat. Dodger, with only a few neurons to work with, wasn't able to realize what was happening fast enough, and kept running for all he was worth, smack dab into the tree trunk with his head down like a battering ram. That staggered him considerable, and he took a couple of jelly leg steps back and then tried to shake the cobwebs out, but with that anvil-like head of his, it warn't five seconds before he was back to barking up the tree at the cat, who was just laying there, calm as could be on the lowest branch, with her tail waving in the breeze and nearly touching his frustrated face with each easy pass. Gracie, on the other hand, went flying through the air like a ragdoll, as Dodger came to his sudden stop, flying clean over the mutt, and after doing a full summersault, landed flat on her back with a thud, just missing an especially nasty looking barrel cactus on the way.

As I raced over to where she was laying with my stomach doing a mean rendition of the rumba, I noticed she was making this high pitched, whimpering sound that was all muffled up on account of the football helmet was now turned completely *backward* on her head. I unsnapped the chinstrap and yanked the helmet off prepared for the worst, but as I did, I realized, thanks be to God, she weren't crying at all, but instead was giggling!

"Wow-wee, Johnny! Did ya see *that!*" she yelled. "That was more fun than the big kid's roller coaster at last year's rodeo. Dodger's the coolest dog ever! Make 'im do it again, will ya! Come on. Make 'im do it again!"

I just sat there dumfounded and counting my lucky stars. I guess you can say what you want about Gracie but most of the time, I gotta admit, she was a pretty tough cookie. I helped her up and dusted her off and told her how brave she was and all, knowing full well how things can change in flash with little kids, and before ya knew it, what was once cool and exciting now was the most horrifying thing they ever did see, and the laughing and giggling all of a sudden turns into sobbing and screaming for, "Mommy!" But, lucky for me, this time she just couldn't get enough.

"I don't think that's such a great idea, Gracie. Sometimes too much fun ain't a good thing, if you know what I mean. Anyways, you're lucky you didn't get your head cracked open the first time around."

"Aw, come on, Johnny, go get the cat and make 'im run around all crazy-like just one more time, would ya? For me, pleeease!"

"Nope, that's it. I don't think Ma would take too kindly to you running the Indy 500 out here in nuthin' but a Radio Flyer and a football helmet."

I picked up my Colts helmet and strapped it back on her, which she immediately pulled down over her eyes and then crossed her arms over her chest with a "Huff!" to protest my decision.

Dodger was standing up on his hind legs against that cottonwood and getting hisself all worked up to a tizzy again over that blasted cat. He even tried jumping at her a couple'a times, but that didn't work on account'a he was too fat to get more than an inch or two off the ground, and he landed back down hard on his honches, and none too graceful, neither. That cat really knew how to push his buttons, too, just lying there like she didn't have a care in the world, stretching and licking herself and yawning, like she was herself all ready for her afternoon nap. I tried calming Dodger down but there was no reasoning with 'im. Like I told ya before, once he got an idea in that peabrain of his, it pretty much took an act of God to pry it out. I finally tried to coax 'im with a handful of treats, and right in front of his nose, too, but that only got 'im to stop long enough to make a quick try for them, and then here comes all the barking and whining all over again.

He was really getting on my nerves by now, and I knew it wouldn't be long before one of the neighbors would come out and give me an earful, and sure enough, right about then the front door to the Cole's place swung open, and I could barely make out the sound of footsteps in between Dodger's barking, coming up behind me. I cringed at the thought of having to deal with Nancy, or any of her mutant family members for that matter, who I heard were still pretty steamed about our surface to air missile assault on their house a few weeks back.

"Well, well, well, if it isn't the great Johnny Caruso, causing another huge scene just to try to bring a little attention to himself. I should have known." Just the sound of Nancy's voice was enough to make the hairs on the back of your neck stand straight at attention, kinda like pulling a rusty wire across a water pipe.

"Hi Gracie," she said, but Gracie didn't say nuthin' on a account'a her still being peeved about not getting another ride, and she just stood there with her arms cross and the helmet pulled down over her eyes. "Are you gonna get that mutt to shut up or what?"

I whirled around to tell her who I thought was the bigger mutt, when I noticed there was someone with her. I caught a quick glimpse of red hair from behind Nancy's oversized head, and then out from behind her stepped the perfectly feminine form of Jenny Darling.

Well, I guess my jaw must'a fell wide open, 'cause Nancy gave me this funny, kinda questioning look, and I felt my body go tingly all over. After realizing how stupid I had to look, I glanced down to the ground with my heart thumping like a tractor engine with a bad cylinder, and managed a,

"Hey, ah, Jenny. How's it shakin'?" I wished right off I would've left off the "shakin'" part, but nuthin' I could do about it now.

Jenny just batted those emerald eyes of hers, gave me a big sweet smile and said, "Hello, Johnny," soft and sweet, and then *she* looked down and started to smooth over the dirt in front of her with dainty little feet.

What was going on? What was it about this girl that made me all giddy instead of wanting to puke like all the rest of 'em? It was really very weird, and a little bit scary, too. Jenny was different, that's all I could say. She was kind and smart instead of dumb and mean, and never talked too much or to little, but always just the right amount, and never in that squeaky, ear piercing girly voice, neither, but in a lovely, kinda sing-songy way. Her eyes were soft and moist and sparkly and her hair and clothes were always just so, and if she had something special in her lunch box she always offered you a taste, instead of stuffing the whole thing in her mouth fast as she could when she saw you coming so she wouldn't hafta share none. It's real hard to explain, but she had this way about her that just made you want to *do* something for her, if you know what I mean, and it could be anything, anything in this whole wide world. I guess that's the best way to describe how I felt about Jenny Darling.

"How's your folks doin', Jenny?" I said, after a long dry spell.

"Just fine. Thank you for asking. We just came back from a two week vacation in San Diego." San Diego was everyone's favorite place to head to when the heat got intolerable around these parts. Pop said he figured half of the state of Arizona was over there at one time or another during the summer. I'd been hoping maybe Pop would see his way clear to take us over someday, too, but so far no dice, seems he just didn't trust nobody else to watch his business for even one day.

"Well, it must've been nice to get out of the heat and go to the ocean and all," I said as earnest as possible, trying to hide any jealousy that might slip out.

"Yes it was, Johnny, very nice. Thank you." She was ever so sweet and lovely and always said "Yes" instead of "Yup" or "Yeah," like most kids, and made sure to sprinkle in plenty of "Thank yous" and "Pleases," and other such polite stuff.

"Excuse me, Romeo," Nancy's voice broke up my peaceful trance like a sonic boom. "Are you going to shut that obnoxious dog's trap or do I have to call Sheriff Mengo? All this racket is giving me a migraine!"

You see, good old Mengo wasn't only the head lawman of Santa Elena, but also doubled as the town Dog Catcher, Justice of the Peace, Head Little League Ump, like you already saw, and Master of Ceremonies at all Santa Elena special events when Mayor Troncoza was "Officially unavailable," which meant he was either fishing down at Patagonia Lake or in real hot water with Mrs. Troncoza again and she wouldn't let 'im outta the house.

Well, I wasn't gonna let old Nasty get to me this time, wanting to show I could keep my cool under pressure in front of Jenny, so I turned to her and said, "Nope, that won't be necessary, ladies. I'll be happy to get 'im outta here for ya and make sure he don't do no harm to your sweet little kitty." Then I smiled big and wide at Jenny and she smiled right back. With that I took the rope off the wagon handle, made sure it was still tied tight to Dodger's collar, who by the way had not stopped yapping for one single second the whole time, and after a couple of good hard yanks, was able to turn his fat head away from the tree. As soon as I did, he completely forgot what he was doing there in the first place and raced over to me and started sniffing my butt all over again. Well, that wasn't somethin' I was particularly interested in Jenny seeing, and I sure didn't want her getting the wrong idea about what he was sniffing at, so I grabbed all the dog treats out of my back pocket and held them out high in front of me as I started to walk away. Sure enough, here comes Dodger right along, drooling and carrying on 'til I finally gave 'im a little taste.

I yelled to Gracie to grab the wagon and get a move on, which, of course, she didn't 'til I was nearly outta of sight, and then, just like always, when she was afraid of getting left behind, she changed her mind. First, she pulled up her helmet just above her eyes and stuck her tongue out at Jenny and Nancy, then pulled it back down, slowly uncrossed her arms, grabbed the wagon handle, and came racing after me with the Radio Flyer bumping along behind.

As I turned the corner I looked back over my shoulder and gave Jenny a big wave goodbye while Nancy Cole stood there with her face all twisted screaming somethin' at me I couldn't quite make out. Gracie was still kinda peeved and giving me the cold shoulder, but that didn't bother me none 'cause it meant not having to listen to her non stop jabbering for a change. I kept right along at a pretty good clip now that we were behind schedule due to Dodger's little adventure, and as we turned up Jag's alley it looked like I was the last one to show. All the gang's bikes were parked nice and orderly outside the clubhouse, all 'cept Jagger's, which was off to the side in a heap, and looked like he had just jumped off it at full speed and let her run 'til she dropped, which was his "signature dismount," and she was almost clean under the oleander hedge that separated his house from the Ashcroft's next door. The Ashcroft's were decent folks, I suppose, though nobody knew for sure seeing that they didn't have any boys to hang around with, but I heard through the Gestapo that this coming Christmas they were thinking of getting a trampoline in their back yard for their two little girls, a decision that was roundly condemned by Ma, but unanimously cheered by us, and Neil said come fall we needed to make sure and start swinging by their place here and there to see if there was anything Mrs. Ashcroft might need help with, in order to put ourselves in position for some invites down the road.

The sun was sitting pretty high up in the sky by now which meant it was getting nice and toasty, and I unsnapped the chin strap and took the football helmet off Gracie and wiped the sweat off her forehead with the end of my T shirt.

"You don't have to wear that old helmet no more, kid. It is only for protection while you're riding," I said as I went over and put it in the wagon.

She just scrunched up her eyes and nose real tight and then without saying a word went over and grabbed the helmet and slapped it back on, pulling it down tight over her eyes the way she liked. She could really be tough when she wanted to be, and *boy* could she ever hold a grudge. She was the queen of grudge holding if you ask me, and don't just take my word for it, you could ask anybody. Heck, one time she wouldn't talk to *Dodger* for a week on account'a he ate her last Milk Dud; the last outta a box of about a hundred!

"Listen," I said. "You stay right here and keep an eye on that stupid dog while I go in and see the guys. Understand? It looks bad enough for me to have you standing out here, but there's a no fooling, honest to God, serious as a heart attack rule about girls being *in* the clubhouse. Got it?"

"Our agreement was that I got to come along on *all* your stuff with the boys. So I'm coming in too. *Got it?*" she said with the sinister sneer, barely visible through the facemask, that showed she knew how much she annoyed me and there weren't one stinking thing I could do about it.

I was fuming after that, and I started stomping around in a circle, clinching my jaw and punching the air. Dodger sat next to Gracie panting, and watching me go round and round like I was nuts. He tilted his head to the side after my third time through, trying to figure out in his little dog brain what the heck I was doing.

Finally, I stopped in front of her and said, "Okay, listen, at least give me a minute or two to let the guys know the score before you come barging in, okay?" She lifted up the helmet just enough so I could see her eyes and gave me a cold stare right back, then pulled it back down and crossed her arms harder.

I walked over to the door of the clubhouse, banged out a few bars of "Wipe Out," which was the secret code this week, and then opened it up and crawled on in.

"'Bout time," Neil said, sitting against the far wall. "You'd think after that fiasco last night that you'd be embarrassed to show up late for a top secret, emergency meeting." Right off I could see Neil was back to his old pleasant, considerate self.

"Tell ya the truth," I said. "I'm kinda surprised, you ever stopped running, considering the way you high tailed it off the porch of that old place like a jackrabbit with a bottle rocket up it's butt! I don't smell nuthin' so you musta changed your underwear when you got home." Neil didn't take too kindly to that, just as I expected, and he started coming for me with nostrils flared and teeth clinched, but Jag put an arm out against his chest to stop 'im and said with a smile, "I g-guess we were all a l-l-little s-spooked last night. B-b-but that's old n-n-news and we gotta p-plan our next step."

"Jag, I gotta tell you guys somethin' and it's important," I started, but he cut me off.

"L-l-later, Johnny. R-right now Rosie's got the floor s-s-seeing he's the one to c-call the meeting. As for me, all I w-wanted to say is that I already t-took the film from my Brownie over to Mr. Cooper (Chicken Coop's pop) at the f-five and dime and he's gonna develop it s-soon as he's able. Now without f-further delay, I give you Mr. Emeliano de la Rosa."

"But Jag!" I blurted out, but he gave me a quick, nasty scowl and I shut myself back up.

Rosie slowly leaned in toward the middle of the circle with Cooper and Creepy sitting right along side, proud as peacocks that their big buddy was in charge of such an important meeting, as Ira and Neil both stared at him trying to figure what the heck an old coward like Rosie could possibly have to say about such a mind numbing, spine tingling, utterly horrific situation like this one, 'cept maybe that he wanted his mommy.

No matter what, we were all ears, and wondering what our next step should be to reel in that no good ghost. Rosie started off by mopping the ever present drops of sweat from his forehead and upper lip, and then took in a deep long breath, but just as he opened his mouth to speak, there was a bang on the door and it didn't sound nuthin' like, "Wipe Out." In fact, I'm ashamed to say, that it sounded a lot more like "Ring Around the Rosie" and there was even some singing along with it! I covered my face with my hands in shame, knowing darn well what was coming next as everyone else stared over at the door in wonder while it opened up wide, and then in crawled Gracie, helmet first, just as easy as pie.

All the guys were thunderstruck and speechless, with mouths open wide, as she squeezed herself in between Coop and me, sat down Indian style and said, "Howdy, boys!" like she'd been doing it all her life. I guess you gotta give her credit. That little twit had moxie.

Well, all eyes were glued on her, amazed, but still no one could say a word, like when something so utterly horrible happens and you get a frog in your throat big as a bowling ball. No girl, and for that matter, no *anyone* but a full fledged S.S.B, had dared ever so much as put a pinky toe in our official clubhouse for the long and storied history of it's existence, a full two years, but there was Gracie, a *little sister* for crying out loud, sitting right in our circle like this was *Romper Room* or somethin'.

After a second or two, when things started to sink in, all the guys stopped staring at Gracie, and started starring at *me*, and I could see through my hands, that were covering my face by now, the anger swelling up in their faces and getting ready to blow like that Mount Kill-a-Whale volcano! I didn't take my hands away just yet on account'a I knew that the worst was still to come, but just as they started coming towards me with Neil in the lead with his fist pulled back and cocked, in ran Dodger like a freight train at full speed, and headed right for Neil! Well, that lead to complete panic as you could imagine, and before ya knew it that mutt had Neil pinned to the wall and was licking his face up and down like there was no tomorrow. The screams were loud and horrifying from everyone 'cept Neil, who was doing his darndest to just keep breathing from all the slobber, and then there was a mad scramble to hide ourselves from that marauding monster. But that got old Dodge even more riled up and he started racing from person to person, licking and barking and biting and jumping, and waging his bristly tail so hard that it stung if it caught ya just right, and pretty much having hisself the time of his life. Since we was packed in there so tight with nowhere to go, it was like shooting fish in a washtub!

Gracie was beside herself with glee, giggling and pointing and every now and then letting out one of those little kids squeals of utter joy, while everyone else was being tortured to within an inch of their lives. I was yelling for Dodger to stop, and tried over and over to grab 'im by the collar, but he was too quick. Pretty soon someone came to their senses and opened the door, causing a mad dash of crawling kids for safety. Dodge wasn't about to give up the goose that easy, and seeing a great opportunity for his favorite sport of all, proceeded to chomp the heck outta any and all rear ends that made themselves available. This added to the already considerable screaming and cursing from the once proud S.S.B.'s as the guys tried, mostly in vain to avoid those razor sharp teeth. Poor Rosie, being the slowest and also the largest and juiciest target got more than his fair share of attention.

Good old mild mannered Emiliano looked none to happy as he finally squeezed his way out, being the last one to do so, rubbing his rear with both hands to try and ease the pain. Dodger on the other hand stuck his head out the door looking pleased as punch, and deciding he liked our clubhouse just fine after everyone had cleared out, promptly laid down and instantly fell asleep. He flat out refused to come out no matter what I did, probably sensing, the way dogs often do, that he was about to get his neck rung if he showed too much of it. Speaking of getting your neck rung, the guys all started circling me now that all the commotion was over with, rubbing their butts and wiping their eyes, and as I looked up to the Man upstairs for deliverance, there seemed to be no one home. Maybe He was busy hiding from his little sister!

# Chapter Twenty

## ROSIE TAKES CHARGE

I was getting mighty hot around the collar as the guys closed in, when Jagger, like he so often did when things were going to hell in a hand basket, jumped into the middle of the circle in front of me and said, "Hold on a sec. L-l-let's give Johnny a chance to explain hisself, b-before anyone g-g-gets too excited. What da ya s-say?"

"Not a chance! I say we pound the little sissy traitor first, and talk later," Neil said, smashing his fist into his hand over and over with more ferociousness as he went, only stopping once in a while to wipe the dog slobber from his face.

They rest of the irritated and injured kept on coming, too, even Creepy and Chicken Coop, 'til finally in a last desperate act to save my skin I yelled out, "Hold on guys, just hold on and listen for one second!" trying not to sound too yellow. "Listen fellas! Just give me a minute and I'll show ya how I had absolutely no choice but to bring that little nuisance along with me and this mangy mutt to boot!" (I was gonna us the old Bible line of "He who has never screwed up may throw the first stone," but I figured all that'd do was give them the bright idea of braining me with rocks as well as their fists!)

That did manage to slow 'em just enough to gave me a chance to let on how Gracie had seen me leave the night before and all, and her underhanded blackmailing of me into letting her come along or else she'd spill the beans on our whole operation and all our plans and future stardom would be worth about as much as a Mexican *centavo*.

No need to tell ya the guys weren't in an especially generous mood after suffering the indignity of being run outta their sacred clubhouse by a mad dog, like so many rustlers outta Dodge, and then being viscously violated on some very personal parts to boot, but they stopped the squeezing just a tad, and I could tell by their blank faces that they were at least willing to mull things over. I was praying my long, loyal devotion and sparkling service record as a founding member of the Seward School Bombers might pull just a little weight to sway my long time pals, and now short time enemies, to make a favorable settlement of this matter in my behalf.

"As president of these here S.S.B.'s, I s-say we have an emergency m-m-meeting of the disciplinary council and d-d-decide on the f-fate of this here f-fellow member," said Jag authoritative as all get out. Now, of course, we didn't have no "disciplinary council," but it sounded real professional and all anyways, and anytime some sorta problem popped up, we just invented whatever committee or whatnot we needed to get the job done. It was a system that served us just swell up to now.

After that the whole lot of 'em crawled back into the clubhouse, grumbling as they went, and shut the door as I stood outside with Dodger and Gracie and wondered if my goose was cooked. There hadn't been much need for discipline in the S.S.B.'s in the past, on account'a for the most part everyone pretty much stuck to the rules, and if we did happen to get caught doing somethin' of "questionable merit," as Ma liked to say, our folks usually found out faster than a wild fire through dry desert brush and there weren't no need for punishing ourselves, we got all we wanted at home. There was this one time when Neil was, "officially reprimanded," for breaking the code of honesty when he stuck one of his own hairs in the last bite of a hamburger over at the El Minuto Market Luncheonette and then raised such a ruckus, the poor soda jerk finally gave 'im a brand new one just to shut his trap. At the official hearing, with Jag as the judge, me as council for the persecution, and Rosie as Neil's handpicked council for the defense since he was the most compassionate when it came to culinary matters, he pleaded in his defense that he was flat broke since his big brother Barry beat his last week's allowance outta him, and he absolutely had to have another burger or his hippoglycemia would'a kicked in causing 'im to have a conniption fit and a half in front of the whole town, and how embarrassing would that be to the proud reputation of all Seward School Bombers and those youngsters who inspired to someday reach such heights themselves. Well, Jag figured who the heck were we to argue with medical science, and anyway, we all saw right off the genius of Neil's idea and thought we might like to give it a try some day ourselves in a pinch, so we let 'im off pretty much scott free, 'cept that he was supposed to bring snacks to our meetings for a year, no questions asked. That lasted a week.

There was also some major grumbling about Jagger after the tennis ball bazooka debacle, but first of all it would'a been downright embarrassing to us all to discipline our own President, and secondly nobody really had the *cojones* to get Jag too ticked off, so we just let it slide.

Well, I was about to jump outta my skin just standing there waiting for my sentence, so after a bit I put my ear up to the door to try and decipher what the mood inside was like. Mostly I heard nasty screams like, "Pound!" and, "Beat!" and even, "Bludgeon!" so I kinda got a bleak picture. I started to think on how *I* would'a felt if someone else brought *their* little sister and obnoxious dog to a top-secret meeting, but that didn't make me feel no better, so I stopped. Gracie and Dodger, on the other hand, they were having a great old time chasing a horny toad up and down the alley, with Dumbger yapping his head off and doing this dorky leap from side to side trying to trap the little varmint but not having any luck, and Gracie screeching at the top of her lungs the way little girls do sometimes for no reason at all, 'til the poor, scared out its wits creature slipped down its hole. Gracie gave up and walked back toward the clubhouse, helmet bobbing back and forth on her head, but Dodger, not one to give up so easy, hunkered down on his belly and stuck his nose down that hole far as he could, sniffing away, and letting out a little moan every once in a while, the way he does at home when his tennis ball gets stuck under the couch and he can't get it out.

I was getting some major colon quivers by then, and started to think that maybe I should just make a run for it now while I still was able, and then just deal with the guys after everyone cooled down a bit, when the door creaked opened and out they crawled. Creepy came out first, being lowest on the totem pole, followed by Chicken Coop, Rosie, Neil, Big I and then Jag. I searched their faces, frantically looking for a clue about my fate, but there was nuthin', just a stone cold stare from the lot of 'em, all 'cept Neil, who was wearing a sickening sneer, and nodding his head assuredly like, "Oh yeah. Now your gonna get yours." They slowly made a circle around me and then Jag motioned to Bampu to go ahead. The Creep had taken to doing all the official talking for the S.S.B.'s lately, our "mouthpiece," Ira called 'im, on account'a the fact that he knew a bunch more words than the rest of us, some more than a mile long, and it gave the club a real sense of style and class that, let's face it, we could use for a change. Right then Dodger came sauntering over to sniff around where he shouldn't, and I noticed all the guys put their hands behind them to protect their rear ends. I tried not to snicker, no matter how silly they looked, seeing how serious this whole shebang was supposed to be, and so I just stared straight ahead at good old Creepy as he started to read the notes he'd taken on the back of a tomato soup can label he must'a found lying around the alley somewheres.

"Here ye, here ye, on the official matter of disciplinary action of one, Johnny Caruso, founding member (I was glad they remembered) and current Vice President (I was *thrilled* they remembered) of the honorable Seward School Bombers," he said in his deepest, authority voice but still all garbled like. "In regards to his knowingly, and willingly (Uh, oh) violating the sacred rules against females in the clubhouse at any time, and especially during times of top secret meetings, and for totally and unequivocally (Huh?) disrupting the aforementioned meeting by introducing his ill behaved canine, known as Dodger into the confines of the clubhouse (After hearing his name called, that stupid mutt raced over behind Bampu looking for a treat) and therefore causing severe bodily and psychological harm to several of his fellow members, (I shot a glance over at Rosie and he was nodding his total agreement with this last part as he continued to rub his sore butt) the disciplinary council of the S.S.B.'s has voted anonymously on the following actions: 1) The offending member shall walk at the back of the group, in shame, and be completely responsible for keeping the aforementioned canine and female in line for the remainder of the day (That sounds fair). 2) The offending member shall not be allowed to speak or offer any opinion at all about the day's business unless first asked to do so by another member in good standing (I could live with that). Bampu started up again. 3) In lieu (Lou?) of the fact that several members of the official council were, in fact, both physically and mentally abused by the said canine, Dodger, who is after all Mr. Caruso's responsibility, it has been wholeheartedly agreed upon that Mr. Caruso himself should suffer the physical consequences of one hunky, hairy pinkie." (Ruuun!)

Unlucky for me I ran smack into Rosie's big blubbery belly, bounced off and landed flat on my back in the middle of the circle, right where they wanted me. For those of you lucky enough to never had a pinkie, it's when a bunch of guys hold you down, lift up your shirt and start to slap your bare stomach so hard and fast that it burns like fire and turns red as hot coal. It's absolutely horrifying, one of the worst pains a kid can experience, and exactly what they had in mind for poor old Johnny C. Before I knew it they were on me like a pack of piranhas on a porky pigmy, slapping themselves silly and just having a great old time. I tried squirming away but it warn't no use, they had Rosie lying across my chest and it took all the energy I could muster just to keep on breathing! Dodger, my faithful companion, didn't do nuthin' to help, and instead started licking my face unmerciful, and then when he realized I couldn't move at all, he started biting me on the ears. I started to wonder all over again what I did to deserve a dog like this. I mean he was definitely defective. If he was a blender you could return him to the store for a full refund, no questions asked.

When the guys were finally satisfied they'd caused enough pain and Rosie rolled off, I just laid there for a minute completely limp, with my eyes closed, not wanting to let on how much pain I was in, when all of a sudden I felt another searing whack against my poor aching belly, and when I jumped up to see what *that* was all about, there was lovely little sister Grace looking over me with a wide grin on her lips.

"What the heck do you think you're doin'?" I yelled as I gave her a stiff shove that sat her on her keister.

"Hey!" She squealed. "Everyone else was doin' it so I thought I'd give it a try. Anyways, it looked like fun...you big poop!" Then she pulled the helmet back down over her eyes, but not before she stuck her tongue out at me hard as she could. It was hopeless. Even my own flesh and blood couldn't wait to take a shot at me when the chips were down. It just wasn't right.

Well I straightened up slow, brushed myself off, and then very gently lowered my shirt down over my poor, burning tummy, trying to keep it from touching best I could, then walked over to the oleander hedge where the guys were gathered to listened as Jagger started up, "N-n-now that that's over, l-l-lets get back to the real reason we called this here m-meeting, and that was for Rosie to tell us his ideas about trapping that old ghost and for us to g-get on with becoming world famous and all. G-g-go right ahead, Rosie, pal," and he motioned for 'im to come on forward as he slid back into the group.

Now it was plain that Rosie just didn't feel at home in such an important position as this, being mostly humble and soft spoken and all, and he started fidgeting and kicking at the dirt and stared straight into the ground and didn't say a peep. This just wasn't his way. For as long as I'd knowed 'im, and that was all his life, he ain't never took charge of nuthin', and all I could say was he must'a had a darn good reason this time to torture hisself so, but I guess we'd all find out.

After a little while more, he looked up, shot a worried glance over at us guys and then one at Creepy and Coop who were all over beaming with pride and trying to encourage 'im to start up with some little hand gestures, but still nuthin' but dead silence. Finally, fed up to here, Big I shouts out, "You gonna say somethin' this year de la Rosa or are we gonna hafta do a Vulcan mind transfusion to know what you're thinking?"

"Give 'im a chance, will ya," I said. "He's just a little nervous."

"Shut your trap, Caruso," Neil said with a snarl. "Did you forget official disciplinary action number two, already?"

Rosie smiled a little smile at me, just to say thanks for trying, looked down at the ground again and started up in a real soft voice, "Well, ah…my plan's to…umm, I guess, try and *talk* the ghost into givin' hisself up." Then, relieved, he let out a loud sigh and looked up at us with a huge grin.

There was complete silence after that, as Rosie's big idea went over like Playboys at a parochial school, (Just ask Wade Sutton) and everyone just stood and stared at Rosie dumbfounded. Even his two silly sidekicks looked confused and more than a little alarmed. Had Rosie finally ate one too many chimichangas and completely clogged all the arteries to his brain? Seemed so, I'm sorry to say.

Finally, Neil said, "You mean to tell me your great plan, the reason you called this top secret meeting and disturbed this sweet summer day, is to waltz right up to the front door of that haunted house, ring the doorbell and ask that monster if he wouldn't mind giving hisself up to us little kids, nice and easy, so as we could show the whole world what famous ghost catchers we were? Wow, now *that's* brilliant! How come I never come up with great stuff like that? 'Cause I'm not a complete ignoramus, that's why!"

Well, Neil had a point, let's face it. I mean, what kinda self respecting ghost, monster, or vampire was ever *talked* outta being a no good, murdering scumbum, but instead had to be put to no uncertain death, kicking and screaming all the while by some brave, but usually not too bright hero, so it was understandable we all had a few doubts.

After a bit, Rosie got up some more courage and said, "Now I know it sounds kinda crazy, but I just gotta a hunch after somethin' Jag said. That's all."

"Listen, I ain't putting my neck on the line for one of your hunches, E-mi-li-an-o," Ira said, as he slowly produced each syllable in Rosie's Christian name for more effect. "You can go have your nice little conversation, heck you two could have a perfect little tea party for all I care, but count me out, and don't expect me to come save your fat ass when you start screaming for you life, neither."

There was a long pause and nobody said nuthin' and I was starting to think how sorry I was for poor Rosie, making such a fool outta hisself during his first big meeting and all, as his upper lip got to beading up just like always when things weren't goin' to good. It was getting to heat up by now, too, which didn't help none, and the guys started to get antsy and after a little bit more of nobody saying nuthin' Jag finally said, "L-l-look, I don't see no harm in g-giving Rosie a shot if he feels like he's r-r-really on to somethin'. I m-mean, anybody else got any b-better ideas?" (Still nothing.) "Well then, I say we l-let Rosie do his thing, and any m-m-member who wants to go up to the M-Mansfield place with 'im, can, and those that d-don't can wait a safe distance away, b-but we're all g-going over there as a group to see what's what 'cause that's the S.S.B. way."

Neil and Ira both opened their mouths to complain but were stopped dead in their tracks by a nasty glare from our esteemed president, and we all fell in line and headed off down the alley with Jagger and Rosie in the front, looking proud as a peacock, and me, bringing up the rear, dragging that old Radio Flyer, and not saying a word.

We made it to the old mesquite fence surrounding the place without too much commotion, except for when a Palo Verde beetle, big as a battleship, crash landed on the top of Chicken Coops blond mop, getting itself all tangled up, and causing Coop to have about five coronaries, and us to almost pee in our pants laughing. Once, a skinny black snake with yellow and red stripes crossed our path causing a pause in the action.

"That's a poisonous coral snake!" Coop screeched. "Look out!"

"No it ain't, you nimrod," Ira growled. "Didn't your ma ever teach you, 'if red touches yellow, he's a mellow fellow.' That there is a harmless king snake."

"I thought that went, 'if red touches black, better jump back, jack,'" said Rosie.

"No, no, no, you g-guys got it all wrong. It's 'if b-black touches red, your g-gonna be dead, Fred,'" said Jag with confident authority.

"You sure it ain't, 'if black touches yellow your insides will be Jell-O?'" I asked. With that, Bampu, unable to get himself to listen to any more of our moronic gibberish, just shook his head and walked off down the alley disgustedly with us finally following, but giving that snake a nice wide berth just in case.

After reaching the gate, we all gathered round to hear what was to come next, but I still stayed in the back, with my trap shut just like I was told. Jag, he started in by saying how we was all in this together, all for one and one for all, and all that jazz, just like them three Frenchies with the swords that had that candy bar named after 'em. He reminded us that if we could pull this mission off we'd be so famous maybe we'd get a piece of candy named after us just the same as those guys, which really got Rosie all fired up. He said all them fellas did was run through a bunch of fruitcakes wearing tights and feathery hats, anyways, and how hard can that be? But we was up against a real live ghost, somethin' even Dick Butkus wouldn't go near with a ten foot pole, so go figure all the awesome loot in store for us! "We ain't afraid of nuthin'! We're the S.S.B.'s!" Boy, that Jag, he sure had a knack for raising the fire in your belly when you were certain there wern't nuthin' in there but a big block of ice, and everyone got to feeling sure and strong, and after that Cooper blurted out, "Never fear, Underdog is hear!"

"Well, Underdog, you better check your underpants, 'cause something stinks!" said Neil.

Then Jag asked who would be willing to back up Rosie on his glorious mission, but he got no takers. Looking pretty ticked off he asked again, thinking maybe we weren't paying attention. But that weren't it, and still nuthin' but a bunch of sissys staring straight down to the ground.

After a long, awkward silence, only broke here and there by a hiccup from Coop or a sniffle from Creep, I saw my chance of getting back in good graces with the guys and raised my hand to volunteer, figuring my life was pretty much over the way things were now, anyways, so getting killed by old man Mansfield wouldn't be such a big deal. Jag smiled big and wide, picket fence wide, and said he was proud to see *someone* show the real spirit of a Seward School Bomber, and then after snarling at all the others, shot me a wink and a grin.

Now I gotta admit I had done some figuring before I spoke up, and seen right off that if push came to shove, Rosie, being so big and juicy and slow, and me, nuthin' but skin and bones, *he'd* be the one on top of that ghost's gourmet list, giving me a chance to slip away with only maybe a nibble outta me here and there. Jag said he figured he would go along too and then told the others to hang tight at the fence and wait for us to holler the, "all clear" signal which was this ridiculous yodeling sound Jag thought was swell, but really made 'im sound like the Swiss Miss with a bad case of the grip.

"Drizzle, drazzle, drezzal, drone. Time for this one to go home!" Chicken Coop said and then turned to go before Neil grabbed him by the neck and dragged 'im back.

"Not so fast, 'Whinnie-the-Poop.'"

The three of us were just getting going when Jag stopped and turned, and after thinking a sec said, "Listen, if things d-d-didn't work out and we don't make it back, then Big I, I want you to run and find Mengo and l-let 'im know what happened to us, and the rest of you guys r-race home, and n-never, ever come back to this place, and forget all about ghost hunting, and t-try and keep the spirit of the gang alive without us and l-live the rest of your life in a way to m-make the memory of the Seward School Bombers proud."

Well, that shook everybody up but good, and there wasn't a dry eye in the house, even Neil, and Creepy and Coop made a move towards Rosie to try and talk their best pal outta putting hisself in such danger, but he stuck his big hand out, stopping them in their tracks as if to say that this was just somethin' that he had to do. I ain't sure what had come over that kid, but *something* sure had. This sure as you know what, weren't the "scared to go to sleep without his Dumbo nightlight," Rosie we had known so well all these years. He was a whole new person, even walking and carrying himself different. I ain't seen nuthin' like it. I just hope to God he had a good reason for his newfound manliness.

Jag, Rosie and I hopped over the fence, Rosie getting a heave ho from Ira and Neil, and then started out on our way back towards the old place. I realized this was the third time in less than a day that I'd be there, some kinda genius, huh, and that in my previous twelve years I'd had the good sense to visit the Mansfeld mansion exactly *zero* times. So I guess I was either getting dumber, or just listening to Jagger too much again, and I had a good idea which one was the winner! But I also know that sometimes things just change. It don't necessarily mean nuthin', it's just the way it is. Like when some new kid moves into town and you think he's the biggest dweeb you ever saw, but before you know it he does somethin' cool and, presto! He's your new good pal. Just look at Creepy for instance. The problem is, things can work out the other way around, too, and someone you knew for certain would always be there for ya, suddenly is gone, practically before your very eyes. That happened to me with my Grandpa last year. One day he was sitting next to Pop eating pumpkin seeds and watching my little league game, looking like a million bucks, and the next day he gets stroked and he's gone just like that. I didn't handle it too good, being only eleven, but Pop, he said there's something called the circle of life, like a race track, I guess, and when you finish your times up, and God waves the checkered flag and that's that. You don't get no extra time for a victory lap or nuthin'. That didn't make me feel a whole heckuva lot better to tell ya the truth. And Pop, he may be all matter of fact and business like when it comes to Grandpa's passing on the outside, but on the inside I think it's a whole different ballgame. One time I peeked in my folks bedroom when he was all alone in there and looking at his dad's picture, the swell one where he's out in front of his old Ford with a big smile on his face with one of them Ben Hogan style hats on his head, and getting all ready to turn the crank, and I could see Pop's deep, strong eyes well up a bit, and some tears trickling lightly down his cheeks. I know that he misses him somethin' awful. Things like that just ain't easy, I don't care what anybody says.

Anyway, we kept moving along, but Jag and me, weren't moving along quick and energetic, like folks anxious to get someplace, but more at a foot dragging, sauntering speed, like guys that ain't quite sure they want to be where they're going once they get there. Jag was kicking rocks and old rusty cans and trying to whistle, which he did about as good as he talked, and I was throwing some mud clods that were of especially good quality this time of year due to the night time rains and then the summer sun baking the earth the next afternoon. Once in a while I'd flick my finger against my cheek while pushing the air outta my mouth to make that same sound ya get when you drop a pebble in a bucket of water. You know what I mean. It took a lot of practice to get it right, but came in right handy during long school days to get your teacher to stop dead in their tracks during a long, boring lecture, and get to focusing all her attention on where the blasted roof was leaking. Rosie, on the other hand, was strutting tall and proud like a game rooster, without a care in the world, and focusing all along on his final destination. I don't know what the heck had gotten into 'im, but it was getting weird, like maybe aliens had taken over his body or somethin'. But don't ya think they would'a tried to pick a little nicer one if they were going to go through all the trouble? And it wasn't just me who was thinkin' it either, Jag was looking at our fat friend like he had three heads.

After a few minutes, we reached the clearing around the place and stopped to look at what the guys were up to. You could see them all, especially Neil being the tallest, standing on the old mesquite fence and straining their necks to get a glimpse of us. Rosie gave 'em all a wave, and not the kinda wave you get from a beauty queen riding in a parade, neither, but a firm, manly wave, like a general, saying goodbye to his troops before a big battle. Neil, Ira, Cooper and Bampu answered back with a very rigid salute, although we could only see the top of old Creepy's curly mop and had to guess about him. After that it was time to get down to business and so we turned back toward the house, crouched down behind an old Palo Verde, and me and Jag, we looked Rosie right in the eyes and waited for our orders.

"Whadaya say, Rosie. You want me and Jag to try and flush 'em out so you can get 'im?" I asked.

"Nope, that ain't gonna be needed," he answered coolly.

"W-w-well you want me and Johnny to t-t-try and corner him inside, so as you c-can do 'em in?" Jagger asked, all excited like.

"Nope, that ain't the plan, neither," he answered, staring at that old house the whole time.

Jag and me looked at each other kinda dumbfounded not knowing what else the plan could possibly be, but Rosie simply said, "You guys just wait here, and I'll holler when I need ya."

Well, that got us looking at each other all over again, this time with noses wrinkled and eyes all squinted up, and mouths open like someone who can't believe what he just heard, 'cause we couldn't!

Rosie stood up, brushed off his big bottom, pulled out a piece of beef jerky he had hidden in his back pocket, and bit off a big chunk. Then he just stood there for a few seconds, looking straight ahead like he was sizing up the place, and after giving us the thumbs up, started walking, or in Rosie's case, more like waddling, right for the front door. We just crouched there, froze stiff, and watched 'im go along in disbelief. Could this be the same scared to death super wusie who was shaking like a leaf last night when we were still a hundred yards from the place? What in tarnation had gotten into 'im? Was there somethin' in that beef jerky that he was always gnawing on that made you brave and strong, like Popeye and spinach? I couldn't figure it out, not in a million years, and couldn't do nuthin' but just sit there and scratch my head with an intolerable feeling of doom circling around me like so many hungry buzzards. Jag watched in amazement along side me, but with Jag it was different. He had this uncanny knack of looking at the bright side of things, even in a hopelessly bad situation, and the look on his face wasn't so much surprise but more like pride, I guess, like a Dad watching his kid hit his first home run or making the game winning basket. If I didn't know better, I would 'a swore I saw Jag's eyes get a little wet as he watched old Rosie walk into such danger all calm and collected.

After a bit, he turned to me and said, "He's really t-turned into something, ain't he?"

"He's somethin' alright," I answered. "Let's just hope it's not that ghost's lunch!"

# Chapter Twenty-One

## WE MEET A "GHOST"

The sun was blistering by then and straight up overhead, and it was setting everything to shimmer off in the distance like a low, rippling river was flowing, but always just outta your reach. Jag and I kept watch along with the rest of the guys that were still standing back on the fence and hadn't dared move an inch closer, as Rosie, the new, courageous, lion-hearted Rosie made his way across the clearing to the front steps of the Mansfield place. At first, it didn't look near as creepy in broad daylight as in the dead of night, but the more ya looked at it and watched it close, the more a fella would start to feel his skin get all bumpy and begin to crawl. The paint was peeling off the upper floor, mostly, from the beating it had taken from the desert sun all these years gone by, and the bottom floor wasn't much to look at, neither. The roof was worn clean through in spots, so as to allow sparrows and an occasional hawk to fly in and out as they pleased. A slow breeze had just started up, not doing a darn thing to cool off our aching heads, but made its way in and out of the broken windowpanes and set the place to creaking somethin' awful. It was almost like it was trying to speak in this low, moaning voice and most probably saying somethin' like, "Stay the heck outta here, you morons, if you know what's good for ya!" Course we didn't pay no mind, that would'a made too much sense.

As Rosie kept on, we watched for any signs of wavering, but there was nuthin'. He'd stop every few yards, but that was only to rip off another piece of jerky and savor its satisfying deliciousness for a second or two. When he started up the steps, and the boards started to creek from the enormous weight, I could 'a swore I heard the pattering of feet moving quickly inside the house, and then a flash of a wispy figure across one of the front windows, and I got a lump in my throat the size of a grapefruit and my heart sunk down to my knees as I watched our chubby pal waddle off to his sure death.

I turned to Jag and said, "Did ya see that?" but he was in some kinda trance as he continued to look on stone faced. I ain't sure what he was thinking right then, but if I know Jag, he was probably starting to feel guilty as sin for letting Rosie go it alone with no one to back 'im up when the sure trouble started. I decided to yell out to try and stop 'im before it was too late, but it was no use. Nuthin' would come out but a pathetic, wimpy wheeze. You know them times when you're so honkin' horrified that you want to scream loud as you could, but you can't even muster a peep? Like someone had ya around the throat and was trying to squeeze your neck into a thin piece of spaghetti. Well, that's just how it was as I watched poor, in for it Emiliano, still chewing his treat, as he made his way down the side of the porch on the south side of the house and then turned the corner around back, like a giant pig off to slaughter.

We were sweating up a storm by now from the hundred-degree heat and the upcoming murder of our old pal, and I listened for all I was worth, even cupping my hand behind my ear the way Granny used to do to eavesdrop on me and Pop talking in the living room, waiting for that first bloodcurdling screech, but there was nuthin'. Not a cricket chirp, not a dove coo-cooing, not even a June bug buzzing, which were a dime a dozen this time of year by the way. Nope. Nothing. Nada. Nothing but dead silence and I was hoping upon hope that dead wasn't the key word here.

Then *I* started feeling guilty and low down for not trying to talk old Rosie out of his hair-brained idea of negotiating with that bloodthirsty creature. I mean, come on! There weren't a chance in hell of him coming out alive, and everyone knew it soon as he opened his mouth back at the clubhouse. But did I say even one word to try to stop 'im? Did I try and be the leader that Pop always told me to be when I knew somethin' was sure to go haywire? Nope. I just stood there, with my trap shut, while my old pal got ready to commit harry-carry. I was worthless and weak, and selfish and untrustworthy, and I wouldn't have myself as a partner in a pay toilet in the middle of a diarrhea epidemic! And what about poor old, broken-hearted Mrs. de la Rosa? What lame excuse were we gonna give her for letting her poor porky pride and joy face that murderous Mansfield all alone? "Sorry, but we were too worried about saving our own skin to try and keep your fine, brave son from going to his surefire death!" It was just plane pathetic, and I for one wouldn't blame Mrs. De la Rosa one bit if she was so disgusted by our sorry selfs that she never again had us over for one of her *chile verde* burros enchilada style. Although, I have to say on this point, I truly hope that she may reconsider her decision in the not too distant future.

I stood up and looked way back up over my shoulder again to make sure Gracie and the mutt weren't causing no trouble, but all I could see was Neil and Ira still stretching for all they were worth on a fence post trying to get a better view of the massacre that was about to happen. When they saw me looking, they both shrugged their shoulders and raised their hands in the air palms up, as if to say, "What's going on?" or in this case, "Is Rosie dead yet?" I just shook my head and then looked past 'em for Gracie and Dodge, and there they were in the middle of the street, just like they weren't allowed to be, playing that game where she'd throw a stick hard as she could and then try to beat the dog to it, which never, ever happened, and then she'd wrestle it away from 'im and he'd bite her in the butt, and then they'd do the whole thing over again about a hundred times. It was a pretty nutty game, but then that kid was absolutely nuts for dogs. I ain't seen nuthin' like it. If push came to shove, I know sure as I'm telling you this, she'd take that fleabag over me in a second and never even think twice. But I was okay with it. I understood how little kids are. They didn't have any sense of reality.

Just then I heard some strange sounds coming from back of the house and whirled back around to listen, my heart pounding like a jackhammer. It sounded a lot like that same Latin gibberish the ghost had blurted out at Jag last night, only the voices were lower and more calm-like, and harder to make out. I'd 'a swore one of the voices was Rosie's and he was talking that same kinda talk right back to the old man. I cupped my hand behind *both* ears this time, but still couldn't make enough out to tell what was what. I looked down at Jag but he was still stiff as a board, concentrating with all his might for a sign of how things were going.

After a few more lively exchanges from inside the house, I looked over at Jag and said, "Well, what da ya think?" Knowing darn well what needed to be done, but looking for some kinda moral support, I guess.

He just turned his head slowly towards me and the look in his face said it all. It was time for the heroes to stand up and do the right thing for a friend in need, and that's just what we both had in mind. We started through the clearing, nice and slow and crouched low, not wanting to spook that ghost into doing somethin' rash and horrible to old Rosie, and the blood was starting to pound in my head as we reached those dried out wooden steps and started to crawl up on all fours. Neil and Big I caught sight of us and started to jump high off the top rung of the fence, trying for a better view.

We dipped down under the front window and then slowly raised up to peer over the ledge, but there was nuthin' to see 'cept a torn up old couch and a broken down butler table, although I did notice what looked like faint footsteps in the thick dust that carpeted the floor from wall to wall. That was odd I thought 'cause everyone knows ghosts, they don't leave no prints, but just float around easy as can be, like those white fuzzy things in a light summer breeze. Maybe they were left over from some other sad sap that wandered in here way back when, not knowing that he'd never wander out. I got to thinking how many poor souls had been the victim of that miserable Mansfield, and hoping that we weren't about to be added to that lengthy list!

I crawled along the south side of the house and shot a quick glance in one of the bedrooms, but still nuthin', when all of a sudden the back door started to open with a ear piercing, "*screeeech!*" like them old hinges hadn't budged in a hundred years, and then the voices started up all over again, but this time, things seemed to have sure taken a turn for the worse. One voice, speaking that ghost talk sure sounded like Rosie, and he was pleading, practically begging, probably for his life! The other deeper and much creepier voice was shooting back, short and sweet but determined, yeah, determined to have our pal for brunch! That horrible talk kept up for a good five minutes, but it seemed like five hours as I couldn't bear to think of poor Rosie in such a mess, but couldn't wring out the courage to try and save 'im. Finally Jag had heard enough, after a particularly pitiful exchange, and he stood up to make his move. I could see in his face that it was do or die, and if *he* was gonna do the dying, then someone or something was gonna feel the big hurt first. Then, all of a sudden, the door slammed shut with a bang and we knew that it was now or never if we were ever gonna be able to look ourselves in the mirror again, and we jumped up and made a mad dash for the back of the house screaming like banshees, but just as we turned the corner we ran head long into a massive, immovable object that knocked us back hard on our butts. Was it some kind of ghostly force field? Nope. It was Rosie's big beautiful belly.

"What the heck are you guys making all the racket about?" he said looking down at us and holding out his hands to help us up.

There he was, good as new, with no horrible gashes or bites or scratches or bruises or any other things you'd expect from a face to face with the most evil creature this side of Transylvania.

"Rosie, you're okay! Thank God!" I said as Jag and I both threw our arms around his huge shoulders to give him a hug. "How'd ya do it? How'd ya get away from old Man Mansfield without getting mutilated?"

"It was nuthin' really, and I'll tell ya all about it in a minute, but first let's call all the guys up here so we can do this together." Emiliano de la Rosa, cool, calm and completely in charge of the most dangerous adventure in the history of S.S.B.'s. Who would'a thunk it? He walked over to the edge of the porch and put his fingers in his mouth to let out one of them loud, shrill whistles that would almost curl your toes, and then waved to the guys to come on in. I peered around him to see the wondering look on Neil and Ira's faces as they started to climb down from their fence posts, but pretty soon here they all came, trudging through the desert with Neil and Ira in the lead followed up by a thoroughly relieved Creepy and Chicken Coop and finally by a slightly bored looking Gracie and Dodger. We watched from the porch as they zig-zagged their way through the cactus and brush, and then came slowly through the clearing towards the house, still not looking completely at ease with the situation. As they came up the steps Cooper and Creep ran for Rosie, each grabbing onto an arm and squeezing for dear life.

"What's up? Did de la Rosa wimp out at the end, as usual, or what?" Neil asked with a smirk.

"No way, Jose!" Jag answered back, "Big Rosie (which was what he would be known as from that day forward) went t-t-toe to t-t-toe with that monster and d-didn't back down an inch. Which is m-more than I can say for you t-tough guys hiding a mile away."

"Oh yeah, well if he's so tough, how come he's out here and the ghost's still in there?" Ira shot back.

But before Jag could answer, Rosie stepped in and said calm as a cucumber, "On account of there ain't no ghost at all, that's why."

There was dead silence as we all just stared out at Rosie, not believing what we'd heard. Of course there was a ghost. Jag and I had seen it with our own eyes, hadn't we? Didn't we all hear that terrible scream last night that still makes my skin crawl just to think of it. And didn't Jag and I hear that strange voice coming from inside the house just now talking to Rosie in that ghoulish ghost gibberish?

"Whadya mean, there ain't no ghost?" I said. "We all heard it, and I seen it with my own eyes."

"Come with me and I'll show you exactly what you saw," he said as he walked to the back of the house with the rest of us huddled close behind. He stood in front of the large window looking into the sitting room where Jag had taken his pictures with the Brownie camera the night before and then pointed into the back corner of the room.

"There's your ghost. Take a look."

We slowly stepped forward toward the window as a group, still not completely convinced it was a great idea, and pretty jittery about what we'd see, but there, huddled in the far corner of the room, hiding in the shadows, was a dirty little man with his head between his knees and his hands clinched over his head. His hair was all bedraggled and knotted up, and his clothes were filthy and torn. He had on one of them cowboy style shirts with the round white plastic snaps, which was all tattered, just the same as the old blue jeans that he wore. He didn't have no shoes or socks, and I ain't even about to describe what his poor feet looked like. Let's just say this poor guy needed a good hosing down in the worst way.

"Who the hell's that?" Ira demanded as he turned to Rosie and then gave me and Jag a nasty look. "Is this what you jackasses have been dragging us out at all hours of the night for, and getting us all in a tizzy about?"

Jag and I didn't have much to say, still trying to figure out what was what.

"Well, well, what a surprise. Another lame brained idea from Howell and Caruso. The Dynamic Duo of Dumbness!" Neil said, more than happy to take this opportunity to kick us when we were down.

"This here is Jesus Orozco Montoya Moreno de la Cruz," Rosie said with pride and authority as he pointed to the man huddled in the room.

"Is that his name or his life story?" Neil asked, still disgusted with the whole situation. Rosie continued, "He's a farm worker from Mexico who got side tracked on his way over to the lettuce fields in California. Unfortunately for him, that makes him right now an illegal alien."

Alien! And an illegal one at that! Maybe we were still on to something here. Jag and I started getting excited all over again, thinking maybe all wasn't lost after all, so we took another hard look at him to see if maybe we had missed some antenna or green scaly skin or something useful. But there was nuthin' to see after all, just an old scruffy Mexican who had been hiding out in the Mansfield place from the border patrol. That was it. No ghost, no monster, no ghouls, no witches and definitely no Saturday morning T.V. show.

We were feeling low and ashamed and plenty embarrassed for having caused such a commotion over nuthin', but how were we to know that somebody would be so crazy as to voluntarily stay in a haunted house? We didn't say a word and tried to avoid eye contact with the guys, 'cause Neil and Ira and even Chicken Coop and the Creep were pretty ticked right about then, and looking at us with the same disgusting look you get when you come across a dog turd stinking up the middle of your bedroom floor. I know. I've been there. I'm the not so proud owner of Dodger, the retarded retriever, remember?

I knew I had to come up with something quick to get the guys minds off maybe wanting to beat our brains in, so I said, "Rosie, how in the heck did ya know it wasn't no ghost in this place at all and only some Mexican fella that had been way laid?"

That did it. The guys were as curious as I was to know just how Big Rosie had figured it out, and immediately gave him their complete attention.

"Well, I'll tell ya," Rosie said with his hands in his pockets and his new found sense of accomplishment. "Remember last night when Jagger said the ghost screamed out something in that secret ghost talk? "*No mi matees?*" Well that sounded kinda familiar to me, like I'd heard that phrase before, so

I kept turning it over in my head last night 'til finally it came to me. That wasn't no secret ghost talk at all, but a saying in Spanish, one I'd heard over and over again in the Cowboy movies they play on Sunday mornings right after Mexican Theatre. No me mates, means, "Don't kill me" in Spanish. Now first of all, I knew for sure that old Man Mansfield weren't Mexican and wouldn't be speaking Spanish, and second, if we were dealing with some kinda ghost or scary monster, even if he happened to know Spanish, why in the heck would he be begging Jag not to kill *him*, it should be the other way around. Right?"

Well, what Big Rosie said was clear as day, and showed some pretty awesome detective work, to boot. He sure had done hisself, his family and his culture proud, and I hope he never again feels outta place being the only brown skin kid in the White Ghetto.

"You are a real stinking genius, de la Rosie, ya know it," Ira said only half kidding, as he smacked Rosie on his back hard. "Only thing is I ain't so certain that you're so darn smart or everybody else in this club is just so damn dumb!" he added, looking right at you know who.

After that, we all took a long look through the window again and Neil asked, "What did you say this here fellas name is, Rosie? Hey soos?"

"Yup."

"How do ya spell that?

"J-e-s-u-s."

"That ain't "Hey Soos," that's Jesus!"

"Yeah, but you pronouce it Hey Soos in Spanish."

"You mean to tell me that Mexican people actually name their kids Jesus?" Ira asked.

"That would be like my folks calling me Moses or something, for crying out loud!"

"It'd be cool if your name was Moses, Big I," Chicken Coop said. "Then you'd have one 'a them big old boats with all them animals in it to play with."

Well no one knew quite what to say to that, but it was pretty obvious that Coop wasn't on the honor roll of Sister Mary Martin's Sunday School class.

We all looked again through the sitting room window and saw poor old *Jesus* still sitting all scrunched up and scruffy in the corner. He kept on whimpering and hadn't looked up once. I started to get this real sad feeling inside, like someone had sucked all the juiced outta me, thinking that there was this real human being, just like any one of us, only poorer and dirtier, of course, and here we were staring at 'im like he was some animal in a cage.

"Why's he hiding out Rosie?" I asked. "What'd he done wrong?"

"Nuthin', just he ain't supposed to be here according to the border police. He says he ain't got no official papers to come across the border legal, but he just couldn't wait no more on account of the fact that his family was so poor that they'd sure starve to death if he didn't make some money soon. Says he decided to sneak across the border down around Nogi, and then light out for the California lettuce fields where he has some amigos that'd lend 'im a hand, but on his way up he hitched a ride on the back of a watermelon truck and was sitting pretty 'til ten miles up I-19, around Rio Rico, they came across a border patrol road block and he had to make a run for it. He decided to head for the Santa Cruz River where he hid in the brush between the big cottonwoods for a day or so, and then made his way up to Santa Elena. He says he came across the old Mansfield place by accident, and thought it looked like somewheres that no one would want to be looking for nobody and decided to give it a try as a hide out. Now he's feeling mighty low on account'a he can't think of any way of getting over to California so he can start to work and make some money to save his wife and kids. He says he knows the police have been looking out for him, and if he tried to hitch-hike again he'd for sure be caught and deported and then his family wouldn't have no hope at all."

That got us to looking over at poor Jesus all over again, and I thought I'd never seen nobody in such a terrible fix. I mean we all had our problems with Nancy and the like, but starving sure warn't one of them. The problem was what could we do about it? Nuthin', that's what. We were just a bunch'a kids, and let's face it, we had our hands full just taking care of ourselves. It was a pretty sad situation.

Well, we all just kinda shrugged our shoulders, shook our heads, and then turned to head on home, I mean, it was lunchtime after all, but as we started to walk away, Jag said with this desperate look on his face, "W-w-wait a minute fellas. We can't j-just leave 'im here!"

"What do ya want us to do, Jag?" Neil asked. "Who are we, anyhow? Nobody, that's who. Just a bunch'a kids horsing around, and I ain't stickin' my neck out for no filthy, illegal Mexican, no how. He shouldn't 'a came here in the first place. There's laws about that ya know."

"D-didn't ya hear what Big Rosie said? His family's s-starvin' to death, you twit. He didn't have no choice. He *had* to t-try to make it to them l-lettuce fields!"

"Yeah, well that's tough," Neil answered. "We all got problems, Jag, know what I mean?"

"I don't know, Jag," Ira added. "Messing with Nancy Cole is one thing, but helping an illegal alien is another. We could all end up in Juvi 'til we're eating our dinner through a straw."

"He's right," said Chicken Coop, licking his lips. "That's called aiding and betting on a criminal. I seen it on this episode of *Perry Mason* a few weeks back. It was the one where a real handsome burglar is trying to escape from the cops, and runs right into this beautiful babe's place to give them the slip. But instead of turning him in right off, the babe *falls* for the guy, just like always, and tries to help him out best she could 'cause that low down swindler tells her he ain't such a bad guy after all, and he's only being framed for something he didn't do. Same old baloney. Well, the poor girl buys the story, hook, line, and sinker, but the cops finally nab him anyway, and then at the trial old Perry rakes her over the coals something awful, and the jury sends her up the river for five to ten!"

Well, that pretty well settled it as far as the guys were concerned, but not old Jag, he was just flabbergasted at how we were thinking, and after a few minutes of looking down at that old wood porch and shaking his head sadly, he said, "You all should b-be ashamed. Here we are, the so-called *honorable* Seward School Bombers whose m-main purpose in life is to help out the p-poor and d-down on their luck folks (Huh?), and you c-can't wait to turn your b-backs on this poor godforsaken alien on account'a it's lunchtime! Or m-maybe you're afraid of m-maybe getting into a little trouble with your mommies! (After that last remark he glared over at Neil) I say we g-gotta do *somethin'* for this fella or we're n-nuthin' but a bunch of s-sniveling little weenies, horsing around the neighborhood and doin' a b-bunch of s-stupid stuff that don't add up to a hill of beans!" (To tell ya the truth, that's pretty much what I thought the S.S.B.'s were about all along, 'cept for the weenie part, of course, but I could see what Jag was trying to do, he was trying to take us to the next level, to *really* stand for something, like Robin Hood and his Merry Men, only maybe we'd be Jagger Howell and his Kooky Kids, helping out all the sorry souls that couldn't help themselves---long as they lived within the four square blocks we were allowed to play in.)

Then all of the sudden after he finished talking, Jag turned to me and said, "What about you, Johnny. What do *you* say? Should we j-just let this poor guy stay here all alone 'til he finally gets arrested and his family b-back in Mexico starves to death, or should we be m-men enough to do what we d-deep d-down know is right?"

Well, I guess that officially meant that my punishment of silence was over, and to tell you the truth I kinda resented being put in such a tight spot after being treated like doggie doo-doo less than an hour before, but I took another long look through that dusty old window at that Mexican man sitting there so pathetic, all crumpled up in the corner. He still had his face buried between his knees, not looking up even once, and I saw that his shaggy black hair was all tussled and matted and hung down greasy over his eyes, and his clothes were somethin' that an old scarecrow wouldn't put on without a fight. I was having a hard time deciding whether this guy was really a person at all, at least not a person like us, and we were getting ready to stick our necks out further than ever before to help him escape from the law.

A bunch of stuff started racing through my head, and I tried to sort it all out, but it was tough, then after a bit I had made up my mind. The whole thing was just too darn risky, especially on account'a us already walking on real thin ice over our earlier screw ups, but as I turned to Jag to tell 'im what I thought, Dodger suddenly pushed his way through the back door and raced right over to that poor wretch in the corner and started licking him something fierce. I guess all that grime on him was a tasty treat old Dodge couldn't resist, but as I yelled at the mutt to get away, which he whole heartedly ignored as usual, that Mexican lifted up his head which made Dodger even more excited as he was now able to get a couple of choice licks flush on the face. It wasn't every day he got this good an opportunity for face licks, which were his all time favorite, and disgustingly dirty ones at that. At first Jesus tried to push 'im away, being gentle all the while, but that weren't no use, and then before you knew it, he was rolling around on the floor with that stupid dog and laughing and giggling and yelling out a bunch more Mexican gibberish, and having just a great old time. It was then that I started to realize that this wasn't some kind of animal or alien or *anything* we were dealing with, but a real live human being, just like the rest of us; only a little dirtier, but not by that much to tell the truth, and from a different place---that's all. And as we all stood there and watched 'im horse-playing in the dust with Dodger, I realized right then and there that we had no choice but to use the whole power and might of the S.S.B.'s, to help this man get to where he was going so he could save his family back in Mexico.

I turned to Jag and the rest of the guys and said, "Men, I learned a long time ago in catechism class that there would be a lot of trials and tripleations for kids like us on this earth over the years, some put up by God almighty hisself and some by that low down devil, but if you chose to do the right thing, then the man upstairs is gonna look down on our sorry group with a big wide smile, and I don't gotta tell ya that right about now we could use all the brownie points we can get after some of the asinine stuff we've been pulling, and after the mess this poor fellas in and listening to what President Jagger has to say, deep down I know the right thing to do for the distinguished order of the S.S.B.'s is to go all out to make sure Heysoos has every chance of getting to the lettuce fields of California!"

A rousing cheer followed my little speech, with big smiles all around, but not from Neil, he just didn't seem to get it, and he shouted out over the others, "You're gone completely bonkers Johnny, and so are the rest of you numb nuts. If you think for one second that I am gonna get myself thrown in the slammer for helping some filthy, flea-bitten, Mexican alien, who broke the law to get here in the first place, then you've got another thing comin'! What's in it for us? And anyways, we don't know nuthin' about this guy at all. He could be some crazy Mexican mass murderer for all we know!"

We all just looked back at him with vacant stares.

"That's it," he said, after a long awkward pause. "You guys can ruin your life if you want, but you can count me out. I'll see you later. *Much* later! Come on, Big I, let's make like a banana!"

But Ira didn't budge. He was still staring through the window watching Dodger and Jesus horsing around, and I could tell by the look in his eyes that he wasn't gonna be able to abandon that poor fella, neither. That really got Neil ticked, and he started yelling how he wasn't gonna bale us out when we got caught and how we were just a bunch of pathetic losers and sad sacks, and how we weren't cool enough to hang out with him anyway, and then he ran down the porch and stairs and off through the desert toward home, not once slowing down to look back over his shoulder.

After we watched him get smaller and smaller in the distance, Jag turned to Rosie and said, "Okay, guys, I guess that's it. Let's go have a l-little talk with our n-new friend."

# Chapter Twenty-Two

## S.S.B.'S TO THE RESCUE

We all stepped into the parlor room, and after I yanked Dodger off by the collar, Jag told Rosie to let Jesus know that we were gonna do everything in our power to help 'im outta his terrible jam. Well, you would'a thought we had given him a million *pesos!* No...wait a minute...that's only about five bucks. Anyways, you get the picture, and I never saw a person so overjoyed and grateful after he heard them lines that Rosie rattled off in Mexican faster than machine gun fire. He got down on his knees and kept saying over and over, *"Gracias a Dios,"* which Rosie said meant, "Thank God," and the tears were flowing down his face harder than the Santa Cruz River after a real snake stripper. Then he went around to each and every one of us and gave us a kiss on the cheek and a big bear hug, which weren't too pleasant to tell you the truth, considering the poor state of personal hygiene he was in at the time, and he kept on calling us, *"Mis salvadores pequenos,"* which meant "My little saviors," giving us all a real warm feeling inside, and there were smiles, big and bright, all around, and I knew right off I'd made the right decision no matter how things turned out.

"Ask 'im what we can do for him first," I told Rosie, so he did, and Jesus thought for a second or two and then rattled off sentence after sentence like *he* was shooting that machine gun right back at Rosie. Boy, Mexican's can talk faster than beans through a boy. We asked Rosie about it one time, but before he could answer, Neil blurts out it was because they were making up for doing everything else so darn slow.

Finally, Rosie said the thing he wanted most right off was some food, seeing that he hadn't had nuthin' to eat for near three days, 'cept for a few

Prickly Pear Cactus fruit, and even they weren't quite ripe. Well, that seemed easy enough, and we decided that each of us would swipe part of his supper and bring it on back here tonight to give that poor starving Mexican a feast fit for a king. To hold 'im over, Rosie gave up what was left of a sausage stick he'd been gnawing on, and without so much as a second thought, I'm proud to say, but I ain't so proud to tell ya that stinking Dodger made such a fuss over it, no matter how I yelled, that poor, half-starved Jesus felt obliged to give him half. That dog, I mean, he's got no conscience what so ever, it's a fact.

So it was settled. We each knew our mission and swore to take our secret about Jesus and his whereabouts to the grave or be banished from the S.S.B.'s for life.

"Yeah, and if we ever saw you walkin' around, then we'd all be obliged to beat you to an inch of your life," Ira added.

"Right," Jag said. "And the only games you could play at recess would be two square with the girls and the retards in special Ed!"

That gave us all a nasty shiver.

"Yes," Creepy added. "And for the ultimate humiliation, next Valentine's day you'd have to be Nancy Cole's date and have to hold hands with her and give her a big kiss on the lips!" Well, that got old Bampu monkey bumps galore on account'a the especially nauseating impressions it conjured up in everyone's heads, plus the fact that it was okay to give a kid a good pounding for something, but it was a whole different ballgame to be scarred for life!

Rosie told Jesus about our plan to get him fed, and he started up with the yelling and crying and praying all over, but knowing what was coming next, we just smiled and waved and then got the heck outta there before the smelly hugging and kissing started up.

It was closing in on five o'clock by then, and we were gonna hafta get it in gear to snatch half our dinner and get back by six like Jag planned. He said we didn't have no time to waste if we were gonna have any chance at all of getting Jesus on his way, safe and sound and in time to save his family, and that planning had to start tonight. We sure had our work cut out for us, and this one wasn't no little kid stuff, neither, but super sensitive spy work, like our masterful plan to spring Coop's stinkin' shit-zoo "Flipper" from the dogcatcher's (Mengo and Pato again). She got her nickname on account'a she made a beeline straight for Highland Vista pool every time she got loose, which was almost daily, and then wouldn't get out of the water 'til our trusty Sheriff and Deputy jumped in after her. In that world famous case, we decided that to set her loose we'd have to cause a distraction, and dressed up a dead drunk Mr. Sistrunk in Rosie's Halloween St. Bernard costume while he was sleeping it off out behind El Minuto. Then when those two dedicated lawmen/dogcatchers came over to investigate in their dog catcher truck, which was nuthin' but an old paddy wagon with a dog bowl in the back, we snuck up, unlatched the door, and took off for home with Flipper close behind. Pure genius, huh? And we heard old Mr. Sistrunk didn't mind too much neither, since he got himself two swell dog treats and a free flea dip.

About then I got to thinking how this whole darn adventure got turned on it's head, and we went from the world's greatest ghost catchers to the world's greatest illegal alien smugglers in nuthin' but about two seconds flat. Funny how things turn out sometimes, and although it looked like our chance for a Saturday morning T.V. show was probably out the window, 'cept maybe an appearance or two on Mexican Theater, it still sounded like a lotta fun and maybe the perfect way to send off summer vacation with a bang. I just hope that "bang" ain't the sound of the cell door at Juvi locking tight behind us!

We were keeping up a pretty quick pace on the way home at first 'til Gracie started to poop out, the way little kids do after a long day in the summer sun.

"Pick it up, Kiddo. We gotta get home soon as we can to figure out how we're gonna steal some supper."

"But I'm tired, Johnny, and I'm thirsty and I'm hungry," she whined as she dragged her feet along in the dirt with every step with that football helmet still bouncing around on her like one of them bobble head dolls.

"Maybe you should think about staying in tonight, sweetie," I said, trying not to sound too hopeful.

"Not a chance!" She screeched, and she pulled the helmet up, threw back her shoulders and started to march on ahead with new energy with Dodger snapping at her heals. She could really be a tough little stinker when she wanted.

Just then something clicked in my head, and I started to remember about that Harriet Tubman lady we'd read all about in history, and how she had helped a whole slew of slaves escape from the south during the civil war, and how they called it the, "Underground Railroad," though it wasn't any speeding black train racing through tunnels at night to snooker them rebels at all, which was the way I had it figured at first, but just a bunch of friendly folks in houses here and there, that let them poor negroes stay over night and maybe give them a meal and a nice pat on the back and then send them on their way to the next house down the line 'til they finally reached safety in the north. Anyway, she was real famous and in all the history books, and there's probably even a statue of her somewheres I bet, and I figure if some old lady could do that for the slaves, why couldn't we do the same sort of thing for all the poor illegal Mexicans in these parts that were trying to get somewheres so as they could make some dough and save their families. We could call it the, "Taco Train," or the "Chimichanga Choo-

Choo," or something catchy like that, and we could hand out fliers at all sorts of places around the border towns where they might be hiding out, and our logo could be a giant sombrero with wheels on a railroad tract with a few border police chasing behind all tuckered out. We could let it be known that we were available to meet with the aliens, but only at top-secret hideouts on account'a the fact that we'd all be on the F.B.I. most wanted list and every lawman worth his weight in horny toad turds would be on the lookout for the notorious Seward School Bombers. I suppose we'd have to stay on the move, going from town to town, and never even sleeping in the same place twice. Of course, we could never go to school again or hang out in any of our usual spots 'cause they would surely be swarming with cops and bounty hunters night and day, and we wouldn't be able to see our folks no more, neither, and only maybe just sneak up and leave 'em a note sometimes at night where they'd be sure to find it to let 'em know we were safe and sound. Pretty soon we'd be in all the papers, and not only around these parts, but the whole country, maybe even the whole world, and everybody would say we were the most famous group of outlaws since the James gang, and since we were just kids helping out poor, innocent Mexicans in need, all the normal folks would be pulling for *us*, making it even cooler, and us into even bigger heroes! Now I know it'd be tough going for us at first, and maybe even tougher on our folks, but just like Pop always says, sometime it ain't easy doing what you know deep down is right. You know, maybe that Saturday morning T.V. show was still a possibility!

Our shadows were starting to grow a little longer, stretching out to the east, and Gracie and Dodger had slowed down to a snail's pace. The mutt still hadn't figured out we were headed home which meant walking through the kitchen and right past his happiest place on earth; the treat jar. There weren't many clouds rolling in for this time of day, and I started getting that same sad feeling I always got at the end of August when the monsoons start to peter out. It meant no real rain 'til at least December, maybe longer, and what's worse, it meant school was right around the corner. It sure was nice to have that afternoon cloud burst to cool things down a tad, if only for a few hours, and the poor, shriveled plants appreciated it too, as they had started to fill out, almost lush, and their offspring, that had waited patiently all year long for just a little sip of water to give them a chance, slowly made their debut.

"Johnny?" Gracie said. Not bothering to lift up the football helmet that had fallen back over her eyes.

"Yup."

"What we gonna do now?"

"We're going home to get some supper."

"No!" she answered, annoyed to have to explain herself. "I mean about

Hey-Soos."

"Oh, well, like I said before, we're gonna do everything we can to help 'im get to California."

After a few seconds Gracie asked, "How do you suppose you're gonna do that? I know you guys are twelve and all, but you still don't have any money, and you can't even drive a car for gosh sakes."

I have to admit those were two pretty important points, and ones I'd been thinking on pretty hard since leaving the guys. "I'll come up with somethin' kiddo. Don't worry," I said, trying to sound reassuring, though far from sure myself.

Dodger stopped dead again, and had to be promised *two* milkbones and *three* bowls of Gravy Train before he'd take another step.

"Johnny?" Gracie asked again.

"Yup."

"You really think there's little kids out there that are so hungry they can get sick and even die?" She asked in a soft voice, this time raising up the helmet to look me square in the face with eyes that were both worried and confused.

"I guess so squirt, now and then," I said, not wanting to worry her little head with what I knew to be true. I'd caught a glimpse or two before of some pitiful pictures of starving African kids all shriveled up and too weak to move on Walter Cronkite, but Pop would quickly turn the channel to something more pleasant.

"What are we gonna do?" She asked again, this time more desperate.

"Well, maybe some day, Gracie, you and me can really do something special to help them poor folks out, but for now, we gotta try and save at least *one* Mexican family whose Pop needs us somethin' awful, and that's a start," I said and gave her a little pat on the back.

We were just about to our garage when Gracie said, once again. "Johnny?"

"Yup," I answered.

"I'm real proud you're my big brother."

Wow, I wasn't ready for that one, and it hit me like a rabbit punch to the solar plexus, stopping me dead in my tracks. I had to blink my eyes over and over, feeling them welling up a bit, and then tried to say something back, but nuthin' would come out, so I finally just gave up and walked on into the garage.

As we went through the back door, there they were just like always; Granny, Ma and Aunt Leah, standing around the kitchen table making cookies, cackling about somethin', and all covered in flower, looking a whole lot like them three witches in the first scene from Shakespeare's "Hamhock," that we'd just studied the crud outta in Ms. Wacker's drama class last year. They were rolling a bunch of dough and unrolling plenty of the town folks' reputations, if you know what I mean.

"Have any of you seen Vada Simpson's new hair do?" Aunt Leah asked as she giggled and grabbed a hand full of flour. "It looks like someone put her head in a blender and set it on puree."

(More cackling)

"What about that eye mascara?" added Ma, as she ran her fingers across her eyes to show how it went. "Looks like it was put on by a blind man with a can of spray-paint!"

(Higher pitched cackling)

"Let me tell yas. She ain't no spring chicken neitha," Granny added with her thick Boston accent. "She should be ashamed'a hah-self. Can you imagine me actin' like that in a million ye-ahs. She looks like a floozy!" she snarled, and then smacked her chewing gum, took a drag from her cigarette, and reached under her dress to adjust her corset.

"Hi Ma. We're home!" Gracie cried out as she raced over to her and hugged her around the waist hard as she could. Ma wrapped her arms around Gracie, too, but only to the elbows since her hands were such a mess.

"How is my little angel?" she asked as she kissed her on top of the football helmet.

"Take that contraption off so as we can see ya beautiful face," Granny said, with a big smile.

"Isn't she lovely?" added Aunt Leah, as Gracie stood there covered in dirt from head to toe with pigtails sticking out every which way. "Absolutely breath taking!"

"In a few ye-ahs yous gonna hafta beat off the boys with a big stick," Granny said as she reached over and gave Gracie's cheek a good hard pinch.

I started to wish someone would beat me with a big stick and put me out of my misery so I wouldn't have to listen to any more of this drivel, when good old Dodger sauntered over, put his front paws on the kitchen table and tried to snatch a piece of cookie dough right out from under Ma's nose. That led to exquisite screaming and hollering and cursing and flour flying, and gave me a perfect opportunity to sneak by, scott free and avoid the third degree.

I was only two feet from the family room and freedom, when I heard, "Johnny Caruso, stop right there, mister!"

"Yes Ma'am" I answered without turning around, not wanting to have to endure the twisted faces of the Commandant and her two SS officers.

"Didn't you forget somethin', young man?"

"Look, I'm sorry, Ma, but I wiped my feet best I could on the door mat, if that's what ya mean?"

"That is not what I mean in the least," she answered. "You have shown no respect at all for your elders and completely forgotten to greet your grandmother and aunt who love you so dearly."

That was the laugh of the century I thought, and then blurted out, "Oh, hi. How's it hanging?" before I could stop myself, realizing too late that probably wasn't the best greeting for a couple of ladies that were getting on in years.

Well, that did it, boy, and they were on me like flies on you know what, yelling about how I needed to learn some proper manners and how a good hiding might be just the thing, and how kids these days ain't nuthin' but a bunch'a hooligans, and how it all started with that rock and roll, devil-worship music, and how the whole of American society was going straight to hell in a handbasket. You know. The usual stuff. And they kept it up, working themselves into such a lather like you never seen in all your days, unless, of course, you lived in the insane asylum I called home where it was pretty much a daily occurrence--and twice on Sundays.

I took advantage of them trying to out "nutcase" each other and eased on out of the kitchen, but before I did I caught a glimpse of Dodger seeing his chance, too, and slurping up a large blob of cookie dough that had wandered too close to the table edge, while Gracie put her hands over her ears and slid under the kitchen table to hide like she liked to do on occasion, pulling the table cloth back over her as she went. It was one of her favorite places to hide out, especially when she was playing spy, which she did a lot, and once in a while, when she got a wild hair, she'd reach up under Granny's skirt and snap her garters hard as she could. Well, that was always quite a show, and I begged Gracie to let me know before she was gonna do it, 'cause the old girl would let out an ear-piercing, "WOOP!" and jump outta her chair like she was shot out of a cannon. Then she'd start dancing around and slapping at her legs and cursing a blue streak, while Ma and Aunt Leah would jump up and down right along with her, trying to figure out what the heck was the matter. Gracie would then sneak out from under the table and into the family room until things cooled off, and only pulled off her stunt every couple of months to keep 'em from ever catching on. That really drove 'em nuts, and they even took Granny all the way to Phoenix to see some big shot nerve doctor, but he couldn't find a thing, so then they took her over to old Mrs. Squatting Squirrel, or something like that, on the Navajo reservation near Wilcox, who was this famous Indian healer women, and after poking and prodding and pinching and hopping up and down on one leg for a while, and then doing the same with the other, she finished up with this never-ending chant that sounded a lot like, "Hey, how are ya?" over and over again 'til she finally snapped outta it and pronounced that what good old Granny had was called "the jimmy leg," and in order to lick it she had to drink tonic water three times a day, which she did, faithfully. And although it didn't completely cure her condition since Gracie couldn't completely control herself, it helped her disposition immensely since she always said, "What good's tonic wata without a little gin to liven it up."

As I went into the den, there was good old Pop, sitting in his favorite chair, just like always, just like you could always depend on, with his shoes off and his gold toed stocking feet stretched out on his footstool and reading the newspaper with those crazy little eye glasses he bought at the five and dime barely hanging there on the end of his nose for dear life. Before he had an inkling I was there, I raced over and jumped in his lap, whipping the paper aside, and started to give him a vicious barrage of body shots.

"It's the fight of the century!" I yelled, as I continued to flail away.

"Hold on there, Rocky Marciano," he laughed, half-heartedly trying to cover up.

Rocky Marciano was his favorite prizefighter of all time on account'a he was Italian, just like us. "Clinch! Clinch!" He yelled out as he grabbed me around the back and pulled me in. "We've got to make some rules up before we can fight for the heavyweight championship of the world, you know. But first, how about some smackos?" and then he started giving me kisses all over my face.

"Aw, come on, Pop, fighters don't never give each other kisses. They want to knock each others blocks off," I said, still squeezed against his chest, his forearms were like steel.

"Okay, Okay," he agreed. "But remember the most important rule in all of boxing is no hitting on the break. Got it?"

"Got it, Pop."

"Break!" he yelled, but before he could get it out, I whacked 'im a good one, square on the belly, which, by the way was getting to be a considerably larger target over the last year or two, but that only made 'im laugh even louder and then get me into another clinch.

"You win, you win!" he said, barely able to get it out. "There is no way I can answer the bell. I'm throwing in the towel," and he grabbed the dishrag he used as a bib off the arm of his chair and tossed it into the air.

"Whatcha listening to Pop?" I asked after some more hugging and kissing. I noticed the Victrola was playing something soft after the big fight was over.

"Why, that's old Frankie," he answered with a real satisfied look, the kind a kid gets after that first delicious lick of ice cream on a hot July afternoon. "He's the greatest there ever was, Johnny, and there won't ever be another one like him. You can mark my words, son." And then he closed his eyes, snapped his fingers and started to sing along, "Fly me to the moon, and let me play among the stars…" Then he opened his eyes again and said, "This here is real music, Johnny, not a bunch of noise like the kids listen to today."

Well, I wasn't gonna argue with that. I couldn't stand the stuff. Plus I already told ya about the ridiculous hairdos most of our moms forced on us on account of them four farts from England.

Pop *loved* good singing, especially Sinatra, and he'd been known to belt one out with the best of 'em when he had a mind to. As a matter of fact, he even majored in voice at the University of Arizona for a year, before going off to war to show them Japs and Krauts a thing or two about messing with the good old U.S. of A., and was sort of a legend in Santa Elena because of his voice. Folks were always hounding him to sing at their son's wedding or their daughter's *quinceniera,* and he did, on occasion, "when the feeling moved him."

Once I asked Pop if it was true that we fought the Italians in the big war, too. "Well kind of, Johnny, but they didn't last long. Everyone knows Italians are lovers, not fighters. Right Frieda?" he said with a little smirk. And then he went over and gave Ma a little peck on the cheek and a pinch on the behind, and she giggled like a schoolgirl and told him he was "encourageable." And if she was ever sore at him for somethin' all he'd have to do was sing a little "I got you under my skin…" in her ear and she'd get all dreamy-eyed and weak in the knees and forget all about it. It was a neat little trick and I figured it might be worth my while to give it a whorl some day.

"Hear that voice, Johnny?" Pop asked, with eyes closed again, drinking it all in. "You gotta be Italian to sing like that. All the great ones are, you know. It's a God given talent." After a few more bars, Pop told me to click off the record player 'cause it was time to watch Huntley and Brinkley, and then he, "clanked" on the T.V. with the remote control.

"Time to see what's happening in the world, Johnny," he'd always say.

"Anything exciting happening around these parts in the newspaper?" I asked.

"Sure," he said. "All kinds of earth-shattering news coming out of Santa Elena as usual," and then he looked at me and gave me a big wink.

Earth-shattering. That killed me. Pop could be real witty when he wanted to be.

"Oh yeah, like what?" I asked, calling his bluff.

"Well, like right here on the front page, I'm reading about how they had to shut down the dog track in Tubac because the owners got caught giving the greyhounds laxatives to make them run faster."

"Wow! How'd they find out about it?"

"Well, besides the fact that the track smelled a lot worse than usual, the dogs started acting kind of crazy, running every which way, and the final straw was when one of them stopped trying to catch the rabbit running around the track and instead jumped into the stands and started to chase the mayor's wife, trying to catch the mink stole hanging around her neck!"

"You mean fat old Mrs. Trancoza had to run for her life?" I said, giggling.

"It seems so," Pop answered trying not to giggle.

"Boy, I sure wish I coulda seen that!"

"Me too, son, me too."

Well, the news started with that corny music they always used that sounded like a million business machines working in the backround all at once, and there was old Chet Huntley, all ready to go. (Pop had sworn off Walter Chronkite last week. Said he was a communist synthesizer.) The first story started off with a bunch of colored folks walking down a street, holding hands, carrying signs and singing songs.

"What are all those Negroes upset about, Pop?" I asked.

"They're protesting so that they can have equal rights."

"What's equal rights mean?"

"It means that everyone should be treated the same in this country no matter if you're black of white, red or yellow, man or woman."

"Ain't that the way it is already?"

"Not necessarily. Some parts of the country Negroes are treated pretty shabbily."

"Like how?"

"Well, for example, some places in the south they're not allowed to stay in the same hotels as whites, or eat in the same restaurants, or even drink out of the same drinking fountains."

"You gotta be kidding, that's horrible! You mean they just turn them away? What the heck does a person's skin color got to do with what he's like inside? Ain't they afraid of hurting somebody's feeling?"

"I guess not."

"That's sad, Pop." And then after thinking a bit, I said, "It kinda makes ya a little embarrassed to be an American."

"Well, Johnny, I never really thought I'd say it, but it kind of does at times."

Right about then Ma yelled out from the kitchen that it was time for supper, which suited me fine, the sooner the better, and then I could head back over to the Mansfield place with my stash.

"What we having, Ma?"

"Fried chicken and corn on the cob. Now come along you two."

Bingo, I thought. Easy to hide in a pocket and not too juicy to leak down your leg, neither.

"I gotta go wash up first," I yelled as I ran down the hall to my room, kicked off my P.F. Flyers and pulled on a pair of cowboy boots Ma had bought me to wear to the rodeo days parade up in Tucson last February. They had plenty of space to hide stuff in, on account'a the fact that my scrawny legs didn't take up much room. Then I threw on an old baggy T-shirt of Pops that I used for sleeping and tucked it in my Levi's to make a kind of pouch in front that I could throw some food into through the collar when no one was looking.

Supper was pretty smooth sailing since Granny and Aunt Leah were heading over to Rio Rico to comfort Mrs. Talmadge whose husband had just passed, and that meant two less sets of prying eyes to have to deal with while I clipped a drumstick here and snatched a cob of corn there, stuffing it all in the top of my boots or down the front of my shirt. It was hard not to wince when some hot Crisco from the fried chicken leaked down between my toes or the melted butter off the corn dribbled into my belly button and started to burn, but I knew I had to be tough for Jesus, and I bit my lip and kept right on eating and stealing 'til my stomach *and* my clothes couldn't hold no more. Ma was real busy in the kitchen cooking and serving and cleaning and was so tickled at how healthy my appetite had become that she didn't notice nuthin' outta the ordinary.

"Boy, this sure is good, Ma. Keep it coming!" I said, licking my lips.

"My stars, Johnny. You must be hitting one of your growing spurts again! I declare I have no idea where you put it!"

Pop was too deep into a newspaper article about a drought down in Mexico that might cause him to raise the price of lettuce, to catch on to our heist. I say *our* because Gracie, was making a fine account of herself in the burglary business too, filling the big pocket on the front of her skirt with so much corn bread and biscuits that when she was finished she looked like a Mama Kangaroo totting a whole gang of babies in her pouch.

Now with Ma and Pop under control, and Aunt Leah and Granny out of the picture, that still left one pain in the rear person to give us a major headache. You guessed it, Dodger, and he was being worse than ever; sniffing and licking at my boots, and practically biting a hole through my shirt, and was close to blowing the whole top secret operation 'til I hauled of and whacked 'im on the nose with the big silver serving spoon which finally got 'im to back off, and he laid back down over at Ma's feet, hoping to catch a falling crumb or two.

"That was one fine meal," I said, patting my tummy, but not too hard. "Thanks, Ma."

"You're welcome, Sweetie. Can I get you some dessert? I picked up some fresh apple empanadas and a few cochitos from La Estrella Bakery this afternoon," she said with a smile as she held up the bag and gave it a little shake. Boy, that was mighty tempting, especially the cochitos which are these little pig shaped cookies that taste a lot like gingerbread, only not so sweet, but I thought I better not press my luck.

"No thanks, Ma. Couldn't eat another bite. I'm full to the brim."

"I'll have one of those empanadas, Frieda, I'm still hungry," Pop said, licking his lips.

"These are for the kids, John. And anyway you are getting way too fat around the middle as it is."

"Aw, come on. I'm starving here!" he pleaded. Pop really liked his dessert and got kinda testy when Ma cut 'im off.

"I'll make you a nice tossed salad in just one second," she answered with a nod.

"Thanks a whole helluva lot," he grumbled disgustedly under his breath and went back to reading the paper.

"I gotta go meet the guys, Ma, we're playing kick the can over at Jag's, and Gracie and Dodger can come along too if they want," I said as I stood up real gingerly, letting my stash settle nice and slow before I tried to take my first step.

"All right Johnny, but not too late, you hear?" she said, not looking up from the sink. "And keep an eye on your baby sister."

"No hay problema," I said as I leaned over to give Pop a kiss on the cheek and then waddled out the back door with Gracie and Dodger close behind.

The sun was starting to set and the western sky was the colors of one of them bullet popsicles, the ones the ice cream man was always running outta first, with the layers of red, yellow and orange floating over the Santa Elena mountain range, and it made me sad about leaving without dessert, knowing darn well that as soon as Ma turned her back Pop would finish off every last one of the *muy delicioso* Mexican pastries. We walked toward the Howell's a ways to keep up appearances, and then doubled back toward the Mansfield place. The going was kinda slow, but hey, you try and walk fast with your belly on fire from hot grease and melted butter running down your ankles!

When we finally made it, Ira met us at the door, "Welcome to the Haunted Hash House. It's all you can eat, or all you can be eaten. We have many devilish delights for what could be your best and last meal on earth!" he said and then let out a loud cackling laugh and opened the door wide.

As we stepped in, I saw that rickety old table sitting in the parlor room, covered from end to end with enough food to feed a *hundred* hungry Mexicans, and there was old Jesus scarfing stuff down like there was no tomorrow, and only now and then stopping to take a breath and blurt out something in Mexican which I'm pretty sure meant, "Thank you very much," only with a lot more emotion like Mexican folks tend to do. All the guys were already there, sitting on the couch watching in amazement as Jesus continued to go through the food like a swarm of locusts through a wheat field. Every once in a while it would be too much for Rosie to stand,

and he'd slowly reach over for a piece of pot pie or a taste of a tater tot, which lead to him getting his hand slapped and a stern look from one of the guys sitting along side.

Dodger, after getting a few good whiffs, figured the feast had to be all for him, and made a quick bee-line for the table. It took me, Ira, and Jagger, who leaped over the table like a gazelle, to keep the mutt from snagging a prize slab of rump roast that was the centerpiece of Mrs. Howell's dinner tonight. But the heartless hairball refused to give up, and kept going for the table from all different directions 'til we had to tie him to the radiator in the corner with a small bowl of Mrs. Cooper's chicken catchatory to shut 'im up.

I emptied my boots and shirt on to the table, which made Jesus' eyes get wide, and my toes and tummy feel a lot better, and Gracie came over and handed Jesus, with a little curtsy, the muffins and cornbread she'd stuffed in her pockets. He stopped munching just long enough to give her a sweet smile and a, "*Muchissimas gracias, Señorita bonita.*"

"I pilfered an ice chest from our garage to properly store the left overs. We wouldn't want him to get salmonella," the Creep said proudly.

"What's wrong with him eating a little fish?" Cooper asked.

"Not salmon, Coop. Salmonella!" Bampu answered, too polite to call 'im a moron.

"Huh?" Was all that Chicken Coop could muster.

After a few more minutes of us watching Jesus go to town, Jagger stood up and said, "W-well, now that starvation is no longer a concern, we g-gotta figure out how in the heck we're g-gonna get Hey-soos off to California without g-getting caught and him deported and us spending the r-rest of our lives in Juvi. Any ideas?"

It didn't surprise anybody that Bampu was the first to stand up, and he said proudly, "It just so happens that after several hours of contemplation and multiple calculations this afternoon, I have resolved the problem very satisfactorily," his voice sounded more like his mouth was full of marbles than I ever remember.

"Great, let's hear it, you Indian Einstein," Ira said.

"Voila." Bampu blurted out as he whipped out a piece of construction paper from his back pocket and unfolded it smoothly on the dusty wooden floor.

We all gathered round to get a load of his drawing.

"What the heck's that?" asked Rosie, confused like the rest of us. "It looks like a big orange with a thimble hanging from it."

"Not quite, my gargantuan friend," answered The Creep. It is a hot air balloon, although a crude rendition of one I will admit."

We looked at each other and then back at Bampu and his drawing, which had all kinds of lines and arrows and math problems written all over, and finally Ira asked, "How in the hell do you expect a bunch of kids like us to build a contraption like that?"

"I have listed all the raw materials needed to complete the project, and I feel certain they can all be located in the near vicinity." And then he started rattling off; "twenty-five large plastic garbage bags to make the balloon itself, three wooden crates for structural supports, five medium sized hibachis to create enough hot air..."

"I think you make enough hot air *yourself* to send that thing straight to the moon!" Ira said disgusted.

"L-L-Let 'im finish," Jag said holding, up his hand.

"We will need three bags of charcoal," Bampu started up again. "Two gallons of lighter fluid, 40 feet of heavy gauged twine, and one 20 gallon plastic trash can to carry our passenger safely to California." Creepy finished, smiled big, and nodded his head firmly as if to say, "And that's that," and then looked up to see all our flabbergasted faces. "If you are concerned about Hey-soos piloting the aircraft, I have plans to acquire a professional air navigation compass and jet stream charts for this time of year, preferably in Spanish," he added quickly.

Now I have no doubts that old Creepy's contraption would probably work just swell if it was put together by someone who had even the slightest clue about what they were doing, but let's face it, he might as well ask us to build one of them Apollo rocket ships they're getting ready to shoot at the moon.

Ira opened his big mouth to let Creepy have it again, but Jagger jumped in again to try and keep the peace and said, "Thanks for the, ah, g-great plan, Bampu, we'll d-definitely think about it. Now anybody else got any ideas?" and then he shot us each a quick glance like he was pleading for someone to say something that made a little more sense.

I looked over at Rosie to see if he had something to say, but he just kept on staring at the table full of food like he was in a trance, not moving a muscle 'cept for licking his lips on occasion.

Suddenly Cooper jumped up and said real excited-like, "How's about we dig a tunnel!" This brought back the same astonished looks all over again.

"No, really. I've seen in one of them war movies where American G.I.'s cut a whole in the floor of their barracks without the German's ever catching on and then all night long when they were supposed to be asleep, they'd be digging their hearts out with sticks or spoons or whatever they could lay their hands on 'til they finally had a tunnel long enough for the whole mess of 'em to high tail it outta there."

"Do you have any idea how far…" Ira blurted out, but was cut off by Jagger one more time.

"That m-might be a little tough, Coop. But good try."

Chicken Coop stuck his lower lip way out and sat back down dejected.

"Okay, anyone else?" Jag asked, shaking his head.

I stood up slowly but none of the guys seemed to pay any mind, probably getting a little numb by now, and said, "Well, I was thinking real hard on it this afternoon and then it hit me like a ton of bricks, Pop has a produce truck that heads out to Salinas, California once a week to pick up a load of lettuce."

"Now we are getting somewheres!" Ira said as he and the gang sat straight up to listen hard to the rest of what I had to say.

"The way I figure it, see, today is Tuesday, right? So alls we gotta to do is hide good old Hey-soos here 'til Saturday morning and then sneak 'im down to El Minuto Market where Chango always makes his delivery around noon, then when old Chango goes inside, and he'll be in there for a good while on account'a I heard he's sweet on Josefina, the new cashier, we'll somehow get Hey-soos in the back of that truck, cover 'im up with some gunny sacks or something, and off he goes for a first-class, air-conditioned ride all the way to the California lettuce fields."

"Johnny C., that's pure genius," Jag said with that big, picket fence grin, while putting his arm around my shoulder.

I was about to say something like, "Aw, it was nuthin' really," when I heard a loud whimpering sound from over my shoulder. It was Dodger, straining at the end of his rope, his face red all over with spaghetti sauce, wanting us to know was ready for his second course.

# Chapter Twenty-Three

## OUR PAL JESUS

The sun was blazing and straight up in the sky by the time I escaped from my house the next morning and made my way to see our new pal. An *escape* was what it took, too, 'cause Ma was sure on the warpath this morning, and had me working harder than a convict on the chain gang at the Arizona State Penn. She set off on a complete rampage after getting a look at my closet before I had a chance to tidy up a bit, and found the last two weeks of dirty clothes stuffed way in back, covered up by my baseball equipment. But jeez, come on! I mean it's not like I wasn't *ever* gonna take 'em down to the wash. After all I've been pretty busy lately, too, haven't I? But she wasn't buying one word of it. Anyway, after I thought about it, I thanked my lucky stars that she hadn't took a peek under the bed! Then she started with the, "You are not *that* busy young man, (uh-oh, "Young man" usually isn't followed by anything good) because I've noticed you have not done a darn thing around the house all summer." Well, I knew where that was going, and realizing I could be in for some real trouble, I tried doing some damage control by reminding her about my successful completion of all the requirements at Old Pueblo Debutantes in near record time, and pointed proudly to my graduation certificate that I purposely placed right up front on my book shelf just for these types of emergencies. She wasn't buying that this time, neither, saying that *real* gentleman do their fair share of the chores around the house like taking out the garbage and picking up the dog poop without there mothers having to beg them.

"The way I figure it, *real* gentlemen probably have people working for 'em to do that sort of nasty stuff," I said, realizing as the last words came out it was a *huge* mistake. Well, that really got her goat, and she started carrying on about how I was turning out to be a spoiled, good for nuthin', lazy lout and how I was never gonna amount to anything, and on and on about how I needed to learn responsibility, and just *who* did I think did all that nasty stuff around here. Her, that's who! It was getting crystal clear, that if I didn't come up with something quick, I was toast for the rest of the day and maybe the week, but just as I was mulling over my options, wouldn't ya know it, but here comes good old, "kick you right in the groin" Dodger, sauntering easy as can be through my door and up to the bed, where he squatted way down, stuck his head underneath, and as I watched in horror, pulled out two dirty socks and a half eaten Hostess cupcake, and then just walked right back out.

Ma just stood there frozen stiff as a statue with her mouth wide open, as she watched that stupid mutt disappear down the hall, and then, against my pitiful objections, got down on all fours and took a look under the bed for herself. That was pretty much the end of it, 'cause after she saw the years of garbage shoved under there, including a boatload of stuff she'd already replaced thinking they were lost for good, my goose wasn't only cooked, but burnt to a crisp! I buried my face in my hands to try to shield myself from the onslaught that was on it's way, and Ma practically had two conniption fits before she was finally finished letting me have it. I didn't say a word, but just sat there and took it, knowing darn well it didn't do no good to try to stop a mother on a rampage before they were good and finished, in fact that just gave 'em something new to sink their teeth into and could prolong your agony considerable. You can quote me on that, I swear, I practically wrote the book. If you need any more convincing you can ask your Pop, he'll tell ya.

Anyway, after she finally tuckered herself out, she grabbed me by the collar and dragged me into the kitchen where she wrote up a list of chores about a mile long for me to do, and then shoved it in my face.

"This should keep you busy for a while, young man," she said in a huff as she walked off.

"I ain't gonna be so young, after I finish all this," I muttered under my breath.

"What was that?" she whirled around quick as a cat.

"I said I ain't gonna yawn 'til I finish all this," I answered polite as can be, and she just gave me one of them piercing glares she liked to use to let you know how much hot water you were in, the kind you could almost feel pinching your skin, and then stomped off through the living room and up the hallway.

I took another long, sad look at my sentence and decided I better get cooking if I was ever gonna meet the guys today. I decided to get the most disgusting job outta of the way first, so I grabbed the little shovel that we used for a pooper-scooper and went to work. It was the one that came with the fireplace set but never got used on account of the fact that it was only cold enough in Santa Elena to light a fire about twice a year, and even when it was, good old Pop didn't have a clue how to start one up. In fact the last time he tried, he used so much lighter fluid that when it finally did catch, it singed off most of his eyebrows and all of his nose hairs. But he said it was actually kinda nice, 'cause for a while he could breath easier than ever before. The only down side was when a gnat flew straight up there and buzzed around his sinuses for a while since there wasn't no hairs to tangle itself up in.

I was just about done degrading myself for that worthless animal, when out of the back door here he comes, happy as a lark, and he proceeds to squat down right in front of me and make a nice big steaming pile of Dodger doo-doo to pick up all over again. I swear as he was doing his business, he looked up at me over his shoulder and gave me a little sinister grin like, "How do ya like them apples?" Well, that did it, and I was just about to cold cock 'im with that shovel when outta the corner of my eye, I saw Ma peering at me through the bedroom window and decided better of it.

I went on in and cleaned up my closet and under the bed and vacuumed all the carpets in the house in a flash. I mowed the lawn and raked the gravel and took out all the garbage, and heck, I even helped Gracie make her bed for a few more brownie points, just to show what a great guy I was, 'cause I was dying to get back over to the Mansfield place and see what was up.

I bided my time 'til Ma was deep into a particularly juicy phone conversation with aunt Leah about the young and innocent new secretary over at the town hall, Miss Pachyderm or something, who apparently wasn't that young or innocent after all. Seems someone saw here wearing a red ribbon around her waist with a key hung on it last month on the night of the lunar eclipse. Now that wouldn't mean much to normal folks, but every Mexican worth his weight in frijoles knows that an eclipse will sure enough cause a cleft lip in your unborn child when your expecting, and the only way to ward it off is to wear the ribbon and key, so you do the math. Don't believe me about this unusual cure? Go ahead and call down to Mexico City and ask for the Minister of Weird-o Mexican Superstitions; you wont believe your ears!

I saw my big chance and just walked right by, fluffing the pillows on the couch as I did, and said, "See ya, Ma. All through. Love ya," and then flew out the back door faster than a F-4 Phantom. I might've heard someone shout, "Johnny!" just as the door slammed, but then again I couldn't be absolutely sure, what with the bang of the door, the cars going by and the neighbors chit-chatting. Heck, that sound could've been just about anything.

I thought I was good and rid of Gracie and her side kick Muttley, too, and was feeling pretty good about myself right about then, when I heard a high pitched "Arf! Arf!" coming from straight behind, which I recognized right off as Dodger's, "Hey, what about me?" bark he used when he thought you were ignoring him, which was almost impossible to do, or say if you had forgotten him outside or something. It was different from his deep, "Woof!" of a bark, he used to sound tough around other dogs or strangers, or his low, moaning, "Haruuumph," he used when he was real sad, like when his favorite toy was stuck under the couch and he couldn't get it out, or when you still had plenty of food on your plate but refused to give him even one more little taste. You really couldn't tell a darn thing about what he was thinking by that sleepy-eyed, droopy-lipped, ain't-nobody-home look on his face, but at least he could communicate with three different sounds, which, come to think of it, was more than most of The Losers could muster.

I turned around just in time to whack the charging Dodger on the nose before he could take a bite outta my butt, which stopped him cold, and he gave out that same low "Haruuumph," I told ya about and then laid himself out flat, dejected.

"Try to keep him in line, will ya!" I pleaded with Gracie, and then started back on my way to the Mansfield place.

When we got there and walked into the parlor room, there was good old Jesus on one side cooking up something that smelt just swell on the hibachi we'd *barrowed* from the Sundt's backyard, and the rest of the guys over on the other side locked in a super serious conversation.

"Who do ya think's better, Johnny. Koufax or Marischal?" Chicken Coop asked, licking his lips all the way up to his nose. "We've been trying to decide for an hour."

"I say Marischal, on account'a he's Mexican just like me," Rosie sat up and said proudly.

"He ain't no Mexican, you twit," Ira answered. "He's from one of them Carribean Islands, like Cuba or Hawaii."

"I don't give a darn. He's got brown skin and speaks Spanish. That's close enough for me. Right, Jesus?"

Jesus just looked up and nodded while he smiled, clueless, as usual.

"Marischal couldn't hold up Koufax' jock strap," I said. Disgusted that I even had to answer such a ridiculous question.

"W-w-wait a second," said Jag, suddenly sitting up straight from where he was lounging on the end of the sofa. "Wasn't he the g-guy that clobbered that c-catcher over the head with his bat last year?"

"That's the one. He's a lunatic," I said, shaking my head.

"Then he's the one for m-me!"

It was obviously no use arguing with such baseball birdbrains.

"Hey, what's Hey-soos cooking up over there? It smells *muy delicioso*," I said as my rumbling belly reminded me that I'd skipped out of the house before lunch.

"Don't know, but he already made up some fresh tortillas this morning. I came a little early and brung him some flour from home that I snuck out in my pant pockets," Rosie said as he glanced down sheepishly at the white powder all over the front of his Levi's. "Now it looks like he's frying up some *carnitas* from last night's left over, left overs, and it's almost ready!" He started smacking his lips and rubbing his big belly.

Sure enough, here comes Jesus smiling ear to ear with a plate, or I should say the top of an old frying pan, full of hot, juicy, chunks of white meat, still sizzling from the skillet.

"*Vas a comer, mis amigos*," he said, as he held 'em out for us to grab, which we did with enthusiasm. They were hot little devils, but I managed to toss one from hand to hand a few times to keep from burning myself, and then popped it into my mouth. Boy-o-boy, was it good! Tender, moist and delicious, but not tasting exactly like any meat I'd ever had before.

"Wow, that is dee-lish, Hey-soos!" Rosie said, rolling his eyes back in utter delight. "*Que es?*"

"*Es carne de cascabel. Anoche, la mate despues que se fueron*," he rattled off with a real satisfied smile.

W-what'd he say?" asked Jag, swallowing his piece down and reaching for another as Rosie just stared ahead, kinda spooked.

"Well, aaah, he said aaah…"

"Spit it out, chubs!" demanded Big I.

"Well, he said he caught it last night. It's rattlesnake meat!"

As you would guess, that kinda put a damper on things to say the least, and Chicken Coop started running every which way, spitting and gagging and bouncing up and down like a drop of water on a hot skillet, and screaming all the while, "Sufferin' Suckatash!" while Creepy turned five shades of green and started rolling on the floor swearing he could feel the snake slithering around inside his belly. Ira was cussing up a blue streak and was just about to stick his fingers down his throat, when Jag stood up and yelled out, "That is so b-bitchin'! Don't you guys see? Think how cool it's gonna sound when word gets out that not only are the S.S.B.'s not afraid of rattlesnakes, but we actually eat them for lunch!"

Well, leave it to old Jag to turn a disaster that would surely have led to a visit to the Emergency Room for all day stomach pumping, into one of the most brilliant successes we'd ever had. Coop got his color back, Creep stopped writhing around, Iceman pulled his fingers outta his throat and we all let out a big cheer and raced over to give Jesus an enthusiastic group hug which he thoroughly enjoyed. No more weenie rich kids; we were the fearless, hard as nails, rattlesnake-eating *hombres* of the white ghetto!

"That's great and all, Jag," Big I said after thinking a bit. "The only trouble is no one's gonna believe a word of it. We're gonna need some cold, hard proof."

He was right. Kids always needed some kinda proof for something this big, like the time Scooter Thompson swore he stole a pair of El Generalissimo's underpants off her clothes line and made a giant parachute for his hamster Harry out of 'em, but then couldn't come up with even a thread of the material to prove it, which ended up getting him pounded more that praised. Well, that kinda dampened our spirits, and we went back to starting to feel a little nauseous 'til good old Jesus held something up in his hand and gave it a quick shake...it was the stinking snake's rattle!

"All right!" We all wailed and ran over to give it a closer look.

"N-now no one can d-doubt us. Our place in Santa Elena history is s-set in stone," Jag said in triumph as he took the thing from Jesus and held it over his head shaking it for all he was worth while the rest of us did a little snake dance around 'im. After that, we decided to hide it in the fireplace in the living room for safekeeping behind a brick that had worked its way loose, and then settled back into the parlor. We laid flat on the floor in the usual order, just staring up at the ceiling and enjoying our new found bravery, and realizing, I think, that things may never be this good again, when Rosie said, "Too bad Neil ain't here. Look at all the cool stuff he's missing."

"Yeah, but it's his own darn fault, ain't it?" I said. "He chose to leave us high and dry when we could have really used 'im, so I ain't feelin' too sorry. He's nuthin' but a Beenadick Arnold."

"I just don't get him," said Coop. "Sometimes he's your best pal, and the next minute he's your worst enemy. Come to think of it, maybe he's Shitso-frantic."

"Shitso what?" asked Ira, bewildered.

"Sounds like some kinda dysentery," said Rosie.

"Naw, you know," Coop said with unusual confidence. "That thing where people have a whole bunch of different personalities all living inside 'em so as you don't know which one you're gonna run into next. We learned all about it in science last year, member? We were studying that weirdo, Sigma Fraud."

"You mean schitzophrenic?" said Bampu irritated again at the ignorance around him. "And it is Sigmund Freud not *Fraud!*"

"Well, that's exactly what I said now, wasn't it?" answered Coop as he looked each of us in the eye so we could acknowledge his brilliance.

Actually, there was a chance that Coop was on to something with this one for a change. I had seen it in this cool movie on Mid-day Matinee one time, when this poor girl who had three completely different people living

# Our Pal Jesus

inside her head; one sweet as pie, one mean as the devil and one scared of her own shadow that would fall completely to pieces at the drop of a hat. I asked Pop about it afterwards and he said it was a real rare condition, and then as he turned away, I could of swore he said under his breath something like it was just his luck that every woman he ever met seemed to have a horrible case of it.

"W-w-well we can't worry about Neil, he m-made his bed and now he's got to s-sleep in it. We n-need to concentrate on sneaking Hey-shoos outta here in an f-few days and keeping him safe and sound in the m-meantime," Jag said, giving the final word on the subject.

That Mexican looked up from the beans he was cooking up in an old coffee can when he heard his name and flashed us another gentle smile.

After some more laying and thinking, Ira pulled an old red, half-flat utility ball outta his pants and started tossing it in the air.

"Where'd ya find that?" I asked.

"Over in the alley behind the Toone's. Someone must've swiped it from The Sewer 'cause it's got S.E.S. stenciled on the side. On the way over I tried to nail a prairie dog with it but the little snot ducked at the last second and the ball got stuck on some jumping cactus and now is leaking air pretty good. I was hoping to have a game of 'ghetto' dodge ball, and break in old Hey-soos with the ways of the S.S.B.'s, but now it's so flat you can't even get a grip on it."

"Ah!" Jesus screamed out when he saw what Ira had, and then took that ball outta his hands and started bouncing it off of his knees and ankles and head over and over, and never once letting it hit the floor. We all sat up and watched, amazed, while he kept up his little dance.

After a bit Chicken Coop asked, "What the heck's he doin'?"

"I d-dunno," answered Jag, not taking his eyes off 'a him. "But it looks like he has done it plenty of times before."

Finally Rosie rattled off some Mexican at 'im and Jesus shot some back.

"What'd he say, Rosie?"

"Well, I think he must be confused, because he said he's playing football."

"Football?" Ira yelled out. "If some football player was stupid enough to do all that silly bouncing and dancing he'd be wearing his ass as a hat in about two seconds, and never be able to show his face on the field again!" Everyone nodded in agreement.

"I believe what Hey-soos is performing so admirably is referred to as juggling," said Bampu. "It is a warm up drill for the game of soccer, which the rest of the world calls football."

"Soccer? Yuck!" I said. I remember trying to watch that lame game one time on "Wild World of Sports" to see what all the hubbub was about, but after about thirty minutes not a darn thing had happened, and I mean

nuthin'! Not only was there no score, but nobody had even got close enough to even take a shot for crying out loud. All they did was kick the ball back and forth and side to side, over and over and over until someone would finally kick the stupid ball outta bounds and everything would stop. Then they'd throw it in and start up all over again. Once in a while, just as one team started making some headway, a player would fall down and start rolling around on the ground like he was in horrible agony, and then some guy wearing what looked like my four year old Easter outfit, would race over and pull a flashcard outta his pocket and shove it in the face of the player who had supposedly done the tripping. Then, I guess, if that player couldn't get the problem on the flashcard right, he was outta the game, and the guy who just a second ago was on the ground looking to all the world like he was about to die, would pop right up, good as new, and start running around like nuthin' ever happened. But the really weird thing about the whole thing was that the thousands of people in the stands who somehow kept from falling asleep, didn't think this was unusual at all, although, to tell you the truth, it looked like they were a lot busier singing songs and doing dances and trying to out shout the other teams fans than they were watching what was going on the field. But then again, I guess you really couldn't blame 'em.

"Well, believe it or not, it is the most popular sport, world wide," added The Creep.

"Yeah, well if that's so it's on account of the guys in the rest of the countries are too retarded to play *real* sports like baseball and basketball, and way too big of weenies to play real football, so they made up this girlie game where all you gotta do is kick the ball back and forth. God forbid you might want to pick it up and throw it down field like a man, that's totally illegal. Don't take no talent at all. The way I see it, long as you can run without tripping over yourself, you could be a big soccer star," Ira said, rolling his eyes and shaking his head.

"My Pop, he says it is a big communist conspiracy," I added. "Says them Reds want everybody in the whole world to play it on account'a it's *so* boring that it puts people to sleep and makes it easier for them to take over the world."

"On the contrary, Johnny C. The crowds at some soccer games get so excited that they have been known to riot."

I thought for a while on how that could possibly be true, and then it came to me, "That's probably on account'a them getting so raving mad for having spent good money for tickets to such a stupid game that they decide to beat the snot outta each other!"

All the while Jesus kept bouncing that ball, over and over, while he listened to *our* gibberish, and then finally said, *"Quiere jugar, mis amigos?"*

"He wants to know if you guys want to play a game of soccer," said

Rosie.

"Sure!" We all screamed and then eagerly followed him outside to a clearing on the side of the house.

"*Primero necesitamos los gols*," he said, and looked around to find some dried out Saguaro ribs. Then he stuck 'em in the ground about six feet apart at each end of the field and tied another one on top with some cattail stalks to make a sorta box to kick the ball through. He found some sticks and rocks to put around the outside for boundaries, stood back, looked it over, rearranged 'em a bit and then finally turned to us with a satisfied look.

We picked out sides using, the old, "Ink a dink a bottle of ink," method and the last ones to "stink" were the first to get the ball. So with Jesus as referee, that ball started to fly and dust filled the air and with screams and curses all around, we gave soccer our best S.S.B. try. It didn't take long for us to see that the other team with Rosie in front of their goal had a huge advantage since he was darn near as wide as the goal was, making it darn near impossible to get the ball by 'im no matter how good an aim, and he must've blocked at least ten shots without so much as moving a muscle, they just bounced right off of him. The last few, I don't think he even noticed 'cause he was so engrossed with a Black Cow Carmel Sucker, that, much to his delight, he had just rediscovered in his back pocket.

On the other hand, we had Chicken Coop in our goal, who hid his eyes, ducked his head and started to hiccup whenever someone even got close to taking a shot, trying his darndest *not* to get hit. So after almost twenty minutes, our team was down eight to zip and needless to say tempers started to flare. Pretty soon there were a lot more shins and butts being kicked than the ball, and players decided to start using their hands after all, but only to slap the stuffing outta the guys on the other side, and finally, with the ball forgotten all together, there was nuthin' but a big pile of boys wrestling in the dirt trying to strangle each other 'til Jesus screamed out, *"Alto! Alto!"* and dragged each of us to our feet, one by one.

*"No mas futbol! No mas futbol!"* Jesus kept yelling as he tried to keep us apart.

"You said a mouthful there, amigo," Ira said, wiping the dirt off his face with the back of his hand. "Another minute and we might've killed each other. That crazy soccer's a lot more violent than you'd expect from watching those pansies on T.V. running around on their tip toes with satin shorts and girly striped T-shirts."

*"No mas futbol,"* Jesus said again, holding out his hands as if to calm us down, and glancing quickly from side to side. Then after a minute or two, when the guys' tempers cooled off a bit, he said, *"Quieres comer?"* with that great, kindly smile.

*"Si! Si!"* we all answered with enthusiasm, remembering from Mrs. Orozco's kitchen that *"comer,"* meant something about eating, and then we raced up the steps and back into the house.

That dear Mexican fella started cooking his heart out all over again to fix us up a feast on that tiny hibachi. Imagine what he could do with a proper kitchen! There were fresh tortillas, a big Folger's can full of piping hot frijoles, and some kinda green vegetable all cut up in a red chili sauce that smelt outta this world. We stood in line waiting our turn and smacking our lips with Rosie slowly but surely pushing his way to the front, not looking from side to side or acknowledging our loud complaints at all, but just staring straight ahead like some starving zombie, as Jesus started handing out bubbling beans in burritos and swell smelling scoops of that red chili stew to boot. We could hardly wait to stuff it in our mouths and started pushing forward for all we were worth, but it didn't matter none. The whole lot of us shoving against Rosie was like an ant pushing against an elephant, and it became plain that we weren't going nowhere 'til he got all his *comida* first.

Well, let me tell ya, it was worth the wait. This was some of the best Mexican food anyone had tasted this side of the Orozco's kitchen, and Jesus nervously watched as we devoured the stuff like a pack of hungry hyenas, another animal I learned all about on Mutual of Omaha's Wild Kingdom last Sunday with Pop. He moved from one to the other of us, trying to get a handle on what we thought, but the problem was that it was so darn good, no one was thinking of nuthin' but their next bite, and he had to wait for quite some time. Finally, I looked up from my burro for just a split second and saw him staring me square in the face from about a foot away, *"Muy bueno!"* I spit out, best I could with my mouth full of frijoles, and then the rest of the guys yelled out, *"Muy Bueno!"* too, and went right back to work.

*"Gracias a Dios,"* Jesus said clapping his hands and looking like a guy who just hit the jackpot on "Bowling for Dollars," and I swear that fella had a tear in his eye as he went back over to his hibachi and started up on his next delicious dish. We all took a short break at the same time, our stomachs bulging and our jaws aching, and Jagger took the opportunity to lead us in a rousing rendition of one of our old favorites:

Beans, beans, the musical fruit,
The more you eat the more you toot,
The more you toot the better you feel,
So eat beans with every meal!"

After a few more joyful verses, Coop licked his lips, wiped his face on his sleeve and said, "Boy, this really hits the spot, Big Rosie, but how'd he make all this stuff? Seems as if none of it's from the left overs we brought from home."

"Well, I grabbed a few pocketfuls of pinto beans along with the flour from my mom's stash this morning, and the red chili sauce is thanks to Bampu, who lifted that old dried out strand that Mrs. Molina had decorating her front porch the last couple years."

"You m-mean you can eat them things?" Jag asked.

"Only way to make *real* red chili sauce according to any Mexican woman worth her weight in menudo. First ya got to pulverize the heck out of it," Rosie said, pounding one fist into his other hand to demonstrate. "Then you add some water, a dash of salt, maybe a splash of vinegar and presto, red chili sauce."

"That's amazing," I said, shaking my head. "All this time I thought them things were just for looking at."

"Mexican folk are pretty clever when it comes to making delicious meals outta stuff you'd never even think was edible. When you're as poor as some of us are, you ain't got no choice, and you sure can't be too proud."

"Hey Rosie, ask Hey-soos what this green vegetable is," said Big I, real excited like. "I think I finally found one I like so I can get my mom off my back."

Rosie looked over at Jesus, pointed to what was left of the red chili dish and asked, *"Que es esto?"*

He rattled off a couple sentences of Mexican back at Rosie, gave us all another big smile and went right back to work.

"Hmmm, that's a new one," Rosie said, almost to hisself.

"What's he say?" demanded Ira.

"It's called *Nopalitos*, and the green stuff is prickly pear cactus."

"Damn! What we gonna eat next, prairie dog poop!"

"I hear they're quite divine in a lovely red wine sauce," I said in my best snooty chef's voice, which got me multiple monkey bumps and a bunch'a laughs, and then Jag said that this made us even tougher than before, eating rattlesnake for breakfast and cactus for lunch!

With my belly full and the warm summer air swirling threw the old house, I found my mind starting to fade the way a combination like that will do to ya sometimes, and I began daydreaming on how swell things had turned out for the S.S.B.'s this summer; first we'd taught Nasty Nancy a lesson or two for making our lives miserable during school year, then we beat those low down Losers at their own game and saved Creepy's life to boot, and now under Jagger's and Rosie's fearless leadership, we'd discovered poor Jesus and were about to help him and his family out of a horrible jam. Not bad if I do say so myself, but I surely knew we were far from home free on this one, and I couldn't help but think it'd be nice to have that no good Neil with us if we got our butt in a bind, which seemed to happen all too often around here.

After lazing around for a bit, Rosie asked, "Now whatdaya want to do?" Patting his stuffed belly and not really caring what the answer was.

*"Quien quiere jugar beisbol?"* asked Jesus, noticing that we were starting to come to life again.

"Sure, Hey-soos, that sounds swell, b-but we didn't b-bring our stuff," answered Jag and then laid his head back down.

*"No hay problema!"* said Jesus, as he pulled out a big cardboard box filled with all sorts of junk and emptied it out on the table.

We all hopped up to check on what he had, and when I saw what was on the table, I could hardly believe my eyes. Jesus had *made* all by hisself a full set of baseball gear from God knows what.

"What's all this?" Ira asked, looking astonished and excited all at once.

Rosie asked and Jesus answered, and then Rosie said, "Seems he wanted to do something nice for us for helping 'im out and all, so after we left last night he went out and found all the stuff he needed to make us baseball mitts, a bat and a ball, just the way the kids do it back in Mexico."

He held up the bat, which was long and thin, a piece of mesquite wood I think, whittled just so, with a nice smooth finish and even a knob on the end, and when I turned it over, carved in big letters right were the trademark would normally be were the letters *S.S.B.*

"Neat-O!" we all yelled.

The ball was near regulation size but just a tad lighter, and even covered in leather that Jesus said he got from some old slippers he'd found in the trash, and stitched all around real professional-like with twine. I picked it up, tossed it in the air a few times to get the feel, and then told Big Rosie to go to the end of the room where he got down in a crouch and I wound up and fired him a strike.

"Cool!" we all shouted.

Then we turned our attention to the mitts, that I gotta tell ya, were nuthin' short of works of art. Each one was cut just right from what looked like old milk cartons, and had spots for your fingers and thumb and even a hinged pocket, and there was a pad in the palm, too; a piece of old sponge I was guessing. In fact the only thing missing was the laces.

"This is absolutely amazing, Rosie," I said, picking up Jesus' creation and slipping it carefully on my hand for a try. "These musta taken him hours."

"That's what I thought, too, but Jesus says he's been making them up so long, he can pump 'em out in no time flat." We all looked up at Jesus in wonder and he smiled and nodded back.

"What about the laces?" Ira asked, getting antsy to try everything out.

"I'll ask." And after Jesus had rattled off a few words, Rosie looked back at us and said, "He says, use the ones in your shoes."

"Great!" we all yelled as we ripped the laces outta our tennies and threaded them through the holes Jesus had already punched. We molded the mitts to our hands a bit, gave the pocket a punch or two and raced out the back door to give 'em a whirl.

We started up a game of pitcher's hand, right off, with Jesus as the proud umpire. All the gear worked out just swell and was a whole lot cooler being made by hand and all. I mean, anyone could just go down to Jack Ellis Sporting Goods over in Tucson and buy a new mitt anytime they wanted, right? After that thought I stopped for a second, realizing the answer actually was no, or else Jesus wouldn't ever have had to make all this stuff outta a bunch of junk. Boy, it was hard to believe that a country only a few miles away could be so completely different; a whole different world, with the only thing separating us is a little border crossing station down in Nogales, right? I just don't get it. I mean, couldn't we maybe just help them out a bit so everybody would be better off? I guess it's just one of those things grown-ups are gonna have to work out for themselves.

Well, the game was going along beautiful, 'cept for one shoe flapping all over the place when you tried to run the bases, but no one really seemed to mind, we were having too much fun. After some experimenting I learned to really make that crazy ball dance on just about every pitch, with a little twist of the wrist here and a bit more pressure there, on account'a it wasn't perfect round to start with, plus the stitching stood up nice and high; a soon to be major league pitcher's dream come true. Any pitcher worth his weight in salt, that is. I had Rosie's team by the throat and wasn't about to let up, their only chincy run coming on a worm burner that got past Chicken Coop in left desert and ended up in a patch of prickly pear he was too scared to go into, turning it into an inside the park homer, or in this case, inside the cactus patch. But with the score tied at one in the top of the sixth, Big Rosie came up with a big swat, and put his team in the lead by flat out annihilating one of my knucklers that didn't, and that ball would still be flying on it's merry way if it hadn't hit the chimney of the Mansfield place to slow it down. We still had a chance with our last ups, but after Creepy's pathetic whiff and a fly out by yours truly, Jeff "zero for the season" Howell was our last hope. Well, he stepped up to the plate like he owned the place, wiggled his stubby arms and legs all over to get loose, and on the Iceman's first offering, laid down a nice bunt down the third base line. But then, to all of his teammates amazement and horror, he just stood like a statue in the batters box and waited for Ira to come tag him out!

"What in the ever loving name of wide world of sports was that?" I screamed, running over and getting right in his face.

"T-t-that, as you should know, Johnny C., was what's c-called a suicide bunt," he answered, nodding his head with certainty and even pride.

"No it ain't, numb-nuts! A suicide *squeeze* is when you bunt to protect a runner on third that's stealing home or else he'd be dead at the plate!"

"Oh," Jag grunted and then frowned. "I thought it was s-s-something you did at the end of the g-game to keep your honor when your team was sure to l-lose. You know, like committing Harry Karry."

Un-be-*leav*able! Why the heck did I even bother? "Ya know Jag, you got a 10 cent brain!"

And without missing a beat he smiled that goofy grin of his and said, "Yeah, but they're having a sale on candy over at El Minuto and 10 cents will get me a giant Sweet Tart and some Sugar Babies, so who's lookin' dumb now!"

We were back inside lying on the parlor room floor, with all the doors and windows open, hoping for even the slightest bit of a cross breeze to take the edge off the stifling heat, and just having ourselves a good old afternoon *siesta*, like Rosie said all of his family down in Mexico did every day.

"You mean to tell me," Ira snapped, "They close the whole darn town down for three to four hours every afternoon just to go home and take a stinking nap? No wonder it still looks like the dark ages down there."

"Heck, my dad used to even work on Sundays up until last year when mom made him stop. She said if he didn't he was sure to have one of those my-own-car-deal infarction," added Coop.

"We may not want to be too quick to criticize the Hispanic lifestyle," said Bampu. "The American Heart Association's latest research indicates that stress is one of the primary risk factors in shortening your life span."

"Yeah, well *you're* the biggest factor in shortening *my* life span, brainiac," Big I growled.

"Well *you're* the end product of peristalsis!" Bampu shot back, uncharacteristically.

"What the heck does that mean?" Ira asked, turning to the rest of us for help but getting only blank looks. "Well, if I find out that means something bad, I swear I'll rip you another…"

"Yes, yes, I understand," said Creepy, figuring he didn't have too much to worry about this time.

"Listen, you guys need to stop fighting, there's already a major battle going on in my stomach between all the red chile and frijoles I scarfed down for lunch," moaned Rosie, rubbing his belly ever so gently.

As soon as he said it, we all started noticing a nasty rumbling coming from our insides we hadn't felt before. It was just like when you're playing outside happy as can be 'til some big mouth says, "Boy, my mouth is so dang dry if I don't get a snow cone quick, I'm gonna die." Then all of a sudden you notice *your* mouth is dry as the Sonora desert, too, and then *you* can' t think of nuthin' else but that darn snow cone, either, which ruins whatever you were having so much fun at before that idiot had to open his pie hole.

Anyway, we were definitely feeling the full fart-forming force of those frijoles but good, when Coop complained, "It feels like someone is lighting off little sticks of dynamite in the middle of my gut!" and began rolling all over the floor, moaning and groaning.

"Funny you should make that remark," said Creepy. "Did you boys realize that human gas is actually flammable? It has the same composition as methane."

I ain't gotta say that that sure got our attention, and everyone stopped bellyaching and sat up straight.

"W-what's he saying, Johnny?" Jag asked real interested.

"He says you can light your farts on fire," I answered. But as soon as the words came outta my mouth I realized it was a mistake, 'cause as soon as he heard, Jag got that same old crazy look in his eye.

"Is it t-true, Bampu? Is it? Can you r-r-really light 'em on fire? Huh?"

"Well, yes, I suppose…theoretically, I mean. But I would seriously warn…"

"Get out!" Jag shouted, pushing the Creep in the chest as he did. "All this t-time having a built in flame thrower and n-not even knowing it! Just think of how f-feared the S.S.B.'s will be now! Quick g-g-give me a match, somebody. I feel a d-doozy brewing!"

"Wait, Jag," I begged, once again trying to keep my screwball friend from causing himself bodily harm. "It might be dangerous. Your innards could explode!"

"Quit whining, Johnny C." Ira snarled, obviously wanting to see if what Creepy said was true. "You'd think you'd be proud of our fearless leader for attempting such a great scientific experiment," and then after sifting through a pocket full of junk he pulled out an old faded match book and handed it over to our new chief investigator of obnoxious gases.

"T-t-thank you, professor," Jag said with a nod.

"Don't mention it, Your Honor," Ira answered with a bow.

Well, that jackass Jagger smiled so wide you could see every darn tooth in his head and every space in between, and then went over to the corner of the room and laid down flat on his back.

"Jag, don't do it! Your butt could explode!" Chicken Coop cried out.

But I knew there was no use trying to stop 'im once he got like this, and especially in this case, when he had a chance to try out a theory that could be so monumentally important to every twelve-year old boy the world over, so I just sat and watched and got ready to run home and call the ambulance once it was over.

So there was Jag, flat on his back with his knees pulled up tight to his chest to get his rear end angled up just right and his legs far apart, "For maximum ejection", and then after looking over at us, he gave the thumbs up, yelled out, "G-g-gas, ready for immediate release!" and then lit the match and held it down between his legs, closing his eyes, blowing out his cheeks and, pushing with all his moronic might.

We all leaned in to get a better view to see if this bodily function fantasy could really be true, and boy did we get an eyeful! Ira started the official count down; five, four, three…but our esteemed president just couldn't hold off no longer and let her rip, and I mean rip, like a king sized sheet tearing straight down the middle! And then there it was, a blue flame streak, two feet long if it was an inch, shooting straight outta the bottom of Jag's Levi's, like a stinking blow torch for gosh sakes, and nearly singed off Ira's eyebrows who had crept in a little too close for a better look.

For a second or two there was utter silence, half from disbelief, and half from awe at the incredible spectacle we had just witnessed, but that was shattered by a hair raising, "Yeeeooow!" as our esteemed president jumped up, started shaking his butt, and then began waving at it from behind like he was, well, on fire. We all froze, not having any experience with anyone with a butt hole burn, 'til finally Jesus came running over with a big pot of water he was gonna use to make vegetable soup, and sat poor old Jag right down in the middle of it. He stopped screaming after that, and as we all gathered around he managed to crack a smile and then, as he gathered up his senses, screamed out, "Great m-mother of God! Wait 'til them b-big shots in Junior High get a load of this!"

# Chapter Twenty-Four

## THE TORO GAME

"Hey, you guys want to go to the Toro game tonight? I heard that nutcase Bobby Booty got thrown out for arguing calls the last three nights straight, and if they toss 'im out again he breaks a fifty year old Cactus League record," Ira said. "And if that ain't enough, it's bat night to boot!"

"Sounds great!" we all answered.

To tell ya the truth, there was nuthin' in the whole world I got more of a kick outta than watching good old Bobby Booty, the scatter-brained skipper of the Single-A Tubac Toros for long as anyone could remember, blow his stack and then practically rupture an aneurysm, arguing with an umpire over some bone-headed call. I mean you would'a thought it was game seven of the World Series every night the way he'd go nuts, but the truth was, the Toros were horrible, always were. In fact they played so bad in a game last week, when a newspaper reporter asked about the execution of his team, Bobby said he was all for it! But still folks came from far and wide and filled those rickety old wooden bleachers of Tubac Field, or the "Bull Rink," as it was known in these parts, just to watch "Bombastic" Bobby go ballistic, and he would, most every night, you could count on it. I mean it got to the point that you started rooting for the Toros to get a bum call just to get old Bobby going.

He was a short, fat, bald guy with a head like a basketball, and a humongous round butt that, unfortunately for him, fit his name to a T, and when he walked fast out on the field, running was out of the question, to give an umpire what for, it bounced along right behind 'im, like too mad hogs fighting in a gunny sack. Whenever he started out of the dugout, all the folks in the stands, 'cept the most modest few, would stand on their seats, facing away from the field and shake their butts as hard as they could to show support for our beloved manager. It was a Toro tradition! So as any fool could see, all that, *plus* free bat night was just too good a thing to pass up on a lazy summer night like this. I mean where else could you go for all that entertainment *and* get a weapon to beat the heck outta the fella sitting next to you while you watched!

"G-great idea, Ice Man, but what about Hey-soos? Can't he g-go too? He's a huge b-baseball fan."

"I don't know about that, Jag," I said. "You know Mengo and Pato are always working security at the Bull Rink. They might spot 'im."

"Are you kidding?" Ira laughed. "Those two wouldn't recognize John Dillinger if he came up and gave 'em a big kiss on the lips."

"Who the heck is he?" asked Rosie.

"Never mind, Big Guy," answered Creepy. "Just an old miscreant."

"Oh," Rosie said, more confused than ever.

"How about a d-disguise?" Jag suggested.

"Man you guys are really pushing it, but if we're gonna try it, it's gotta be good. No eye glasses with fake noses or something asinine like that," I said, as Rosie looked away, dejected that I already shot down his big idea.

"How about a woman?" asked Coop, real proud-like.

"What about a woman?" I answered.

"No, how about we disguise him like a woman?" said Coop

"Oh, come on, that's ridiculous. What about his mustache?" I asked.

"I know!" said Rosie excited to support his little friend. "We could tell everyone he had a glandular problem just like my Aunt Isabella, her mustache is so dang thick you can't even see her upper lip. It looks like a darn caterpillar's living on her face! I tell ya, I still get nightmares about her kissing me all over my face last winter at cousin Josefina's quincéniera!" And then he gave a big shudder, which made his blubber jiggle all over, and stuck his tongue out in disgust.

"You and your families "glandular problems," Ira said. "Maybe you should all check in at Johns Hopkins so someone could finally figure out what the hecks wrong with you all."

"I don't know Rosie," I said, trying to comfort him a bit. "That might be stretching it pretty darn thin, even for us."

"Hold on there a sec, John John," Ira said rubbing his chin. "Maybe that *Señora* idea ain't so far fetched as it seems. I could swipe my dad's electric razor, and with a little buzz here and a snip there, Hey-soos' face would be soft as a baby's behind," and then he turned around, pulled his pants down and mooned us as he finished.

After a few attempted kicks, we looked over at Jesus, who seemed more puzzled than usual, but then started laughing himself, even though I know for a fact that he didn't have the slightest idea of what we had up our sleeve for 'im.

"What about those hairy legs?" I said pointing. "Look like they should be on a gorilla!"

"That ain't no p-p-problem," said Jag. "Have you s-seen most of the l-ladies in Santa Elena? He'll fit right in."

"Okay, Okay," I said, finally giving in a bit. "Where the heck we gonna get some woman's clothes?"

"I saw a housedress and some stockings flapping in the breeze on Mrs. Redondo's clothesline over on Paseo del Norte just this morning," said Coop.

"Sounds good to me. Why don't you and Creepy run on over and try to lift that dress for Hey-soos, and keep a look out for a scarf or a shawl or something, we're gonna need to cover his head up, too. Got it?"

"Si Señor," they both said and gave me a little half-assed salute and then jumped on their stingrays and split.

"Big I, why don't you try to snatch your Pop's Remington and then we'll all meet back over here around five. First pitch ain't 'til seven o'clock so that'll give us plenty of time to get our new pal all dolled up. Heck by the time we're finished with 'im, he'll be a shoe in for this year's La Señorita de Santa Elena beauty pageant, which, quite frankly ain't saying much. Remember who won last year?"

"Sure do," Jag answered. "Scary" Carrie Lemis, the "Santa Elena Sea Bass." I heard Mayor Trancoza whisper to his w-wife that anything with a m-m-mouth that big should have a hook in it," and then he put his hands on each side of his face and waved 'em back and forth like fish gills while bulging his substantial lips out far as possible.

"That actually looks more like an orangutan than a fish, butt face, but we get your point," Ira laughed. "Let's make sure we get there before they run outta the free bats, I know a few ushers that deserve a little pay back from last game we were at, then we'll just grab some grub at the bullrink for dinner."

"Oooh, that sounds mighty good," said Rosie, rubbing his stomach up and down.

"Relax, big guy," Ira said. "It's only two o'clock, so you've got a long, painful wait for those *gorditas*, you *gordito*."

Rosie shot him a dirty look, pulled out some mangled beef jerky from his pocket and gnawed off a big bite right in Ira's face. Then he turned to me and asked, "How we gonna get there, Johnny?" He sounded a little worried, as usual, although his words were real garbled trying to talk around that big clump of beef.

"Santa Elena Express, of course," I said with a smile. "I heard good old

Señor Villaseñor is back in commission as of this week."

The Santa Elena Express is what we called the 1957 Chevy Bel Air station wagon the Señor drove to shuttle people around in greater metropolitan Santa Elena. It was the closest thing to mass transit we had. There was no city bus, obviously, and no taxis neither. Just Señor Villaseñor and his turquoise and white Chevy with the swell stainless steel panel along the fin, which suited us and the whole town just fine. Problem was, he was kinda getting along in years and had this knarly case of trench foot he brought back from the big war, which kept 'im from doing much of anything 'cept driving, and then only on days when there were no storms brewing. He used to say his big toe could pick up a real frog stripper all the way over in El Paso! Not that he would ever let it get him down, he was about the happiest, most satisfied human being I ever met, always singing or whistling a tune, and waving to folks as he drove on by with a big fat smile on his face, and not one of them phony ones neither, but a real sincere one, like the kind your pop gets when you nail a homer. Plus, he always made sure to honk his horn for us kids, the special one he bought down in Nogales that played "La Cucaracha," over and over. All in all, he was one swell *compadre*. He had this perfectly round face, and an even rounder belly, his hair was always slicked down just right, and he wasn't chintzy with the cologne, neither. He said a man always had to look his best for the *Señoritas* because you never knew when an especially *bonita* one might show up, and ever since Mrs. Villaseñor passed on a few years back, he was back on the look out for the next *"Meesis Right."* He tried to explain to us how every man needed a good woman, but only got a bunch of blank stares in return, and then said we'd understand when we got older.

The best thing about that old Chevy wagon of his, and there was plenty to like about it from the fluffy dice hanging from the rear view mirror to the miniature statues of Jesus and Mary he had glued all over the dash board, was that you could stuff about twenty kids into the back and the price for a ride was always the same; twenty-five cents for anywhere in town and fifty-cents for outta town, all the way to the border if need be, per car load. The only *bad* thing about it was there was no stinking air-conditioning, making it pretty brutal on a hot summer day, but Mr. Villaseñor had that covered, too, by keeping a squirt bottle full of cold water in the front seat at all times to spray down his passengers when asked...absolutely free! That was a lot more refreshing than air-conditioning, anyhow, and a thousand times more fun. To top things off, he always kept a cooler up front chock full of cervezas and whatnot for him, and sodas and popsicles for us kids. All in all, getting a lift from Mr. Villaseñor was more like an amusement park ride than sitting in a taxi, and we used his services anytime we could scrape up the dough, even if we were only going a few blocks.

Anyways, after hashing out a few final details we headed on home to grab our ball caps and some cash. I got outta dragging Gracie along by telling her dogs weren't allowed into Tubac Field and she'd have to leave Dodger behind, which I knew she'd never go for, and that was that. This, of course, was a big fat lie. Heck, some nights it seemed like there were more darn dogs at the park than there were humans. Now *officially*, pets weren't allowed in, but old Mr. Tassi, the head grounds keeper, was such a softy when it came to animals that folks would bring their dogs along anyhow and he'd never have the heart to say no, as long as you agreed to clean up when they did their duty and kept 'em off the infield. On top of the ones he let in the front gate, a mess of strays were always squeezing through holes in the outfield fence to see what all the ruckus was about, and then made themselves right at home under the wooden bleachers, waiting patiently for a stray sopapilla or maybe a loose frijole or two. You learned real quick not to lay your food down by your feet while watching the game 'cause before you could say Carl Yazstremski it'd be gone, with half of your foot right along with it!

But those dogs didn't cause any major problems, mostly, and were pretty much just part of the whole atmosphere, 'cept on the occasion when a tomcat happened to wander in by mistake; and then all hell broke loose. The whole lot of 'em, and there might be fifteen at a game, twenty for a double header, would start to barking and yapping and whining their heads off, so you knew something was up, and then all of a sudden here they'd come, like one of those wild west stampedes, chasing that cat down one side of the stadium and up the other, and then through the stands, knocking over the vendors and patrons alike, and making such a spectacle that they'd have to actually stop the game. But that didn't upset the fans none, since it was usually a lot more fun to watch those dogs going nutso than the two-bit Toros blow another game on the field. In fact, folks would actually get kinda upset if there *wasn't* a full-blown dog show that night, feeling they really didn't get the most for their entertainment dollar.

When I reached the Mansfield place I was feeling like a million bucks, going to the ballgame and not having to drag Gracie and the mutt along for a change, and then as I walked around to the parlor and peered through the window I almost busted a gut! There was poor old Jesus, slouched on the sofa all decked out in Mrs. Redondo's finest housedress and looking none too happy about it, neither. Rosie was jawing at 'im in Mexican, trying to explain what we were up to and why he had to wear that get up, while Creepy and Coop were doing their darndest to hoist up some nylon stockings past his knobby knees. Ira was bent over in the corner, laughing so hard he could barely catch his breath, and I, after composing myself for a bit, took a deep breath and walked in the back door.

"So, what do you think, Johnny C?" said Rosie, proudly, as he and the two fashion designers stopped what they were up to and looked over at me with a smile.

"I think he looks lovely, fellas. Just lovely," I answered as I patted Jesus on the shoulder, his eyes looking up at me and pleading for help.

"Oh yeah," Ira said, still chuckling. "Forget Miss Santa Elena, we're going all the way to the Miss Universe Pageant!"

"I wonder if they have a 'Miss Out of this Universe' contest?" I asked.

"Come on now, Big I," Rosie said. "Remember this was partly your idea, too? Now grab your pop's razor and see what you can do with that mustache."

"Okay, okay," he said, as his laughing fits slowly faded away and he

335

pulled out the Remington from his pocket, gave it a few whacks on his knee to set the battery just right and clicked it on.

"I'll put it on the nose hair setting and see if I can just thin that thing up a bit first."

That razor was buzzing like a hornet's nest as Ira held it out straight, squinted his eyes up to take aim like he had a pistol or something, and came right for Jesus. Well, that poor Mexican man started shaking like a leaf, apparently never having seen an electric razor before, and then let out a big yelp, hiding his face in the sofa cushions and started screaming, "No me mates!" all over again. It took Rosie a good twenty minutes of negotiating, he had no clue how to say "electric razor," in Spanish, before Jesus finally sat back up and let Ira do his duty, all the while Rosie kept saying in his ear, *"No quieres ir al jugo de beisbol?"* and poor Jesus would whimper back, *"Si, yo quiero,"* wincing in pain as the razor pulled and tugged at his wire-like whiskers.

After about fifteen minutes of chopping and yanking and yelping, Ira finally stepped back and blurted out, "Behold my masterpiece!" as Jesus, more or less clean shaven but looking like he had just sat through the worst horror flick of his life, tried his darndest to work up a little grin. There were still a few stray hairs sticking out here and there, but that was pretty common with the ladies of Santa Elena, too, so he was definitely passable, maybe too good.

After Ira slapped on a few drops of Aqua Velva he'd brought along for good measure, Coop tied a big pink scarf around our new friend's head, and yelled out, "Now for the crowning touch," and stuffed two pair of rolled up tube socks down the front of Jesus' dress.

"What the heck is holding them up?" I asked.

"That would be old Mrs. Redondo's brassiere. I swiped that along with all the other stuff," he said proudly.

"That's disgusting!" Rosie said and spit on the floor. "How could you even touch that thing?"

"Well actually, I didn't. I carried it over here on the end of a long stick and then gave it up to Jesus who seemed to know exactly what to do with it. He didn't even have any trouble with those tricky hooks on the back."

After looking our new creation up and down for a while, we realized we didn't have any girly shoes for him to wear, so we didn't have no choice but to pull on his old work boots over the nylon stockings that were already starting to sag considerable, and decided to tell any nosey body that asked that he had this horrible foot problem and needed to wear these special designed orthopedic boots at all times or become cripple for life.

We were all ready to head out when Rosie said, "Ain't you guys forgetting the most important thing?" and as we turned away from the door, he whipped out a baggie from his back pocket and unsnapped the top to reveal a bunch of different colored powders and two or three little brushes to boot. Out of the other pocket he pulled a plastic case with some hairy looking flat things inside that looked like a couple of squished brown caterpillars and a contraption that looked like scissors on one end and a guillotine on the other.

"Now I know that one pack is full of different types of make up, Rosie," I said, pointing, "But what the heck is that fuzzy stuff and that scary looking tool ya got in the other."

"Why Johnny C.," he said, flitting around like some girly man. "I'm appalled you don't recognize the latest in ladies beauty accessories from gay Pari!"

"Just spill the beans, chubs or I'll turn you into gay purée!" snapped Big I.

"Well, these are false eyelashes," he said pointing at the hairy things, "and this here is the finest in twentieth century eyelash crimping technology," he added holding up the other and giving it a little squeeze.

"Looks more like some kinda torture tool," said Chicken Coop, wincing.

"Funny you said that. I heard my mom scream out in pain on more that one occasion while using this little devil."

Then Rosie went to town on that poor Mexican fella all over again, patting on a pile of the red powder so thick it sent Jesus, and most of the rest of us into a serious sneezing fit, and then slathering on a mess of this bright and shiny green, gooey junk all over the top of his eyelids. After stepping back and admiring his work several times, he glued on those eyelashes all half cocked, but good enough for government work and a Tubac Toros baseball game I guess, looking for all the world like two angry monarch butterflies had come home to roost smack dab on Jesus' peepers. Bampu, wanting to lend a hand, spread on the cherry red lipstick that was half melted by then, doing a commendable job of staying inside the lines, mostly. Then Rosie tried going after our lovely lady with that crimper thing, but it was more than Jesus could take and he covered up his face and pleaded, "No mas! No mas!" causing Rosie to backed off.

"He don't look half bad if I do say so myself," Rosie said with a smile as we all looked on, and being flat out amazed at what women will do to themselves in the name of vanity.

"Okay, okay," I said trying not to laugh, and thankful there weren't no mirrors for Jesus to get a load of hisself. "First pitch is in thirty minutes. Let's get a move on. Hey, where the heck's Jagger, by the way." I had just noticed he wasn't around.

"He went on over to the town square to try to flag down Mr. Villaseñor and the Santa Elena Express," answered the Creep. "He said to meet him in front of the courthouse at 6 o'clock sharp."

"Then we better get make like a leaf," I said, and we all headed toward the door with Ira in front and the dragon lady bringing up the rear. We used as many back alleys and secret passageways as possible to avoid any unwanted attention and formed a ring around Jesus, standing on our tippy-toes as we did, to shield him best we knew how. We came across little Pukey Porter just before the town square, but as he opened his mouth to ask why we were walking like that, Big I gave him the "scram punk, I'm not in the mood," look, and he just shut his trap and stood still as a statue as we passed by.

As we came into sight, Jag raced up and said, "M-m-man, I am glad you g-guys made it. Another five minutes and we'd b-be walking to the game. Seems Mr. V has g-got hisself a hot d-date with the Señora Valdez tonight down in Nogales and he's g-gonna knock off early."

"Señora Valdez?" Ira blurted out. "She's gotta be eighty years old if she's a day. That's totally rancid. What're they gonna do, sit and watch their dentures soak together? Yuk!"

"I really d-d-don't think we want to…" Jag stopped short like someone had reached in and grabbed his tongue as he looked up and spotted Jesus for the first time. His jaw almost hit the floor and his eyes bulged clean outta his head as he looked 'im over from head to toe. Then all of the sudden as if someone had turned on a switch he started laughing hysterical, much to the chagrin of poor old Jesus. "Good God almighty!" He spit out while gasping for air. "You g-guys really did it this t-time."

"Shut your trap, Jag," barked Ira, taking offense that Jagger didn't appreciate his expert trim job.

"You think you could'a done better?"

"Who's the m-make up artist?" Jag asked, taking a closer look.

"That'd be me," Rosie answered as he stepped forward, pulled out his mom's lipstick, gave it a curious look, took a little lick, and then put it back in his pocket, disappointed.

"Absolutely b-b-breathtaking," Jag said, and then turned to Rosie and gave 'im a quick wink.

Jesus, starting to sense he looked like some side show freak, began walking around in circles, muttering to hisself and acting like he was gonna rip off that dress and wipe his face clean any second.

"No, no. You l-look great, b-b-big guy!" Jag said, composing himself and giving Jesus a big pat on the back. "Don't forget about baseball." And he swung an imaginary bat while Jesus looked on. "Heck he l-l-looks so good, Señor V-V-Villaseñor might just forget all about Señora Valdez!"

Well, that gave us all a good laugh, all except Jesus, of course, and we tore over to where the Santa Elena Express was waiting to whisk us away to the Bull Rink.

"Hola, Señor Villaseñor!" We all said, as some of us slid in the back seat, and the rest crammed in through the tailgate.

*"Hola muchachos! Mis amigos! Que tal?"* he answered looking back at us in the rear view mirror, his voice deep and gravely from years of sucking on the unfiltered Camels he had sitting on the dash next to a miniature statue of the Virgin Mary. As he spoke, he made that funny lip smacking sound like old folks sometimes do, but you couldn't really see what caused it, his bushy, gray "Zapata" mustache covered too much of his face for that.

"Bien gracias, y usted?" Rosie answered, as our official Mexican spokesman.

"Asi, asi," he answered, still looking at us through the mirror. "Pero what can choo eekspek por un viejo," he said, shrugging his shoulders. Choo boys quiere ver un beisbol game, huh? Too bad Los Toros jugar como caca!" Even with our limited Mexican vocabularies we knew what *that* meant, and nodded our agreement.

With that, he pumped the gas, turned the ignition, and after five or six cranks that old Chevy V-8 fired up as a massive cloud of black smoke blew outta the tail pipes, most of it circling back and into the car through the open rear window and straight into our lungs. We started hacking and gagging as Señor V. yelled out, "Arriba! Arriba!" and then, looking back at us once again, "Choo boys will be okay. Abra las windows, pero don't breeth in too deep antes conmenzando, comprendes? Shee'l clear up in un minuto."

Creepy and Coop were turning a sickening shade of blue, and we all were feeling kinda nauseous 'til the Santa Elena Express got a good head of steam and the fresh desert air started to stream in and push the gray, musty stuff out. We bounced along through the outskirts of town, ("Chingala los shock absorbers!" Señor V. screamed with every bump) as the blazing sun, looking like a huge fireball jaw-breaker in the sky, began to slowly sink behind the Tortalita Mountains, dragging the daylight right along with it, and then pulled onto the I-19 on ramp heading south. Señor V. gunned the engine to pick up steam, sending a wicked shudder through the old girl from the hood ornament to the tailfins, and an ear splitting backfire out the exhaust and up our spines, and just like the gun that starts a track meet, our adventure had officially begun.

We were too busy singing, "Do a didi, didi dum, didi do," to notice it getting pretty toasty inside from all the smushed bodies, not to mention the rank smell, but Señor sure did, and while still checking us out through the rear view mirror he grabbed the spray bottle and asked, "Quien quiere un spray?" Already knowing the answer, he reached over the seatback finished in a bright turquoise vinyl tuck and roll with big silver buttons, and started squirting away to his, and our heart's content. He's a certified sharpshooter with that thing, front and back and side to side, never even once looking over his shoulder, and hitting each one of us with a sweet, cooling spray square in the face, even the guys stuck behind Rosie. He soaked Jesus so well that his darn eye make up started to run, causing 'im to look like a sad raccoon with lipstick, but not all that much worse off than when he started, to tell ya the truth. The welcomed water made things a lot more comfy, and got us to singing with added enthusiasm, and Señor Villaseñor, after stopping for a pack of javelinas to cross the road, turned to ask if any of us wanted a soda outta the ice chest. That's when, for the first time, he realized there was a "lady" along for the ride.

His whole manner changed in an instant, going from just one of the guys, to the suave and sophisticated hombre about town, and he asked with a smile so wide you could almost catch a glimpse of gold underneath his mustache, "Quien esta la Señorita, muy bonita?"

"Es mi tía," answered Rosie, somehow not cracking up as he did. "Come up from Hermasillo para visitar. Es loca para baseball, so we brought her along."

"Si, si, bien idea," he said enthusiastically and continuing to smile, while he shot a glance at Jesus and started moving his eyebrows up and down. They were almost as bushy as his mustache.

The guys began to snicker but I shot 'em a nasty look and they straightened up pretty quick.

"Que es su nombre, chiquita?" he asked as Jesus glared back at him, shaking his head in disbelief but keeping his trap shut.

"His, ah, I mean *her* name is Sereslinda," sputtered Rosie. "But she's got this nasty goiter growing in her vocal cords that makes her voice real deep and rough like a man's. She's kinda touchy about it so she don't talk much." He finished and sat back with a sigh of relief for getting Jesus off the hook, at least for now, and we were all impressed by the big guy's ability to lie so well under pressure.

"Es no matter," said Señor Villaseñor. "Nada could take away from her eeksquisite beauty."

Jesus, he just rolled his eyes and shook his head, apparently catching enough of what old Mr. Villaseñor meant to realize what was what, and after that javelina family finished crossing the road, there must'a been twenty of them hairy pigs, including two or three babies that would'a been cute if they didn't stink to high heaven, the Señor gunned it and that Bel Air Wagon backfired twice this time to the delight of all the guys, and then started to roar down the freeway towards Tubac and the Bull Rink.

After five miles or so, which was half way there, Ira started us off, just like always, with his own rendition of "Take Me Out to the Ballgame," one he personalized just for our own beloved Tubac Toros, and before long we were all enthusiastically joining in:

Take me out to the ball game,
Take me out to the sham,
Buy me some tacos and machaca,

Better hide your eyes 'cause they play like caca,
So it's ha ha ha at the Toros,
If you think they can play you're insane,
So it's one, two, three beers and pass out at the old ball game.

We sang and sang that old song at the top of our lungs 'til our throats hurt, with every now and then someone making up a new line or two to try out just to jazz things up. But God forbid it was a real boner, the guy who came up with it would be covered with monkey bumps before he got the last syllable out. For example, poor old Creepy was just certain it'd be laugh out loud hilarious to change, "if you think they can play you're insane" to "if you believe they are skilled you have encephalomalacia." Well, I don't have to tell you how hard we beat the little foreigner now, do I?

When we finally reached the Bull Rink we tried to settle up with Señor V., but he wasn't having any of it. He said it was his pleasure to drive us around anytime we wished, since we were becoming such fine young men and all, but considering the way we'd been acting for the last twenty minutes, no one was quite sure what he meant.

Then it all became crystal clear when he looked over his shoulder, stared a hole through Jesus, or, I mean, Sereslinda, and said, "Hanyway, yo pienso I'd rather estay con chu boys y tu tia magnifica than espend la noche con una vieja." After that he blew a kiss towards Jesus who shot a down right frightened look over at Rosie, and then leaned back in his seat as far as he could. We all started chuckling all over again at that and then one by one, slid outta the Santa Elena Express.

It was plenty dark by now and the big field lights cast a soft yellowish glow over the whole stadium from the top of their wooden poles, with just enough spilling over into the parking lot to light our way to the gate. Because of all the rains we'd been having, there was a mess of grasshoppers and moths and other flying vermin swirling all around, and when you looked overhead you'd swear it was a full blown blizzard moving into town, that is if you lived somewheres that it snowed more than once a century, and it wasn't the dead of summer to boot, I guess.

Tubac Field was a real throw back to a time gone by, Pop would always say, made totally outta wood, and I mean totally: the bleachers, the grandstands, the dugouts, the fence and even the restroom and snack bar, and the whole shebang painted the same shade of dark green, like a Christmas tree, a fresh one, I mean, not after it gets all dried out and crunchy. The backstop was nuthin' but chicken wire, not that fancy chain link stuff, and it formed a kinda mangled curly-Q on top, so any foul balls that made it up that high would roll around and fall back behind home plate instead of going over the roof and into the parking lot and landing just about where we were still standing. The game was just about to start, and Mrs. Holmes, the only woman in these parts who could play the organ and sit through a Toros game at the same time, was banging out her rendition of "Las Mananitas," just like always, to honor all the fans who were unlucky enough to have been brought to a Toros game on their birthday. As she played Señor Villaseñor and Rosie started singing along;

Estas son las mananitas,

Que contar El Rey David…

Jesus opened his mouth to sing along too, knowing the words and all, but I snapped one of his garter things hard to get his attention, which it did right quick, and he clammed up after that. Mrs. Holmes started right in with the "Star Spangled Banner," which we always started with the line "Jose, can you see?" since about ninety percent of the men in these parts were named Jose anyways, and it just seemed to fit. We didn't mean no disrespect by it. Finally she started playing something real jazzy, "Rock Around the Clock," I think it was, to try to get the Toro fans all riled up for the first pitch, but from the sound of things, she wasn't having much luck.

Just as we reached old Mr. Tassi, who was smoking his corncob pipe, just like always, and sitting there in his ticket booth, that was also made outta wood, and painted that same green hue, there was a loud *crack!* Rosie, looking up at the sky yelled out, "Thar she blows!" Which got us all to looking up, and there it was, a tiny white dot moving just different enough from the thousands of assorted flying bugs to make it out coming over the grandstands. A foul ball, the Holy Grail of baseball souvenirs to any kid who's ever been to a professional ballgame, although "professional" is pushing it more than a bit when it came to a bunch'a turds like the Toros. And it was heading straight for us! Well, it smacked down on that hard baked dirt and bounced fifty feet if it was an inch, and we all took off after it, even Jesus, who was quite a spectacle racing across that parking lot in his house dress and work boots, and getting the Señor more interested by the minute, but Ira, being by far the fastest, was way out in front of the pack. There was a mad scramble as kids from all over darted in and out of cars, around curbs, hopped over pot holes, and pulled at each others T-shirts to get at the prize, but Rosie managed to block three or four of the liveliest ones by just being his old, wide self, and the rest of us were able to slow the others down enough to give Ira the chance to dive under a red Apache pick-up where that ball had come to rest, and gather it up.

He walked back towards us in triumph, holding the ball above his head for all the other sulking losers to see, and said, "Boys, looks like we got ourselves a ballgame tomorrow." You see, we hadn't been able to play for the last two weeks on account'a Big Rosie hit a screaming liner with our last ball through the second grade classroom window, and after Cooper cut his arm but good on the broken glass while trying to scoop it up with Mrs. Howell's old butterfly net, we gave up the goose. It had been tough. I'd been going through withdrawals. I swear.

Big I got pats on the back all around, and we headed back toward the front gate where the Señor was waiting on us, "Well done, mis amigos. Well done!" he said joyfully and then with dreamy eyes, looked over at Jesus and said, "Muy especial effort, Señorita."

We each handed over a quarter to Mr. Tassi for general admission bleacher seats, which was the only place to sit as far as we were concerned.

Not only were they cheaper than the grandstands, but a lot more fun, 'cause you couldn't get any balls with that chicken wire up in front, plus, the bleachers is where all the cranks, screwballs and drunks sat, making for a much more lively night at the ballpark. Speaking of finding the right place for foul balls, we'd completely taken luck outta the equation, and instead, now had the power of physics and Creepy's analytical mind to guide us. First, he'd analyze the pitcher to see what he was made of. If they threw mostly heat, then we knew the lame right-handed batters on the Toros would surely swing late, fouling the balls down the right field line, so that's where we'd hang out. The Creep would try and gauge the bat speed against the pitch velocity and position us along the most likely twenty feet of fence. If the pitcher was a junk baller, there was more of a chance the batter would pull the ball, and so the left field line is where we'd head. If the guy at the plate had power, Creepy would move us farther down toward the fence, and if he was a punch and judy hitter, he'd move us closer in. We found The Creep's program gave us our best shot at success, and I'd strongly recommend it to any kid the next time they were at a ballgame. Heck, we were averaging five to ten balls a year, and that was with only really paying attention a couple of innings a game. Any more, with the way Bobby's team played might be hazardous to your health after all. It was easy running our system at the bull rink, too, since there were none of them pesky ushers always sticking their nose in your business and ordering you around, but only good old Mr. Tassi, strolling about all night long, making sure everyone at his park was having a grand old time.

Well, we each bought our own ticket 'cept for Jesus, who the Señor insisted on treating, and that was just fine by us since our cash was running short and we all still needed something to eat for supper. Jesus, or should I say Sereslinda, kept whispering all nervous in Rosie's ear, and then would look back at Señor who would bat his eyebrows, lick his hand and then slick back his hair over and over. Rosie would whisper something back, trying to reassure 'im, but to tell ya the truth, he didn't look all that convinced. We walked up to the front gate and gave out tickets to Mr. Tassi, who had just raced over from the ticket booth to perform another one of his jobs as ticket taker. By the way, he was also grounds keeper, maintenance man, head of security, and substitute umpire when need be. He loved that old ballpark like his own home. Come to think about it, it really *was* his home. Pop said he slept in the clubhouse in winter and in the first or third base dugout during summer, depending on which way the coolest breeze was blowing that night. Seems he didn't have no family around here anyhow, only a sister who lived back east, but after he found out she was a Yankee fan he swore he'd never have another thing to do with her 'til she changed her evil ways. Seems Mr. Tassi was originally from Boston. And that's the God honest truth, straight from the horse's mouth. You could ask 'im yourself.

He handed each of us a miniature Louisville Slugger in honor of "Bat Night," and then said in his creaky, stuffy nose voice, "Now you boys be real careful with these, remember they ain't weapons."

"You don't have to worry about us, Mr. Tassi," Ira said. "We know *exactly* what to do with 'em." Then Big I smacked that bat in his hand, turned to us and winked and then stuck it in his back pocket.

One thing, and come to think of it, the only thing good old Mr. Tassi wasn't in charge of at the Bull Rink, was the concession stand. He left that in the very capable hands of the Rodriguez family, and all the Toro's fans were darn happy he did. Martha and her daughters Alma and Alina were the best cooks this side of the border, hands down, and everybody knew it, including them. They called their food stand, "Mi Nidito" or "My Little Nest," and the Mexican food they cooked right there in the back on big black griddles and in huge metal basins filled the park from baseline to baseline with the mouth watering aroma of chile colorado, enchiladas de la bandera, caldo de queso, and piping hot tortillas to boot. Heck, the food at Mi Nidito was as much a part of Toro tradition as finishing last every stinking year, and a lot more enjoyable. I'd betcha ten pesos straight up, that if it ever closed down, them good for nuthin' Toros would be playing in front of nobody but their own moms and dads and maybe a sucker of a girlfriend or two, but that's it, and then maybe only on "Massacre the Mascot Night!"

Although everything on the menu, which was nuthin' but an old chalkboard hanging from the roof by a rusty nail, was a Mexican food lovers dream come true, the frijoles, creamy but not too thin, and spicy but not enough to drown out the mouth watering flavor, were pretty much agreed to be Mrs. Rodriguez's masterpiece. Word was she added just a pinch or two of brown sugar and a cup of jalapeño juice to each batch to make it just right, but you'd be more likely to get the secrets of the A-bomb from the C.I.A. than for Mrs. Rodriguez to let you in on her private recipes. Problem was, with those frijoles being so popular and all, there was another, much less pleasant aroma hanging over the whole of the ballpark, if ya know what I mean.

There weren't no peanuts, popcorn, or crackerjacks to be seen so you could just forget it. But you could get a hot dog if you had an inkling, only it wasn't no *American* hot dog like you'd get at any other ball game in the country, but one of Mrs. Rodriguez's special Sonoran style hot dogs where the wiener itself was barbequed nice and crisp, and then wrapped in a thick piece of bacon and nestled in a hot outta the oven bun and topped with chili beans, jalapeños and a nice fresh saladito for dessert. Believe me, you ain't never tasted nuthin' like it in your whole life, and you better have a big, ice cold drink to go along with it too, if ya knew what was good for ya. In fact, all the food was so good that lots of folks paid the price of admission just to order at "Mi Nidito," and then headed back home without ever seeing a pitch. That was cool with Mr. Tassi, too. He didn't care what got ya to his ballpark, long as you came. All the vendors in the stands sold Mrs. Rodriguez's *comida*, too. Toros fans wouldn't have it no other way. Mostly they just had finger foods like chips and salsa, chicken flautas, or sopapillas drenched in honey, but if the tip was right, you could get yourself a full combination plate with beans and rice and the works hand delivered right to your seat. Heck, that lady even made her own soft drinks! My favorite was jamaica, a delicious red punch made from some flower that grows wild down in Mexico, that has just the right amount of sweet and sour to make the taste buds on the tip of your tongue jump up and do a little Mexican hat dance with every sip.

We all raced over to the counter where Mrs. Rodriguez was waiting to greet us, "Hola, mis amigos. Que quieres?" she said with her arms open wide, pointing at the piping hot food on the stovetops behind her. She was a large round faced lady with a genuinely friendly smile that never seemed to leave her face, and although she always looked real plain herself, in her house dress, apron and slippers, Alma and Alina, her two little girls, always looked just right in their colorful Mexican party dresses, the ones with the puffy sleeves and lace sewn on all over, their perfectly braided pigtails tied at the ends with ribbons the same color as their dresses, and their spotless white tights and shiny black patent leather shoes.

"I'll have a carne seca burro, enchilada style and two chicken flautas, por favor," I yelled out, beating the other guys to the punch.

*"Ay! El nino tiene mucho hambre,"* she laughed and then turned and rattled off something to the girls which sent them scampering.

"She said you must be very hungry," Rosie whispered to me.

"Oh, si, si, mucho," I said back as she chuckled at my attempt to speak Mexican.

Alma smiled real sweet at me as she handed over my burro and then looked away as I said, "Gracias," but Alina, the younger but more spunky of the two, just rolled her eyes at me as if to say, "What a retard!" and then slid my plate of flautas, that were still sizzling from the deep fryer, across the counter in my direction.

After getting all our mouthwatering *comida*, we sat down on the wooden picnic tables out in front of "Mi Nidito," and after piling on the fresh cut green onions, radishes and cucumbers, which were the only condiments available, we inhaled our Mexican feast like we hadn't ate in a week. After that we squeezed our bloated bellies outta our seats and slowly trudged toward the left field bleachers. Señor tried to hold Jesus' hand as they walked side-by-side, but just then Jagger, "accidentally" stepped of his foot to take his mind off things for a bit. As we went by the table that said

"Programs. 10 cents. Honor system," Big I grabbed one, stuck it in his back pocket, and we headed for the gate.

"Gracias, Señora Rodriguez!" we all shouted as we ran off.

"De Nada, mis amigos!" she yelled back as she waved, her smile still unchanged.

Then from the back of the pack Rosie said, "You guys go on ahead, I'll catch up in a bit." And when we turned to look over our shoulder we could see what changed his mind. Mrs. Rodriguez had just taken outta the oven a fresh batch of apple empanadas, and like a Mexican bloodhound, Rosie had caught the sent.

Well that did it. Now we all had to have some dessert, and boy did it hit the spot! One hundred percent *delicioso!* I mean Rosie's mom was great and all, but Mrs. Rodriguez was in a league of her own. And although she was real sweet and soft-spoken and all, you could tell deep down she knew she was the best, and was darn proud of it. That was saying a lot, too, 'cause in these parts, to a Mexican lady, her cooking was probably the most important thing next to her family and the Catholic Church. But, I'll tell you another thing I noticed about Mexican women and their cooking, if you ever want to see somebody change from a saint, to Satan in about a millionth of a second, all ya gotta do is make some off the cuff remark that could be taken as the least bit unflattering about her food, and run for your life! You ain't never seen anything like it, I guarantee. Someone should do some kinda sikiatree paper on it or something. And believe it or not, those kinda fights happened all the time, on account'a every Mexican women in Santa Elena thinks *her* food is the top, and everybody else's ain't fit for a dog. I remember one game last season, when Pop and I were waiting in line for some chile rellenos, a special treat that Mi Nidito only had on special occasions like "Our Lady of Guadalupe Day," when a lady up in front of us made some wisecrack about the meatballs in the albondigas needing a little more cilantro. Well, you would'a thought she had cussed the Rodriguez family up one side and down the other, 'cause before you could say, "Adios amigo," Mrs. Rodriguez' face turned from its normal pleasant pink to bright red, and her kind, soft eyes turned to fire, nearly bulging outta her head, and then she gave it to that other lady with both barrels, screaming out in Spanish things that I'm sure weren't too complimentary, 'cause all the Mexicans in line proceeded to cover up their little kids ears and whisked them off, pronto. After that, Mrs. Rodriguez reached out and grabbed that big mouth lady by the hair and darn near pulled her across the counter and right *into* the pot of hot boiling albondigas soup so she could get a real close look at those same meatballs that were causing all the commotion, before four or five men, including Pop and Mr. Tassi managed to finally pull them apart. That wasn't the end of it, neither. They kept jawing at each other for another ten to fifteen minutes 'til finally the one lady got in her car and drove off, still yelling out the window as she went. It was really quite a spectacle, and one of those things as a kid that I'll probably never forget, like the first time I put on my shoe and there's was a scorpion inside.

Anyways, after eating our share of conchitos, them cookies I told you about earlier that are always in the shape of little pigs for some reason, pan de huevo, a kind of sweet Mexican bread, and more empanadas, we washed it all down with big glasses of horchata, which looks like watered down milk but tasted terrific, and decided it was time to watch the Toros play ball, if you can call it that.

After some thought, Creepy calculated we should start out on the third base line, on account'a he heard both pitchers were junk ballers and the righties would be pulling everything our way. We found ourselves a perfect spot in the first row, right behind the Toros Bullpen, which was nuthin' but a wooden bench for the relief pitchers to sit on about half way down the left field line. Ira immediately pulled out his souvenir bat and whacked Bampu across the back for absolutely no reason, causing his glasses to fly off onto the field, and getting the whole game off on the wrong foot, just like we like it. Before you could say, "hit and run," there were bats flying and bones cracking and kids yelping, and all before we'd seen our first pitch. The bullpen guys, most of 'em not more than teenagers themselves, turned around to see what all the hubbub was about, and then started cheering us on. Before long Jagger had Big I in a head lock and was beating him on top of the noggin for all he was worth, Rosie, using his most effective defense, was sitting on poor Creepy and Chicken Coop who were screaming that they were about to suffocate, and I was running from one to the other, pleading for them to quit horsing around before we all got tossed out. Up in the stands a few rows, Señor Villaseñor was being real "Suave," acting like he was protecting poor old Jesus from us no good roughnecks. After a few more minutes of chaos, sure enough here comes Mr. Tassi to break things up.

"Could ya t-tell us one of them swell w-war stories, Mr. T-Tassi? Huh, could ya?" asked Jag, as he started to walk away.

Pop said Mr. Tassi's one of the only G.I.s from the big war to have landed in Africa, Sicily, and Normandy and lived to tell about it. He said that people like us owe men like him a debt of gratitude. Funny thing, Mr. Tassi didn't look like no war hero. He just looked like an average Joe from where I was standing. Maybe sometimes that's enough. Seems he had half his ear blowed off and the left side of his face paralyzed at the Battle of the Bulge while we were fighting the krauts, and it left 'im with that trademark gravelly voice of his. Every once in a while, if his mood was right, you could get 'im to tell ya what it was like, although sometimes he wouldn't get too far before he would get kinda teary eyed and start to sniffling and have to excuse hisself. He'd say he was suffering from some awful hay fever, but

348

none of us could ever remember seeing 'im sneeze. Not even once.

"Not tonight, boys, sorry," he said. "Too busy. Gotta go help a kid that's stuck in the out house behind the first base bleachers. No more horse play, now. Got it?" And then off he went on his next mission. He never stopped.

On the mound tonight for our beloved Toros was Eddie "Big City" Wilson, a tall lanky southpaw from New York or Boston or one of them monstrous east coast towns, who always had this horrible scowl on his face that Pop said was probably on account of the fact that he was none too happy about being sent out here to the middle of nowhere. He had an average curve ball, a *very* average slider, and a fastball, if you could call it that, that wouldn't scare a pee-wee leaguer with double vision. The Mexican fans all called 'im "El Blanco," on account'a his skin was so white, but the players on the team mostly called 'im a lot less friendly things. The guy who truly detested Wilson the most was "Shin Bone" Shanie Buckmore the third baseman, who got nuthin' but rockets hit at 'im all night long down at the hot corner each time Wilson pitched. He'd have so many bruises on his legs and everywhere else for that matter, after one of Wilson's games, he looked more like a Dalmatian than a ball player. You could practically see the daggers shooting outta old Shanie's eyes as he glared at Wilson after each vicious shot. In fact, two weeks ago, after an especially nasty one hopper that beat him up like a weed whacker, Shin Bone had finally had enough and right in the middle of the inning threw down his mitt and went after Wilson for all he was worth. It took most of the players and coaches plus the mascot, Tuffy the Toro to yank 'im off. No kidding. It made national news, too, which didn't happen much around here, on account'a it was the first time anyone could remember that a player charged his *own* pitcher and tried to beat the snot outta 'im!

As we sat down on the wooden bleachers and leaned back to rest on our elbows, we all took in a deep breath as the sweet smell of the freshly cut grass was almost as satisfying as the one coming from Mi Nidito. It was the one thing that really said, "baseball," more than the crack of the bat or the bark of the umpire or the sales pitch of the vendors, and I always took a minute to soak it all in whenever I came to the park.

"I wonder if the Toros are gonna lose again tonight?" Cooper asked as he looked out to the field.

"What kinda stupid question is that? Of course they're gonna lose," Ira shot back. "The only question is, what kinda bone headed, asinine play is gonna cost them the game and drive poor old Bobby Bottom to his next nervous break down in the process. After all, that's the real reason we're here. Ain't it?"

Well, it looked to all the world that Big I was right, as the team from Benson, Owensville, Orton and Bisbee that we, and just about everyone else, simply called BOOB 'cause of the initials they wore proudly in red across their chests, were already stomping our hapless heroes, but good. They'd already scored four times in the top of the first, still had the bases loaded and only one out, that just so happened to be a line shot right at Buckmore, and our seats weren't even worm yet. Wilson was looking a bit shaky, to say the least, and it didn't help none that besides having to worry about the batters from BOOB, he also was shooting some pretty worried looks over his shoulder at his own third baseman. The boo-birds were starting early tonight, already all over Wilson and good old Bobby Bottom, with a lot more anger than usual this soon from the start. Jees, there was even some old guy in the top row cussing poor old Tuffy, for crying out loud.

"What the heck's going on?" I said, turning to Jagger. "I've seen 'em mad before, but this is ridiculous."

"D-d-didn't ya see the sign?" he said, pointing to the back of the Toro dugout.

And there it was, clear as day, in big capital letters, "TEN CENT BEER NIGHT." Well that explained it. I mean ten cent beer night was practically a national holiday around here. It only happened once a season, and sports minded drunks from all around would come to do their two favorite things; drink as much cheap beer as they could before they passed out, and yell obscenities at the Toros and their skipper, Bobby Bottom. I'm pretty darn sure it wasn't one of Bobby's favorite days, though, and now with his team getting shelled and looking more pathetic than ever, he was already up and pacing in front of the fence in shallow left field. Jagger, seeing his chance to help rile up the fans even more, ran over to where Bobby was, stuffed some random trash down his shirt so his belly hung way out over his belt, puffed his cheeks up as far as they'd go, stuck his butt out best he could, and then started walking right along next to Bobby copying every move that he made. First, Bobby would stomp along about four or five steps and then turn towards the field and shake his fist, and then Jagger would do exactly the same. Then Bobby would jump up and down after a bad call and throw his cap on the ground in disgust, and then so would Jag. Then after a particularly bone headed play by his catcher, he reached up to the sky like he was pleading for God to give him strength, and then put his hands on the side of his head like it was about to explode, and then so did Jag. Well, all the folks in the left field stands caught on right quick what was happening, even the ones that were already half-sloshed, and pretty soon they were all busting a gut, laughing hysterical at Jag and rooting 'im on, totally forgetting about what was going on in the game, and saying how he was better at being Bobby than Bobby hisself, and how maybe he should manage the team 'cause he couldn't hardly screw things up any worse! After a bit longer the folks behind home plate and the right field seats started looking over at what all the hubbub was about, and then *they* started laughing and screaming and egging Jagger on as he continued to put his hands on his hips and shake his fist at the field and hold his nose when there was a bad call and do every little thing that good old Bobby did, right to the T.

Well, before ya knew it the umpires and then the ballplayers themselves stopped and looked over at was up, and then *they* started laughing and pointing 'til it seemed the *only* person in the whole darn ball park that didn't know what was happening was poor Bobby hisself. Finally, after realizing the whole place was going nuts, he stopped and looked slowly over his shoulder and sees Jag there right behind 'im with his stomach sticking out and his cheeks all puffy, and gets so ticked off that he lunges over the fence to try to get a hold of our pesky president. But Jag, being too quick for that, just took a couple of steps back, then turned, and with the tubby Toro manager stuck half way over the fence, bent over, stuck his butt way out, and shook it hard as he could right in Bobby's face. Well, that man turned red as a turnip, and I swear there was smoke coming outta his nose, just like what's supposed to happen with the Big Toro on the center field fence soon as one of our players hits a home run, which apparently hasn't happened since the Truman administration. By now, the whole place was going ballistic, and Bobby, who was about to blow an aneurysm, found hisself stuck on that fence, like a fat worm on a hook, and he couldn't get loose an inch, no matter how hard he kicked his legs and flailed his arms in the air. Well, the whole ballpark was shaking with laughter so hard that it started to creek, and I thought for sure it would start to splinter any minute, 'til Mr. Tassi came over with some pruning sheers and cut out the fabric around Bobby's private parts to set 'im free, and he stomped off the field with his hands over his groin, and didn't come out again 'til the seventh inning, which as it turned out, wasn't such a good idea, neither.

We were just having ourselves a swell time after Jag got everyone in such a tizzy, and a bunch of little kids started milling around and asking him for his autograph and adults were patting him on the back and saying how he should be in show business and move to Hollywood and maybe even get on the "Ed Sullivan Show." Even the guys in the bullpen got together and gave Jag a signed ball that said, "To Little Bobby. You're Better Than The Real Thing!" but after thinking about it a bit, they asked him if he wouldn't mind not letting on where he got it.

Things settled down a little after that and we were back to swatting bugs outta the air with our bats, (a single for a brown beetle, a double for a grasshopper, a triple for a June bug, and a homer for a Palo Verde beetle,) eating Mexican pastries, and drinking ice cold jamaica and pretty much just enjoying a lovely summer night at the ball park watching the Toros stink up the place. There was a botched pickle play that turned a sure out into an easy run, a worm burner that rolled through an outfielder's legs like a croquet ball through a wicket, a line drive that hit our first baseman square in the caboose while he was talking to a pretty girl down the first baseline, and even a suicide squeeze bunt with nobody on third base. And that all happened in just the fourth inning! So, it was pretty much your usual day at the bull rink with the Tubac Toros.

In the middle of the fifth, a bunch of barking and yelping started to boil up from down in the left field corner and we decided to go on over and have a look see. Seems a pack of dogs had once again outsmarted old Mr. Tassi and somehow squeezed themselves through gaps in that ancient wooden fence, and now they had some poor stray cat cornered up in the bleachers and were letting her know they were none too happy about her being around. Well, all of a sudden that cat, she decides to make a break for it and shoots down the bleachers like a bat out of hell and streaks in front of the stands with about a dozen raving mad dogs in hot pursuit. Then, with them dogs biting at her heels, she raced down behind home plate and up the right field side, and then back again, over and over. The whole time them dogs kept on barking up a storm and chasing her for all they were worth. Right away the people in the stands forgot all about the game again and started cheering for the cat or dogs, depending on which way their favors went, and before you knew it the whole place was going berserk once again. The players stopped playing and the umpires stopped umpiring and the vendors stopped hawking their stuff and everyone started to watch the show, until Mr. Tassi, seeing what was up, climbed up on the visitors dugout with a big old fishing net and calmly scooped up that cat as she scampered by, holding up his prize as he did, and then taking a little bow amid joyous cheers from the cat lovers in attendance and horrible hoots from those who preferred dogs. Boy, good old Pop was sure right when he said going to a Toro game was better than a three ring circus, and that went double on ten cent beer night!

The fans settled down to a low rumble once again, and us guys went to work to find out the most sensitive spots on the human body you could hit someone with a souvenir bat. Turns out it's either on the bone just under the knee cap, or right across the nose a hair or two below the bridge, which had the additional benefit of causing your eyes to tear up almost immediately. So we wasted no time inflicting as much pain as possible on each other until we looked like a bunch of gimpy old men bawling their eyes out.

After that highly sophisticated scientific experiment, we took aim at the bullpen guys, trying to bat some pebbles at 'em, but found it took considerable talent to even come close. Finally Rosie got in a lucky shot that knocked Doofus McDuffy's hat clean off, (he was known as doofus on account'a he couldn't remember the signs and kept throwing pitch-outs when there weren't no runners on base,) getting 'im pretty ticked and he said if we didn't cut it out he'd hit us on top of the head so hard we'd be talking outta our butts the rest of the summer. That kinda put a damper on things and we decided to try to find a new way to entertain ourselves.

The game had turned kinda ordinary I'm sad to say, 'til in the top of the sixth BOOB's clean up hitter, Ronnie "The Wrecker" Redhouse, a full blooded Cherokee Indian with legs the size of tote-em poles, hit a major league pop up directly over the mound that Wilson never saw. All five infielders raced towards where he was still standing on the rubber, and formed a little circle around him. They were all looking up in the sky at the ball, and then looking at each other, and then looking up again, and then at each other, trying to figure out who was gonna make the catch. All the while Wilson was looking at each and every one of *them* like, "what the heck are you all doing here?" Well it turned out, which was no surprise to anyone, that none of the Toros had the *cajones* to take charge, and that ball came down about a hundred miles an hour and hit Wilson square on the top of the head, dropping him like a hundred pound sack of potatoes. Then all them infielders started pointing at each other, and shouting at the top of their lungs as to whose fault it was, and whose ball it should have been, and who did or didn't call it, and not once did any one of 'em pay any mind at all to poor old Wilson who was lying there in the dirt in the middle of the mound out cold. To make things worse, Ronnie "The Wrecker," seeing his chance, made a mad dash around the bases without any of those ranting and raving lunatics ever even bothering to take a look no matter how loud everyone in the stands was yelling, and he didn't stop 'til he crossed home plate with the screwiest inside the park home run that we, or anybody else in the universe for that matter, had ever seen. Heck, maybe our Toros would get on national news all over again! Sammy "The Stick" Perlich, the long drink of water pitching coach, came outta the dugout, motioned to the bullpen that he wanted the lefty, and then he, Mr. Tassi, and Tuffy, grabbed Wilson by the collar and dragged him off the field and into the dugout.

"I sure hope he doesn't have a subdural hematoma, " Creepy said, looking on. "Sometimes they can make one side of your body act completely different than the other."

"Heck, that sounds like just the ticket to help that stinking Wilson's control," Ira said, and none of us could honestly disagree.

We were sure we'd already seen just about anything you could possibly see at a ball game in one night, and feeling a little sad about it, when in the bottom of the seventh with BOOB leading eleven to one, Ducky Dobson, the chubby second baseman for the Toros, came waddling into third base and was called out on a bang-bang play. I guess that was when old Bobby had reached the end of his rope, and he came racing outta the dugout to argue the call, face red as a beet this time, and eyes bulging out like a tree frog with a thyroid problem. He and that ump were jawing at each other toe to toe, even turning their caps around so that their noses practically touched, and we all ran up to the fence, leaning over far as possible, with our hands cupped behind our ears to try and make out was being said, but all I could catch was a bunch of stuff about each man's family that didn't have the slightest thing to do with the call on Ducky that I could see. This, however, got the fans, who were three sheets to the wind by now, going worse than ever, and then *they* started ragging on that poor umpire's family in nuthin' but the most unflattering terms, which I also thought was plenty unusual, since I recognized just about every one of the people in the stands, and to tell ya the truth, I'm pretty certain none of them had ever set eyes on that umpire before in there whole life.

Well, Bobby wasn't about to back down and neither was that ump, and pretty soon Bobby was stomping around, flinging his arms and kicking up dirt, and even trying to rip the third base bag right out of the ground, but that weren't no use since it was stuck like cement and you could tell old Bobby kinda wrenched his back after an especially violent yank, which put a damper on things for awhile 'til he could work the kinks out a bit, and then he was right back at it. Everybody started beating their souvenir bats against the wooden bleachers to make as much ruckus as possible, and with no sign of Bobby letting up an inch, Ira reached back and swung his bat forward to whack that fence as hard as he could, when it slipped outta his hand and instead went hurdling towards the field. Just like with that new *slow motion* they show on, "Wide World of Sports," we watched his bat float through the air, turning end over end as it sailed right to where Bobby was standing. Our eyes got big as the harvest moon up in the sky, and our mouths fell wide open as we could see what was about to happen, and before ya knew it, there was a sickening "Clunk!" like when you drop your bowling ball on your foot, as Big I's souvenir bat whacked the Toro manager square on the back of the skull! Well, Bobby stiffened up for a second, spun around real slow to face the crowd, and then with his eyes rolling back in his head fell flat on his face, out cold, just like Wilson.

There was complete and eerie silence in all of the stadium as me and the guys looked straight ahead, too shocked to move, and then all of the sudden, like a tidal wave, there arose from the stands the loudest laughing and screaming and cheering you've ever heard. Why even that umpire looked like he was about to wet hisself right then and there. The problem was, Mr. Tassi, didn't think it was all that funny, and it seems he'd seen everything right from the get go from where he was standing behind home plate, and was now making a bee-line through the crowd right for us!

I quickly got the guys attention and we were off like a shot, first all the way down the third base line and then doubling back behind the stands to throw 'im off our scent. Jesus was right behind us, dress and all, running for his life, and the Señor, not wanting to let his lovely lady friend get away that easy, was trying to keep up best he could, limping along with that bum leg of his. We raced past Mi Nidito, waving to Mrs. Rodriguez and the girls as we did, and then were through the front gates in a flash, even Rosie. We was all sitting in the Santa Elena Express before you could say, "Juvenile Center," and the Señor slid in the driver's seat as Jesus dove in the back, pumped the gas three times and turned the key to bring that old V8 to life with a loud *Ka-pow!* Then, showing off for his new sweety, he stomped on it hard, peeling outta that dirt parking lot, and leaving Mr. Tassi shaking his fist at us as he slowly disappeared in a huge cloud of dust.

# Chapter Twenty-Five

## THE GREAT SCUMBAG SCARE-A-THON

Jag and I leaned on the old wood railing surrounding the porch of the Mansfield Place, being careful not to get any splinters, and looked out over the desert. There was a slow cool breeze in the air left over from a late night rain, probably one of the last of the monsoon season, and the soon to be blistering sun was just peeking up behind the Rincon Mountains to the east, still hidden mostly behind some thin clouds, the last stragglers from the storm. A few bright rays poked through here and there, streaking down to earth like a good morning welcome from the Big Man Hisself. Off in the distance I could see the red tile roof of my house, barely visible above the tops of the Chilean mesquites that lined the small arroyo on the southern border of the old homestead.

We looked on as dust devils, ten, maybe twelve feet high, would pop up outta nowhere every now and then, kicking up dirt and twigs and leaves and any other stuff in their path that wasn't tied down for a minute or two until they slowly died away. Gracie and Dodger would chase them down for all they were worth, staying in the middle long as they could with their eyes closed as Gracie's hair and Dodger's ears and tail would get blown straight up, and they'd wait to be sucked up into the sky and transported off to some enchanted land like that other little girl and her dog from Kansas. They were real disappointed every time they opened their eyes up to find they were still in plain old Santa Elena, and to tell ya the truth, so was I.

We were all getting real used to the place by now, and it was amazing how in just a few short days it had gone from a horrifying haunted mansion to a comfy cozy clubhouse, practically a home away from home.

"I don't know about you Jag, but I just can't remember the last time I felt quite this swell," I said, now looking out to the east past the row of cottonwoods along the Santa Cruz River.

Jag just looked at me with that big toothy grin and sighed his agreement. We weren't just feeling on top of the world on account'a the rare, cool morning in the middle of summer, or the fact that we were gonna help a poor fella save his starving family, or even because we hadn't ran into that rancid Nancy "The Nuisance," for over two weeks. Nope, we were mostly feeling like this 'cause our bellies were filled with a piping hot breakfast of *chorizo con juevos* that Jesus had cooked up for us, and had washed it all down with a big glass, or jelly jar I should say since that was all we were able to swipe form home, of *abuelito*, a kinda Mexican hot chocolate that was so thick and creamy you'd swear he'd just melted a full Hershey bar in each glass and then added some milk. We got in the habit of not asking no more about what was in the stuff Jesus made, and to tell ya the truth, we really didn't care. We were all still amazed that he could take just about anything, and I mean *anything*, and fix it up into a mouth-watering delight. Pop said a lot of the folks down in Mexico were so dirt poor they had to be pretty clever just to feed their families, and they had this uncanny knack for fixing up things that you'd never guess were even edible. Ever heard of *menudo*?

So with our stomachs full, a cool breeze in our face, and no thought of school or having to put up with tattletales, teachers or too big kids for at least another few weeks, things were about as perfect as they were gonna get. The only thing that was muddying up my thoughts at all was that sweet Jenny Darling. I couldn't stop myself from thinking on her every once in a while no matter how hard I tried. You know. What she was wearing. What she was up to. How milky white her skin was. That sort'a stuff. 'Course, I'd never let on to the guys about it. Not even Jag. I mean how were they gonna help me out when I didn't have a clue myself what kinda terrible disease was going on in my head! Maybe after school starts, if I didn't come to my senses, I'll catch the Greyhound up to Tucson one Saturday and try and see a shrink or maybe even a palm reader or someone.

Like I said before, everything else couldn't of been better, not if Dodger stadium burned down and they had to play the rest of the season at the Bullrink...well, okay. Maybe then. But then outta the blue, here comes Chicken Coop riding through the desert all frantic and crazy like he had Ben-Gay in his Jockey shorts. But even more wild and hysterical, like he had Ben-Gay in his Jockey shorts *and* he was being chased by a pack of sore-jointed javelinas that wanted some of it! He was kicking up this monstrous cloud of dust in his wake as he came roaring towards us without paying no mind to nuthin' 'cept getting here fast as his scrawny little legs would let 'im. Jag and me looked on dumbfounded, as he sped right through the middle of jumping cactus, prickly pear patches, and a particularly nasty bunch of cholla, so by the time he was finished he looked like a human pin cushion, and the whole time not so much as a flinch! And remember, this is a kid that has a double hissy fit if a cattail so much as brushed his uncovered arm.

"Johnny C.! Johnny C.!" we could hear him screaming as he got about fifty yards away. "They're coming! They know! Oh God! Oh God! Ahhh!" He continued to holler out, loud enough to make a deaf man cringe.

Dodger, never a mutt to let a good chance go by, made a valiant attempt to bite Coop on the butt as he sped by but just missed, falling flat on his back, and then he laid back down, dejected at the foot of a tall mesquite tree.

As Coop reached the house, he jumped off his bike, a Lady Schwinn, no less, with no cross bar, an embarrassing hand me down from his big sister but somehow fitting old Coop to a T, and he raced up the stairs to where Jagger and I were standing, and up to now enjoying the peaceful morning.

He continued to bellow, "They're coming! They know!" over and over, as tears ran down his cheeks leaving long brown streaks as they mixed with the dirt he'd picked up from his rambunctious ride, and he kept his eyes glued shut, like he was too scared to see what might happen next.

"Who's c-coming?" Jag asked, as calm as can be.

"They are!"

"Who?"

"Pound us!" Cooper shrieked.

"What?" I asked.

"Make us pay!" he blurted out.

"Huh?" Jag asked.

"Poor Hey-soos!" he cried.

"What the hell's all the commotion out here?" Ira barked, coming around the corner with the rest of the guys close behind. "Sounds like 5th grade girls bathroom break for crying out loud!"

"They will ruin everything!" Coop screamed and then fell to his knees like a hundred pound sack of Pop's potatoes, pulling at his hair and blubbering like a little baby.

"What's with him?" Ira asked as he pointed to Cooper lying in a heap on the porch.

"Beats me," I said. "He came riding through the desert like a loon, and has been screaming all hysterical every since."

Big I reached down an pulled Cooper up by the collar, gave 'im a few slaps across the face with a quick back and forth motion, a la Moe of the Three Stooges, while saying, "Snap out of it, dammit, and tell us what's up 'cause you're giving me a migraine from all your screeching, and I get real violent when my head starts to hurt!"

That brought Chicken Coop around quick and he started telling this story about how he was riding down Camino Principal on his way over here this morning when all of the sudden out of the alleyway jumped a group of Losers who knocked 'im off his bike and slapped 'im around awhile. Then, Loser Lane asked what we'd all been doing up at the old Mansfield Place lately. He said he had heard we'd been hanging out there real nice and cozy and he meant to find out for himself just what was going on.

"What did ya tell 'em?" I asked, scared to death he'd spilled the beans about Jesus, and knowing darn well that if The Losers found out about him they'd go straight to Mengo just for spite.

"I didn't tell 'im nuthin'. I swear. I just kept agreeing with whatever he said," Cooper cried out through a bunch of sniffles.

"W-w-what else did he say," Jag asked, putting his hand on Coop's shoulder to try to calm 'im a bit.

"He said (big sniffle) he heard that the old man (deep inhale) had hidden a huge treasure in the house somewhere when he died, (rapid in and out breathing) and he wanted to know if we had found it. (More sniffling and a wipe of the nose on his sleeve) I told 'im I didn't know nuthin' about no treasure, and then he and Crater Face started slapping me around but good to try to make me talk. (Bawling started all over again) But I didn't Jag, I swear. Finally, he says, 'Go tell all your pissant pals that we're coming up to that old house tonight, haunted or not, to take a look around for ourselves, (head now down and barely audible) and if we see hide nor hair of any of you dweebs, you'll wish you'd spent the night in bed with your mommies like you usually do."

"Then what?" I asked.

"Then they all took one last punch at me as I got back on my bike, and I rode as fast as I could back here. I'm sorry Jag, but I did the best I could."

"D-don't sweat it pal. You d-did just fine."

"Now what?" Ira asked, disgusted, as he looked at me and Jag. "We've better make like a tree, pronto, before they show up and clean our clocks."

"What about Jesus?" asked Rosie.

"Look, Rosie, kid," Ira said. "If those butt faces get any wind at all that we're helping an illegal alien, they'll make a bee line to the Sheriff and we'll all be in Juvi 'til we're toothless and drooling all over ourselves, comprende?"

"But we can't just abandon him," Rosie pleaded, looking over at me and Jag. "Can't we hide him somewhere else for a few days 'til everything blows over?"

"The more a fugitive moves, the higher the chances of him being apprehended. It's basic criminology," the Creep answered, matter of factly.

"First of all, there ain't no other place in all of Santa Elena that's better for hiding than this," I said. "Second of all, we're running outta time to get 'im over to California as it is, and third, them Losers will be back here every stinking night for the rest of the summer if they think there's a treasure to be had, so we'll never be able to get Hey-soos back over here."

"Okay then, what the heck are we gonna do?" Ira asked.

"Well, the way I see it, there's only one way to get rid of them Losers once and for all and not have to move Hey-soos even one inch."

"How's that?"

"Look, The Losers haven't been up here 'til now on account'a they thought the place was haunted, right? Well, I say when they show up tonight, we make their worst nightmare come true. I mean we give 'em the most hair-raising, barf up your guts scary haunted house the world has ever known, so heart stoppingly horrendous they'd sooner put on little pink dresses and have a tea party in front of town hall before ever thinking of coming within a country mile of here again."

"N-n-now you're talking, Johnny C.!" Jagger shouted and threw his fist in the air.

"I like it. I *like* it!" added Ira with a grin.

Rosie, Cooper and the Creep didn't look so enthusiastic, but only slowly nodded with a kinda sick grin on their faces.

"Okay, listen up," I said, tryin' to give the three nervous Nellies some confidence. "These yahoos are all into acting macho as possible, right? But what happened down at the schoolyard the other day when we pelted 'em with our wrist rockets? I'll tell ya. They rolled around on the grass yelping like a bunch'a puppies outta milkbones, that's what. I say, if we do this thing just right, meaning it's no chinsey second grade Halloween play, we could scare the bejeesus outta the whole lot of 'em and they won't show their ugly mugs around here for the rest of the century."

"What if they see through it and realize it's nuthin' but a hoax?" asked Coop, poking his head around Rosie's big belly.

"Well, then, it'll be curtains for us, Hey-soos, and his family, and the whole stinking summer will be flushed straight down the toilet. That's why it's gotta be the real deal. *No* excuses. Are you with me?"

Rosie leaned over and whispered in Jagger's ear, "I sure wish Neil were here. He's got a real knack for this kinda stuff."

"Yeah, m-m-me too, big guy," answered Jag. "I'm still hoping he'll c-come around soon."

We all gathered in a circle and Jag put his hand out in the middle with everyone else doing the same, and then Ira screamed out, "All for not!" and we answered back, "Not for long!" and the planning for, "The Great Scumbag Scare-a-Thon," began.

We all moved on into the parlor room where Jesus was cleaning up the breakfast dishes as well as the knives and forks that I'm sure our moms will be missing real soon, and I gotta say I'm right proud how the new furnishings were turning out so nicely, already including two magnificent milk carton "chairs" we lifted from out back of El Minuto Market, a terrific telephone wire spool "table" we borrowed off a Mountain Bell truck parked out in front of Poco Loco Cantina, and the crowning jewel of our impeccable interior decor, a remarkable red velvet couch that was hardly stained at all and only torn in two places, that we were able to sneak off with from the Goodwill truck across the freeway while Mr. Morales, the volunteer worker, was taking his afternoon siesta. Let me tell ya, it weren't easy dragging that thing across I-10, dodging traffic, and then through every alley and side street in town to reach the Mansfield Place without getting busted, but it was worth it to see the look on good old Jesus' face when he got a load of his new place to sleep. Strikes me sometimes how one man's junk is another man's treasure, and it ain't just men, neither. Take my ma for example, she thinks the sun rises and shines on this collection of dirty old combs she got all set out in nice, tidy rows on her dressing table. How disgusting is that! I mean a bunch of old codgers combed their greasy mops with them and instead of having them incinerated, like any sane person would do, she's gotta put them in a place of honor. She's got straight ones and curved ones and some with jewels and some with bows and one that's even got a stinking horsefly stuck on it! Says they're *dainty* and have *sentimental* value, and all the uppity ladies back east collect them, too. Says she read all about them in Vague magazine. I say their nuthin' but digesting pieces of plastic, covered in grease and grime from some old lady's hair that has accumulated in sickening amounts over decades. It's not like they were something *really* special, like, say, old MAD Magazines.

We all sat around that big spool table, and huddled in tight to start to work out the details of the make or break plan of the year. "Creep, you still got that tarantula collection at home?" I asked.

"Sure do."

"How many of them things you got left?"

"Only three. One got out in the house the other day and snuck up my mother's skirt while she was making breakfast. She smashed it to smithereens with a spatula before I could stop her."

"Well, that ain't near enough for what I got in mind," I said, shaking my head. "How many of them Losers you say jumped you, Coop?"

"Five, I think, maybe more. It's kinda hard to count when you're getting your brains bashed in."

"Okay, we're gonna need at least seven, maybe eight to do the job," I said. "Bampu, you and Coop try and snag some more tonight after dark. I saw some promising holes out back. Ira, how's Zorro doing?"

"Eight feet long and meaner than snot," he answered, with a sly smile. Zorro was this especially nasty old bull snake that Ira found in the desert behind The Sewer one day. He had a permanent kink in his back from wear some crazy mom probably whacked 'im good a couple times with a shovel and it caused 'im to spell out the letter "Z" as he slithered along. He lived in Ira's back yard in an old doghouse, and the Goldstein's never had to worry about pack rats or any other varmints for that matter ever since.

"Great, bring the big guy and a roll of tape with ya tonight. We're also gonna need that rattle that was attached to Hey-soos' surprise snack the other day, too. Oh, and grab that set of castanets your ma has hanging on the wall in your den."

"Got it."

"One other thing, Iceman. Make sure old Zorro is plenty hungry."

"No problema."

Jesus, every once in a while would look up from the dishes, smile at us and nod, without a clue what we were talking about.

"Rosie, you still got that florescent body paint we used to put all over ourselves after slumber parties and then scare the heck out of your pop when he'd stumble in late?"

"Yep, I got tons of that stuff back in my storeroom, all different colors."

"Great. Grab a whole mess and bring it back this afternoon with your black light, alright."

"Sure thing."

Black lights were really cool, and used to light up florescent posters that every kid that wasn't a complete dweeb had hanging in his bedroom. I had one of this bad old green dragon with fire coming outta his mouth that was fighting to the death with this purple knight on horseback. There was a castle in the background with a waterfall on the side, and a volcano behind that was spewing lots of flaming lava, and it hung in a place of honor on my wall, smack dab between Sandy Koufax and Carl Yastremski. At night when it was pitch black, I'd turn on my black light and watch as the colors of that poster would jump out like it was on fire or something. It was bitching! Of course, I had to hide the black light from Ma, on account'a she was convinced that if you looked at it too long it would burn your eyes out, fry your brain and make you into a vegetable.

"Coop, you still got that toy treasure chest we used to bury when we played pirates?"

"Yep, my mom's got me using it as a clothes hamper. It's kinda embarrassing."

"Well bring that along too, okay? Let's see. What else could we use for a grand finally? I know, got any bottle rockets left over from the commando raid on the Cole's house, Jag?"

"I'm sure I g-got a few in my r-rainy day stash."

"Grab 'em with some matches. They should make the perfect send off for our unwelcome guests. Alright, well…oh yeah, Jag, you think you can snatch that portable reel to reel tape deck from your pop's study?"

"Does a bear do "do-do" in the woods?"

"Sure, if you say so, fearless leader. Okay, everybody got their assignments?" I asked taking a quick look around. Coop had his eyes closed and was mumbling to himself, but everybody else seemed to have their part down.

"Alright then, grab your stuff and check back here no later than two o'clock."

As the guys started to filter out I grabbed Rosie, "Tell Hey-soos to lay low 'til we get back, and if he sees any of them scumbags heading this way, have 'im hightail it out the back and hide in the desert 'til they're gone."

"Okay, Johnny." So he rattled off some Mexican, as Jesus got this terrible worried look on his face.

Then Rosie must'a said something like, "Don't worry pal, we ain't gonna let you down," and that seemed to calm 'im a bit, at least for now.

Gracie, Dodger and I made our way home, Gracie asked, "Johnny, you forgot about Dodger and me. What are we gonna do to scare them no good creeps out of their wits?"

"You're not doing a darn thing, 'cause you and that stupid mutt aren't gonna be nowhere near that house tonight. Got it? It's way too dangerous. I don't care what kinda deal we had going."

"But I taught Dodger how to growl and bark real mean. All I got to say is "Spooky" and he goes ballistic." Spooky was the neighbor cat and Dodger's mortal enemy. "Watch, I'll show ya," and she proceeded to have that peabrain sit down and then she bent over and whispered in his ear, and in an instant he was transformed from harmless goofball to stark, raving mad beast. It was amazing. His eyes glared and his teeth showed and his nostrils flared and he growled and barked so vicious it made *my* skin crawl. Boy, did he ever hate that cat.

That gave me an idea and I said, "Okay, Gracie, you changed my mind. Snatch a bottle of ketchup from the fridge and you and Dodge can come along after all." She reached down and gave that big lug such a tight squeeze around the neck his eyes bulged outta his head, and she was all smiles the rest of the way. As we got close to the back door, Gracie stopped and looked at me, "Hey Johnny, what are *you* gonna bring?"

"Well, you know that disgusting angel hair stuff that Ma wraps so darn thick around the Christmas tree every year that it looks like an eerie cocoon?"

"Yeah, boy I hate that stuff."

"Well, that's what I'm after."

# Chapter Twenty-Six

## SCARED STIFF SCOUNDRELS

After wolfing down a supper of silver dollar fried potatoes and very well done pork chops, the only way Ma fixes 'em so we don't get any, "intentional parasites," I said, "Me and the guys were thinking about playing some kick the can tonight. Okay Ma? But don't worry, we won't be out too late."

"I don't know Johnny, you haven't been home one night all week. What do you think dear?"

"Huh?" Dad asked, peering over the sports section, his mouth full of bread he was using to sop up every last crumb of stuff on his plate.

"Could you please pay a little more attention when I ask you questions about your only son's well being, please?" She said like *he* was one of the kids, too.

Aunt Leah and Granny sitting across from each other at the kitchen table just rolled their eyes at the same time as if to say, "That man is simply worthless."

"What now, Frieda?" Pop asked. "Can you please stop hounding the boy and let him have a little fun. It's summer vacation for gosh sakes."

That's my Pop, pure common sense.

"I don't know, Johnny," she said, turning back toward me after seeing she wasn't gonna get any help from her husband in making my life miserable. "You are just asking for trouble one of these nights, gallivanting around the neighborhood like a bunch of hoodlums."

Aunt Leah and Granny both nodded their absolute agreement.

"Aw, come on, Ma, we never do nuthin' but just horse around a little.

What the heck's gonna happen?" I pleaded.

"Well, you just never know who you might run into after dark. What would happen if those horrible, delinquent kids from the south side decided to pay our neighborhood a visit? What then?"

She was talking about The Losers. See what I mean about mothers' sixth sense. It's scary.

"There ain't a chance them morons would come all the way up here. Why in the heck would they? Anyhow, we'll probably just hang out at Jagger's. Maybe play some Yatzee or something." She didn't look too convinced.

"Did I mention that I would like to invite Gracie along with me," I said as I eagerly watched the expression on her face. "Her and I've been getting real close lately, and I'd sure enjoy having some extra time to spend with my baby sister," and then I went over and gave Gracie a little hug as she tried to kick me in the shins.

Well that did it. Ma got this huge smile on her face and her eyes lit up like two high beams on a Hudson as she ran over and gave me a big sloppy kiss on the cheek and told me what a great young man I was becoming, and how proud she was of me and how nice it was that I appreciated having a wonderful little sister like Gracie, and how someday when her and Pop were dead and gone it would only be me and Gracie to look after each other, and a bunch of other sappy stuff like that. Finally, she said the words that I was waiting for, "Now you two kids run along and have yourselves a wonderful time together."

I saw my chance and went with it, and giving Ma a big hug said, "Don't worry, we'll be back before ya know it. See ya, Pop."

"Be careful, Johnny," he said without lowering the paper.

As I walked toward the back door, I turned and gave Aunt Leah and Granny a big snotty grin and they sneered back at me, and then outta the corner of my eye, I saw Gracie snatch the Heinz ketchup bottle off the table and stick it under her dress. Then, sweet as can be, she and Dodger followed me out the back door. She really was starting to crack me up, and hard as it is to say, I gotta admit she was turning into a pretty decent little S.S.B. For a girl I mean, of course.

As we walked through the garage I motioned to Gracie to follow me down the street a ways like we were heading towards Jagger's, and as I said it I looked over my shoulder, and sure enough there were the three Gestapo commandants watching our every move through the kitchen window. I told Gracie to wave and smile real nice, which we both did and then walked on outta sight.

"You're the smartest big brother a little sister ever had," she said, squeezing my arm for all she was worth. "I can't wait to here those nasty Losers scream, "Uncle!" And as she said it, she jumped up in the air with her hands over her head, the way little kids do when they're real excited about something. But that got Dumbger excited too, and he gave out a yelp and then bit Gracie in the butt. "Ouch! You stupid dog!" She screamed, and then socked him in the jaw with all her might, which was kinda like hitting a bowling ball with a wet noodle, and had about as much effect.

It was only about six o'clock by now, and there was still plenty of light as we doubled on back, careful to stay out of view of the house. I circled around leaving Gracie and Dodger at the mesquite fence, and picked up the garbage bags full of Ma's beloved angel hair that I'd stashed behind our house earlier, then crawled through the fence and made our way toward the old mansion.

As we got closer I heard lots of laughing, and a bunch of clapping and tapping sounds coming from the parlor, and as I got near enough, I could just make out through the big, hazy pane window what all the commotion was about. There in the middle of all the guys was Jagger, clacking some castanets in each hand like mad and doing this crazy flamingo dance. His feet were going a mile a minute, stomping the dusty floor over and over with a wilted old wildflower stuck between his teeth, and Ira was shaking his mom's prized maracas to beat the band, sitting on the old cantaloupe crate that Zorro called home. It had these slats along the sides which were good to get air in, but bad because Zorro was always trying to squeeze out of 'em and then getting hisself stuck. That meant someone had to tug on a real ticked off bullsnake from the inside to spring 'im loose and them leap outta the way before he took a bite out of you!

Rosie was making a pathetic attempt at a Mexican Hat Dance right next to Jag, using his filthy old Little League cap to dance around, and bowing here and there and holding out his arms like he had the prettiest Señorita in all of Mexico for his partner. Jesus, who was starting to fit right in with our group of goofballs, was standing in the corner, slapping his thigh and singing a rousing rendition of *Rancho Grande* with all the high pitched, *"Ah ha's!"* in just the right places. Creepy and Chicken Coop were sitting on the couch, clapping their hands and whistling along.

As Gracie, Dodger and I watched, I couldn't help but think the whole shindig looked like something you'd see on *Mexican Theatre,* a local T.V. show that came on live outta Tucson every Sunday morning at nine, right after the *Reverend Tommy Thompson's Family Crusade for the Redemption of your Soul Hour.* It was hosted by these two brothers, Tony and Henry Villalobos, that is 'til old Henry got hisself killed in a car crash around midnight last year on I-10. It was a real tragedy. I heard Pop telling Mr. Bradley he'd been coming home from a "Cat House" down in Nogales, and I couldn't help but think he must'a been quite an animal lover to be out at that hour trying to help out some kitty in need. The show featured mostly locals, who had, or at least *thought* they had some kind of talent; singing, dancing, acting, juggling, you name it, they weren't too picky. It was kinda like our own little *Ed Sullivan Show* for Mexicans, and it was actually pretty entertaining 'cause even though the talent was usually more than lame, unlike the big network shows, on Mexican Theatre you never knew what the heck was gonna happen next. Sometimes the T.V. picture would go all over the place because the cameraman would forget that his camera was the one that was actually on, or once in a while a piece of the background set would fall over making a loud bang and scaring the snot outta whoever was performing at the time. And once I even saw the overhead microphone fall outta the sky, knocking the guitaron player out cold as the rest of his mariachi buddies kept right on playing "Coo-ca-roo-ca-coo," without missing a beat! I watch it pretty regular, to tell you the truth. Hey, it's still better than the Sunday morning preacher shows, and since just about every Mexican in southern Arizona watched it too, its got quite a following, and anyone from Santa Elena lucky enough to get on the show become an instant celebrity with the local Hispanic community. After that you'd be guest of honor at all Quincineras, Baptisms or First Communion parties, asked to say a few words on Cinco de Mayo, and maybe even be M.C. at the biggest event of the year, Mi Nidito's "Bean Burrito Blowout!" on Poncho Villa's birthday. Plus your advice would be sought on all kinds of stuff, from who'd be the best Godfather for some Mexican baby, to who had the best cow intestines for New Years Day menudo.

Anyways, after a while more of watching the entertainment, I opened the door and walked in followed by Dodger, Gracie and her bottle of ketchup.

"Hey, Johnny," Rosie hollered out, not missing a step and shaking his big butt in my face. "You're just in time. I need a dance partner."

"I don't think so, Big Guy, but go ahead and ask Dodger there, he looks a lot more like the girls you're gonna end up dancing with anyway," giving him a big "chop low."

"What the heck do ya call that, Jag?" I asked, watching him twist and contour hisself in all kinds of hideous ways. "You look like a spastic monkey walking over a bunch of hot coals!"

"Ooh, k-kiss me where the s-sun don't shine!" he answered, not missing a beat, neither, with them castanets or his heels. "This here is r-real, authentic flamingo d-dancing. I seen 'em do it on T.V."

"Yeah, I seen it, too, on *Gunsmoke*. The one where Marshall Dillon is shooting at the feet of some low down bushwhacker," I said, using my fingers as pistols.

After a few more minutes of clapping and stomping, and now barking and howling since big mouth Dodger had joined right in, I told everyone to pipe down so we could get down to business.

"Okay, listen up, you embarrassing bunch of bone heads," I said, to no one it seemed, 'cause Jag and Rosie kept on dancing and clapping and Dodger kept on yapping and trying to bite Rosie's rear end as he passed around the hat in front of him. "Look!" I screamed out loud as I could which was a little embarrassing, too, on account of my voice cracked, but it happened to do the trick. "You ding-dongs can goof off as much as you want, but in case you forgot, if we don't pull this thing off just right, it's gonna be the biggest butt wooping party of the century and we're gonna be the guests of honor, got it! Not only that, but Hey-soos will be deported back to Mexico faster than you can say, "Speedy Gonzales!" After that they all settled down kinda sheepish, and shut their traps.

"Alright now, timing is absolutely crucial in any battle plan, as we learned earlier with our wildly successful operation against Nasty and her family of fartfaces in "Castrate the Coles," (I just came up with that off the top of my head, no kidding) so pay attention to your job and don't mess up, cause this here campaign's gonna make that look like a tangle with the toddlers on Romper Room!" I didn't say nuthin' for a minute, but just paced back and forth with my head down for effect, hoping that these chumps would get it through their hard heads how hairy this plan was gonna be, and then started, "Here we go. Jag, you got that tape recorder?"

"R-r-right on," he said, as he pulled out the contraption from under the couch.

"Okay, I want you to record the scariest, most spine tingling haunted house sounds you can come up with, got it?"

"Like what?" he asked.

"You know. Deep and long 'Oohs' and 'Aahs' and weird howling, and doors creaking and a lot of slow, low pitched laughing like this, 'Muuuaaah!' 'Muuuaaah!'"

"That ain't no scary ghost laugh," Ira said, disgusted. "That sounds like a sissy hyena with laryngitis! This is how its gotta sound," and he stood up, took a deep breath and blurted out his best ghostly moan.

"You gotta be kidding!" said Big Rosie, shaking his head. "You laugh like that, and those Losers will think a bunch of little baby girls have haunted the place. It has gotta sound like this!" and then he gave it his best shot, too, which sounded like a cross between a Moose in heat and a Crow with constipation.

Anyway, it went around the room like that 'til everyone had their chance, even Jesus, who I'm sure once again didn't have a clue what was going on, and had to be wondering if maybe he'd hooked up with a bunch of escapees from the Arizona State Mental Hospital.

"Anyhow, you get the picture," I said, not sure what else to say after that pathetic display. "But I'm telling ya it's gotta sound *authentic*, not corny, and the tape's gotta last about twenty minutes or so. I figured that should be plenty of time to scare the snot outta them jackasses. We'll start it up nice and low, soon as they're within ear shot, got it?"

"Si, Señor," said Jag. "I b-brought one of my m-ma's Beatle's tapes, and n-nuthin' will make m-me happier than recording over it. B-boy do I hate them g-guys."

"Tell me about it!" I said. "Look at these ridiculous hairdos! What about them bottle rockets?"

"Right here in my p-pocket," he said, patting his butt.

"Great. Set them up along the trail in the desert leading up to the house, and you and I will be in charge of setting 'em off as The Losers come running out of here crying for their mommies as the grand finale!"

"Creepy, you got your furry friends?"

"Looking more terrifying than ever, if I do say so myself," he answered as he whipped off the top of the shoe box in front of him to reveal three of the largest, hairiest and creepiest looking tarantulas you ever laid eyes on.

"Ah...great," I said, a little queasy just from the site of them things. "You can put the lid back on now Bampu. But like I told ya before, we're gonna need another three or four, so you and Coop try to dig up a few more out back soon as the sun goes down. Use some brown beetles as bait. Okay Coop?"

"I don't know Johnny C., them hairy things scare the tar outta me," he said kinda soft as Creepy dangled one of the biggest ones in front of his face.

"What's scarier, a little spider or the Surgeon coming at you with his pocket knife?" Ira barked. "All right then, suck it up and try and be a man. The Creep will show ya how to sneak up on 'em. Right Bampu?"

"It would be my pleasure. But what do we do with them after that?"

"I want ya to take 'em up to the second story bedroom window and tie some of that twine on one of their legs so you can dangle 'em down over the porch to reach right about shoulder height to a Loser. Okay? And when they walk down the porch to take a look at Coop's treasure chest, go ahead and let 'em go, along with a bunch of this angle hair crud for their webs. That should give 'em a good case of the heebee-jeebees!"

"Utter genius," Creepy answered. "It's nice to see that someone besides myself is at least attempting to use his mental capabilities for a change," then he smiled widely, and adjusted his glasses.

"Ira, how's Zorro feeling today?"

"Mad as hell 'cause I haven't fed 'im for two whole days."

"Perfect! See if you can tape that rattle to his tail to make him look more like a Diamondback, then curl him up and put him in Coop's treasure chest. We'll put him at the end of the porch and shine a flashlight on it from inside so The Losers won't miss it when they come looking for old man Mansfield's gold. Shake them maracas like crazy when they open the chest to give it the full effect, okay?"

"It would be my pleasure," Ira said, and then picked up the maracas and gave 'em a whirl.

"Now, Rosie, this might be the most important part of all," I said, turning to the big kid and reaching up to put my hands on his massive shoulders. "I want you to use those florescent paints of yours to make the most god awful looking, grotesque faces possible on you and Hey-soos." Jesus looked up and gave us a pleasant little smile after hearing his name, not having a clue what we had got him into.

"In fact," I said, after thinking a bit. "Why don't you guys strip down to your jockey shorts and paint your whole darn bodies. The more gross the better. Got it? Then I want you both in the front room 'cause I figure that after them weenies get a load of Zorro, that's the direction they'll be scrambling. Have Jesus all painted up sittin' against the wall facing the door and you just inside the doorway. Put the black light on the ground in the middle of the room, one side facing Jesus and the other facing you."

"When do I turn it on?"

"Well, wait 'til you hear The Losers run towards the front of the house and then slowly open the big door from inside. That should get their attention. And when they walk into the middle of the room, slam the door behind them and flick on the switch. When they get an eye full of Hey-soos sitting there glowing like some radioactive zombie, and then turn to run out and see you sitting there looking even more hideous, it should be enough to put 'em over the edge and off and running like jackrabbits with their tails on fire into the desert. That's where Gracie and Dodger will be waiting for one last horrifying surprise, and Jag and I will proudly shower them with a barrage of bottle rockets on their way off!"

After I finished, and the guys saw the big picture, they all said it was the best plan ever, and if we pulled it off it was something our grandkids would be telling *their* grandkids about and it would surely go down in history as the greatest achievement ever of kids against creeps, and they gave me a standing ovation and a big cheer, all except Jesus, who still didn't understand what the heck was going on, and Chicken Coop, who was surely thinking about what would happed it we *didn't* pull it off.

Just then Rosie rattled off some Mexican at Jesus, who looked perfectly happy with what he had heard.

"What did ya tell 'em?" I asked when he finished.

"I said we were gonna scare a bunch of old friends tonight, just for fun."

"Good thinking. I wish it were true."

And with that we headed off to start preparing for operation, *"Horrify and Glorify,"* which was the best name we could come up with in a pinch without Neil to help us out. To tell ya the truth, I was getting to think we could sure use that little weenie right about now, also. I mean, even though he was usually such a butt wipe and mostly full of crapola, he was *our* butt wipe, and a pretty valuable kid to have around when in a jam on account-a he wasn't ever about to let someone get the upper hand on him no matter who was right or who was dead wrong.

So off the guys went to do their duty; Creepy and Coop grabbed the shoe box, some twine and a flash light and headed out back in search or the biggest, hairiest tarantulas they could find, Rosie took the florescent body paint, a black light and Jesus and headed on down the hall to the front room to start his master art work. Big I tore off a piece of electrical tape to add Jesus' rattle to the tail of Zorro, who didn't look none too pleased at the whole situation of being humiliated and hungry all at the same time, and Jag and I fired up his Pop's reel to reel and took turns making authentic horrifying haunted house howls and moans without sounding silly, which is actually a lot harder to do than it seams. First Jag would do a high pitched "Aaaah!" holding it long as he could, then I would do my best old door creaking, then we'd do a long and low "Wooo!" and a sinister, "Ah-ha-ha-ha!" laugh, and it kept going like that for a while, each of us trying to outdo the other. The problem was, although the sounds might be scary, watching someone make them with all their crazy facial expressions and all, was really pretty hilarious, and we had to keep rewinding and starting over on account'a one of us would always start to crack up and ruin the whole darn thing. On one especially nice, make your legs turn to jelly and colon constrict screech, Jag's eyes rolled back in his head and his nostrils flared something fierce, and I just couldn't control myself and busted up so bad I almost peed my pants. That got 'im really ticked on account'a me ruining what he thought was sure his masterpiece of the day, so he jumped me and held my nose and mouth closed 'til my head started to swim, and made me promise to show him more respect from then on before he'd let up.

After our tape was finished, the last part completely covering over our least favorite Beetles song, *Love Me Do*, which made it all the more satisfying, we headed out to the desert to set up the bottle rockets along the trail. I motioned over to Gracie, who had her little hands full trying to keep the ketchup bottle away from Dodger, to follow along. We took a good look around and within a few minutes had already found about ten old Coke bottles to use as launchers. If there was one thing you could depend on in this life, it was finding an old Coke bottle when ya needed one, no matter where in the heck you were. There's gotta be millions of 'em scattered all over the world, 'cept maybe in the Amazon jungle or some God forsaken place like that. But, come to think about it, I bet even there you'd find some cannibal with an old Coke bottle on his kitchen table using it as a flower vase or salt shaker or somethin' while he sat down to his nice warm dinner of unwanted visitor. That was the thing about Coke bottles; you could use them for all sorts of stuff. Not only were they great as bottle rocket launchers and flower vases, but also for storing all kinds of junk like sand rubies or those nice round pebbles for your wrist rocket or even earthworms, 'til one very determined one somehow escapes and ends up as an unwanted ingredient in your Mom's linguine a la Caruso she made special for the Santa Elena Sisters of the Poor and Hungry Gala, but that's a whole other story. Gracie used 'em for beads and ladybugs, and Ma for different spices and Pop for everything from small nails to motor oil. They were the perfect design, if ya think about it; things went in easy, but it took some doing to get them back out again. Just the ticket if you wanted something to stay put. It was really a shame to waste something so practical, and I think that's why nobody ever threw 'em away. Now I know you could get a few cents for 'em over at the grocery store, but let's face it, that didn't happen all that much, but just because of the fact that they *were* actually worth something made folks feel guilty about tossing them out, and so they pretty much just left them wherever they finished their drink; alleyway, ballgame, desert, you name it. You've probably have done it a thousand times yourself and didn't even realize it.

Anyway, it was getting good and dark by the time we had set up a row of rockets on each side of what we hoped would be the trail of tears for The Losers, and not us, and I figured we had at least another half hour or so before our honored guests would show up. It was about seven-thirty judging by the sliver of light peeking over the Tucson Mountains, and I knew them Losers would never be caught dead out before eight 'cause that wouldn't be very *cool*, God forbid. After Jag and I went over a few last details he went back to the mansion to get the tape recorder ready and I called Gracie and Dodger over for their official briefing. She sprinted over fast as she could with her chubby kid knees rubbing together all the way like they always did when she ran.

"Gracie Caruso, reporting for duty, sir," she barked in her best grown up voice as she stood at attention and gave me this real lame salute. She killed me sometimes. She really did.

Just then, here comes Dodger running up behind her, and seeing a golden opportunity gave her a chomp right on her little rear end, causing her to wince just a bit, but she did her best to keep her eyes front and center and continued to stand at attention.

"At ease, soldier," I said to her. "You too, Captain Ass Bite," I said to Dumbger as he laid down in the dirt and rolled over with his legs wide open completely exposing himself. "Okay, here's the deal. You and Dodge stay way back outta sight in the desert 'til The Losers pass by and go on up to the house, then when I give you the signal, move up to right about here next to the trail, and pour a whole mess of that ketchup all over yourself so it looks like you're covered with gory blood. Got it?"

Gracie smiled wide and said, "You mean to tell me you are giving me permission to pour ketchup all over my new sundress?"

"That's right."

"And you will tell Mom it was your idea?"

"Right again."

"That's *so* boss!" she screamed while smiling even wider, and then gave Dodger such a hug his nose turned blue. "What about Dodgie, does he get the ketchup treatment, too?"

"Nope. Here's the thing. When ya see them fellas come running from the house, you lie down flat on the ground here next to the trail and let Dodger lick that ketchup off of you to his heart's content so he gets it all over his stupid mutt face but good. Get it? I want it to look like he's some kinda raving mad dog and he's trying to eat you alive!"

"Cool!"

"Are you sure you can still get Dodger to growl real mean and go all berserk, just by mentioning the stupid cat's name?"

"Sure, watch." And she just leaned over easy as pie and whispered ever so softly in his ear again, "Spooky."

Well ya would'a thought she had stole a big juicy T-bone from 'im or somethin', 'cause he started growling real low and nasty and baring his teeth something vicious, and drooling all over, and then he started barking and growling at the same time as the hair on his back stood straight up and his eyes blazed like fire. Heck, he even sent chills down *my* spine. Boy, did he hate that cat!

"Perfect," I was able to utter, still a little creeped out. "So when them guys come running by, scream out at the top of your lungs, 'Help me! Help me! I am being attacked by a wild animal!' and then flick this here flashlight on so they can get a real good look at you two, okay? Then as they start coming closer lean over and whisper in Dodger's ear and let him scare the you know what outta them!"

"Awesome!" she said with her eyes big and bright and a smile from ear to ear.

I walked back up to the house to see how the other guys were making out with their assignments, and as I went in the front door there was Rosie with his paints out, going to town on poor old Jesus who just sat there up against the far wall, stripped down to his jockey shorts, looking real confused.

"*No te mover!*" Rosie said as he slapped some green goop over his cheeks and purple on his nose, and then, "*Cierra sus ojos,*" as he smeared on a glob of pink goo all over his forehead. He kept this up for a while, adding a little touch here, and a little dab there; so deep in concentration he didn't even notice I was watching. Every once in a while he'd step back and shout, "You are my masterpiece!" and then kiss his fingertips like one of them crazy foreign film directors when they really knock themselves out with a scene nobody else in the world can make heads or tails outta. Then he grabbed the orange and made big rings around Jesus' belly button and man breasts so they looked like targets at a shooting gallery and all the while that Mexican he just sat there still as can be, like he was ordered, not complaining even once. After painting up his arms and legs in yellow with red polka dots, Rosie finally turned to me and in a real cheesy French accent said, "Voila, my work is done," and flicked on the black light.

Well, like magic, that poor Mexican fella lit up like some psycho Christmas tree looking absolutely hideous, and *exactly* what I was hoping for. Then I looked over at Rosie and realized that he was all painted up, too, but his job looked like a *real* artist had done the work. On his big fat belly was painted this bitchin' face that was screaming out in pain, with his nipples as the eyes and his belly button the mouth, and you could see all the teeth and even that thing that hangs down in the back of your throat. There were deep wrinkles in the forehead and the nose was all scrunched up and flared out. The eyes were bloodshot as all get out with each vein present and bulging to beat the band, and the pupils were a deep green and glowed especially fierce. Rosie's real face was all painted black so it didn't light up at all. It was really outta sight!

"Did Jesus do that to you?" I asked, astonished.

"Yep. Seems he's a pretty famous artist in his little town. Does mostly murals on neighbor's walls of the Mexican Revolution or the Virgin Mary and that kinda stuff. He said he did a portrait once of the President of Mexico's daughter, and he liked it so much that he invited Jesus down to Mexico City as his guest."

"Wow! How'd he like it?"

"Oh, he didn't go. He says he couldn't afford the twenty pesos for the train ride."

"How much is twenty pesos?"

"About a buck and a half."

I looked over at Jesus, feeling kinda sad about how poor he was all over again, but he just smiled back at me with his glowing purple teeth against the black light and pointed at Rosie's big belly as if to ask how I liked it.

"Muy bien!" I said real enthusiastic. "Me gusto mucho," and then I gave 'im a big thumbs up.

I walked back outside and there at the end of the porch towards the back of the house sat Chicken Coop's treasure chest with Big I busy duck taping a flashlight to the window sill and aiming it right down at it.

"How's it going?" I asked.

"Perfect. Big Z is now officially a rattler, and he's so stinking pissed about being starved that he's all ready for a big fat plate of fresh Loser."

"Hope you got a big bottle of animal Alka-Seltzer at home. Poor guys gonna need it," I said pretending to upchuck.

Just then I felt something warm and fuzzy brush across the back of my neck making my skin crawl horrible, and when I whirled around to see what was what, there staring right back at me was the biggest, hairiest, and creepiest tarantula in all of the Sonoran Desert.

"AAAh!" I yelped, and covered my face with my hands.

"How do you like Godzilla, Johnny C.?" Creepy laughed from the upstairs window, as his sidekick Coop reeled the gigantic spider back in.

"He's t-t-terrific, I guess," I said with a shudder. "How'd ya catch 'im?"

"Peanut butter. They can't resist it. If you can find a moth or two to stick in it, they like it even better."

"How many did ya get?"

"Five more, just like him. Want me to send them down for you to take a look at?"

"No! I'll take your word for it," I said real quick. "Good job, guys. Now we'd better get set. I expect the low lifes to show up any time now."

I walked slow along the old wood porch and down the front steps, past the spot that Jag and I ended up after being spooked by that rattler in the cactus patch that started this whole stinking mess we were in. It seemed like months ago that it happened, but in really was only a few days, and I thought again that if things didn't come off right tonight, not only was Jesus and his family done for, but maybe us, too. But it was worth it, right? I mean we couldn't just let his family starve, could we? Or should little kids like us just mind our own business and let the adults take care of the rest? I guess we were gonna find out just what the guy upstairs thinks about *that* real quick.

The last orange rays of sunlight had faded to plum purple when I met up with Jag again. "All set?" I asked as I took a long look around, straining for any sight of their gang coming up the street.

"R-r-roger," he answered with that big, toothy, picket fence grin.

"Got your lighter for them bottle rockets?"

"Check."

"Where the heck's Gracie?"

"L-last I saw her, she was r-running toward the back of the house with D-dodger in hot pursuit trying to g-get that ketchup bottle away from her."

"I swear I'm gonna murder that dog! I'll go find 'em and get 'em back set. You better head down the street and keep a sharp look out for The Losers. Soon as ya spot 'em, kick butt back here and start up the tape player. Got it?"

"Right arm!" He said, gave me a wink, a thumbs up, a cock-eyed salute and ran off toward the old mesquite fence.

By now the sun had completely set, and the lovely pink and purple streaks it had lit up on its way down faded to black. At the same time an enormous harvest moon of bright yellow was rising fast over the Rincon Mountains to the east, and shining bright over our little valley. I heard the "*Hoo-Hoo,*" of a barn owl as I looked up to catch him taking off from the highest peak of the Mansfield Mansion, flapping his gigantic wings in long slow motions to gently gain altitude with what looked like a pack rat in his claws. It gave me the heebee-jeebees at first, but then I realized that anything that made this night more creepy would actually work to our advantage. I gathered up Gracie and Dodger and headed to the most southern part of the homestead, as far out of the way of the trail as possible, and there I waited to hear from Jag. I yelled out to the house to see if everything was ready to go and got back, "Yep," "Sure," "Quit asking!" "Absolutely," and a "Si." Then a warm summer wind started blowing through the Palo Verdes and Mesquites coming from the south, and Dodger instinctively turned to face it and started sniffing away like a madman. I hoped that would keep 'im occupied long enough to miss the stink of them Losers coming up, and keep his trap shut for a change so as not to blow our cover.

"We're gonna show them bad fellas, aren't we Johnny?" Gracie whispered while gritting her teeth and wrinkling up her little pug nose to look tough as she could.

"I sure hope so, kid. A man's family might depend on it."

She looked at me kinda bewildered for a second or two and then went right back to grimacing to try and look tough as nails, or at least, say, straight pins.

As I glanced back toward the trail, I heard the patter of feet hitting the pavement and quick, and as I squinted up my eyes to get a better look, I could start to make out the silhouette of Jagger's head, crazy hair and all, in the moonlight as he came tearing through the old gate at the edge of the property.

"The Losers are coming, The L-losers are coming!" he yelled out, clear as a bell as he flew down the trail and scampered up the front steps. Dodger turned quick to see what was up but I grabbed his muzzle just in time and then distracted 'im with that ketchup bottle. I heard some scrambling about inside and then here comes a low moaning sound through every window, which was pretty darn eerie, if I do say so myself, as our tape player started up. My heart was racing a mile a minute as I realized that this was it, and Jag came tearing out the front door, down the steps and right towards where we was hiding.

"Over here," I whispered loud, waving my hand.

"This is g-gonna be g-great," he said as he squatted down, but having a hard time trying to contain hisself.

Dodger sensing his excitement, jumped on top of 'im and started licking his face and biting his ears.

"Knock it off!" he said, as I yanked the dog off of 'im.

"Will you two morons put a sock in it. They'll be here any second!"

I was able to calm Dodger down one more time, but Jag was a hopeless case. He was fidgety as a ground hog in heat and he couldn't help hisself no matter what he did.

We all crouched down behind a big barrel cactus to watch the show, and after a few more minutes, there they were. At first, all you could here was the light clink, clink, clink of the metal buckles and taps on their square toed, tough-guy Dingo boots against the asphalt, and then the scraping of hard baked dirt as they hit the desert and dragged their feet along as they walked in classic *pachuco* style. As their pack came closer we could make out in the moonlight the tops of their heads jutting out above the creosote bushes with Loser Lane in the lead, his greasy mop of hair plastered down the side of his face like always, with the rest of the good Samaritans, wearing their customary hairnets, falling in behind.

"Johnny C.," Jag whispered in my ear, sounding concerned for the first time tonight.

"What's up?" I answered, afraid maybe he spotted something wrong.

"W-well, you're k-kinda sitting on my m-moon shadow."

The Losers were laughing and joking and having a grand old time as they went, and all the Eagle Scouts were in attendance; El Raton, Chile con Carne, El Estupido, R. I. P. and of course, that great humanitarian himself, Leroy "The Surgeon" McKnight. I guess nobody wanted to miss the golden opportunity to find the treasure of old man Mansfield, and kick some puny upper east side butts all at the same time. They were all puffing on something or other and blowing the smoke in each other's faces, elbowing each other in the ribs, and spitting on their nearest neighbor. Pretty much what you'd expect from such a group of fine young gentlemen, when all of the sudden they stopped dead in their tracks and shut their traps as they came within earshot of Jag's tape player.

"Que es esto?" I heard one of 'em say.

"No se."

"No me gusta."

"Shut up you weenies. It ain't nuthin' but the wind. What's wrong with you?" I recognized Loser Lane's voice saying in disgust.

"Ees creepy. That's all," El Estupido answered.

"Come on now, ladies. Or maybe you don't wanna be millionaires after all!"

Loser Lane started into the clearing around the house and the others began to follow, but they had lost the cocky spring in their step, and no one was saying a darn thing now. The Surgeon whipped out his trademark stiletto and held it in out in front, and El Raton's eyes began to dart back and forth and he started to crouch down just a bit like someone expecting to get whacked on the head any second. Even Chile Con Carne and R.I.P. were getting a tad uneasy and had their hands straight out with bent elbows like they were ready to give someone a karate chop, leaving only Loser Lane himself to look cool and collected as he motioned disgustedly to the rest of his gang to catch up.

"We've g-got 'em now," Jag whispered in my ear. "They're doomed."

"What the heck are you talking about? Nuthins happened yet," I whispered back.

"Didn't you n-notice? They're stepping all over each other's m-moon shadows."

"Oh, for the love of Pete, will you please shut up!"

When they reached the front steps, they stopped and looked from side to side, and just then the sound of a high pitched laugh came from inside the house. Jag and I chuckled to ourselves and gave each other the thumbs up as we saw the effect our tape was having on the baddest guys in all of Santa Elena.

"Holy cheet! That ain't no freecking wind, Amigo," said El Estupido, quickly looking over his shoulder to make sure nuthin' was sneaking up on him. The other Losers were doing the same, and looked none too happy to be there.

"Aaah, it was probably just an old window squeaking. Yeah, that's it," Loser Lane stammered out, not all that convincing. "Come on. We came this far. Don't wimp out now. Anyway, them little fruitcake fairies have all been hanging out here the last couple of days. The place can't be too haunted. Right?"

The rest of The Losers seemed to agree with this latest point made by their brilliant leader, and got just a little of their swagger back. They moved up the steps and slowly down the wood porch with the old boards creaking under their weight with each step. The further they went the closer they huddled, like a bunch of ducklings swimming around their mother, and their eyes kept darting suspiciously from side to side. Every once in a while The Surgeon would slash at an imaginary attacker, while R.I.P. would do a couple of karate chops on someone that wasn't there. After a few more steps, Loser Lane took a long hard look down the side of the house and then screamed out, "There it is! Just like I said, you little sissies. We're rich! We're rich! The old man's gold is right there in front of us!"

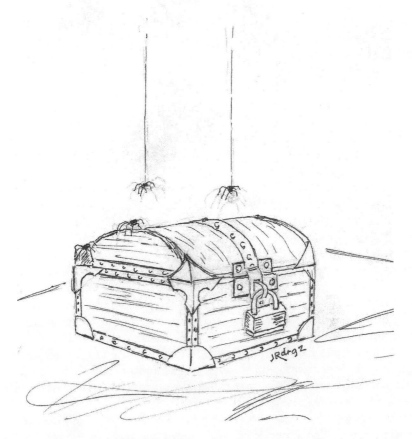

They all rushed forward, pushing and shoving each other to the side to get a closer look at good old Chicken Coop's "Little Petey the Pirate" treasure chest.

"Gracias a Dios!" all the Mexican Losers yelled out and started dancing a little jig, right then and there and then once again crowded around the chest that Big I had lit up so swell. None of them geniuses seemed to notice the flashlight taped to the windowsill, they were already way too busy thinking about what they were gonna buy with their share of the loot.

"First thing I'm buying es mi cousin Chango's seexty-two Chevy Impala. Es un sweet chort, con curb feelers and one of them, *que dice*, esteering wheels made outta chain, and diamond tuck and roll seats," explained El Estupido.

"You can't even drive yet, *Cabron*," snapped Chile con Carne. "And don't choo remember what that *bendejo* sheriff said after that leetle crash at the Casaus Quinciniera last summer? He'd only let choo drive in Santa Elena over hees dead body. Pero, that could be arranged!" he said holding up his knife and smiling. "Yo voy a Nogales por unos lovely eswitchblades de oro con mother of pearl handles," he said, closing his eyes like he was thinking about a beautiful woman.

*"Imbeciles!"* El Raton spit out, disgusted. "You guys don't know cheet."

"Oh yeah, well what you gonna do with your share, smart guy?" asked The Surgeon.

"I'm gonna buy el rancho mas grande een todo Arizona and then I will plant the *marijuana* and be the happiest man een los Estados Unidos for the rest of my life."

"Ooh, good thinking!" they all nodded in agreement.

Jag and I leaned forward and cupped our ears so as not to miss any of the brilliance being shown, and heard Loser Lane say real sharp, "Quit yapping like a bunch of old ladies and help me get this trunk open."

None of this group of intellectuals was near bright enough to notice that the padlock on Cooper's chest was nuthin' but a plastic toy that any of them could have ripped off with their pinkie, so they all looked for some huge rock to smash it with. We watched for a bit longer, shaking our heads as they searched and searched, as our tape continued to fill the air with ghoulish sounds that they didn't seem to even notice any more since they caught sight of the treasure. I figured it was pretty hard for guys like them to concentrate on two things at once, like when your dog is barking his head off at some stranger outside like he's ready to rip the guy's throat out, and then all you have to do is say, "Treat!" and he immediately shuts his trap and races into the kitchen, totally oblivious to what he was doing just a second before.

"Well, I guess we'd better get in position," I said to Jag, and he made his way around to the far side of the trail toward his row of bottle rockets, and Gracie, Dodger and I moved to a spot just outside the clearing around the house 'til it was time for our next move.

As The Losers gathered back around the chest with their boulder they were all smiles, and some were still dancing around and clapping their hands. I noticed the second floor window start to slowly open and could barely make out the shadows of Creepy and Chicken Coop as they carefully leaned out and lowered their furry friends into position above the porch. I didn't hear no hiccupping at all, and could'a swore I saw the moonlight shine off the lenses of the Creep's glasses, meaning they were still on his head, and I smiled to myself feeling mighty proud at how manly the guys were acting, so far, anyways. With the tarantulas all dangling in place and Ira positioned just inside the house with his maracas ready on each hand, I hoped that the next few minutes would be some of the proudest moments in all the storied history of the S.S.B.'s, and I gotta tell ya, I wasn't disappointed.

As soon as Loser Lane broke open that lock and yanked back the top with the rest of his gang looking on in excitement right over his shoulder,

Big I started to shake them maracas so loud you could hear 'em up in Tucson, and when they got a load of a plenty ticked off and half starved Zorro, they let out a hair-raising screech and jumped back like a bunch of greasy kangaroos, all at once. Then, too bad for them, but really cool for us, they ended up right on the spot that Cooper and the Creep's eight-legged furry friends were quietly waiting to greet 'em, and as they slowly backed away, step by step, from that slimy snake, I could see them reach back behind their necks at something tickling, and when they quickly whirled around to see what it was, all hell broke loose.

"Jesus, Maria y Jose!" "Ay, mi madre!" and plenty of other choice sayings that ain't fitting for a kid to repeat, they screamed out as they swatted wildly in the air above their heads and then covered their faces to avoid the huge insects and the angel hair spider webs, and then ran to the end of the porch where they stopped to catch their breath, all huddled together like a bunch of terrified football players waiting for their quarterback to tell 'em what to do next.

"Come on, Gracie, time to get you and the mutt ready," I said as we walked over to a clear spot at the front of the trail. I laid her on her back, grabbed the ketchup bottle and poured it all over her face and chest which she thoroughly enjoyed, and then smeared some over Dodger's face for added effect and let him go to town licking it off of her, which he obveously got a real kick outta, too. I knew Ma was gonna have about three hemorrhages when she got a load of the mess Gracie was, but, hey, I can only worry about one life-threatening situation at a time. That's just the way I am.

"Now, listen, remember what to do and, please, try not to giggle. Understand?" I said.

"What do you think I am, some little kid or something?" she shot back, all indignant- like, pushing Dodger away from her just long enough to give me a real dirty look. She could really crack me up sometimes. No kidding.

I flicked on the flashlight and laid on the ground, aiming it at her at the creepiest angle, and then got out the Chesterfield cigarette lighter, a souvenir from Pop's smoking days that I snatched from his top drawer, and walked over to my position next to the bottle rocket launchers. I looked across the trail and could barely make out Jagger, his hair stickin' up every which way as usual, hiding behind an old Ocotillo. I turned my attention back up to the house, just as the front door slowly creeped open, all by itself. I squinted up my eyes so as to get the clearest picture possible, and could see those punks standing their staring straight ahead, scared stiff, with their jaws dropped and their eyes bulging, and then slowly creeping away from the door. But Loser Lane not ready to throw in the towel yet, tried to rally his troops for one last chance to find the old man's gold, and after a stern talking to, finally convinced 'em to take a look inside. They all crammed together like one big mass of disgusting dog doo, and slid along the porch and into the parlor room.

When the whole mess of 'em were finally all the way in, I heard Jesus yell out, happy as he could be, *"Buenos Noches, Amigos!"* and then, all at once the room became flooded with an eerie blue glow and before you could say, "Yellowbelly Sapsucker," such a wailing came up for outta that room that the dead could'a used some ear plugs. But before they could escape, the door slammed shut and then another even more bone chilling screech pierced the air as they must'a gotta load of old Rosie with Jesus' amazing artwork all over his blubbery body.

Well, that did it, and that doorknob started to rattle and twist and turn like all get out, and the door itself was shaking so ferocious it was sure to splinter into a million pieces any second, when finally it sprang open and out they flew. They were pale as sheets, and not on account'a the soft moonlight, neither, and ran all crazy, flailing their arms and legs, and yelling out a, "Wooooh!" that started kinda low, but quickly built itself up to a howling roar as they bolted down the steps and raced headlong for the trail as fast as their Loser legs could carry 'em. When they got close to where Gracie was lying, she flipped on the flashlight right on cue, and started screaming at the top of her little lungs, "Help! I'm being eaten by a wild dog!" When they slowed down a bit to take a gander at what sure looked like good old Dumbger chomping her to bits, Grace whispered into his ear and out came the most hellacious growling and barking and carrying on you ever heard this side of *Abbott and Costello Meet the Werewolf!* Boy, did Dodger ever hate that cat. Anyway, that put them Losers completely over the edge, as if they weren't already, and they let out *another* yelp along with an assortment of Mexican and American cuss words I'm sure would've made old Poncho Villa and Genaral George Patton blush, and then tore off down the trail.

I waved to Jag to get his attention and we started lighting the bottle rockets one by one along the path so they exploded right over our uninvited guests heads as they tried to escape and save their skins. They leaped in the air all together with a screech, and covered their heads with their hands like a bunch of little girls trying to avoid a rainstorm as each pair blew up, lighting up the sky for a split second, and giving the rest of the guys back in the mansion a good view of our enemy's repugnant retreat. The last rockets exploded together in a massive "Ka-Bang!" a fitting final send off as the hysterical hard-asses hit the pavement screaming like banshees and not daring to look back even once. Jag and I ran up the trail to the edge of the desert and watched as they disappeared up Chantilly street, but it was a good long while before their screams would die down, and it would be even longer before we saw the likes of them around these parts again.

# Chapter Twenty-Seven

## ALL FOR ONE OR THE POTTY-GAL-SON

Next morning I slept in nice and late. I guess scaring the bejesus outta the toughest gang in Southern Arizona takes more energy outta ya than you realize. I lay there in bed for a long while thinking about how well things had gone and how satisfying it had been to watch them hooligans running for their lives and begging for their mommies. Maybe after seeing how it felt to be scared to the point of pooping your pants they might reconsider their life's work of doing just the same to every little kid and feeble old lady in town. I doubt it though. I mean they didn't have a wing named after them at the newly expanded Cochise County Juvenile Center for nuthin'. But if we, the proud and righteous S.S.B.'s, have in some small way helped them poor delinquent Losers turn over a new leaf, and maybe someday become responsible adults and members in good standing in Santa Elena society, then all our hard work to scare the snot outta 'em would be worth it. And that's not even considering the fact that we saved old Jesus from going to the slammer.

Speaking of Jesus, this was his big day. The day we'd been planning to put 'im on that truck for California where he'll meet up with his *amigos* and get to work picking lettuce and making enough money to save his poor family. Now don't get me wrong, no one was happier than me about helping out and all, but I gotta tell ya the truth, now that the time had come, I was getting to feeling kinda blue about him leaving. Now I know he'd only been one of the gang for a week or two, but we'd spent nearly every waking hour with him since the first day Big Rosie rousted him out. And he has been so swell, cooking us all kinds of crazy but delicious stuff, making us cool baseball equipment outta a bunch of garbage, going to the Toro game as Señor Villaseñor's "date" and not complaining even once, and even doing his best to teach us that numbskull game of soccer. I mean who else did we know that would do all that? No one, that's who, plus we just met the guy! In just a few short days he had become just like one of the gang, only older. Like a really cool big brother, or something. Come to think of it, none of us had an older brother 'cept Neil, and maybe that's the reason we took such a liking to old Jesus right off the bat, *except* for Neil. Let's face it, Neil's relationship with his brother Barry wasn't what you'd call warm and fuzzy, if ya know what I mean. Speaking of Neil, that big fat fart face, he was really ticking me off. I always knew he didn't have the same, deep down feeling for the Seward School Bombers that the rest of us guys did, but I still couldn't believe he just abandoned us like this, especially in a pinch like last night, when any little mistake meant a slow, painful death for us all. I guess it's just like Pop says, some people think they're the center of the universe, but that's a real lonely place to be, on account'a only one person can really be in the center of anything at any one time.

I kept lying there in bed, staring up at the ceiling and thinking, with the sun already big and bright and shining its piercing rays through my Superman curtains, the same ones Ma had made me when I was four. One of these days I gotta come up with some way to break it to her gently that it might be time for a change. I didn't hear any commotion from down the hall so I guess Ma hadn't found Gracie's ketchup stained jumper we'd stashed last night under the huge pile of dirty clothes in the washroom. I was working on a possible reason for a ketchup bottle to explode in your hand right outta the blue, but was so far coming up empty. You gotta give that squirt credit, and maybe even the mangy mutt, for doing a pretty decent job last night. It was the first time in a long time, maybe even forever, that I can remember I didn't absolutely despise the fact of having a little sister. The jury's still out on Dodger, though.

All in all, I suppose it's been a pretty swell summer, and although it was coming to an end real quick, I'd have to look back and say I got no real regrets. There was the happy humiliation of Nancy Cole and the entire Cole family early on, and then the great victory over the South Siders for the Little League Championship of Santa Elena, the terrific triumph over the Nazi Mrs. Houseman and her Pueblo Junior Debutantes, and the most glorious accomplishment of all, the complete and utter defeat of The Loser Lane gang…twice. I mean, that ain't too shabby for a bunch of goofballs just hanging out and trying to keep from getting beat to a pulp, no matter how ya cut it. Of course, to be honest, we did have our fair share of, let's say, less than spectacular moments that have already been pretty well documented, and I don't see no need to drudge up old dirt at this point.

But of all the swell stuff we've done these last few months, what we've got going today, saving good old Jesus and his starving family, should be the crowning glory to the S.S.B.'s summer of 1968. Now, compared to some of the other adventures you already heard about, I figure this is gonna be a piece of cake. I worked out all the details over and over in my head, and double-checked with Chongo, Pop's number one driver, about his delivery time to El Minuto Market on the town square at exactly twelve noon today. I mean what could possibly go wrong? After Chongo dropped his stuff, it was off to Los Angeles in Pop's Ford three-quarter ton truck, the one with the new refrigerated box, to pick up the weekly produce order from L.A.'s Farmer's Market. All's we hadta do was get our pal there in time without getting spotted, wait for good old Chongo to go on inside with Señor Lopez' produce, slip Jesus in the back of the truck and, *Sayonara,* he's off to California in air-conditioned comfort. Easy as pie. End of story.

I sat up in bed and stretched big as the sky. I got a quick tinge in my left shoulder, still sore from all the innings I threw this summer, but if I was gonna be a major leaguer some day I guess I would just have to get used to that kinda stuff. It was about time to get a move on since we was all set to meet at the Mansfield Place around ten and then head on out. Dodger, the big lummox, was lying on my slippers just like always, and also just like always he refused to move an inch for me to get 'em loose as I tried to shove him off, so I had to yank with all my might and push against his back with my feet to finally wiggle them free. He slowly lifted up his head and looked over his shoulder at me like, "What's all the fuss about?" as I gave it my last mighty tug. Then he yawned real big, flopped his head back down on the floor, let out a big, "Haruuumph," and went back to sleep. Just then I heard the phone ring in the den, and then that unmistakable swishing sound of Ma's apron against her dress as she walked on down the hall towards my room.

"Johnny, dear, it's time to get up," she said as she swung the door open.

"I'm already up, Ma."

"Phone's for you. It's Jeffrey and he sounds quite excited about something. His stuttering is so bad that I can hardly make a word out edgewise."

Well, I didn't like the sound of that, so I raced on down the hall lickety-split and picked up the receiver. "What's up, Jag?"

"J-J-Johnny C. y-y-you g-g-gotta g-get over there, quick!" he screamed so loud it nearly blew out my eardrum.

"Settle down, will ya? Get over where?"

"M-m-mansfield's. Mango and P-P-Pato are coming to g-get him!" I felt myself go all stiff and the blood drained down into my toes, "Get who?" I asked, hoping what I was already thinking was wrong.

"Hey-soos! You m-m-moron!"

"Oh, my God! Oh, my God! Oh my God! How in the heck did they find out? Who ratted us out?"

"It was m-my mom. She f-f-found the p-picture I took that f-first night with my b-b-brownie!"

"You mean to tell me that you kept that picture, you idiot! Oh my God! Oh my God!" I yelled out unable to control myself. But then trying to settle down and think, I said, "Okay, listen, call Lipshitz and tell 'im we need his mini-bike, and call all the other guys and meet me over at the old mansion, *pronto*! I'll take off right now and see if I can beat 'em to the punch."

I slammed down the phone, ran to my room, threw on some clothes and flew out the door with my PF Flyers practically smoking under my feet. It was downright hot already at just past nine, with the sun a ball of orange flame rising full over the Rincon's as I raced towards the mesquite gate, and I could feel the sweat beading up on my forehead and upper lip; partly from the heat and partly from being a nervous wreck! My heart was pounding harder than the drumbeat of one of them new acid rock bands, but a quick look around didn't show no sign of Santa Elena's finest, meaning Mango and Pato, of course, so maybe it was just a false alarm after all, or maybe they was just taking their good sweet time which was pretty much par for the course for our top notch police force.

I kept on tearing through the desert regardless, not paying no mind to rattlers, gila monsters, tarantulas or centipedes, and as I got closer there didn't seem to be nuthin' out of the ordinary. Pretty soon I could even smell fresh tortillas cooking on the hibachi on the back porch, which eased my mind a tad, and I slowed down the pace a bit to give my aching chest and legs a break. I climbed up the front steps and threw open the front door and hollered out, "Hola! Buenos Dias!" and then listened real keen, but there was nuthin'. Maybe he was just taking a siesta. "Jesus!" I said, even louder this time with my hands cupping my mouth, as I quickly walked down the hall to the parlor room, checking the other downstairs rooms as I went. Still there was no sign of 'im. On the back porch I could see the hibachi, coals still red hot, with a stack of fresh tortillas neatly stacked right next to it, part of what was gonna be our last meal together. Then I started to panic and ran upstairs to the bedrooms, the last place he could possibly be, but still no dice. He was gone!

I walked slowly back down stairs and plopped myself into the sofa trying to hold back the tears, but still a few of the more insistent ones managed to seep out. Now what? You knew Mango and Pato would hand 'im over to the Border Patrol faster than you could say, "Baby Face Nelson," on accout'a they were always sucking up to those guys with their official uniforms and decked out patrol cars, and trying to impress them with their uncanny investigation ability. How could this happen? Everything was going so smooth, maybe *too* smooth, and especially today, the last day of his time with us. The day all our planning and hard work had lead up to. The day we were finally gonna put 'im on that truck, wave good-bye and know we'd done all we could to help out a poor, pathetic fella and his poor pathetic family down in Mexico. But now what? Was it all a mistake and a waste of our time like Neil said it would be at the beginning? Would The Losers rat us out and send us all up the river to Juvi for the rest of our lives, or maybe something even worse, something so horrible you'd rather die than have to put up with it. Something so disgustingly grotesque that the rest of your life would be ruined no matter what you tried to do in the future to make it right. Something so degrading that you'd have to move to some far off foreign country like Mongolia or Minnesota and live in a tent in the middle of nowhere just so you wouldn't have to hear about it ever again. Something like forcing you to be Nancy Cole's date to the seventh grade mixer the first week of school, and maybe even make you dance the bearhug with her in front of the whole school! They couldn't do that, could they? They wouldn't dare, would they? That would surely fit under that cruel and unusable punishment law, wouldn't it? And what would Jenny Darling and her folks think about having a common criminal as the guy who likes her? Oh, it was all too horrific to even think about!

As I sat there feeling like one of them punching dummies that someone had just knocked half the stuffing outta, I heard off in the distance the high-pitched exhaust note of a Briggs and Stratton engine. Not thinking too clear, I just blew it off as some poor kid stuck mowing his lawn, but as the sound got closer I suddenly snapped out of it, and raced back upstairs to have a look see. I threw open the window of one of the bedrooms on the southeast corner of the house and peered off into the distance in the direction of the noise. Flying up the street, only still just a tad bigger than a spec, was Jagger, his hair blown straight back against his head, riding good old Lipshitz' minibike like Tom Slick with hemorrhoids! As he got closer in, I could see he was leaning way down low over the handlebars, trying to cheat the wind, and his eyes were peeled open wide to big ovals, and his lips pulled way back showing his teeth clinched tight, making his faced look a lot like the front end of Pop's old '55 pick-up, only with eyebrows. Close behind was Big I, at a full sprint, pumping his arms and legs like there was no tomorrow, and then just turning the corner was Coop, hiccupping so loud I would hear 'im from hear, The Creep, in an all out fidgeting fit, and then Big Rosie, huffing and puffing, with sweat pouring down his face, about twenty yards behind.

The minibike did a nasty fish-tail as Jag came off the asphalt and on to the soft dirt of the desert edge, but he managed to keep control and headed through the gate and on down the trail at full throttle. He was kicking up a mighty dust cloud in his wake, which was hitting Ira square in the face, making it brown as mud, but he didn't slow down a step, like a man on a mission. It lifted my sorrowful soul considerable to see the S.S.B.'s racing to the rescue in this time of trouble like the third cavalry or the eighty-second airborne or Batman and Robin! I just hoped we didn't end up acting more like Dudley Doo-right.

"Is he okay!" Jag yelled above the *brat-brat* of the bike as he got in closer and seen me in the upstairs window.

I just shook my head. "He's gone," was all I could muster.

Jag came to a slow stop and shut down the bike and slumped his head down over his arms that he had folded on the handlebars.

Ira, seeing the expressions on our faces, knew the jig was up, and his whole body went limp as he kicked the dirt hard. "I can't believe it!" he yelled, as if in agony. "We only needed two damn more hours!"

I slowly made my way back down the stairs, and as I did the guys filed in one by one through the back door. Rosie was chomping on one of the fresh tortillas Jesus had left, and had another one in his hand.

"How in the heck can you eat at a time like this, Emiliano?" Ira asked as he came closer.

"To tell you the truth, I've noticed there ain't much that can really affect my appetite, besides, Jesus wouldn't've wanted them to go to waste, now would he?" he said as he took another bite, proud of his common sense comeback.

"I can't believe it's over," I said, as I plopped myself back down on the sofa.

"We were so close to doing something really important for a change," Chicken Coop added a little teary eyed.

"Often times, events of the heart transcend those of the mind," the Creep said, I imagine trying to comfort us, but no one really had a clue.

Nobody made a peep for what seemed like forever, and then with a loud group sigh we slowly headed toward the door to go home to spend the rest of our summer thinking about nuthin' but what a bunch of failures we were and probably always would be, when all of a sudden Jag raced over to block the door, pounded his fist into his hand and yelled, "We ain't g-giving up that easy, or I'm sure m-mistaken about everything it m-means to say you're a m-member of these here Seward School Bombers!"

"What are you blabbing about, you bonehead," said Ira. "We got no idea where they even took poor Hey-soos. For all we know he's already back across the border, and even if he wasn't, Mr. C's truck leaves for California in less than an hour!"

"W-well, we d-d-don't know for sure where he's at," Jag shot back, "But one thing we d-do know is Mengo and Pato are n-n-never in a hurry about nuthin'. Heck, if I know them, they just l-locked 'im up down at their office and are g-gonna wait 'til after lunch to m-mess with them Border Patrol g-guys and all their p-pain in their b-butt paperwork."

"Jag could be on to something, guys," I said, seeing a glimmer of hope. "If they was too lazy to take 'im straight down to Nogales, he might just be locked up down at the Pig Sty (which was Neil's name for the Santa Elena sheriff's office over on the town square.) Let's face it, if there was one law those two really believed in, it was 'wait 'til manana.'"

"But even if he is in the Pig Sty, how are we gonna spring 'im and get 'im on that truck in such a short time?" asked Ira.

"I don't know Johnny C., helping a guy that's run away is one thing, but breaking 'im out of jail is another," said Chicken Coop, starting to tremble, and then sure as you know what, "Hiccup! Hiccup! Hiccup!"

"I believe that is a Class III felony," added Creepy starting to fidget like mad, and reaching for his glasses.

"Do I have to remind you all of what's at stake here?" I asked, staring them all down, hard as I could. "I guess it comes down to, are the S.S.B.'s men or mice? Huh? Are we little girls who should be wearing petticoats under our jeans 'cause we ain't got nuthin' in there to hold up anyhow? Are we the pathetic, weenie, rich kids that The Losers always said we were after all? Well are we? What do *you* say, Big Rosie?" I asked, looking over at the big guy with pleading eyes.

Rosie took a deep breath and let it out nice and slow, then wiped the sweat off his forehead, chewed up the rest of the tortilla in his mouth, and after swallowing hard yelled out, "Let's bust 'im out, boys!"

Everyone let out a whoop and a holler, all except Coop who just let out a bit of a whimper, and we all got down to business.

"Okay, first things first," I said. "Jag, you hop on Lipshitz' minibike and haul butt down to the town square to see if they got Hey-soos there in the first place. Big I, you race down there along with 'im since you're the only one who can probably stay up with Jagger, and help scope out the situation. I'll follow along with the rest of the guys and try to cook up some scheme to spring Hey-soos loose if he really is locked up at the Pig Sty. We'll all meet behind El Guero's in twenty minutes, got it?"

"Got it," Jag and Ira blurted out as they flew out the back door.

"Remember," I yelled after 'em, "The truck leaves at 12 o'clock sharp!" As I turned back to the rest of the crew, still standing in the parlor, I said "Okay, boys, anybody got any good ideas for a jail break?"

We decided we'd better discuss it on the fly since time was short, and Creepy started right in on this elaborate plan of dropping in through the roof using the ventilation ducts and then with a sophisticated pulley system and ropes that N.A.S.A. would'a been proud of, we could lift Jesus clean out of his cell and to freedom without nobody even knowing he was gone. He said he saw it work easy as pie in one of them flashy spy movies once and he felt certain he could make a replica of the system if he just had the time. I hated to break the news to 'im that it may just be a tad too

complicated for the mess we were in right now, and we probably needed
something a little more simple and quick, and he just hung his head low and
wouldn't say a word the rest of the way.

We were walking double-time through the desert when I heard someone
call my name, and when I turned to look, I saw Gracie and Dodger running
right for us.

"What's going on, Johnny?" she asked, a little hurt at not being included
right off.

"They got Hey-soos. They arrested 'im and took 'im to jail."

"What!" she yelped as she started to cry. "How could they do such a
thing? He is such a nice man. He made us stuff to eat and everything! He
wouldn't hurt a fly. Why don't they just let him be?" Tears were flowing
down her face pretty good by then and Dodger nuzzled up against her to
give her some comfort. She threw her arms around his neck, almost
knocking him over, and started blubbering even worse.

"Look, Gracie, kid, we don't have no time to waste. We gotta see if
there's anything we can still do to save 'im, so why don't you just go on
home and I'll tell ya all about it when I get back. Okay?"

"No, Johnny. I *gotta* come. Hey-soos is my friend too, ya know. Maybe
me and Dodger can help."

"No, Gracie. You and that mutt will just be in the way. And anyhow, we
could really get into some trouble for this. It ain't just kids stuff no more,
and I don't want you involved, got it?"

We didn't have no more time to waste so me and guys just turned and
walked off, but after a few seconds, sure enough, I heard them following
from behind. Once in a while I would stop and look over my shoulder and
Gracie would try and slide behind a tree or garbage can or something to
hide, like little kids will, even though they ain't no good at it. I really
couldn't get too ticked off at her, I mean, for a little kid, she was turning
into quite a trooper, sticking up for what she believed was right.

We had to cut through the Barrio on our way, which was the oldest and
poorest Mexican part of town, on account'a the fact that it was the shortest
way to the town square. All the houses were no more than big square
boxes, maybe fifteen foot by ten, and made outta adobe and mud with tin
roofs and dirt floors. There was small patches of stucco still hanging on the
walls here and there, the last remains of what once covered the whole place,
and they all had a little door in front and another one just like it directly
behind that one in back, which were always open, so any cool breeze, which
was few and far between these days, could make its way on through. Some
of the swankier places had a window or two, with an old floor fan stuck up
on the sill, and every last one of 'em had a big wooden barrel, the kind that
wine settles in, out in front to catch any rain water from the monsoons that
could be used for drinking and washing and cooking. They all had

outhouses out back, too, since indoor plumbing still hadn't made it's way into the barrio of Santa Elena. *None* of the houses had air conditioning, something we all took for granted these days, and in fact only one place, Señor Acosta's, even had a swamp cooler, an old rusty one, stuck up on top, groaning away to beat the band, but that automatically made it the most popular gathering spot of the neighborhood on hot summer days. The Acosta's were pretty well off considering, something of barrio royalty, I guess, on account'a the fact that Señora Acosta made extra *dinero* with her world famous green chili salsa that she put up in pint jars and sold off her cart at an amazing rate to all the *gringo* ladies out in front of the Fox Theatre each Sunday morning after church.

There was actually a lot of strange and wonderful things about the barrio, if you thought about it, a whole different world from where we lived just a few blocks away, but the most wonderful of all were just the folks that lived there. First off, for some completely unknown reason, they just didn't seem to care one second, or even have the slightest clue, about how poor they were. I don't remember once in all my life, after walking through that neighborhood hundreds of times, ever seeing one of 'em, from the littlest tykes to the oldest great grandparents having nuthin' but a great big, contented as you could be, smile on their face every minute of the day. And another thing, the whole darn place was always alive, with everybody outside, laughing and joking and visiting, not all cooped up inside like they were afraid of their own shadows like everyone in *our* neighborhood. There was all the time mariachi music blaring from transistor radios at nearly every house, and people singing along out loud no matter how good their voices, and the women, in their house dresses and slippers, with colorful bandanas covering their heads would always be out in front, grinding corn or washing their families clothes in a giant tin basin, and always at the same time keeping an eye on *los niños*, theirs and everyone else's that happened to be playing out in the street. It was like one big happy family.

The sumptuous smell of home cooking filled the air of the barrio no matter what time of day, and as we passed by the Rodriguez' we took an extra big whiff of what must'a been a fresh batch of chorizo con papas, and it was all we could do to keep Rosie from making an uninvited visit. We waved happily at Alma and Alina who were out front roasting coffee beans in the biggest tin pan you ever saw on an old adobe stove, while their aunt Angelica was grinding 'em up on a worn out stone *metate* for tomorrow morning's pot. Alma waved back, Alina just snarled.

Kids were everywhere, like ants at a picnic, and though they were dusty and dirty, and had no more clothes on than an old pair of hand me down underpants that by this time in the morning were already riding pretty low, they didn't seem to mind, and were having themselves a ball chasing dogs, playing duck-duck-goose, and pushing each other along in an old broken down wheelbarrow up and down the dirt road. The men were all out working on their pick-up trucks or patching up the house or just lying in the shade drinking a *cerveza,* and pretty much just enjoying watching the day go by. And every one of 'em seemed as content as could be, considerably more happy than the folks that lived around us, and it made ya wonder about who was fooling who when it came to being a success.

They all seemed genuinely glad to see us there, too, although I think we were more of a curiosity than anything else to the littlest ones who'd every once in a while gather up their courage and run right over and take a long hard look at us, and then scamper off fast as they could go. We had all kinds of offers from perfect strangers to come and join them *para comida* as we walked along, and though it was mighty tempting, we had to say "thanks but no thanks," and kept on moving.

As we turned to wave good-bye, we hit open land between the Barrio and town square with about five minutes to spare, and made it to El Guero's right on time. Jag and Ira were nowhere to be seen, so we sat down in the shade on the side of the taco stand against its wooden wall that was painted in wide red, white and green stripes, just like the Mexican flag.

"Hola, Joe-nee C.," I heard a small child's voice from directly above me. I looked up to see the smiling face of Chuy, El Guero's little boy.

"Hola, Chuy. Que tal?"

"Nada mucho. Tienes hombre, mis amigos?"

"Si. Tengo mucho hombre!" Rosie answered as he began to stand up.

"Not now, man. We've got work to do!" I said as I grabbed 'em by the back of the pants and yanked him back down.

But that gave me an idea and I asked, "Tienes menudo, hoy, Chuy?"

"Si! Te gusto menudo, Joe-nee?" He asked, more than a little surprised.

"Un pocito," I said, lying through my teeth. "Pero es el favorito de Mengo and Pato, right?" I asked, straining the limits of my knowledge of Mexican.

"Oh si, si!" he answered, nodding his head enthusiastically. "Ellos son loco para menudo."

Menudo was that disgusting soup that I told ya about earlier that was made outta cow innards and who knows what else, and God only knows why, but every Mexican I ever met would practically kill for it, but it had to be fresh and done just right, and nobody had better menudo than El Guero.

Just then Jag and Ira raced around the back of the building and plopped themselves down beside us.

"Whatdaya got, boys?" I asked, itching to hear the news.

"Well guys, we got good news and we got bad news," said Ira mopping the sweat from his forehead with the end of his T-shirt. "The good news is that Hey-soos is safe and sound over at the Pig Sty and there ain't no sign of any Feds around yet."

"That's great!" we all said. "What's the bad news?"

"The b-b-bad news," said Jag, shaking his head, "is that they g-got 'im in the f-freaking f-front cell, the one with the n-new lock that's a lot harder to pick!"

"Dang it!" I'd been depending all along on Jag's uncanny ability to pick simple locks to maybe help spring Jesus, there weren't many that could keep 'im out once he set his mind to it. He said he learned his "art" from breaking into the cheap metal cash boxes his ma used to hide her money in. It was truly amazing to watch what he could do with some spit and a simple hair pin.

"Any other inmates?" I asked.

"Just El Guapo, as usual," Ira answered. "But he's still sleeping one off from last night. Seems he had a little too much Mescal and then went over to visit Señora Bustamonte uninvited. The problem was, I guess Señor Bustamonte got home from Albuquerque earlier than expected, and then all hell broke loose. Mengo threw 'im in the slammer for public drunkenness, and for his own protection. I overheard Pato say he'd go and try and smooth things over with Señor Bustamonte this afternoon, but it probably wouldn't do no good in the long run. He said the next time he went on the road there'd sure enough be some other bird dog sniffing around his chicken coop all over again, but I ain't quite sure what he meant by that."

"So where are our fearless fighters of crime now?" I asked.

"Sitting at their desks looking at girlie magazines and sucking on *saladitos*, just like always," Jag said, with a smirk.

"*Quieres saladitos?*" Chuy said leaning out of the window with an open jar of the salted prunes. "Ees on the house," he said with a smile.

"Don't mind if we do, Chuy, my fine boy," said Rosie as we each grabbed one and popped it in our mouth and began to suck on it until our lips puckered up and our eyes started to water.

"Alright, here's the deal," I said, getting down to business. "We've got about half an hour to get them two out of the Pig Sty, spring Hey-soos from his cell, and get 'im on the back of Chongo's truck. Let's get on over there and try to distract 'em, which shouldn't be too difficult, while Jag, you try to find the keys to the cell, and Rosie, you try to sneak over and whisper to Hey-soos about our plan. Got it?"

"Got it."

"Alright then, let's gather round and get ourselves a cheer."

The S.S.B.'s, about to set out on their most difficult and dangerous assignment of all time, made a circle, shoved their hands in the middle, and yelled, "All for naught and not for long!" maybe for the last time as free men, and then headed as a group on down the street, determined to keep their promise to a poor Mexican fella who had put all his hope and trust into a group of twelve year old boys he hardly knew.

We walked along Camino Primero, which was the street that the Pig Sty was on, and was bordered on the town square by Camino Segundo, Camino Tercero and Camino Quatro. We were already directly across from the old Courthouse that sat smack dab in the middle, with the statue of good old Father Kino, like I told ya before, who was the Spanish Missionary who managed to not get hisself scalped as he tried to learn the Indians all about Christianity in what is now the western United States. It was the only statue around these parts, and it weren't half bad looking, to tell ya the truth, with the padre in his big, round brim hat, and long robes, and his horse's head raring back with nostrils flared and tail at full salute, which Neil said meant he was about to drop a load, but good! In fact, just for the heck of it one week last year, Neil went around collecting all the dog poop he could find every night and then around midnight would dump a tall steaming mound of it right under the horse's butt! Every day they'd clean it up, and every night Neil would dump another fresh batch. No one could figure out how or why it was happening, and it caused quite a stir for a while, 'til the Reverend Mother from St. Augustine's Nunnery near Aravaca came up with the idea that it had to be a message from God, seeing that the statue, after all, was of a famous Spanish missionary, and that maybe the mayor and town council needed to think about just what kind of message the Almighty might be sending them with this act. After that, Pop said he hardly ever saw Mayor Troncoza's or any of the other Santa Elena dignitary's cars out in front of Poco Loco Cantina, and all of a sudden there seemed to be a lot more money left in the town treasury to run things.

The shop owners were out sweeping the wooden walkway in front of their stores and other folks were starting to set up their small tables on the grass around the courthouse to sell their trinkets, artwork and canned goods, just like always on Saturday morning. Dan Dunn was out in front of the Fox Theater checking the marquee to make sure no kids last night had changed the order of the letters to make any cuss words. Hard to believe anyone would stoop that low. Dunn had just been promoted to chief usher after his commendable handling of the end of the Marshall KGUN fiasco, and he gave us a great big goofball wave when he saw us across the square. I shot a glance on down to the street corner and was happy to see there was no sign of Chongo or his truck out in front of El Minuto Market.

We came up to the Santa Elena Sheriff's Office, another old adobe building with patchwork stucco and mesquite beams sticking out along the top, with a narrow arched front door with two well worn steps leading up to it, and two small windows out in front covered over with iron bars. It said, "Sheriff Office" in black painted letters above the door, but a couple of months ago, someone, who will remain nameless, erased the "ice" at the end of office, and added an "'s" at the end of sheriff, so now it said

"Sherrif's Off." The heavy wood plank door with big black nailhead studs was wide open, and I heard Pato chuckle, "I might jus veesit Señora Bustamonte myself la proxima ves que el viejo ees gone," as we sauntered

on in.

"Hola, Sheriff! We just decided to stop by to let you know how happy we are that you and your deputy here are keeping the people of Santa Elena safe and secure," I said as I walked around behind Mengo and gave 'im a big pat on the back, and then sat down on the edge of his desk. Ira plopped down on the opposite side, and Creepy and Chicken Coop walked over to visit with Pato, who just stared at 'em with a wary gaze. You could hear "El Guapo" snoring in the cell down the hall.

"The peeple of thees here town deserve a good keek in the ahs," he grunted disgustedly, as he and Pato quickly put their magazines away. "What chu boys want, anyways? Can't chu see we're beesy?"

"Of course you are," I said. "Police work, especially in a bustling town like Santa Elena, is tough, and nobody really appreciates everything you two highly trained officers do."

"Chu can say that again, seestar!"

I looked over at Pato, and good old Creepy and Coop were keeping him well occupied by pulling on his pistol and taking off his badge, and then taking turns pinning it on themselves.

"Geeme that, chu little cheet!" he yelled as Bampu pulled the pistol clean out of the holster and said, "Put 'em up!" By that time Coop was wearing his cap *and* his badge and was blowing his police whistle for all he was worth right in his ear. "Ay, carumba!" Pato squealed as he lunged for Chicken Coop.

I watched outta the corner of my eye as Jagger riffled though Pato's desk in search of the keys, and Rosie slowly made his way back to Jesus' cell. Ira got Mengo's attention by swiping the baton from his belt and then played, "Whip Out" with it on the back of his chair.

"Ay, Mi Madre!" Mengo yelled as he swerved around and wrestled the stick out of Ira's hand.

After a few seconds I saw Rosie slip back into the room and then Jag gave me a wink as I looked over his way.

It was time to put the rest of our plan into action, so I licked my lips and rubbed my belly hard and said, "Boy, I'm sure getting mighty hungry for lunch. How about you guys?"

"Why don't chu keeds *vamos a su casa* and have chore mommies make chu *alguna comida? Comprendes?*" Pato said abruptly with Mengo nodding in agreement.

"Nope," I said, scratching my chin. "I'm feeling more like Mexican food today. Say, come to think of it, I heard El Guero just made up a fresh batch of menudo. I think we'll high tail it over there and get some before it's all gone." Santa Elena's finest perked up their ears at that, stood up quick, pushing their chairs out from under them and said, "Deed chu say menudo?"

"I just saw Chuy and he said it's going faster than brownies at a Weight Watchers convention!"

"Come to theenk about eet, why don't chu boys hang around here for a while and cool off. Wee'll be right back." Before we could answer they were out the door and running down the street, holding on to their hats and pistols as they went.

I watched them head over to El Guero's, but as I turned my head the opposite direction, my heart sank with a thud. Chongo had just pulled up in front of El Minuto Market!

"Holy sh!#" I yelled out as I turned back around, and then, "Oops."

"Congratulations, Johnny C. That's your first official cuss word of all time," Ira said with a pat on the back. "I'm real proud of ya, kid."

"Quit screwing around, Big I. Chongo just pulled up!"

"Holy sh!#" Ira yelled, right back at me. "Why the hell's he here already! He's fifteen stinking minutes early for Gosh sakes. What's he doing, trying for a raise or something?"

The guys raced over to the door and we all stuck our heads out, one on top of the other like some scared stiff totem pole, and we looked down the street as Chango opened the back of his truck and started to gather up the produce for his delivery. Then, all together, we turned our heads quick to look the opposite direction and saw Pato and Mengo standing in the order window line at El Guero's behind old lady Ledesma with her three bratty grandkids in tow up from Hermosillo, smacking their lips and looking mighty antsy in anticipation of their steaming hot bowl of stewed cow intestines.

"Thank God we got them two outta here when we did," I said, turning towards Jag. "Alright, where's the keys? We gotta spring Jesus, pronto!"

"T-t-hat's a problem, Johnny C.," he answered with a worried look. "They're still in P-pato's p-pocket!"

"Gees! What else! I guess you'll just hafta pick the darn thing, Jag."

"N-not a chance," he answered, dejected. "They m-must'a gone up to Tucson and g-got one of them new b-bullet proof Master Locks. Houdini couldn't open that thing if his life depended on it!"

"O, my God! O, my God! O, my God!" I yelled out, and there followed a few seconds of silence, with a lot of hair pulling and hand wringing and pacing up and down but then as the panic passed we tried to come up with a quick solution to our humongous problem. I looked each and every one of the S.S.B.'s in the eye and got nuthin' in return but a blank stare, and when I finally came to the Creep and even he just shook his head and dropped his eyes to the ground, I realized it was up to me to come up with something and *fast* or Jesus and maybe his whole family were sure goners.

I poked my head out the door and took a quick look from side to side again. Chongo was stacking a lug of tomatoes, a carton of lettuce and a box of lemons on his hand truck and getting ready to drag the whole load inside. That gave us ten minutes, twelve max, I figured before he got it inside, had Mr. Jacobs look over the stuff, have him sign the invoice, and then back out to get set to shove off for L.A. Over at El Guero's Mengo and Pato were totally engrossed in their lunch, sprinkling a tad of cilantro here and squeezing a little lime there, but totally oblivious to everything else around them. They weren't going nowhere for a while. Thank God for menudo!

"Okay, listen up," I said as I turned back into the room. "The way I see it, our only chance is to get Pato back in here and take them keys from 'im."

"Johnny, are you nuts? He may be a doofus, and all, but he's still a police officer!" Chicken Coop cried out. "Even if we could somehow wrestle those keys from 'im, and that's a pretty big if, we'd be busted so hard that Juvi wouldn't be good enough. They'd send us straight to Elevenworth!" Rosie and the Creep nodded their heads in full, frantic agreement.

"Now just hold on," I said. "I think I got a plan that can get Jesus to L.A. and keep us outta prison, too."

"How do you propose to do that?" asked Bampu, doubtfully.

"Here it is," I said. "And listen up good, 'cause we're running outta time and I'm only gonna say it once. First. Creep, you and Cooper run down and tell Pato that Mrs. Bustamonte's on the phone and she's acting real excited to talk to 'im. Got it? That should get 'im away from his menudo. Jag, you and Big I grab the bullwhip Mengo keeps draped over that velvet painting of the Virgin Mary behind his desk and get ready to pull it tight across the doorway as Pato comes rushing in. Make sure he falls flat on his face hard so as he won't know what the heck hit 'im. Okay?" Jag and Ira gave each other a big thumbs-up and a nasty smirk.

"What about me, Johnny C.?" Rosie asked, all hurtful. "Don't I get to do nuthin' good?"

"Sure you do, Big Guy. You've got the most important job of all, in fact, and what's more, it's something that no one else in this room could do. Heck, maybe no one in the whole town."

"Wow! Really? What's that?" he asked, all excited and with a new sense of pride.

"You're gonna jump smack dab on top of old Pato soon as he hits the floor, and pin 'im down so hard he won't be able to move a muscle. Ain't that neat?"

"Yep. Real neat-o," he answered, not near as enthusiastic.

"After Pato's down and out, I'll grab the keys, spring Hey-soos, and get 'im down to the truck."

"That's a pretty cool plan, Johnny C., I gotta admit," Ira said. "But let's face it, we're gonna get busted, sure as snot. Even those two bozos are gonna figure out that it was us that did it. I mean who else is there?"

"El Guapo," I answered with a big smile.

"What!" They all asked at once.

"After I bust out Hey-soos, I'll let El Guapo out, too, and tell 'im to head to the mountains for a week or so 'til things blow over between him and Señor Bustamonte. Then when Mengo asks what the heck happened, we'll blame the whole thing on him. We'll tell Mengo that while we were sitting around minding our own business, keeping an eye on things best we could, El Guapo somehow jimmied the lock on the old jail cell door and then, although we did our darndest to stop 'im, he tripped Pato when he heard 'im coming in the door. We can say Hey-soos asked him to let him out too, and El Guapo, feeling sorry for the poor guy, took Pato's keys and set him free."

Nobody said a thing, but just looked at each other, then at me and then at Jag for his approval. He thought for a second, scratching his head, and then got that big toothy grin on his face, wrinkled up his eyes and said, "I like it. I *like* it!"

"Okay, great," I said, relieved. "Everyone remember your part, don't screw up, and let's get moving!"

Bampu and Coop took off running full tilt to El Guero's and I looked out at the corner market to see Chongo pushing his hand truck through the front door. I hid behind Mengo's desk as Ira and Jag got into position with the bullwhip on each side of the doorway. I blessed myself and said a little prayer that our plan would work, though I guess I could understand if the Big Guy upstairs might not look all that kindly on a bunch of kids helping a guy escape from jail. Hopefully, in this case, he'll make an exception.

"Rosie, go tell Hey-soos that as soon as I let 'im out he's gotta follow me fast as he can. There ain't gonna be no time for good-byes." After I said that, it hit me for the first time, that if this nutty plan really did work, we weren't gonna never see old Jesus again, and it made me kinda sad. I wonder if the rest of the guys were starting to feel the same, too.

Well, sure enough, here comes Pato racing down that wooden sidewalk looking like a kid coming down the hall on Christmas morning, and I whispered to Jag and Big I to get ready to pull that bullwhip tight soon as he hit the front steps.

"Ay!" He screamed as he flew through the air and landed hard, face first, with a sickening crunch on the red cement floor. He just laid there for a second making slow moaning sounds as we stared down at him, which gave Rosie a chance to race over, or should I say waddle, and then do a little hop and come down with full force, square on the deputy's head, like he was doing a cannonball in a swimming pool, so his chubby thighs were straddling poor Pato's shoulders and back.

"Dios mio!" I think I heard him say from underneath Rosie's immense rear end, and then after a long sigh, he laid completely limp. I quickly sifted through his pockets and pulled out the keys, the problem was there was about fifty different ones on his ring.

"Any idea which is which?" I asked the guys, but no one had a clue.

Just then there was another slight mumbling sound coming from underneath Rosie.

"Now what's he trying to say?" I asked. "He says he can't breath," answered Rosie, a little embarrassed.

"Okay, let 'im up just a bit," I said. "After all, we don't want to suffocate the poor fella. But if he starts squirming too much, squish 'im but good."

"No problema," Rosie said and pushed hisself up just a tad. I ran over to Jesus' cell and started working the keys one by one.

"How's it looking, Big I?" I asked as he and Jag kept watch down the street.

"Mengo's still slurping up his soup. I swear it looks like he's in a daze or something."

"How about Chongo?"

"Nada." So we still had say a minute or two, but we needed that stinking key!

"Ees the one *con el rojo*," I heard a voice from over my shoulder say. It was El Guapo, all sobered up from his big night out.

"Thanks, Señor Gomez," I said as I slipped the red topped key into the slot and opened the door with a clang.

"Don't mencheen eet," he answered, smiling. "After all, I should know."

I turned around and opened his cell up too. "*Muchas gracias, mi amigo,*" he said as he patted me on the back. "Chu es berry nice boys."

"My pleasure, Mr Gomez, but I gotta tell ya, I heard Mengo and Pato talking, and they said they were really ticked off and gonna throw the book at you this time."

"No sheet," he answered, looking a bit worried.

"I was thinking maybe it wouldn't be a bad idea for you to high tail it out to Ventana Canyon or somewheres and lay low for a week or so."

"*Tu eres muy intelligente, tambien,*" he said. "I theenk I'll do jus that!"

With that, he tucked in his shirttail, smoothed down his hair, straightened his jacket and then spat on the floor as he walked by where Pato was being "guarded" by Rosie and grunted, "*Pendejo!*" under his breath as he wiped his mouth. Then he grabbed his hat off the peg by the window, stuck his head out the door to make sure the coast was clear, and then nonchalantly strolled down the steps, across the street, and past the courthouse out of view.

"*Andale! Andale!*" I yelled at Jesus as I grabbed him by the hand and started for the door.

"B-b-better boogey, Johnny. I think I see Chongo at the door."

"Not yet!" I said and stuck my head out to see what was what.

"Johnny C.?" I heard Rosie's voice from behind me.

"What is it?" I said, kinda irritated, and not pulling my head back in.

"I think I gotta cut one loose."

Well, Jag and Ira almost fell over backwards laughing and even I started to chuckle at the thought, despite my serious predicament.

Man, that is cruel and unusual punishment for poor old Pato, I said to myself.

"Listen, Rosie," I said, "Try and hold it, 'til he starts to really squirm and then let her rip. I gotta believe one of your gas bombs at close range is a better sedative than a truck full of ether!"

"Got ya," he said with a big, wide smile on that chubby face of his.

"Come on!" I said to Jesus as we tore down the front steps and toward the open back of the truck. I could make out Chongo standing in the doorway as we got a little closer. I could tell he was making time with

Josefina, the new checker at El Minuto, and she was batting her eyes like all get out and smiling up a storm, and I was hoping that might give us the extra minute or two we needed to get old Jesus loaded up. We reached the truck without a hitch and I started to give Jesus a leg up, when outta nowhere came a loud barking noise to my left that could blow our cover all to bits. I looked over my shoulder in horror to see that mongrel Dodger running towards us, yapping his fool head off like we was playing a game or something. Gracie was screaming at him to shut his trap from over on the courthouse lawn where they'd apparently been hiding out, but that just made for *more* commotion. I shot a quick glance down the street to see Mengo stand up from his bowl of menudo to see what all the racket was about, while Jagger and Ira were now out in front of the Pig Sty standing next to Bampu and Cooper, and all of 'em had their hands over their eyes, not wanting to see what might happen next! Mengo, first looked over at Gracie, then at Dodger and then at me behind the truck. He seemed to relax for a second, thinking it was just us guys and Dodger horsing around, but then as Jesus climbed up and into the back of the truck, he squinted his eyes up in our direction again for a second or two, and then flung his chair back, ripped off the napkin he had tucked into his shirt, and started running full tilt towards us, yelling, *"Alto! Alto!"* at the top of his lungs. I stood there froze stiff, unable to move a muscle, and just then heard the truck door slam, the engine come to life, and the grinding or gears as it started to pull away. I managed to turn and look up at Jesus who was standing on the edge of the van, and then I smiled and said, "Buenas suerte," as my eyes started to well up a bit and I swallowed real hard. He smiled back real big, too, said in a low voice, "Muchas gracias, mi amigo," and then waved to me and the guys as the truck slowly moved out on down the road.

*"Alto! Alto!"* Mango kept on yelling as he ran, but then stopped when he realized he couldn't catch the truck on foot and quickly jumped into his squad car parked right in front of where the guys were standing. After a few cranks that old Chevy engine turned over with a big cloud of blue smoke out the back, and he slammed it into gear and peeled out, the whole time talking to himself and weaving all over like a mad man. I started to get that horrible feeling of doom that I had this morning all over again, as I realized it would only take a minute for him to catch Chongo and pull 'im over, sending Jesus back to jail, and probably us along with 'im, when outta the corner of my eye I caught a glimpse of something moving fast this way from across the courthouse lawn. At first it was just a flash in the sun's reflection, but when it hit the shade of the big cottonwood tree, I could start to make out that it was a kid on a Stingray, riding like the wind. As I turned my head and squinted up my eyes to get a better look, my jaw dropped like a rock as I couldn't believe what I was seeing. It was *Neil,* that dirty rat, and he had his teeth clenched tight and his eyelids peeled back and

this look on his face of sheer determination. But what in the heck was he doing?

Well, Mengo kept coming like Mario Andretti, all the while his head was out the window as he kept on yelling to beat the band. The guys were all in a tizzy, too, having made Neil out by now, and they jumped up and down and pointed, and then ran towards the corner market where I was standing to get a better look. Just then *Pato* comes staggering out of the Pig Sty, guns pulled and yelling best he could in this real raspy voice, something like, "*Escapando!*" and "*Ay, que fregado!*" As Neil started getting closer, I realized he wasn't coming towards us at all, but was gunning straight for where Mengo's squad car was heading. Had he gone nuts? What was he trying to pull? Was that Benadick Arnold trying to ruin things for us once and for all? All I knew for sure was if Mengo hit him at this speed, we'd be scraping pieces of Neil off the sidewalk with a spatula for weeks. None of that seemed to effect old Neil one bit, though, and he just kept on peddling so fast that his legs were nuthing but a blur, getting lower and lower against his monkey bars, staring straight ahead, and then suddenly it hit me. Neil wasn't trying to mess up our plan at all, he was gonna risk his life and head off Mengo to help Jesus escape!

Well, Mango wasn't letting up none, neither, hell bent on catching Chongo's truck and coming hard, right toward where I was taking the whole crazy scene in, but when his squad car was no more than ten yards from the corner, he must'a caught a glimpse of old Neil and his Stingray outta the corner of his eye and then turned sharp right to try to miss smacking him to smithereens. With tires squealing and the horn blowing, and all of us yelling, he smashed head on into the fire hydrant on the sidewalk, and came to a sliding stop no more than five feet from where I was standing! A long tube of water shot sky high as Neil slammed on his brakes, but still caught a piece of Mengo's front fender, and went head over heels over his monkey bars, doing one of the nicest somersaults with what might'a been one of those half gainers, you ever did see, landing almost square on my chest, and knocking me flat. There weren't no time for hellos, as Pato came running up to the squad car best he could considering the position he had most recently been in, gave Mengo a hard slap across the face which he didn't seem to appreciate much, to make sure he was okay, and then with a mighty shaky hand, took aim with his pistol at Pop's delivery truck that was at least two blocks down the road by now making its way to I-19. But before he could get off the shot that could still ruin all of our plans and doom Jesus' escape, I saw a large, low, yellow blur through the wall of water that was falling all around us, coming hard straight for 'im, and then just before he pulled the trigger, I heard a loud "*Chomp!*" and then a horrifying scream.

"Ay, mis *hungas!*" (I'm pretty sure hungas meant butt in Mexican, but I could be wrong)

It was Dodger, the ass-biter, finally using his only real talent to do hisself proud for a change! Well, Pato's pistol went flying in the air, landing in a puddle about five feet in front of the fire hydrant as he sunk to the ground stunned and sore, and then Mengo came staggering out of the squad car, still a bit woozy, and sat down in the street dejected next to his cousin, their brown uniforms both dripping wet, one of them rubbing his head and the other one rubbing his butt.

Neil and I stood up and looked down the road as Chongo and Jesus drove out of site, and I waved one last big good bye that I'm pretty sure they couldn't see, let out a deep sigh and then turned towards Neil.

"What the heck were you doin' you nimrod! You could've been killed!"

"Well, I had nuthin' better to do today," he said, showing no emotion at all. "And anyway, I knew you pea brains were gonna need me to bail you outta your screwball scheme sooner or later."

I reared back and punched 'im in the shoulder hard as I could, trying to give 'im the most monster monkey bump of all time, but he didn't even flinch, and then we both started laughing and pushing each other 'til the rest of the guys raced up. They started slapping Neil on the back and telling 'im what a hero he was and all, and how much we missed 'im and how he was the bravest S.S.B. that ever lived and how what we did today would be remembered forever in the history of Santa Elena as the "Great Jail Break of '68."

Dodger got his share of attention, too, with everyone agreeing he was surely the most brilliant and loyal dog since "Lassie," or maybe even "Rin Tin Tin," and how he helped to save the day just like them dogs always did, and how we couldn't've done it without 'im. Gracie watched, proud as a peacock as Big Rosie took out a piece of beef jerky from his pocket and gave it to Dodger as a reward, after breaking off a small piece for himself, and said he'd be happy to share his snacks with Dodger any time from now on, which we all found hard to believe, but didn't want to say nuthin' to ruin the moment.

By now the sidewalks were full of town folk, come out to see what all the ruckus was about, and little kids were already crowding around the fire hydrant, stripping down to their skivvies to play in the cool water. We all started to walk off, shoulder to shoulder, with our arms around each other, heading back towards the white ghetto and home, not wanting to press our luck too much by hanging around the Santa Elena police force any more than need be, and Gracie and Dodger, Dodger the Great, from then on, ran circles around us as we walked along.

"I c-can't believe summer is almost over," Jag said, after a bit, real dejected like.

"No kidding," I answered. "Before you know it we'll be back in school

with Nancy Cole and the rest of them twits."

"Shut up, will ya. You're making he sick!" said Neil, pretending to up-chuck.

"At least sweet little Jenny Darling will be there to make things more peachy for you. Right Johnny C.?," said Ira in a screechy girl voice while he batted his eyes wildly.

"Why don't you bite me, Big I?"

"You'd like that, wouldn't ya, Johnny C.?" Chicken Coop said with a big smile, proud of hisself for such a quick come back.

"Chopped low!" everyone yelled out and gave me the tomahawk sign.

We walked on past the courthouse and turned up the street headed back through the barrio on our way home. The afternoon sun was blazing like fire down on our heads and them squiggly lines started rising from the street in the distance. As we got close to the old Mansfield homestead, I could see the mansion off in the distance and thought to myself how I would never think of that old place the same. I laughed to myself, thinking about how we all thought it was haunted, and I caught a quick glimpse in my mind's eye of them Losers running away from it for dear life, but now, even knowing different, I still didn't think I'd ever go back there, on account'a it just wouldn't be the same without Jesus. That was *all our place* for a short but special time and I guess some places and memories are best just left alone. I bet you a Butterfinger the other guys were thinking the same way, too.

"What do you guys want to do tomorrow," asked Bampu in that nutty sing-song voice of his as he kicked an old *Delaware Punch* can in front of 'im.

"I don't know, but how about something fun and exciting for a change!" Neil barked as he raced in front of Creepy and gave his can a kick.

"That's the problem with this town, nuthin' cool *ever* happens," added Rosie.

"You said a mouth full there, seester," said Ira as we all cracked up thinking about old Pato squished like a bug by Rosie over at the Pig Sty. "Did ya ever cut that one loose you were saving up, big guy?"

"Sure did. And it was atomic!" Rosie answered proudly.

"Grotty!"

"Hey, how about another b-b-bazooka war tomorrow?" asked Jag, getting real excited.

"Shut the heck up, will ya," we all turned and yelled at the same time.

Jag just grinned his goofy grin and chuckled to hisself.

"I heard there is a neat science fair in…" Creepy started out, but Neil slugged 'im a good one right in the breadbasket before he could even finish. "I guess that's a no," he managed to spit out in between gasps.

"Hey Neil," I said, thinkin' of something. "What you did today was just like that potty-gal son old Bishop Moreno was talking about a few weeks back in his sermon."

"What the heck are you yapping about, Johnny?" Neil turned toward me and asked.

"You know, that bible story about that no good son who takes off and leaves his friends and family high and dry for no good reason but that he was just a selfish turd, and then finally he makes his way on back after realizing his terrible mistake."

Well, that didn't sit too well as ya might'a guessed, and he reached over, grabbed me by the collar and yanked me towards 'im and said, "Look, you ever compare me again to one of them weenies in those bible stories of yours and I'll turn *you* into a potty-gal. Got it?"

"Got it," I answered, quick, and thought it best to just let the whole dumb idea drop.

After a few more minutes we were making our way through the alley behind my house when I asked, "Hey, Rosie, how did Pato manage to get out from under ya, anyhow?"

He didn't answer right off, but quick looked down at his feet like he was ashamed or something, and we all stopped and stared at him, wanting to know the answer. We all knew for certain there was no way that scrawny deputy was gonna *throw* Big Rosie off his back.

"Well," Rosie said real low, almost a whisper. "You know that big jar of lemon drops Mengo always keeps on his desk?"

"Stop right there!" Ira yelled. "You mean you almost screwed up the whole day and got us sent down the river because you had to have a lemon drop?"

"But I was getting hungry, and Pato hadn't moved a muscle the whole time I was squishin' him, anyhow," he pleaded. "I thought he was for sure passed out!"

"What about that jerky you had in your pocket." I asked.

"I was in the mood for somethin' sweet."

"You got a real problem there, Sugar Bear," said Neil, as he turned and started to walk on. "You really need to see a shrink."

"Yeah, you need to see a shrink so *you* can shrink. Get it?" Coop blurted out, proud all over again for being so clever.

"Good thing Dodger was there to save your butt," said Ira bending over and giving the dog a pat.

"That's r-right," Jag said. "D-dodger saved your butt by b-biting Pato's!" Then he ran up a few steps, grabbed his butt with both hands and jumped into the air screaming, "Ay, mis hungas!"

We all busted out laughing and then one by one started copying Pato and grabbing our butts and yelling out, while Dodger ran circles around us, barking like a lunatic and trying to sink his teeth into anyone he could sneak up on. We kept that up for quite a while and I suppose we probably looked pretty darn silly right about then, but hey, we were just a bunch'a kids in Santa Elena, Arizona, having some fun during a hot summer day, and if people didn't like it, then I guess they just could lump it.

# THE END

# ABOUT THE AUTHOR

J. E. Tooley is a family physician born and raised in Tucson, Arizona. He has three very bright children (all gone from home now, unfortunately) and four very dumb dogs (all still around, unfortunately!). He likes restoring old muscle cars, collecting civil war stuff, and coaching little league. His wife Paula puts up with him because as far as he can tell after 30 years she doesn't know any better. They live in the Santa Catalina Mountains just north of Tucson, where, when not in his office seeing sick people, he spends most of his time picking up after the dogs and dodging assorted tarantualas, rattlesnakes, and gila monsters.

Made in the USA
San Bernardino, CA
01 May 2014